TRAVELS IN TRANSLATION

Judaic Traditions in Literature, Music, and Art
Harold Bloom and Ken Frieden, *Series Editors*

Samuel Dunn, *Map of the World with the Latest Discoveries*, Eastern Hemisphere, from Samuel Dunn, *A New Atlas of the Mundane System* (London: Sayer, 1788), plate 1, detail. Courtesy of the New York Public Library.

Travels in Translation

SEA TALES AT THE SOURCE OF JEWISH FICTION

Ken Frieden

Syracuse University Press

The author acknowledges the College of Arts and Sciences and the B. G. Rudolph Endowment in Judaic Studies at Syracuse University for their generous support of his research and the production of this book.

First Edition 2016
16 17 18 19 20 21 6 5 4 3 2 1

∞ The paper used in this publication meets the minimum requirements of the American National Standard for Information Sciences—Permanence of Paper for Printed Library Materials, ANSI Z39.48-1992.

For a listing of books published and distributed by Syracuse University Press, visit www.SyracuseUniversityPress.syr.edu.

ISBN: 978-0-8156-3457-7 (cloth) 978-0-8156-3441-6 (paperback)
978-0-8156-5364-6 (e-book)

Library of Congress Cataloging-in-Publication Data
Names: Frieden, Ken, 1955– author.
Title: Travels in translation : sea tales at the source of Jewish fiction / Ken Frieden.
Description: First edition. | Syracuse, New York : Syracuse University Press, 2016. | Series: Judaic traditions in literature, music, and art | Includes bibliographical references and index.
Identifiers: LCCN 2016005456| ISBN 9780815634577 (cloth : alk. paper) | ISBN 9780815634416 (pbk. : alk. paper) | ISBN 9780815653646 (e-book)
Subjects: LCSH: Hebrew fiction—History and criticism. | Jewish fiction—History and criticism. | Sea stories—History and criticism. | Sea in literature. | Translating and interpreting.
Classification: LCC PJ5029 .F67 2016 | DDC 892.43/509–dc23 LC record available at https://lccn.loc.gov/2016005456

Manufactured in the United States of America

In
memory
of my father,
Julian Frieden *(1924–2003), a man of science*
who loved to go down to the sea in ships

We Jews live without geography!

מיר יידן לעבן אָן געאָגראַפֿיע!

—Provincial Jew in I. L. Peretz, “The Dead City”

Contents

Illustrations

Portraits, Maps, and Facsimile Pages

Table

Graphs

Note on Transliterations and Quotations

Transliteration of Hebrew and Yiddish

Transliteration of Hebrew and Yiddish is, at best, an imperfect art. The goal is to convey adequate information to the reader about the Hebrew words that are represented by an inevitably flawed transcription into Latin characters. To this end, I have used a simplistic, straightforward system, following current pronunciation norms—even though this system is anachronistic and flawed. It might be preferable to represent Hebrew as it was pronounced at the time and place of writing, yet such a representation could confuse twenty-first-century readers who are accustomed to Israeli Hebrew.

In transcribing words that begin with the letter 'Aleph, I have usually placed an apostrophe (') to differentiate 'Aleph from `Ayin, with the latter indicated by the grave accent mark (`). In the case of the omnipresent word *oniya* (ship), however, I have assumed that readers will not need all of those extra apostrophes to be reminded that this Hebrew word is spelled with an 'Aleph.

Transcribed Hebrew words that include the letter Ḥet benefit from the use of a subdot under the *h*. When these words occur in Yiddish, however, the YIVO guidelines call for *kh*. Transcribed words that include the letter Tzadi use *tz* for Hebrew but, following YIVO guidelines, *ts* for Yiddish. In Hebrew titles, acronyms are sometimes indicated by the use of a quotation mark before the final letter.

In most cases, I have dropped the word *Sefer* ("Book of") when it appears at the beginning of Hebrew titles because it has little significance and distracts from the true title. In a few cases, however, the word is an essential part of the title (e.g., *Sefer ha-middot*). It is worth noting that Mendel Lefin's *Sefer Mase`ot ha-yam* (1818) and Joseph Perl's *Sefer Megale temirin* (1819) include this word in order to foster the illusion that they are traditional books.

A Note on German, Hebrew, and Yiddish Quotations

Throughout this book, except where otherwise noted, I quote German, Hebrew, and Yiddish passages as they were originally printed in the first edition of the works under discussion. Because orthography was fluid and inconsistent in the eighteenth and nineteenth centuries, however, this approach may create the impression of typographical errors. Segev Amossi, Erella Brown-Sofer, Ora Wiskind-Elper, Rebecca Wolpe, and I have proofread all passages numerous times in an effort to ensure that the quirks of spelling reflect the original source and not current misprints. A particularly glaring instance is Joachim Heinrich Campe's original decision in 1781 to publish his book about Columbus under the title *Die Entdekkung von Amerika*. In that case, I have opted to refer to the book under its usual appellation since 1782, *Die Entdeckung von Amerika*. All translations of passages quoted from German, Hebrew, and Yiddish are my own, except where otherwise noted.

Preface

Wandering for millennia through space and language, Jews have been travelers in translation. Ancient Jewish communities moved from Hebrew to Aramaic and Greek, and while Hebrew remained the sacred and literary language, modern Jewish culture also emerged in translation. From the Middle Ages to the nineteenth century, most central and eastern European Jews spoke Yiddish as they migrated among German, Polish, and Russian speakers. Influenced by the local languages, an avant-garde group of educated Jews remade Hebrew as they entered the modern world, discovering new vistas and imprinting novel forms onto Hebrew literature.

Following the destruction of the Second Temple in Jerusalem in 70 CE, Jews began their long wanderings in exile. Dispersed throughout the world, for centuries Jewish pilgrims returned to Palestine and were buried on the Mount of Olives. These pilgrimages fired the imagination of many Diaspora Jews, who engaged in far-flung trade, fled persecution by land or sea, and continued to long for Zion. In spite of their tendency to be bookish and estranged from nature, traditionally educated Ashkenazic Jewish men were often attracted and captivated by sea travel. For centuries, the Land of Israel was a prime destination, both real and imagined.

As Jews entered the modern period in Germany and eastern Europe, Hebrew travelogues became an increasingly important genre that conveyed new values. Around 1800, European Hebrew authors expanded horizons by writing and translating narratives of wide-ranging world travel. Accounts of sea voyages marked a turning point in Hebrew literature and modern Jewish identity. Translations of Joachim Heinrich Campe's book *The Discovery of America* were especially popular, preparing the way for mass immigration to *di goldene medine*, the Golden Land of the New World.

This collective history of travel is also part of my family history. My ancestors traveled to the United States in the century before I was born, and I grew up on these shores, watching the tides rise and fall in a harbor of Long Island Sound. The influence ran deep: in those waters we sailed, paddled canoes, explored desolate islands, watched yachts and speedboats beyond the breakwater. My family experienced hurricane tides that covered the yard, filled our basement, and flooded the furnace. These adventures and crises were some of the most exciting events of my childhood.

One summer I sailed my father's catamaran alone when a black flag was flying in the harbor—and came face to face with the power of nature when the upper pontoon lifted so high out of the water that the boat capsized. After my glasses fell off and sank, I encountered adversity half-blind, sitting on the twin hulls of the overturned boat and waiting to be rescued. Decades later, this book became a way to revisit my childhood by exploring Jewish literature of sea travel, shipwreck, and survival. Since then, although my lenses have thickened, my childish enthusiasm remains. When I had almost completed revisions of this manuscript, I was caught in another storm—on Skaneateles Lake in central New York, surrounded by thunder, lightning, and sheets of rain—but by then I knew that shipwreck is always the best part of sea narratives.

This journey in literary history is also a quest for what it means to be (a Jew) in the modern world. Looking at early-modern Jewish life, we recognize later patterns of immigration and acculturation among other ethnic groups. Persecuted and expelled, Jews involuntarily tested the waters for those who migrated later. Other immigrant groups, if they survive their perilous sea journeys, still encounter the consequences of exile and immigration that have characterized Jewish life and literature for two millennia.

Growing up in the greater New York City area, I never felt that I was living in exile from the Land of Israel. More than half of our neighbors were Jewish, and in that miniature shtetl I was oblivious to any residual anti-Semitism. And yet, despite our thorough assimilation, some kind of alienation from American culture eventually took me abroad. I lived and traveled in Europe, where I learned more about our roots. During the past two decades, I have traveled to connect the texts I study to my ancestors' real-world geography.

In search of remnants of history, I traveled back in time—to the Rhineland, a center of Jewish life during the Middle Ages. My grandmother's ancestors lived in Beerfelden, in the Odenwald, during the period of the wonder-working Ba`al Shem of Michelstadt (1768–1847). One day, after I had sifted through the records of the Moses family's births, deaths, and marriages, an archivist in the Beerfelden Town Hall threw open his window curtain and pointed to the site where they had lived, House 122. Most of the Jews in Beerfelden were horse and cattle traders. In 1855, the young Wolf Moses and his family sailed across the Atlantic and settled in Baltimore, where they sold horses to several American presidents. His granddaughter was my grandmother, Evelyn Gutman Frieden. When I visited the Jewish regional cemetery in Michelstadt with my father, he said, with the sly irony of a scientist, "Some of our DNA is in there!"

From Rügen, Germany, I took a ferry across the Baltic Sea to Klaipeda (near former Prussian Königsberg) and then drove to Kvatki, Lithuania, which the locals call "Kvetkai." In that predominantly Jewish shtetl, Avraham (Milner) Żyw raised nine sons and one daughter. Around 1908, my grandfather Sender Żyw (later Alexander Frieden) went on a hunger strike in Kvatki when he was a schoolboy, refusing to continue Hebrew and Bible lessons in the local one-room heder and demanding to study in a real school. His parents sent him to receive a secular education in Warsaw, where he lived with his favorite brother, Jakob, and his wife (figure 1). After the family—except for the ill-fated Jakob Żyw and Leonie—moved to the United States (under the name Frieden), Alexander finished high school and studied at the University of Virginia. By the time he received a PhD in chemistry at Columbia University, he had transformed himself from an Orthodox shtetl boy into a secular American scientist. He was proud to have squelched his foreign accent, and he refused to speak the Yiddish, Hebrew, Russian, and Polish he knew from childhood.

I returned to see Kvatki in 1995, but not to reclaim those shtetl roots. In that still impoverished town, consisting of little more than a dozen wooden houses near a slow-moving stream, I understood why my

Fig. 1. Leonie and Jakob Żyw in Warsaw, ca. 1930. Courtesy of their grandson, Michael Żyw.

grandfather had so desperately wanted to leave.[1] And yet once assimilation had been achieved in America, what was the next step?

In Vienna, Budapest, and Odessa, there were traces of our forebears on my mother's side—some of whom had left Austro-Hungary around 1860 and others had fled Russia in about 1882. My most illustrious ancestor, Solomon Mandelkern (1846–1902), came from the small town Mlynov, near Lvov. He studied Semitic languages in St. Petersburg, lived in Odessa, and taught Oriental languages in Leipzig. In 1875, he published a three-volume history of Russia, and later he wrote Hebrew poetry in the outmoded maskilic mode, sometimes translating from Byron or Heine. In 1896, he published a seminal concordance to the Hebrew Bible, which I used while writing this book.

Solomon's philological bent resurfaced in my passion for words, concordances, and literature. At some point, I took this identification beyond texts and decided to relive some part of what my ancestors were. Being American in the 1980s seemed too bland, lacking in cultural depth, and so I learned to hear and to help my students hear the eloquent voices of Jewish writers.[2]

I did not try to turn back the clock. Nevertheless, my wife and I reconstructed a simulacrum of European Jewish family life in Syracuse, New York.[3] I have enjoyed doing research in Hebrew and Yiddish, living in Israel, reading and teaching Judaic literature, playing Klezmer clarinet and performing at weddings, holding Passover Seders, and building a sukkah in the backyard for family and friends. After decades of life and learning, I feel that I have become who I am or, rather, who I chose to be: my knowledge and travels have enabled me to reclaim my European Jewish affinities. Like the heroine of the film *Woman in Gold* (Simon Curtis, 2015), who reclaims Jewish art looted by the Nazis, I have revived masterpieces of European Jewish literary culture that had disappeared from view.

Literary scholars have sometimes tried to separate literary meaning from mundane reality and world geography. Literature can offer an escape because fiction creates an alternate reality, which is part of its power and charm. Formalism, New Criticism, and Structuralism contributed a deep understanding of literary form, but we should not be content to immerse ourselves in textuality and the play of signifiers. Without turning to New Historicism, we need to change how we understand literary studies. Discipline is important, and we can count on the historians to go on writing and rewriting history without us; however, literary history is another discipline, told for different reasons and with distinctive goals.

I propose a new approach, textual referentialism: an orientation toward texts that emphasizes the interrelationship between literariness and world reference. Modernist abstraction, pure poetry, and verbal fireworks still have the power to fascinate and create a virtual reality in our imaginations. But the time has come to travel beyond the text because in some contexts and for very good reasons we want to reunite them with real sites in the world. Hence, travel narratives could become the flagship genre for this return to referentiality. Leaving aside fantastical travels, we can focus on narratives that represent human travel to actual places. Distinct from chronicles, memoirs, or diaries, which typically focus on events and people, travelogues describe places. This book takes a fresh look at travel narratives—especially German, Hebrew, and Yiddish sea narratives—and focuses on some extraordinarily innovative prose written early in the nineteenth century.

When Yiddish studies were reawakening in the United States in the 1970s and 1980s, it was still virtually impossible to visit most of the sites of Yiddish literature in eastern Europe. As a result, my peers and I had to imagine Jewish life in the city, in the shtetl, and on the road, with Yiddish films from the 1930s providing real and staged scenes that seemed to give a foothold for American Jews who did not know the language or the geography. Like Jews described by a character in I. L. Peretz's story "The Dead City," we lived our eastern Europe "without geography."[4]

A decade ago, in my advanced seminar on parody and allegory, students sometimes wondered what these literary forms have in common. I showed that parodies and allegories embody a radical textualism: they are texts that refer primarily to other texts. Literary parodies usually refer to prior texts, in contrast to satires, which refer to people and situations in the world around us. Religious allegories refer back to sacred texts while referring beyond the material world to a "higher" order of spiritual meaning. I still believe all this to be true but have supplemented my intertextual focus with referentialism. Travel narratives, along with real travel, may help us reunite texts and their world references. My effort to reclaim literary geography has inspired me to incorporate historical maps in this study of sea tales.

When people ask how long it took me to write this book, I usually answer that it is based on a decade of research. Nevertheless, the underlying framework in literary theory brings together my studies and scholarship over several decades. In New Haven, Chicago, and Berlin, I was in the right place at the right time—fortunate to be educated by leading scholars of literature and philosophy. Most influential to my thinking have been Harold Bloom, Wayne Booth, Leslie Brisman, Paul de Man, Peter Demetz, Jacques Derrida, Shoshana Felman, Geoffrey Hartman, J. Hillis Miller, Dan Miron, Fred Oscanyan, Paul Ricoeur, Gershon Shaked, Khone Shmeruk, Michael Theunissen, and Ernst Tugendhat. I am grateful for the generous support of graduate and postdoctoral fellowships at Yale University, the University of Chicago, the Hebrew University of Jersualem, and the Freie Universität Berlin. I thank Yale University for several doctoral fellowships, the University of Chicago for a Special Humanities Fellowship, and the German Academic Exchange for supporting two years of study in Freiburg and Berlin. Postdoctoral studies were generously funded by the Lady Davis Trust, Yad Hanadiv, Jim Ponet and the Yale Hillel Foundation, the YIVO Institute for Jewish Research (now at the Center for Jewish History), the American Council of Learned Societies, the Memorial Foundation for Jewish Culture, the National Endowment for the Humanities, the Oxford Centre for Postgraduate Hebrew Studies, and the Alexander von Humboldt Foundation.

It gives me pleasure to thank several other fellowships and institutions that supported my research over the past dozen years: a Harry Starr Fellowship at the Center for Jewish Studies, Harvard University, 2003–4; a Lady Davis Visiting Professorship in Hebrew and Comparative Literature at the Hebrew University of Jerusalem, 2007–8; and a Faculty Fellowship at the Humanities Center, Syracuse University, spring 2013.

I also wish to express my gratitude to the journals and essay collections that have permitted me to print revisions of sections of articles that first appeared in their pages, especially *AJS Review: The Journal of the Association for Jewish Studies* (2005 and 2009). I also explored some of the ideas expressed here in *Poetics Today* (2014–15), *Dappim le-mehkar be-sifrut* (2006), *Studia Rosenthaliana* (2007–8), and two essay collections: *Leket: Jiddistik heute | Yiddish Studies Today | yidishe shtudyes haynt* (2012) and *Arguing the Modern Jewish Canon: Essays on Literature and Culture in Honor of Ruth R. Wisse* (2008). Completion of the Yiddish component of this research project will have to await a future book.

Among many colleagues who helped to make this book possible, Naomi Seidman virtually took the journey with me in conversations by Skype. Erella Brown assisted me by reviewing my translations of Hebrew passages. Rebecca Wolpe, who audited my seminar in Jerusalem in 2008 and wrote an excellent dissertation on Hebrew and Yiddish sea narratives, shared her expertise with me and checked the completed manuscript, helping me acknowledge the many debts to her research and that of other scholars. Chana Kronfeld and her many talented former students at the University of California, Berkeley, encouraged me to believe that Hebrew literary studies has a future alongside Yiddish literary studies. Edward Mooney's intelligent remarks gave encouragement and inspiration during late stages of revision. David Ruderman critiqued my preface and introduction, helping me to strengthen the presentation. David Ehrlich spoke with me in Hebrew about the twenty-first century, and Dovid Katz spoke with me in Yiddish about the nineteenth century. My friends and colleagues Fred Beiser, Brooks Haxton, Steven Kepnes, Marc Safran, and Harvey Teres helped to keep my brain working through the long Syracuse winters.

Robert Alter's books on modern Hebrew literature, Nancy Sinkoff's work on Mendel Lefin, and Ghil`ad Zuckermann's studies of Hebrew and Israeli linguistics paved the way for my own contributions. During the course of this journey, Hannan Hever joined me, following in my wake in the pursuit of Hebrew sea narratives. Jonatan Meir lent his astute eye to some preliminary drafts. Marion Aptroot worked with me on the mysterious *Oniya so`ara*. I also thank all of my colleagues who have commented on pertinent conference papers that I have given over the past decade. My bibliography lists dozens of other scholars whose writings preceded mine and charted a course for me to follow. Matthew Kudelka and Ora Wiskind-Elper offered editorial suggestions on the nearly completed manuscript. Kerry Wallach and Eric Berlin made trenchant comments on early drafts of the introduction. Yonat Klein assisted me by typing the text of Mendel Lefin's *Mase`ot ha-yam* and by analyzing the history of Hebrew nautical terms based on data we culled from the Bar Ilan Judaic Library, from DBS (*Ha-Taklitor ha-Torani* [The Computerized Torah Library]), and from Google Books. Veronica Maidel helped with questions of author attribution, using computer analysis of Hebrew texts. Joseph Stoll assisted me by transforming two Google Books Ngram Viewer graphs from color to black and white for use in my conclusion. This book has been enhanced also by the addition of maps he helped me modify to include the travel routes discussed in these chapters.

Deborah Manion, like Jennika Baines before her, has been an outstanding acquisitions editor for the Syracuse University Press series Judaic Traditions in Literature, Music, and Art. She was particularly helpful during the final stage of revision, when I was completing the manuscript and working with Joseph Stoll to add and modify historical maps.

Finally, completing the research required for this book would not have been possible without the professional assistance of many librarians—especially those who fill interlibrary loan and scanning requests—at the Syracuse University Library, the YIVO Library at the Center for Jewish History, the British Library, the Bodleian Library, the University of Munich Library, the Bavarian State Library, and the National Library of Israel. Tracking down rare Hebrew travel narratives sometimes resembles detective work, although digital scans available online in Google Books are making this process easier. As I was checking the copyedited manuscript of this book, for example, I discovered a formerly unknown complete copy of Mendel Lefin's *Mase'ot ha-yam* (1818; see chapter 7, note 2).

The images included in these pages have been made available by and are being reprinted with permission from the British Library, the Tate Museum, the New York Public Library, the Map Collection at Yale University Library, and the National Library of Israel.

At the final phase of copyediting and proofreading, Susan Wright unexpectedly and unselfishly stepped forward to join me on this journey. She also helped me navigate the sea of virtual reality by discovering the available domain travelsintranslation.org and by helping me populate this website with texts and images that accompany the chapters of this book.

I owe the profoundest debt to my children for their inspiration. For figurative in-house editing, I thank my mother, Nancy Mandelker Frieden, and my brothers, Jeffry A. Frieden and Thomas R. Frieden, who are among the best friends and readers I have ever known.

I hope that the coming generation, including my children, Tal and Maya, will understand why this literary and geographical journey is important to our collective future. May every generation have the good fortune to make a voyage to Jerusalem and, realizing that the Temple Mount is not the navel of the world, also travel beyond Zion.

TRAVELS IN TRANSLATION

Introduction

Hebrew tales of far-flung sea adventure began to appear during the Jewish Enlightenment (Haskala), supplementing traditional narratives of pilgrimage to the Holy Land. In contrast to premodern Jews, who often viewed the Land of Israel as the center of the world and dreamed of going there, Jews of the Enlightenment (*maskilim*) broadened their horizons by reading and writing about travels far beyond Zion. Pilgrimage narratives since the Middle Ages expressed a devotion to the scriptural Zion before there was political Zionism, whereas the new adventure stories challenged sacred geography and may have encouraged the mass migration of Jews to the New World.

This book traces the emergence of modern Hebrew literature from 1780 to 1825, when Jews gradually moved beyond their traditional, Torah- and Zion-centered worldviews. Ashkenazic Jewry had undergone a collective trauma during the Chmielnitzky massacres of 1648; Jewish communities had been splintered by the messianic claims of Shabbetai Tzvi (1626–76) and Jacob Frank (1726–91); and the Ba`al Shem Tov and his hasidic followers had challenged the authority of mainstream rabbinic Judaism. Following these unsettling developments, as European Jews began to modernize and secularize during the Jewish Enlightenment, their perspective began to shift. Writing in Hebrew, some authors changed their focus from spiritual pilgrimage to worldly travel and affirmed their Diaspora identities. Enlightened Jews in Berlin and their followers shattered boundaries, diverging from pilgrimage traditions and appropriating—mostly from German sources—stories of travel to America, the Indian Ocean, the Pacific, and the Arctic. Yet many of these Hebrew translators continued to rely on scriptural traditions, inserting quotations from the Hebrew Bible instead of translating more literally from their German sources.

Jews have often seen themselves as diasporic, living in exile from the presumed homeland—and influenced by ancient and medieval sources, they sometimes considered Zion the center of the world. (The precise geographic locus of this lost "Zion" has never been definitively mapped, however, and its meaning in the Hebrew Bible is ambiguous.) There were exceptions to the Zion-centered norm, but travelers such as Benjamin of Tudela—who traveled far beyond the Holy Land to explore western Asia—and some Italian Jewish merchants, who voyaged across the Mediterranean, only underscore the rule. One persistent dream of a landlocked, persecuted, wandering people was to board ships and make a pilgrimage to the Land of Israel.

The Jewish literary imagination took the Torah as the blueprint of the world or mapped the Torah onto the world: pilgrims to Zion sought out sacred places and tombs using the Bible and Talmud as their travel guides. For hasidic Jews who traveled to the Land of Israel, the journey became a spiritual ascent. The earthly Zion or "Jerusalem Below," alluding to a "Jerusalem Above," brought the shadow of a higher reality or sacred space into play, which seemed to justify subjecting oneself to the dangers of sea travel. One of the most remarkable pilgrimages of this kind was Nahman of Bratslav's journey in 1798–99, as narrated in a detailed account published by Nathan Sternharz in 1815. Then in 1822 Sternharz followed in the Rebbe's footsteps with his own pilgrimage to the Land of Israel, which he documented in a new Hebrew narrative that was published half a century later. The style of Sternharz's Hebrew was rabbinic, Mishnaic, and at the same time influenced by Yiddish.

Jewish writers' expanding worldview found expression in the modernization of Hebrew, and their modernizing Hebrew in turn fostered a broader view of the world. As Jews moved away from traditional education, they started to break away from the Zion-centered world and simultaneously to reject rabbinic Hebrew writing. Hence, it is possible to trace the rise of modern Hebrew literature in tandem with the shift from narratives of pilgrimage to narratives of secular travel.

The German Jewish Moses Mendelsohn-Frankfurt (1782–1861; no relation to the renowned Moses Mendelssohn of Berlin) turned away from narratives of sacred pilgrimage in 1807. Translating from a popular German source, he launched a new genre of travel narrative in Hebrew. This nascent genre was intended to teach the reader history and geography as well as openness to other peoples of the world. From a specifically literary perspective, Mendelsohn-Frankfurt began to unfetter Hebrew style from the neobiblical limitations imposed on it by the Haskala. Several other Hebrew authors followed his example in eastern Europe, and Mendel Lefin reached new heights by using a rich vocabulary drawn from various historical phases of Hebrew.[1]

Devotion to sacred texts has been both a strength and a weakness in Jewish cultural history. Commentaries, midrashic retellings, and legalistic arguments ensured the continuity of textual traditions, yet this recycling of ancient texts may have hindered the development of an original literature in response to everyday life. If the Torah was the blueprint of the world, what need was there to assert originality or explore distant lands? For almost two millennia, although Hebrew was no longer a spoken language, Hebrew writers continually referred to classical Hebrew texts, emphasizing their ongoing and evolving relationship to the Hebrew Bible and the Talmud. This commitment to the past complicated these Hebrew writers' efforts to produce a modern literature. Dominant textual sources so influenced perceptions that they limited writers' capacity to see reality in new ways; it was difficult to convey immediate perceptions. Traditionally educated Jews tended to interpret experiences in relation to familiar, sacred texts; quotations from and allusions to these texts often took precedence over original expressions.[2]

Writing and translating sea narratives played a significant role in early-modern Hebrew literature because these tasks required a concreteness—an empirical, naturalistic approach—that was at odds with the textual focus that typified rabbinic culture. Instead of making fresh observations, Hebrew authors frequently fell back on clichés from the Book of Jonah, such as "the boat was on the verge of breaking up" (*ha-oniya ḥishva lehishaver*). This was especially the case among the early *maskilim*, who consciously strove to emulate biblical Hebrew. For different reasons, hasidic authors such as Sternharz also described sea journeys in relation to scriptural sources, often with Psalm 107 as a central reference point. For these writers, the spiritual meaning of the journey outweighed its tangible details.

Translated sea narratives played an important role in early-modern Hebrew writing, in part because the challenges posed by translation exerted pressure on authors to develop concrete language. In order to express the specificity of the events described in prior travel accounts, they had to invent new descriptive language in Hebrew. Thus, a few enlightened writers strove for more vivid, immediate, and original expressions, overcoming their tendency to introduce biblical phrases and quotations at every turn. In this manner, they anticipated the later accomplishments associated with the "revival" of Hebrew at the end of the nineteenth century.

When we compare hasidic accounts of pilgrimage to Zion to travel narratives translated by the enlightened Hebrew authors in Germany, Galicia, and Russia, we notice a literary and cultural parting of ways. Hasidim described their pilgrimages in scriptural and Mishnaic Hebrew, with a Yiddish subtext, and often expressed their Zion-centered worldview. In contrast, maskilic writers began to develop a new kind of Hebrew that described the modern world at a distance from rabbinic sources. Their subtext was German, and they no longer placed the Talmud and Land of Israel at the center. At odds with traditional texts, some enlightened Jews began publishing European travel narratives and translating non-Jewish travel narratives. Travel accounts by traditional and secular Jewish authors thus exposed a clash of worldviews. From hasidim to *maskilim*, from Sternharz to Lefin, these diverse and talented authors tried to reach the widening circle of Jewish readers.

As Hebrew writers reshaped Jewish literature, they attempted to influence their readers. New literary forms arose within the hasidic movement and the Jewish Enlightenment. These forms energized the Hebrew literary tradition, and the resulting battle of books made a modern literature possible. At the same time, as the opponents tried to vanquish one another, their conflict fostered the creation of an original literary culture.

The antagonists, without setting out to do so, fashioned a new narrative literature that became increasingly capable of representing everyday life in Hebrew. Even more remarkably, they re-created Hebrew as a language that sounded spontaneous and spoken after centuries when it had been primarily textual and ritual. The interdependence of Hebrew and Yiddish enhanced these languages, and both were enriched by German, French, Polish, and Russian. Hasidic authors commonly worked in a Yiddish-speaking context, whereas authors associated with the Enlightenment often translated from German. Whereas the hasidim reached the masses by writing in simple Hebrew and accessible Yiddish, the *maskilim* attempted to exalt Jewish literature by emulating the European culture they so admired. One author who emerged victorious from this fray was Mendel Lefin (1749–1826), who was influenced by the Berlin authors but chose to write accessible Hebrew and Yiddish. This book concludes with a chapter about Lefin's synthesis, which may be found in his translations from German into Hebrew and from Hebrew into Yiddish.

Travel, Translation, and Cultural Transfer

Writers in Germany, Austrian Galicia, and Russian Ukraine charted a world of Hebrew and Yiddish translations that changed Jewish history, historiography, and literature. In their efforts to educate Jewish readers, several translators remade the genre of the travel narrative and contributed to the rise of modern Jewish literature.

Until about 1800, Jewish geography centered on the Land of Israel—the despoiled homeland of the Jews' ancient forbears, according to the accepted canonical narratives. Exalted by diasporic Jewish writers in medieval psalms, poems, and prayers, Zion inspired pilgrimages and dreams of redemption. Premodern Jewish communities around the world reaffirmed their bond to the Land of Israel in prayers and at the annual Passover Seder.

Most notable early Jewish travel narratives were written in Hebrew: the narratives by Benjamin of Tudela (dating from about 1173), Ovadia of Bertinoro (who sailed the Mediterranean in 1486–88), and Shmuel Romanelli (who traveled in 1787–90 and published a book about his travels in 1792). Other travel stories, such as the fantastical Hebrew "Tale of a

Jerusalemite," sometimes ascribed to Maimonides's son Abraham (1186–1237), also exist in later Arabic and Yiddish versions. During the medieval and Renaissance periods, Hebrew remained the primary language of Jewish literacy, although Jewish communities in different regions read and spoke Aramaic (or Judeo-Aramaic), Arabic (or Judeo-Arabic), Ladino (Judeo-Spanish or Judezmo), Persian (or Judeo-Persian), or Yiddish. The genre of the travelogue was dominated by pilgrimage accounts in Hebrew, yet descriptions of travel began to emerge in other languages as well. Moreover, the spoken vernaculars influenced how Hebrew was written.

Jewish travel narratives have been intertwined with a history of exile, migration, and immigration. Modern Jewish migration has its roots in the late eighteenth century, when western European Jews began to embrace a worldview that no longer revolved around the Land of Israel. Following Moses Mendelssohn (1729–86) and his disciples, a new cohort of Jewish writers broke with tradition by urging Jews to learn formerly unfamiliar subjects. As secular education and modernization reached more Jewish Europeans in the nineteenth century, the Jews' geographical horizons widened as well. Palestine under the Ottoman Turks remained a pilgrimage destination for pious Jews, but Jewish travel narratives moved beyond the ancient longing for Zion. By 1880, more than one hundred thousand German Jews had migrated to the United States, and in the subsequent four decades almost two million Jews from eastern Europe traveled to "the Golden Land."[3]

In 1782, Naftali Hirsh Wessely—a leader of the Berlin Jewish Enlightenment—argued vehemently that Jews should learn history, geography, ethnography, mathematics, and other secular subjects.[4] He specifically recommended reading travel books, probably alluding to works such as Joachim Heinrich Campe's *Die Entdeckung von Amerika* (The Discovery of America), which had recently become a best seller in German.[5] Wessely also praised the study of biblical Hebrew grammar, which would enable Jews to write "pure" Hebrew. Although many traditional communities rejected Wessely's arguments, some Hebrew writers did respond by translating travel literature into Hebrew. Their translations became part of a broad project of "modernization via translation," which Yaacov Shavit describes as "an intensive, ongoing attempt at transfer and adaptation, to enable the new Hebrew reader to find the knowledge he or she needed about the 'world around them' and its culture, through Hebrew."[6]

Many enlightened Jewish writers in Berlin, influenced by German classicists who idealized the Greeks, returned to the biblical prophets for inspiration; they opposed centuries of linguistic evolution in rabbinic and literary circles. Spoken Hebrew had waned in Palestine at the start of the Common Era, supplanted mainly by Aramaic and Greek. After the period of the Mishna (ca. 200 CE), rabbinic Hebrew continued to evolve in writing, though not in spontaneous speech. Alongside Aramaic, it was used by educated men for prayer, study, poetry, correspondence, and legal decisions. The religious associations of Hebrew were so prominent that the Hebrew used by the rabbis, often incorporating Aramaic from the Talmud, was referred to as *leshon ha-kodesh*, the Holy Language (or "language of sanctity"). Many early Enlightenment Jews had learned the Talmud in traditional yeshivas, but they generally avoided Aramaic and scorned the long history of rabbinic Hebrew, viewing it as a degradation of the best or "purest" biblical Hebrew. Moreover, many educated Jews rejected vernacular Yiddish as a barbaric jargon unsuited to serious literature and an obstacle to modernization.

After 1807, a radically new travel literature arose in Hebrew. Under the star of the Berlin Enlightenment, authors such as Moses Mendelsohn-Frankfurt and Mendel Lefin published books that charted a new literary route through the world and in European history. Without being explorers or seafarers themselves, they took up the western European fascination with travel. A century or more after narratives of sea travel became popular in Dutch, French, German, and English, Jewish authors imported the genre into Hebrew (and later Yiddish). The "plain style" of captains' accounts was one characteristic that challenged Hebrew translators to develop new resources.[7]

Literary history shows how original works of travel literature have creatively transformed preexisting forms. When Daniel Defoe published *Robinson Crusoe* in 1719, he alluded to past narratives about sea travels and shipwrecks and helped inaugurate a literary era with roots in earlier models. Although European ship captains and their ghostwriters had been publishing travelogues in several languages for centuries, Defoe made an original contribution with his fictionalized prose narrative that centered on an individual's survival, far from civilization, following shipwreck. Defoe's novel was published in hundreds of editions and in dozens of languages, spawning imitations, adaptations, and even philosophical worldviews.[8]

The nineteenth century saw at least seven Hebrew and Yiddish versions of *Robinson Crusoe*, some of them adapted from J. H. Campe's adaptation, *Robinson der Jüngere* (*Robinson the Younger*, 1779). Contrary to expectations, Jewish travel writers achieved both popularity and originality when they adapted the travel genre to their needs and goals in Hebrew and Yiddish. Only a handful of the modern Jewish authors discussed here—such as Isaac Euchel and Shmuel Romanelli—published accounts based on their own journeys. More often, the new Jewish writers were armchair travelers who adapted narratives from other languages. They were travelers in translation.

Readers sometimes assume that translations lack originality. Yet the resulting texts can be highly original and significant in their own right. Obvious examples include many of the time-honored translations of the Hebrew Bible—for example, into Greek, Latin, German, and English. Other classic works such as Shakespeare's plays were the source of groundbreaking translations into several languages. Some literary historians have argued that Charles Baudelaire's French translations of Edgar Allan Poe's stories surpassed the originals and influenced the subsequent advance of French short fiction.

At an early stage of literary development, exemplified in modern Hebrew after 1800, translation often plays a decisive role. Itamar Even-Zohar explains this phenomenon in general terms, writing that "in such a state when new literary models are emerging, translation is likely to become one of the means of elaborating the new repertoire."[9] In this case, the new repertoire included narratives of sea travel, carried over from German. According to Even-Zohar's analysis of translation in literary history, "through the foreign works, features (both principles and elements) are introduced into the home literature which did not exist there before." Sea narratives illustrate his theory: they showed the way to a new naturalism and at the same time explored new "compositional patterns and techniques."[10] The period around 1800 was a turning point, a time when modern Hebrew writing was in the process of redefining itself in relation to German, Yiddish, and rabbinic culture.

George Steiner has written that from one perspective "the translator invades, extracts, and brings home."[11] With reference to travel narratives, this metaphorical language of mining is especially suggestive: in the same way that the explorer may invade, extract, and bring home goods from a foreign land, so a pioneering translator may bring home literary techniques from a foreign language. And so it was when Hebrew (and Yiddish) writers adapted travel narratives from German. Steiner's image is especially apt in connection with Columbus's obsessive search for gold, as described in Campe's German narrative, which was repeatedly translated into Hebrew and Yiddish.

Naomi Seidman and Seth Wolitz have shown how a translation can sometimes become a "second original" that surpasses the source.[12] Some readers have claimed, for instance, that Isaac Bashevis Singer improved his Yiddish stories when working with translators on English versions. Elie Wiesel transformed his Yiddish account of his Holocaust experiences into the more effective French autobiographical novel *La nuit* (*Night*, 1958).[13]

Hasidic authors also made unparalleled advances in literary narrative, especially in their use of oral-style language and folk motifs. Hebrew and Yiddish authors—compilers, scribes, and translators—disseminated *Shivḥei ha-Besht* (*In Praise of the Baal Shem Tov*, 1814–15). Within three years of the publication of these hagiographic stories about the founder of Hasidism, several Hebrew reprints and three different Yiddish translations were printed. Shortly after *Shivḥei ha-Besht* appeared, Nathan Sternharz of Nemirov (1780–1844) published a groundbreaking Hebrew/Yiddish edition of Rabbi Nahman's *Sippurei ma'asiyot* (*Tales*, 1815), bound together with his Hebrew account of Nahman's journey to the Land of Israel in 1798–99. These popular narratives have withstood the test of time in spite of efforts by envious rivals of the hasidim to suppress and lampoon them.[14]

Opponents of the hasidim were another essential source of innovation: by satirizing and parodying the hasidim and their writings, they helped import folk Hebrew into the literary mainstream. The sharp ideological rift between hasidim and their antagonists led nonhasidic Hebraists to be skeptical of hasidic writings. After Joseph Perl (1773–1839) mocked hasidic circles, it became commonplace to say that their Hebrew was riddled with errors and thus "barbaric." Yet the ultimate victors were, against all odds, the hasidim. Most of Perl's highly educated friends, who wrote poetry in the ornate, neobiblical style called *melitza*, have been forgotten. And although Perl's intent was satiric, his greatest literary success came when he emulated hasidic writing. Today's modern Hebrew readers—most of them living in Israel—find it almost impossible to read the high *melitza* mode espoused by the Enlightenment Hebraists. In contrast, hasidic sources have over the past two centuries garnered an increasing number of readers and devotees around the world. By working from Yiddish, the hasidim anticipated the creation of a modern Hebrew vernacular.

A central problem for modern Hebrew writers was how to break through the stylistic limitations that had been established by Enlightenment literati. Perl escaped their excessive reliance on biblical quotations through his parodies of hasidic writing.[15] This book contends that translation in connection with travel narratives was another essential literary strategy used by *maskilim* such as Mendel Lefin.[16]

Rewriting Hebrew Literary History

Hebrew writers faced an arduous task in adapting to new literary fashions during the nineteenth century. The high literary style, widely preferred in the eighteenth century, became outmoded early in the nineteenth. At a time when European romanticism was turning toward everyday lives and vernacular speech, the biblical Hebrew of the prophets no longer served the needs of prose authors.

Mendel Lefin, associated with the "moderate Haskala" in Galicia, led the development of a more accessible Hebrew literature. He was an early proponent of using Mishnaic Hebrew, expanding stylistic options beyond the biblical Hebrew of the prophets.[17] His goal was to write clear, simple Hebrew that could be understood by a wide readership. His works thus questioned the dominant position of *melitza*, the quasi-biblical Hebrew of the Berlin Haskala. Lefin's discursive books—*Refu'at ha-'am* (Healing for the People, 1789/1794) and *Ḥeshbon ha-nefesh* (Moral Accounting,

1808)—moved in this direction, and his translation *Mase`ot ha-yam* (Sea Voyages, 1818) showed how effective his postbiblical style could be in narrative literature. Translation played an essential role in Lefin's contribution: translating from German exerted a pressure to match in Hebrew the effects that were possible in a culturally dominant, living language.

The modernization of Hebrew occurred in several phases. First, the Berlin writers tried to limit the influence of rabbinic (and hasidic) writing by favoring biblical Hebrew. Second, a few notable followers of the Berlin Haskala loosened their leaders' narrow, puristic demands. Hasidic writing intervened, competing for readers and provoking responses from the *maskilim*. In 1818, Lefin brought together the traditions of biblical and rabbinic writing in a new synthesis. This book follows an arc that culminates with Mendel Lefin's translated sea voyages, in which he demonstrated that modern Hebrew literature could be written by translating from German sources and drawing upon different historical layers of Hebrew. At the same time, he retained many traditional Jewish ideas, such as the belief in Divine Providence.[18]

The rise of modern Hebrew travel writing contributed to a growing freedom from biblical models and fostered graphic descriptions instead of pilgrimage clichés, fantasies, allegories, and parables. Where the hasidic pilgrim found spiritual meaning in every storm at sea, secularizing writers worked toward more immediate representations of the everyday world. As Rebecca Wolpe commented to me, the *maskilim* were "trying to show that all natural phenomena can be explained by science and that they are not all omens and signs."[19]

Moshe Pelli ends an essay on Enlightenment Jewish travelogues with an astute comment on the prominent literary-historical role of travel writing: "In its literary devices, its story development, characterization, the portrayal of the protagonist, and many other literary traits, Hebrew travel literature may be said to have paved the way for the development of the Hebrew novel, as is the case in European literature." Pelli then comments that "Romanelli's travel to an Arab land may be construed as a metaphor of a *maskil*'s voyage to, and his exposure of, the unenlightened segment of the Jewish people, not only in Morocco, but in other places closer to home."[20] This metaphorical resonance may explain why Jewish readers were so drawn to travel narratives involving encounters with foreign cultures. Nancy Sinkoff follows Pelli and writes that Mendel Lefin "appears to be comparing the 'noble savages' with east European Jewry and the British and their world with Western, non-Jewish culture."[21] Many of the meetings with indigenous people could, therefore, represent some of the elite authors' dealings with the less-educated members of Jewish society. Sinkoff adds that "by the second decade of the nineteenth century, the image of the east European Jew as culturally backward was already well on its way to becoming an immutable stereotype among Germans, German Jews, and east European Jewish maskilim who moved in German cultural circles."[22]

Europeans' ambivalence toward indigenous people—whom they perceived variously in different contexts as "noble savages" or ignorant barbarians—resembles enlightened Jews' ambivalence toward uneducated Jews. Moreover, when the European conquerors and colonizers mistreated the natives, Jewish readers in czarist Russia could easily identify with the victims. In some respects, the Jews of Russia were a disenfranchised, colonized people who saw their plight reflected in the distant lands they discovered in Hebrew and Yiddish translations. Travels in translation were, for all of these reasons, central to the rise of early-modern Jewish literature.

This book tells a story, in three movements, about the creation of secular literature in Hebrew. We begin with *premodern* and *hasidic accounts of pilgrimage*. These texts express the traditional, Zion-centered worldview. As an extraordinary outgrowth of this tradition, Nathan Sternharz writes rabbinic Hebrew based on the Bible, Talmud, and commentaries, but his grammar often follows that of Yiddish. Second, in a short interlude, we turn to *Enlightenment prose writing* by the Berlin *maskilim*. Isaac Euchel, when describing travels in Europe, sets his sights beyond the traditional Jewish world while keeping his language close to Hebrew scriptural traditions. Finally, we turn to *translations by moderate maskilim*, starting with Moses Mendelsohn-Frankfurt. Translating from German, Mendelsohn-Frankfurt and others travel beyond the traditional Jewish world; their grammar continues to be shaped in part by biblical conventions. Mendel Lefin's language moves away from reliance on Hebrew scripture, and his works show how translating into Hebrew helped him create a more flexible language.

Both the hasidim and *maskilim* contributed to the modernization of Hebrew. Unlike the early *maskilim*, the hasidim had an expansive view of Hebrew, using all layers of the language and allowing influences from Yiddish. It remained for moderate *maskilim* such as Lefin to create a new synthesis with the help of translations. Together and in opposition, the hasidim and the *maskilim* moved from sacred pilgrimage to secular Hebrew literature.

The chapters in this book do not follow chronological order. The first chapter provides background by returning to biblical, Renaissance, and early-modern sea narratives. The subsequent two chapters analyze hasidic texts of pilgrimage that were published in 1815 or later, representing a traditional worldview. Chapters 4 and 5 turn back in time to 1785–1807 because the German Jewish authors of that period express a modern sensibility. The last two chapters shift to eastern Europe, where moderate adherents of the Jewish Enlightenment synthesized some of the achievements of the hasidim and the early *maskilim*. We could view this movement as one from thesis and antithesis to synthesis, but the more sensible model would be a hermeneutic circle: by the end of the book, it becomes evident that we must cultivate a new approach to Hebrew literary history. My hope is that by moving through these chapters, readers will come to appreciate these authors' remarkable writings. Two centuries ago a small number of innovators opened up new prospects for modern Hebrew prose. The hasidim made contributions that have too often been ignored; the early *maskilim* have been praised to the detriment of their successors.

Zion and Beyond

What does "Zion" mean? What is the etymology of the Hebrew word ציון (Tzion or Zion)? There are no simple answers to this question, but lexicographers raise several possibilities. This is Ernest Klein's full entry for the word צִיּוֹן, *Zion*: "Of uncertain etymology. Some scholars derive it from צוה in the sense 'to erect' (cp. צִיּוּן). Others connect it with base צין, appearing in Arab. *ṣāna* (= he protected), so that צִיּוֹן would lit. mean 'fortress, citadel.' Scholars, with reference to Syr. צֶהְיוּן (= Heb. צִיּוֹן), derive these words from base צהה or ציה; according to them the orig. meaning of צִיּוֹן would be 'bare hill.' Other scholars regard Syr. צֶהְיוּן as the older form." Originally, then,

"Zion" may have meant "something erected," "fortress," or "bare hill." In the subsequent entry, Klein further notes a connection to the word צִיּוּן, adding three more related meanings: "1 monument. 2 landmark, signpost. 3 gravestone [Related to Syr. צְוָיָא (= heap of stones). . . . These words prob. derive from base צוה in the sense of 'to erect']."[23]

All of this suggests that "Zion" is something that is constructed or that serves as a marker or monument (*tziun*). In biblical texts, the term frequently appears in the name "Mount Zion" (*har Tzion*; e.g., Isaiah 1:8, 10:32), in reference to Daughter/s of Zion (*bat Tzion*, *banot Tzion*; e.g., Isaiah 3:16–17, 4:4), and as another name for the City of David (*'ir David*; e.g., 1 Kings 8:1). If "Zion" can be synonymous with "Jerusalem" or a synecdoche referring to the Land of Israel, then the biblical word *Zion* has no exact geographical referent.

We might speculate that in literary texts the name "Land of Israel" is the more literal designation of a geographical place, whereas "Zion" is more heavily weighted with biblical, Talmudic, and later rabbinic significance. A sober description of the place, then, would sooner refer to "the Land of Israel," but a nostalgic recollection is more likely to refer back to "Zion." This distinction is confirmed by one of the most prominent exilic texts ever written, quoted here from Robert Alter's translation of Psalm 137:

> By Babylon's streams,
>   there we sat, oh we wept,
>   when we recalled Zion.
> On the poplars there
>   we hung up our lyres.
> For there our captors had asked of us
>   words of song,
> and our plunderers—rejoicing:
>   "Sing us from Zion's songs."[24]

In this poem from the Babylonian Exile after 586 BCE, the speaker refers to a collective nostalgia for Zion, with all of the biblical associations to that name. Recalling "the Land of Israel" would not have had the same resonance.

The rise of modern Hebrew literature required that writers strip away some of the excessive reliance on biblical allusions. Moving "beyond Zion" also required moving away from undue dependence on biblical texts. In other contexts, it was essential that travel writers see what they actually encountered instead of projecting their expectations and familiar biblical quotations onto the landscape. As Wallace Stevens writes in the poem "The Snow Man," a distinctive sensibility is required to see "nothing that is not there, and the nothing that is."[25]

Secular writers such as S. Y. Abramovitsh and H. N. Bialik, who helped reinvent modern Hebrew at the end of the nineteenth century, thereby heightened the possibility of creating a state in which Hebrew would become the national language.[26] If we acknowledge the importance of the forerunners discussed here, however, it is necessary to push back the date of the *teḥiya*, the so-called revival of Hebrew, by about a century. This suggests that the rise of a secular, modern Hebrew did not necessarily imply a connection to the Land of Israel; the modern point of view did not always place Zion at the center of the world. A post-Zionist thinker might argue that Zionism returned to a premodern conception and biblical associations for support.

Since 1948, many literary scholars working in Israel have overemphasized the "revival of Hebrew" that took place alongside the Zionist movement since the 1880s. After the decline of the Haskala, territorial Zionism reappropriated the premodern belief in the centrality of the Land of Israel. In spite of this deliberate anachronism, most modern Zionists did not try to reverse the secular worldview that had become widespread, and Theodor Herzl envisioned a secular state. Nevertheless, Zionist rhetoric inevitably drew strength from religious assumptions and echoes of biblical sources. In short, we need to remember that early-modern Hebrew literature preceded Zionism and that one of the primary goals of this literature was to expand horizons beyond the limitations of biblical prose and beyond pilgrimage (or messianic) narratives of returning to Zion.

PART ONE

Pre-Zionist Pilgrimages to the Holy Land

1

Narratives of Sea Travel from Jonah to Yosef Sofer

Biblical and postbiblical representations of sea travel show the gradual development of Hebrew maritime language and literature, marked by the Jewish cultural context. From ancient times until the medieval period, many literate Jews lived in a text-centered world with Zion as the imaginary geographic center. Pilgrims to the Land of Israel searched for scriptural remnants, following biblical narratives, which superimposed a higher reality on the world. They carried the Torah as a guide in their search for sacred places and as the basis for tales of their journeys. Biblical models provided seminal Hebrew phrases that permeated accounts of sea travels and pilgrimages to the Land of Israel.

As modernization enabled Jews to perceive a world that was governed by laws of nature, one challenge for modern Jewish literature was to dispense with theological underpinnings. Because the Bible and the Talmud emphasized God's omnipresence, rabbis were often suspicious of scientific conceptions of nature. In some circles, realistic description was readily associated with a heretical worldview.[1]

Narratives of sea travel illustrate perceptions of the natural world. The two parts of this book juxtapose hasidic pilgrimages to maskilic sea travels, showing the gradual shift toward concrete, naturalistic depictions of the sea. This change in emphasis becomes evident in the extreme circumstances of storms at sea, especially when shipwreck threatens. Modern descriptions rely less on the idea that storms at sea are sent by God or that Divine Providence saves sea travelers from them. Some authors showed

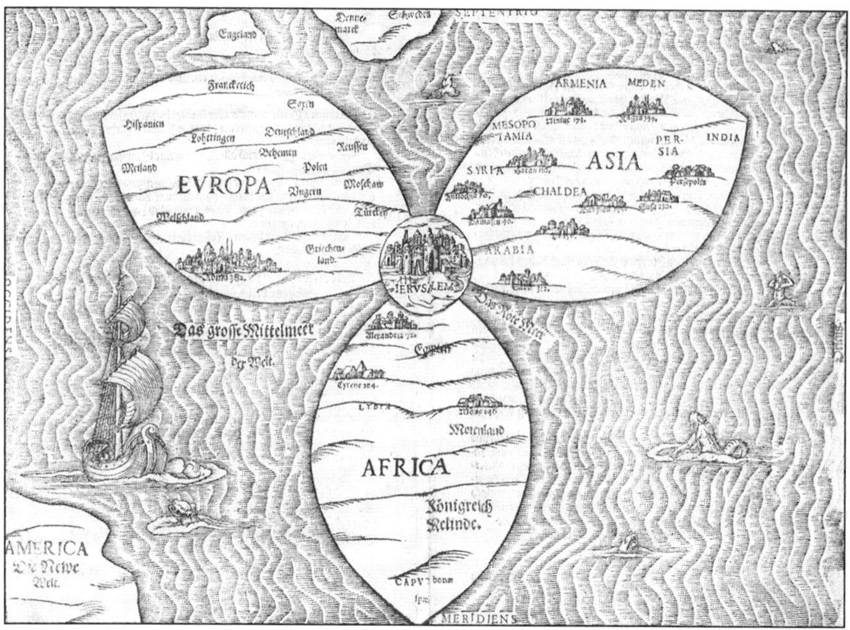

Fig. 2. Heinrich Bünting, *Die gantze Welt in ein Kleberblat* (The Whole World in a Clover Leaf), from *Itinerarum sacrae scripturae* (Helmstadt: Siebenburger, 1581). Courtesy of Map Collection, Yale University Library.

their modern worldview when they moved away from beliefs regarding God's role in bringing about miracles.

At the same time as this book looks at a changing worldview, it examines the rise of modern Hebrew by focusing on the very specific genre of sea travel narratives. Many real-world objects and experiences surrounding ships and the Mediterranean Sea have remained relatively constant since ancient times. Nevertheless, linguistic shifts brought about changes in even the relatively technical maritime vocabulary. Hebrew nautical language reveals how authors related to the European world and to the literary tradition in different ways.

To understand the language of sea travel in early-modern Hebrew narrative, then, one must be aware of the passages relating to sea travel in the Hebrew Bible. To a lesser extent, the Babylonian and Palestinian

Talmuds and the Midrash added to the language of sea travel, making new terms available to medieval authors. Renaissance-era accounts written by Italian travelers echo biblical language but also show the influence of Italian culture. After discussing these precedents, I turn to representative eighteenth-century Hebrew travel narratives. Biblical descriptions of the sea and sea travel cast a long shadow over early-modern Hebrew sea narratives: storms at sea were frequently treated as metaphors of God's power, and the belief in Divine Providence was prominently associated with the topos of sea travel. In these accounts, it was virtually impossible for Hebrew authors to resist the temptation to imbed biblical phrases in their descriptions.

Sea, Ship, and Storm in Biblical Texts

A few seminal biblical phrases that refer to sea travel are quoted repeatedly and adapted in modern Hebrew writing when the sea is mentioned.[2] Analyzing representations of sea travel thus provides a kind of modified carbon dating, showing whether a Hebrew author uses the neobiblical *melitza* style and inlaid biblical phrases (*shibbutz*) or instead tries to invent novel ways to describe sea travel. The most important biblical passages are in Jonah and Psalms. Here are the most essential verses from Jonah 1:4–5 and 1:12:

וַיהוָה הֵטִיל רוּחַ־גְּדוֹלָה אֶל־הַיָּם וַיְהִי סַעַר־גָּדוֹל בַּיָּם וְהָאֳנִיָּה חִשְּׁבָה לְהִשָּׁבֵר׃
וַיִּירְאוּ הַמַּלָּחִים וַיִּזְעֲקוּ אִישׁ אֶל־אֱלֹהָיו וַיָּטִלוּ אֶת־הַכֵּלִים אֲשֶׁר בָּאֳנִיָּה אֶל־הַיָּם לְהָקֵל מֵעֲלֵיהֶם
וְיוֹנָה יָרַד אֶל־יַרְכְּתֵי הַסְּפִינָה וַיִּשְׁכַּב וַיֵּרָדַם׃ . . . .
וַיֹּאמֶר אֲלֵיהֶם שָׂאוּנִי וַהֲטִילֻנִי אֶל־הַיָּם וְיִשְׁתֹּק הַיָּם מֵעֲלֵיכֶם כִּי יוֹדֵעַ אָנִי כִּי בְשֶׁלִּי הַסַּעַר הַגָּדוֹל
הַזֶּה עֲלֵיכֶם׃

4. God cast a great wind upon the sea, and there was a great storm in the sea, and the ship was on the verge of breaking up.
5. The sailors were afraid and each man called to his god, and they cast the ship's vessels overboard to lighten their load, and Jonah went down inside the ship, lay down, and fell asleep. . . .
12. He said to them: lift me up and cast me into the sea, and the sea will become quiet before you, for I know that this great storm is because of me.[3]

One essential element of this narrative is its emphasis on God's role in bringing about the storm. The passage refers to both a divinely inspired wind (*ruaḥ*) and the resulting storm (*sa'ar*). In this influential text, then, the storm is a kind of theophany, an expression of God's displeasure.

A distinctive theological conception emerges. First, God is the ultimate cause of storm winds and waves (the narrator asserts unequivocally, "God cast a great wind upon the sea, and there was a great storm in the sea"). Second, God sometimes brings a storm as a punishment (Jonah admits to the sailors, "I know that this great storm is because of me"). Third, appealing to divine powers and using petitionary prayer can bring relief or at least is thought capable of bringing relief ("each man called to his god"). Thus, a storm at sea can present a microcosm or metaphor of God's interventions in human experience and of human efforts to elicit God's aid in adversity.

Several Psalms also present the sea's power as a manifestation of God. The fundamental representation of divine power at sea occurs in Psalm 107. The poetic verses 23 to 29 present an extended metaphor that illustrates God's omnipotence:

יוֹרְדֵי הַיָּם בָּאֳנִיּוֹת עֹשֵׂי מְלָאכָה בְּמַיִם רַבִּים:
הֵמָּה רָאוּ מַעֲשֵׂי יְהוָה וְנִפְלְאוֹתָיו בִּמְצוּלָה:
וַיֹּאמֶר וַיַּעֲמֵד רוּחַ סְעָרָה וַתְּרוֹמֵם גַּלָּיו:
יַעֲלוּ שָׁמַיִם יֵרְדוּ תְהוֹמוֹת נַפְשָׁם בְּרָעָה תִתְמוֹגָג:
יָחוֹגּוּ וְיָנוּעוּ כַּשִּׁכּוֹר וְכָל־חָכְמָתָם תִּתְבַּלָּע:
וַיִּצְעֲקוּ אֶל־יְהוָה בַּצַּר לָהֶם וּמִמְּצוּקֹתֵיהֶם יוֹצִיאֵם:
יָקֵם סְעָרָה לִדְמָמָה וַיֶּחֱשׁוּ גַּלֵּיהֶם:

23. Those who go down to the sea in ships, making it their trade in vast seas,

24. They have seen God's works and His wonders in the depths.

25. He speaks, and a storm wind arises and lifts up the waves.

26. They rise to the heavens and fall into the abyss, their souls melt away in calamity.

27. They circle and lurch like a drunk, all of their wisdom is swallowed up.

28. They shout to the Lord in distress, and from their affliction [He] removes them.

29. He makes the storm become silent and the waves become still.

Consistent with the Jonah narrative, this poetic reframing suggests that mariners experience God's might and wonders ("They have seen God's works and His wonders in the depths"). Describing Psalm 107, A. Cohen writes that it presents "four word-pictures"—including sea travel—"as circumstances of distress in which man is dependent upon God's mercy."[4] The Psalm opens by mentioning God's everlasting mercy and then provides scenarios that show why human beings need divine succor.

The storm at sea in Psalm 107 is presented as one exemplary instance that shows God's power and benevolence.[5] The key verse for the overall theological message is repeated four times almost verbatim in four different contexts, with variation only in the final word:

וַיִּצְעֲקוּ אֶל־יְהוָה בַּצַּר לָהֶם מִמְּצוּקוֹתֵיהֶם יַצִּילֵם׃ (Ps. 107:6)
וַיִּזְעֲקוּ אֶל־יְהוָה בַּצַּר לָהֶם מִמְּצֻקוֹתֵיהֶם יוֹשִׁיעֵם׃ (Ps. 107:13)
וַיִּזְעֲקוּ אֶל־יְהוָה בַּצַּר לָהֶם מִמְּצֻקוֹתֵיהֶם יוֹשִׁיעֵם׃ (Ps. 107:19)
וַיִּצְעֲקוּ אֶל־יְהוָה בַּצַּר לָהֶם וּמִמְּצוּקֹתֵיהֶם יוֹצִיאֵם׃ (Ps. 107:28)

6. They shout to God in distress, from their affliction [He] rescues them.
13. They shout to God in distress, and from their affliction [He] redeems them.
19. They shout to God in distress, and from their affliction [He] redeems them.
28. They shout to God in distress, and from their affliction [He] removes them.[6]

This apparently simple notion—that when people cry out to God, they are saved from danger—raises a question: If prayer can bring salvation, does petitionary prayer have the power to alter nature? That might contradict a Talmudic dictum, often repeated by rabbinic sources, that "we do not rely on miracles" (*ein somkhin `al ha-nes*).[7]

In the middle of Psalm 107, there seems to be a turn from physical description to a psychological dimension: "They rise to the heavens and fall into the abyss, their souls melt away in calamity [*nafsham be-ra`a titmogeg*]" (Ps. 107:26). This change leaves room for a metaphorical or allegorical interpretation associated with the Ba`al Shem Tov, which many hasidic readers accepted.[8] But the description is also sufficiently graphic to influence descriptions of actual sea travel. Although hasidic authors often referred back to Psalm 107 as a prooftext showing the supernatural power of prayer, enlightened authors such as Mendel Lefin resisted this interpretation. Psalm 107 thus became a literary touchstone and the locus of a theological debate.

As part of a broader belief in God's Providence (*hashgaḥa*), the Psalm reasserts God's influence over human encounters with the hazards of the sea. Recalling Jonah 1:4, Psalm 107 asserts: "He speaks, and a storm wind arises and lifts up the waves" (verse 25). It also emphasizes the importance of prayer as a means of appealing to God's kindness and mercy (*ḥesed*): "They shout to the Lord in distress, and from their affliction [He] removes them" (verse 28). A storm at sea may be understood as an expression of God's displeasure or chastisement, and prayer may be effective in bringing it to an end ("He makes the storm become silent and the waves become still"). In the context of the Psalm, the sea narrative creates a metaphorical sequence that characterizes the fraught relationship between human beings and God.

Theologically charged storm winds in later Hebrew texts often derive from Psalm 107 and from biblical passages in Job and Ezekiel. A theophany, God's appearance to human beings, occurs in Job 38:1, when "God answered Job out of the storm wind" (ויען־יהוה את־איוב [מנהסערה] מן הסערה). There is also a long exegetical tradition that finds mystical secrets in Ezekiel 1:4, where "I looked, and I saw a storm wind coming from the north" (וארא והנה רוח סערה באה מן־הצפון). Rashi (Rabbi Shlomo Yitzḥaki, 1040–1105 CE) comments on this passage from Ezekiel:

> והנה רוח סערה באה מן הצפון—היא מרכבת כסא כבוד השכינה כמה שנאמר בענין ולפי שבאה בחימה להשחית את ישראל לכך נדמית לרוח סערה.
>
> And behold, a storm wind is coming from the north—This is the chariot of the Throne of Glory of the Divine Presence [Shekhina], as is said on the matter; and because she came in anger to destroy Israel, for this reason she appeared as a storm wind.

Rashi's commentary suggests that the "storm wind" encountered in pilgrimage narratives also often conceals higher meanings. Commenting on

Psalm 148:8, which refers to a *ruaḥ se`ara* that "does His bidding" (literally, "doing His word," עשה דברו), Rashi adds that beyond executing God's command, the storm wind carries out His mission (*shliḥuto*):

> העושה את דברו ושליחותו, ואמרו רבותינו שהדברים הללו היו תחלתם גנוזים בשמים ובא דוד והורידן לארץ לפי שהם מיני פורעניות ואין נאה להם להיות גנוזין במגוריו של הקב״ה:

> Doing His bidding and His mission: our rabbis said that these words were originally hidden in the heavens, and David came and brought them down to earth, because they are species of troubles, and it is not suitable for them to be hidden in the dwelling of the Holy One, blessed be He.

The "storm wind" is thus an example of how, in the Hebrew literary tradition, a theological vision permeates natural phenomena.

Psalm 24 also typifies later descriptions of nature and the sea in Hebrew writing. It offers a metaphysical description, set apart from any human existence, referring to the Creation:

> לַיהוָה הָאָרֶץ וּמְלוֹאָהּ תֵּבֵל וְיֹשְׁבֵי בָהּ
> כִּי־הוּא עַל־יַמִּים יְסָדָהּ וְעַל־נְהָרוֹת יְכוֹנְנֶהָ:

> The earth and all that it holds belong to God,
> the world and those who dwell there.
> For He founded it upon the seas,
> set it upon the rivers. (Ps. 24:1–2)

These verses emphasize that God, as Creator, controls the world and "those who dwell there." Metaphorically or literally, God established our world "upon the seas" (*`al-yamim*). This psalm, then, supports the idea that sea travel may be understood as a metaphor of all human life. Human society may be likened to a "ship of fools," as in Hieronymus Bosch's allegory (ca. 1510–15).

Representations that link the sea and divine intervention sometimes refer back to Exodus 14:21–23 and 14:26–28. Relevant here is the story about the miraculous parting of the Red Sea (or Sea of Reeds, *yam suf*):

> וַיֵּט מֹשֶׁה אֶת־יָדוֹ עַל־הַיָּם וַיּוֹלֶךְ יְהוָה אֶת־הַיָּם בְּרוּחַ קָדִים עַזָּה כָּל־הַלַּיְלָה וַיָּשֶׂם אֶת־הַיָּם לֶחָרָבָה וַיִּבָּקְעוּ הַמָּיִם:

וַיָּבֹאוּ בְנֵי־יִשְׂרָאֵל בְּתוֹךְ הַיָּם בַּיַּבָּשָׁה וְהַמַּיִם לָהֶם חֹמָה מִימִינָם וּמִשְּׂמֹאלָם׃
וַיִּרְדְּפוּ מִצְרַיִם וַיָּבֹאוּ אַחֲרֵיהֶם כֹּל סוּס פַּרְעֹה רִכְבּוֹ וּפָרָשָׁיו אֶל־תּוֹךְ הַיָּם׃ . . . .
וַיֹּאמֶר יְהוָה אֶל־מֹשֶׁה נְטֵה אֶת־יָדְךָ עַל־הַיָּם וְיָשֻׁבוּ הַמַּיִם עַל־מִצְרַיִם עַל־רִכְבּוֹ וְעַל־פָּרָשָׁיו׃
וַיֵּט מֹשֶׁה אֶת־יָדוֹ עַל־הַיָּם וַיָּשָׁב הַיָּם לִפְנוֹת בֹּקֶר לְאֵיתָנוֹ וּמִצְרַיִם נָסִים לִקְרָאתוֹ וַיְנַעֵר יְהוָה אֶת
מִצְרַיִם בְּתוֹךְ הַיָּם׃
וַיָּשֻׁבוּ הַמַּיִם וַיְכַסּוּ אֶת־הָרֶכֶב וְאֶת־הַפָּרָשִׁים לְכֹל חֵיל פַּרְעֹה הַבָּאִים אַחֲרֵיהֶם בַּיָּם לֹא־נִשְׁאַר בָּהֶם
עַד־אֶחָד׃

21. Then Moses stretched his hand out over the sea—and the Lord drove back the sea with a strong east wind all that night, made the sea into dry ground; and the waters were split.
22. The children of Israel went into the sea on dry ground, the waters forming a wall for them on their right and on their left.
23. The Egyptians pursued them and came after them into the sea, all of Pharaoh's horses, chariots, and horsemen.
26. Then the Lord said to Moses, "Stretch out your hand over the sea, so that the waters will come back upon the Egyptians and upon their chariots and upon their horsemen."
27. Moses stretched out his hand over the sea, and at daybreak the sea returned to its usual strength, and the Egyptians fled at its approach. But the Lord shook the Egyptians into the sea.
28. The waters turned back and covered the chariots and the horsemen—Pharaoh's entire army that came after them into the sea; not one of them remained.[9]

The Exodus, including the parting of the Sea of Reeds, is one of the founding narratives embraced by modern Judaism. Hence, a crisis at sea can potentially be viewed in relationship to that primal scene in which God saves the Israelites from the sea and from their Egyptian pursuers.

Based on these associations, sea travel narratives readily evoke a multifaceted textual and theological context, which makes the sea especially suggestive in narratives of pilgrimage. A storm that arises during travel to the Holy Land is often understood to have spiritual meaning. The travelers may conclude that they are not worthy to make the voyage, or they may need to show their piety and perseverance in order to arrive safely. All of these elements return, along with many of the same key words, in modern sea narratives.

Because the Hebrew scriptural tradition typically invests storms at sea with theological meaning, it was a challenge for modern Hebrew writing to convey contemporary scenes, speech, and nature with an air of immediacy. Modern descriptions of sea travel reveal authors' attempts to move Hebrew beyond the traditional religious contexts.

Postbiblical and Premodern Narratives of Sea Travel in Hebrew

On one level, the Talmud presents concrete, mundane descriptions of ships, thus providing realistic terms that will be used in later rabbinic writing. For example, a Mishnaic passage in Baba Batra lists the parts of a ship that are included when it is sold: "A person who sold a ship also sold the mast [*ha-toren*], the sail [or banner, *ha-nes*], the anchor [*ha-`ogen*], and all of the means of steering it [the rudders or oars, *ha-manhigin oto*]."[10] Talmudic passages show some ambiguity, however, about the meanings of nautical terms. A curtain in the Temple is "like the sail [*kel`a*] of the ship."[11] Metaphorically, sin "is like the thread of a spider web, and in the end it becomes like the sheet [or rope, *kel`a*] of a ship."[12] Elsewhere the Talmud provides more technical terms in Hebrew and Aramaic, some taken from Greek. Baba Batra 73a gives Hebrew–Aramaic equivalences, such as תורן = איסקריא, meaning "mast" or "sailyard," and נס = אדרא, meaning "mast" or "sails."[13] The Talmud also contains fantastic tales of sea travel attributed to Rabba bar Hana. But these passages were not the primary influence on later Hebrew descriptions of sea voyages.

For centuries, narratives of sea travel in Hebrew referred back to biblical sources. The heavy reliance on biblical models paralleled a worldview that had been shaped by Judaic traditions. One may distinguish between pilgrimage narratives and other travel narratives that did not have the Land of Israel as their goal. Linguistically, there is a tension between authors' use of biblical quotations and their reliance on words or translations from their vernacular, such as Italian or Yiddish.

Postbiblical Hebrew narratives of sea travel represent distinctive literary styles. For our purposes, it is possible to discern the extent to which early-modern Hebrew texts of this kind (1) create and use what may be called neobiblical *melitza*, with frequent quotations; (2) are influenced by a contemporary vernacular such as Italian or Yiddish;[14] and (3) incorporate various stages of postbiblical Hebrew and Aramaic (Mishnaic Hebrew, Aramaic, medieval Hebrew, Renaissance Hebrew, post-Renaissance rabbinic Hebrew).

My approach combines a linguistic, stylistic approach with a diachronic analysis of periods in premodern European cultural history. Because many travel manuscripts were not published during an author's lifetime—indeed, many of them remained obscure for centuries—it is difficult to show a direct lineage that links these travel writers. Several of the authors worked independently, influenced by their foreign literary milieu as well as by the existing norms of Hebrew writing in their time and place. Hence, the examples in this chapter are representative and symptomatic, not comprehensive. This brief overview of premodern Hebrew travel narratives draws primarily from Yehuda Eisenstein's and Avraham Ya`ari's collections of travel narratives to Palestine.[15] In English, the reader may consult Elkan Nathan Adler's collection *Jewish Travellers in the Middle Ages*.[16]

Italian Jewish Travelers

Italian Jews wrote at a high point of Hebrew literary culture in the fifteenth and sixteenth centuries, and some travelers left distinctive, memorable narratives. Their writings show how heavily they relied on biblical models and traditional ideas. They were also indebted to Italian culture, however, which left its mark on their Hebrew writing. An example is Meshullam of Volterra, who wrote an account of his journey to Egypt and Palestine in 1481. He was a wealthy jeweler who traveled for commerce, but he also made a pilgrimage to Palestine. He expresses the Zion-centered worldview when he writes that on reaching Hebron, he "saw the Cave of Ha-Machpelah, which is in the navel of the land [*tabur ha-aretz*]."[17] Like some other pilgrims, Meshullam appears to have viewed the Land of Israel as the center of the world. This image also occurs in medieval Hebrew sources, usually associated with the Temple Mount in Jerusalem. Radak (1160–1235) writes in his commentary on Ezekiel 38:12 and elsewhere that *tabur ha-aretz* means that the place is at the center of the world, as the navel is at the center of the body. Spiritual geography supersedes mundane geography.

On seeing Jerusalem, Meshullam follows a tradition linked to mourning the destruction of the Temple on the Ninth of Av: "when I saw its ruin, I made a tear in my garment a hand's breadth long, and with bitterness of heart I recited the suitable prayer from a small booklet that I had at hand."[18] The pilgrim experiences reality mediated by the scriptural tradition. He describes the Temple Mount in detail, including a legend that illustrates the power of the place: every year on the Ninth of Av, lamps in the area go out and cannot be relit.[19] He restates the traditional view that the Temple Mount was the site of Abraham's binding of Isaac, visits the sites of tombs of biblical prophets, and locates the place where David killed Goliath. There is little that is original in Meshullam's account of Jerusalem, where his main purpose is to rediscover biblical and rabbinic sites in the Holy Land.

Descriptions of sea travel also show how Meshullam's Hebrew invariably borrows from biblical sources. As noted earlier, pilgrimage narratives of sea travel tend to echo biblical phrases, investing the experience with spiritual significance. To focus the analysis, I concentrate on the descriptions of storms at sea and shipwreck. Extreme experiences may sometimes push an author toward greater concreteness, but here Meshullam seems unable to express the concrete details in Hebrew and turns to Italian.

Meshullam combines secular and scriptural elements in his narrative. (In the Hebrew passages quoted throughout the book, I set transliterated non-Hebrew words in italics and biblical phrases in bold; in the English translation, biblical phrases are given in bold also.)

נכנסנו בחוף אליסנדריאה. ובהיות כי מת הפילוטו שלנו במלחמה, והנוקיירי היה מוכה ופצוע והיה שוכב במטה, הוכרחנו לעשות נוקיירי אחד מהמלחים. ויהי בהכנסנו בחוף הנזכר, הספינה נתכה בארץ **והאונייה חשבה להשבר, ותהי צעקה גדולה** בספינה, ובאו היינוביסי מאליסנדריאה לעזור לנו, וזרקו האנקורי, ואח״כ מכח ארגנלי היו רוצים להוציאה חוצה, ויחתרו המלחים ונשבר החבל מהארגנילי.[20]

We entered the coast of Alexandria, and because our helmsman [*piloto*] had died in the battle, and the captain [*nocchiere*] was struck and injured

> and lying in bed, we were forced to make one of the sailors into captain. And it happened that, when we entered the aforementioned coast, the ship ran aground and **the boat was on the verge of breaking up** [Jon. 1:4]. **There was a great outcry** [Ex. 12:30] on the ship, and the *Genovese* of Alexandria came to help us and lowered the anchors [*ancore*]. Afterward, with the help of levers [*arganelli*], they wanted to pull us out, and the sailors rowed, but the cable of the levers broke.

This Hebrew passage is laced with Italian words that have been transliterated into Hebrew characters. It attests to the author's familiarity with the contemporary world, including basic Italian seafaring vocabulary, but it also shows that the author lacks appropriate seafaring terms in Hebrew. Meshullam's "helmsman" is a *pilota*; "the captain" is a *nocchiere*; "anchors" are *ancore*; and "levers" or "winches" are *arganelli*.[21] The author interweaves biblical words such as *ḥof* (shore, coast), *oniya* (boat), *malaḥim* (sailors), and *ḥatar* (to row). The Mishnaic noun *sefina* (ship), which occurs only once in the biblical corpus (in Jon. 1:5), is used interchangeably with the biblical word *oniya*. The grafting of Italian onto Hebrew is facilitated by grammatical devices such as adding the definite article *ha-* to the Italian loan words.

In recounting his journey, Meshullam of Volterra inserts biblical phrases and uses some biblical grammar. He quotes Jonah 1:4, "the boat was on the verge of breaking up," a reference that most Hebrew readers would have recognized. This leads to "a great outcry" (Ex. 12:30), reminding the reader of ancestors who were persecuted in Egypt in a story that subsequently displays God's power over the Egyptians. The text places the narrated events in biblical context by resorting to phrases from Jonah and Exodus. In contrast, when describing the concrete scene, Meshullam relies on mariners' Italian.[22]

Meshullam's description falls back into biblical language when he tells of a storm striking his ship near Corfu:

> בו ביום בערב, **ויהי קולות וברקים וענן כבד על ההר**, והמטר נתך ארצה עם **רוח קדים חרישית**, כי כמוהו לא ראיתי מעולם. . . . וה׳ היצילנו מהסער ההוא, יהי שמו מבורך לעד. וכמה מעלות טובות למקום עלינו.[23]

That evening **there was thunder and lightning and a heavy cloud over the mountain** [Ex. 19:16], and the wind sliced the ground with **a deafening wind from the east** [Jon. 4:8], the likes of which I have never seen before. . . . God saved us from this storm, may He be blessed forever, and how many kindnesses has He shown us.[24]

The first part of this passage is a direct quotation from the Revelation on Sinai (Ex. 19:16), followed by a reference to the Book of Jonah; the closing phrase is an expression of piety that is familiar from the Passover Haggadah. Even when Meshullam tries to convey direct observations, he mixes his descriptions with scriptural quotations.

Ovadia of Bertinoro follows similar patterns from his visit to the Cave of the Machpelah to his visit to Jerusalem, where he, too, makes a tear in his garment to mourn the destruction of the Temple.[25] He provides some concrete details about his visit to Jerusalem, while adding mythical details about the River Sambation. Like other Jewish pilgrims, he visits the tombs of prophets and biblical sites such as Sodom and Gomorrah, recording that among the pillars of salt near the Dead Sea he is unable to locate Lot's wife. He seems to vacillate between descriptions of what he actually saw and descriptions recycled from the Bible.

Like other Italian Jewish travelers, Ovadia of Bertinoro uses Italian words liberally. The first part of this description is vivid in spite of using some familiar language about storms at sea:

הלכנו ברוח מצויה ארבעה ימים, וביום הרביעי לעת ערב הפך ה׳ רוח הים והשיבנו אחור **בסופה וסערה**, ונסתרנו מזעף הים באי אחד, במקום אשר בין ההרים, כעין נמל עשוי בידי שמים, וההרים האלה מלאים חרובים והדס, ושם ישבנו שלשה ימים. מקצה שלשת ימים, ביום הראשון בי״ח במרחשון, נסענו משם ובאנו עד ששים מיל קרוב לרודוס; ובכל הדרך ראינו איים מפה ומפה, גם הרי התוגרמא נגלו לנו. ובהיותנו כמו ששים מיל קרוב לרודוס, נהפך עלינו רוח, ושבנו אחורנית **בזעף** כשמנים מיל, ותקענו האנקורי מהדוגיאה סמוך ליבשה באי ששמה לונגו, והיא תחת ממשלת רודוס.[26]

We went with an ordinary wind for four days, and on the fourth day in the evening, God turned the sea wind, and it pushed us back **in the storm and tempest** [or **storm and whirlwind** (*sufa u-se`ara*)], and we

> took refuge from the sea on an island, in a place among the mountains, a kind of harbor made by the hands of Heaven, and these mountains are full of carob trees and myrtles, and there we dwelt for three days. At the end of three days, on Sunday, the 18th of Marḥeshvan, we departed from there and came within sixty miles of Rhodes; all along the way we saw islands here and there, and also the mountains of the Turk were visible to us. When we were about sixty miles from Rhodes, the wind turned on us, and in **the raging storm** [*ba-za`af*] we returned about eighty miles, and we dropped the anchors from the boat near to the coast of an island called Longo, which is under the rule of Rhodes.

This description at first appears to be a straightforward, naturalistic account of sea travels. A closer look at the language, however, reveals its significance from both linguistic and theological standpoints. The descriptions are often realistic until storms arrive, at which point they become biblical, apparently for theological reasons. The religious worldview is evident when Bertinoro states that "God turned the sea wind" and interprets a natural harbor as having been made "by the hands of Heaven."

Especially the language used to describe the storms—first *sufa u-se`ara* and later *ba-za`af*—connects the description to biblical sources, which often link such events to God's anger. *Sufa u-se`ara* is a biblical turn of phrase found in Isaiah 29:6: "You [Ariel, or Jerusalem] will be remembered by the Lord of Hosts in thunder and in a mighty sound, storm and tempest, and a blaze of consuming fire."[27] The phrase *sufa ve-se`ara* also occurs in Nahum 1:3, describing God's attributes: "The Lord is slow to anger and of great strength, and yet He does not remit all punishment; His path is in storm and whirlwind [*be-sufa u-vi-se`ara*], and clouds are the dust at His feet." The phrase "storm and tempest" (or "storm and whirlwind") often suggests divine intervention. Moreover, when the word *se`ara* stands alone, it is associated with a climactic moment in the Book of Job 38:1, when God answers Job "out of the storm [or storm wind, tempest, whirlwind]" (*min ha-se`ara*, scribal correction for *minhase`ara*). Just as important is the reference to a *se`ara* in 2 Kings 2:1: "When the Lord was taking Elijah up to the heavens in a storm wind" (or whirlwind, *be-se`ara ha-shamayim*). A natural storm that is described in biblical texts as a *sufa* or *se`ara* often takes on the theological significance of a divine epiphany. This line of analysis is confirmed by biblical uses of the word *za`af*, meaning "storming, raging."[28] In Jonah 1:15, this term is associated with the sea and with the storm that God has cast upon it. Similarly, a chastising passage in Isaiah 30:30 associates *za`af* with God's punishing anger, which will appear in a fiery blaze.

These biblical passages make a strong statement that God expresses His anger through nature, specifically through storms, winds, tempests, thunder. In connection with theophany, rabbinic passages inevitably refer to the revelation on Sinai: "On the third day, in the morning, there was thunder and lightning, and a heavy cloud upon the mountain, and a very loud blast of the shofar" (Ex. 19:16). Later that morning "the sound of the shofar became louder and louder, with Moses speaking and God answering him in thunder" (Ex. 19:19). This primal moment of revelation comes in a storm, which embodies God's presence and communication to Moses. In the Hebrew scriptural tradition, theophany is most often loud and tempestuous.

Linguistically, Ovadia of Bertinoro's travel account resembles Meshullam of Volterra's. This is not surprising, for they were acquaintances; indeed, Bertinoro's narrative indicates that he and Meshullam traveled on the same ship in 1488 (seven years after the journey described in Meshullam's sea narrative). Bertinoro even describes an incident that involved Meshullam, and although it is not a storm description, its graphic quality is significant. It is also unusual because it characterizes the relationship between Jewish travelers and sailors. The unresolved antagonism is typical of the premodern world, and the author makes no effort to smooth over this unpleasant encounter with non-Jews:

> ושם היינו עשרה ימים, חונים על הים, כי היה הרוח לנגדנו. ובהיותנו שמה קרה מקרה, כי אחד מתופשי משוט אשר בדוגיא, הטיח דברים כלפי הנכבד הר׳ משולם מווֹלְטֵירה הנזכר; וקבל עליו הר׳ משולם הנזכר לפני הפאטרוני מהדוגיא, וירד הפאטרוני בעצמו לבקשו, והשתדלו חבריו להסתירו ולהצילו מידו ולא יכולו, וצוה לאסרו על העץ אשר באמצע הספינה ולהכותו מכה רבה; ובראותו כי נתרשל המכה להכותו, לקח הוא בכבודו החבל אשר יכו בו והכהו כדי רשעתו, ורצה שיבקש מחילה מהר׳ משולם הנזכר לעיני כל העם. ויקנאו כל העם מאד על אשר עשה האדון ככה לאיש ההוא, ר״ל בגלל דברי קנטורין בלבד אשר דבר כנגד היהודי, ומהיום ההוא והלאה החלו אנשי הדוגיא לשנוא אותנו, ולא היו אלינו כתמול שלשום.[29]

> We were there for ten days, moored at sea, because the wind was against us. While we were there, an incident occurred because one oarsmen in the small boat [*dugiya*] made some remarks about the honorable Rabbi Meshullam of Volterra, mentioned above; so Rabbi Meshullam complained about him before the owner of the boat.[30] The owner himself went down looking for him, and his friends tried to hide the oarsman and save him from his hands, but they could not. He commanded that he be bound to the mast [*etz*] that is at the center of the ship and that he be beaten harshly; when he saw that the man who was whipping was slacking off from beating him, the owner himself took the rope they used for beatings and beat him with all his might, and he wanted the oarsman to apologize in front of everyone to the aforementioned Rabbi Meshullam. And all of the people were very incensed that the owner did this to the man, just because of some provocative words he had spoken to the Jew. From that day on, the crew of the boat began to hate us and did not act toward us as they had formerly.

Bertinoro gives a crisp picture of the relations between the crew of the small boat and the Jewish passengers. (The word *dugiya* seems to refer to the launch or lifeboat that is used to take people from the ship to shore because few harbors could accommodate the docking of seaworthy schooners.) Like Eliahu of Pesaro, discussed later in this chapter, Bertinoro uses a Hebrew word for tree (*etz*) to designate the mast because in Italian *albero* means both tree and mast. Where Bertinoro uses the biblical term *etz*, however, Pesaro chooses the postbiblical word *`ilan*. Both cases show how translation from the vernacular played a part in Hebrew writing.

Meshullam's and Bertinoro's writings were representative of Hebrew prose available to educated Jews at that time. On the one hand, these authors frequently refer back to scriptural phrases; on the other, they epitomize the phenomenon of writing implicitly in translation—in this case, thinking Italian and writing Hebrew. Whenever Jews came in contact with the non-Jewish world, beyond the horizons of Jewish communal life, words failed them. Their willingness to import foreign words was the same impulse that brought Greek into the language of the Talmud and that later gave birth to Yiddish, with its complex use of Germanic, Semitic, and Slavic vocabulary.

In 1521–23, Moshe Basola also traveled from Italy to Palestine. Like Meshullam and Bertinoro, he injected Italian words into his Hebrew text. His descriptions are precise, as befits a merchant, but they, too, incorporate biblical phrases. The account begins,

> בשם ה׳ אלקי ישראל נכנסתי בגליאה יום ג׳ י״ז אלול רפ״א [1521] פ׳ **ברוך אתה בצאתך**. ה׳ למען רחמיו יגיעני למחוז חפצי לשלום וישיבני לביתי לשלום ויקיים בי קרא דכתיב **ה׳ ישמר צאתך ובאך** . . . . בששי בשבת לי״ו שעות נסענו מוויניציאה ונלך כל היום וכל הלילה ברוח מצויה עד יום שבת לי״ב שעות. באה אז רוח חזקה נגדנו וסערה בים.[31]

> In the name of the Lord, God of Israel, I entered the *galea* on Tuesday, the 17th of Elul [1521], [during the week of] the parsha [containing the verse] **Blessed are you in your going out** [Parshat Ki Tav'o, passage found in Deut. 28:6]. God, for the sake of his mercy, will bring me in peace to the place of my longing, and will return me to my house in peace, and will fulfill what is written: **God will guard your going out and coming home** [Ps. 121:8]. . . . On Friday at 16 hours [4:00 p.m.] we departed from Venice and traveled all day and all night with an ordinary wind until the Sabbath at noon. Then a strong wind came against us and a storm at sea.

Although Basola's Hebrew is heavily influenced by Italian, his ideas are traditional. For example, he imagines that his travels are protected by a biblical passage in that week's synagogue Torah reading and Psalm 121. This selection illustrates both the allusions to Hebrew biblical verses and the use of Italian. In his account, Basola includes the Italian words for ship (*galea*), storage room, and hold (*gebba*), along with many other words describing the merchandise on the ship. From a linguistic standpoint, the use of the Mishnaic past tense is significant. In some places, Basola uses the biblical consecutive Vav, as in the word *ve-nelekh*.

Eliahu of Pesaro, another Italian Jewish traveler, made his pilgrimage to the Holy Land in 1563 and gives greater detail on nautical matters, but—like Meshullam of Volterra and Moshe Basola—he inserts Italian words:

> על הגליאה הקאפיטנה הולך תמיד שם אחד מגדולי וויניזיאה, נקרא אלקאפיטאנו ועל האחרת או האחרות, נקרא לקונסרוא. על הקאפיטנה תמצא א׳ מטרונית גדול מזהב על הפופא שקוראין

אותו פולינא כי בו יתנכר היותה הקודמת, והנגיד שעליה מצוה גם לאחרות. על פיו יחנו ועל פיו יסעו.[32]

One of the grandees of Venice, called *ilkapitano* [Italian *il capitano*], always goes on the *galea ha-kapitana* [Italian *capitana*]; and the second or others are called the *konserva*. On the *kapitana* you will find a *matronit* on the *poppa*, which is called *polena*, because from this one recognizes that it is the leading ship, and the commander on it is also in charge of the others. They dock or cruise at his command.

That is: on the flagship is the captain; the other ships are for supplies. On the stern of the flagship there is a gilded carving called a figurehead.

Pesaro grafts Italian words onto his Hebrew, sometimes fusing them grammatically. In the subsequent passage, he refers to sailors as **גליאצים** (from Italian *galeazzi*), giving a Hebrew ending to the Italian word.[33] He then intersperses a wide range of other, mainly Italian nautical terms:

שלש משמרות עומדות תמיד בכל גליאה, אחת בראש האילן, ואחת על הפופא, ואחת על הפרוא, ומשמשין שלש שעות. . . . ויש גם הסקאלקו והאופה. לצורך הגליאה יש ג״כ אדם אחד בקי ברוחות, נקרא אל פילוטה, מקום מושבו תמיד על הפופא, והוא בקי בשבילים הנמצאים בים ובכל מקום שיש שם חוף. ומסדר הנהגת הגליאה אל האדמיראליו, והאדמיראליו מצוה לקומודו, והקומודו מצוה לפארונו, ופארונו מצוה לעם. נמצא ג״כ אנשים שהם כתות כתות, כל כת עושה המלאכה המזומנת לו, אך בהצטרך להסיר הוילי, או להחליפן מצד אל צד, או לעסוק איזה מלאכה כבדה, כלם מצטרפים יחד לעשות מלאכתם.[34]

On every ship [*galea*] there are always three watches: one at the top of the mast, one in the stern [*poppa*], and one in the prow [*prua*]. They serve for three hours. . . . There is also the carver [*scalco*] and the baker. For the needs of the ship there is also one man who is an expert in the winds, called *il piloto*, whose place is always at the stern, and he is an expert in the routes at sea and everywhere there is a coastline. The *admiraglio* arranges the leadership of the *galea*, and the *admiraglio* oversees the *comodo*, and the *comodo* oversees the *parono*, and the *parono* is in charge of the people. There are also men who are arranged in teams, with each team assigned to a specific task, but when it is necessary to bring down the sails [*veli*] or to shift them from one side to the other or to do some heavy task, all of them join together to do their task.

Most of the technical terms are given in Italian, as glossed by editor Avraham Ya`ari, with only a few in Hebrew. When Pesaro refers to the sails as הויילי, he is probably transliterating the Italian term *vela* (plural *vele*), meaning "sail." The Italian derives from the Latin term *veli* (plural form of *vēlum*), cognate with French *voile* and English *veil*.[35] Pesaro then lists the Italian names of the different groups of sailors: *calafati*, *marangoni*, *proveri*, *cordinai*, *concari*, *balestrieri*, *palombai*, *scandoleri*, *portolatti*, *navicellai*. He transliterates these terms instead of finding or inventing Hebrew equivalents.

Pesaro's approach to writing about sea travel is epitomized by a short passage that describes a storm:

> בחצי הדרך עמד עלינו נחשול של ים לטבענו עם סערה גדולה, ועמדה בתוקפה ג׳ ימים וג׳ לילות. צפו מים על ראשנו עד אשר היינו יראים לנפשותינו. קראנו אל אלהינו בחזקה, ושמע קול תחנונינו בשוענו אליו, **ועמד הים מזעפו ויחשו גליו**, וברוח טוב הלכנו אל קורפו ביום ה׳, י״ט אגוסטו, ר״ח אלול. ברוך אשר הפליא חסדו לנו ביום מצור.[36]
>
> In the middle of our journey, a high sea arose to drown us with a mighty storm [*se`ara*], and it surged for three days and three nights. Water lay over our heads until we feared for our lives. We called forcefully to our God, and He heard our supplications as we cried out to Him; **the sea fell back from His rage** [Jon. 1:15] and **the waves became silent** [based on Ps. 107:29]. With a good wind we went on to Corfu on Thursday, the 19th of August [1563], on the new moon in the month of Elul. Blessed is He who works wonders with His kindness to us in a day of distress.

Within the limits of his Hebrew nautical vocabulary, Pesaro describes the scene, albeit laconically. The three days, fear, prayer, and salvation fit into a predictable pattern; as did other Italian Jewish travelers, Pesaro frames the concrete description within biblical phrases, and he ends with a familiar encomium to God for working wonders. Grammatically, Pesaro uses the Mishnaic past tense form instead of the biblical consecutive Vav.

To sum up the analysis of these Renaissance period sea narratives, the accounts written by Italian Jews such as Meshullam, Bertinoro, Basola, and Pesaro in the fifteenth and sixteenth centuries show their frequent use of both Italian and biblical quotations. They also draw from Mishnaic

Hebrew and other rabbinic influences. To express piety, they resort to familiar Hebrew prayers or biblical passages.

These travelers' perceptions were often colored by their traditional views as pilgrims. This tendency posed one of the main challenges facing Hebrew writers who sought to tell about sea travel. Because of their traditional belief in Divine Providence (*hashgaḥa*), Jewish travelers often interpreted storms as punishments for wrongs they had done, on the model of Jonah's guilt. Many of them also believed that supplicatory or petitionary prayer could soften the judgment against them. When a storm at sea became a symbol of divine disapproval, the author's descriptive language tended to lose its concreteness. A scientific worldview was more conducive to concrete descriptions of nature than a religious worldview, which tended to turn real-world objects into symbols and to make travels into allegories.

Premodern Travelers

Hebrew style in the premodern era often reflected the writer's spoken language. Premodern Hebrew writing by Jewish speakers of Italian, Yiddish, and German usually show the influence of implicit translations or calques from their mother tongues.

Rabbi Haim Yosef David Azulai (ca. 1724–1807)—also known by the acronym חיד"א or HYD"A—is an exceptional case because his multilingualism gave him a broader perspective.[37] According to Ya`ari, Azulai descended on his father's side from "a famous Sephardic family." His mother, however, was Ashkenazic, apparently having arrived in Palestine with the group led by Yehuda ha-Hasid in 1700. Azulai must have known Yiddish and German in light of his many travels around central Europe, and during his travels in the Ottoman Empire he would have gained some ability to converse in Arabic, Turkish, and Ladino. This wide-ranging linguistic exposure probably enriched his Hebrew. His travels were not pilgrimages; rather, they were fund-raising missions as an emissary on behalf of the Jews in the Land of Israel. As a prominent member of the Jewish community in Palestine, Azulai lived and actively sustained the Zion-centered worldview.

Unlike the Italian writers, Azulai seems to avoid calques from the other languages he knows when he writes in Hebrew. Instead, he relies heavily on biblical allusions and later rabbinic usage. Even his description of a storm he experienced in 1758 shows his erudition:

> עברנו בים צרה מכל הסער הגדול יתר מאד, **והמים להם חומה גבוהה** נפקין בריש גלי **הפלא ופלא**, וכל אשר לנו, חפצים **וכלים מכלים שונים**, אף נעים ונדים, **וכל גבר ידו על חלציו**, **עני וכואב** נד ונבדל, הולך וחוזר **ושב על קיאו**. ורב החובל אז יסיר הוילאות ועשה המצאות לבלתי לכת הספינה. ונפשנו מאד נבהלה.[38]

> At sea we underwent distress from all of the exceedingly mighty storm, and **the water was a high wall unto them** [Ex. 14:22]; they [the Israelites] go out at the head of the waves [Targum Onkelos to Ex. 14:8], **wonder upon wonder** [Is. 29:14]. Everything we had—**vessels of different kinds** [Esther 1:7]—was rocking and shaking, and **every man's hand was on his loins** [in fear, like a woman in labor, as in Jer. 30:6], **poor and in pain** [Ps. 69:30], **shaking and separate** [Rashi on Ex. 28:6], coming and going [as a dog] **returns to his vomit** [Prov. 26:11]. The Captain then let out the sails [*vila'ot*] and found contrivances so that the boat would not go. Our souls were much affrighted [cp. Ps. 6:4].

The patchwork of quotations seems to obstruct the representation of a specific, mimetic scene—although the biblical references do add other memorable images to the portrayal of seasick sailors and passengers. Amid the biblical *shibbutz*, one also finds rabbinic Hebrew vocabulary, phrases, and grammar.

The extensive quotations were made possible by a culture of memorization and communal performance of biblical readings: rabbis such as Azulai were steeped in sacred texts. One exception in the passage just quoted is the nautical term *vila'ot*, which Azulai uses to describe sails (similar to Pesaro's use of וילי). As mentioned earlier in this chapter in connection with Pesaro's use of the term *vele* or *vili*, this medieval Hebrew usage derives from the Latin term *vēlum* or plural *veli* but also draws on the Italian term *vela* (plural *vele*), meaning "canvas" or "sail." Later, *vilon* and *vilonot* would be more commonly used in Hebrew to describe a curtain and curtains, heightening the need to find another Hebrew word.

The following quotation from Simḥa ben Yehoshua of Zalozitsh (Założce, near Brody), who traveled to Palestine in 1764–65, expresses the familiar belief that storms at sea have spiritual significance. This patchwork of quotations portrays the scene vividly in spite of the heavy burden of textual allusions. By incorporating so many biblical phrases, Simḥa ben Yehoshua is able to keep Yiddish influences at bay:

> **אבל אשמים אנחנו** וחטאנו לה׳ **ויאמר ויעמוד סערה ותרומם גליו** . . . **הים הולך וסוער** כל הימים והלילות . . . **עלו שמים ירדו תהומות, יחוגו וינועו כשיכור וכל חכמתם תתבלע,** והספינה שטה על הצד, פעמים הפכה עצמה לצד זה ופעמים לצד שני, **והלחם אזל מכלים, ומים אין לשתות,** וכמעט אמרנו: **נגזרנו הן גוענו אבדנו, כלנו אבדנו.**[39]

> **But we are guilty** [Gen. 42:21], for we have sinned before God, **and He speaks, and a storm arises and lifts up the waves** [Ps. 107:25] . . . **the sea storms** [Jon. 1:11] all of the days and all of the nights. . . . **They rise to the heavens and fall into the abyss, their souls melt away in calamity. They circle and lurch like a drunk, all of their wisdom is swallowed up** [Ps. 107:26–27]. The ship turned to the side—sometimes it tipped to one side, and sometimes to the other. **The bread ran out** [1 Sam. 9:7], **there is no water to drink** [Num. 20:5], and we almost said: **We are doomed. We are perishing; we are lost, all of us are lost** [Num. 17:27].

As indicated by the prevalence of bold type, this passage is a pastiche of biblical phrases. With some modifications, these verses are quoted accurately. Simḥa ben Yehoshua's account ends with an allusion to Numbers 17:27, when the Israelites are in the desert and complain to Moses, "Lo, we are perishing. We are lost, all of us are lost" (וַיֹּאמְרוּ בְּנֵי יִשְׂרָאֵל אֶל מֹשֶׁה לֵאמֹר הֵן גָּוַעְנוּ אָבַדְנוּ כֻּלָּנוּ אָבָדְנוּ). To this grim outcry, Simḥa ben Yehoshua adds a rare usage (*nigzarnu*, "we are doomed") from Ezekiel 37:11, where the Israelites say, "our bones are dried up, our hope is lost; we are doomed [or cut off]" (יָבְשׁוּ עַצְמוֹתֵינוּ וְאָבְדָה תִקְוָתֵנוּ נִגְזַרְנוּ לָנוּ). There is also a phrase from 1 Samuel 9:7 saying that "the bread ran out" (כִּי הַלֶּחֶם אָזַל מִכֵּלֵינוּ). The traveler describes what he sees mainly by association to prior texts. Intertextual references seem to take precedence over references to the real world.

To what extent does a travel writer describe a concrete scene, and when does the scene become subsumed under a biblical precedent? These premodern descriptions of sea travel show how a passage can be overburdened by its biblical quotations, to the point of blocking out the specifics of the narrative. Intertextuality sometimes interferes with the way in which these Hebrew writers refer to their surroundings.

Precursors to Hasidic Style

The mid-eighteenth century glimpsed a new kind of writing by traditionally educated men such as Yosef Sofer of Safed, who anticipates the hasidic writing discussed in chapters 2 and 3. They wrote in the shadow of several collective traumas—the Ukrainian massacres of 1648–49, followed by the fervor, strife, and disillusion surrounding the false messiahs Shabbetai Tzvi and Jacob Frank.

Narratives by the new eighteenth-century Hebrew writers reflected social changes that enabled Jews outside the rabbinic elite to express themselves in folksy, Yiddish-inflected Hebrew. They were not as well versed in postbiblical Hebrew as were established rabbinic authors, who usually limited the influence of Yiddish. In spite of their shortcomings—which sometimes included a shaky grasp of Hebrew grammar—these new authors provided an alternative to the quasi-biblical *shibbutz* championed by the Berlin *maskilim*. They preceded and heralded the coming boom in hasidic writing.

Yosef Sofer of Safed was a Torah scribe who lived in Safed under Ottoman rule. Avraham Ya`ari notes that Yosef Sofer, beginning his journey to Palestine, left Beresteczko (north of Brody) in 1758 and traveled by ship from Galatz to Istanbul. Sofer's writing, as Ya`ari states, is "written with simplicity and innocence, in a folksy language influenced by the Yiddish that he spoke."[40] This was an important, innovative moment for Jewish writing. A new stream began to broaden the traditional Hebrew prose genres of biblical commentary (*parshanut*), narrative Midrash (*aggadah*), legalistic tracts (*pilpul*, halakhic discussion of the Talmud), ethical teachings (*musar*), and mysticism (Kabbalah).[41]

A letter by Yosef Sofer of Safed reflects the messianic ideas that circulated in the wake of Sabbateanism, Frankism, and the rise of Hasidism. Writing in 1762, Yosef Sofer begins by mentioning his belief that "in this age are really the birthpangs of the Messiah, based on the great miracles and wonders that have happened in these times, as I will write you. May God, blessed be He, grant that it shall begin today, with great mercy, and He will send us redemption speedily and in our days. Amen."[42] He reiterates his belief in God's miracles that were performed on his behalf on the Mediterranean Sea after he left Istanbul. This is his account of how the storm began:

> נתרחש לילה אחד ויום אחד שהיה רעש ארץ גדול תחת הים שהים נשאו ומגביהו למעלה והולך וסוער וזרק הספינה מלמטה למעלה ומלמעלה למטה ולא היתה מנוחה אף רגע אחד, ותמהו כל אנשי הספינה ואמרו: **מה זאת עשה אלקים לנו**, והיינו בצרה גדולה מאד. ורב החובל היה מתמיה מאוד ואמר: מיום שעמד על דעתו, וגם שנתגדל ממש על הספינה, לא נתרחש זאת וגם לא שמע כזאת מאבותיו.[43]

> It happened one night and day that there was a huge earthquake beneath the sea, so that the sea surged and was lifted upward, and it continued to storm, and it threw the boat from down below to up above, and from up above to down below. There was no rest for a single moment, and all of the people of the boat were dumbfounded and said: **What is this that God has done to us?** [Gen. 42:28], and we were in great distress. The Captain was astounded and said: From the day he reached maturity [*'amad 'al da'ato*][44]—although he really grew up on ships—this had never happened, nor had he heard of anything like it from his ancestors.

This passage illustrates a rising linguistic trend among traditionally educated Jewish men in the eighteenth century: they often wrote Hebrew that seems translated from an unwritten Yiddish source. The source might be oral or internal, but as in the everyday life of this population it would have been in Yiddish. Structurally, for example, the long first sentence parallels the word order and breathless cadence of a spoken Yiddish phrase. In the midst of that stream of words, the connective use of ש for Yiddish אז is typical (*she-ha-yam nasa'o*, so that the sea surged). Moreover, the passage shows quirks—such as the absence of the particle את, where biblical grammar calls for it to precede every direct object that bears the definite article ה. For example, Sofer writes that the sea *zarak ha-sefina* ("threw the boat"), leaving out the particle preceding the noun. Because these authors made no effort to master or mimic biblical style, grammatical differences of this kind arose naturally.

The omission of the letter Heh, marking the definite article, combined with the omission of the particle *et*, was typical of Mishnaic Hebrew. Aba

Bendavid notes in his classic study of Mishnaic Hebrew: "One of the clear signs that change the language of the [Mishnaic] Sages from the Scripture is the reduction of the definite article Heh, especially in the Babylonian Talmud." He provides numerous examples by comparing the Palestinian Talmud with the Babylonian Talmud, where the Babylonian parallel text has dropped the ה־ or the את ה־.[45]

Eighteenth-century authors such as Yosef Sofer of Safed relied more on Mishnaic grammar than on biblical grammar. This is to be expected because the focus of traditional study was on the Talmud, and rabbinic writing of ancient times had followed more closely to Mishnaic Hebrew. After touching on the small group of *maskilim* who tried to write "pure" biblical Hebrew, Bendavid notes that "the remaining branches of the river did not stop writing Hebrew in their own ways."[46]

In the subsequent, nearly apocalyptic storm description by Yosef Sofer, there are further markers of Mishnaic Hebrew and Yiddish. Alongside the omission of the particle את before a definite article is a Yiddish-inflected use of the word *efshar*:

> ואמרו אפשר שהקב״ה רוצה להחריב העולם, אפשר רוצה להביא התהום מלמטה למעלה, וראה בעל הספינה שאר תחבולות שלא יזרק כל כך עם הספינה והיה משליך על היסוד הברזלות הגדולות מכל צד הספינה הנקרא בלשון אשכנז אַנקרש ונגרעו האַנקרש מן היסוד וזרק למעלה ולא הועילו כל התחבולות.[47]

> They said, Maybe the Holy One, blessed be He, wants to destroy the world, maybe He wants to bring the abyss up from the depths. The Captain ["Master of the Ship"] saw to all of the means so that the ship would not rock so much, and he was throwing down the huge irons [*barzelim*]—called anchors [*ankers*] in Yiddish [*leshon Ashkenaz*]—from the sides of the ship to the bottom of the sea. And the anchors were dragged from the sea floor and thrown upward, and all the measures were ineffectual.

Descriptions of storms at sea raised the broader question of what was appropriate for modern Hebrew writing; the apocalyptic intimations of this short passage reveal its author's cultural milieu. This text exemplifies many aspects of Hebrew written by Yiddish-speaking, Ashkenazic Jews in the eighteenth century. There is postbiblical Hebrew in the use of *efshar* (possibly, maybe) in the primary position of a phrase. The word *efshar* and its negation *i efshar* are found in the Talmud; when used to begin a sentence, however, both reflect Yiddish usage (thus, this phrase could derive from the Yiddish: *efshar vil Got khorev makhen di velt* [maybe God wants to destroy the world]). As Ya`ari notes, at least one other phrase in this passage shows the influence of the author's mother tongue, Yiddish: "so that the ship would not rock so much."[48] This seems to have been translated from the Yiddish idiomatic phrase *es zol zikh nit azoy varfn mit dem shif.* Another linguistic feature in the phrase *ve-haya mashlikh* (he was throwing) shows the influence of the compound past tense verb formation in Yiddish (*hot . . . gevorfn* or *hot mashlikh geven*)—unless the author is trying to convey an action that occurred repeatedly or over a continuous past time ("he would throw") by using something analogous to the imperfect in other European languages. This quasi-imperfect usage may be found in Rashi's commentaries, which is logical because in Worms the medieval commentator Rashi spoke Old French. Israelis use this form today, although it is foreign to the ancient system of verb aspects. Israeli Hebrew's grammar synthesizes many historical layers of biblical and postbiblical language, just as its vocabulary blurs the distinction between words derived from the Bible—such as *oniya* (ship) and *yareaḥ* (moon)—and those derived from the Mishna—such as *sefina* (ship) and *levana* (moon). There is seldom a significant difference in semantics or linguistic register, which could motivate the word choice; these varied usages instead sometimes reflect the ways these words were altered by their use in Yiddish.

As we have seen, Hebrew writers typically borrowed biblical phrases or foreign terms when describing sea travels. This practice would continue into the nineteenth century, including a vast tradition of rabbinic commentaries, responsa literature, and hasidic narratives that used postbiblical Hebrew. The movement beyond biblical pastiche happened in several ways, whereas biblical *melitza* and *shibbutz* remained maskilic norms of supposedly "pure" Hebrew style.

The Yiddish speaker Yosef Sofer, as discussed earlier, dabbled in writing Hebrew prose and was a harbinger of things to come. Innovating in translation from his Yiddish thought process, he moved away from biblical *melitza*.

Excursus on Key Words in Nautical Hebrew

Authors' uses of certain key words are often symptomatic of their intertextual sources. In nautical writing, for example, the ancient Hebrew root פ-ר-שׂ generated many meanings as Hebrew evolved over the millennia. Today Israeli Hebrew uses מפרשׂ (*mifras*) to mean "sail." This usage goes back to a somewhat dubious interpretation of an obscure biblical word that could mean "banner" or "sail" in the context of Ezekiel 27:7 and possibly Job 36:29.[49] The word מפרשׂ (*mifras*) derives from the root פ-ר-שׂ, "spreading out," as in unfurling a banner. Because of influence from Aramaic, however, the homophonic roots פ-ר-שׂ and פ-ר-ס sometimes interact.[50] The Aramaic term פרס or פרשׂ (*paras*, with the final letter either Samekh or Sin) means "to split," "to divide," or "to break";[51] thus, it is linked to the noun פרס, meaning "curtain."

It is necessary to reconsider all of this in the light of diachronic linguistics; that is, one should be aware of mixing usages from different historical periods. But that is precisely the problem for modern Hebrew users, whether they are aware or not of the linguistic shifts that have occurred. In postbiblical Hebrew, a מְפָרֵשׁ (*mefaresh*) is a sailor or navigator, one who spreads the sail, מִפְרָשׂ (*mifras*), whereas in medieval Hebrew a פַּרְשָׁן (*parshan*) or a מְפָרֵשׁ (*mefaresh*) is a commentator, one who opens or spreads out a text. After a sailor sets sail, someone spreads out the story of the voyage. In an unexpected turn of language, the sailor and the scholar come together in the four-letter word מפרש; "booking passage" has something in common with passages in books.[52] Tradition tells us to immerse ourselves in the sea of Torah.

Reviving Hebrew through Translation

Around 1800, two facets of style—naturalistic description and the everyday cadences of speech—were particularly difficult for Hebrew to develop. Narratives of pilgrimage and storms at sea reveal how authors struggled to represent nature; they often quoted biblical descriptions even when allusions obstructed the graphic character of the represented scene.

In premodern sea travel narratives, authors relied heavily on biblical prooftexts, reflecting their Torah- and Zion-centered worldview. Many also used words and phrases that were borrowed from their mother tongues, especially Italian and Yiddish. The unquestioning reliance on biblical passages tended to obstruct more creative, original uses of post-biblical Hebrew. Calques from Italian and Yiddish, however, sometimes made interesting inroads into Hebrew grammar and lexicon. In many ways, it seems that these early-modern Hebrew authors thought in their mother tongues while writing in Hebrew. There is often a kind of implicit translation from Italian or Yiddish into Hebrew, which created the echo of an oral style. Something similar happened later with translations from German, which helped to transform Hebrew into a living language.

Hebrew writing that strung together biblical quotations was like a gradually changing ship in a bottle. By itself, the ancient Hebrew ship was inert; the language of the Bible was powerless to represent modern life in Europe. Speakers of modern Italian, Yiddish, and German breathed life into Hebrew when they translated their descriptions, thought processes, and dialogues from their vernaculars into Hebrew. The direction and destination could be determined by pilgrimage, commerce, or adventure, but only speakers could pull the ship out of the bottle and give modern Hebrew narrative the breath of life.

Thus translation, explicit or implicit, became a powerful force in the rise of early-modern Hebrew writing. Recent translation theory has emphasized the importance of "foreignizing" as distinct from "domesticating" translation. Foreignizing is often associated with Walter Benjamin, who quoted Rudolf Pannwitz: "The basic error of the translator is that he preserves the accidental state of his own language, instead of allowing it to be powerfully affected by the foreign language."[53] In this vein, premodern Hebrew writers benefited from foreignizing translation of their own thoughts when it enabled them to introduce vernacular expressions into Hebrew. Instead of simply accepting the state of Hebrew, they allowed it to be transformed by Italian, Yiddish, and German.

The next two chapters turn to hasidic writing in Hebrew that was implicitly or explicitly translated from Yiddish. Hasidic writing embodied the rough, foreignizing style that was influenced by Yiddish and that made it unacceptable to the maskilic authors who cultivated the supposedly "pure" neobiblical style. Much as the Italian Hebrew writers sometimes grafted Italian onto Hebrew, so the hasidim grafted Yiddish onto their Hebrew texts.

2

Nahman

THE REBBE'S PILGRIMAGE

A turning point in Rabbi Nahman of Bratslav's life (1772–1810) came when he made a pilgrimage to the Land of Israel in 1798–99. The Baʿal Shem Tov—Nahman's great-grandfather, usually considered the "founder of Hasidism"[1]—is said to have attempted a pilgrimage, but he abandoned it after reaching Istanbul.[2] Nahman aspired to complete the voyage that the Baʿal Shem Tov was unable to finish. After Nahman's return, several of his followers and descendants also made the journey, and some remained in the Land of Israel.[3]

Hasidic accounts of journeys to the Land of Israel expressed a Zion-centered and Torah-centered worldview. As Nathan Sternharz writes in *Likutei halakhot*, "The Land of Israel and the Torah are all one, because the essential existence of the Torah is in the Land of Israel."[4] Hasidic pilgrimages, also known as "ascents" (*ʿaliyot*) to the Land of Israel, and their underlying ideology deserve close attention.[5] Since ancient times, the Hebrew word for "pilgrim" has been *ʿole regel*; that is, in Hebrew the pilgrim was someone who walked—literally, ascended on foot—up to Jerusalem and the Temple Mount (usually at the time of three week-long festivals—namely Sukkot, Passover, and Shavuot).

In studying the life and works of Nahman of Bratslav, one must remember that nearly all of the most important texts were written by his scribe, Nathan Sternharz.[6] This chapter examines Nathan Sternharz's story of Rabbi Nahman of Bratslav's pilgrimage, first published in 1815. Like many other rabbinic and maskilic authors of his time, Sternharz uses numerous biblical quotations, but he innovates when he adds a colloquial

Fig. 3. Chart of Rabbi Nahman's pilgrimage to the Holy Land in 1798–99, based on Samuel Dunn's map *Turkey in Asia*, in *A New Atlas of the Mundane System* (London: Sayer, 1788), plate 23, with approximate route added by Joseph Stoll, Syracuse University Cartographic Laboratory, in collaboration with Ken Frieden and by consulting the map in Nahman of Bratslav, *Rabbi Nachman's Wisdom: Shevachay HaRan and Sichos HaRan*, trans. Aryeh Kaplan, ed. Zvi Aryeh Rosenfeld (Brooklyn, NY: Breslov Research Institute, 1973), p. 32. Dunn's original map courtesy of the Lionel Pincus and Princess Firyal Map Division, New York Public Library, Astor, Lenox and Tilden Foundations.

dimension by inserting Yiddish into his Hebrew narratives.[7] This colloquial quality reflects the genesis of Nahman's writings: although Rabbi Nahman's teachings and tales were published by Sternharz in Hebrew, almost all of them were based on oral Yiddish sources.[8] Similarly, Sternharz's account of Nahman's pilgrimage was derived from oral reports by other Bratslav hasidim.

Bratslav (or Breslov) Hasidism assigned particular importance to the Land of Israel.[9] In *Likutei Moharan*, Nahman of Bratslav states, "It is known that the atmosphere of the lands of the nations of the world is impure, and the atmosphere of the Land of Israel is holy and pure."[10] Continuing Nahman's tradition, Nathan Sternharz writes that "the entire sanctity of the people of Israel is the Land of Israel, and through everything that a person does to sanctify and purify himself, and to serve God, he conquers a part of the Land of Israel and engages in the repair of the path to the Land of Israel."[11] Despite Sternharz's use of the verb *conquer* (כבש), on the surface the essence of a pilgrimage to the Land of Israel was spiritual ascent, as part of a larger messianic process. One of the prayers written by Sternharz asks God to "help me to go and arrive soon in the Holy Land" because "all of our Jewishness depends on the Land of Israel."[12]

In many of Nahman's fantasy tales, the ultimate, messianic goal is to rescue the exiled Shekhina (Divine Presence) and return Her to Zion. This goal establishes a link between mystical, kabbalistic ideas and pilgrimage to the Land of Israel.

Nahman of Bratslav said that he had fulfilled the entire Torah in his pilgrimage to the Land of Israel,[13] and he described a process of initial descent followed by spiritual ascent that was essential to the journey. He expressed his intense spirituality by saying that he would make every step of the journey with complete devotion.[14] He believed that only by overcoming great obstacles and by descending to insignificance (literally "smallness" or "diminution," *katnut*) could he rise to greatness and reach the Land of Israel.[15] Nahman also believed that the teachings he conceived while in the Land of Israel were vastly superior to those he conceived while outside the Land of Israel.[16]

Descriptions of hazards during the sea journey link Sternharz's account of Nahman's pilgrimage to biblical sources. Arthur Green emphasizes that the journey, as a rite of passage, had even greater significance than the destination.[17] The meaning of pilgrimage narratives often revolves around the hardships encountered along the way and how people respond to adversity. One key reference in most Hebrew pilgrimage narratives is therefore to the frightening and awe-inspiring storm wind (*ruaḥ se`ara*), with all of its accompanying biblical echoes, when God controls the traveler's fate. Nahman also based one of his basic teachings on God's promise in the verse "When you pass through water, I will be with you" (Is. 43:2).[18] A sea voyage is never just a sea voyage when it tests the pilgrim's faith and connection to God.

Nathan Sternharz, Scribe and Author

Nathan Sternharz told the story of Nahman's pilgrimage to the Land of Israel twice: in "Seder ha-nesi`a shelo le-Eretz Israel" (Order of His Journey to the Land of Israel, 1815) and in "Nesi`ato le-Eretz Israel" (His Journey to the Land of Israel, written sometime after 1822 and first published in 1874). The focus of this analysis is the development of a Hebrew style, but I hope to strike a balance between presenting the narrative of sea travel and the style of the narrative. Simply retelling the story misses the point, but analyzing only the style would be tedious. The two narratives of Nahman's pilgrimage are gripping, and part of the effect derives from their innovative literary form.

Translation was essential to the creation of almost all of the texts ascribed to Rabbi Nahman. In his autobiographical work *Yemei Moharnat*, Nathan Sternharz describes his method of writing down Nahman's teachings in 1803:

> וכך הי׳ דרך כתיבתי לפניו שהתורה שאמר באותו העת כמו בשבת חנוכה חזר אח״כ בעת הכתיבה ואמרה לפני פיסקא פיסקא שאמר לפני כמה דיבורים בלשון אשכנז ואני ישבתי לפניו וכתבתי הדברים בלשון הקודש עד שגמרתי כתיבת כל התורה וע״פ רוב חזרתי וקריתי אותה לפניו אחר שגמרתי כתיבתה.[19]

> And this was the manner of my writing before him. The Teaching (*torah*) that he spoke at a certain time, such as on the Shabbat during Hanukkah, he would afterward repeat when I was writing it down, saying it to me sentence by sentence. That is, he would speak before me a few

> phrases in Yiddish [*leshon Ashkenaz*], and I sat before him and wrote the words [or "things," *dvarim*] in Hebrew [*leshon ha-kodesh*] until I had finished writing the entire Teaching. And usually I read it back to him after I finished writing it.

After Nahman dictated his teachings to his scribe in Yiddish, Sternharz translated them into Hebrew. The Yiddish was undoubtedly already interspersed with Hebrew from various sources, while the resulting Hebrew texts echoed Yiddish. This scene of dictation makes explicit the dynamics of translation that are typical of Hebrew writing by Yiddish speakers.

According to Nathan Sternharz, Nahman once said to his followers: "Each one of you has a part in my teachings. But Nathan has a greater part than all of you." He continued: "You know that, if not for him, you would not have even a single leaf of the book [*Likutei Moharan*]. He said in Yiddish, 'ven nit er volt ir nit gehat a bletl shemos' [If not for him, you wouldn't even have even single torn page]."[20] Nahman was the inspiration, but Sternharz transformed Nahman's oral Yiddish teachings into Hebrew texts. Thus, both dictation and translation were essential parts of the creative process. Once when Nahman returned home and did not find his scribe, he commented that he had no one to receive what he needed to reveal: "I can hold in very much and not speak until the waters overflow the banks and it goes out by force. (In Yiddish he said: 'nor az es geyt iber di zastavkes' [Only when it overflows the dam].) And now, even so, I have no one before whom to speak."[21] He thought that most people were incapable of grasping what he said, and the words were lost on them. Nahman's teachings and tales resonated powerfully in Sternharz's Hebrew and became part of literary history.

Although Nathan Sternharz (1780–1844) may not have wished or expected to be remembered as a literary innovator, he was one of the most interesting and original Hebrew writers at the start of the nineteenth century.[22] The Russian Hebrew writer Eliezer Steinman admired Sternharz as "master of a sublime style."[23] Along with the popular hasidic hagiography *Shivḥei ha-Besht* (*In Praise of the Ba`al Shem Tov*), ascribed to Dov Ber of Linitz, Sternharz's narrative writings made a remarkable contribution to early-modern Hebrew prose. Like Nahman's more abstract teachings, his tales were translated from his oral Yiddish. Sternharz's method of translation from Yiddish into Hebrew helps to explain the tales' vitality and originality.

Much of what Nahman of Bratslav has become for readers over the past two centuries derives from a masterful hagiography that is inseparable from Nathan Sternharz's literary gifts.[24] Nahman of Bratslav was a charismatic leader who inspired his disciples though his sermons and stories; by selecting Sternharz as his scribe, he ensured that his legacy would be passed on in the most favorable light.

Sternharz was utterly devoted to Nahman of Bratslav, and he remained obsessed by him long after the Rebbe's death in 1810. From the time he met Nahman in 1802 until the end of his life in December 1844, he was first and foremost a disciple of the Rebbe. Nahman of Bratslav evidently had an inkling of this when he selected his amanuensis. Probably because he understood that Sternharz's Hebrew writing was exceptional, he appointed Sternharz to the position and dismissed a previous scribe.[25] Above all, Sternharz shared Nahman of Bratslav's vision of himself as a divinely inspired leader who would help bring the Messiah. For the initiated, Nahman's charisma turned everything he said and did into gold, and Sternharz tried to record everything. After serving him for eight years until the Rebbe's death, Sternharz spent the next thirty-four years of his life continuing his effort to write down everything that Nahman said and everything that was known about Nahman, as if the position of the Rebbe's scribe were a lifetime appointment.

Sternharz's nonhasidic family and in-laws were scandalized in 1802 when he began visiting Nahman in Bratslav. The opponents of the hasidic movement, the *mitnagdim*, tended to be wealthier and better educated than the hasidim. Many looked down upon Hasidism both because it flaunted some nonstandard practices (for example, it called for the use of a different knife for ritual slaughter) and because its adherents were usually poorer and less educated. Mainstream rabbinic leaders had good reason to oppose hasidic rebbes, who challenged their authority, whereas powerful Jewish leaders commonly supported the status quo, which favored them. So it is no surprise that Nathan Sternharz, from a wealthy family in Nemirov, met with opposition when he broke ranks and started visiting Rabbi Nahman.

After Sternharz became Nahman's disciple, he traveled often to Bratslav (about ten miles from Nemirov, which probably took about two hours by horse and carriage). The situation at home worsened when Sternharz became Nahman's scribe in 1803: his in-laws threatened him with divorce. Sternharz was somehow able to preserve the balance, however, living his family life in Nemirov and traveling to stay with the Rebbe on Shabbat and holidays.

Sternharz's narratives share a distinctive quality with some of the other effective Hebrew narratives of the time: they sound more idiomatic because they bear traces of having been translated from a living language. Whereas Moses Mendelsohn-Frankfurt translated from German (see chapter 5), the hasidic narratives are implicitly or explicitly translated from Yiddish. Although the Bratslav literature emerged from a strictly traditional, Orthodox world, Sternharz uses biblical references less often than the Berlin Hebrew authors, avoiding some of the pitfalls of maskilic *melitza*.

Prelude to Rabbi Nahman's Sea Voyages

Nahman of Bratslav had apparently long been attracted to traveling by water. About a decade before his journey to the Land of Israel, he had childhood experiences with boating on a river. Internal Bratslav sources indicate that Nahman lived with his father-in-law in Medvedevke between the ages of thirteen and eighteen—that is, from 1785 to 1790. This practice was commonly part of the marriage agreement: young newlyweds were often supported for a year or more at the house of the bride's parents. The groom was usually expected to continue his studies in a yeshiva or House of Study (*beit midrash*). In this case, besides keeping up his studies, Nahman followed the example of his great-grandfather, the Ba'al Shem Tov, and practiced solitary meditation in nature.

The following story, which describes Nahman's childhood experiences while boating, emphasizes his awareness of the fragility of human existence. His response to boating in extremis also brings up the hasidic emphasis on meditation and fervent prayer. Adrift on a river,[26] Nahman turns to God. In most of Sternharz's writings, as was typical of printing in his time and place, the punctuation is minimal. It consists of only periods—actually printed as bullets—which may also function as commas;

the ends of paragraphs are sometimes marked with what looks like a colon but is actually the cantillation sign marking the end of a verse (*sof pasuk*).[27] Sternharz describes the scene vividly:

> בכפר אסאטאן סמוך לעיר מעדווידווקע שם הי׳ דר חמיו ז״ל · ושם הי׳ עיקר גידולו · ושם הולך נהר גדול ועליו גדלים קנה וסוף הרבה למאד מאד : הי׳ דרכו בקודש של אדומו״ר זצוק״ל [אדוננו מורנו ורבנו זכר צדיק וקדוש לברכה] · שהי׳ לוקח לפעמים ספינה קטנה ושט עמה בעצמו לתוך הנהר הנ״ל · אעפ״י [אף על פי] שלא הי׳ יכול היטב להנהיג ספינה זאת · אעפ״כ [אף על פי כן] הי׳ שט עמה עד אחורי הקנה וסוף · עד המקום שלא הי׳ רואין אותו עוד · ושם עשה מה שעשה בעבודת הש״י [השם יתברך] בתפלה והתבודדות אשרי לו · כי באמת זכה למה שזכה כנראה בחוש בספריו הק׳ [הקדושים]:[28]

> In the village of Osiatyn, near the city Medvedevke, there lived his father-in-law, may his memory be blessed. And there was the main part of his upbringing. There a great river runs, in which grow very very many reeds and bulrushes. The way in holiness of our Master and teacher, our Rebbe of blessed memory, was that he sometimes took a small boat and sailed alone in the aforementioned river. Although he was not able to manage [or steer, *lehanhig*] this boat very well, nevertheless he sailed on it beyond the reeds and bulrushes, until one could no longer see him. There he did what he did in service to God, blessed be He, in prayer and solitary meditation, happy was he! For he truly merited what he achieved, as is clear from his holy books.[29]

While boating, Nahman placed himself at the mercy of forces beyond his control. He experimented with difficult circumstances and achieved his early spiritual breakthroughs in that place, on that river, while he was sailing a boat to serve God in prayer and solitary meditation (*hitbodedut*).[30]

As it continues, the passage about Nahman's early boating in Osiatyn anticipates how he would later conceive the sea journey to be an apt metaphor for the human condition. This reminds us of the phrase and song that are associated with him: "The entire world is a narrow bridge, and the main thing is not to be afraid."[31] In this case, however, the precarious position is rendered more extreme by stormy weather:

> וכשבא בתוך הנהר רחוק מהיבשה · ולא ידע כלל מה לעשות · כי הספינה מתנודדת וכמעט שיטבע ח״ו [חס ושלום] · ואז צעק להש״י [להשם יתברך] והרים ידיו אליו כראוי · [32]

> When he went into the river far from land—and didn't know at all what to do, because the boat was rocking [or reeling, *mitnodedet*] and he was almost going to drown, God forbid—then he cried out to God, blessed be He, and raised his hands up to Him, as is fitting.[33]

Feelings of helplessness and fear bring Nahman closer to God. This scene reminds the narrator, Nathan Sternharz, of the story of Nahman's flight from Tiberias when plague broke out and the city was closed. While hanging over the Sea of Galilee, Nahman calls out to God:

> וכן כשהי׳ תלוי בידיו על החומה בטבריה כשרצה לברוח מהעיפוש ר״ל [רחמנא לצלן] וכו׳ · וראה תחתיו הים כנרת וכמעט כמעט שיפול כמבואר במ״א [במקום אחר] בסיפור הנסיעה שלו לא״י · אז ג״כ [גם כן] צעק בלבו להש״י כראוי · והי׳ רגיל לספר זאת · ורצה להכניס בלבינו שכך צריך כל אחד ואחד לצעק להש״י ולישׂא לבו אליו ית׳ [יתברך] כאלו הוא באמצע הים תלוי על חוט השערה והרוח סערה סוער עד לב השמי׳ [השמים] · עד שאין יודעין מה לעשות וכמעט אין פנאי אפילו לצעוק · אבל באמת בודאי אין לו עצה ומנוס כ״א [כי אם] לישא עיניו ולבו להש״י:[34]

> Similarly, when he was hanging by his hands on the wall in Tiberias, when he wanted to flee from the plague, God save us, and he saw the Sea of Galilee beneath him and almost, almost was going to fall (as is explained elsewhere, in the story of his journey to the Land of Israel), also then he cried out in his heart to God, blessed be He, as is fitting. He used to tell us about this because he wanted to impress upon our hearts that this is how every single person must cry out to God, blessed be He, and raise his heart up to Him—as if he were in the middle of the sea, dangling by a hair's thread [*talui `al ḥut ha-se`ara*], and the storm wind is raging up to the sky to the point that one doesn't know what to do, and there is barely even time to cry out. Yet in truth, without a doubt, there is no way out [literally, no counsel and no refuge, *ein `eitza ve-ein manos*], other than to raise one's eyes and one's heart to Him, blessed be He.

The childhood experience in a boat thus anticipates Nahman's journey to the Land of Israel.[35] The hagiography transforms these moments of crisis on a river or at sea into an intensified contact with God through prayer. Reading back from the pilgrimage to Nahman's childhood, Sternharz finds a pattern.

This descriptive scene of calamity and prayer supports the claim, on the title page of *Magid siḥot*, that the book is written in simple and clear language (*be-lashon kal ve-tzaḥ*) that is accessible to all, "great and small." This was the stylistic genius of Nathan Sternharz, as illustrated even by manuscript passages like this one, which he did not publish and which had to wait decades to appear in print.

Sternharz's biographical passage and commentary explain what sea travel meant in Nahman's thought and tales. A youthful experience of terror repeated later in life during storms at sea—and again by the Sea of Galilee during his pilgrimage to the Land of Israel—became for Nahman emblematic of all human existence. "All the world is a narrow bridge"; or, to shift the metaphor, we all are dangling over the sea, hanging by a thread, in a storm. In Nahman's worldview, the sea traveler in distress becomes a figure for the storm-tossed individual at any time.

Nahman Prepares for His Pilgrimage

Nathan Sternharz's narrative of Nahman's journey, titled "Seder ha-nesi`a shelo le-Eretz Israel" (Order of His Journey to the Land of Israel), is one of the most detailed hasidic accounts of pilgrimage. Originally published in 1815, it was inconspicuously slipped into the back part of the book *Sippurei ma`asiyot* (*Tales*) in Rashi script, with a new pagination, yet with misleading running headers that continued from the prior hagiographic portion of *Sippurei ma`asiyot*.[36] There is also an extant manuscript of "Seder ha-nesi`a shelo le-Eretz Israel" included in the manuscript of what became known as *Shivḥei ha-Ran*.[37]

The description of Nahman's journey to the Land of Israel, "Seder ha-nesi`a shelo le-Eretz Israel," is the high point of Sternharz's biographical narrative about the Rebbe.[38] This narrative forms the second part of the book, which has often been reprinted as *Shivḥei ha-Ran*. (The title *Shivḥei ha-Ran* apparently was not given by Sternharz, however, for it was not used as the title of a self-contained book until 1864.[39]) Because this trip took place several years before Sternharz met Nahman, Sternharz gathered the details from various sources, including Nahman himself, Nahman's fellow traveler Reb Shimon, and other disciples.[40] Sometime after

1822, Sternharz wrote a second version, "Nesi`ato le-Eretz Israel" (His Journey to the Land of Israel), in which he added new details and left out many others; this later version was included in *Ḥayei Moharan* when it was published posthumously in 1874. In the background of Nahman's sea journey is his awareness of the Ba`al Shem Tov's failed journey to the Land of Israel and Nahman's deliberate attempt to accomplish what his great-grandfather did not.

Shivḥei ha-Ran is significant both as a spiritual biography of Nahman and as Nathan Sternharz's first independent work. Unlike Nahman's previous discursive publications in 1808 and 1811 and the tales published in 1815, most of which had been dictated by Nahman, *Shivḥei ha-Ran* compelled Sternharz to develop his own narrative voice. He had served as Nahman's scribe for seven years, translating the master's sermons and tales from Yiddish into Hebrew; after the Rebbe's death in 1810, Sternharz completed preparations to publish Nahman's stories. In order to retell Nahman's journey to the Land of Israel, Sternharz had to develop beyond his role as amanuensis and become an autonomous narrator. Although he received all of his information second- or thirdhand, he invented a convincing literary voice that often sounds like that of an omniscient narrator.[41]

When Sternharz describes how Nahman decided to travel to Palestine in 1798, he places this decision in the context of a conversation. This choice also reflects Sternharz's reliance on sources other than Nahman himself: "On Passover Eve (in the year 1798), our Master and teacher, our Rebbe of blessed memory, left the ritual bath and said to the one who was walking with him that in this year he would certainly be in the Holy Land."

> בערב חג הפסח · (שנת תקנ״ח לפ״ק) יצא אדומו״ר ז״ל מהמקוה · ואמר לזה שהלך עמו שבזאת השנה יהי׳ בוודאי בארץ הקדושה.[42]

The Hebrew style is accessible in part because the syntax follows Yiddish. It is possible to reconstruct an implicit Yiddish original for this phrase, one that retains much of the Hebrew that was already present in Yiddish:

> ערב פסח (אין יאָר תקנ״ח) איז אדמו״ר ז״ל ארויס פונעם מקוה און האָט געזאָגט צו דעם, וואָס איז געגאנגען מיט אים, אז אין דעם יאָר (הײַנטיקס יאָר) וועט ער אוודאי זײַן אינעם הייליקן לאנד.

The clumsy Hebrew phrase *'amar le-zeh she-halakh `imo* (said to the one who walked with him) sounds more idiomatic when we hear behind it the implicit Yiddish *hot gezogt tsu dem, vos iz gegangen mit im.* In 1815, Sternharz apparently was reluctant to acknowledge the disciples who were close to Nahman before Sternharz met him in 1802. It is possible that a power struggle was taking place following Nahman's death. Ada Rapoport-Albert points out that in his later account Sternharz refers to Nahman's fellow traveler to the Land of Israel as ר"ש, an abbreviation of the name "Reb Shim`on."[43]

The narrative builds suspense as Nahman prepares for his journey and his family learns of his plan. Nathan's direct style makes his response to their dismay appear callous:

> וכאשר שמעה אשתו זאת · שלחה בתה אליו לשאול אותו איך אפשר לו להניח אותם מי יפרנסם · והשיב כך · אתה (!) תסע למחותנך · אחותך הגדולה יקח אחד אותה להיות בביתו משרתת קטנה שקורין נאינקע [ניאנקע] · אחותך הקטנה יקח אחד אותה לביתו מצד רחמנות · ואמך תהי׳ משרתת קעחירין · וכל מה שיש בביתי · אמכור הכל על הוצאות הדרך · [44]

> And when his wife heard this · she sent her daughter to him to ask him how he could leave them who would support them · and he replied thus · you will travel to your in-laws · your elder sister someone will take to be a little servant in his house that is called a *nianke* [nurse] · your younger sister someone will take into his house out of pity · and your mother will be a servant *kecherin* [cook] · and everything there is in my house · I will sell everything to cover travel expenses ·

This rough translation retains Sternharz's minimal, bullet punctuation. Adding punctuation, as most modern editions in Hebrew, Yiddish, and other languages have done with Nahman's work, produces a more readable passage:

> And when his wife heard this, she sent her daughter to him to ask him how he could leave them—who would support them? And he replied: You will travel to your in-laws. Someone will take your elder sister to be a child servant, which is called a nurse, in his house. Someone will take your younger sister into his house out of pity. And your mother will be a servant cook. And everything there is in my house—I will sell everything to cover travel expenses.

Perhaps this cleaned-up rendition is too tame, however, diminishing the raw drama of Nahman ruthlessly planning to break up his family. Sternharz's narrative conveys the bluntness and sparseness of Nahman's pronouncement: he is preparing to sell his house and all its contents, with little regard for the consequences. As Nahman remains starkly indifferent to the plight of his family, letting nothing stand in the way of his spiritual journey, Sternharz's narrative does not soften the force of this decision. And so it continues:

> וכאשר שמעו זאת בני ביתו געו כולם בבכיה · ובכו כמה ימים ולא הי׳ לו שום רחמנות עליהם · ואמר כי לא סגי בלאו הכי יהי׳ איך שיהין[ה] הוא יסע בודאי · כי רובו כבר הוא שם ומיעוטא בתר רובא אזלי (ואמר בזה״ל [בזה הלשון] · ווארין דיא גרעסטי העלפט איז שון [!] דארט וכו׳).[45]
>
> And when the members of his household heard this, they burst into tears. And they cried for several days, and he showed them no mercy. And he said, it's not enough, anyway [Aramaic: *ki lo sagi be-lav hakhi*], whatever will be, he would definitely travel. For most of him is already there, and "the smaller part follows the larger" [Aramaic: *ve-mi'uta batar ruba azli*]. (And he said in these [Yiddish] words: Because the greater part is already there, *vorin di greste helft iz shoyn dort.*)

As Sternharz was himself considering a pilgrimage to the Land of Israel by 1815, this scene may have been important to him in making the difficult decision to travel in spite of the obstacles. Here his Hebrew includes an unusual combination of embedded Aramaic and Yiddish, alongside influences from those languages. For instance, "he showed them no mercy" (*ve-lo' haya lo shum raḥmanut aleihem*) is a calque from the Yiddish *er hot nit gehat keyn rakhmones af zey.*[46] This passage exemplifies how Yiddish speakers picked up the postbiblical Hebrew word for mercy or compassion, *raḥmanut* (originally and usually found in commentaries on Lamentations 4:10). They appropriated the Hebrew word, naturalizing it into the Yiddish term *rakhmones* in popular texts such as the *Tsene-rene.*[47] *Raḥmanut* was also linked to the more common attribute of mercy (*raḥamim*), which—based on biblical sources (*'el ḥanun ve-raḥum* [Ex. 34:6, Deut. 4:31, Ps. 86:15, Ps. 103:8][48])—was often ascribed to God in medieval poetry and prayer.

The final line of Nahman's reply reminds us that all of the dialogues were spoken in Yiddish, which is directly quoted in many places, both in this text and in other writing by Nathan Sternharz. The narrator also seems to quote Nahman's own Aramaic phrases, which would have been familiar mainly to scholars who were well versed in Talmud.[49] Perhaps Nahman quoted Talmud to underscore his authority, deliberately speaking over the heads of his wife and daughters, and making it more difficult for them to protest.

The Rebbe's Pilgrimage Begins

Rabbi Nahman's pilgrimage begins with what appear to be aimless, spontaneous wanderings.[50] The narrator intimates, however, that the Rebbe was carrying out a divine plan. His initial trip to Kamenetz-Podolsk sets the scene by suggesting that Nahman was able to overcome an anti-Jewish decree that prohibited Jews from remaining inside the city overnight. Nevertheless, the first impression is mystery and wonder:

> קודם שנסע לא״י [לארץ־ישראל] · הי׳ בקאמיניץ · והנסיעה שלו לקאמיניץ הי׳ פליאה גדולה · כי פתאום נסע מביתו · ואמר שיש לו דרך לפניו לנסוע · ונסע מביתו על הדרך שנוסעין למעזיבוז · ואמר שהוא בעצמו אינו יודע עדיין להיכן הוא נוסע · ונסע למעזיבוז ·[51]
>
> Before he traveled to the Land of Israel, he was in Kamenetz. And his trip to Kamenetz was a great wonder. For suddenly he left his home, and he said that before him was a route to travel, and he traveled away from his home on the road that people take to Medzebozh, saying that he himself didn't know yet where he was going, and he traveled to Medzebozh.

Yiddish inflections are present in Sternharz's writings from the beginning of his story of Nahman's journey. This account—by one Yiddish speaker for other Yiddish speakers—is based on traditional Hebrew writing in a rabbinic, Mishnaic guise. The narrative uses short phrases, loosely connected by the repeated letter Vav ("and," but also blurring into other meanings), and the word choices rely heavily on the Hebrew that was present in everyday Yiddish. The phrase אינו יודע עדיין להיכן הוא נוסע (he himself didn't know yet where he was going), using *`adayin* and *le-heikhan*, draws from the Hebrew of medieval rabbinic commentaries, which was familiar to hasidic writers.

The simplicity of this style, involving repetition and short phrases, corresponds to the simplicity of Nahman's travel. The verb נסע (to travel) occurs many times in this passage, supplemented by the noun נסיעה (trip, journey). Hebrew narrative since the Bible has employed repetition, possibly because it emerged from an oral tradition. In particular, there are many biblical passages in which virtually every sentence begins with "And" (the connective letter Vav). Sternharz follows this model, which is especially evident here because the Hebrew phrases are so short. Yet even with this characteristic of biblical style, without the grammar of the consecutive/conversive Vav (*vav ha-hipukh*), the passage does not sound biblical. It sounds like Yiddish translated into Hebrew because short phrases take the place of linked hypotactic clauses.

Even apart from the literal presence of Yiddish phrases, one can almost hear the Yiddish inflections—and imagine the implied Yiddish narration—crying out from inside the Hebrew. The Hebrew opening sounds like Yiddish syntactically; furthermore, the word choices are based almost entirely on Hebrew roots that were present in Yiddish speech. For instance, to begin at the beginning of the Hebrew passage: *koydem* is used in Yiddish; *nas'a* is the root of *nesi'a*, a Yiddish word (pronounced *nesiye*) that occurs in the next sentence; the Hebrew/Yiddish names "Eretz Israel" (Erets Yisroel), "Kamenetz," and "Medzebozh" are identical in Ashkenazic pronunciation; *pli'a* is familiar from the Yiddish *pele*; and so on.

The narrative continues with the suggestion that Nahman received guidance from a heavenly source:

> ובמעזיבוז נתוודע לו מן השמים · שהוא צריך לנסוע לקאמיניץ ונסע לקאמיניץ · וכל נסיעותיו היו בפשיטות כדרך אנשים פשוטים · בלי שום התנשאות ובלי שום פרסום · אע״פ [אף על פי] שאז כבר הי׳ מפורסם בעולם אעפ״כ [אף על פי כן] הזהיר מאד לאנשיו שנסעו עמו שיזהרו לבלי להודיע בשום מקום שהוא נוסע · [52]

> And in Medzebozh it was made known to him from Heaven that he must travel to Kamenetz, and he traveled to Kamenetz. And all of his travels were in simplicity, in the manner of simple people, without any haughtiness and without any public knowledge. Although he was already renowned in the world, in spite of this he forcefully warned his

> followers who traveled with him to take care not to make it known anywhere that he was traveling.

There is a characteristic ambiguity here, combining Nahman's sense of carrying out a heavenly task while expressing humility in this world. On the one hand, Nahman is presented as acting with divine guidance; on the other hand, he puts on no pretenses. One could say that this high and low double register permeates Sternharz's Hebrew, with its Yiddish subtext. For example, *kvar haya mefursam* (was already renowned) is not Yiddish, but here it corresponds to the Yiddish phrase *iz shoyn geven mefursem*; the verb *hizhir* (to warn) is used in the compound Yiddish verbal form *mazhir zayn*, just as the earlier term *hodi`a* (to make known) occurs in Yiddish as *modiye zayn*. Almost every word is already familiar from spoken Yiddish vocabulary. The result is a Hebrew that sounds less literary and more spoken than almost any other Hebrew written at the time, a Hebrew easily understood by less-educated readers. Sternharz constructed a Hebrew idiom that usually stayed within the confines of the Hebrew already present in Yiddish.

Sternharz emphasizes that no one understood why Nahman began his trip in Kamenetz and that people always erred with regard to things the Rebbe did: *ha-`olam to`in `atzman*.[53] For several reasons, this phrase exemplifies Sternharz's Yiddishized Hebrew. First, *`olam* (with the non-temporal meaning "earth, world") is a late usage that appears at most in a single, disputed passage in the Hebrew Bible (Eccles. 3:11).[54] Based on this postbiblical sense, in this context *ha-oylem* has assumed the Yiddish (linked to medieval Hebrew) meaning of "people"; the verbal form *to`in `atzman* calques the reflexive in the Yiddish verb construction *zikh toe zayn* (they err) in Yiddish. Nahman might have said, *zey zaynen zikh toe* or, in the past tense, *zey hobn zikh toe geven*. As discussed toward the end of this chapter, the Hebrew stays as close as possible to the Rebbe's Yiddish, including its grammar.

Many hasidic teachings and practices revolved around a rebbe's (or *tzaddik*'s) ability to change an outcome, reverse an evil decree, or bring desired results. Along these lines, Sternharz writes that "not a creature knows what he did there," but somehow Nahman changed the evil decree:

"from that time on, permission was given to [Jewish] people of Kamenetz to dwell within the city."[55]

Nahman Encounters Storms at Sea

The pilgrimage narrative is structured around three major storms at sea,[56] which are represented as life-threatening moments that tested Nahman's faith. At climactic moments, Sternharz uses long, run-on phrases that create a breathless effect. The basic grammar is Mishnaic, with frequent use of connective Vavs but without the biblical Vav consecutive (ו' ההיפוך). Although Sternharz received all of the details secondhand, he successfully evokes the intensity of the experience:

> ובבואם לספינה והתחילו לילך על הים השחור · תיכף במעת לעת הראשון הי׳ פרטינע גדולה דהיינו רוח סערה · עד שהגלים קפצו על הספינה · והוכרחו להיות בחדר סגור ומסוגר מחמת המים שלא יבואו עליהם · והיו ברקים ורעמים ורוחות גדולות בלי ערך · והי׳ פחד גדול מרעש הרעמים והגשמים ושאון הגלים · ומחמת פחד לא הי׳ באפשרי לישן בלילה וכו׳ ואחר ד׳ ימים באו לסטאנבול וישבו על הספר · [57]
>
> And when they came to the ship and started to go on the Black Sea · immediately on the first day there was a great *firtina* that is a great storm · until the waves leaped onto the ship · and they were forced to be in a closed and sealed room because of the water so that it wouldn't reach them and there were thunder and lightning and high winds without measure [*bli `erekh*, from the Yiddish *on an erekh*] · and there was great fear from the sound of the thunder and the rain and the roar of the waves· and because of fear it was not possible to sleep at night and so on and after four days they came to Istanbul and sat on the shore [*ha-sfar*, from Aramaic *sfara*]·[58]

The narrative traps the reader in this storm experience, moving briskly from phrase to phase without a break: from the storm to the waves to the sealed room to the thunder, lightning, winds, and fear. Then, in what seems like an anticlimax, four days have suddenly passed, the travelers have arrived safely, and they are sitting on the shore in Istanbul.[59] Sternharz describes a tangible scene without inserting biblical references, in contrast to most of the earlier Hebrew storm descriptions. Either lacking sufficient storm terminology in Hebrew beyond the words *ruaḥ se`ara* or quoting the language of the sailors, Sternharz has recourse to the word *firtina*. In modern Turkish, this word means "storm, gale, tempest, hurricane"; it could be etymologically related to the Greek word φουρτούνα, meaning "storm, rough sea."[60] The use of this term shows Sternharz's openness to outside linguistic influences.

Yiddish is implicit behind these phrases, both in syntax and vocabulary. "Immediately on the first day" uses four words that were also common in Yiddish: *teykef*, *meys leys*, and *rishon*. The phrase almost doubles as Hebrew and Yiddish. "Because of fear it was not possible to sleep" also uses several common Yiddish words: *makhmes*, *pakhed*, *efsher*. Sternharz's Hebrew was as accessible as possible to Yiddish speakers.

As discussed previously, the biblical Psalms influenced many early-modern Hebrew descriptions of sea travel. Biblical phrases are less common in Sternharz's narrative writings, but in "Seder ha-nesi`a shelo le-Eretz Israel," he uses Psalm 107 to frame the description of a second storm and how it subsides (with biblical phrases highlighted in bold print):

ובלכתם על הים · היה רוח סערה גדולה מאד מאד שקורין (אפרטינע גדולה מאד) והיתה הספינה בסכנה גדולה · **יעלו שמים ירדו תהומות** וכו׳ · ולא הי׳ עוד בלב איש מהם להנצל מן המיתה · והיו צועקים כולם אל ה׳ · והיתה לילה אחת כמו יוה״כ [יום הכפורים] ממש שהכל בוכים ומתוודים ומבקשים כפרה על נפשם · ואמרו סליחות ושאר דברי תפילות ותחנונים · ורבינו ז״ל הי׳ יושב ודומם · והתחילו כמה אנשים לומר לו מפני מה הוא שותק בעת צרה כזאת ולא השיב · אך אשת הרב דק׳ חאטין שהיתה מלומדת ובכתה וצעקה כל הלילה והתחילה היא ג״כ לומר לו כאלה · מפני מה הוא דומם · וכמדומה שקילל אותה · ואמר לה · הלוואי הייתם שותקים גם אתם הי׳ טוב לפניכם · **ובזאת תבחנו** · אם אתם תשתקו · **ישתוק הים מעליכם** ג״כ · וכן הי׳ · ופסקו מלצעוק ושתקו · ואזי מיד כשהאיר היום · **יקם סערה לדממה ויחשו גליהם וישמחו** וכו׳ · [61]

When they went onto the [Mediterranean] sea, there was a very great storm (which is called a very great *firtina*), and the ship was in great danger. **They rose to the heavens and fell into the abyss** [*ya`alu shamayim yerdu tehomot*, Ps. 107:26]. And not a person among them expected to be saved from death. And they all cried out to God. And one night was just like Yom Kippur, when everyone was weeping and confessing and begging forgiveness for their souls. And they said the

> Penitential Prayers and the rest of the prayers and supplications. And our Rebbe z"l [may his memory be for a blessing] was sitting and was silent. And some people began to ask him why he was silent in such a time of distress, and he didn't reply. But the wife of the rabbi from the community of Hattin, who was educated and wept and cried out all night, also began to say things like this to him. Why was he silent? And it seems that he cursed her. And he said to her, If only all of you would also be silent, it would turn out well. **By this you will be tested** [*be-zot tibaḥenu*, Gen. 42:15]: if you will all be quiet, **the sea will become quiet before you** [*yishtok ha-yam me`aleikhem*, Jon. 1:12]. And that is what happened. They stopped crying out and became quiet. And then immediately when daylight came, **He makes the storm become silent and the waves become still, and they rejoice** [*yakem se`ara li-demama va-yeḥeshu galeihem va-yismeḥu*, Ps. 107:29].[62]

In a departure from Sternharz's usual narrative practice, this scene of prayer and salvation becomes densely biblical. The beginning and end of this passage quote Psalm 107, framing the dramatic scene with biblical verses. Even Rabbi Nahman's words—as conveyed in Sternharz's Hebrew rendering—draw phrases from Genesis 42:15 (*be-zot tibaḥenu*) and Jonah 1:12 (*yishtok ha-yam me`aleikhem*).[63] Here Sternharz's narrative stands out from the straightforward, Yiddishized style of his more typical Hebrew narrative prose.

At odds with his fellow travelers' expectations, Rabbi Nahman does not cry out to God. Instead, he calls for silence. Sternharz's narrative asks us to believe that in this instance silence was a more effective response than outcries. The climactic phrase, "He makes the storm become silent," refers to God in Psalm 107. In this passage, however, there is a hint that the powerful "he" who calms the storm is Rabbi Nahman. None of the crying out to God is effective; only the silence Nahman calls for leads to a diminution of the storm. The allusion to Jonah 1:12 is more complicated because in that passage Jonah tells the sailors, "Lift me up and cast me into the sea, and the sea will become quiet before you, for I know that this great storm is because of me." The biblical source suggests that the man who speaks these words is the cause of the storm. An alternation between grandiose claims and self-blame is a recurrent motif in Nahman's biography.

Describing the approach to Ottoman Palestine, off the coast of Yafo, Sternharz's narrative again places the pilgrimage in biblical context. The captain finds that strong waves make it impossible for the ship to moor outside the harbor. He asks, "What is this, and why is this?" Then some Sephardic Jews answer that they have an oral tradition according to which, "in this place, Jonah ben Amitai the Prophet was thrown [into the sea]."[64] It almost seems as if Nahman's quotation from Jonah anticipated this discovery. In the perception of these traditional Jews, natural phenomena could be explained by biblical narratives.

Arrival is climactic and anticlimactic. Nahman arrives in Haifa the day before Rosh Hashanah in an exalted state: "the great strength of the joy that he felt at that moment, when he entered and stood on holy soil, it is impossible to imagine with the mind." He said that "immediately, when he walked four paces (*'amot*), right away he achieved what he wanted to accomplish." His high spirits continue through a Rosh Hashanah dinner. But upon entering the synagogue the next morning, "worry and an immeasurably broken heart were awakened in him, and he did not speak a word to anyone."[65] The description of alternating states like these led Arthur Green to speculate that Nahman suffered from a mood disorder, possibly manic depression.[66]

During Sukkot, the Rebbe goes with the Jewish community to the cave of Elijah the Prophet, "and there everyone made a big celebration with dances" (*`asu kol ha-`olam simḥa gedola ve-rikudin*). Again there is a Yiddish subtext: *der gantser oylem hot gemakht a groyse simkhe un tantsn*. Both *der oylem* (the people) and *a simkhe* (a celebration) are examples of Hebrew words that took on new meanings in Yiddish, meanings that Sternharz retains in his Hebrew texts. When Yiddish is grafted onto Hebrew, it produces new life.

Nahman chose a particularly dangerous time for his trip to the Land of Israel. As he was attempting to return to Europe from Acre, Napoleon's fleet besieged the port. Sternharz explains that Nahman and his fellow traveler searched for a neutral ship, which enemy ships "do not take into captivity" (*she-lo lokḥin le-tokh ha-plen*).[67] This phrase exemplifies

Sternharz's use of Hebrew, as it is calqued from the Yiddish phrase *nemen in plen* (to take into captivity).[68] It also illustrates Sternharz's traditional use of Aramaic forms, in particular with verbal endings ין– in place of ים– and plural nouns, using ין– in place of ים–. The ין– ending links Sternharz's writing to traditional rabbinic Hebrew texts while preserving a distance from the neobiblical style of maskilic authors.

The first traumatic part of Nahman's journey home is a close encounter with the war between the French and the Turks. The following passage is the beginning of a detailed account in *Shivḥei ha-Ran*, quoted in the original with minimal punctuation:

> ובבוקר באו אל הספינה אנשי חיל שקורין בראנד וואך ורבינו ז״ל עם האיש שלו הנ״ל רצו עוד לבא להתנפל לפני רגלי הקאפיטאן ולהתחנן לו שיניח אותם לשוב אל הספר · אך בתוך כך עקרו האנקיריס וברחו לצד שהרוח נשאם מחמת פחד · כי המלחמה נתעוררה מיד · ונשמע קולם מאד · ושמעו שם על הספינה קול גדול מאד של ההורמאטיס והבאמביס ושאר קולות כאלו מעניני מלחמה · כי קולם נשמע למרחוק מאד · וגודל הסכנה והאימה והפחד שהיה להם אז אין לשער · ונפלו למשכב שניהם יחד · ולא הי׳ להם אפילו מים לשתות · כי לא הכינו להם כלום כנ״ל · וד׳ ברוב רחמיו וחסדיו נתן להם חן בעיני ישמעאל אחד שהוא היה קעכיר אצל הקאפיטאן · ונתן להם בגניבה א׳ שאל קאווי שחורה לכל א׳ וא׳ בבקר ובערב · ומחמת החולשה שלהם שהיו מוטלים על ערש דוי ר[חמנא]״ ל[צלן] · [69]

> In the morning, soldiers called *Brandwache* [fire guards] came to the ship, and our Rebbe—of blessed memory—with his man, mentioned above, still wanted to come and fall at the feet of the Captain and beg him to let them return to the shore · But in the meantime they pulled up the anchors and fled in the direction that the wind carried them, out of fear, because the war was awakened suddenly · And their sounds were very much heard · On the ship they heard the very mighty sound of cannon and bombs and the rest of the sounds, like those, from the stuff of war. For their sound is heard at a great distance · One cannot imagine the greatness of the danger and panic and fear they felt · So both of them together fell onto their bed · They didn't even have water to drink, because they hadn't prepared anything for themselves, as mentioned above · God, in His mercy and kindness, enabled them to find favor in the eyes of a certain Arab, who was the Captain's cook · He secretly gave each of them a bowl of black coffee in the morning and in

the evening. Because of their weakness, they were stretched out on their sickbed, God save us.

As usual, the syntax of Sternharz's Hebrew follows the implicit Yiddish original. For example, the entire opening sentence, *u-veboker ba'u el ha-sefina anshei ḥail she-korin brand vakh*, seems to follow Yiddish, word for word: *un in morgen zaynen gekumen af der shif soldatn, vos men ruft zey brand vakh*. The continuation offers more of the same effect of Hebrew calquing Yiddish; the Rebbe and his attendant wanted to "fall at the feet of the Captain." The expression *faln tsu di fis fun* (to fall at the feet of) was a widespread nineteenth-century idiom.

To reiterate, much of Sternharz's Hebrew narrative is a transparent reframing of Yiddish. The implicit, underlying Yiddish may derive from Nahman himself, from Nahman's fellow traveler Shimon, or from other hasidim. In this case, the specific oral sources are unspecified and therefore less important than the method of writing. Sternharz has perfected a Hebrew style that remains close to the implicit Yiddish. As narrator and editor, he keeps the narrative easily comprehensible to less-educated readers at the same time as he conveys his Yiddish vernacular thought processes.

In a later storm description, Sternharz includes biblical references, when the foundering ship once more reminds the narrator of Psalms:

ואח״כ [ואחר כך] אחר חצי היום נתעורר עוד הפעם רוח סערה גדולה · ונשא את הספינה · והיתה הספינה מטרפת ומבולבלת כמה ימים ולילות רצופים · **יעלו שמים ירדו תהומות** · ולא היה לבעלי הספינה שום עצה איך להמלט · **ויחוגו וינועו כשכור וכל חכמתם תתבלע** ·[70]

Afterward, after noon, once again a mighty storm was awakened and lifted up the ship. The ship was raging and foundering [*haita ha-sefina metorefet u-mevulbelet*] for a few days and nights in a row. **They rise to the heavens and fall into the abyss** [Ps. 107:26]. The masters of the ship had no idea how to find refuge. **They circle and lurch like a drunk, all of their wisdom is swallowed up** [Ps. 107:27].

The phrase *ha-sefina metorefet u-mevulbelet* suggests an interesting personification of the boat, making it appear deranged and confused. The spiritual sea voyage is often linked to volatile states of longing and euphoria, confusion and madness. Sternharz combines his Yiddish-inflected narrative with biblical allusions, especially Psalm 107. He begins with the same reference as in the previous passage, "They rise to the heavens and fall into the abyss," possibly alluding to Nahman's own psychological descent. Sternharz continues with the unresolved description, "They circle and lurch like a drunk, all of their wisdom is swallowed up."

During a situation of extreme danger, Nahman asks God to save him because of the merit of his ancestors. But in the midst of the storm, he also mentions that he cannot pray because he is in "the state of mental diminution" (*ha-moḥin de-katnut*). There is even a comic moment in the midst of the storm when they expect the ship to sink and the Rebbe tells his attendant what to do: "Take all of the money, until the last coin, and divide it in two. Half—tie onto your body, and the other half—I will tie onto my body. The man asked him: Why? The fish in the sea will be able to swallow us without the coins." And then Nahman refers to Exodus 14 for reassurance: "Do as I say. The Israelites were upon the sea and did not drown [alluding to Ex. 14:22, 29], and we are still in a boat."[71] In other words, God saved their ancient forebears from the sea without any boat to help them, and Nahman and his fellow travelers still had a boat to guard them from the sea. This tragicomic scene has some of the cartoonish qualities of Nahman's fantasy tales, which are discussed in the next chapter.

A miracle apparently rescues them. In passages like these, the narrative combines the otherworldly aura of Nahman's tales with the hagiographic genre of miraculous stories contained in *Shivḥei ha-Besht*:

> ואחר זה ראו מרחוק כמו ענן גדול אפל מאד · ונפל עליהם עוד פחד גדול · מחמת שלפעמים כשהענן מתאסף ומתקשר לשאוב המים מהים · נעשה שם כמו בקעה וכשהספינה יורדת לשם · אזי נטבעין שם והתקנה לזה · לירות בקני שריפה והורמאטיס כדרך המלחמה כדי לשבר העננים · ולהם לא הי׳ להם פנאי לזה מחמת שהיו צריכים לשאוב המים מהספינה כנ״ל · והיו הצרות צרורות זו לזו כמו זיבורא ועקרבא [חגיגה ה] · אך בחמלת ה׳ מחמת תוקף הרוח סערה היה הליכת הספינה במהירות גדול ופרחה הספינה כמו חץ מקשת ממש · ובאה הספינה למקום הנ״ל שהענן שותה משם · והי׳ שם כמו שער והרים סביב לה · ועברה הספינה משם בשלום ובתוך כך האיר ה׳ עיניהם ומצאו החור שדרך שם נכנסין המים בספינה ·[72]

After this they saw from afar something like a huge, very dark cloud, and again fear fell upon them. Because sometimes when the cloud is

> gathering and connects to draw water from the sea, there is formed something like a breach, and when the ship goes down there, they drown. The remedy for this is to shoot guns and cannon in the manner of war, to break the clouds. As for them, they didn't have time for this because they had to pump water from the ship, as mentioned above. So their troubles were bound together like a wasp and a scorpion [Tractate Ḥagiga 5].[73] But thanks to God's compassion [cp. Gen. 19:16], because of the power of the storm wind, the course of the ship was exceedingly fast, and the ship flew just like an arrow from a bow. The ship came to that place where the cloud was drinking from, and something like a gate surrounded by mountains was there. The boat passed from there in peace, and at the same time God opened their eyes, and they found the hole through which the water was entering the ship.

This storm seems to dissolve the boundaries between seafaring customs, mystical occurrences, and natural phenomena. Sternharz mentions the usual "remedy," referring to maritime practice. But this remedy is impossible to carry out in this case, leaving only "God's compassion." There are intriguing parallels between the actions of nature—a storm cloud drawing water from the sea and a whirlpool opening up in the water—and the sailors' actions, pumping water from the ship and discovering the hole that threatened to sink the ship. As in Nahman's allegorical tales, where the human realm refracts a higher realm, mundane events parallel cosmic reality.

Again a storm (*ruaḥ se'ara*) creates a spiritual drama that ultimately confirms Nahman's power through his ancestors' merits and closeness to God. When the mariners are saved, Nahman "said the Psalm, **Give thanks unto the Lord** [Ps. 107] with great joy."[74] This conclusion to the episode returns us to where we started: Psalm 107, with its description of stormy sea travel and God's Providence.

In contrast to his procedure when transcribing Nahman's tales, Sternharz was not taking dictation when he artfully shaped the story of Nahman's voyage. He brought together the vivid accounts of sea travel he had gathered from Nahman's contemporaries with the story of Nahman's spiritual journey and mystical ascent. His most remarkable accomplishment was fusing them into a coherent pilgrimage narrative, guided by overarching themes from Nahman's teachings.

The Development of Sternharz's Style

A comparison of the two accounts of Nahman's journey shows how Sternharz's writing changed between 1815 and his composition of *Ḥayei Moharan* in the 1820s. He realized that some readers would know the first account and refers to it occasionally in the second. The condensation in the later text may reflect his efforts to avoid redundancy. The later account adds dialogue, which sometimes creates more vivid scenes. This chapter has already analyzed the earlier account, and thus only the differences between it and the later one concern us here.

In the 1815 version, Sternharz mentions Nahman's attendant only as "the man who was with him," whereas the later version retelling refers obliquely to "Reb Sh[imon]." Some scholars have speculated that this change may be connected to a leadership battle following the Rebbe's death. Mendel Piekarz has written about the opposition to Sternharz's leadership among other followers of Nahman.[75]

The posthumously published description of Nahman's pilgrimage in *Ḥayei Moharan* acknowledges the prior version and then continues more graphically. Sternharz has perhaps by this time become a more skillful narrator, including details that enable us to imagine Nahman starting his trip: "In the beginning, before he traveled to the land of Israel, he traveled to Kamenetz, as explained in the published book. And on his trip to Kamenetz he said to Reb Sh[imon], There is a trip ahead of me and I don't know where, and Reb Sh[imon] laughed, How do we travel if we don't know where we are going? and he answered, I truly don't know. And Reb Sh[imon] went and prepared a wagon and horses and all of the travel necessities and traveled with him."[76] The shift to directly quoted dialogue from third-person, indirect representation of speech is accompanied by a shift to present tense. Instead of presenting sketchy details, the text gives a vivid conversation with Shimon and new details about their preparations for departure.

The later account continually provides more graphic details and dialogue. The early version says that "in Medzebozh it was made known to him from Heaven that he had to travel to Kamenetz." In the later version, when Nahman reaches Medzebozh, his mother says to him, "My son, when will you go to your grandfather the Besht—that is, to his holy grave? Our Rebbe, of blessed memory, replied, If my grandfather wants to see me, he will come here. Afterward at night he lay down to sleep, and in the morning his mother got up and came to him, and said to him: Hasn't your grandfather already been with you? When will you go to him—that is, to his holy grave? Our Rebbe, of blessed memory, replied, Not now, I will be at his grave on my return; if God so wills it, I will be at his grave. And so it was."[77] In place of the vague information that "it was made known to him from Heaven," there is a faint suggestion that the Besht visited Nahman at night, perhaps in a dream vision. In a subsequently quoted conversation with Shimon, Nahman makes this explicit: "On that night the Besht was with me and made known to me where to travel."[78] Nahman's pilgrimage became a kind of fulfillment of the journey that the Ba`al Shem Tov did not complete. It also illustrates Sternharz's greater use of dialogue in the later version.

Writing Yiddish in Hebrew

Sternharz contributed a lively style to modern Hebrew by working from Yiddish, sometimes echoing Yiddish phrases, grafting Yiddish words or meanings onto the Hebrew. The first storm at sea in Nahman's pilgrimage, as shown earlier, illustrates Sternharz's Yiddish-inflected Hebrew.

Certain aspects of Sternharz's Yiddishized Hebrew style, relating to the grammar he applies to verbs, deserve special attention. The Yiddish verbal compound זיך מxxx זײַן, consisting of the reflexive *zikh*, a Hebrew present participle, and the Yiddish verb of being, made it possible to import innumerable Hebrew nonreflexive verbs into Yiddish, with or without a shift in meaning. By the same token, Yiddish speakers sometimes exported the Yiddish syntax into Hebrew. For example, Sternharz writes that as a child Nahman didn't despair or torment himself—לא היה מיאש עצמו,[79] which is probably a translation of the underlying, implicit Yiddish in the past tense: ער האט זיך נישט מיאש געווען. This Yiddish form זיך מxxx זײַן is clearly in the background of some hasidic Hebrew usages.[80] For instance, the reader learns that Nahman would compel himself to pray: *hu z"l haya makhriaḥ `atzmo*, translating from the Yiddish *er z"l hot zikh makhriekh geven*.[81]

At the end of Nahman's stay in Palestine, he was in a hurry to leave, Sternharz writes: he *zirez et `atzmo me'od*—literally, he "hurried himself very much."[82] This illustrates another prominent stylistic quirk, parodied by Joseph Perl in *Megale temirin* (1819), involving the frequent use of a verb plus עצמו, corresponding to the Yiddish reflexive זיך. There are hundreds of examples of this quirk in Sternharz's Hebrew, often relating to Hebrew verbs that had become common in Yiddish. *Shivḥei ha-Ran* includes expressions such as "he would exert himself" (היה מיגע עצמו), "to afflict himself" (לסגף עצמו), "he accustomed himself" (הרגיל עצמו).[83] This feature stands out especially when the verb is already in a reflexive form, as in the case of "he distanced himself" (התרחק עצמו), "he overcame himself" (התגבר עצמו), and "he boasted himself" (התפאר עצמו).[84]

Rabbinic writers commonly took Mishnaic Hebrew as their foundation, as did Maimonides in *Mishneh Tora*. It became the basis for traditional study, ensuring that rabbinic norms remained at odds with the Hebrew of Enlightenment authors, who most often emulated the prophets. Another aspect of rabbinic writing was the use of Aramaic and some elements of Aramaic grammar, such as the plural ין– endings of nouns and verbs. Because Sternharz continued in the rabbinic tradition, he sometimes uses Aramaic plural forms. This use could have been a nod to Talmudic norms. In the eyes of enlightened Hebrew writers in Berlin, the use of a Mishnaic or later postbiblical style represented a corruption of "pure language"; however, this shift in the level of discourse kept the tone familiar to traditional readers.

Conclusion

From opponents of the hasidim in the nineteenth century to modern scholars, it has long been argued that hasidic writing in the nineteenth century was defective. According to some scholars, this imperfection resulted from "intentional ignorance" fostered by the faulty educational system of eastern European Jewish communities. Iris Parush presents this argument, explaining that because the Hebrew Bible was seldom studied beyond the early years of heder, it was inevitable that traditionally educated Jews were unable to write Hebrew in the manner of ancient biblical texts. Instead, she notes, postbiblical rabbinic Hebrew became a model. She argues that Jewish communities in nineteenth-century eastern Europe "worked to preserve the ignorance of grammar, of Scripture, and of the Hebrew language." One aspect of this agenda was the "taking of rabbinic language as a model worthy of imitation." Parush also states that the situation differed between hasidim and *mitnagdim* as well as between Ukrainian hasidic leaders and Lithuanian nonhasidic rabbis: "among the hasidim, the ignorance of grammar was great, whereas among the Lithuanians there were students, teachers, and rabbis who knew grammar."[85]

Parush possibly overstates her thesis when she writes that ignorance of biblical Hebrew grammar resulted from "the minimizing of teaching Scripture and the system of teaching it."[86] Although that was often true, this explanation plays down the fact that traditional Jews, and especially rabbis, were reading, chanting, and hearing Torah and Haftara at least three days of the week, on Mondays, Thursdays, and Saturdays. Because men who were frequent readers in synagogue had memorized large portions of the text and trope (the system of cantillation), the text and tropes were easily accessible to them at least as possible allusions or direct quotations. This is evident in the first section of *Shivḥei ha-Besht*, which quotes scripture extensively and parts of which are clearly modeled on the Joseph story in the Book of Genesis. The question arises: To what extent were rabbinic writers able to transform known biblical phrases into newly shaped sentences?

In Hebrew writing, allusiveness often ran the risk of leading to dry imitation or obscurity. One of the most successful authors in the mode of *shibbutz* was the medieval poet Yehuda Ha-Levi. His poem "'Al ha-yam" (Upon the Sea) is a masterpiece of this kind, although its poetic language distances it from the texts studied in the present work. *Shibbutz*, the practice of embedding scriptural phrases in newly written Hebrew, takes many different forms. Sometimes, in maskilic writing, the quotations seem to overwhelm the text, whereas elsewhere they provide the text with a meaningful underpinning and resonances. Modified allusions to scriptural phrases, as opposed to direct quotations, afford more freedom to the author.

Nathan Sternharz's main innovation was that he allowed Yiddish to guide his Hebrew narrative style. Instead of mimicking biblical grammar and vocabulary, he combined Mishnaic Hebrew with Yiddish to create an accessible alternative. His approach resembled other hasidic writing of the time, such as *Shivḥei ha-Besht*. The result was greater immediacy.

Although vividness and immediacy are often unquestioned objectives for modern narratives, this was not always the case for hagiographic writing, inspirational literature, or pilgrimage accounts. Moreover, Nahman himself had a clear preference for parables and allegorical tales. For a Torah-centered imagination, the intertextual relationship to scripture or Kabbalah was often more important than the specificity of a mundane scene. Thus, descriptions of concrete events had to be invested with meaning, as when a storm during a sea voyage had to be withstood in the course of a pilgrimage. This suggests an alternate reason for hasidic authors' frequent references to biblical contexts, which is distinct from the maskilic efforts to return to biblical Hebrew.

Turning to Nahman's tales in the next chapter, we find fictionalized sea travels that are included in adventurous quests, representing spiritual processes. Like the hero of his tale "The Master of Prayer," Nahman often subordinated the mundane world to a higher purpose. Every nation has a central goal, *takhlit* or *takhles*; in Nahman's worldview, the only true purpose is to serve God. To help bring the Messiah, Nahman indicated, devotion to the true purpose must conquer other goals such as wealth and beauty. The kabbalistic notion of the *sefirot* (emanations of God) cast our world as a refracted expression of the higher spheres. Nahman's intent was to raise his disciples to a higher level, not to leave them immersed in everyday insignificance.

So it is that Nathan Sternharz's writings evoke a tension between abstraction and concreteness, between allegorical meanings and the material world, between mystical Hebrew and mundane Yiddish. His accomplishment was to break down this barrier, thereby infusing Hebrew with Yiddish. Sternharz raised Yiddish to the level of Hebrew by writing a Hebrew that lowered itself to Yiddish. In this way, he helped turn Hebrew into a modern vernacular.

3

Nahman's Fantasy Travels and Sternharz's Pilgrimage

Nathan Sternharz's worldview was traditional, but his Hebrew was ahead of its time. This chapter juxtaposes Nahman of Bratslav's fantasy tales of sea travel with Sternharz's account of his own pilgrimage in 1822. Whereas Nahman's fantasy travels usually avoid concrete detail, emphasizing instead a higher level of meaning, Sternharz's pilgrimage narrative is vivid and includes many graphic details. In Nahman's tales, the mundane level remains vague, with the plot subordinated to a mystical, allegorical meaning. Sternharz's pilgrimage narrative to the Land of Israel invests travel with meaning by following in the wake of Rabbi Nahman. As discussed in chapter 2, the influence of Yiddish enabled Sternharz to convey spontaneous impressions and an oral style, using easily accessible language.

Nahman's purpose in telling stories was to teach his disciples indirectly because many of them were simple men who had difficulty understanding his abstract teachings. His metaphorical method was familiar to yeshiva-educated Jews from their study of Midrash, with its use of parable (*mashal*) and narrative (one of the meanings of *aggadah*, sometimes also referred to as "legend"). In ancient and medieval Midrashic passages, for example, many phrases and short parables explain attributes of God (the King of kings) metaphorically by telling stories about worldly kings. Nahman's matter and manner of storytelling deviated sharply, however, from the rabbinic norms of his milieu.

Sternharz wrote a preface to the 1815 edition of *Sippurei ma'asiyot* (or *Sippurey mayses* in the Ashkenazic Hebrew and Yiddish pronunciation).

The preface notes that a few of the narratives resemble folktales: "sometimes he would tell a story [*ma`ase*] from among the folktales [*ma`asiyot*, not *ma`asim*] that the people of the world [*ha-`olam*] tell." Sternharz continues: "But he added a lot to them, changing and fixing the order. Until the story of the tale [or "plot"; *sippur ha-ma`ase*, not *sippur ha-ma`asiya*] was completely different from what people tell."[1] In this passage, Sternharz slides almost imperceptibly between calling Nahman's narratives "stories" (*ma`asim*) and linking them to "folktales" (*ma`asiyot*), as in the title of the book.

It is not clear to which folktales Sternharz is comparing Nahman's tales. The sentence "sometimes he would tell a story from among the folktales that the people of the world tell" is open to varying interpretations. Stories told by "the people of the world" (*ha-`olam)* are literally, in modern Hebrew, told by "the world"—but this really means stories told by *ha-oylem* in Yiddish. As discussed in chapter 2, the Yiddish usage of *ha-oylem* means "the people, the public," usually referring to "people of our group" (*anshei shlomenu*). Nevertheless, in the context of folktales, "stories told by *ha-`olam*" probably denotes folktales told by both Jews and non-Jews in different areas of Europe. This is important because some of Nahman's tales do resemble widely dispersed European folktales. Intriguingly, the Grimm brothers collected what became their book of *Märchen* (*Fairy Tales*, 1812–15) at the same time that Sternharz collected and retold Nahman's tales.

Like Nahman, Sternharz inhabited a Torah-centered world; the Rebbe's teachings and the Land of Israel were the foci of his spiritual world. Sternharz followed Nahman's example by making a pilgrimage to the Land of Israel, thus uniting these two foci. He accepted the spiritual importance of pilgrimages to Zion, for, as Nahman said, "the essential sanctity of the Jewish person depends on the Land of Israel."[2] When Sternharz asked for clarification on this point, Nahman told him: "My intention is literal: I mean the literal Land of Israel with the rooms and houses. And he said in Yiddish, in these words: *ikh meyn take dos Erets-Yisroel mit di shtiber mit di heyzer*. That is, my intention is literal, that every Jewish person must go to the material Land of Israel."[3] Nahman's goals combined the individual's spiritual ascent with a broader goal of repairing the world (*tikkun ha-`olam*).[4] The essence of the holiness of the Land of Israel, Nahman added, is that "God's Providence [or supervision, *hashgaḥa*] is always there."[5] One of Nahman's mystical goals was to draw sanctity from the Land of Israel into the Diaspora.[6] The Rebbe's involvement was essential to this goal: "When the *tzadik* [righteous man, hasidic rebbe] speaks in Torah or in prayer, it is called Eretz-Israel."[7]

Chapter 2 showed that in writing the first narrative of Rabbi Nahman's voyage to the Land of Israel (published in 1815), Nathan Sternharz began to develop as an independent author. His own pilgrimage took that development a step further: he emulated Nahman's journey and wrote his own narrative. Sternharz wrote several manuscripts about his life and pilgrimage, which were edited and published long after his death in 1844. The first, published in 1876, is primarily a memoir of his years with Rabbi Nahman (1802–10), edited by Nahman of Tcherin.[8] Near the end of this posthumously published work, though, several pages are clearly based on Sternharz's contemporary diary from the years 1824–35.[9] This distinction between memoir and diary is pertinent to an understanding of Sternharz's emergence as the author of original travel narratives.

The Style of Nahman's Tales (*Sippurei ma`asiyot*)

Nahman told his tales in Yiddish, and as his scribe, Sternharz wrote them down in Hebrew. There has long been a debate over which came first, the Hebrew version or the Yiddish version, but for our purposes the issue is moot. No one doubts that Nahman originally told his stories in Yiddish—interlaced with essential Hebrew loan words—and Sternharz reports that he translated them into Hebrew as he recorded them. In an interesting bilingual hybrid, Yiddish is present explicitly and implicitly in all of Sternharz's Hebrew texts. This is perhaps the most important means, albeit a controversial one, by which the hasidic authors broadened the scope of Hebrew writing. By allowing Yiddish to inform their writing, they influenced the evolving grammar and vocabulary of written Hebrew.

Sternharz helped create a more accessible alternative to the staid Hebrew of the Enlightenment Hebrew authors. Yet for ideological reasons, most Hebrew critics have kept hasidic writers at a distance and have mistrusted their contributions to literary history. Discussions of

Nahman's tales have generally neglected their formal aspects, as embodied in Sternharz's Hebrew. One of the few scholars to shed light on Sternharz's style, Isaiah Rabinovitch, placed greater emphasis on narrative than on language.[10] Yosef Klausner also recognized some merits of folk Hebrew, as represented by Sternharz's writings, but he never let this influence his version of Hebrew literary history.[11] From a linguistic and literary perspective, the study of Sternharz's Hebrew writing is largely uncharted territory.

Shmuel Werses took some pioneering steps into the linguistic realm of Nathan Sternharz's Hebrew and Yiddish texts, exploring relationships between one Hebrew tale and its Yiddish version. In his analysis of Tale 9, "The Sophisticate and the Simple Man," Werses discusses interlinguistic features of Sternharz's writing. In particular, he cites salient Hebrew–Yiddish commonalities as well as calques from the Yiddish.[12] He also points out that Tale 9 is one of the most worldly, incorporating realistic details from Warsaw. Werses's contribution helped prepare the ground for the present analysis.

Nathan Sternharz, an innovative Hebrew stylist, eschewed both Enlightenment norms and the dominant style of the rabbinic opponents of the hasidim (the *mitnagdim*). He made a fresh beginning, moving beyond the narrow, conventional realms established by *melitza* and rabbinic responsa (*she'elot ve-tshuvot*, letters answering halakhic questions). To match the Hebrew texts as closely as possible to their oral Yiddish sources, as we saw in chapter 2, he used a simple Hebrew style that bore the mark of having been translated from Yiddish.

The clearest expression of Sternharz's literary intentions is found in the second preface to *Sippurei ma'asiyot*, which was published sometime around 1845–50, a few years after his death. The first edition was the object of controversy and criticism after it was printed in 1815. In *Megale temirin* (Revealer of Secrets, 1819), Joseph Perl mocked many aspects of the book; another unpublished manuscript he wrote around 1816 attacked *Sippurei ma'asiyot* and Sternharz even more directly.[13] Moreover, as is evident from the second preface to Nahman's tales, some traditional readers closer to home in Podolya objected to what seemed like idle fantasies. In the second preface, to counter these objections, Sternharz and a later editor carefully explained the spiritual, kabbalistic significance of stories that might otherwise seem profane.

The end of the second preface tries to dispel concerns about stylistic and other issues. An editor—presumed to be Nahman of Tulchin (1814–84)[14]—introduces Sternharz's final lines with the words "And this we found in the bag of writings and it concerns an apology that he, of blessed memory, wrote the *Sippurei ma'asiyot* in such a simple language, and this is it."[15] After this sentence come the telling lines that are attributed to Sternharz from his unpublished manuscripts:

> עוד ראיתי להעיר לבב המעיינים בספר זה של המעשיות לבל יהיה בלבם עליו על אשר נמצאים לפעמים שיצא מתחת לשונו לשונות גסים בס׳ ספמ״ע [בספר סיפורי מעשיות] כגון ונעשה ברוגז עליה בסי׳ א׳ [בסיפור מספר 1] ולקח א״ע [את עצמו] אל השתיה בהמעשה של הבנים שנחלפו ועוד באיזה מקומות כי ידין אותו לכ״ז [לכף זכות] שזה היה כשגגה היוצא מלפני השליט ע״פ [על פין] הכרח גדול. כי, ע״כ [עד כאן] מצאנו והעתקתי אות באות לשונו ז״ל.[16]

> What is more, I have seen the need to awaken the heart of those who read this book of stories, lest they become incensed at him that in the *Tales* there are sometimes found, as if they had slipped from his mouth, coarse expressions—such as, "he was *brogez* at her" in Tale 1, and "he took to drinking" in the story of the children who were switched, and in a few other places. Let the reader judge him leniently, for this was unintentional, like an error that comes from a ruler [using an expression from Eccles. 10:5], in accordance with great necessity. For so we found it, and I translated his words letter by letter.

In the last sentence, Sternharz seems to be insisting that he has faithfully translated Nahman's Yiddish narratives into Hebrew. An example is *ve-lakaḥ et 'atzmo 'el ha-shtia* (he took to drinking), a Hebrew phrase that literally translates a Yiddish idiom.[17] In the face of criticism, Sternharz contended that his rendering was accurate because it precisely followed the Rebbe's Yiddish, and he also defended Nahman against complaints of vulgarity.

Equally interesting is the further expansion of this defense by the editor (presumably Nahman of Tulchin), referring to Nathan Sternharz's intentions. The editor opens a new paragraph with the words

> והנה נראה בעליל שרצונו הק׳ [הקדוש] היה לכתוב טעם על זה אך לפי הנראה שפסק באמצע מחמת איזה אונס ושוב לא זכינו שהש״י יסבב הדבר שיכתוב בעצמו. ת״ל [תודה לאל] אשר זכינו ברחמיו ית׳ [יתברך] שנכתבו דברים אלה.[18]

> It is evident that his holy wish was to explain the reason for this, but it appears that he stopped in the middle because of some compulsion, and we were never privileged to have God, blessed be He, change the matter so that he himself would write it. Thank God that we were privileged by His compassion, Blessed be He, that these things were written.

The editor then explains that psychological, spiritual, or even demonic obstacles blocked Sternharz's efforts to write and to reveal Nahman's presence in the world:

> כי על כל דיבור ודיבור שרצה לכתוב שיתגלה בעולם היה מניעות על זה הרבה ומחמת זה היה זריז מאד מאד בכתיבתו כאשר ראינו בעינינו כי היה רגיל לומר לנו תמיד שאם אינו מזרז א״ע [את עצמו] לשבר המניעות לכתוב מיד אינו יודע אם יכתוב עוד מכמה טעמים הכמוסים אצלו.[19]

> For regarding every word and phrase that he [Nathan] wanted to write in order to reveal him [Nahman] in the world, there were many hindrances to this, and because of this he was very quick in his writing, as we saw with our own eyes—for he was always accustomed to tell us that, if he did not hurry himself [mezarez et `atzmo] to overcome the hindrances to writing immediately, he did not know if he would write any more, for several reasons he did not disclose.[20]

Enlightenment authors concluded simply that hasidic writers wrote bad, "barbaric" Hebrew. In a less-judgmental mode, it is possible to see that Sternharz refashioned Hebrew grammar in a way that—by following Yiddish—made it more familiar and comprehensible to Yiddish-speaking readers.

Sternharz alluded to his belief that by writing about the Rebbe, he was acting to repair the world and bring the Messiah. The hindrances were, at least in part, satanic forces that were trying to prevent this reparation—a struggle made explicit in some of Nahman's stories (e.g., Tale 7, "The Rabbi's Son"). The pace of Nathan's writing and the obstacles to its completion are not, however, the main point of this passage; the editor raises this issue to explain why Sternharz did not complete his explanation. Next he elaborates on the question of style in *Sippurei ma`asiyot*.

The editor (again, probably Rabbi Nahman of Tulchin, publishing the second edition of the *Tales* around 1845–50) elaborates on the account that Sternharz left incomplete:

> ועתה בשביל ששמעתי גילוי דעת ממנו ז״ל שרצונו כשידפיסו עוד הפעם לכתוב איזה טעם על זה אמרתי לא אכחד מלכתוב טעם אחד מטעמים הרבה אשר היו גנוזים וכמוסים אצלו ז״ל וזהו ששמעתי ממנו ז״ל כי אדמו״ר מוהר״ן זצוק״ל סיפר המעשיות בלשון אשכנז הנהוג במדינתינו ומו״ר הרב ר׳ נתן זצ״ל ראשון שבתלמידיו היקרים ז״ל העתיקם על לשון הקודש והוריד א״ע [את עצמו] בכוון ללשון פשוט בכדי שלא ישתנה הענין אצל הקורא אותם בלה״ק [בלשון הקודש] מכפי מה שסיפרם הוא ז״ל על לשון אשכנז הנהוג בינינו וזה סיבה אשר נשמע מלשונו הק׳ [הקדוש] לשונות פשוטים כאלה בכמה מקומות.[21]

> And now—because I heard him [Sternharz] state openly that, when it was reprinted, it was his intention to write an explanation of this—I said [to myself] that I would not refrain from writing one reason among many that were secret and concealed by him. And this is what I heard from him: that our Master and Teacher Rabbi Nahman (may the memory of a righteous and holy man be a blessing) told the stories in the language of Ashkenaz [Yiddish], which is customary in our country, and our teacher and rabbi Reb Nathan of blessed memory, who was foremost among his dear students of blessed memory, translated them into the Holy Tongue and lowered himself intentionally to a simple language in order that the matter would not be changed for a person who reads them in the Holy Tongue, in accordance with how he [Nahman] told them in the language of Ashkenaz, which is customary among us. And for this reason, some common language of that kind is heard, in several places, from his holy tongue.

This is the clearest description and explanation of Nathan Sternharz's literary aesthetic of simplicity: in writing Hebrew, he "lowered himself intentionally to a simple language." It makes explicit that, at least in *Sippurei ma`asiyot*, Sternharz strove to create a Hebrew style that would most closely correspond to the Yiddish original, even where the latter verged on vulgarity. Writing quickly, too, had deeper psychological or mystical justifications.

This explanation has far-reaching significance. Diametrically opposed to many of the *maskilim*, who attempted to write in a high biblical register, Nathan Sternharz aimed for a common, Yiddish-inflected style. The closer it stayed to the Yiddish original of Nahman's narration, he believed, the more faithfully it would convey the sense. There is an apologetic tone in this final page of the second preface, suggesting that there were secret reasons, never explained, for the presence of low or coarse Hebrew in *Sippurei ma'asiyot*. The editor is at pains to assert that the low style must have been deliberate because "it is known from his holy books that he was a great master of language [*ba'al lashon gadol*]"—and yet, in spite of this, "he lowered himself to simple language."

Nahman narrated his tales in Yiddish, and when Sternharz transcribed them in Hebrew, he stayed as close as possible to the oral version, so that many Yiddish phrases refract and show their impact on the Hebrew. Opponents of the hasidim mocked this aspect of their Hebrew, but it is not necessarily a problem. Ultimately, their Yiddish-inflected Hebrew was more successful than the archaic biblical Hebrew of the *maskilim*. As discussed in chapter 1, Walter Benjamin and some contemporary translation theorists might call this "foreignizing translation,"[22] where the Hebrew target language allows the Yiddish source language to show. The resulting Hebrew can be disdained as bad Hebrew only if one accepts the premise that good Hebrew must sound biblical and follow biblical grammar. In the case of represented dialogue, drawing from Yiddish locutions gave life to an ancient language that was becoming modern.

Allegory in Nahman's Fantasies of Sea Travel

In 1806, when Nahman became frustrated by his followers' inability to understand his abstract teachings, he told allegorical tales, which often seem to embody Lurianic Kabbalah. Sternharz's biography of Nahman first quotes a translated phrase in Hebrew and then reports the sentence parenthetically in the original Yiddish: "Now I'm going to start telling stories [*'ata atḥil lesaper ma'asiyot* (*ikh vel shoyn onhebn mayses dertseyln*)]."[23] The situations that arise in Nahman's tales sometimes require concrete descriptions of characters and places, natural-sounding dialogue, and even some crude language.[24] At the start of the nineteenth century, few authors wrote

Hebrew that conveyed these qualities. Naturalistic language—for instance, in descriptions and dialogue—was exceedingly rare in Hebrew of the time because to achieve that quality it was necessary to emulate Yiddish or another living language. There was some tension between the mundane details and the allegorical method, which favored abstraction.

This analysis focuses on Nahman's two canonical tales that revolve around sea travel. Sea narratives play a significant role in Tales 2 and 10, but the language used to describe them is limited. Because they are fantasy tales with allegorical leanings, the descriptions are minimal. Nahman could have drawn on his own travels in 1798–99 to give more vivid depictions of ships and stormy seas, but he instead sketches cartoonish characters and scenes. Translating from the oral Yiddish storytelling, Sternharz uses just a handful of key nautical terms and phrases: *storm wind* (רוח סערה), *they set sail* (פרשׂו בים), *ship* (ספינה), and *mast* (תורן). In referring to sailors, anchors, and a tempest, he follows the Yiddish, using the transliterated terms *matrosin*, *ankers*, and *impet*. He also draws from Talmudic and medieval Hebrew (and Yiddish) when in Tales 2 and 13 he reaches for a way to describe unfurling the sails: the princess *pirsa ha-vilonot (haynu ha-leivintin)* (פירשׂה הוילונות [היינו הלייווינטין]). Also typical, following Mishnaic Hebrew, is the omission of the particle את preceding the direct object. *Maskilim* often scorned both these characteristics in hasidic Hebrew writing.

There has been some disagreement over the allegorical nature of Nahman's tales. Although they are not simple allegories with obvious, univocal equivalences, Nahman undoubtedly intended to include allegorical elements. The characters seem to represent aspects of God, the kabbalistic emanations (*sefirot*), the Creation, spiritual discipline, and Messianic ideas. The plots often seem to allude to "practical Kabbalah," when characters work to advance the process of *tikkun*, or repair, by rescuing a princess. Interpretations of these allegorical elements are available in English and other languages.[25]

Tale 2, "Of the King and the Emperor," tells of two destined lovers who are separated and try to reunite. It goes a step beyond Tale 1, where a king's wise man searches for the lost princess. In Tale 2, the emperor's daughter is the active force, probably representing the Divine Presence or female aspect of God (the Shekhina); she achieves her self-liberation, in part, through sea travels and cross-dressing. Alongside the other thematics and stylistics, some fascinating issues relate to gender and disguise.

In the descriptions of this quest narrative, Nahman seldom goes into the nitty-gritty detail because of the fairy-tale aura. There is a pertinent sequence of episodes at sea; as the destined couple elopes and sets out in defiance of the emperor, they express their spontaneity and elusiveness:

> אח״כ [אחר כך] התיעצו שיניחו לפרוש עצמם על הים · ושכרו להם ספינה ופרשו בים · והלכו על הים · אח״כ רצו לקרב עצמם אל הספר · ובאו לספר · והי׳ שם יער · והלכו לשם · ולקחה הבת קיסר הטבעת ונתנה לו · והיא שכבה שם · אח״כ ראה הבן מלך שבסמוך תעמד · והניח הטבעת אצלה · אח״כ עמדו והלכו אל הספינה ·[26]

> Afterward they consulted and decided to set off to sail on the sea · They rented themselves a boat and set sail · And they went on the sea · Afterward they wanted to approach the shore, and they came to the shore · A forest was there, and they went there · The emperor's daughter took the ring and gave it to him · She lay down there to sleep · Afterward the king's son saw that soon she would get up · So he placed the ring next to her · Afterward they got up and went to the ship.

This passage describes no specific details about sea travel because in this context sailing is a plot element that assumes a primarily symbolic meaning. Going to sea is associated with a consummation of the couple's marriage; Nahman presents a thinly veiled sexual scene, in which the exchanged ring takes on an allegorical meaning before it is forgotten and the two are separated.

In Nahman's intricate plot, all of the main characters travel on ships: the king's son and the emperor's daughter; a merchant's son; eleven daughters of government ministers; another king's son; and twelve pirates. The emperor's daughter is the dominant character, guiding events that eventually lead to her reunion with her destined mate, the first king's son. The romantic journey seems to represent some aspect of cosmic repair, *tikkun ha-`olam*, in which the Shekhina returns home (to God, to Jerusalem).

Subsequent scenes in this tale follow the pattern of combining sketchy details about sea travel with sexual overtones. When a merchant's son finds the emperor's daughter hiding in a tree, "she said to him that she didn't want to board the ship unless he promised her that he wouldn't touch her until after he came to his house and married her in accordance with religious custom. So he promised her. She entered into his ship" (*SM*, pp. 8a/12). In every sexually charged encounter with a man, the emperor's daughter deflects his sexual desire by demanding that he marry her first. After they reach his country, and before he can marry her, she escapes him by getting the sailors drunk and setting sail again:

> הלכה היא והתירה הספינה מן הספר · ופירשה הווילונות (היינו הלייווינטין) והלכה לה עם הספינה · והם באו אל הספינה (היינו כל המשפחה של הסוחר) ולא מצאו דבר · (*SM*, pp. 8b/13)
>
> She went and untied the ship from the shore, and she spread the sails (that is, the *leivintin*) and went her way with the ship. They came to the ship (that is, the merchant's whole family) and didn't find a thing.

Because the emperor's daughter already knows her destined match, she confidently repulses all others. This pattern repeats itself with a king she meets. As soon as she arrives at the king's palace, the first thing she says is that "he should swear to her that he will not touch her until he marries her in accordance with custom" (*SM*, pp. 9a/14). Again, she immediately assumes the prospect of a sexual encounter.

The next episode gives us the inevitable storm at sea while the princess is sailing with eleven daughters of government ministers: "Afterward a storm wind came up and they said, Let's go back to our houses. She informed them that the ship had already left the shore. They asked her why she did this. She said that there was a fear that the ship would break because of the storm, and so she was forced to release the ship and spread the sails [*lifros ha-vila'ot*]. So they went on the sea" (*SM*, pp. 10a/16). Nothing of the storm is described; the only noteworthy nautical detail is the spreading of the sails, where instead of the term *ha-vilonot* Sternharz uses the alternative plural form *ha-vila'ot*. These words appear in the Talmud.[27] As shown in chapter 1, *vilon* also meant "curtain" in Hebrew, although it may have shifted toward "sail" under the influence of the Latin word *vēlum*, which came to include the meaning "sail."

The sea carries riotous behavior with it. In two instances, the sailors get so drunk they fall down; a strong combination of desire, violence, and greed typifies the male sea travelers. These forces come together in the next encounter, when the princess vanquishes twelve pirates. If she represents the Shekhina, on the allegorical level she is also defeating the disruptions caused by drunkenness. Here the sexual connotations are close to the surface: "Afterward they saw a kind of sea island and approached it. Twelve pirates [*gazlonim*] were there, and they wanted to kill them. She asked who was the greatest among them, and they showed her. She said to him, What do you do? He said to her that they were pirates. She said to him, We're also pirates. It's just that you are pirates with your might, and we're pirates with our wisdom, because we are learned in languages and musical instruments. So what do you achieve by killing us? Isn't it good that you should take us as wives, and you'll also get our riches? She showed them what was in the ship. They agreed [*nitratzu*, using a postbiblical sense[28]] to her words" (*SM*, pp. 10b/16). Translated from Yiddish, this naturalistic dialogue effectively shows that, using her wisdom, the emperor's daughter is able to sublimate the pirates' murderous impulse into a combination of sexual desire and greed. She says she wants to give them wine that she has been saving until "the day when God, blessed be He, would send her destined mate [*ziveg*]." Resorting to the wine trick a second time, she gets the pirates drunk, and then "she said to her girlfriends: each one of you, go and slaughter her husband, and they went and slaughtered all of them" (*SM*, pp. 10b/17). At this point, she and the eleven ladies decide to dress as men in European clothing.

One point of retelling this tale is to emphasize that Nahman's language, as represented in Sternharz's Hebrew version, uses a basic nautical vocabulary. Nevertheless, with the help of Yiddish words and an intricate plot, the story commands attention. The center of attention is the journey of the emperor's daughter, now dressed as a man. This leads to a particularly strange scene, brought to us in a cartoonish, dreamy atmosphere. After a prince sets sail with his wife and government ministers, they give free rein to their impulses:

> והלך עם אשתו עם השרי מלוכה ופרשו בספינה והיו שם שמחים ומשחקים מאד · אח"כ [אחר כך] אמרו שיפשטו כולם בגדיהם (היינו ה[בן] מלך עם השרי מלוכה שהיו שם בספינה התייעצו מחמת שמחה שיהיו כולם פושטים את בגדיהם · וכן עשו) ולא נשאר עליהם כ"א [כי אם] הכתונת. (*SM*, pp. 11a/17–18)

> He [the prince] went with his wife and government ministers, and they set sail [*parsu be-sefina*], and there they were very happy and playful. After that they said that all of them would take off their clothes (that is, the prince and the government ministers who were there on the ship conferred and decided that because they were having so much fun they would take off their clothes. That's what they did) and nothing remained on them except their undergarments.

This erotic fantasy about sea travel is surprising because it forms part of a tale that is supposed to convey mystical ideas. Thinly veiled sexual content comes to a head when they decide to try to climb the mast (*ha-toren*), and the prince does so himself. The princess, who may represent the Shekhina, then punishes the prince:

> המתינה עד שעלה אל ראש התורן ממש ולקחה הזכוכית ששורף נגד החמה (שקורין ברען בריל) וכונה נגד מוחו עד שנכוה מוחו ונפל לתוך הים. (*SM*, pp. 11b/18)

> She waited until he had climbed to the very top of the mast and took a magnifying glass (called a *bren bril* [burning lens]) up against the sun, aimed it at his brain until his brain was burned, and he fell into the sea.

The princess kills this prince, the instigator of lawless sensuality. Perhaps it is necessary to defeat raw desire in order to make possible her sought-after reunion with another prince, the first king's son.

Although most of the narrative takes place at sea, its drama has almost nothing to do with the literal sea. Instead, the sea becomes the scene of a battle between the emperor's daughter and all of the obstacles she confronts in trying to find her bridegroom. The sea descriptions are generic because this is all Nahman needs for his allegorical purposes. Associated with sexual and violent impulses, the sea must be overcome to bring repair or redemption to the world (*tikkun `olam*). A storm wind (*ruaḥ se`ara*) appears to have mystical meanings, which have little to do with actual storms at sea.

The innovative quality of Sternharz's Hebrew derives primarily from Yiddish. Tale 2 uses many examples of Hebrew phrases with a definite connection to Yiddish. At the start of the tale, the emperor wanders the earth to "seek and maybe he will find some advice" (*levakesh ulai yimtza eze `etza*) to overcome his childlessness. This phrase calques the parallel Yiddish version: *zukhen tomer vet er gefinen epes eyn eytze*. Similarly, when people look for a doctor to give them advice, the Hebrew phrase *liten lahem `etza* comes from the Yiddish *gebn an eytze* (*SM*, pp. 6b, 11b/9, 18–19). The emperor later has a daughter, and people start to talk about possible matches for her: *medabrim shidukhim*, from the Yiddish *men hot geret shidukhim* (*SM*, pp. 7a/9). When the king's son catches sight of the emperor's daughter, the narrator tells us that "he fainted" (*nafal ḥalashot*), echoing the Yiddish expression *iz gefaln* or *iz geblibn khaloshes*. They confer and decide to go to sea (*lifros `atzmam `al ha-yam* [*SM*, pp. 7b/10]) in a reflexive verbal form that copies the Yiddish, *zikh avek lozn af dem yam*.[29] The emperor's daughter considers a matter (*yishva `atzma*) in another reflexive that calques Yiddish, *hot zi zikh meyashev geven* (*SM*, 7b/11). Going astray is *to`eh `atzmo*, from the Yiddish *zikh toe zayn* (*SM*, pp. 8a/14). When she tells him the right thing to do (*ha-yosher*), this comes from Yiddish *der yosher iz* (*SM*, pp. 8b/12). In these cases, the idiomatic Yiddish includes a Hebrew word and inspires a Hebrew phrase that gives a new coloration to the Hebrew.

Sternharz's nautical terminology follows postbiblical prototypes, including his overwhelming preference for the Mishnaic term *sefina* over the biblical term *oniya*.[30] Sailors are *matrosin*, a term derived from Yiddish and Slavic languages. Sails are *vilonot* in the medieval sense that is usually used by Rashi and other commentators to mean a screen or curtain.[31]

One grammatical peculiarity in Sternharz's Hebrew versions of Nahman's tales is a compound past tense that seems to calque, or replicate, the imperfect past continuous from Slavic languages. For example, where the king "did not know," Sternharz's Hebrew says that he "wasn't knowing"—*lo haya yode`a* rather than the usual past form *lo yad`a*. Perhaps, with his Hebrew locution *lo haya yode`a*, Sternharz tried to capture an imperfect aspect—as in Russian—because this not knowing did not occur at a single moment but was a continuing state.[32] As Ora Wiskind-Elper pointed out to me, this phrase occurs in Mishnaic Hebrew; according to Ghil`ad Zuckermann, however, this connection does not rule out the later influence of Yiddish or Slavic grammar. Under the rubric of "use intensification,"

Zuckermann argues, "A writer chooses an ancient form simply because it corresponds with his/her mother tongue."[33]

Nahman's allegorical tales seem to negate or at least minimize the physical world, for they point to a higher level of the cosmos and a mystical process of redemption, linked to the kabbalistic ideas of the thirteenth-century *Sefer ha-zohar* (*The Zohar*). Emphasizing spiritual meaning through allegorical elements, the tales often cast aside mundane details. In Tale 2, "The King and the Emperor," the princess states a central motif when she says that pirates steal by means of their might, whereas she steals by means of wisdom (*ḥokhma*). The heroine shows how to use intelligence, persistence, strength of will, and devotion to overcome obstacles—including sexual temptations—in order to move toward a mystical union (literally with her beloved but allegorically also with God). The allegorical tales are usually interpreted as having moral messages as well as kabbalistic meanings.

Tale 10, "Of the Burgher and the Pauper," also combines sea travel with the attempted reunion of a destined bride and groom. In this case, in the midst of violence and frustrated sexuality, the discrepancy between rich and poor is an additional obstacle. A nouveau-riche emperor decides not to marry his daughter to her destined groom because the groom's family is not sufficiently rich. The drama includes kidnappings, which are motivated by other characters' desire for sex and money.

Sea voyages take travelers to lawless places where base impulses are exposed and expressed. In connection with seafaring and shipwreck, Hans Blumenberg aptly writes that although the sea is "a naturally given boundary of the realm of human activities," it is also demonized "as the sphere of the unreckonable and lawless."[34] Similarly, as W. H Auden writes, "the sea, in fact, is that state of barbaric vagueness and disorder out of which civilization has emerged and into which, unless saved by the effort of gods and men, it is always liable to relapse."[35] The lawlessness of sea travel has continued to hold sway until the present time: a recent series of articles on "the outlaw ocean" describes "lawlessness on the high seas, and how weak regulations and lax enforcement allow misconduct to go unpunished."[36]

Punishment catches up with one misbehaving character in Nahman's seafaring tales. At sea in Tale 2, the travelers encounter a hedonistic prince who takes off his clothes and climbs the mast. The emperor's daughter, on witnessing this lawless sensuality, punishes him by using a glass to "burn his brain," but this action does not free her from ongoing situations in which men desire her. She repeatedly wards them off by saying that they must wait until after they marry her or by getting them so drunk that they fall unconscious. In another ruse common to these tales, the central female characters cross-dress as men, which enables them to blend in with the male-dominated maritime world and to escape the role of the weak dependent that was commonly associated with women.

In Tale 10, sea travel and storms are prominent yet receive short shrift. The destined, sought-for union is between the emperor's daughter and the burgher's son. The emperor, formerly a poor man, refuses to make a match with a mere burgher. Greed, like sensuality, obstructs the match, which represents a transcendent union in the higher spheres. The emperor's wife sees beyond wealth, however, and tells her daughter that the burgher's son is her destined match (*hu ha-ḥatan shelakh*); the girl accepts her mother's words because "she also was God fearing" (*SM*, pp. 48a/95). She sends the burgher's son a map and writes to him that she "holds with him" (*meḥazeket `atzma bo*, parallel to the idiomatic Yiddish *zi halt zikh in im*). The emperor plans to murder the boy, who escapes and "went [*va-yilekh*] and passed over [*va-ya`avor*] until he came to the sea, so he sat [*va-yeshev*] in a boat and crossed the sea. A mighty storm wind came and lifted the ship up to the shore where there was a desert. From the mighty storm (called an *impet*), the ship was broken. But the people in it were saved and went out [*ve-yatzu*] to dry land" (*SM*, pp. 48ab/95).[37] This passage epitomizes the paradoxical quality of Nahman's tales and Sternharz's texts: on the one hand, they are built on short, simple phrases, using unpretentious vocabulary; on the other, they often seem to point toward a transcendent, ethereal level that is abstracted from the material world. One surprising feature in this passage is that the narrative uses the biblical Vav consecutive (the so-called *vav ha-hipukh*), though not consistently. Perhaps the sporadic use of biblical grammar is deliberate, to raise the register of the narrative voice at certain points in the story.

As the emperor's daughter encounters other obstacles, including a murderer who pretends to be a merchant and captures her on his boat, the linguistic register plunges. This kidnapper is characterized by coarse language, greed, violence, and implicit sexual desire. The narrator hastens to reassure us that "he didn't need her, because he was a eunuch" (*SM*, pp. 52a/103), but this only serves to underscore the sexual role that is repeatedly imposed on women in these tales. Instead of taking advantage of her sexually, he wants to sell her to a king for a vast sum of money.

The emperor's daughter goes to the kidnapper's ship to see his wares. Perhaps she is distracted and seduced by beautiful objects. Again, the ship's journey is less important than the drama on the ship. An array of artful, golden, singing birds that the kidnapper has created beguile the emperor's daughter into entering an inner chamber of the ship (*SM*, pp. 52b/103–4). Aryeh Kaplan associates those birds with evil forces,[38] which connects them to Nahman's dream of soldiers and poisonous birds.[39] This encounter is the tale's climactic moment, and it is remarkably sexualized, considering that the kidnapper is a eunuch:

> Once she came to him. He went and opened the room for her, in which stood the golden birds, and so on. She saw that it was a wondrous innovation. . . . She came in by herself. He also went into the room and locked the door. He did a vulgar thing [literal, simple, direct, *ke-pashuto*] and took a sack and put her by force into the sack. And he took off [*pashat mi-mena*] her clothes. He dressed a certain sailor in them, covered his face, pushed him outside, and said, Go. That sailor didn't know at all what was being done with him. When he suddenly went out with his face covered, the soldiers didn't recognize him, so they started to walk with him. It appeared to them that this was the Emperor's daughter. . . . The murderer took the Emperor's daughter because he knew that they would certainly chase him. He left the ship and buried himself with her in a pit, where there was rain water, until the tumult would pass. He ordered the sailors on his ship that they immediately cut the anchors and flee. . . . The murderer hid himself with her in a pit of rain water and they were lying [*munaḥim*] there. He threatened her so that she would not cry out, so that no one would hear. He would say to her, I devoted myself completely to you, in order to catch you. And if I lose you, my life won't be worth anything to me. . . . So as soon as you cry out, I'll strangle you right away. (*SM*, pp. 53ab/105–6)

The narrator reminds us that the kidnapper doesn't really need her because he's a eunuch, but this seems like a ploy to temper a scene that is obviously charged with sexuality and violence. The text tells us that before he undresses her, *hu `asa ke-pashuto*, he did the simple, vulgar thing: he put her in a sack and took off (*pashat*) her clothes. This phrase *hu `asa ke-pashuto* uses the same verbal root as "taking off" clothes, getting down to the naked truth. These words are linguistically related to the simple, literal meaning of a text (the *pshat*).

The metaphor of garments often plays a role in Nahman's writing, as it does in some kabbalistic works. Nahman could fulfill his goals in Bratslav, he told his friend and disciple Reb Yudl, but he believed that in the Land of Israel he would have a greater effect by working to achieve his goals "with garments" (*al yedei levushim*).[40] In the tale of the murderer kidnapping the emperor's daughter, the murderer has to disguise her in order to get her away, "so he went and dressed her in sailor clothes, and she appeared to be male. He went with him on the sea" (*SM*, pp. 54a/107). The text explains parenthetically that Nahman began to refer to the emperor's daughter in the masculine at this point because she was dressed as a man. In the debased world of the story, appearances deceive nearly everyone.

When the murderer takes the princess to sea, the narrative gives a typical, simplistic description of shipwreck, as is found elsewhere in the tales: "A storm wind came and lifted up the ship to the shore and broke the ship" (*SM*, pp. 54a/107). Tale 13, "The Seven Beggars," repeats the sketchy description of sea travel that is familiar from Tales 2 and 10. The first beggar tells a tale that begins, "Once people traveled in many ships on the sea. A storm wind came and broke the ships, but the people were saved and came to a tower":

> פעם אחד הלכו אנשים בספינות הרבה על הים. ובא רוח סערה ושיבר את הספינות והאנשים
> ניצלו ובאו אל מגדול א׳ [מגדל אחד]. (*SM*, pp. 96b/199)

This tale incorporates some of the usual maritime words: *sefina* (ship), *yam* (sea), and *ruaḥ se`ara* (storm wind). Nahman's oral tale may have been more detailed than this written version; however, this analysis does not focus on the Yiddish source, but on the Hebrew transcription and its place in literary history. It is clear that Sternharz uses a meager vocabulary to describe a sea voyage.

In Nahman's tales, as in other folktales, the sea is a place of transgressions and transformed identity.[41] The disguises, deceptions, abductions, and naked men and women are, according to Sternharz, the misleading outer garments of spiritual allegories. Indeed, the second preface to *Sippurei ma`asiyot* emphasizes that the tales are full of wisdom and moral teachings.[42] To forestall criticisms regarding the superficial actions, Sternharz hints at the tales' true purposes. Basing his comments on *The Zohar*, he writes that a princess is an expression for the Shekhina or Congregation of Israel. In this interpretation, he explicitly follows the rabbinic, allegorical reading of the Song of Songs, where the bridegroom represents God.

Insisting on the allegorical level of meaning allows Sternharz to shield Nahman from the accusation that he told immoral tales using coarse language (*leshonot gasim*). Moreover, the editor of the second edition added a paragraph at the end of Sternharz's preface, stating that he "lowered himself intentionally to simple language [*lashon pashut*] in order that the matter would not be altered for one who reads them in the Holy Tongue."[43] To accommodate readers and convey the implicit Yiddish source, the scribe needed to bring Hebrew down from its sacred heights. Sternharz apologizes for the simple language, which leads in one scene to the simple nakedness of a princess lying with a murderer. But if the Holy Tongue has been degraded by being used to describe vulgar, mundane realities, Nahman's scribe asserts that this serves a higher purpose. As in the Song of Songs, there are unions that represent the coming together of God and the People of Israel, or the return of the Shekhina to the Holy Land, or the coming of the Messiah. Don't look too closely at the princess, Sternharz seems to be saying, because the naked truth is just a metaphor. Simplicity and abstraction, presenting yet concealing other layers of meaning, characterize Nahman's tales.

Yemei Moharnat and Storms at Sea

Sternharz's own pilgrimage narrative conveys a far stronger impression of reality because the narrator frequently describes mundane details. There are no naked princesses, but there are remarkable scenes at sea, including terrified hasidim encountering storms and a lively portrayal of Sternharz and his friend dancing with sailors.

Yemei Moharnat (The Days of Our Teacher, Rabbi Nathan) was published posthumously in two parts, the first in 1876 and the second in 1903 (Lemberg) and 1904 (Jerusalem). Because these editions are extremely rare, I refer primarily to a later edition of both parts (New York, 1970). The second part, edited by Israel Heilprin, deserves special attention because it contains a genuine Hebrew travel narrative by a Jewish traveler.[44] In it, rather than reporting on Nahman's pilgrimage or translating Nahman's fantasy narratives into Hebrew, Sternharz records his own impressions of traveling to the Land of Israel.[45] This distinguishes his travel writings from most of the other narratives discussed in this book—with the exception of Isaac Euchel's brief letters from 1785 and Shmuel Romanelli's work, to be discussed in the next chapter. Perhaps the unfamiliarity of this genre among Hebrew readers contributed to the delayed publication of *Yemei Moharnat*, about eighty years after Sternharz wrote it.

The second part of *Yemei Moharnat* revolves around a journal that Nathan Sternharz kept during his travels.[46] Its centerpiece is his pilgrimage to the Land of Israel, when he was accompanied by Yehuda Eliezer in 1822. Sternharz's text shares many stylistic features with eighteenth-century narratives by Jewish travelers to the Land of Israel (see chapter 1). Yet his narrative is far more extensive and detailed than most others that have been preserved, and it is guided by the framework of Nahman's teachings and precedent as a spiritual traveler. The journey becomes a series of trials and tribulations, with Sternharz and his fellow traveler struggling to overcome mental and physical obstacles (*meni'ot*). Sternharz becomes convinced that he must be willing to endanger his life, exposing himself to shipwreck, in order to elevate his soul. This returns us to the topos of the storm at sea as the epitome of placing oneself in God's hands during a spiritual journey.

The narrative of *Yemei Moharnat* is structured by sacred time, sacred space, and sacred language. Many of Sternharz's accounts refer to the date in accordance with the weekly Torah reading, using the Hebrew calendar. The goal of this pilgrimage is not Ottoman Palestine but rather the Holy Land, in particular the sacred tombs of Jews. Once Sternharz reaches the

Land of Israel, he turns his attention from fellow travelers and natives to deceased Jews, taking it for granted that the graves of saints are imbued with holiness. Sacred language permeates the Hebrew narrative: as Sternharz frequently refers to prayers and holidays, he quotes scriptural passages, speaks words of Rabbi Nahman's teachings whenever possible, and sells copies of the Rebbe's books wherever he goes. Moreover, he presents the entire journey as having been favored by Divine Providence. He firmly believes that his pilgrimage takes place sheltered by God's protection, notwithstanding the omnipresent dangers of sea travel during the Greco-Turkish war.

The Schocken Library in Jerusalem holds many manuscripts of Sternharz's Hebrew writings, some of them in his own hand.[47] They reward close study, for they shed light on his process of composition and his casual approach to punctuation. All of the published editions of *Yemei Moharnat* have taken liberties with the author's manuscripts—adding punctuation and paragraph breaks, providing section numbers, changing the orthography, expanding the abbreviations, and adding diacritical voicing marks (*nikkud*). Some recent editions have returned to the manuscripts, restoring omitted passages but without clearly demarcating the textual variants.[48] In any event, the Schocken manuscripts confirm that part 2 of *Yemei Moharnat* is based primarily on entries from a journal that Sternharz kept during his voyage to the Land of Israel.

Sternharz's travel narrative illustrates his attempts to establish a safe realm of sanctity with the help of sacred sources and memories of the Rebbe. Reality is less threatening when it is mediated by textual traditions. When encountering difficulties, Sternharz repeatedly renews his confidence by speaking and writing about Rabbi Nahman. In a foreign setting, the most reassuring social context is a meal during which he is able to speak about the Rebbe's teachings.

Sternharz's pilgrimage follows the route that Rabbi Nahman had taken twenty-four years earlier. The disciple is happy to spend some time in Haifa, because "our Rebbe, of blessed memory, when he entered the Land of Israel, came first to Haifa, and there he immediately accomplished what he accomplished, and he remained there for all of the holidays, from Rosh Hashanah until after Sukkot. Thank God that we have been privileged to tread on holy soil, in a place where our awe-inspiring Rebbe trod."[49] Referring back to the prior account of Nahman's travel, Sternharz infuses his reality with sanctity at every turn.

Yemei Moharnat is explicitly based on Sternharz's travel diary, often written in the present tense. This immediacy is a distinguishing feature. One entry reads: "Now we are traveling, on this Wednesday, from Alexandria in Egypt to Tzidon, which is the border of Eretz-Israel. And I am writing all of this on the boat" (*YM*, p. 178).[50] Similarly, while crossing the Black Sea, he writes: "On Tuesday, while I was writing all this, the German [*ha-Ashkenazi*] scribe came into the cabin and didn't disturb me at all. Afterward he showed me the map [*ha-land kart*] of the sea we're traveling on, and he showed me where are Odessa, and Kherson, and Nikolaev, and Atshakov, and Istanbul, and the rest of the places. He showed me that now we are about a third of the way from Odessa to Istanbul." This basic geography lesson was helpful to Sternharz because of his limited secular education and worldly knowledge. He closes the entry with a prayer: "May God guide us in peace, so that we may be privileged to come to the Land of Israel safely" (*YM*, p. 225).

Although Sternharz tries to keep the narrative within the confines of an uplifting spiritual pilgrimage, the world intervenes in several ways. Most obvious and most threatening in this regard are storms at sea. Another disruption occurs in a meeting with *mitnagdim*, referred to as *prushim*, from Vilna. And an element of ethnography slips in when he describes the exotic customs of Jews in Turkey and Palestine. Finally, encounters with non-Jews occasionally threaten to pierce the bubble of Sternharz's sacred journey.

Hebrew narratives of sea travel reach climactic moments during storms. For the devout pilgrim, nature does not appear to present insurmountable obstacles because God's Providence is believed to be stronger. In the evolution of Hebrew style, there was an uneasy tension between original, descriptive language and biblical quotations or allusions. Sternharz's language often captures a concrete scene, but it also relies on Hebrew commonplaces.

Sternharz describes the responses to a storm that strikes after the ship leaves Istanbul:

> there was a bit of a storm wind while I was praying in our small room down below. Reb Yehuda Eliezer was on deck cooking, and a great fear fell upon him because he saw that the ship was tilting very much to the side, so that the upper side of the ship was very close to the water, and the wind went on getting stronger. The captain and all of the sailors were busy, in fright and haste, pulling ropes and the rest of the adjustments that were necessary in accordance with this wind. (*YM*, p. 241)

Sternharz evokes the travelers' emotions, but descriptive language is limited; in general, his sea travel descriptions rely on a small vocabulary: *sefina* (ship), *vilon* and *vilaot* (sail, sails), *anker* (anchor), *kapitan* (captain), *matros* or *malaḥ* (sailor). His travel narratives seldom dwell on worldly details because they assume that the meaning of the events lies elsewhere.

A later storm description resembles others because it draws from the Psalms, with added detail:

> A great storm wind was awakened, getting stronger and stronger, and there was a great tumult on the ship because it was a lot of work and great toil for the sailors, for they were constantly forced to do different work. For the wind went on storming, not turned in our direction, and it circled and went from every side, in the way of great storms. So every time they were forced to spread the sails to a different side. Once they were forced to take down some sails, and other such things, but from the greatness of the powerful storm **all of their wisdom was swallowed up** [*kol ḥakhmatam titbal`a*, Ps. 107:27]. And the ship tilted and rocked to all sides, and it went at a very sharp slant; at one time it leaned very far to this side, really close to the sea, and at another time to the other side. (*YM*, p. 243)

At times, Sternharz moves beyond the abstractness and fantasy of Nahman's tales when he narrates the story of his own voyage. He includes vivid descriptions, but under duress he also resorts to commonplaces from Psalms. He writes that later "some other ships were traveling near us and we saw all of them, how the wind lifted them up and turned them, **rising up to the heavens and falling into the abyss** [*ya`alu shamayim, yerdu tehomot*, Ps. 107:26]" (*YM*, p. 243, cp. p. 247). It could be reassuring to link a life-and-death situation to a biblical prooftext.

Description sometimes merges with prayer. Later "they were forced to drop anchor, lower the sails, and stop the ship at the time of afternoon prayers. And we gave praise and thanks to God, may He be blessed, that they stopped the ship and now there's no great danger." At the end of this passage, the continuation of the Psalm becomes a prayer: "Our strength has not yet returned, may God have mercy, **and He makes the storm become silent** [*ve-yakem se`ara le-demama*, Ps. 107:29], and He will quickly restore our strength, Amen, so may it be" (*YM*, p. 246).

Encounters with Opponents and Natives

Sternharz meets a wide range of people and is happiest when he encounters those who listen to him discuss Rabbi Nahman and his teachings. This happens on occasion, but there are some significant failures. One of the most striking failed dialogues occurs when Sternharz meets a group of Jewish travelers from Vilna—*prushim*, literally "abstinents"—who are opponents of the hasidim.

While meeting with these travelers, Sternharz starts an argument about faith in religious leaders. He knows that *mitnagdim* are critical of the way hasidim follow their rebbes, and he provokes them by raising the subject of "faith in the wise." He conveys his dispute with them using direct and indirect speech:

> I would think that, in any case, they have some faith in the Vilna Gaon, whom they call by his name, but they replied to me immediately. One of them was the main one who spoke, and all of them agreed with him. He said . . . I should have faith in a man? (with surprise). . . . I started to argue with him, if so, what is faith in the wise? But they didn't listen to me at all and responded with nonsense [*divrei shtut*, an interesting postbiblical expression shared with Yiddish]. . . . Then I saw clearly the difference between hasidim and *mitnagdim* because I saw that they don't even have faith in their own scholar [*talmid ḥakham*]. . . . I told them openly, I would have thought that if you have no faith in the great hasidic *tzadikim*, at least you would have faith in your own scholar, but now I know your level, that you have no faith at all. (*YM*, pp. 214–15)

This argument fails to convince his opponents, and "while we were talking, they wanted to push me out of the house, and there was almost a big fight between us" (*YM*, p. 215). The narrative effectively conveys dialogue and the conflict between the Lithuanian *mitnagdim* and the Ukrainian hasidim.

Sternharz has very different encounters with Sephardic Jews in Istanbul and Alexandria. He notices some of their unfamiliar customs, especially those relating to their practice of Judaism. It seems to reassure him that even if he and the Sephardic Jews cannot communicate in Arabic or Yiddish, they all share the Holy Tongue and the Torah. Even there, however, he notices extreme differences in pronunciation, so that his efforts to communicate in Hebrew usually fail. With astonishment he notices the hard Sephardic Torah case, as opposed to a fabric cover, and their different way of standing it upright while reading.

Among the Sephardim (*frenkin*), "it is very very hard to find a house to lodge in, especially for people from Poland, who are comical, mocked, and scorned in their eyes" (*YM*, p. 229). Without passing judgment, Sternharz comments that "their wives never receive house guests, especially not Ashkenazim" (*YM*, p. 231). Communication is difficult: "No one understands a single word in our language, and even in the Holy Tongue it is rare to find a person who understands our words" (*YM*, p. 230); or, again, "I couldn't tell them anything about it because they don't understand our Hebrew [*leshon ha-kodesh shelanu*]" (*YM*, p. 232). Sternharz notes that when they ask for the synagogue or House of Study, no one understands "because they call the synagogue *kahal kadosh*, and they don't have any House of Study there. There the place where they learn is called a yeshiva, and there's a place where *batlanim* say Psalms, which is called *hesger*" (*YM*, p. 230). Some people understand when they ask for the *ḥakham* or the *rav*, but "all of the boys who saw us laughed at us very much and chased us, each time, as they do to the madman [*meshuga*], God forbid" (*YM*, p. 230). All of these travel setbacks are incorporated into a successful narrative.

Sternharz's efforts to communicate in Hebrew are significant in light of disagreements about the use of Hebrew as a spoken language in the early nineteenth century. T. V. Parfitt disputes the idea that Eliezer Ben-Yehuda "revived" Hebrew in 1882, suggesting that it was previously used for communication among Jews from different cultures: "The Ashkenazim for the most part were able to converse together in Yiddish, while the Sephardim could communicate together equally well in Ladino. However, on the frequent occasions when Jews from different parts of the world met together without one of these languages in common, it was usual for Hebrew to be spoken."[51] Sternharz's account confirms that he tried to communicate in Hebrew, but without much success. In Arab lands, according to Sternharz's testimony, "even in the Holy Tongue it is rare to find a person who understands our words" (*YM*, p. 230).

Sternharz observes different Jewish practices. He hears a reading of the weekly Torah portion "in their melody and pronunciation" (*YM*, p. 254). During a gathering on Shavuot, "some Sephardim began to chant prayers [*shirot ve-tishbaḥot*], some known to us, and some others in their strange melodies [*be-nigunim meshunim shelahem*], and they also chanted 'Ya Ribon Olam' in their melody and strange pronunciation" (*YM*, p. 258). In spite of their foreign-sounding chant, Sternharz writes, "I was happy to hear that everywhere people sing praises to God's great name" (*YM*, p. 258). Open to seeing and describing Jews from other communities, he seldom passes judgment on the unfamiliar customs he encounters.

Through much of his journey, Sternharz experiences the non-Jewish world as incomprehensible or hostile. In the harbor of Alexandria, "some of the boats were war ships, where a lot of Arab soldiers were sitting, and when they saw me they laughed and made fun of me, but with God's help none of them hurt me" (*YM*, p. 252). In Istanbul, the language barrier in trying to communicate with sailors is virtually insurmountable because "most of them speak in the language of Italy or in the language of Ishmael [Turkish or Arabic]" (*YM*, p. 216). When "the two of us are alone in the boat in which everyone else is not Jewish," it is a gift of God when one of the others knows German (*leshon Ashkenaz*) (*YM*, pp. 214, 217). In a dispute with the captain over the cost of travel from Odessa to Istanbul, "I didn't want to argue with him very much, and also I don't know how to speak that language well, not even the language of Russia" (*YM*, p. 220).

The world may have been hostile and foreign, but it becomes familiar and manageable when Sternharz sells Rabbi Nahman's books. Besides, he needs to sell the books to help cover expenses. He imagines that it is God's wish that he distribute the Rebbe's books: "How is it possible that I will be in Istanbul without leaving a single book there, God forbid?" (*YM*, p. 229). This becomes his new task: "My entire intent was to find buyers for our Rebbe's books. . . . On Wednesday in the morning I sold six copies of the large *Likutei Moharan*" (*YM*, p. 232). In Alexandria, when a Jewish acquaintance expresses interest in new Hebrew books, Sternharz is in his element: "and with this he revived me, and immediately I replied to him that I have a new book with me, which you have not yet seen in this country, and its title is *Likutei Moharan*" (*YM*, p. 253). Being able to spread the Rebbe's teaching makes all of his troubles worthwhile:

> I said to myself that for this alone, all of the torments and wanderings are worthwhile—that I am now as if in the Egyptian exile, that I am dragging myself from one place to another and am bewildered in Alexandria, Egypt, although it never occurred to me that I would be here. But when I have the privilege to mention, in the marketplace of Alexandria, the name of our awe-inspiring Rebbe's book, for this everything is worthwhile. For I believe and know a little of the greatness, holiness, and awesomeness of this book and of the greatness of the favorable and awesome effect that it has in the world, and so on. And who knows, if I weren't here, when this book would be mentioned here. If I had come only for this, it would have been enough, especially as I understood right away that by means of this question I would certainly be able to sell some book here (and so it was), and this is more precious to me than all wealth. (*YM*, p. 253)

When Sternharz concentrates on the Rebbe's books, under duress away from home and on his way to the Holy Land, he feels confident because he can continue to inhabit a structured, Torah-centered world. Often beset by depression, he strives to live under the sheltering protection of the Rebbe's teaching, which calls for a life of continual happiness. Nahman, who understood depression, developed teachings that satisfied Sternharz's needs, becoming his primary concern for the rest of his life. Even when voyaging to Zion, he emulated the Rebbe.

Anxiously contemplating his journey to the Holy Land, Sternharz receives encouragement from the weekly Torah reading. Shabbat Shira (*Be-shalaḥ*) includes the Song of the Sea, following the Israelites' departure from Egypt. Sternharz thinks about how leaving Egypt is a prelude to coming to the Land of Israel. This passage in *Yemei Moharnat* shows Sternharz drawing strength from a patchwork of quotations.

> For the *parsha* begins, "And when Pharaoh sent forth the people . . ." [Ex. 13:17]. That is, when the Israelites left Egypt. And it is known that every departure from Egypt was to come to the Land of Israel. As it is written, "I will bring you up out of the affliction of Egypt" [Ex. 3:17] to a good land, and so on. And so this *parsha* speaks right away of the path to the Land of Israel, as it is written there . . . and in Rashi's commentary. And the entire matter of that *parsha*, in it I found the entire matter of my journey to the Land of Israel. For that *parsha* comments that we need to lengthen the path and come to the Land of Israel. As it is written, "God did not lead them through the Land of the Philistines" [Ex. 3:17], but "God led the people around through the desert by the Sea of Reeds" [Ex. 3:18]. For God also led us around, because our straight path to the Land of Israel is through Odessa . . . but I was forced to lengthen my path to Odessa. (*YM*, pp. 187–88)

Sternharz is reassured that his circuitous journey is providential and correct because it conforms to the passage in Exodus, and, according to Jewish tradition, the Torah is the blueprint of the world.

The overwhelming impression of *Yemei Moharnat* is that Nathan Sternharz strove to live in a textual universe, where everything was subordinated to the Torah and to the Rebbe's teachings. It was not always easy to maintain this worldview, however, in the face of arduous travels, exotic cultures, and uncomprehending people. It helped to believe firmly in Divine Providence and to see God's clues and encouragements along the way. At one point, Sternharz writes: "I understood that God, blessed be He, in his mercy, was hinting to me with this that I must travel to the Land of Israel" (*YM*, p. 195). After speaking about one of Rabbi Nahman's teachings about the path to the Land of Israel, Sternharz concludes: "I saw that this, too, was a hint for me to travel to the Land of Israel" (*YM*, p. 197).

Dancing with Sailors

One passage in *Yemei Moharnat* illustrates the tension between concrete experience and the attempt to invest events with meaning. Sailing from Odessa to Istanbul, Sternharz and his companion, Yehuda Eliezer, enjoy a lively evening with the captain and sailors. Sternharz subordinates the experience to their goal of visiting the Holy Land and juxtaposes it with a hasidic parable from Ya`akov Yosef of Polonne's collection *Toldot Ya`akov Yosef* (Generations of Jacob Joseph). The description begins with a vivid scene:

> בתחילת הלילה התחיל הקאפיטאן לנגן על איזה כלי זמר ושאל אותי אם אני יכול לנגן השבתי לו לא ודיבר עמי מענין כלי זמר והתחלתי לדבר עמם מענין ריקודין שבינינו מרקדין ביו״ט [ביום טוב] ועל חתונה. (*YM*, p. 226)

> In the early evening the captain began to play on some musical instrument and asked me if I can play. I answered him No, and he spoke with me about the matter of instruments. I started to speak with them about the matter of dances among us, that we dance on a holiday and at a wedding.

Sternharz gives a natural-sounding description of a scene on board, including a discussion of Jewish customs. The inclusion of small details creates the effect of a modern travel narrative:

> בתוך כך ירדתי אל הבית בתוך כך נתעוררו הם והתחיל א׳ מהם לרקד הרבה ואזי נתעורר רי״א [רב יהודה אליעזר] לרקד ג״כ [גם כן] קצת ואח״כ [ואחר כך] ירד לשמש אותי בסעודה כי אני כבר ישבתי לאכול והוא לא אכל עדיין וגמרתי סעודתי לבדי. (*YM*, p. 226)

> Then I went down into the cabin, and meanwhile they were roused and one of them began to dance a lot, and so Reb Yehuda Eliezer was also roused to dance a little. Afterward he came down to attend me during the meal because I had already sat down to eat, and he had not yet eaten, and I finished my meal alone.

At first, the scene of dancing appears to have no particular significance, enhancing the graphic quality of Sternharz's narrative:

> ואח״כ אמר רי״א [רב יהודה אליעזר] שיש לו חשק לרקד עוד ועלינו על הספינה והקאפיטאן עם עוד א׳ היו מנגנים באיזה כלי שיר פשוטים ורי״א היה מרקד הרבה מאד עד שאח״כ [שאחר כך] רקדתי גם אנכי עם רי״א הרבה וגם שני מטראסין רקדו. (*YM*, p. 226)

> Afterward Reb Yehuda Eliezer said that he wanted to dance some more, and we went up to the boat [deck], and the captain and one other were playing on some simple musical instruments. And Reb Yehuda Eliezer was dancing very much, until afterward I also danced a lot with Reb Yehuda Eliezer, and also two sailors danced.

But Sternharz goes on to explain that their dancing did have a spiritual meaning that was not apparent to the sailors:

> הם רקדו ושמחו ולא ידעו מה שמחתם ואנחנו ת״ל רקדנו ושמחנו שאנו זוכים לילך לא״י לאה״ק להכיר את מי שאמר והיה העולם. (*YM*, p. 226)

> They danced and were happy and didn't know what they were happy about, while we, thank God, danced and were happy that we were privileged to go to the Land of Israel, to the Holy Land, to become acquainted with the One who spoke and created the world.

Sternharz's account separates sharply between the sailors and the two hasidim, who have a higher reason to be joyful. Their happy dancing has meaning because it is connected to a spiritual goal. This reminds him of a parable in the early hasidic text by Ya`akov Yosef of Polonne, *Toldot Ya`akov Yosef*:

> וכמו שמובא משל בשם הבעש״ט ז״ל (בספר תולדות יעקב יוסף) מענין בן מלך שהיה בשביה והגיע לו אגרת מאביו ורצה לשמוח והשקה את כל מי שהיה עמו עד שנשתכרו ורקדו ושמחו הם רקדו ושמחו בהוללות ושיכרות והוא רקד ושמח בתוכם על שהגיע לו ידיעה מאביו. (*YM*, p. 226)[52]

> This is like a parable that is brought down in the name of the Ba`al Shem Tov, of blessed memory (in *Toldot Ya`akov Yosef*), regarding a prince who was in captivity, and he received a letter from his father. He wanted to celebrate and served drinks to everyone who was with him, until they became intoxicated and danced and celebrated. They celebrated and became joyful out of unruliness and drunkenness, and he danced and celebrated among them because he had received word from his father.

Ya`akov Yosef of Polonne gives this parable a clear message (*nimshal*): true rejoicing in this world derives from closeness to God. Everyday life appears shallow if it is not linked to a spiritual goal or higher meaning. The same assumption often characterizes Sternharz's narrative in spite of its many concrete details.

As Sternharz continues his description of the scene on deck, he expresses surprise that the non-Jewish sailors can share their exalted moment without understanding it:

> והיה זה בעינינו לפלא גדול שזכינו לרקד ולשמוח על הספינה שהיו כולם עכו״ם ולא היה ביניהם שום יהודי כ״א אנחנו שנינו לבד כי זה ידוע לנו שעיקר התחזקות הוא שמחה כי חדוות ה׳ הוא מעוזכם כמבואר בדברינו פעמים הרבה בלי שיעור. (*YM*, p. 226)

> And this was a great wonder in our eyes, that we were privileged to dance and celebrate on the boat, where all of them were idol worshipers, and not a single Jew was among them except for us two alone. For we know that happiness is the main thing in strengthening oneself because "the rejoicing in God is your strength" [Neh. 8:10], as is explained in our writings many, countless times.

This passage reflects Sternharz's consistent view that worldly pleasures have no meaning unless they are harnessed to a spiritual purpose.

Although Sternharz tends to subordinate reality to the teachings of Rabbi Nahman and spiritual goals, his travelogue successfully describes concrete scenes. Unlike Nahman's fantasy tales, which are larger than life and contain magical events, Sternharz's *Yemei Moharnat* powerfully evokes the real drama of a dangerous sea voyage. He captures both the emotions and the realia, sometimes even surprising us with vivid ethnographic accounts.

The Contribution of Hasidic Hebrew Literature

Histories of modern Hebrew literature have generally bypassed the contributions of hasidic authors such as Nathan Sternharz. Ideological biases have combined with idées fixes to render hasidic Hebrew texts nearly invisible to literary history. Their existence was, however, immortalized by their enemies—in particular, by Joseph Perl's antihasidic writings.

A premise of this book is that the *maskilim*, the *mitnagdim*, and the hasidim all inhabited the same cultural space, notwithstanding their geographical spread and mutual animosities. That space included their publications in Hebrew and Yiddish, addressed to the relatively small market for Jewish books (leaving aside prayer books, Bible, and Talmud). Hasidic stories broke established norms, especially as departures from the standard rabbinic genres of textual commentary and halakhic treatise. There had previously been a small number of books of hagiography (*shevaḥim*), such as *Shivḥei ha-Ari* (in praise of R. Isaac Luria, the kabbalist associated with Safed) and some popular story books such as the *Mayse bukh* in Yiddish. But there were few precedents for Nahman's collection of thirteen allegorical fantasy tales.

Prior to 1814, most hasidic books were homiletical commentaries or moralistic treatises, which were familiar and accepted genres. Skeptical readers, therefore, questioned the validity of the innovative hasidic narratives. Joseph Perl was especially critical of hasidic books and, having read almost everything that had been published by hasidim since the 1780s, he set to work debunking the new movement. After Perl had firsthand experience of charismatic hasidic leaders and their palatial courts, in 1816 he wrote a polemic that sharply criticized all of the deficiencies of the hasidic "sect," as he called it.[53] His critique was so extreme that the authorities blocked its publication, presumably to circumvent the conflict that would have ensued. Next, Perl began to write a parody of Nahman's collection *Sippurei ma'asiyot*.[54] Finally, he found his voice in *Megale temirin* (Revealer of Secrets, 1819), an epistolary novel that enabled him to parody (mimic) and satirize (critique) the style of the hasidic writings he so intensely scorned.

Hasidic authors were not constrained by the limitations that the *maskilim* placed on themselves in trying to write "pure," biblical Hebrew. The Mishna, Midrash, and medieval commentators had developed a range of postbiblical Hebrew that served them well in various contexts. Having emerged from this tradition of commentary, rabbis saw no reason to exclude the many postbiblical linguistic resources that had evolved over the centuries. Hasidim and other rabbis continually quoted the Tanakh, alluded to biblical verses, and explicated scriptural passages, but their active vocabulary was closer to the Mishna, and they usually followed the grammar of Mishnaic Hebrew. Because early maskilic writing reached only a small audience, few Hebrew and Yiddish readers were aware of the scorn that the *maskilim* such as Perl showered upon the language of hasidic texts. Hasidic narratives were more accessible than maskilic writings, presented interesting real-world scenes, and were far more popular.

Rabbi Nahman's thirteen tales in *Sippurei ma`asiyot*, along with shorter parables and dreams ascribed to him, form a fascinating corpus. In the twentieth century, many secular authors retold, translated, or borrowed from them: they inspired I. L. Peretz to write neohasidic tales; Martin Buber rewrote them; Franz Kafka read them; and many other writers and scholars have translated them. Nevertheless, although much has been said about Nahman's intriguing plots and characters, and although there have been multiple interpretations of his allegories, little has been written about the place his texts hold in literary history. The sea narratives in *Sippurei ma`asiyot*, when analyzed using techniques that function almost like carbon dating, situate Nahman's tales in a broader linguistic and literary context.

Not only have the tales received too little attention from literary historians, but their true author has also often been ignored. Rabbi Nahman was a charismatic, inspirational storyteller, but the literary task of shaping *Sippurei ma`asiyot* in Hebrew fell to his scribe, Nathan Sternharz. Between 1806 and 1815, Sternharz labored to record the Rebbe's stories in Hebrew, using the skills he had developed as a well-educated Jewish man from a wealthy family in Nemirov.

Nahman's tales and Sternharz's pilgrimage narrative express a Torah-centered and Zion-centered worldview. In this sense, they are premodern, yet their language transcends their ideology. By allowing Yiddish to assume a significant role, these two authors counterbalanced the traditional biblical and rabbinic Hebrew. Members of the Jewish Enlightenment had moved beyond the Zion-centered world, rejected postbiblical Hebrew, and attempted to reestablish ancient Hebrew as a linguistic model. Later, the second generation of moderate *maskilim* took the next step and synthesized these trends by writing Hebrew narratives of travel that expanded the geographic and linguistic boundaries of biblical Hebrew.

In the movement toward modern, naturalistic narrative, one impediment was a tendency to see God's hand in the world, to the point of eclipsing descriptions of nature itself. In this vein, Nahman's tales often abstract the characters from concrete reality. As a result, his fantasy texts sometimes appear to be simplistic, kabbalistic allegories, linked to a fairy-tale style of narration that avoids meticulous descriptions of the real.[55]

Nahman's allegories are well suited to conveying his religious messages, but allegory has drawbacks in terms of the associated Hebrew literary qualities. In particular, Hebrew that relies heavily on moralistic messages or that draws attention to miraculous deeds can lose its moorings in reality. The *maskilim* also sometimes weakened their literary creations by depending excessively on biblical quotations; some hasidic writers diminished their literary effects by failing to appreciate the value of immediacy and vivid detail. Only when Sternharz moved away from fantasy and abstract teachings, as in his account of Nahman's voyage (and his own pilgrimage) to the Land of Israel, did he transcend the limitations of Nahman's allegorical tales. But he maintained a worldview circumscribed by the Torah.[56]

Hasidim and *Maskilim* in Uman

The *maskilim* and hasidim had well-known ideological differences, and they engaged in a battle of books during the early 1800s. From a literary perspective, Mendel Lefin (1749–1826) and Nathan Sternharz (1780–1844) were two leading figures in the intertextual battleground of early nineteenth-century Hebrew prose. Their competing narratives of sea travel tested the ability of each to convey concrete descriptions of nature in Hebrew as well as their proclivity for doing so. Travel writings express far-reaching attitudes toward natural science, geography, and the non-Jewish world.

However obvious their differences, Lefin and Sternharz had much in common. Sternharz was raised in an antihasidic family in Nemirov, which meant that his early Hebrew education was not so different from Lefin's in Satanov. Neither was primarily an original thinker; both responded to inspiration from other sources. The turning point for Lefin came when he met Moses Mendelssohn and his circle in Berlin in 1780–84; Sternharz's life changed after he met Nahman in 1802. Their goals were entirely different, as were their intellectual and religious milieux, yet their literary means were similar.

Links can be discerned between the Hebrew narratives of sea travel written by Sternharz and Lefin. As Haim Liberman and Mendel Piekarz have showed, hasidic authors left compelling accounts of Rabbi Nahman's and Sternharz's connections to the *maskilim* in Uman. Before and after 1810, Nahman and Sternharz met with Khaikl Hurwitz (1749–1822) and his son Hirsh Ber Hurwitz (1785–1857).[57] The most astonishing record of these meetings is to be found in Avraham Hazan's work *Kokhevei 'or* (Stars of Light). Hazan writes:

> ואחרי פטירת רביז״ל היו [המשכילים] ידידים אהובים לאנ״ש ומכ״ש למהרנ״ת ז״ל. ומהרנ״ת ז״ל היה לו ציווי מרביז״ל שידבר עמם. ע״כ בכל פעם שהיה באומין היה לו וויזיט אצלם ודבר עמם, ופ״א נכנס עמם בחקירות גדולות כ״כ עד שצעק ואמר מה רצה רביז״ל ממנו.[58]

> After the departure of our Rebbe, of blessed memory, they [the *maskilim*] were beloved friends of our Breslov circle, and especially of R. Nathan z"l. And R. Nathan had a command from our Rebbe z"l that he should speak with them, and so every time he was in Uman, he had a visit at their house and spoke with them. And once he entered into such deep philosophical questions [*hakirot gedolot*] with them that he cried out, What did our Rebbe want from him?

Around the time of these meetings, sea travel became a popular genre in Hebrew literature, and the Jewish community of Uman provided a direct link between maskilic and hasidic travel writing. In 1817, two years after Sternharz printed his first account of Nahman's pilgrimage to the Holy Land, Khaikl Hurwitz published a Yiddish translation of Joachim Heinrich Campe's narrative *Die Entdeckung von Amerika*.[59] There are unconfirmed accounts that Hurwitz's son Hirsh Ber (later known as Hermann Bernard at Cambridge University) translated Campe's book into Hebrew around 1810.[60]

Although the *maskilim* and the hasidim were opposing camps, they were well aware of each other's actions. There were also family connections and other matters of lineage (*yikhes*). For instance, Khaikl Hurwitz was a descendant of Isaiah Horowitz,[61] author of *Shnei luḥot ha-brit*, which gave him some standing among hasidim. Khone Shmeruk and Shmuel Werses have pointed to evidence that Nathan Sternharz knew that his opponents were reading and scrutinizing what he wrote. He cautioned his son to guard his letters "because they are forbidden to strangers, who make a mockery of truthful words";[62] also, the second edition of *Sippurei ma`asiyot* corrected an error that Joseph Perl had mocked in *Megale temirin.*[63] A manuscript including omitted passages from the letters that was printed as *'Alim le-trufa* contains additional evidence of Sternharz's fear that his letters might be read by people outside the Bratslav community. He repeatedly urged his son to keep many things secret and asked him to send a special stamp to seal his letters.[64] In one excised letter from 1841, Sternharz wrote to Shmuel Weinberg, "For God's sake, carefully warn anyone who is informed about this matter that he should conceal and hide the thing away, lest strangers learn of it, God forbid."[65] And at the end of a letter to his son in 1841, Sternharz wrote: "Hide these things away from the mockers."[66]

Shmuel Feiner mentions intriguing accounts of Nahman's and Sternharz's meetings with *maskilim* in Uman. He then demonstrates that Sternharz responded to the ideology of the Haskala, specifically attacking works such as Shmuel Romanelli's *Mas'a ba-`arav* (1792).[67] Although Romanelli was a Sephardic Jew from Italy,[68] he published his travel narrative in Berlin at the press affiliated with the Jüdische Freischule (or Knabenschule, 1778–1825).[69] The same press—Ḥevrat ḥinukh ne`arim—had published Lefin's book *Mod`a le-vina* in 1789. Sternharz expressed his complete rejection of the Berlin Jewish school in *Likutei halakhot* when he referred to groups of "completely wicked and notorious people, who have made for themselves a Society for the Education of Youth."[70]

One even finds evidence of a literary rivalry in the choice of titles. For example, the title *Sefer ha-middot*—which appears as the title of a Yiddish book in the sixteenth century—was adopted by Isaac Satanov in 1784 (as well as again for his book-length translation of Aristotle's *Ethics* in 1790) and by Naftali Hirsh Wessely in 1786 and 1818–19. In 1811 and 1821, Sternharz—or, previously, Nahman himself—recycled the title as a second title for *Sefer ha-Alef-Beit*. It is no coincidence that the books by Satanov and Wessely (like the books by Romanelli and Lefin) were published by the Ḥevrat Hinukh Ne`arim Press at the Jüdische Freischule.[71]

Sternharz undoubtedly knew of the books published in Berlin under the title *Sefer ha-middot*. The *maskilim* and the hasidim even fought over the title *Mase`ot ha-yam* (Sea Voyages), as the publication history shows: after Lefin's book was published under this title in 1818 and 1823, Sternharz's account of Nahman's journey to Eretz Israel—originally called "Seder ha-nesi`a shelo le-Eretz Israel" when it was included in the 1815 edition of *Sippurei ma`asiyot*—was reprinted under the title *Mase`ot ha-yam* in 1846 and 1850. Lefin's sea narratives were then republished in 1854 and 1859, followed by reissues of Sternharz's *Mase`ot ha-yam* in the 1870s.

Between the Hasidim and the *Maskilim*

There was no unbridgeable geographical or literary chasm between the hasidim and their opponents. Indeed, as previously noted, there is a clear intertextual link between Sternharz's account of his charismatic leader's pilgrimage and the details of Joseph Perl's epistolary novel *Megale temirin*. I quote again from Sternharz's narrative of Nahman's pilgrimage:

> ובבואם לספינה והתחילו לילך על הים השחור · תיכף במעת לעת הראשון הי׳ פרטינע גדולה דהיינו רוח סערה · עד שהגלים קפצו על הספינה · והוכרחו להיות בחדר סגור ומסוגר מחמת המים שלא יבואו עליהם · והיו ברקים ורעמים ורוחות גדולות בלי ערך · והי׳ פחד גדול.[72]

> And when they came to the ship and started to go on the Black Sea · immediately in the first day there was a great *firtina* that is a great storm · until the waves leaped onto the ship · and they were forced to be in a closed and sealed room because of the water so that it wouldn't get in to them · And there were thunder and lightning and high winds without measure · and there was great fear.[73]

Sternharz often used Yiddish grammar, and Perl parodied this feature by exaggerating it—for example, by replacing "when they came to the ship" (*be-vo'am la-sefina*) with "we came on the ship" (*banu `al ha-sefina*), mimicking the Yiddish prepositional phrase in "we came onto the ship" (*mir zaynen gekumen afn shif*). Perl's parody eliminates much of the description, which makes Sternharz's account sound simplistic rather than vivid:

ובאנו על הספינה, והתחלנו לילך על הים השחור, ובמעת לעת הראשון, היה רוח סערה גדולה, עד שהגלים קפצו על הספינה, והיה פחד גדול.[74]

> And we came on the ship, and we started to go on the Black Sea, and in the first day there was a great storm, until the waves leapt onto the ship, and there was great fear.

This passage is from the final letter in Perl's epistolary novel, written by "The Travelers to the Holy Land" (letter 151). There is no doubt that it uses parody and satire by emulating the account of Nahman's pilgrimage. Apart from Perl's omissions, another difference is that his description purports to be a first-person plural narrative by the travelers themselves, whereas Sternharz's description uses third-person narrative. Perl's parody eliminates the charm and suspense of the original by paring it down to the point of vagueness in short independent clauses. Whereas Sternharz combines the phrases into a powerful narrative, Perl chops them into separate units.

In contrast to Nahman's pilgrims, Perl's hasidic travelers are fleeing punishment after their corrupt deeds have been exposed. Perl's satire turns their spiritualized journey into a ploy to escape imprisonment. As Jonatan Meir writes in a note to this passage, in his critical edition of *Megale temirin,* the letter is "a parody of the immigration of hasidim to the Land of Israel, a place which was transformed in Perl's eyes into a refuge for those who have broken the law, and as a shelter for opponents of the Haskala and of the enlightened State."[75]

The remaining chapters of this book examine how *maskilim* wrote and translated narratives of sea travel. Chapters 4 and 5 go back in time to German Jewish narratives from 1785, 1790, and 1807. I have discussed the hasidic writings first because they represent a more traditional worldview. Chapters 6 and 7 move forward to narratives dating from 1815–24. There was undoubtedly some degree of competition between factions in this battle of books. The most conservative group comprised hasidic men such as Sternharz who strove to live within the confines of Torah. The hasidic authors unabashedly drew inspiration from Yiddish speech, which sometimes made their literary expressions more original than those of the neo-biblical writers in Berlin. But one moderate *maskil* had particular success, beyond what early *maskilim* and hasidim had attempted: when Mendel Lefin translated sea narratives from German, he achieved a meaningful synthesis of styles and produced the highest level of narrative Hebrew for his time. This book builds toward the final chapter, with an appreciation of Lefin's accomplishment as a leading Hebrew stylist of his day.

Interlude

4

Euchel

SEA TRAVELS AND STORM WINDS FROM BERLIN

In the second half of the eighteenth century, Enlightened Jews in Berlin promoted Jewish modernization. The *maskilim* fostered Western ideas and education by publishing in German and Hebrew and by creating the first modern Jewish schools.[1] Although some of these educated Jews favored secularization—and their world no longer centered on Jewish practice, the prospect of messianic redemption, or a return to Zion—they tried to take Hebrew back to its ancient scriptural sources. Their secular worldview and literary goals implied no internal contradiction: the choice of biblical Hebrew was their enlightened way of distancing themselves from postbiblical Hebrew writing, which for centuries had been dominated by mainstream Orthodox rabbis.

In the circle of Moses Mendelssohn (1729–86), most maskilic authors differentiated themselves from rabbinic authors by trying to write what they considered to be "pure" Hebrew, emulating the language of the biblical prophets.[2] To justify this choice, they pointed to grammatical errors and improper vocabulary in postbiblical Hebrew. The *maskilim* were not, however, successful in imposing linguistic purism on the invention of a modern Hebrew literature. The long tradition of rabbinic writing made it impossible to circumvent the established norms that were familiar to Jewish men who had studied in yeshivas.

The *maskilim* followed the example of the German neoclassicists when they returned to ancient sources. They encouraged the Berlin Hebrew authors to emulate biblical models—as one part of the culture war they were fighting against outmoded features of Jewish life. Separating themselves

Fig. 4. Isaac Euchel's route from Königsberg to Copenhagen by way of Gdansk (Dantzick), 1785, based on Samuel Dunn, *The Northern States*, in *A New Atlas of the Mundane System* (London: Sayer, 1788), plate 10, detail, with Euchel's approximate route added by Joseph Stoll, Syracuse University Cartographic Laboratory, in collaboration with Ken Frieden. Dunn's original map courtesy of the Lionel Pincus and Princess Firyal Map Division, New York Public Library, Astor, Lenox and Tilden Foundations.

from the rabbinic tradition, they dismissed much of postbiblical Hebrew as a precipitous decline from the heights of the Hebrew Bible. By rejecting the rabbis' postbiblical Hebrew, however, they rendered their writing less accessible to most readers of Hebrew. They also limited their range of expression by eliminating a large descriptive vocabulary that could have added greater detail to their narratives. Moreover, their biblical pastiches and patchworks raised their poetry and prose to a high register that was not always appropriate to the material at hand. The maskilic use of biblical grammar, as in the treatment of verbs, exalted their writing and often made it appear alien to the existing Hebrew readership.

To some extent, the Berlin *maskilim* saw themselves as continuing the development of Hebrew poetry since the "Golden Age" in medieval Spain. This view explains in part their somewhat one-sided emphasis on writing poetry and philosophy to the detriment of narrative forms. But whereas the Hebrew poets in Spain were heavily influenced by contemporary Arabic writing, the Hebraists in Berlin followed the German literary fashions of their day. The German models fostered neoclassicism, which tended to diminish naturalistic portrayals.

The *maskilim* were extremely influential in Jewish intellectual history, but most of their Hebrew poetry has aged poorly. By the time these new Hebrew writers belatedly found inspiration in German neoclassicism, European authors were already moving on to what became known as Sturm und Drang and romanticism. For this reason, most of the Berlin authors' Hebrew poetry was destined to become obsolete in a few decades. As the florid neoclassical style withered, another style emerged among unpretentious prose writers. Jacob Emden and Ber of Bolekhov (Birkenthal) had explored the potential for new modes of Hebrew narrative in their autobiographical works, and hasidic texts such as those discussed in the previous chapters drew wider readership.

It is worthwhile to consider briefly the path not taken by the *maskilim*. Without abandoning their biblical predilections, the Berlin *maskilim* could have also found inspiration in other more recent sources; some Hebrew authors did in fact work within the time-honored norms of rabbinic texts. Jacob Emden's autobiography *Megillat sefer* (Scroll of the Book) embodies those norms and transcends them, showing that exceptional rabbinic authors were able to produce strong, readable prose narratives. Ber of Bolekhov's memoir, *Zikronot*, demonstrates that a well-educated merchant, combining rabbinic Hebrew models with the influence of other languages and literatures, could write effective narrative prose.[3] The literary impact of these pathbreaking autobiographies was not felt until long after their authors' deaths because there was not yet a modern literary milieu of publishers and readers to embrace them.[4]

Twentieth-century scholars of Hebrew literary history often assumed that modern Hebrew literature began during the Haskala. They thought that the *maskilim*, by returning to biblical models, had made a fresh start and laid the foundations of a modern literature.[5] Although the *maskilim* were an elite group with a small readership—so this version of literary history explains—they paved the way for the revival of Hebrew at the end of the nineteenth century. This account represents only part of the story, however, because innumerable precursors provided diverse models to modern Hebrew writers. Although the Berlin *maskilim* rejected most of their forerunners, they were unable to prevail over them. The maskilic preference for ornate biblical *melitza*, in particular, limited the possibilities for realistic narrative; other sources, especially from German and Yiddish, were needed to breathe life into revivified Hebrew prose.

The limitations of the Berlin Hebrew writers have been widely recognized. Israel Zinberg shows that the authors who published in the journal *Ha-me'asef* "collected Biblical metaphors and expressions in heaps, and in this way created the pretentious, florid, diffuse style that is so typical of their generation." He points to Isaac Euchel as "the renewer of the *artificial* and *rhetorical* prose that was regarded as a model by the *maskilim* of the generation of the Meassefim."[6] Yosef Klausner noted in 1930 that the beginnings of a broader conception of Hebrew may be found among other Berlin writers such as Isaac Satanov, who was more open to Mishnaic language.[7] Klausner traced a line of influence from Satanov to Mendel Lefin, from Lefin to Mordechai Suchostober and Eliezer Tzvayfl, and from them by way of the Zhitomir Rabbinical Seminary to S. Y. Abramovitsh.[8] This is a more accurate genealogy of "*nusaḥ* Mendele" (Mendele's style) than the myths spread by Y. H. Ravnitzky, H. N. Bialik, and S. Y. Abramovitsh between 1907 and 1911.[9] According to Bialik, Abramovitsh's mature Hebrew fiction written after 1886 almost single-handedly established the dominant style for modern Hebrew literature.[10] For the past century, literary historians have tended to accept this questionable notion because Abramovitsh never acknowledged his debt to bilingual Hebrew/Yiddish authors such as Mendel Lefin, the subject of chapter 7.

The decision to privilege biblical Hebrew—especially the poetic language of the prophets—proved to be counterproductive for modern

Hebrew narrative. As Moshe Pelli notes, "An eighteenth-century writer of a travel account in Hebrew faced a unique problem that inherently limited authenticating an actual experience." Discussing this problem in connection with Shmuel Romanelli's travel writing, Pelli comments that the use of biblical language "tended to generalize the experience rather than depict it accurately or portray it singularly."[11] From the Mishna to modern rabbinic writing, a larger vocabulary and more flexible postbiblical Hebrew grammar had developed. A few decades later, around 1815 to 1825, moderate *maskilim* and hasidic authors in Austrian Galicia and Russia advanced Hebrew literature in ways that had seemed nearly impossible for the Berlin authors.

Maskilim in Berlin were attracted to German travel narratives, ascribing educational value to them in that they exposed readers to world geography.[12] Hence, the German writings of J. H. Campe, which inspired the Hebrew works discussed in chapters 5, 6, and 7, were popular reading material among *maskilim* and their students at the Jüdische Freischule (Jewish Free School) in Berlin.[13] There was resistance to fictional narratives; as Rebecca Wolpe notes in reference to the German works that *maskilim* chose to translate, "only very rarely were *belles lettres* and fictional texts utilized; love stories are nonexistent."[14] In contrast, travel accounts had a realistic aura and may have seemed innocuous to traditional readers and rabbinic authorities. Ostensibly beyond the sway of ideological biases, travel writing expressed immediacy and concreteness in plain, descriptive language.

Two interrelated literary topoi—sea voyages and storms at sea—provide an opportunity to analyze the language used by successive authors and to distinguish clearly between various uses of biblical and postbiblical phrases. Chapter 1 presented the distinctive approaches to biblical quotation and allusion as well as the different shades of biblical and postbiblical style. Because the traditional language of sea travel is specific and limited, many of the same key words recur. Narratives by the *maskilim* Isaac Euchel (1756–1804) and Moses Mendelsohn-Frankfurt (1782–1861) highlight early efforts to transcend biblical *melitza* through more spontaneous-sounding sentences. Also at stake in the Hebrew sea travel narratives were methods of translation and adaptation; contemporary norms encouraged translators to rewrite the source rather than to translate word for word. Mendelsohn-Frankfurt, for example, openly acknowledged in 1807 that he did not translate Campe's *Entdeckung von Amerika* word for word, instead opting to adapt the content using idiomatic biblical Hebrew.

The rise of modern Hebrew literature has often been represented as a straight line from Enlightenment authors' flowery, neobiblical *melitza* style to "Mendele's *nusaḥ*" in S. Y. Abramovitsh's fiction, leaving aside other influential writers.[15] Beyond this two-dimensional geometry, however, there were additional stages of development, from traditional rabbinic writing in post-Mishnaic Hebrew to hasidic narratives, parodies of hasidic Hebrew, and mitnagdic tracts, all of which contributed to the emergence of a vernacular Hebrew style. The older approach to Hebrew literary history was not adequate and culminated in Bialik's hyperbolic claims for Abramovitsh's short stories (1886–96). A more complete picture includes authors as diverse as Nathan Sternharz and Mendel Lefin as well as their successors.

Scholarship on the Jewish Enlightenment and Hasidism has often emphasized their conflicting ideologies. As noted in the previous chapter, however, the literary contribution of the hasidim has been undervalued and is seldom understood in its proper literary-historical context. The accepted wisdom in Hebrew literary studies is that the *maskilim* favored a neobiblical style, which they considered to be "pure"; by contrast, the hasidim wrote a kind of "low Hebrew" or "folk Hebrew," which many nonhasidic readers have scorned over the past two centuries because it is based on postbiblical Hebrew, has grammatical errors, and is tinged with Yiddish.[16] This simplistic dichotomy has seldom been questioned, although some linguists have challenged the claim made by the *maskilim* that they were returning to "pure" biblical Hebrew.

Intellectual historians have emphasized the antihasidic polemics[17] and have studied maskilic satires in depth,[18] but other literary genres have been neglected. Moreover, not all *maskilim* embraced biblical Hebrew and *melitza*; Isaac Satanov and Mendel Lefin, for example, favored Mishnaic Hebrew and influenced Joseph Perl. Chapters 6 and 7 show that moderate *maskilim* in Galicia and Russia contributed to the invention of a modern Hebrew style.

A passage by Jacob Emden written around 1760 illustrates some of the issues surrounding linguistic choices in premodern Hebrew (as in previous chapters, bold print indicates biblical passages in both the Hebrew extracts and the English translations):

> ושלחתי שתי בנותי הי״ל [השם ישמרן לנצח] בבת אחת, בשילהי קייטא תקי״ז דרך ים כה לדנציג, והייתי בדאגה גדולה בעבורן, כי עמדו רוחות סערות חזקות מאד בעודן על הים; אח״כ נודע לי שהיו בסכנה גדולה מאד, כי בהיותן כבר סמוך לדנציג השליך הרוח את הספינה הרבה פרסאות הרחק מן העיר, ואבדו התורן, ו**האניה חשבה להשבר**.[19]

> At the end of the summer 1757, I sent my two daughters together—may God protect them always—by sea from here to Danzig, and I was very worried for them, because very strong storm winds came up while they were still on the sea; afterward I was informed that they were in very great danger, because when they were already close to Danzig, the wind threw the ship many miles away from the city, and they lost the mast, and **the ship was on the verge of breaking up**.

Emden was an important voice in early-modern Hebrew writing because he was an independent-minded rabbi whose writing preceded that of the *maskilim*. This short account exemplifies the clarity of Emden's prose and his use of synthetic language, with pronominal suffixes of verbs (e.g., *be-heyiotan*) and nouns (e.g., *bnotai*).[20] But the passage has a somewhat limited descriptive quality. Emden overuses the words *very* and *great* instead of expanding the vocabulary. It is not clear what is meant by the vague phrase "they lost the mast" (*'ibdu ha-toren*), though the phrase does show Emden's openness to the Mishnaic dropping of the particle *et*. Although Emden resorts to the best-known commonplace of biblical shipwrecks from the Book of Jonah, "the ship was on the verge of breaking up" (*ha-oniya ḥishva lehishaver*), this passage is refreshing in its naturalness.

Isaac Euchel as Travel Writer

Modern Hebrew narrative owes a debt to the editors of the journal *Ha-me'asef*, Isaac Euchel and Aharon Wolfsohn of Halle (1754–1835). Although they produced no narrative masterpieces, their best Hebrew prose is impressive. One instance is a remarkable play by Wolfsohn, *Kalut da'at u-tzevi'ut.*[21] Euchel, as an admirer of letters written by Moses Mendelssohn, Montesquieu, and other precursors, made small but significant advances in the genres of epistolary writing and travel narrative in Hebrew. He wrote mainly in neobiblical language but usually without relying excessively on quotations. For nautical terminology, he most often employed the terms that appear in Jonah and Psalm 107.

Euchel was born in Copenhagen in 1756 and later lived in Berlin, where he studied in a yeshiva from 1769 to 1773.[22] After receiving this traditional education, he was at a loss regarding his future, recalling later that "I was like a man who goes down to the sea in a boat, without an oar or a compass; I would go wherever the wind took me, and when a storm came up and waves arose, I would capsize and come to nothing."[23] The nautical metaphor reflects Euchel's preoccupations in the 1780s; he wrote these lines in the years between the publication of his two sea narratives. From 1776 to 1778, Euchel was a student in Hamburg, after which he became a tutor in Königsberg. At the University of Königsberg (where Immanuel Kant was a professor and later rector), he studied Oriental languages and philosophy with such success that in 1786 he was nearly appointed a lecturer there.[24] His appointment to teach Hebrew was blocked, however, because he was a Jew. Meanwhile, Euchel founded the landmark journal *Ha-me'asef* in 1783. In the spring of 1784, he traveled from Königsberg to Copenhagen, a journey that provided the material for one of his early Hebrew narratives.

Euchel's letters to his student Michael Friedländer, "'Igrot Yitzḥak Euchel," contain traces of a modern Hebrew sea narrative, although they are brief and lack literary force. Published in the second volume of *Ha-me'asef* (1784–85), these letters include a short account of the author's European travels by ship from Königsberg to Copenhagen by way of Gdansk.[25] In a footnote, Euchel apologizes that the contents are sometimes insignificant, commenting that they have been published for proponents of the Hebrew language. He indicates that his main goal is to show "how our Holy Tongue could serve us, to speak of whatever we wish, from small to great."[26] This aim is outlined in the first letter, which states that "I agreed to write you all my letters in the Hebrew language, to test whether we could write about whatever we wish in it."[27] In fact, no striking events are described in this account, and apart from the linguistic experiment, the content of Euchel's trip is scarcely sufficient to hold the reader's interest. (One particular limitation is that the motivation for the voyage is left unclear; according to Andreas Kennecke, Euchel's trip was connected to his failed effort to receive a teaching position in Kiel, which was then ruled by Denmark, or in Berlin.[28])

As indicated to his student, the son of the wealthy community leader David Friedländer, Euchel's travel writing was an experiment in using Hebrew for everyday experiences. (It is pertinent that literary efforts of this kind had the backing of benefactors such as the Friedländer family.) Moreover, because Euchel wrote while traveling, he had limited access to his books, which may have had the unintended effects of diminishing his use of biblical quotations and setting the letters apart from most of the overly erudite Berlin Hebrew writing. By virtue of their inability to use reference works, travel writers sometimes achieved a "plain style" like that associated with captains' logs.

Euchel's most pertinent maritime description is embedded in a static scene, starting with an address to God, quoted from Psalm 36:8: מה יקר חסדך אלהים! (How dear is Your mercy, O God!).[29] Euchel expresses his wonder at the beauty of the world and the creatures of the earth. Following this outburst of piety, he addresses an imagined person who dares to think himself superior. For Euchel, sea travel illustrates how utterly weak human beings are in the face of God's power, which is embodied in forces beyond our control. Hence, the overall theme of this letter is wonder, emphasizing a devout worldview.[30]

To what extent does Euchel succeed in representing a concrete scene? In describing a ship, he uses familiar biblical vocabulary, including the words *oniya* (boat), *rav ha-ḥovel* (captain), and *malaḥ* (sailor). He also falls back on well-known biblical phrases:

> הבט פה, וראה זה **הים גדול ורחב ידים**, שמה אניה גדולה תהלך, רב החובל וכל מלחיו כלמו גבורים; בהרימם קול ידמו לך כבני אלים; בנחה תהיה בעיניך כעיר גדולה ובצורה בשמים, ובפרוש עליה את נסה לנסוע, תדמה שמוע **קול רעש גדול וחזק**; יגל כבודך לאמור: מה רבו מעללי איש! מה גדלו תחבולות בני אדם! — (כי תתפאר ברוחך לאמור: אני אדם כמוהו·) — אמנם זכור! לו חסד ה׳׳ החפץ בתחבולות תבונה, יוליכם **אל מחוז חפצם** מה כחם ומה גבורתם? תחבולתם אפס ומעלליהם מאפע! — רגע ישב רוחו, יחלופו ואינם, **ישלח דברו** והיו כלא היו![31]

> Look here and behold this **great and broad sea** (Ps. 104:25). There a great ship sails, and its captain and all of its sailors are mighty men; when they lift up their voices, they will seem to you like children of gods; at rest it will appear to you like a huge city and a fortress in the sky. When they spread their sails to journey forth, you will imagine that you hear **a great and powerful voice** [Ezek. 3:12, quoted in the traditional Ashkenazic prayer book]; it will announce God's glory, saying: How great are the deeds of men! How great are the schemes of men!—(For you will boast to yourself, saying: I am a man like them.)—And yet remember! If not for the kindness of God, who looks favorably upon the schemes [*taḥbolot*] of intellect, what power and might do they have to take them **to where they wish to go** (Ps. 107:30)? Their schemes are nothing, and their deeds are naught!—If for a moment His wind [or spirit, *ruaḥ*] is still, they vanish and are gone; if **He sends His word**, they will be as if they never were!

This passage begins with a kind of humanistic pride in the accomplishments of people but then submerges this feeling under a humble acknowledgment of the ultimate weakness of human beings when confronted by greater forces such as wind sent by God. The rhetorical flourishes, European punctuation, and biblical choice of words make it typical of Hebrew from the Berlin Enlightenment. Looking back from a distance of 230 years, and aware that Euchel would later become one of the notorious reformers in Berlin Jewish circles, we might not expect such an emphasis on the divine. Sea travels repeatedly expose people to extreme situations in which they reexamine their beliefs. Also, Euchel may have adopted a pious and moralistic tone because he was writing to his pupil.

Euchel's travel letters illustrate many distinctive linguistic features. Like most other Berlin *maskilim*, he attempted to use neobiblical style, called *melitza*, a word usually translated as "rhetorical language" or "flowery language." (The term *melitza* derives from the biblical root ל-י-צ, which has an array of meanings that range from "scorn" and "scoff" to "recommend," "interpret," and "translate.") Hence, in the midst of his graphic description of a ship, Euchel throws in the biblical phrases "great and broad sea" (Ps. 104:25) and "a great and powerful voice" (Ezek. 3:12). A subsequent passage in the travel letters further illustrates Euchel's tendency to insert biblical language into the flow of his narrative. Describing a rainstorm, he writes that "the waters prevailed and came up to our souls."[32] Allusions of this sort lift the text to a high register, although not always by quoting directly. In a similar way, he uses biblical terms in his phrase "the captain and all of his sailors [*rav ha-ḥovel ve-khol malaḥav*]." Elsewhere he creatively alludes to and modifies other biblical precedents.

Yet Euchel's writing was not as consistently biblical as he and other *maskilim* intended.[33] He could have described the moon using the noun *yareaḥ*, the usual biblical word. He refers instead to the *levana*, a rare word in the Bible, more closely associated with Mishnaic usage. The word *taḥbula* (scheme) is a rare biblical word found only in the Book of Proverbs, becoming more important in medieval commentaries. Yet because it does occur in a biblical book, the *maskilim* could justify using it, even if its main source was postbiblical. In a related way, Euchel uses the word *ḥayat* (tailor) even though it does not appear in the Bible, but rather in the Mishna;[34] he adds a footnote to justify this usage based on a biblical Hebrew root.[35]

Euchel later wrote an extensive and fictionalized epistolary travel narrative entitled "'Igrot Meshullam ben Uriah ha-Eshtemo`i" (Letters of Meshullam ben Uriah the Eshtomoite), which was published in *Ha-me'asef* 6 (1790).[36] Pelli refers to Euchel's text as "the first epistolary publication in Hebrew *belles lettres* in the modern period."[37] One should note that some *maskilim*—like influential early settlers in the Land of Israel—considered the Sephardic pronunciation of Hebrew to be more authentic than Ashkenazic pronunciation, which was thought to have been tainted by Yiddish. Perhaps to underscore their claim to authenticity, Euchel's letters are presented as if they were written by a Sephardic Jew who leaves Aleppo and travels through Spain, Italy, and the Ottoman Empire during 1769. The purported author's name, "Meshullam," links him to the fifteenth-century Italian Jewish traveler Meshullam of Volterra, yet there are other fictional precedents. Euchel's short work has been compared to Montesquieu's full-length epistolary novel *Lettres persanes* (Persian Letters, 1721, with a second revised edition published in 1759),[38] which Euchel probably read in a German translation. Like Montesquieu in *Lettres persanes*,

Euchel introduces a fictional, foreign narrator as a way of representing European cultures from an imaginary, outside perspective. As such, the book comments on European and European Jewish mores. Euchel did not give the Land of Israel any place in his text because his purpose was to explore Jewish identity in Europe.

The letters' minimal plot does little to structure the epistolary text.[39] Euchel relies heavily on generalized accounts of places and ideas, and it resembles other travel narratives that describe the sea, the captain, the sailors' activities, storms, and shipwrecks. In the first letter, the captain and sailors appear:

> רב החובל וכל מלחיו שומרים את מלאכתם בחבל וסדניהם, וכל האנשים אשר על הספינה סוחרים ישמעאלים ונוצרים אנשי ספרד וצרפת, כומרים ומשוררים איש איש יושב בחדרו, ואין אתנו יודע מי אנכי ומאיזה עם אני. כן נסענו שני ימים. . . . ותשבות הרוח לא יכולנו ללכת עוד. ויתירו המלחים את הסדינים, וישליכו את הוו הגדול אל הים ותעמוד הספינה כאי מוצק בתוך הים מבלתי פנות אנה ואנה.[40]

> The captain and all of his sailors ply their craft, with ropes and sails [*sdinim*], and all of the people on the ship are Arab and Christian merchants from Spain and France or monks and choir boys, each one sitting in his room. No one among us knows who I am and from what people I come. Thus we traveled for two days. . . . The wind rested, and we could not go farther. The sailors pulled down the sails, threw the great anchor [*vav*] into the sea, and the ship stood like a cast metal island on the sea, turning neither this way nor that.

How original is Euchel's use of Hebrew? Moshe Pelli notes that Euchel introduced significant nautical terminology in this text and in the "Letters of Isaac Euchel" (1785), but he overstates the case because Euchel relied heavily on biblical terms. Pelli writes that "some unique seafaring terminology is used."[41] From "The Letters of Meshullam," Pelli cites the phrase *rav ha-ḥovel ve-khol malaḥav* (the captain and all his sailors); however, the term *rav ha-ḥovel* occurs in the Book of Jonah 1:6 (and in rabbinic commentaries on that passage), and the term *malaḥim* is given in Jonah 1:5, Ezekiel 27, and many commentaries. Pelli also mentions Euchel's simile *ke-ish yored ha-yam be-oniya* (like a sailor in a boat; literally, like a man who goes down to the sea in a boat) in Euchel's biography of Mendelssohn.[42] But the term designating "sailor" is no innovation because it occurs in the plural form, referring to sailors as *yordei ha-yam*, in Psalm 107:23. The continuation of Euchel's last-mentioned phrase, *yored ha-yam be-oniya u-ve-yado ein mashot ve-ein meḥugah* (like a sailor in a boat, and in his hand there is no oar and no compass), uses rare biblical vocabulary from Ezekiel 27:29 (*mashot*) and Isaiah 44:13 (*meḥugah*). Euchel did sometimes innovate in his use of Hebrew, although less by inventing terms than by shifting meanings and creating unique combinations of words. Possibly more original (although sometimes found in medieval rabbinic writing[43]) is Euchel's use of the term *sdinim* to denote sails instead of the rare biblical term *mefarsim* or a rare use of the overdetermined word *nes* (usually meaning "banner"). The biblical word *sdinim* refers to sheets or linen in Genesis 38:26, Numbers 19:2, and Proverbs 31:24. It may be that Euchel's usage was influenced by the German word *Segelleine* (literally, "sail linen"), meaning "sail sheet" or "mainsheet," which suggests that *sadin* is a translation or calque from German. (The mainsheet can also be a rope that controls the main sail.) This extension of meaning from *sadin* = sheet to *sadin* = sail did not catch on in modern Hebrew. Another interesting, postbiblical choice is the use of the word *vav* (hook)—that is, the name of the Hebrew letter—to mean "anchor." In Exodus 27:10 and in some medieval commentaries, *vav* means "hook," apparently based on the vague resemblance of the letter Vav (ו) to a hook. Euchel inventively transforms that biblical usage into a maritime term.

Euchel's lyrical description of the sea also draws from nautical vocabulary in the Bible:

> בערב יום השלישי אחרי אשר שקט הים ופניו כראי מוצק מבלי שוא גל והרים דכיו, ואנחנו על הספינה שלוים ושקטים . . . ואנכי לבדי קמתי להשתעשע על גג הספינה להביט אל הים הגדול הזה, אשר ירגיע לב רואה להביט את פועל ה׳ ולהגדיל שמו בקרבו, והנה הירח עולה מאחורי ההרים.[44]

> In the evening on the third day, after the sea had calmed and its surface was like a cast iron mirror, without surging waves or pounding waters, and we on the boat were tranquil and undisturbed . . . and I alone got up to amuse myself on the deck [*gag*] of the boat, to look at this great sea,

> which calms the heart of one who sees it and observes the action of God, and to exalt His name inwardly. And behold, the moon is rising behind the mountains.

In notes to this passage, Yehuda Friedlander points out that the phrases "surging waves" and "pounding waters" draw on terms that appear in Psalms 89:10 and 93:3. By limiting himself to borrowing a few words rather than importing complete phrases, however, Euchel seems to avoid a pitfall of *melitza*. As seen in the case of the word *sdinim*, another technique he uses is to take biblical Hebrew words and give them new meanings. Here he again uses the ancient Hebrew word *sadin*, meaning "sheet," to designate "sail."[45] Modern Israeli Hebrew has limited *sadin* mainly to the meaning "bedsheet," and, following Ezekiel 27:7, it has settled on *mifras* to designate the sail of a sailboat.[46] This usage was not yet established, however, when Euchel was writing in 1790. Euchel also refers to a sail as a *nes*, a biblical Hebrew word usually meaning "banner" or "flag." Regarding one unclear biblical passage (Isa. 33:23), Rashi and some lexicographers state that *nes* signifies a sail.[47] Euchel sometimes derives his originality from transforming or transcontextualizing biblical words, influenced by medieval sources. For example, he uses the term *gag* (roof) to refer to the deck of a ship. The phrase he uses, *gag ha-sefina*, "deck of the boat," is not biblical but appears in at least one midrashic passage (see Lamentations Rabba) and in later responsa literature.[48] Euchel provides unmistakable examples of postbiblical usage in maskilic writing; even his use of the term *sefina* instead of *oniya* for "ship" brings this passage closer to Mishnaic Hebrew.

In "Letters of Meshullam," Euchel's obligatory description of a storm begins with a reference to the Book of Jonah. It may be that because of the difficulties inherent in successfully describing a storm at sea, he falls back on biblical phrases. The author seems to want to include all of the available biblical prooftexts, which sometimes interferes with his descriptions:

> **והאלהים הטיל רוח סערה על הים** לא יכולנו לגשת אל היבשה, ונלך ברוח קדמה חזקה **מבלי מצוא מנוח**, והמלחים יראו לבל יתקרבו אל שפת חלק אפריקא ויפלו ביד **אנשי חמס** העושקים אשר בארגיל פעס וטוניס ויאמצו את כל כחם לשמור דרך שפת אייראפא, וכה נסענו שני ימים מבלי דעת אנה נפנה כי הרוח הולך וחזק, ומטר וקולות וברקים רב נפלו מן השמים, לא יכול איש לראות את ידו, וביום השלישי **חתרו המלחים לבוא אל היבשה**.[49]

> **God cast a storm wind upon the sea** [*ve ha-'Elohim hetil ruaḥ so'ara 'al ha-yam*, cf. Jon. 1:4] and we could not reach the shore [cf. Jon. 1:13]; we went with a strong easterly wind **without finding a place to rest** [*mi-bli matzo manoaḥ*, cf. Gen. 8:9]. The sailors saw to it that we did not approach the shore of Africa and fall into the hands of **violent men** [on *'anshei ḥamas*, cf. several verses, such as Ps. 18:49, 140:12, and Prov. 3:31, 16:29], the oppressors [pirates] who are in Argil, Pas, and Tunis. They exerted their utmost powers to keep along the coast of Europe, and so we traveled two days without knowing where to turn, for the wind kept on blowing strongly, and great rain and thunder and lightning came down from the sky; no one could see his own hand. On the third day **the sailors rowed and came to the shore** [*ḥatru ha-melaḥim la-vo 'el ha-yabosha*; cf. Jon. 1:13].

Euchel has patched together much of his description from passages in Jonah, Genesis, Psalms, and Proverbs. Can this pastiche of biblical phrases successfully describe an actual storm at sea? For a reader who recognizes the allusions, it superimposes the story of Jonah onto the narrative. Nevertheless, Euchel modifies each phrase slightly to make it his own. For example, here are three of Euchel's phrases, paired with their biblical precedents:

1. והאלהים הטיל רוח סערה על הים לא יכולנו לגשת אל היבשה
   Compare to Jonah 1:4, ויהוה הטיל רוח־גדולה אל־הים ויה סער־גדול
2. וביום השלישי חתרו המלחים לבוא אל היבשה
   Compare to Jonah 1:13, ויחתרו האנשים להשיב אל־היבשה
3. ונלך ברוח קדמה חזקה מבלי מצוא מנוח
   Compare to Genesis 8:9, ולא־מצאה היונה מנוח

Euchel wanted to show that Hebrew was capable of expressing anything that a travel writer wanted to express, but he could not resist basing his innovative writing on biblical models.[50] For learned readers of his time, part of the effect of such passages was admiration of Euchel's ability to echo biblical language without simply copying it.[51]

In sum, the Berlin *maskilim* made great advances in the use of Hebrew, but they were sometimes hampered by their commitment to emulating biblical sources. Even Euchel often breaks the immediacy of his travel descriptions with biblical allusions and direct quotations. One of the greatest challenges for modern Hebrew writers of that time was to capture the vividness of an immediate scene such as a storm at sea or a shipwreck. Only by moving away from biblical *melitza* could they rise to that task.

Shmuel Romanelli, an Italian Jew, published his travel narrative *Mas'a be-`arav* (Travail in an Arab Land) in 1792 in Berlin at the publishing house associated with the Jewish Free School and the journal *Ha-me'asef*.[52] This publication history establishes a clear connection to Isaac Euchel, who was one of the principal editors of the Ḥevrat ḥinukh ne`arim (Ḥinukh Ne`arim Press), and it directly links Romanelli's travelogue to Euchel's travel narratives. Sea travel is only a minor component of *Mas'a be-`arav*, but even two short passages enable us to characterize Romanelli's style.

In the first passage, Romanelli boards a ship to cross the Strait of Gibraltar: "One day a sailing ship [*'oni shait*] arrived, going to Tetuan; the merchant paid its fee, and we boarded to travel with it."[53] There is little to discuss here. The term *'oni shait* is biblical, occurring in Isaiah 33:21. The second passage gives no more maritime detail. Using the later, more commonly Mishnaic word *sefina*, Romanelli notes that "boats [*sefinot*] were traveling back and forth from the citadel."[54] Then Romanelli sees a boat and hopes to set sail, but the ship is not allowed to dock. He provides this description:

> עוד אניה באה, רוח צח נופח בכנפיה **ומרחפת על פני המים**,. . . . לא הניחוה להשליך הברזל.[55]
>
> Another ship was coming, a clear wind was filling its sails and **hovering over the face of the water**. . . . They did not let it drop anchor.

These two phrases reveal that Romanelli, like Euchel, did not know what technical terms to use for "sail" and "anchor." Neither *kanaf* (usually meaning "wing") nor *barzel* (usually meaning "iron" but perhaps meaning "ax head" in 2 Kings 6:6) is a traditional term used to denote "sail" or "anchor" in the Bible or Talmud. As if to make up for this deficiency, Romanelli includes a well-known biblical phrase about the wind "hovering over the face of the water" (Gen. 1:2). After this, bemoaning the lack of ships, he quotes and then transforms a biblical phrase. Hosea prophesies that for a long time the Israelites will have "no king, no ministers, no sacrifice" (Hos. 3:4); Romanelli quotes and then transforms this prophecy into his own lament: "no merchant, no speeches, no man from Vienna, no consul, and no English ships."[56] This is a humorous transformation of the biblical phrase.

In sum, Romanelli did little to enhance the concreteness of sea travel descriptions; throughout his narrative, learned quotations intercede. Moshe Pelli explains the problem well: "As a result of language constraints and literary conventions, an eighteenth-century writer of a travel account in Hebrew faced a unique problem that inherently limited authenticating an actual experience by its very description. Like other Hebrew Haskalah writers, Romanelli utilized biblical phrases as literary and linguistic conventions. These biblical expressions tended to generalize the experience rather than depict it accurately or portray it singularly as a unique experience."[57]

Few early-modern Hebrew descriptions of sea travel dispensed with biblical allusions. Either their authors could find no other suitable words, or they considered it most appropriate to borrow the biblical phrases, following the Berlin writers who deliberately attempted to write in biblical style.

The Berlin *maskilim* sought to expose Jews to secular European education, yet their Hebrew remained archaic. They were committed to Hebrew but wanted to exclude much of the rabbinic tradition of Hebrew writing, which they considered inferior. They thus walked a fine line, trying to preserve Hebrew while separating themselves from the rabbinic mainstream.[58] Their decision to adopt the Hebrew of the Bible limited their linguistic resources and their readership and ultimately became untenable.

Chaim Rabin rightly questions the established story of the "Hebrew revival." In an important article titled "The Continuum of Modern Literary Hebrew," he writes that according to the "official" version of linguistic history, "Hebrew was 'dead' from late antiquity till 1880 or thereabouts, when it was revived. . . . The language itself was reconstituted from the ancient sources (the Hebrew of the Bible and the Hebrew of early rabbinic literature)." Rabin then counters this version by pointing out that "the ability to express nineteenth-century thought in Biblical Hebrew had been built up in a long process, going back to the early middle ages, in which each generation benefited from the 'discoveries' of its predecessors. . . . While the forms of the words were Biblical, the syntax of *haskalah* literature—except for the Biblical idiomatic phrases—is that of a European language, and probably also the result of a development in which each writer developed sentence types he found in the earlier writers he read." The one-sided effort to base Hebrew writing on biblical Hebrew during the Haskala may be traced to the "classicism of all literary activity in western Europe in the seventeenth and eighteenth centuries."[59] Rabin notes that the reliance of the *maskilim* on neoclassical models weakened their appeal to readers in the nineteenth century, which was increasingly influenced by romanticism. He is an unusual voice in Hebrew studies because he emphasizes the influence of European languages on modern Hebrew.

Isaac Euchel and his contemporaries at *Ha-me'asef* limited their range of expression and their readership by attempting to write in an archaic style. They often overused biblical quotations, but their Hebrew was never a "pure" expression of biblical style. By juxtaposing Euchel's narratives of sea travel with other Hebrew sea travel narratives, it is possible to recognize both the traditional elements and the originality of his language.

PART TWO

Travels in Translation beyond Zion

5

Mendelsohn-Frankfurt

REDISCOVERING AMERICA IN HEBREW

Moses Mendelsohn-Frankfurt opened a new chapter in maskilic Hebrew writing in 1807, when he translated a travel narrative by Joachim Heinrich Campe (1746–1818). The task of translating helped to free him from biblical *melitza*: working from the prose of a popular German author, he depended less on biblical allusions and quotations. As is often the case in the development of a young literature, translation played a decisive role by introducing new genres and inspiring new styles. Moreover, the German source provided a riveting plot, the absence of which had weakened Isaac Euchel's travel writings (see chapter 4). Translating from Campe inspired Mendelsohn-Frankfurt to rise to the challenge of writing a modern narrative in Hebrew. Stylistic originality distinguished his Hebrew writing, in spite of its seemingly derivative status as a translation.

Moses Mendelsohn-Frankfurt (1782–1861) was an unlikely muse for modern Hebrew literature.[1] Throughout his life, he lived in Hamburg and Altona, where Shalom Ha-Cohen launched the attempt to revive the journal *Ha-me'asef* in 1809. Although he visited Berlin and was a follower of the Berlin Haskala, he continued to practice Orthodox Judaism and opposed the liturgical and halakhic changes introduced by German Jewish reform rabbis.[2] Notwithstanding his conservative views on religious reform, he read widely and valued some of the secular Hebrew poetry and prose written by other *maskilim*.

In 1807, Mendelsohn-Frankfurt spurred a fresh trend in Hebrew writing with an innovative style that diverged from the reigning *melitza* associated with Berlin, *Ha-me'asef*, and Isaac Euchel. He later translated German

Fig. 5. Portrait of Joachim Heinrich Campe, engraving by J. G. Seiffert, in Samuel Baur, *Charakteristik der Erziehungsschriftsteller Deutschlands: Ein Handbuch für Erzieher* (Leipzig: Fleischer, 1790). From the copy at the Duke University Library and available online at https://archive.org/details/bub_gb_IhwWAAAAYAAJ.

prose and poetry into Hebrew and contributed to Hebrew journals. A multifaceted collection of his original poetry and prose was published posthumously under the title *Penei tevel* (The Face of the Earth, 1872).[3]

While living in Hamburg, Mendelsohn-Frankfurt felt the strong gravitational pull exerted by the writers of the Berlin Haskala, epitomized by the Hebrew journal *Ha-me'asef*. He admired the new model of Jewish literary activity established by Isaac Euchel and Aharon Wolfsohn in *Ha-me'asef*, which appeared during the years 1783–97. After Shalom Ha-Cohen revived *Ha-me'asef* in 1809, it published a review of Mendelsohn-Frankfurt's first book—his translation of Campe's adaptation *Die Entdeckung von Amerika*—in 1810. Mendelsohn-Frankfurt never met Moses Mendelssohn (1729–86) yet chose to live in his sphere of influence. So impressed was he by the founder of the Berlin Haskala that he assumed the name "Moses Mendelsohn-Frankfurt" even though there was no family connection to the Mendelssohns in Berlin and his father's surname was simply "Frankfurt." (This latter-day Moses could justify the appellation because he was the son of another Mendel.) Mendelsohn-Frankfurt's closest direct connections to the Berlin writers were Shalom Ha-Cohen and Naftali Hirsh Wessely, who advised and influenced him in Hamburg. Before Wessely died, he read the first part of Mendelsohn-Frankfurt's first book manuscript and made suggestions. Ha-Cohen may have been the second, anonymous editor of this first book and its reviewer for *Ha-me'asef*.

As a traditional Jewish man, Mendelsohn-Frankfurt was devoted to traditional study of the Hebrew Bible and the Talmud and to the practice of Jewish law. In 1805, he founded a Talmud Torah, a traditional school for poor children in Hamburg. He was interested in educational reforms and no doubt depended heavily on the curriculum developed by the Jüdische Freischule (Jewish Free School) in Berlin. Before he was born, his father, Menaḥem Mendel Frankfurt, was well acquainted with and admired Moses Mendelssohn in Berlin.[4] Both father and son adhered to the school of *maskilim* who taught "Torah with respect,"[5] unlike some of the more radical reformers, who incurred the wrath of traditional rabbis.

Although Mendelsohn-Frankfurt lived a traditional Jewish life, he benefited from an unusually promising era for modernizing Jews, when their opportunities and citizenship rights advanced quickly in Germany, Austria, and France. Unlike many other Jews, Mendelsohn-Frankfurt was critical of Napoleon, in part because he recognized that Napoleon's liberal policies encouraged Jews to assimilate: "His entire tendency," Mendelsohn-Frankfurt wrote about him, "was to intermix the Jews with the nations of the world."[6]

Differences between Mendelsohn-Frankfurt and the older Shalom Ha-Cohen came to light in a debacle during the Napoleonic wars. When the French army occupied Hamburg in 1812, the Jewish community was offered payment for the composition of a Hebrew poem to be read publicly in honor of Napoleon. Mendelsohn-Frankfurt relates that he never accepted money for writing poetry and that for this reason—not to mention his opposition to Napoleon—he suggested that Ha-Cohen be asked to do the job. The French were apparently satisfied with the result, but Mendelsohn-Frankfurt himself was scandalized by a line in Ha-Cohen's poem that proclaimed, "God in the Heavens and Napoleon on Earth."[7] In a counterpoem written after Napoleon's defeat, Mendelsohn-Frankfurt quoted Ha-Cohen's line and then modified it to make a new couplet:

"אֱלֹהִים בַּשָּׁמַיִם וְנַפֹּלֵיוֹן עַל הָאָרֶץ."
אֱלֹהִים בַּשָּׁמַיִם וְעַל הָאָרֶץ גַּאֲוָתוֹ,
וְנַפֹּלֵיוֹן לִקְבָרוֹת יוּבַל, יִבְאַשׁ גְּוִיָּתוֹ.[8]

"God in the Heavens and Napoleon on Earth"
God in the Heavens, and on Earth His pride.
And Napoleon will be brought to burial, his corpse disgraced.

He seems to have been genuinely appalled that Ha-Cohen would exalt Napoleon to such a degree. His political and pedagogical ideas fostered modernization but not assimilation.

Mendelsohn-Frankfurt did, however, share the general excitement over world exploration and sea travels. In the 1780s and 1790s, educated German Jews read about remarkable sea voyages in the Pacific, such as those of Captains James Cook and Henry Wilson. Following the American and French Revolutions, many Jewish intellectuals were fascinated by the rapidly evolving history of Europe and the Americas. Their knowledge of world geography and modern history was shaped by German editions of travel narratives and history books, some of them written or adapted by J. H. Campe. Because of his involvement with the Talmud Torah in Hamburg, Mendelsohn-Frankfurt was also interested in Campe, who was a leading educator.

In 1807, Mendelsohn-Frankfurt self-published his first book, *Metziat ha-aretz ha-ḥadasha* (The Discovery of the New Land). Although it was not a material success, its originality and significance are evident from a literary-historical perspective two centuries later. Following the pedagogical bent of the Enlightenment circles, he introduced the practice of translating German travel writings into Hebrew.[9] His pathbreaking translation *Metziat ha-aretz ha-ḥadasha* was based on the first volume of Campe's wildly popular book *Die Entdeckung von Amerika* (The Discovery of America, three volumes, 1781–82).[10] Mendelsohn-Frankfurt could not have expected that his earliest work would attain independent literary importance decades later. Over the next twenty years, several Hebrew and Yiddish writers followed his example with their renderings of Campe's travel narratives. Although unappreciated, he had launched a new fashion that had wide-ranging implications.

No Hebrew novels and few extended prose texts had been published in modern Hebrew before 1807. The most familiar Hebrew narratives were from biblical and midrashic sources; Shmuel Romanelli's travel account was unusual. Another rare exception, coming out of Berlin, was the opening pages of Isaac Satanov's work *Nevu'at ha-yeled* (The Prophecy of the Child, 1789), but this was a parody of a religious text rather than a secular narrative. Secular novels such as those published in the early and mid-eighteenth century by British authors—Defoe, Swift, Richardson, Fielding, Sterne—did not appeal to the enlightened, late-eighteenth-century German and Hebrew writers. In eighteenth-century Germany, poetry and drama were more highly respected than fictional prose narrative. Enlightened authors would have associated contemporary novels with Johann Wolfgang von Goethe's fiery best seller *Die Leiden des jungen Werthers* (*The Sorrows of Young Werther*, 1774), which was in turn linked to the proto-romantic movement called "Sturm und Drang" (storm and stress). In contrast to such shocking tales of passion and despair, historical works and travel narratives had clear pedagogical value and matched the tastes of rationalistic authors.

Highly literate in Hebrew and German, Mendelsohn-Frankfurt no doubt read Campe's German travel accounts as a young adult. When he was about twenty-two years old, around 1804, he decided to publish the first Hebrew version of a book by Campe. Can a translation of a translation—or an adaptation of an adaptation—qualify as a major literary event? Mendelsohn-Frankfurt's source was derivative because Campe based his three-volume work *Die Entdeckung von Amerika*, intended for young adults, on William Robertson's best seller *The History of America* (1777). Readers were eager to learn the history of the newly independent United States of America. The loose copyright laws of the time enabled Campe to publish and profit from his own German version even though Johann Friedrich Schiller's two-volume authorized translation had already appeared in German.[11]

Metziat ha-aretz ha-ḥadasha was thus a second-order translation and adaptation based on the first volume of Campe's German text. But neither the reliance on translation from Campe nor the connection between Robertson's original and Mendelsohn-Frankfurt's Hebrew rewriting diminishes the importance and originality of the Hebrew work. In an analysis of the origins of modern Hebrew narrative, it is sufficient to focus on the most significant cultural transfer, which occurred from Campe's German to Mendelsohn-Frankfurt's Hebrew. Mendelsohn-Frankfurt diverged from prevailing literary norms and in part freed himself from the oppressive demands by linguistic purists in Berlin.

Although Mendelsohn-Frankfurt inaugurated a significant new fashion in maskilic circles, his youthful literary ambition must have been curbed by a dearth of purchasers and the critical response. The anonymous review of *Metziat ha-aretz ha-ḥadasha* that appeared in *Ha-me'asef* in 1810 was, on the whole, favorable; even so, the author published no continuation. The review noted that "the author, in his excessive modesty, did not hurry to distribute [*lehafitz*] his book over the face of the earth, and many copies of it lie in his storage rooms [*ḥadrei maskioto*; *ḥadrei maskito* is probably intended]."[12] The preface to the first volume announced that the author hoped to publish two more Hebrew volumes based on the second and third parts of Campe's *Die Entdeckung von Amerika*, but he abandoned that project. He published some poetry, translations of work by the Swiss poet and painter Salomon Geßner,[13] in the journal *Der Orient* in 1818. But he did not publish another book until decades later, when he released a two-volume commentary on the Book of Genesis titled *Schuschan `edut* (1840–42); and, as previously noted, most of his original writings were published posthumously. In many ways, he was a derivative author, choosing to translate or emulate the precursors he admired. Nevertheless, he brought something new into Hebrew.

Between 1815 and 1824, as secular Hebrew literary activity moved eastward, other writers paid tribute to Mendelsohn-Frankfurt when they followed in his wake. The small audience for secular Hebrew writing in 1807 could not support large-scale publishing projects, yet other writers continued to make new Hebrew and Yiddish adaptations of Campe's works. Secular Hebrew books faced a limited potential readership, the audience for *Ha-me'asef* was dwindling, and the prospects for books such as *Metziat ha-aretz ha-ḥadasha* were further diminished by their attempt to reach a narrow, young-adult market.[14] The youthful readership may have been limited to pupils in schools such as the Hamburg Talmud Torah and the Jewish Free School of Berlin. Yet many of those pupils could and did read Campe's German source texts, which rendered the Hebrew translation superfluous to them.[15] As a consequence, the front lines of avant-garde Hebrew writing were pushed eastward. The reviewer for *Ha-me'asef* recognized this demographic and geographical fact, writing that *Metziat ha-aretz ha-ḥadasha* was especially well suited to Polish Jews, who did not read "books by other nations [*sifrei `amim*]."[16]

Mendelsohn-Frankfurt's posthumously published work *Penei tevel* (1872) includes poems, prose essays, and mixtures of verse and prose organized in fifty-five *maḥbarot* (pamphlets, notebooks, or collections) following the *Taḥkemoni* by Yehuda Al-Ḥarizi and the *Maḥbarot* by Immanuel of Rome.[17] He narrowed his potential for expression by forcing most of his work into outmoded literary forms, such as rhymed prose in the style of Immanuel of Rome. Aside from these unusual choices, his Hebrew style sometimes follows contemporary norms in Berlin, with some neobiblical *melitza* and its accompanying drawbacks. In spite of these problems,

Mendelsohn-Frankfurt was an innovator; he had no qualms about resorting to Mishnaic Hebrew and Aramaic, as when he pushed beyond the biblical canon and quoted Talmudic dicta. In one of his most surprising prose works, he anticipated the satiric fiction of Joseph Perl and I. B. Levinsohn: he lampoons an ignorant rabbi in "ʿAvon ha-doresh ha-ḥadash" (The Iniquity of the New Preacher, 1809) in Notebook 41 of *Penei tevel*. This work refers to the hypocritical preacher somewhat ambiguously as a "hasid" and a "rebbe."[18] The story takes place in some unnamed capital city, but the author seems to be referring to a contemporary hasidic rebbe in what is now Ukraine. Mendelsohn-Frankfurt wrote this satire in German before translating it into Hebrew, which may explain why the Hebrew sounds more natural than it does in most of his other writing. If this notebook circulated in manuscript, it could have influenced the next generation of antihasidic Hebrew writers in the East.

Mendelsohn-Frankfurt also wrote literary criticism in which he candidly praised and critiqued all of the leading authors of his time. Nurit Govrin, referring to Notebooks 45, 46, and 47, calls this criticism "a first effort to write the history of the Haskalah and of Hebrew literature from the end of the eighteenth century until the beginning of the nineteenth."[19] Though Mendelsohn-Frankfurt had acquired a broad knowledge of the Hebrew writing of his time, the combination of his modesty, the muted critical reaction, and a failure to appreciate the value of translation precluded wider recognition of the importance of his first book.

Importing Sea Travels into Hebrew

Accounts of sea voyages had been a popular genre[20] for more than a century when Mendelsohn-Frankfurt contributed his translations, and the lines between nonfiction and fiction were frequently blurred.[21] Daniel Defoe's novel *Robinson Crusoe* (1719), probably based in part on the experiences of Alexander Selkirk, gave sea adventure a potent fictional expression. Accounts that derived from historic explorations also captured the imagination of eighteenth-century readers. Captain James Cook's accounts of his expeditions to Australia in the 1770s evoked widespread interest, as did Johann Reinhold Forster's and Georg Forster's accounts of Cook's second voyage in English (1777) and German (1778–80), respectively.[22]

In 1777, William Robertson's magisterial and elegantly written work *The History of America* inspired Campe's narrative of Columbus's voyages, *Die Entdeckung von Amerika*. Another of Campe's English sources, George Keate's *An Account of the Shipwreck of the* Antelope, was published in 1788. In addition, a red-letter date for writing about maritime events was 1790, for in this year "Lieutenant William Bligh miraculously returned to London . . . and published *A Narrative of the Mutiny on HMS* Bounty."[23] The time was ripe for importing famous European narratives of sea travel into Hebrew.

Metziat ha-aretz ha-ḥadasha, based on *Die Entdeckung von Amerika*, expresses typical maskilic ideological views, but in an original Hebrew style. The book expresses definite pedagogical goals because it is designed to educate readers about geography and history. On the title page, Mendelsohn-Frankfurt states that the Hebrew he uses is "clear and simple, to teach the youth of the Children of Israel the beauty of this language."[24] He wanted to serve the needs of young Jewish readers, using Hebrew (*sfat `Ever*) in a "refined language [*lashon mezukak*]" (p. v). Nevertheless, Mendelsohn-Frankfurt took an important step forward in literary history by not insisting on purity as an overriding ideal.

Metziat ha-aretz ha-ḥadasha extended the genre of maskilic travel narratives by importing the model provided by Campe.[25] But, like most of the later Hebrew and Yiddish translators, Mendelsohn-Frankfurt retained only Campe's main narrative, omitting both the frame narrative in which a father tells the story to his children and the father's didactic commentary.

Although removing Campe's framework and dialogue form, Mendelsohn-Frankfurt follows Campe's pedagogical program and even part of his theological bent. Campe's didacticism is evident throughout his copious works; for example, in the introduction to his early work *Robinson der Jüngere* (*Robinson the Younger*, 1779–80), he mentions his hope that it will "sow in young hearts the seeds of virtue, piety, and contentment with the ways of Divine Providence."[26] Mendelsohn-Frankfurt also strikes a pious tone on his own title page when he writes that the book should "make known to them [the young children of Israel] the greatness of God, and the wonders He will perform in all the land."[27] Showing his piety, Mendelsohn-Frankfurt deliberately tried (yet evidently failed) to appeal to traditional Jewish readers. His epigraph underscores a biblical connection by linking the book's title to a phrase in Isaiah 65:17, כי הנני בורא שמים חדשים וארץ חדשה, "for behold, I am creating a new heavens and a new earth." He anachronistically conflates God's "new earth" with the New World.

The preface to *Metziat ha-aretz ha-ḥadasha* includes a kind of limited *ars poetica*. Mendelsohn-Frankfurt writes that he tried to use refined language and that "the educated reader will understand how difficult is the work of writing matters like this in a simple and clear language in our Holy Tongue." He adds that he did not attempt a word-for-word translation of Campe's narrative, but he instead tried to convey the content using "our Hebrew and the *melitza* that is specific to it" (p. v). He then describes a conversation with Naftali Hirsh Wessely in 1805, not long before the older man's death, and quotes Wessely as having warned him against piling up biblical verses that are not pertinent. Wessely, who had quoted biblical phrases to excess in his own poetry, advised the young translator to "write the things as they rise up from the walls of your heart, without exaggeration and riddles. Then they will flow from your mouth, like a stream that flows out from a ceaseless spring" (pp. viii–ix).

Finally, Mendelsohn-Frankfurt mentions a letter from J. H. Campe, who encouraged him to publish the book. In the Hebrew rendering of the letter that is included in the preface, Campe writes, "How you have gladdened me, Sir, with your words! My heart rejoiced on hearing the good news that a man from the Children of Israel will, for the benefit of his brothers, make known among them something of what I have written. Almost all of my books, in almost all of the regions of Europe, are translated for every nation in its language; but I have not yet had the privilege to see them in a Hebrew garb, for the benefit of the youth of this people" (p. x). Following Wessely and Campe's advice, Mendelsohn-Frankfurt "toiled very hard to do what my heart wished and write in a way that is easy to understand. And I did not mix in the language of the Talmud more than a little bit, which was necessary" (p. x). His effort to avoid Talmudic language (i.e., Mishnaic Hebrew and Aramaic) was typical of his time and place, given that *maskilim* associated with *Ha-me'asef* aspired to write poetic Hebrew similar to that of the biblical prophets. He used postbiblical Hebrew when "necessary" (*min ha-tzorekh*); without any dogmatic intention, he asserted that it is acceptable to include rabbinic Hebrew alongside biblical Hebrew.

Following his preface, Mendelsohn-Frankfurt also provides a six-page glossary, listing difficult terms for each chapter. It is indicative of his expected readership that he translates his challenging Hebrew words into German, which he writes in Hebrew characters. In the glossary, he lists the terms *maḥat magnet* (magnetic needle, p. xii), which he uses to mean "compass"; *ḥevel* or *`oferet ha-mida* (measuring cord or lead, p. xiii), his equivalent for the German term *Senkblei*, the lead-weighted line for sounding the depth of the water; and *nes* to denote *Segel* (sail)—or *vilon*, "in the language of our Sages [*ba-leshon Ḥaza"l*]" (p. xiv).[28] He was willing to fall back on vocabulary used by Talmudic and later medieval sources for clarification. In his glossary, *tofes ha-keresh* (literally, "holder of the plank") is used for "helmsman"; the biblical term *mishberei yam* refers to "breaking waves" or "breakwater" (וואגען ברוך, p. xvi); *briaḥ ha-yam* (בריח הים)—which occurs biblically only in Isaiah 15:5 with the meaning "runaway, fugitive"—is a sea current (German *Meerstrom*, p. xvi); and *briaḥ ha-aretz* is used for "isthmus" (*Erdenge*, p. xvii), possibly based on a second meaning of *briaḥ* as "bar."[29] To describe a small boat (*eine Kahne*, p. xiv), Mendelsohn-Frankfurt reaches for the rare term *dovra*, a hapax legomenon, occurring biblically only in 1 Kings 5:23 and possibly meaning "raft" in that context.

The reviewer of *Metziat ha-aretz ha-ḥadasha* in *Ha-me'asef* quibbles over some entries in the glossary and other new coinages. These objections reveal the extent to which Mendelsohn-Frankfurt was an innovator, stretching the accepted limits of maskilic Hebrew usage. Difficulties naturally arose in connection with efforts to translate technical nautical terms and to name navigational instruments. The anonymous critic disputes six glossary entries; for clarity regarding what the Hebrew is supposed to mean, the critic parenthetically provides German equivalents in Hebrew characters. This critique illustrates how Mendelsohn-Frankfurt was a linguistic pioneer, albeit in an unassuming way. The six terms are קשתות צהרים (literally "midday arc," used to translate the term *meridian*), אופן ההיפוך or אופן הסיבוב (literally "wheel of turning," used to translate *Wendezirkel*, "tropical circle"), ריפת (Britain) , ארץ מכוננת (solid, dry land),

גבעות קצוי ארץ (literally, "hills at the end of the earth," to translate "Vorgebirge der guten Hoffnung"—that is, the Cape of Good Hope), and כומר רומי (the pope).

In the last and simplest case, the reviewer argues that *komer Romi* (a Roman priest) is an imprecise way to describe the pope; perhaps Mendelsohn-Frankfurt deliberately chose to be vague regarding Christian matters. To translate the German word *Papst*, the reviewer recommends writing "the Head of the Priests" (*rosh ha-komerim*). Similarly, ארץ מכוננת does not seem like an apt equivalent for "dry land" (*festes Land*), and the reviewer notes that the biblical word *yabasha* would be a more suitable choice (cf. Jon. 1:13 and 2:11).[30]

More complex and difficult to decide is the most appropriate translation of German term *Wendezirkel*, meaning "tropical circle."[31] Mendelsohn-Frankfurt tries אופן הסיבוב (circling wheel) or אופן ההיפוך (turning wheel), but the reviewer prefers מחוגות הסבוב, which means "turning or circling dividers."[32] Is this German *Zirkel* a circle, a wheel, or a divider? Here Mendelsohn-Frankfurt seems to have received the imprimatur of linguistic history: in the past two centuries, official, academic Israeli usage settled on calling the tropics המהפך, using the same root (ה-פ-כ, "to turn") as Mendelsohn-Frankfurt's choice אופן ההיפוך.[33]

Another objection by the reviewer is that Britain should not be called ריפת, although he acknowledges that Bin Gorion (reputedly the medieval author of *Yosippon*) used the word in this way.[34] The broader question is whether in 1807 a modern Hebrew writer should avoid postbiblical words and usages even when referring to things that did not exist in the biblical period. Mendelsohn-Frankfurt was more open to Talmudic and later medieval usage than was the reviewer for *Ha-me'asef.*

Mendelsohn-Frankfurt and his successors had unusually helpful resources in translating Campe's works because Campe was a lexicographer who published German dictionaries. Translators could consult Campe's own definitions of difficult or ambiguous words in his narrative works. Campe's underlying nationalist bent motivated him to exclude or "Germanize" foreign elements; in 1801, he published a dictionary that was specifically designed to replace foreign expressions, *Wörterbuch zur Erklärung und Verdeutschung der unserer Sprache aufgedrungenen fremden Ausdrücke.*[35] For example, Campe rejected the romantic key word *Genie*, from French *génie.*[36] Mendelsohn-Frankfurt may have referred to Campe's 1801 dictionary in translating his travel narrative. Campe's five-volume *Wörterbuch der deutschen Sprache* (1807–11) subsequently became available and was most likely used by some of his translators. Because it was printed too late for Mendelsohn-Frankfurt to use it in making his first translation, he probably used Johann Christoph Adelung's dictionary, which appeared in 1774–86 and was reprinted countless times.[37] (Incidentally, Campe followed in Adelung's footsteps both as a lexicographer and as a publisher of travel works; decades before Campe, Adelung achieved recognition for his extensive publication of sea travel narratives in 1767–68.[38])

One of Campe's linguistic peculiarities is his intriguing use of the word *Vorgebirge* to mean not "foothills," as in today's usage, but "mountains at the edge of the sea."[39] His idiosyncratic usage was part of his broader effort to Germanize foreign names for places such as the Cape of Good Hope. Previously it had been known as the "Kap der guten Hoffnung," translated from the Dutch name "Kaap de Goede Hoop," but in the eighteenth century German lexicographers—such as Adelung and Campe—tried to wean German speakers from the loan word *Kap*. For that reason, they attempted to impose a shift from *Kap* to *Vorgebirge*. (Google Books' Ngram Viewer attests, however, that by 1900 this effort in linguistic prescriptivism had failed.[40]) In the late eighteenth and early nineteenth century, then, Campe and some other authors switched to the name "die Vorgebirge der guten Hoffnung."[41] This usage sometimes confused the Hebrew and Yiddish translators of Campe—for example, where Campe's unusual usage of *Vorgebirge* occurs in the narrative of Captain Willem Bontekoe's journey (contained in volume 5 of Campe's multivolume work *Reisebeschreibungen* [Travel Descriptions], discussed at length in chapter 6). When Bontekoe's ship nears the Cape of Good Hope, Campe refers to this area as "die Gegend des Vorgebirges der guten Hofnung" (the region of the Cape of Good Hope).[42] The Hebrew tranlator of *Oniya so`ara* (ca. 1815) seems to have been at a complete loss, rendering this phrase using a parenthesis that implies that *forg geberg* is a proper name:

בבואם קרוב אל מקום (פארג גבערג).[43]

This vague translation means "When they came to the place (*forg ger berg*). . . ." In the reprint of *Oniya so`ara* in 1823, the editors unaccountably and inaccurately revised the Hebrew translation of Campe's phrase to read

בבואם אל אי (פארג גיבערג).[44]

When they came to the island (*forg giberg*).

In short, based on the two editions of *Oniya so`ara*, it is clear that some Hebrew translators were ill prepared to deal with the real-world reference suggested by words such as *Vorgebirge*.

Among the glossary entries that precede the narrative of *Metziat ha-aretz ha-ḥadasha*, Mendelsohn-Frankfurt gives a Hebrew equivalent of the German term *Vorgebirge* (written פֿארגבירגע : גבעת קצוי הארץ) (*giva`at kitzvei ha-aretz*, literally meaning "hill at the end of the earth," p. xv). This is a clever choice because the German word calques the Latin term *promontorium*, the source of English *promontory*, a mountain ridge.[45] The Hebrew phrase *giva`at kitzvei ha-aret* occurs in Mendelsohn-Frankfurt's Hebrew translation (p. 45); the reviewer of *Metziat ha-aretz ha-ḥadasha* questions this translation, however, and prefers *harei ha-safa* (mountains of the shore).[46] One might say that the issue here is whether to translate the signifier or the signified and referent; although the passage does not refer to the Cape of Good Hope, it uses the German word *Vorgebirge* in a context that links it to the new German name for the Cape of Good Hope (supplanting "Kap der guten Hoffnung"). Hence, the more accurate translation might have to be compared to the implicit referential object, and Mendelsohn-Frankfurt's phrase "hills at the ends of the earth" was apt—more so than *Vorgebirge*, which essentially means "foothills." This is an example of textual referentialism: writing that points to a real-world reference instead of remaining within intertextual literary history.

The reviewer follows the Berlin norms, arguing for word choices that are closer to biblical usage. In contrast, Mendelsohn-Frankfurt usually translates the German more literally, sometimes creating a new coinage instead of reviving or reappropriating biblical words. He shows originality in his willingness to calque the German when necessary, but without slavishly mimicking German vocabulary or syntax.

The broader significance of Mendelsohn-Frankfurt's glossary and preface is that he provides a lesson in geography, probably motivated in part by Wessely's call for such studies in *Divrei shalom ve-emet* (1783). Although Mendelsohn-Frankfurt remained an Orthodox Jew, he favored Wessely's pedagogical initiatives. He saw no contradiction between the practice of Orthodox Judaism and broad exposure to science. In his review of Haskala literature, therefore, he does not limit himself to belletristic works and includes scientific works such as Baruch Linda's *Reshit limudim* (1789). He also refers to books on Hebrew grammar by Judah Leib Ben Ze'ev and others—at odds with many Orthodox Jews of the time, who disapproved of studying Hebrew grammar.[47]

Mendelsohn-Frankfurt's immediate inspiration came from Campe's best-selling books. Although it is clear that an extensive cultural transfer occurred from German to Hebrew, including the adaptation of travel narratives into Hebrew, it is less evident how that extraordinary trade route was established. It is helpful to know more about the author of the very popular twelve volumes of *Reisebeschreibungen* that appeared between 1786 and 1793.

Who was Joachim Heinrich Campe?[48] "Something of an enigma," writes Cendric Hentschel. He was both "a prosy windbag, sententious and complacent," and a "staunch pillar of the Enlightenment—the apostle of Rousseau and the French Revolution . . . a lifelong pedagogue and author of best-sellers."[49] He was a moralistic, rationalistic, eighteenth-century neoclassicist, yet there is perhaps a paradox here: Campe embraced the Jean-Jacques Rousseau of "natural man." Following the lead of Johann Bernhard Basedow, Campe helped popularize the Philanthropismus movement, which aimed to transform educational methods based on a more natural, universalistic, nondenominational approach.[50] In 1774, Basedow opened a school in Dessau called the Philanthropinum, and for a short time Campe was director of that school.[51]

Joachim Heinrich Campe, the influential German pedagogue, author, philologist, and lexicographer, was admired in Moses Mendelssohn's circle.[52] In 1775–76, he tutored the brothers Alexander and Wilhelm von Humboldt,[53] who in turn developed close connections to the world of Jewish salons. (For instance, Wilhelm von Humboldt corresponded with Henrietta Herz, one of Berlin's trend-setting salon hostesses, in German written in Hebrew characters.) After publishing his adaptation of the English novel *Robinson Crusoe*, Campe became a well-known author of books for young German readers. His adaptation, titled *Robinson der Jüngere*, was intended to enhance the pedagogical value of the work by reconciling it with Rousseau's ideas about education. Campe's rewriting embeds the story of Robinson Crusoe in a pedantic frame in which a father narrates the story to his family. As noted earlier, most of the Hebrew and Yiddish translators subsequently eliminated the framing device that Campe used in *Robinson der Jüngere* and elsewhere. In any case, Campe's writings influenced generations of German readers, including Jewish scholars such as the historian Heinrich Graetz (1817–91).[54]

German children's literature exerted deep influence on the Berlin Haskala,[55] which was advanced by Campe's friendship with Moses Mendelssohn and by Mendelssohn's with Mendel Lefin. As Israel Bartal has written, Campe's works allowed authors such as Mordechai Aaron Günzburg "to convey to his readers geographical and historical information in a moderate maskilic vein. The German author, moreover, was an intimate of Moses Mendelssohn, and in the maskilic consciousness was stamped as a proponent of the universal brotherhood of the enlightened intellectuals of all nations."[56] Hence, Campe's books for young adults were prime candidates for translation into Hebrew and Yiddish.

In the early nineteenth century, European languages provided modern literary models for describing sea travel; eighteenth-century British and German travel literature was an essential source. Zohar Shavit has shown that early Hebrew children's literature—including stories of sea travel—was heavily influenced by German children's literature. She also notes that Campe "was regarded by Jewish writers as the most important German writer for children of the Enlightenment."[57]

In the wake of the European craze for Goethe's novel *Die Leiden des jungen Werthers*, Campe attacked central components of Sturm und Drang. He anticipated and scorned the spread of European romanticism, with its exaltation of *Genie* (individual genius) and *Phantasie* (fantasy). In his travel books for young readers, he criticized the reading of novels because they encouraged idle fantasy. Just as he opposed the new attraction to genius and fantasy, he wrote vehemently against *Empfindsamkeit* (sentimentality) in his preface to *Robinson der Jüngere*.[58] These ideological underpinnings of Campe's work became part of the Enlightenment movement that so inspired German Jews at the end of the eighteenth century.

Campe's friendship with Moses Mendelssohn enabled him to exert influence on the Jewish Free School in Berlin. There was a productive, reciprocal affection between the Philanthropists and the enlightened Jews, including Wessely. Thus, the Dessau Philanthropinum (Philanthropist School) began accepting Jewish students and teachers in 1778, just a few years after opening.[59] It was not easy to find Jews who wanted to send their children there, however—a point on which Campe complained to Mendelssohn, providing the occasion for a piqued response by Mendelssohn, which was published in 1783.[60]

Campe's educational ideas motivated his decision to translate a series of travel narratives (*Reisebeschreibungen*) rather than fiction. Although his adaptation of *Robinson Crusoe* had achieved popularity, Campe was critical of the original novel and favored nonfiction. In the 1788 preface to the fifth volume of *Reisebeschreibungen*, Campe broadly rejected novels and proposed travel narratives as a substitute.[61] He criticized romances that evoked fantasy and emotion, preferring pedagogically useful books about the world. Followers of Mendelssohn and the Jewish Enlightenment tended to agree that novels had dubious educational value. Travel narratives seemed acceptable because they familiarized readers with real-world geography.

Campe's attitudes were typical of his time and place. He advised against "the reading of novels as well as generally all books that aim only to arouse fantasy, imagination, and sentiments, out of full conviction of their great harmfulness."[62] To compensate for this prohibition, he offered other, harmless reading delights. For the sake of "pleasurable instruction" in his series of travel narratives, then, Campe decided "not only to select the most interesting of this type, but also beyond this—to intersperse, now and then, one or another of those completely extraordinary travel accounts, whose story completely matches the charm and splendor of novels without thereby leading us, as in novels, away from reality into the world of fantasies and whims."[63] His rationalistic bias was far-reaching but not entirely convincing or consistent. Campe rejected the "Arkadische" vision of an idealized, rustic paradise,[64] but he romanticized the "noble savages" that appear in George Keate's version of Captain Henry Wilson's travel narrative, which (as discussed in chapter 7) Campe translated for volume 9 of *Reisebeschreibungen*.[65] Moreover, it is possible to question the authenticity and accuracy of some accounts that Campe perhaps naively considered factual and trustworthy. The Enlightenment rationalism of the Philanthropinum School founders was not entirely consistent with their Rousseau-influenced beliefs about natural education.

When adapting travel narratives for young adults, Campe borrowed closely from his sources, even those written in German, and today he could easily be accused of plagiarism.[66] Percy Adams notes, however, that "one of the distinctive features of eighteenth-century literature of all sorts was the quite liberal attitude to the borrowing of other writers' works. Travel writers were the most 'liberal' of them all."[67] Especially when Campe quoted Bontekoe's first-person narrative in volume 5 of *Reisebeschreibungen*, he often copied verbatim from the prior German translation—which was based on the French version by Antoine François Prévost, which was in turn adapted from Melchisedec Thévenot's earlier French translation, based on the Dutch.

So it was that Campe became a major influence on *maskilim* associated with Mendelssohn's disciples in the Berlin of the 1780s. The Campe connection became even more prominent early in the nineteenth century following Mendelsohn-Frankfurt's translation of the first part of *Die Entdeckung von Amerika* into Hebrew. Between 1807 and 1824, Moses Mendelsohn-Frankfurt, Mendel Lefin, Khaikl Hurwitz, Mordechai Aaron Günzburg, and David Zamość all produced Hebrew and Yiddish adaptations of travel narratives that had been published by Campe.[68]

A distinctive characteristic of Campe's literature for young adults is his use of a dialogue framework, which derives from the pedagogical ideas of the Philanthropist movement. Susanne Barth provides a useful introduction to the issues in her book *Mädchenlektüren: Lesediskurse im 18.*

und 19. Jahrhundert (Girls' Reading: The Discourse about Reading in the 18th and 19th Centuries).[69] Her third chapter turns to "the discourse about reading in pedagogy."

The story begins with a belief that some kinds of reading can be harmful to children and young adults. Books associated with fantasy, such as *Don Quixote* (1605), were viewed as spreading a pernicious influence, leading children away from reality by drawing them into an imaginary realm.[70] Some pedagogues, including Campe, argued that reading this kind of fiction could cause a *Realitätsverlust*—a loss of (connection to) reality. Rousseau's *Émile* (1762) tells of other dangers associated with reading, and *Confessions* (1781) describes Rousseau's excessive reading habits during adolescence.

Campe embedded the narrative realm in what he considered to be a pedagogically sound dialogue, with a father narrating and his children responding. Two of his most famous books for young adults—*Robinson der Jüngere* and *Die Entdeckung von Amerika*—use the dialogue form in a manner that now seems tedious, pedantic, and disruptive. It requires great patience on the reader's part to follow Campe as he mediates the narrated world through a scene in which a father tells his children the story of Robinson or Columbus, frequently interrupting the narration with explanations and judgments. Later, in the *Reisebeschreibungen*, Campe dropped the dialogue form, though he continued to insert strong moralistic and educational sentiments. Moreover, he included long ethnographic digressions (as in volume 9, about Palau) that distracted from the narrative. In *Mase`ot ha-yam* (see chapter 7), Lefin recognized this shortcoming in Campe's book and moved the ethnographic explanations to the end to allow the narrative to flow more smoothly.

Metziat ha-aretz ha-ḥadasha (1807)

In the preface to *Metziat ha-aretz ha-ḥadasha*, Mendelsohn-Frankfurt writes that before Naftali Hirsh Wessely died in 1805, he read the first part of Mendelsohn-Frankfurt's translation of *Die Entdeckung von America* and suggested improvements (p. ix). This work includes both the neobiblical *melitza* that typified the Hebrew of Berlin *maskilim* and some interesting deviations from the norm. Typical of the reliance on biblical quotations is one passage when, encountering danger, Columbus's sailors express despair. In Campe's German, they say, "We are lost . . . if we do not turn around within the hour."[71] Mendelsohn-Frankfurt expands on their outburst:

> ויהי ביום השני, ופתאום נשבר קרש האניה · ויראו האנשים יראה גדולה כי אמרו **הן אבדנו כלנו אבדנו** (p. 15)

> On the second day, the boat's rudder broke. The people were very afraid, for they said, "**Behold, we are lost, all of us are lost**."

Mendelsohn-Frankfurt puts a phrase in the sailors' mouths that has been taken almost exactly from the Israelites' words to Moses: הן גוענו אבדנו כלנו אבדנו ("Behold we perish, we are lost, all of us are lost" [Num. 17:27]). Simḥa ben Yehoshua of Zalozitsh used the same Hebrew phrase in the eighteenth century (see chapter 1); over the next two decades, most Hebrew accounts of a shipwreck refer to this passage from Numbers. This phenomenon of verbal borrowing shows how intertextuality sometimes supplants real-world references.

Previous chapters have shown that describing storms at sea posed difficult challenges to Hebrew translators of sea narratives. Indeed, all naturalistic sea descriptions presented problems. Mendelsohn-Frankfurt's extensive poetic works also show his struggles to represent nature. He rose to the challenge when he translated Campe's detailed descriptions of storms in *Die Entdeckung von Amerika*, although he did not suppress the impulse to draw from biblical prooftexts. Two storms occur early in Campe's narrative, and Mendelsohn-Frankfurt introduces the first of them with an ominous quotation from a traditional Hebrew source. He gives even greater detail than does Campe:[72]

> **ויהי בחצי הלילה**, וגלי הים מתנשאים ורועשים ברעש גדול הלוך וסוער · והנה זרם מים כבירים הולכים ונושאים את האניה לאט לאט על שפת הים, ופתאום נשמע קול רעש גדול, ו ת ת פ ו צ ץ האניה!— **ויחרד** הנער מקול השאון, ויפול המשוט מידו אל תוך המים, **ויצעק צעקה גדולה**. . . . ויקיצו האנשים כלם ויזעקו לאמור, **הן אבדנו כלנו** · וירוצו **ויחוגו כשכור** כי לא ידעו מה יעשו. (pp. 45–46)

> **And it was in the middle of the night**, sea waves rose up, creating an uproar, with a great noise, and became stormier. And behold, a powerful

stream of water came and lifted up the boat very slowly toward the sea coast. Suddenly a great noise was heard, and the ship burst open!—The boy trembled from the sound of the tumult, and the rudder fell out of his hand into the water, and he **cried out a great cry**. . . . And all of the people awoke and cried out, **Behold, we are all lost**. They ran and **circled around as if drunk**, for they knew not what to do.

The opening establishes a portentous tone by alluding to Exodus 12:29, where God strikes down the first-born in Egypt. That passage would have been familiar to all Jewish readers from the Passover Haggadah (and the phrase recurs in Ruth 3:8). Then the middle section alludes to Genesis 27, quoting from the description of Isaac and Esau after Jacob has stolen his father's blessing. Isaac is seized by a "great trembling" when he realizes what has happened, and Esau "cried out a great cry" (Gen. 27:34). Finally, the familiar phrase recurs: הן אבדנו כלנו, "Behold, we are all lost," from Numbers 17, with the addition of ויחוגו כשכור, "they . . . circled around as if drunk," from Psalm 107. The storm description is laced with biblical passages, but this does not necessarily spoil its vivid impression.

The second storm scene also incorporates biblical idioms. Mendelsohn-Frankfurt uses all of the existing biblical vocabulary in describing the stormy sea:

ויהי עד כה ועד כה, והשמים התקדרו עבים, ורוח גדולה באה מעבר הים, **ואימה חשכה נופלת עליהם** · וכל איש עומד על מקומו מחריש ומשתאה, ואך אל קלומבא עיניהם לאמור, ה א י ש אשר עזרינו עד הנה, ה ו א יוציאנו מצרת נפשינו גם הפעם · —וגלי ים הולכים וסוערים על מלא רוחב הים הנורא, ויעמד הרוח, וירעם בקולו נפלאות בין התורן ומפרשי האניה, **ויחוגו וינועו** מקצה ועד הקצה · ויהי כרגע האירו ברקים כל פני השמים; וברגע נהפך לחשכת לילה · ויהי **קולות וברקים**, וקול המון הגשם גדול למאוד, **ולהבות אש** מתהלכים כחצים ומחרידים לב העם · **וימס לבבם ויהי למים** ·

(p. 56; wide spacing for emphasis in original)

Meanwhile, the skies darkened with clouds [1 Kings 18:45], **a mighty wind came from across** the sea [Job 1:19], and **a great dark dread fell upon** them [Gen. 15:12]. Every man stood in his place, silent and amazed, with their eyes directed at Columbus, saying: T h i s m a n, who has helped us until now, also this time h e will deliver us from our distress.—The sea

> waves began storming across the entire breadth of the frightful sea. The wind arose and thundered wondrously between the mast and the sails of the ship, and **they circled and lurched** [Ps. 107: 27] from side to side. One moment the lightning brightened the entire sky, and another moment it turned into the darkness of night. There was thunder and lightning, and the sound of a vast multitude of rain, and **flames of fire** [Ps. 29:7] traveled like arrows and brought anguish into the hearts of the people. **Their hearts melted and became water** [Joshua 7:5].

Mendelsohn-Frankfurt's art and technique as translator come into clearer focus from a comparison of this passage to the original German: Mendelsohn-Frankfurt seldom translates sentences literally; there are no biblical allusions in Campe's description.[73] Mendelsohn-Frankfurt acknowledges that he has taken liberties when he states in his preface that

> לא העתקתי כל הספר אות באות, כי אין בו מועיל כי אם אריכות דברים ולא שמרתי המלים רק הענין והמעשה פעם קצרתי פעם הארכתי, והדברים אשר לא יתכנו דרכם בלשון עברי בחרתי תחתם העתקה הנאותית ללשונינו ומליצה המיוחדת לה. (p. v)

> I did not translate the entire book word for word, because there is no use in that, for it would bring only long-windedness. I did not retain the words, but just the matter and the action; sometimes I shortened, and sometimes I lengthened. For things that were not possible in the Hebrew language I substituted [*baḥarti taḥatam*] the suitable translation into our language and the phrasing or rhetoric [*melitza*] that is specific to it.

Mendelsohn-Frankfurt does not claim to have attempted a literal, word-for-word translation; he states that he has instead translated Campe's German into suitable Hebrew idioms, focusing on the matter (*ha-ʿinyan*) and the action or story (*ha-maʿase*). In itself, this approach shows a kind of referentialism, placing the translation of the narrated, worldly events above an effort to convey the exact language used by the original.

In translating Campe's *Die Entdeckung von Amerika*, Mendelsohn-Frankfurt transformed the German text by borrowing from biblical sources, giving the passage the appropriate "phrasing or rhetoric" (*melitza*).

For example, the opening sentence of the description of the second storm starts with a tacit quotation:

> **ויהי עד כה ועד כה, והשמים התקדרו עבים, ורוח גדולה באה מעבר** הים, **ואימה חשכה נופלת עליהם** · (p. 56)
>
> **Meanwhile, the skies darkened with clouds, a mighty wind came across** the sea, **and a great dark dread fell** upon them.

Almost the entire opening phrase is biblical: "Meanwhile, the skies darkened with clouds" (ויהי עד כה ועד כה, והשמים התקדרו עבים) is taken from 1 Kings 18:45; "a mighty wind came from across" (ורוח גדולה באה מעבר) echoes Job 1:19 (והנה רוח גדולה באה מעבר המדבר); and "a great dark dread fell upon them" alludes to Genesis 15:12 (אימה חשכה גדלה נפלת עליו). Mendelsohn-Frankfurt moves deftly between translating words and inserting biblical phrases. On the one hand, the task of the translator pushed him to invent original sentences and to use Hebrew words in new ways; on the other, he resorts to familiar phrases, even when the meaning differs (and certainly the context does). To express the sailors' fears in the final sentence of this passage (וימס לבבם ויהי למים, "their hearts melted and became water"), he quotes from the Book of Joshua 7:5, וימס לבב־העם ויהי למים ("the hearts of the people melted and became water").

It seems that Wessely cautioned Mendelsohn-Frankfurt on his tendency to use biblical phrases instead of translating the German words. In his preface, Mendelsohn-Frankfurt quotes Wessely's advice to him after he saw part of the manuscript in 1804: "Don't give up, for you have done well and will succeed. But listen to me and guard your words, lest you bring out falsehoods and lest you distort your writing, wearying yourself with idle and inferior work, gathering and collecting [biblical] verses that are not apt and not proper. When people dress themselves in unfamiliar clothing, they speak words that have already been said; they seek thoroughly to find deep thoughts, and ancient words, to show themselves as wise in the eyes of a fool" (p. viii). As noted earlier, Wessely then urged Mendelsohn-Frankfurt not to rely on ancient verses but instead to "write the things as they rise up from the walls of your heart, without exaggeration and riddles" (p. viii). Despite Wessely's advice, the translator was clearly unable to dispense with biblical phrases.

Stylistic analysis of Mendelsohn-Frankfurt's translation requires a comparison of his text with the original German. In the first shipwreck scene, Mendelsohn-Frankfurt expands Campe's passage. In Campe's German, the shipwreck occurs when the boat is "gradually driven to the coast by a current [*Meerstrome*]."[74] The Hebrew version dramatizes this scene by adding stormy seas and by alluding to Exodus:

> **ויהי בחצי הלילה**, וגלי הים מתנשאים ורועשים ברעש גדול הלוך וסוער · והנה זרם מים כבירים הולכים ונושאים את האניה לאט לאט על שפת הים. (pp. 45–46)

> **And it was in the middle of the night** [Ex. 12:29], sea waves rose up creating an uproar, with a great noise, and becoming stormier. And behold, a powerful stream of water came and lifted up the boat very slowly toward the sea coast.

At this point in the narrative, Campe briefly describes how the boat strikes the coast: "Plözlich erhielt es einen so gewaltigen Stoß, daß dem erschrokkenen Schifsjungen das Steuer aus den Händen fuhr" ("Suddenly it [the boat] received such a powerful blow that the rudder fell out of the terrified ship-boy's hands").[75] The Hebrew is more graphic:

> פתאום נשמע **קול רעש גדול**, ו ת ת פ ו צ ץ האניה!—ויחרד הנער מקול השאון, ויפול המשוט מידו אל תוך המים, **ויצעק צעקה גדולה.**
>
> (p. 46, widely spaced word for emphasis in original)

> Suddenly there was heard the sound of **a great rushing noise** [Ezek. 3:12], and the ship b u r s t o p e n!—The boy trembled from the sound of the tumult, and the rudder fell out of his hand into the water, and he **cried out a great cry** [Gen. 27:34].

Again Mendelsohn-Frankfurt reaches for biblical allusions to add resonance to the description, taking from Ezekiel's mystical revelation and from Esau's reaction to losing his father's blessing, when he "cried out a great cry." When the sailors see that their ship has run aground, "all of them fell into a despairing confusion" (*alle geriethen in verzweifelnde*

Bestürzung).[76] Mendelsohn-Frankfurt dramatizes the scene while incorporating familiar biblical precedents:

> ויקיצו האנשים כלם ויזעקו לאמור, **הן אבדנו כלנו** · **וירוצו ויחוגו כשכור** כי לא ידעו מה יעשו. (p. 46)
>
> All of the men awoke and cried out, saying, **Oh, we are all lost** [Num. 17:27]. **And they ran in circles as if drunk** [Ps. 107:27] because they didn't know what to do.

Then Mendelsohn-Frankfurt augments the sailors' plea to Columbus by adding direct speech:

> פדה נא את נפשנו מצרותינו, ואסוף אותנו אליך, פן נאבד כרגע. (p. 46)
>
> Redeem our souls from our misfortune, and gather us unto you, lest we soon be lost.

Mendelsohn-Frankfurt represents the scene more vividly than does Campe, even to the point of inserting dialogue, but in a tangle of quotations and allusions he is hard pressed to represent spontaneous-sounding speech.

Mendelsohn-Frankfurt similarly adds to Campe's description in a later scene, after he switches to first-person from third-person narrative. Campe's frame narrator (the father) tells his listeners that a storm is approaching and that "the ship's crew stands in anxious expectation of what shall come."[77] Mendelsohn-Frankfurt quotes their words in direct speech:

> ויאמרו: הנה ה א ו ת כי קרוב הסער לבוא בים, ואיה נחישה לנו מפלט מסוער?
> (p. 56; wide spacing for emphasis in original)
>
> They said: This is the s i g n that the storm is nearing in the sea; where will we find refuge from the storm?

Here, as elsewhere, Mendelsohn-Frankfurt dramatizes scenes that Campe leaves vague.[78] When he writes that "the wind becomes stormier, and breakers lift the ships up toward the heavens," his description of breakers borrows the term from Psalm 93:4:

> ועוד הרוח הולך וסוער, **ומשברי הים** נושאים את האניות עד השמים, ומשם ישליכון תהום רבה. (p. 57)

Although the term used to describe breakers is taken from Psalm 93, and there are echoes of other biblical language, the sentence translates Campe's German: "die schwankenden Schiffe werden von mächtigen Wogen bald hoch in die Luft und bald in den tiefsten Abgrund hinabgeschleudert" ("The tottering ships are first tossed high into the air, and then down into the deepest abyss, by mighty waves").[79] Here Campe seems to be echoing Psalm 107:26, and Mendelsohn-Frankfurt translates without yet returning to the Hebrew source. He saves this for a later scene.

In the next storm description, Mendelsohn-Frankfurt again adds biblical references. In the case of certain phrases, instead of translating Campe's words, he inserts standard Hebrew descriptions. Referring to Columbus's experiences, Campe lists many hardships connected by semicolons:

> Bald hatte er die schrecklichsten Stürme in den gefährlichsten, ihm noch völlig unbekannten Gegenden des Meeres auszustehen; bald sah er sich von Klippen und Sandbänken eingeschlossen, die seinen Schiffen in jedem Augenblicke den Untergang droheten; bald rannte er wirklich auf Untiefen, und die Schiffe wurden dabei so leck, daß die Kräfte der ganzen, unaufhörlich mit Pumpen beschäftigten Mannschaft kaum hinreichten, sie flott zu erhalten.[80]

> At times he had to withstand the most frightful storms in the most dangerous regions of the sea, which were still completely unknown to him; sometimes he saw himself locked in by reefs and sandbanks, which threatened to sink his ships at every moment; at other times he ran upon shoals, and the ships became so leaky, that the efforts of entire crew, pumping incessantly, were barely sufficient to keep them afloat.

Mendelsohn-Frankfurt's Hebrew translation omits much of the detail and moves in a different direction by adding quotations from two biblical passages:

> פעם נשאו אותם רוח חזק על גפי מרומי הגלים; ופעם **השליכם במצולות** · **ויעלו שמים וירדו תהומות** · (p. 78)

> At one moment, a mighty wind lifted them up onto the heights of the waves; at another moment **it threw them down to the depths. And they rose to the heavens and fell to the abyss.**

Being thrown "to the depths" recalls Jonah 2:4 and Exodus 15:5, which describe how the Egyptians were drowned. Once again, the sentence "they rose to the heavens and fell to the abyss" directly quotes the quintessential prooftext for all Hebrew shipwrecks, Psalm 107:26.

Mendelsohn-Frankfurt's translation of Campe was a vital first step in the emergence of modern Hebrew travel prose. Following Euchel and Wessely, he usually relied on standard practices among the Berlin *maskilim*, including the use of biblical language, familiar phrases, and grammar. He intimates that to include appropriate idiomatic expressions, he needed to take them from biblical sources. To him, *melitza* was not so much ornament as idiomatic language. His predecessors discouraged him from using postbiblical Hebrew, but he did introduce it when necessary, and in his glossary for *Metziat ha-aretz ha-ḥadasha* he states that he sometimes had recourse to the Mishna, "the language of the sages" (p. xiv). This option broadened his creative potential, expanding the range of vocabulary and pushing him beyond the use of biblical quotations. His inspired decision to translate Campe and his innovative approach influenced later translators and contributed to the gradual advances toward a more flexible Hebrew style.

The literary historian H. N. Shapiro, writing in Kaunas, Lithuania in the 1930s, recognized Mendelsohn-Frankfurt's and his generation's accomplishment. Although Shapiro identified Mendelsohn-Frankfurt as one of several marginal authors in relation to the Berlin literary center (בשפולי המרכז), he noted that these often derivative authors accomplished some things that the original *maskilim* could not do. In particular, they incorporated the element of folksiness (עממיות), which had no place in their forerunners' classical aesthetics: "As is known, to the extent that the world of the Haskalah was classical, it ignored all folksiness in life, and all folkloristic basis in creative work." With the decline of the German Haskala and the eastward movement of modernizing trends in Jewish life, the later *maskilim* were able to introduce the folksy element.[81] Other literary historians were less generous. For example, Fishl Lachover stated that *Penei tevel* was entirely imitative in relationship to works by Immanuel of Rome and Yehuda Al-Ḥarizi. Nevertheless, he admitted that *Penei tevel* was "the most important of the Hebrew books that were written in Germany during this period of decline."[82]

The Berlin authors were often at odds with the rabbinic tradition, and this rivalry led them to criticize writing that fell short of their standards. They renounced postbiblical Hebrew instead of recognizing the manifold ways in which it could enrich their prose. As a consequence, they created an opening for popular Hebrew writing in a more familiar style. With his greater openness to Mishnaic Hebrew, Mendelsohn-Frankfurt began to break away from the excessive reliance on biblical language.

In the Wake of Mendelsohn-Frankfurt's Translation

Campe's writings inspired many Hebrew and Yiddish authors after Mendelsohn-Frankfurt.[83] (See table 1.) Other translations of *Die Entdeckung von America* appeared in Hebrew and Yiddish, and a complete Hebrew version of Campe's adaptation of *Robinson Crusoe* was published. A brief look at other Hebrew writers who translated from Campe increases our respect for Mendelsohn-Frankfurt's achievement. For example, Mordechai Aaron Günzburg (1795–1846), a Lithuanian *maskil* who was the author of a respected autobiography entitled *Aviezer*, also translated *Die Entdeckung von Amerika*, publishing Hebrew and Yiddish versions in 1823 and 1824.[84] Although Günzburg may have tried to improve on Mendelsohn-Frankfurt's translation, his Hebrew frequently falls back on the standard biblical prooftexts.

Maskilim tended to emulate the Prussian sources they admired, and thus Mendelsohn-Frankfurt was not alone in drawing from German. Bartal writes, for example, that Günzburg "saw the influence of German as a major factor in the expansion of Hebrew."[85] In one metaphorical passage, Günzburg describes the difference between his father and himself: "I conceive German ideas and clothe them in the purity of the Holy Tongue, and he gives birth to his ideas in the lap of that language."[86] The older generation was literate primarily in Hebrew, but when the younger generation wrote Hebrew, they implicitly translated from German.

Glot ha-aretz ha-ḥadasha `al yedei Kristof Kolumbus (The Discovery of the New Land by Christopher Columbus, 1823), Günzburg's Hebrew translation of *Die Entdeckung von Amerika*, uses several of the biblical

Table 1. Early Judeo-German, Hebrew, and Yiddish Versions of J. H. Campe's German Sea Narratives

Date	*Author*	*Title*	*Place*	*Language*
1784	Anonymous	*Historiye oder zeltzame und vunderbahre begebenheiten eines yungen zee fahrers*	Prague	Judeo-German*
1807	Mendelsohn-Frankfurt	*Metziat ha-aretz ha-ḥadasha*	Altona	Hebrew
1813	Anonymous	*Historiye fun den zeefahrer Robinzohn*	Frankfurt an der Oder	Judeo-German*
1817	Khaikl Hurwitz	*Tsofnas paneakh*	Berdichev	Yiddish
1815–18?	Anonymous	*Oniya so`ara*	Zholkva?	Hebrew/Yiddish
1818	Mendel Lefin	*Mase`ot ha-yam*	Zholkva	Hebrew
1823	Anonymous and Mendel Lefin	*Oniya so`ara* (reprint), including the second, Heemskerk narrative from Lefin's *Mase`ot ha-yam*	Vilna	Hebrew
1823?	Anonymous	*Historiye: oder, fun shif brokh* (lost), Yiddish text only from the Hebrew/Yiddish *Oniya so`ara*	Vilna	Yiddish
1823	M. A. Günzburg	*Glot ha-aretz ha-ḥadasha*	Vilna	Hebrew
1824	M. A. Günzburg	*Di entdekung fun Amerika*	Vilna	Yiddish
1824	David Zamość	*Robinzohn der yingere*	Breslau	Hebrew
1825	Anonymous and Mendel Lefin	*Oniya so`ara* (reprint), including the second, Heemskerk narrative from Lefin's *Mase`ot ha-yam*	Vilna	Hebrew
1820s?	Yosef Vitlin?	*Robinzon: di geshikhte fun Alter Leb*	Lemberg/Lvov?	Yiddish
1851	Yosef Vitlin?	*Robinzon: di geshikhte fun Alter Leb* (reprint?)	Lemberg/Lvov	Yiddish
1859	Mendel Lefin	*Mase`ot ha-yam* (reprint)	Lemberg/Lvov	Hebrew

*German written in Hebrew characters

passages we have already encountered. In the first storm and near shipwreck, already familiar to us from Mendelsohn-Frankfurt's translation, "there was great commotion among the sailors, and they called in a loud voice, **We are lost! All of us are lost**!" The Hebrew translation here repeats Mendelsohn-Frankfurt and others' use of biblical precedents:

> ותהי מהומה גדולה בין המלחים, ויקראו בקול גדול **אבדנו! כולנו אבדנו!**[87]

In another crisis, Günzburg's Hebrew follows Job, Psalms, and Jonah:

> קאלומבוס **נשא בשרו בשניו** וישב אחור אל קובא, בראותו כי התגעשו מי הים **ויתרוממו גליו** והאניות **חשבו להשבר**.[88]

> Columbus **took his flesh in his teeth** [bit his lip, overcame his pains; based on Job 13:14] and turned back to Cuba, seeing that the waters of the sea were raging, **and they lifted up its waves** [alluding to Ps. 107:25], and the boats **were on the verge of breaking up** [Jon. 1:4].

Günzburg's Hebrew rendition preserves a strong link to biblical sources. One longer passage illustrates this in great detail, when the second and most extensive storm description shows most clearly that Günzburg filled his translation with biblical *melitza*. The account is vivid but scarcely breaks out of the neobiblical tradition, relying heavily on quotations and allusions:

> המה עושים הנה והנה והשמים התקשרו בעבים שחרחרות. הארץ נחשכה והגלים התרוממו. האניות יחוגו וינועו והרוח הומה בין המפרשים ומרתיח מצולה כסיר.[89] **העבים זורמים מטרות עוז** עלי גיווס **וקול שאון הרעם נשמע בגלגל: הברקים חותים גחלי אש עלי ראשם** ומשברי ים אדירים[90] סוחפים ברעש על צפוי האניה, **ומרוח סועה וסער יעלו שמים ירדו תהומות:** ותהיינה האניות לחרדת אלקים.[91] וגם מלחים לא עצרו כח לעמוד על משמרתם, אלה עזבו את פקודתם לשפוך לבבם לפני ה׳: ואלה נודרים נדרים ללכת **ערום ויחף** על מקום נועד למקדש למו כאשר יעלם ה׳ מבין שאול: ואלה שוכבים כבול עץ באין **דעת ומזימה**, כי לא נותרה בם כל נשמה: ורק לב השליש לא עזבו: כי **כארז בלבנון** עמד על עמדו לבקש מועצות ותחבולות לחזק לבב המלחים לשוב אל עבודתם. אך לשוא קרא אל אזנים אטומים משמוע! כי מרבית אנשיו כפגרים מובסים היו אשר לא יצלחו לחזק תורן ולאחוז משוט.
>
> והים הולך **וסוער ברעש ורוגז לגמא** את האניות, עד כי ראה השליש כי **שוא תשועת אדם**. ויפקיד את האניות ביד אלקי השמים והים, וירד אט אל חדרו:[92]

> They go here and there, and the heavens have become overcast with dark clouds. The earth has darkened, and the waves have risen. The boats circle and founder as the wind roars between the sails and scalds the depths like a pot. **The clouds discharge torrential rain** [Job 37:6], and **the roar of the thunder is heard in the whirlwind** [Ps. 77:19]. **The lightning bolts heap coals of fire on their heads** [Prov. 25:22], mighty breaking waves crash loudly on the hull of the ship, and **from the sweeping wind and tempest** [Ps. 55:9] **they rise to the heavens and fall to the depths** [Ps. 107:26]. The boats are struck by the fear of God. The sailors could not summon up the strength to stand at their posts but instead left their orders to pour out their hearts before God. Some made vows to go **naked and barefoot** [Is. 20:2–4] to a church in an appointed place if God diverts them from Sheol. Others lie like blocks of wood, without **understanding and purpose** [Prov. 1:4], **and not a soul was left** [Josh. 11:11] in them.[93] Only the captain's head did not leave him. For **like a cedar of Lebanon** [Ps. 92:13] he stood in his place, seeking council and means to strengthen the hearts of the sailors, so that they would return to their work. But it was in vain that he called to ears that were sealed! For most of the men were like defeated corpses that could not lend strength to the mast or hold an oar.
>
> The sea continues to **rage and storm in wrath** [alluding to Job 39:24], to swallow up the ships, until the captain sees that **man's efforts are in vain**.[94] He entrusted the ships into the hand of the gods of the heavens and the seas, and he slowly went down to his room.

A reader who recognizes the biblical quotations and allusions is continually reminded of other scenes and contexts, which could deepen the effect but more likely distract from the immediate seascape. Günzburg's high-register translation of Campe did not significantly expand the potential of Hebrew writing in the early nineteenth century. This lack of originality does not negate the accomplishment of Günzburg's three-volume translation of *Die Entdeckung von Amerika*, although it does suggest that Günzburg contributed less to the progress of modern Hebrew style than did Mendel Lefin, discussed in chapter 7. His clever echoes and transformations of biblical phrases are fascinating, but they show his virtuosity more than his ability to move in the direction of nineteenth-century realism.

The same may be said of David Zamość, who learned from prior Hebrew translators of Campe's sea narratives. In *Robinzohn der yingere* (1824), a Hebrew translation of Campe's *Robinson der Jüngerer*, Zamość describes a storm using a patchwork of familiar biblical phrases, following the example of Mendelsohn-Frankfurt and others:

> פתאום קול קרקר בעלית הספינה נשמע, יהי ה׳ בעזרנו! קראו המלחים ופניהם יחורו, פרשו בידיהם. **מה היה הדבר**? שאל ראבינזאן אשר מ**קול פחדים** כמעט **לא נתרה בו נשמה**.
>
> אהה! ענו כלם, **אבדנו! כלנו אבדנו!** הרעם שבר את החבל הגדול וגם התרן התיכון נפרק, **יהי לנו לשטן** אם בל נורידו ונשליכו.
>
> **אבדנו כלנו אבדנו!** קרא הקול מ**ירכתי הספינה**, הנה בדק באניה.[95]

> Suddenly the sound of shattering is heard at the top of the ship, May God help us! the sailors called, and their faces became pale and spread out their hands. **What was it?** [1 Sam. 4:16], asked Robinson, who almost **had no breath in him** [1 Kings 17:17] from the **fearful sound** [Job 15:21].
>
> Aha! all of them answered, **We are lost! We are all lost!** [Num. 17:27]. The thunder has broken the main line and also the center mast has split**; it will become our downfall** [1 Sam. 29:4] if we do not bring it down and throw it off.
>
> **We are lost, we are all lost**, the voice called from **the depths of the ship** [Jon. 1:5], here is a split in the ship.

After Robinson faints, a sailor comes and says to him, "מה לך נרדם" (How can you be sleeping?), echoing the same phrase in Jonah 1:6.

There are many things to admire in Zamość's translation of *Robinson der Jüngere*, including his attempt to convey dialogue. He was perhaps the only Hebrew translator of Campe to retain the father–children dialogue format in which *Die Entdekkung von Amerika* and *Robinson der Jüngere* are narrated.[96] But both Günzburg and Zamość learned from and emulated other Hebrew translations based on Campe's travel narratives. And both of them—to a greater extent than Mendelsohn-Frankfurt—weakened the naturalistic, referential aspect of their narratives by relying excessively on biblical *melitza*.

Mendelsohn-Frankfurt's original accomplishment in his translation of Campe was twofold. First, he developed the genre of Hebrew sea travel narratives, extending them beyond pilgrimages to the Land of Israel by introducing Campe's travel narratives into the Hebrew literary tradition. Recognizing the educational importance of geography, he contributed to secular Jewish writing. Second, he exceeded the limitations of maskilic Hebrew by using a larger postbiblical vocabulary (as in his gloss on *nes*, referring to the word *vilon*, "in the language of our Sages"). His openness to postbiblical Hebrew may have derived from his closer connection to traditional Jewish life and rabbinic writing.

Unlike the more radical *maskilim*, who deliberately broke off from what they saw as outmoded rabbinic practices, Mendelsohn-Frankfurt did not burn his bridges. He lived in both worlds, venturing into the realm of secular literature where traditional Jews had seldom journeyed, but without severing his ties to Hebrew learning. He saw no need to renounce centuries of rabbinic writing because he thought that traditional Hebrew writing could continue to exist alongside secular writing, with ongoing points of contact that enriched both.

The hasidim remained focused on pilgrimage to the Land of Israel, whereas the Berlin *maskilim* tried to limit themselves to biblical language. Mendelsohn-Frankfurt moved beyond Zion by translating Campe's book about the discovery of America and at the same time beyond a Torah-centered approach to Hebrew style. This made him an important precursor to Mendel Lefin, whose collection *Mase'ot ha-yam* (1818) would become a high point in Hebrew sea travel literature.

Moses Mendelsohn-Frankfurt showed a sense of humor in his satires, especially in his parodic portrayal of a sermon by a fictional Rabbi Arsela (Rabbi Hammock?!). His humor extended to himself beyond the grave. According to Eduard Dukesz, he requested in one manuscript that his tombstone include this couplet:

חכמה בקשתי ולא מצאתי
מנוחה לא בקשתי ופה מצאתי.[97]

I sought wisdom but did not find it
I did not seek repose, yet here I found it.

Mendelsohn-Frankfurt lived to see other Hebrew writers follow his example of translating German travel narratives, but he could not have foreseen that his first book would achieve a lasting position in modern Hebrew literary history. *Metziat ha-aretz ha-ḥadasha* did not find a wide readership, but a decade later it inspired successors.

6

Bontekoe

STORM-TOSSED SHIP IN THE INDIAN OCEAN

This chapter turns to the remarkable narrative entitled *Oniya so'ara* (Storm-Tossed Ship), which recounts Captain Willem Bontekoe's ill-fated journey from the Netherlands to Java in 1619.[1] (See figures 6 and 7.) Translated and adapted from the shortened version of Bontekoe's book for young adults published by Joachim Heinrich Campe in 1788, *Oniya so'ara* appeared in a bilingual Hebrew/Yiddish edition around 1815–18.[2] Unlike Moses Mendelsohn-Frankfurt's earlier translation *Metziat ha-aretz ha-ḥadasha* (1807), this translation from Campe took into account the needs of less-educated readers by supplementing the Hebrew with a Yiddish version. *Oniya so'ara* may thus be called the Rosetta Stone of modern Jewish literary history because it enables scholars to decipher the literary codes by which German narrative was carried over into modern Yiddish and Hebrew writing. Like the trilingual Rosetta Stone that helped experts decrypt Egyptian hieroglyphics, *Oniya so'ara* solves some mysteries hidden within modern Jewish languages and cultural transfer. Instead of reflecting light backward onto the prior German source, however, this bilingual translation is a gem that refracts light forward onto modern Yiddish and Hebrew literature, showing how they developed in relation to one another. Most importantly, the retelling of sea travels in *Oniya so'ara* reveals the powerful impact of Yiddish on Hebrew. Campe's narrative appears to have been translated first from German into Yiddish and then from Yiddish into Hebrew; the Yiddish rendition stays closer to the original German, yet without using excessively Germanic phrasings or word choices. The Hebrew version, in contrast, takes

Fig 6. Chart of Captain Willem Bontekoe's ill-fated voyage, 1619, based on Samuel Dunn, *A New Chart of the World on Mercator's Projection* (London: Sayer, 1789), detail, with approximate route added by Joseph Stoll, Syracuse University Cartographic Laboratory, in collaboration with Ken Frieden.

Fig. 7. Portrait of Captain Willem Ysbrantsz Bontekoe van Hoorn, from Willem Bontekoe, *Memorable Description of the East Indian Voyage, 1618–25*, trans. C. B. Bodde-Hodgkinson and Pieter Geyl (New York: McBride, 1929), plate II.

liberties and innovates freely by inserting biblical quotations and other pious language.

Maskilic Hebrew authors rejected the traditional, Torah-centered worldview. Seeking to broaden their readers' horizons, they pushed beyond Zion, translating non-Jewish sea travels. There was a growing market for Hebrew and Yiddish books; the challenge was to write accessible Hebrew (and readable Yiddish, before the orthography had been standardized), while moving beyond Jewish traditions and describing the wide world. Authors' primary obstacle was their dependence on biblical sources, Talmudic allusions, and other textual commonplaces that often distracted from real-world references. The author of *Oniya so'ara* partially overcame these obstacles, but his bilingual narrative illustrates how difficult it was to create modern Hebrew. Although translation from German facilitated the process, mediated by Yiddish, the author often depended on the ancient Hebrew textual tradition, which injected piety and archaisms into Bontekoe's narrative.

Intertextuality has long been a distinctive feature of Judaic literature: it links the Talmud to the Hebrew Bible, later rabbinic commentaries to the Talmud and Bible, and codified Jewish law to Talmudic and biblical sources. Intertextuality enabled medieval Hebrew poets to quote and transform biblical language. In the modern period, however, reliance on texts from the past hindered more immediate representations of the world. Expressing a scientific worldview required a less allusive Hebrew—something that may have seemed impossible to many Jews who continued to conceive of Hebrew as the Holy Tongue.

Hasidic writers such as Nathan Sternharz unintentionally contributed to the modernization of Hebrew with works that were based, implicitly or explicitly, on translations from Yiddish. Thus, in the second preface to Nahman's *Tales*, Sternharz apologized for "coarse language," explaining that it was the result of his effort to keep the Hebrew as close as possible to the Rebbe's Yiddish. Nevertheless, Nahman's allegorical bent pushed his fantastic stories away from everyday reality. Sternharz, in his pilgrimage narratives, was more adept at conveying the unfamiliar world that he encountered during travel. It remained for other travel narratives in Hebrew to move beyond pilgrimages to Zion while developing a Hebrew that moved beyond the limits of biblical precedents.

The author or authors of the Hebrew/Yiddish *Oniya so'ara* remain unidentified.[3] The author-translator(s), place of publication, and publisher of the first printing are unknown because the only extant copy of the book, at the National Library of Israel, is missing the title page and the opening pages of the Hebrew/Yiddish text. Fortunately, the first part of the Hebrew version can be reconstructed based on later editions printed in Vilna in 1823, Vilna and Horodna in 1825, and Warsaw in 1854 and 1878. Unfortunately, the Yiddish text was never reprinted except in a single known edition, *Historiye: oder, fun shif brokh*, now lost, and so the opening pages of the Yiddish translation have not yet been recovered.[4]

The first printing of *Oniya so'ara* (1815–18?) provides the Hebrew translation at the top of the page and the Yiddish translation at the bottom.

Until that time, most Hebrew/Yiddish bilingual books had been scriptures and works of ethical teachings, or *musar*. For example, Rabbi Baḥya's work *Ḥovot ha-levavot* (Duties of the Heart, which originally appeared in Judeo-Arabic and Hebrew in the eleventh and twelfth centuries) was reprinted several times in Hebrew/Yiddish editions in the eighteenth century. Also popular were Hebrew/Yiddish editions of Tsvi Hirsh Koidanover's book *Kav ha-yosher* (1705).[5] Then in 1815 Nahman's tales appeared in a Hebrew/Yiddish edition. Like *Kav ha-yosher* and other popular books, Nahman's *Sippurei ma`asiyot* illustrated the potential marketability of Hebrew/Yiddish editions. In 1814, emulating the Hebrew/German editions of the Bible that were launched by Moses Mendelssohn, Mendel Lefin published an edition of *Mishlei* (The Book of Proverbs), with Hebrew and Yiddish on facing pages. All of these books had sacred content and could be published as traditional *sforim* within the European Jewish religious realm. The Hebrew texts were revered, and the Yiddish translations were intended for women and less-educated men.

Oniya so`ara* innovated by combining secular content with the Hebrew/Yiddish format. Mendelsohn-Frankfurt had contributed to literary history by translating Campe into Hebrew, and *Oniya so`ara took another step forward. Because a Hebrew adaptation of Campe's German work had no sacred status, the book could have been printed in Yiddish alone, yet the unidentified author-translator apparently did not want to abandon Hebrew even when narrating an essentially secular voyage. Although the Berlin *maskilim* had championed Hebrew writing, most of them also wrote in German and avoided Yiddish. Thus, although *Oniya so`ara* was adapted from Campe, it represented a novelty. The author (or authors) shared the tastes of the Berlin *maskilim*, who admired Campe's writings, while taking into account the needs of Yiddish readers. Notwithstanding its relative obscurity, *Oniya so`ara* is a milestone in Jewish literature. By transforming a German narrative into Hebrew and Yiddish versions, it served as a bridge from the Berlin Haskala to readers in Galicia and Podolia.

A decisive vector in the rise of Hebrew and Yiddish writing was the movement of the Jewish Enlightenment eastward as it declined in Germany. Because Jewish assimilation into German society (and language) had shrunk the audience for Hebrew books, modern Hebrew publishing followed the spread of Haskala eastward—initially to Vienna and Austrian Galicia and later to centers in Russia. Hence, *Oniya so`ara*, which is thought to have been printed first in Zholkva, near Lemberg/Lvov in eastern Galicia, was well situated to reach Yiddish-speaking readers. Its content and ideology derived from Germany, but its audience was in the East.

Oniya so`ara* was thus a remarkable hybrid. It followed the pedagogical bent of the Berlin Hebrew writers even while it supplemented their Hebraism with an unusual acceptance of Yiddish. It is possible that the success of Nahman's *Sippurei ma`asiyot and several Yiddish translations of *Shivḥei ha-Besht* in 1815–17 encouraged the publication of the Hebrew/Yiddish *Oniya so`ara* (which would suggest that it was published around 1817–18, later than sometimes assumed). From a commercial standpoint, there was an obvious motive for printing Yiddish narratives. But why include a Hebrew version of Bontekoe's sea tale? This seems to have reflected a continuing acceptance of the ideology of the Berlin Haskala, the influence of which hovers over *Oniya so`ara*.

These considerations lead toward our central literary-historical question: What kind of Hebrew did the author-translator of *Oniya so`ara* write? If the Berlin Enlightenment was such a strong influence, did the translator follow the norms established there? Who was this writer who so clearly admired his Berlin predecessors, who did not reject Yiddish, and who acted as a bridge between the Berlin Enlightenment and the Yiddish-speaking population in Galicia and Russia? Is it possible to learn more about and even to identify the anonymous Hebrew author-translator? In Vilna in 1823 and 1825, the Hebrew narrative from *Oniya so`ara* was reprinted together with the shorter of Mendel Lefin's two stories from *Mase`ot ha-yam* (1818), leading to some speculation that Lefin also was responsible for *Oniya so`ara*. Although I previously accepted this idea, on the basis of further study I have concluded that it is unlikely (see chapter 7).

Like other sea narratives discussed in this book, the Hebrew version of *Oniya so`ara* often uses biblical allusions and elaborates on the story's religious elements. It also shows the influence of Campe's German book and retains a number of maritime terms from that source. Some technical terms are used in the body of the text, whereas others are provided as parenthetical glosses: שאלופע, *Schaluppe* (sloop); באאט, *Boot* (boat); קיסטע, *Küste* (coast); שטייאר מאן, *Steuermann* (helmsman); מאטראזין, *Matrosin* (sailors); זגל טוך, *Segel tuch* (sail, to gloss the Hebrew נס); and לאנד קארט, *Landkarte* (map, to gloss the Hebrew מפת הים). The Hebrew translation also shows influence from the Yiddish translation, which seems to have been made first. The glosses in the Hebrew text employ Slavic words, most of which are also present in the parallel Yiddish passage, including *smand*, *tshad* (smoke); *khvalies* (waves); *tshilns* (canoes); *hormates* (cannon); *slabode* (colony); and more.

The biography of Mendel Lefin (1749–1826) makes him a candidate for authorship of *Oniya so`ara*. He lived in Berlin in the early 1780s—when Campe's books were best sellers there—but then returned to Podolia. In addition, he had recently shown his openness to Yiddish writing when he published his Hebrew/Yiddish edition of the Book of Proverbs (*Mishlei*, published at Joseph Perl's Jewish school in Tarnopol in 1814). One might speculate that Lefin chose not to acknowledge his authorship of *Oniya so`ara* in the wake of Tuvya Feder's attack on Lefin's Hebrew/Yiddish edition of Proverbs.[6] Yet the authorship of *Oniya so`ara* remains uncertain, although some scholars such as Nancy Sinkoff (following Samuel Poznanski and Yitzhak Yudlov) have indeed attributed it to Lefin.[7] Because this attribution has not been proven, however, I will not assume that it is correct. Indeed, literary analysis has convinced me that Lefin was *not* the author of *Oniya so`ara*, and I return to this question in the next chapter. In any event, the text's importance does not depend on Lefin's authorship; this remarkable book calls for a revision of Hebrew and Yiddish literary history, regardless of whether the author was Lefin or someone else in the maskilic circles of Tarnopol and Brody.

In the next chapter, I turn to two similar Hebrew sea narratives that have been definitively ascribed to Mendel Lefin. In 1818, Lefin published the unpretentious but pathbreaking secular Hebrew book *Mase`ot hayam* (Sea Voyages), lightly concealing his authorship behind the initials M. L. (מ** ל**).[8] The two parts of this book are based on volume 9 (1791) and volume 1 (1786) of Campe's *Reisebeschreibungen*, respectively. The ninth volume offers Captain Wilson's account of shipwreck on the Palau

Islands in 1783; the first tells of the search for a Northeast Passage in 1596 by Captains Jacob Heemskerk and Willem Barents. In these narratives, Lefin moved away from Enlightenment *melitza* and created an almost colloquial Hebrew style, marking him as an innovator who was leagues ahead of his contemporaries. Juxtaposing *Mase`ot ha-yam* with *Oniya so`ara* helps to underscore their innovative force.

Until a complete copy of the bilingual *Oniya so`ara* is located, including the title page—to supplement the copy in the National Library of Israel, which is missing the opening pages—we can only guess that it was printed in Zholkva around 1815–18.[9] The first edition was bilingual; the revised, Hebrew-only version was published in Vilna in 1823 and was popular enough to be reprinted several times thereafter.[10] The title *Oniya so`ara* or אניה סוערה is a play on words in relationship to Isaiah 54:11, where the phrase עניה סערה refers to a storm-tossed, poor woman—sometimes interpreted as a metaphor for the people of Israel.[11] But *Oniya so`ara* avoids turning Bontekoe's voyage into an allegory; this account of a storm-tossed ship instead conveys the immediacy of a captain's memoir.

As discussed throughout this book, biblical models heavily influenced early-modern Hebrew descriptions of sea travel. Like most other travel books written before and during the early nineteenth century, *Oniya so`ara* and *Mase`ot ha-yam* emulate some aspects of biblical Hebrew, while to varying degrees they also introduce elements of postbiblical Hebrew. There are important ideological considerations when modern authors state or assume ancient or medieval theological views. This occurs in relationship to the Book of Jonah and Psalm 107, which present the storm at sea as an exemplary instance in which God's power and Divine Providence are revealed: "They shout to the Lord in distress, and He takes them out of their affliction" (Ps. 107:28). The verses may be read as a general description of what continually happens in a kind of recurring present time of crying out for God's salvation.

The Psalm asserts that when people cry out to God, they are saved from danger. This claim raises a fraught question: Does petitionary prayer have the power to alter nature? In his commentary on Psalm 107, verse 17, Ibn Ezra implies that human efforts are futile because only God can save us.[12] In the background for nineteenth-century readers were disputes over the status of miracles, which were widely claimed by the followers of charismatic hasidic leaders. *Oniya so`ara* seems to support traditional belief in Divine Providence, which is consistent with both Campe's narrative and Bontekoe's source text.

Psalm 107 was popular among hasidic leaders and readers. Verse 26, "They rise to the heavens and fall into the abyss, their souls melt away in calamity [*nafsham be-ra`a titmogag*]," encouraged an allegorical interpretation that was well known among the hasidim. That interpretation may have derived from a commentary ascribed to the Ba`al Shem Tov (discussed later in this chapter). But in spite of its poetic quality, this biblical description was also sufficiently graphic to serve as a model for modern descriptions of actual sea travel. Hasidic authors often referred back to Psalm 107 as a prooftext showing the supernatural power of prayer, whereas modern authors did not. In a more modern view, abstraction and allegory, like excessive reliance on biblical models, distracted from the reality of concrete representations.

When describing a storm in a later chapter, *Oniya so`ara* relies on Psalm 107 and cites the Book of Lamentations:

> **כי עמד רוח סערה ותרומם גלי הים** · עד כי **נפשינו ברעה תתמוגג**, ויך לבי אותי על אשר יעצתי ככה, **חסדי ה׳ כי לא תמנו**: האניה הקטנה (שאלופע) אשר לנו עמדה נגד הרוח **כמטרה לחץ**, ולא נגע בו רע · **הוקם סערה לדממה ויחשו גליהם**, תודה לאל נתננו, ונברך את ה׳ אשר יעצנו.[13]

> **For a storm wind arose and lifted up the waves of the sea,** until our **souls melted away in calamity** [Ps. 107:25–26]. My heart rebuked me that I had advised [thought] this. **God's kindness has not ended** [Lam. 3:33]; our small ship (*shaluppe*) withstood the battering wind, **like the target of an arrow** [Lam. 3:12], and no evil came to it. **The storm becomes silent, and the waves become still** [Ps. 107:29]. We gave thanks unto God, and blessed God, who advised us.

These biblical contexts are nowhere evident in Campe's German text on Bontekoe's journey.[14] By inserting phrases from Jonah, Lamentations, and

Psalm 107, *Oniya so'ara* follows recurring precedents in Hebrew narratives of sea travel since the Middle Ages.

Another strong biblical echo arises from the words *ruah se'ara* (storm wind). This phrase occurs in Psalms 107 and 148, but, as shown in chapter 1, an equally important prooftext is the Book of Ezekiel. At the beginning of that book, the prophet Ezekiel gives his account of how "the heavens were opened, and I saw visions of God" (Ezek. 1:1). This opens a well-known passage that became the basis for "Merkava mysticism,"[15] a mystical tradition that later became central to the Zohar and its use by hasidic authors. The vision begins, "And I looked, and behold, a storm wind [*ruaḥ se'ara*] came from the north" (1:4). (Rabbi Nahman discusses this passage in *Likutei Moharan*, section 82, and the *ruaḥ se'ara* is a recurring motif elsewhere, such as in section 8; see also Nahman's Tales 1, 2, 10, and 12 in *Sippurei ma'asiyot*.) When is a storm just a natural phenomenon, and when does it have higher meaning?

Chapters 2 and 3 showed that *ruaḥ se'ara* was a key phrase in Nahman's tales and Sternharz's writings. The theological underpinning of *ruaḥ se'ara* suggests a rationale for Sternharz's detailed descriptions of the storms in *Shivḥei ha-Ran*, *Ḥayei Moharan*, and *Yemei Moharnat*. In the eyes of pilgrims to the Holy Land, these storms were neither random nor natural, but rather significant encounters with God and His awe-inspiring power. In a sense, the storms were theophanies, for when the pilgrims survived a *ruaḥ se'ara*, they often took it as evidence of God's benevolent Providence. Campe and Lefin appear to agree with Nahman's and Sternharz's general belief in Divine Providence: Campe frequently refers to *das Vorsehen*, while Lefin refers to *ha-hashgaḥa*. Sternharz finds allegorical meaning in salvation from storms at sea, and some of his descriptions take on the aura of mystical events.[16] For instance, during Nahman's return sea journey from Palestine, a storm strikes with such force that "the waves rose almost to the heavens" (ומגודל התגברות הרוח סערה עלו הגלים כמעט עד לב השמים).[17] When Nahman expresses confidence that they will be saved, he echoes Moses leading the Israelites in their miraculous crossing of the Red Sea: "Israel was on the sea and did not drown," he says, just before Passover arrives. Without saying so explicitly, Nahman implies that their fate will be the same as that of the Israelites.

Reconsidering *Oniya so`ara*

In *Oniya so`ara*, Captain Bontekoe tells the story of his ill-fated voyage commanding a Dutch merchant ship, the *Nieuw-Hoorn*. Campe worked from prior German translations of Captain Bontekoe's sensational tale of disaster and survival at sea. Based in part on Bontekoe's log book but not printed until 1646, the original Dutch narrative portrays Bontekoe's fortitude both in dealings with his crew and in encounters with savage tribes. (See figure 8.) Bontekoe recounts that his sailors, nearing starvation, were on the verge of cannibalism before they reached land; later, he tells of close brushes with cannibals on the island of Sumatra. Bontekoe comes across as a hero who upholds the norms of civilization in the face of adversity. Some *maskilim* valued travel narratives precisely because they illustrated virtuous actions and admirable personality traits. Moral treatises had been popular among enlightened Jews since the 1780s; a generation later, some travel narratives became showcases of exemplary behavior.

The Hebrew and Yiddish translations in *Oniya so`ara* are relatively literal. Especially in Yiddish, the translator achieved a close, word-for-word rendering, but without losing the Yiddish idiomatic character. He heightened the religious dimension, adding a more pious perspective than is found in the original.[18] For example, where Campe tells us that "the departure took place with good wind and weather," *Oniya so`ara* provides a devout viewpoint:

> והנה בעת החלו לנסוע מהאי (טעקסל) אשר (בהאלאנד), וה׳ הניח להם **ברוח צח שפיים**.[19]

> When they began to travel from the island Texel in Holland, God gave them **a pure wind**.

The phrase *ruaḥ tzaḥ shefaim*, taken from Jeremiah 4:11, places the wind in a biblical context.

Storm sequences test the descriptive powers of Hebrew authors as well as their ideology. Comparing the opening storm in the German of Campe's version and in the Hebrew of *Oniya so`ara* further illustrates the translator's tendency to add some details and to incorporate biblical quotations or allusions:

IOVRNAEL

OFTE

Gedenckwaerdige beſchrij-
vinghe vande Ooſt-Indiſche Reyſe van
Willem Ysbrantſz. Bontekoe van Hoorn.

Begrijpende veel wonderlijcke en gevaerlijcke
ſaecken hem daer in wedervaren.

Begonnen den 18. December 1618. en vol-eynt den 16. November 1625.

Tot: HOORN, Ghedruckt by Iſaac Willemſz.

Door Ian Ianſz. Deutel, Boeck-verkooper op 't Ooſt in Bieſtkens
Teſtament / Anno 1646.

Fig. 8. Title page of Willem Ysbrantsz Bontekoe van Hoorn, *Journael ofte Gedenckwaerdige beschrijvinghe vande Oost-Indische Reyse* (Hoorn: Willemsz, 1646). From the image available on Google Books, which was scanned from the collection of the Bavarian State Library, Munich.

Es entstanden nämlich plözlich ganz ausserordentliche Windstöße; Berge von Wasser wurden dadurch gegen das Schiff geschleudert; einige dieser Wasserberge überwältigten das Schiff, zerplazten auf dem Ueberlaufe desselben, und füllten einen Theil der obersten Räume mit Wasser an.

“Wir sinken! Wir sinken!”—So erschollen hundert ängstlich Stimmen.[20]

בפתע פתאום נתעוררה רוח גדולה וחזק משבר משברי ים (ווינט שטויסן) וכח הרוח ההוא הי׳ להעשות בים הרי מים, ולהגביהם עוף עד נוכח ראש הספינה, עד אשר גם היושבים בעליות הספינה ראו מים רבים נטוי על ראשיהם מלמעלה, ואחר כן נפלו המים על ראש האניה וישברו, ומלאו כמה חדרים עליונים מים עד לרוב:

הן גוועני אבדנו כולנו אבדנו, נטבענו, נטבענו, חרדו כל העם וזעקו. . . .[21]

Suddenly there arose extraordinary wind currents, from which mountains of water were thrown against the ship; some of these water mountains overcame the ship, broke on its deck, and filled some of the upper rooms with water.

“We’re sinking! We’re sinking!”—Thus rang out a hundred anxious voices.

Suddenly there arose a great wind and strengthened the waves of the breakers. (Wind currents) and the force of that wind made mountains of water in the sea and raised them up over the top of the ship, until those sitting on the upper deck of the ship saw great waters hanging over their heads, and then the waters fell onto the front of the ship and broke it and filled some upper rooms with a great amount of water.

Behold, we perish, we are lost, all of us are lost, we are sinking, sinking, shouted the people in fear.

The term *mishberei yam* in biblical Hebrew refers to “breakers” (Ps. 93:4), but as used here it expands on the description of wind currents and mountains of water. The Hebrew version renders the scene more vividly by moving us into the perspective of the sailors who “saw great waters hanging over their heads." Another contribution by *Oniya so'ara* lies in its efforts to convey speech. For example, when the ship is endangered early in *Wilhelm Isbrand Bonteku's merkwürdige Abentheuer*, the sailors cry out simply: "Wir sinken! Wir sinken!"[22] *Oniya so'ara* expands Campe's version, imagining the sailors in extremity saying:

הן גוועמו אבדנו כולנו אבדנו, נטבענו, נטבענו.[23]

Behold, we perish, we are lost, all of us are lost, we are sinking, sinking.

The translator goes a step beyond Mendelsohn-Frankfurt's use of this biblical passage. Through repetition, the writer suggests a chorus of voices and the pathos of trying to come to terms with imminent death. He also quotes the first part of this phrase from the complaint of the Israelites in the desert: "Behold, we perish, we are lost, all of us lost" (הן גוענו אבדנו כלנו אבדנו, Num. 17:27). *Oniya so'ara* succeeds in using a biblical phrase and making it sound more expressive and modern.[24] In the midst of this scene, the translator also adds the classic phrase from Jonah: the boat was on the verge of breaking up (*ha-oniya ḥishva le-hishaver*).[25]

In a second storm description, the translator both emphasizes the sailors' emotions and adds a theological dimension supported by numerous biblical references:

Der Sturm tobte indeß unaufhörlich fort. Wind, Wellen und Regen, der sich stromweise ergoß, brausten so gewaltig durch einander, daß man weder sehen und hören, noch festen Fußes stehen konnte.[26]

אך **לא שב חרון אף ה'** מהם והרוח הולך וחזק, שלשה אלה גברו מאד, רוח, משברי הים, וגשם שוטף, ומאלה **פור התפוררה** כל האני' כמעט: **ויתמהו** האנשים איש אל רעהו, **וימס לבב העם**, כלו עיניהם מראות.[27]

Campe's German is concrete: "Meanwhile, the storm raged on. Wind, waves, and rain—which poured down like a stream—stormed together so powerfully, that one could neither see nor hear, nor could one stand firmly on one's feet." The Hebrew of *Oniya so'ara* may be rendered (with biblical phrases in bold): "But **God's fury did not turn back** from them, and the wind kept getting stronger, and these three were mighty: wind, breakers, and streaming rain, and from these the whole ship almost **fell to pieces**. **The people looked at one another, stunned**, **the hearts of the people melted**, and their eyes stopped seeing." Campe's German describes the seascape without shifting to a high register or using obvious biblical verses. One could argue that in the Hebrew version this passage illustrates the maskilic writers' unoriginal reliance on biblical quotations, but closer examination reveals that the Hebrew transforms its source texts. For example, when the Hebrew alludes to passages from the Prophets, there are subtle changes. "But God's fury did not turn back from them" alludes to Jeremiah 4:8 ("For God's fury has not turned away from us," כי לא שב חרון אף יהוה ממנו), where *Oniya so'ara* shifts from Jeremiah's first-person voice to the narrator's third-person voice. Next, "the whole ship almost fell to pieces" draws from Isaiah 24:19 ("the earth has fallen to pieces," פור התפוררה ארץ), shifting the context from land to sea. The next phrase, "the people looked at one another, stunned," echoes Isaiah 13:8 ("people will look at one another, stunned," איש אל רעהו יתמהו), where using the conversive Vav enables *Oniya so'ara* to change an imperfect aspect (and future sense) into past tense. Finally, "the hearts of the people melted" displaces this phrase from the aftermath of a military slaughter in Joshua 7:5, thereby adding complexity to the scene of a storm at sea. On the one hand, one could argue that the inlaying of biblical phrases (*shibbutz*) is a distraction from the scene; perhaps reading the passage without emphasizing the borrowings would allow it to seem more effective. On the other hand, someone who hears the biblical echoes could reason that these particular uses are apt and do not distract from the concrete scene. In any case, it is clear that the Hebrew writer inserts biblical language using an associative method, instead of directly translating from the German.

Alongside the biblical references are many examples of Judaizing in the Hebrew version, sometimes breaking free from the German original. Describing the sailors' pleasure on an island they visit, the narrator uses several biblical phrases. Quoting Joel 2:3, he writes that "before them the land was like Gan Eden" and alludes to Jeremiah and Kings when he adds,

> אין שם כי אם **קול ששון וקול שמחה** · שבע ורויה, **אין שטן · ואין פגע רע**. . . . אכלו ושבעו ויותירו.[28]

> There was nothing but **the sound of joy and rejoicing** [Jer. 33:11], satisfaction and satiation · **No adversary** · **and no evil occurrence** [1 Kings 5:18]. They ate and were satisfied and there was some left over.

The joyful scene invokes biblical precedents. Finally, perhaps with some intended humor, the translator inserts an idiomatic phrase that suggests a traditional description of Jews completing a meal: "They ate and were satisfied, and there was some left over" (*akhlu ve-sav`u ve-yotiru*).[29] This sentence alludes to Deuteronomy 8:10: "you will eat, you will be satisfied, and you will bless God" (ואכלת ושבעת וברכת את יהוה; in *Oniya so`ara*, the grammatical switch changes the phrase from imperfect aspect, with a future meaning, to past time). By following biblical language, *Oniya so`ara* Judaizes Bontekoe's sailors.

The Hebrew translation sometimes enhances the dramatic power of the original. Chapter 2 describes the calamity that besets the ship because of the steward's lack of caution. He allows a wick from a candle to fall into one of the barrels of brandy, which ignites. Campe's version is graphic, and the Hebrew version intensifies the effect:

> Der erschrockene Kellermeister rief Feuer! Und Feuer! Feuer! schallte es fürchterlich aus allen Winkeln wieder. Man stürzte in den Raum; sahe mit Entsetzen wie der flammende Branntewein den Boden des Fasses zersprengte, und wie ein brennender Schwefelbach nach dem Steinkohlenhaufen lief, der in eben diesem Raume sich befand. Allen standen bei diesem schreklichen Anblicke die Haare zu Berge: aber Bonteku, welcher auch herbei geeilt war, behielt noch Gegenwart des Geistes genug.[30]

> אש!, אש!, צוח המשרת **ואין מציל**: כרגע, פחד ורעדה וזעקה נשמע בכל האני׳ · אש!, אש!, וירוצו מהרה אל מרתף האניה והנה האש את החבית ריצץ (צו זעצט), נשבר לבם בקרבם בראותם כי הי״ש אחז דרך ויתהלך על תחתית המרתף · והולך ושורף עד קרוב לגחלים עוממות ויתלהבו הגחלים: רעדה אחזתם שם עד כי נבהלו כי תהלך אש ארצה, והגחלים התלהבו, עד כי מגודל פחדם לא ידעו לשית עצות בנפשם: אך (באנטעקו) התאמץ מאד, אף אם פחד קראהו ורעדה, עם כל זה גבר שכלו על פחדו.[31]

The terrified steward called out, Fire! and from every corner there echoed Fire! Fire! People plunged into the room; they saw with horror how the flaming brandy burst open the bottom of the barrel, and how a burning, sulfurous stream ran toward the pile of coal, which was also found in this room. This frightful sight made everyone's hair stand on end; but Bontekoe, who had also hurried to the scene, kept his presence of mind.

"Fire! Fire!" shrieked the steward, **and there was no one to save him** [*ve-ein matzil*]. In a moment, there was fear and trembling, and shouting was heard all over the ship. "Fire! Fire!" And they ran quickly to the lower hold of the ship. And behold, the fire had burst the barrel, and their hearts broke inside them when they saw that the brandy took a path and went along the floor burning until it was near to a pile of coal, flickering and lighting up the coals. Trembling seized them there, and they panicked, for the fire would catch and the coals start to burn—until, in their great fear, they were at a loss [literally, did not know what advice to give their souls]. But Bontekoe made great efforts, and in spite of his fear and trembling, his reason overcame his fear.

In the midst of this vivid scene, the Hebrew translator limits the use of biblical allusions. The Hebrew seems to flow smoothly, although at one point it seems to follow German word order: "der flammende Branntewein den Boden des Fasses zersprengte"—a word-for-word equivalent to the awkward construction of the sentence "the flaming brandy the bottom of the barrel burst open"—is conveyed similarly in Hebrew with והנה האש את החבית ריצץ.

The crew succeeds in putting out the fire, but, as the tale continues in German and Hebrew,

Nach einer halben Stunde das fürchterliche Geschrei: Feuer! Feuer! von neuem durchs ganze Schiff erscholl.[32]

אבל לא עברה חצי שעה, והנה רעש גדול שנית בכל האניה קול רגשת האנשים יזעקו בקול מר, חמרמר [המרמר?], אש, אש: איש אל רעהו יתמהו ויאמרו **מה זאת עשה אלקים לנו.**[33]

Half an hour later, the frightful cry: Fire! Fire! rang out again through the entire ship.

Half an hour had not passed, when again there was a great noise all over the ship, the commotion of people's voices, shouting in a bitter voice, aggrieved, Fire, Fire. The people looked at one another in astonishment and said: **What is this that God has done to us?**

Here the Hebrew writer expands this climactic moment and conveys the crew's response by using a phrase that Joseph's brothers speak when they are surprised (by Joseph's ruse) that their money has reappeared with the grain in their sacks: "What is this that God has done to us?" (*ma zot `asa Elohim lanu*, Gen. 42:28). When this Hebrew adaptation moves beyond literal translation by adding a biblical allusion, it superimposes another context that mentions God (when, in fact, human actions have caused their surprise and fear).

Subsequently, there is a shift to first-person narrative in Campe's version of Bontekoe's account, and *Oniya so`ara* follows suit as the story comes to a climax. Campe and the Hebrew translator state this explicitly.[34] In the text of the first Hebrew edition, this statement is attributed to the translator:

אמר המעתיק עתה נספר תוכן המעשה במליצת רב החובל באנטעקו כאשר כתב הוא עצמו ככתבו ולשונו אות באות וזה פתשגן כתב באנטעקו.[35]

The translator [or copyist, *ha-me`atik*] says: now we will relate the content of the story in the language [*melitza*] of Captain Bontekoe, as he himself wrote, according to his writing and speech [*leshono*], word for word, and this is a copy [*patshegen* (= late biblical Hebrew, from Persian, found in the Book of Esther)] of Bontekoe's writing.

The second Hebrew edition of 1823 includes the same sentence in a footnote, preceded by

אמר המעתיק עד כה ספרנו את המאורע כפי מה שמצאתי כתוב בסיפורי מסעות הים אשר לאיזה מאסף מסעות.[36]

> The translator [or copyist] says: until now we told the occurrence in accordance with what I found written in the stories of sea travels in some collection of travels.

Assuming that the original Hebrew/Yiddish translator of *Oniya so`ara* was not involved in the 1823 Hebrew reprint, this added sentence is an acknowledgment—by the editor, author, or printer of the Vilna edition—that Bontekoe's narrative is based on a prior edition (probably without permission of the original translator or publisher). The wording is intriguing because it suggests that the original was contained in a *collection* (מאסף); if this is true, all copies of that collection seem to have been lost—unless this statement is referring to *Wilhelm Isbrand Bonteku's merkwürdige Abentheuer auf einer Reise aus Holland nach Ostindien*, volume 5 of Campe's *Reisebeschreibungen*, which includes both Captain Bontekoe's and Captain James Cook's narratives. The bilingual *Oniya so`ara* from about 1815–18 is not really a collection, although the travel account is followed by a short story, "Eyn sheyne mayse" (A Beautiful Tale), in antiquated Yiddish.

At this point, then, Campe and the Hebrew translator give the narrative to Bontekoe. The Hebrew reads:

פחד פחדתי אמר באנטעקו בספרו קורות נסיעותו ומיד ירדתי.

> I became frightened, so says Bontekoe in his book Chronicles of his Travels, and immediately I went down. (*Oniya so`ara*, 1815–18 ed., p. 18)

As the translator has Bontekoe recollect the scene, he adds intensifying phrases. After they pour water on the fire, Bontekoe writes, in the Hebrew rendering, "we went from bad to worse, from **calamity to calamity** [*hova `al hova*, Ezek. 7:26], from **disaster to disaster** [*shever `al shever*, Jer. 4:20]." Yet the German original merely mentions that a new misfortune occurred ("nun ereignete sich ein neuer Zufall").[37] Again the translator expands the narrative through the associative method, adding biblical allusions.

When Bontekoe recalls that he let the sailors take shifts, the Hebrew dramatizes the scene by quoting his command to the sailors in direct speech:

> כה תעשון אחי, הייעפים והמוכים מן הריח ילכו אל האויר לשאוף רוח חדש ולהחליף כח ואחר ישובו לעבודתם למען יכבה האש.[38]

> Thus you will do, my brothers [*ko ta`asun aḥai*]: those who are tired and beaten down from the smell will go outside to breathe fresh air to regain their strength, and afterward they will return to their work in order to put out the fire.[39]

Campe's shift to first-person narrative challenges the Hebrew translator to match Captain Bontekoe's colloquial, vernacular style. The German also includes some direct speech, as when Bontekoe appeals to the second in command to throw the kegs of gunpowder overboard: "laßt uns das Pulver über Bord werfen!"[40] The Hebrew elaborates on when Bontekoe says,

> הנה כה עצתי, נשליכה את עפר השריפה (פולוויר) אל תוך הים פן נבא ח״ו לידי סכנה.[41]

> Here is my advice, we will throw the gun powder [*Pulver*] into the sea, lest we come into danger, God forbid.

The translator Judaizes the text by throwing in the words "God forbid" (*ḥas ve-shalom*, abbreviated *Ḥet"Vav*), which do not appear in the German source.

The subsequent passage describes the chaos that ensues as sailors begin to abandon ship. Again the Hebrew elaborates on the German, adding biblical language:

Die allgemeine Angst wuchs unterdeß mit jedem Augenblicke; denn man sähe nichts wie Feuer und Wasser vor sich, und keine Hofnung, sich zu retten. Das Schifsvolk fing an, sich auf die Seite zu machen, ließ sich	בכל רגע רבתה **תאניה ואניה** נפל **עליהם אימתה ופחד** עד כי נמסך בם רוח עועים, לא הופנו איש אל אחיו מרפיון ידים לא ידעו אנה ילכו ואנה מזה יברחו, אם ימלטו באניה הנה האש ואם יחבאו בקרקע הים יראו פן יכללו בעופרת <יצללו כעופר' 1823>, **וימס לבבם** רבים מהם נשמטו אחד אחד שטו העם

vom Schiffe hinab und schwamm nach der Schaluppe oder nach dem Boote.[42]

כאשר יפרש השוחה לשחות אל השאלופע או אל הבאאט, כי ראו **כי באש ה׳ נשפט** עמם ויאמרו נברח מן האש אל המים, אולי **יחביאנו צל ידו** כאשר יאמרו המושלים, אם ראית שונאך מתגרים איש ברעהו במלחמה מלא שחוק פיך כי אם יקום האחד למוליך להפילך, השני יהיה בעוזריך.[43]

Meanwhile, the general anxiety increased; for one saw nothing ahead but fire and water, and no hope of saving oneself. The ship's crew began to make off to the side, let themselves down from the ship, and swam to the sloop or the lifeboat.

Every moment the **moaning and groaning** [Is. 29:2, Lam. 2:5] increased. **Terror and fear fell upon them** [Ex. 15:16], and **a spirit of dizziness** [Is. 19:14; hapax legomenon]. No one turned to his brother; in exhaustion, they did not know where to go and where to flee from this. If they fled on the ship, the fire is there; and if they hid below, the sea would find them, and they would sink like lead; **and their hearts melted** [Josh. 7:5]. . . . Many of them slipped off, one by one; they went off **as a swimmer spreads out his hands to swim** [Is. 25:11] to the sloop or to the lifeboat, for they saw that **they had been judged by / were contending with the fire of God** [Is. 66:16]. And they said, We will flee from the fire into the water; perhaps **the shadow of his hand will conceal us** [part of the Neila prayer], as the writers of parable say, if you see your enemies fighting against each other in a war, your mouth will be filled with laughter [echoing Ps. 126:2], because if one comes to strike you down, the other will come to your aid.

The Hebrew is an extensive elaboration, with strong biblical motifs and theological overtones. (The 1823 version places the last part of the addition in a footnote on page 12.) The final reference to a parable is a nod to midrashic authors with their use of parable (*mashal*). This shows an openness to features of Hebrew literature that are postbiblical (even if there are elements of parable in some biblical passages such as 2 Samuel 12). The Yiddish version stays far closer to the German, suggesting that whereas the translator of the Yiddish strove for literalness, the translator of the Hebrew had other ideological goals and literary methods.

The Hebrew translation also adds to the immediacy of the text in its portrayal of the merchant overseer, the supercargo Rollin. Campe's narrator uses indirect speech and the German subjunctive to convey dialogue in free indirect style;[44] the Hebrew transforms this into direct speech:

> ראלין צעק אליהם מה אתם עושים, ויען העם אותו קשות ויאמרו אליו, אם יקרה נפשך בעיניך **קום רד מהר** ובא אצלינו, אל השאלופע או אל הבאאט, ונמלטה כי האניה תשרף, **הטרם תדע כי אבדה** האניה, וימהר וירד אליהם, ויאמר להם, **אל נא אחי אל תרעו נא**, אל תעזבו את אדוניכם הקאפיטאן, <נעידה נא> חוסו נא ונקרא אותו · כי הוא הלא שומר ראשינו ומחמד עינינו **והיה לנו <לעניים> לעינים.**[45]

Rollin shouted to them, What are you doing? The people answered him harshly, saying to him, If your life is dear to you [lit. "If your soul has value in your eyes"], **come quickly and go down** [Deut. 9:12] and come with us into the sloop or the lifeboat. We're fleeing because the ship is going to burn up. **Don't you know yet that** the ship **is lost** [Ex. 10:7]? So he hurried and went down to them and said to them, **Please, my brothers, don't do evil** [Judges 19:23]—don't leave your master, the Captain; let us cross over and call him. For is he not our guardian, the delight of our eyes—**and he will be our eyes** [Num. 10:31].

Here the Hebrew version expands on the dialogue between the supercargo, Rollin, and the crew. Campe's German is succinct, saying that when Rollin saw sailors deserting ship, he "expressed his astonishment over this" (*seine Verwunderung darüber äußerte*). To this the sailors reply that "he could climb in with them" (*er möchte mit einsteigen*).[46] In Hebrew, Campe's third-person paraphrase becomes a directly quoted and expanded dialogue. The Hebrew author reimagines an exchange that could not parallel the third-person German passage because the German uses a grammatical form that did not exist in Hebrew. Furthermore, the author-translator inserts a number of direct biblical quotations, which sometimes give rise to comic juxtapositions. For example, when the sailors tell Rollin to "come quickly and go down," they are echoing God's words to Moses in Deuteronomy 9. When they continue, "Don't you know yet that the ship is lost?" they transform the words of Pharaoh's servants to Pharaoh, "Don't you know yet that Egypt is lost?" in Exodus 10. These instances of biblical *melitza* illustrate the way in which *maskilim* undermined the literalness of their translations and the mimetic effect of their narrative writing. The play of the Hebrew signifiers seems to take precedence over the representation of the worldly adventure.

At this climactic moment, the theological dimension assumes a greater role in the Hebrew text. On hearing that some sailors have abandoned ship in the sloop and lifeboat, the German version has Bontekoe say, "If they leave us, they won't come back again" ("wenn sie uns verlassen, so wollen sie nicht wiederkommen").[47] In the Hebrew, however, Bontekoe responds in a dignified phrase that employs typical biblical verb suffixes: "If they have left me, God will leave them" (אם הם עזבוני יעזבם ה').[48] When the ship the *New Horne* comes to its cataclysmic end (see figure 9), Bontekoe's original tone is pious, as quoted in Campe's German: "I reached my hands toward Heaven and cried: God, show me grace and mercy!" ("Ich rekte die Hände gen Himmel, und rief: Herr sey mir gnädig und barmherzig!").[49] In this moment when Bontekoe raises his hands in prayer, the Hebrew author is inspired to compose a new prayer. The first line in Hebrew follows the German: "With my hands stretched out to Heaven, I said: Oh, God, show me your compassion and kindness." Then the Hebrew author adds:

Avontuurlyke Reyſe. 9

ſſen-hoofden op ſtaken opgerecht / daer door zy (ſo wy bemerken konden) ne- 1619.
vielen en aenbaden / ſcheenen heel vreemd te weſen en ſonder gevoel van den
ren God. Den 9 dag dat wy daer gelegen hadden / 't volk als geſeyt friſ en
ſond weſende / kreegden wy ons ſchip op zy / ſo veer als wy konden / en maek-
't onder ſchoon / met verkens en ſchrobbers en gingen 't zeyl / liepen om de Z.
op de hoogte van 33 graden / wenden als doen weder Ooſtwaert over / en ſtelden
ſe cours doe na de Straet van Sunda toe / en gekomen zijnde op de hoogte van
f en een halve graed / zijnde de hoogte van de voorſz. Straet van Sunda , weſende
19 dag van November 1619 / ſoo is door 't pompen van Brandewijn de
nd in de Brandewijn gekomen / want de Botteliers-maet / ging na ouder
woonte / met zijn Vaetjes 's achtermiddaegs in 't Ruym / en ſoude dat vol
mpen / om alſo 's anderdaegs ſmorgens aen de Gaſten yder een half mutsje
t te deelen. Hy nam een keers mede / ſtak de ſteeker in de boom van een Vat /
t een laeg hoger lag als 't Vat daer hy uyt pompte. Zijn Vaetje vol gepompt
bbende / ſoude hy de ſteker daer de keers op ſtond uyt halen / en alſo hy die wat
ſt hadde geſteken / haelt hyſe met een force uyt / daer was een dief aen de keers /
e vielder doen af / en viel juyſt in de ſpond van het Vat / daer hy uyt gepompt
dde. Hier door ontſonkten de Brandewijn / en vloog terſtond op / tot 't Vat uyt /
booms borſten uyt het Vat / en de brandende Brandewijn liep beneden in het
chip daer de Smits-kolen lagen / ſtraks wierden 'er geroepen: brand! brand!

Het Schip raekt in brand.

Ik lag doen ter tijd op het Boevenet en keek door de tralien: dat gerugt hoo-
rende / liep datelijk beneden in het Ruym / daer komende / ſag geen brand :
vraegde /

Fig. 9. Explosion of the *New Horne*, from Willem Bontekoe, *Journaal ofte Gedenckwaardige Beschrijvinge van de Oost-Indische Reyse van Willem Ysbrantsz Bontekoe, van Hoorn* (Amsterdam: Brouwer, 1722). From the image on Google Books, which was scanned from the library of Aloysius College, the Hague.

ידעתי ה׳ כי ידך בכל משלה, בידיך, אם עת פקודת נפשי הגיע, אסוף נפשי אליך, בלהב האש, השמים אעלה, או אם במים אצלול, גם משם ידך תנחני אם למות אם לחיים.[50]

> I know, God, that Your hand is upon everything; it is in Your hands, whether the time for me to give up my soul has come, in the flaming fire, and I will rise to the heavens; or if I shall sink into the watery depths. Also from there, your hand will determine whether I shall die or live.

In this expanded account, Bontekoe's prayer concludes: "Show me, God, Your compassion, and bring me salvation. . . . I will recount Your name to my brothers, and I will praise you among the congregation."

הראיני ה׳ חסדיך וישעך תן לי, אם באתי באש ובמים, לרויה תוציאני, אספרה שמך לאחי בתוך קהל אהללך.[51]

The Hebrew version not only incorporates biblical references but also adds traditional Jewish piety to Bontekoe's language.

In the source text from 1646, Bontekoe wrote as a pious Christian; the equally pious Campe, in his 1788 retelling, followed Bontekoe's lead but with a greater emphasis on the benevolent guidance of Providence. When the captain and one other sailor survive the explosion that destroys their ship, Campe quotes Bontekoe saying to Hermann, "My son, here all hope is lost! It is becoming night; the sloop and the lifeboat are far from us; it is impossible for us to hold out all night. We must call to God and give ourselves over to His will."[52] Bontekoe and Campe see God's hand in a response to their prayer: "We began to pray, and—our pitiable prayer was heard! For we had scarcely finished with it, and the sloop and the lifeboar were nearby."[53] "We began to pray" is all that Campe's Bontekoe tells us, whereas the Hebrew translator spins out a full prayer that incorporates quotations from Proverbs and Psalms. The translator brings the petitionary prayer into the Judaic tradition by having Bontekoe say,

הלא טוב לנו, כי נשמע לקול אבותינו הקדמונים, דבר יצא מפיהם **כל אשר יקרא בשם ה׳ ימלט**, עינינו למרום נשאנו, ענינו ואמרנו אנא ה׳ **הצל לקוחים למות**, ועשה עמנו ככל נפלאותיך, כל דבר ממך לא יבצר, אם אחרנו עד כה לשחר פניך, הלא ידעת כי בשר אנחנו, אתה [עתה] הראנו חסדך, **ונשירה ונזמרה גבורתך**, לקול בכייתנו ועתירתינו רוחמנו מאת יוצר הכל, טרם כלינו להתחנן, והנה השאלופע והבאאט באו עדינו.[54]

> It is good for us to listen to the voice of our ancient ancestors, to a phrase they expressed: **Everyone who calls in the name of the Lord will escape** [Joel 3:5]. We raised our eyes above, concentrated, and we said: Please, God, **save those who are on their ways to death** [Prov. 24:11], perform all of your wonders with us; nothing is out of Your reach; if until now we have tarried in seeking You out, you know that we are just flesh; show us now your compassion, and **we shall sing and chant of Your might** [Ps. 21:14]. The Creator of all things had mercy on our cries and supplications. Before we had finished our pleas, behold, the sloop and the lifeboat came to us.

The Hebrew translator turns Campe's vague indication that "we began to pray" into a direct address to God that recalls the *seliḥot* prayers. The expanded Hebrew prayer combines faith in God's power with a plea for God's wondrous assistance and a promise of future prayers. Campe's version is more focused on accepting God's compassion while hoping that a prayer for His aid will succeed.

Campe's attention to matters of Providence (*Vorsehung* in German, literally "seeing ahead," based on the Latin compound *pro* + *videre*) continues in a later passage, when his narrator mentions that Providence helped the shipwrecked seafarers by sending "flying fish" for them to eat. Campe's phrase "it pleased Providence" (*es gefiel der Vorsehung*)[55] becomes a more traditional reference to the Jewish God in the Hebrew version:

> **ממכון שבתו ית׳ השגיח** עלינו, להראותינו כי ידו לא קצרה מהושיע.[56]

> **He watched over us from His dwelling place** [Ps. 33:14], may He be blessed, showing us that His hand was not too short, incapable of saving us [cp. Isa. 59:1].

Other passages that describe prayer follow this pattern. For example, in a later call to God, trying to stop his sailors from resorting to cannibalism, Campe's Bontekoe narrates and addresses his crew: "I called to God, that He should not allow our need to rise beyond what He knew we could bear. . . . Consider the inhumanity and the godlessness of what you are planning, and restrain yourselves! Call upon the almighty God; He will have mercy on you."[57] In Hebrew, Bontekoe addresses God directly and adds a rhetorical question taken from one of the minor prophets: "Did not a single God create us?" Then the turn to God is modified slightly from the beginning of Psalm 120:

> **אל ה׳ בצרתי לי קראתי** יצילינו מן הדבר הרע המר והנמהר הלז. . . . **הלא אל אחד בראנו**, קראו אליו בכל לבכם אולי יתעוררו רחמיו עלינו.[58]

> **Unto God, in my distress, I called** [Ps. 120:1]: Save us from this evil, bitter, rash thing. . . . **Did not a single God create us?** [Mal. 2:10]. Call to him with all your hearts; perhaps His compassion for us will be awakened.

The Hebrew develops the motif of calling out to God in a later passage, drawing again from the Psalms:

> **בלב נשבר ונדכה** קראתי אל ה׳ **מן המצר**, ישמור אותנו מבוא בדמים.[59]

> With a broken and oppressed heart I called to God, from difficult straits, that he should guard us from shedding blood.

The phrase "with a broken and oppressed heart" (*be-lev nishbar ve-nidke*), translating Campe's term *Verzweiflung*,[60] quotes from Psalm 51:19, and the words "from difficult straits I called to God" allude to Psalm 118:5.

What at first seems like a secular sea narrative turns out to be infused with religious sentiment and biblical quotations. Although Bontekoe's original account from 1646 includes many pious passages, no doubt influenced by his religious background, *Oniya so`ara* expands them, adds more, and incorporates many direct biblical quotations. The unknown author of the Hebrew *Oniya so`ara* was a worthy successor to the Berlin *maskilim* and Moses Mendelsohn-Frankfurt. But because this bilingual book was written for Yiddish speakers, it also expands the language to include Slavic components. The Hebrew translation reaches back for traditional quotations while also looking sideways at the relationship to Yiddish. With the help of Yiddish, Hebrew moves closer toward creating the illusion of being a spoken vernacular.

The next chapter explores one of the turning points in modern Hebrew literature. Mendel Lefin also injects biblical language into *Mase`ot* *ha-yam*, but to a far lesser extent than other maskilic authors of his time. By broadening Hebrew beyond biblical references and by limiting quotations, he took a giant step toward the creation of modern Hebrew writing. Following the teleology implied by this book, he simultaneously moved beyond pilgrimage and beyond scriptural language because a modernizing worldview required a modernized Hebrew.

7

Lefin

VOYAGES TO THE PACIFIC AND THE ARCTIC

In the early nineteenth century, British and German travel literature provided an essential source for innovative Hebrew narratives. As discussed in chapters 5 and 6, the works of J. H. Campe exerted a particularly strong influence on enlightened Hebrew authors in Moses Mendelssohn's circle. Mendel Lefin of Satanov, having lived among the *maskilim* in Berlin in the 1780s, shared their favorable opinion of Campe's works. Lefin advanced Hebrew literature with two compelling accounts of sea journeys based on Campe's multivolume series *Reisebeschreibungen* (Travel Descriptions).[1] *Mase`ot ha-yam* (Sea Voyages, 1818) is the culminating expression of early-modern Hebrew travel writing.[2] (See figure 10.)

Lefin's translated sea narratives have a fresh quality, contrasting sharply with most of the early maskilic writings. His approach to translation and limited use of scriptural quotations ran counter to the prevailing style of neobiblical *melitza*. Lefin was not the only writer at the time to draw from German; many *maskilim* admired and emulated Prussian sources. For instance, Mordechai Aaron Günzburg "saw the influence of German as a major factor in the expansion of Hebrew."[3] Günzburg acknowledged that his Hebrew was essentially translated from German, writing that "I conceive German ideas and clothe them in the purity of the Holy Tongue."[4] But Lefin advanced a step further in his far more compelling translations from Campe.

Lefin's translation of Campe's books led him toward a more varied Hebrew prose style: sophisticated yet unpretentious, based on Mishnaic Hebrew but also incorporating Aramaic, using Hebrew that was familiar

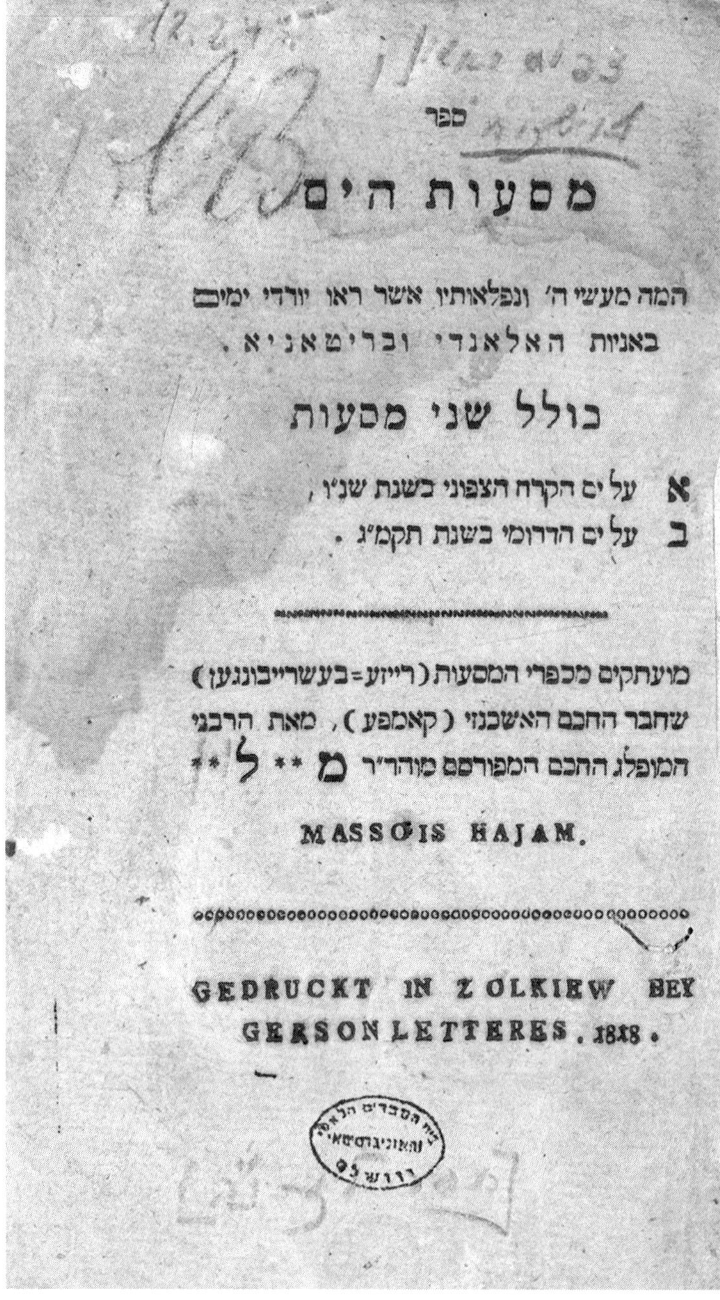

ספר

מסעות הים

המה מעשי ה' ונפלאותיו אשר ראו יורדי ימים
באניות האלאנדי' ובריטאניא .

כולל שני מסעות

א על ים הקרח הצפוני בשנת שנ"ו ,
ב על ים הדרומי בשנת תקמ"ג .

מועתקים מספרי המסעות (רייזע=בעשרייבונגען)
שחבר החכם האשכנזי (קאמפע) , מאת הרבני
המופלג החכם המפורסם מוהר"ר מ** ל**

MASSOIS HAJAM.

GEDRUCKT IN ZOLKIEW BEY
GERSON LETTERES. 1818.

Fig. 10. Title page of Mendel Lefin, trans., *Mase'ot ha-yam*, 1st ed. (Zholkva: Gerson Letteres, 1818). Reprinted by permission of the National Library of Israel, Jerusalem.

in Yiddish, and including German glosses where necessary. The sentences are direct, often simplifying the German syntax, and also employ the Vav consecutive (or "conversive," ו' ההיפוך) and hypotaxis.

Lefin in Literary History

Mendel Lefin (1749–1826) was a mentor to many leading authors and educators, including Joseph Perl, I. B. Levinsohn, Avraham Gotlober, Eliezer Tzvayfl, and Mordechai Suchostober. Nevertheless, few literary historians or general readers have recognized the high value of Lefin's narrative writings. His prose narratives have not been reprinted since the nineteenth century and have been neglected by scholars. Only his philosophical, ethical work *Ḥeshbon ha-nefesh* (Accounting of the Soul, 1808) is widely available because Israel Salanter reprinted and popularized it in connection with the Musar movement. Lefin was a linchpin, facilitating the emergence of modern Hebrew fiction through the mediation of travel narratives. Some scholars have admired Lefin's pathbreaking translations into modern Eastern Yiddish, but his translated Hebrew narratives remain relatively unknown.

In spite of the relative obscurity of Lefin's writings, a few critics have considered his work. Israel Zinberg writes that "Lefin very successfully employed the rich treasures of the clear, pithy Mishnaic Hebrew, and thereby his writing became fresh and vivid."[5] Yosef Klausner and a few other critics have recognized in Lefin an important Hebrew stylist who offered an alternative to maskilic *melitza*.[6] Uriel Ofek notes that "Lefin dared to undermine the attachment of his friends, the maskilim, to the 'pure' biblical style, and he created a flexible, narrative style that includes early and late linguistic layers."[7] By way of his friend Mordechai Suchostober, Lefin was a guardian spirit to Avraham Gotlober, S. Y. Abramovitsh, and the "revival" (*teḥiya*) of Hebrew literature at the end of the nineteenth century.[8]

Mase`ot ha-yam is a neglected masterpiece of early-modern Hebrew writing. Secular Hebrew narrative comes into its own with Lefin's translations from Campe's *Reisebeschreibungen*, which transport Hebrew readers to the Arctic and the Pacific, far beyond the traditional, Zion-centered world. Moreover, the process of translation helped Lefin limit his reliance on biblical quotations. Hence, *Mase'ot ha-yam* is a landmark, or watermark, of the modernization process for Hebrew literature. His language is flexible, moves beyond biblical allusions, includes Talmudic usages, and refracts his translations from German. Yet in *Mase'ot ha-yam* Lefin continues to assert the relevance of traditional religious ideas such as Divine Providence (*hashgaḥa 'Elohit*).[9]

Mase'ot ha-yam consists of two accounts, translated from volumes 1 and 9 of Campe's *Reisebeschreibungen*, describing the ill-fated voyages by Captains Jacob Heemskerk and Henry Wilson. With Willem Barents, Captain Heemskerk led the doomed expedition that searched for a Northeast Passage in 1592. While stranded in Nova Zembla (this is the Dutch spelling; the Russian name is "Novaya Zemlya") during the Arctic winter, his crew battled polar bears and overcame the cold by building a house made of timber taken from their boat. Some of Heemskerk's crew survived through heroic perseverance.[10] Nearly two centuries later, under vastly different conditions, Captain Wilson's boat was shipwrecked on the previously unknown Palau Islands, where the British met and admired the Pacific Islanders. (See figure 11.) Captain Wilson's story (written by George Keate) includes many anthropological details about the natives, showing the disparities between European culture and a completely dissimilar, aboriginal society.[11] Lefin sets up the Dutch and British sea travelers as models of worthy behavior, indicating in his unpublished introduction that he values their bravery, ingenuity, perseverance, and openness to foreign cultures.[12] Like Campe (who was influenced by Jean-Jacques Rousseau's educational ideas), Lefin seems to have admired the native islanders' values and unpretentious virtues.

Few Hebrew narratives written before 1820 are as compelling as the two travelers' tales in *Mase'ot ha-yam*. Lefin's style is direct and clear, with few ornaments or allusions. He improves the flow of Campe's texts by eliminating extraneous details and discussions. For instance, in one polemical digression from the story, Campe vehemently rejects the notion that a miracle saved the mariners; Lefin omits the passage, choosing to keep his book focused on the action.

Most of the Hebrew sea narratives already examined allude to Jonah, Psalms, and other biblical sources. In contrast, Lefin streamlines the text,

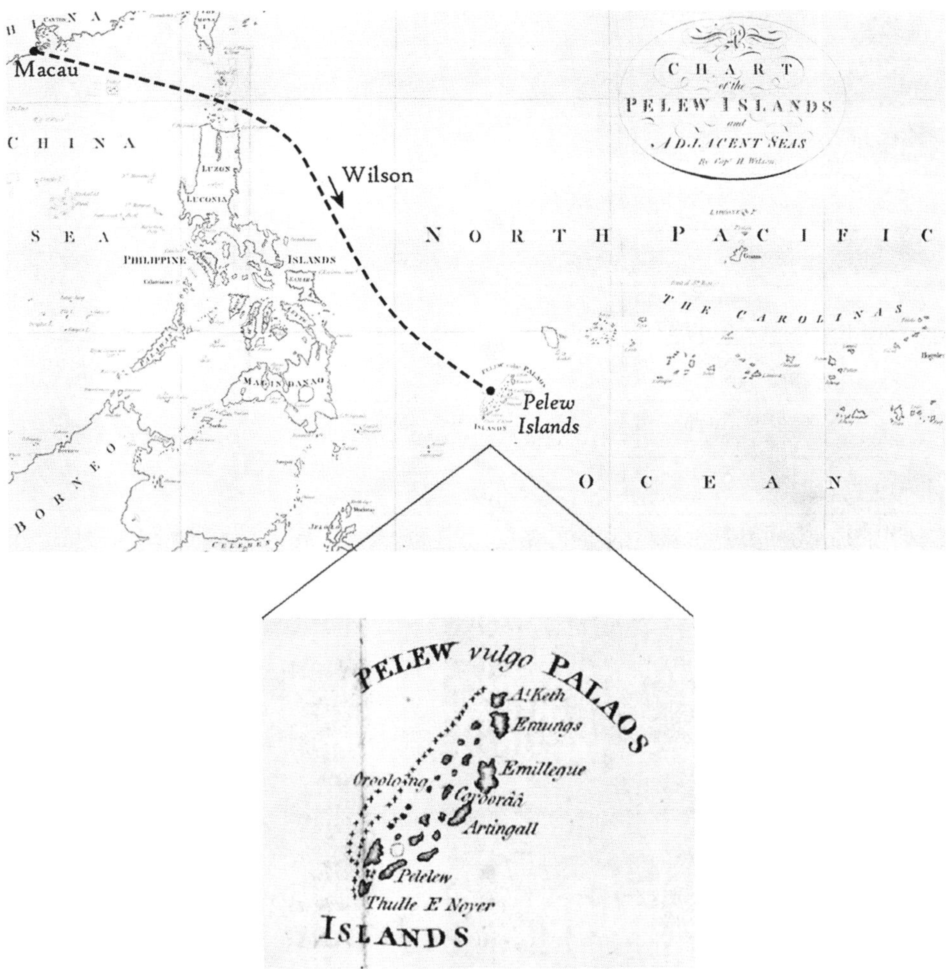

Fig. 11. *Chart of the Pelew Islands and Adjacent Seas*, and detail, from George Keate [and Henry Wilson], *An Account of the Pelew Islands, Situated in the Western Part of the Pacific Ocean*, 2nd ed. (London: Nicol, 1788), with Captain Wilson's approximate route added by Joseph Stoll, Syracuse University Cartographic Laboratory, in collaboration with Ken Frieden. Original map courtesy of the British Library, © The British Library Board, W.7164 Map of Pelew Islands.

works for vivid translation, generally avoids quotations from Hebrew sources, and creates a sharp-edged naturalism. In translating from two of Campe's *Reisebeschreibungen*, he omits almost all of Campe's moralistic commentary and many of his long explanations; he deletes unnecessary minutiae and relegates some of the anthropological material to the last two chapters of the book. *Mase`ot ha-yam* is less obviously pious than *Oniya so`ara*, but Lefin's adaptations do not lack a religious dimension. Where Campe emphasizes the role of a benevolent Providence, for example, Lefin usually changes the wording to refer instead to God. Although Lefin expresses some traditional Jewish attitudes, he minimizes biblical allusions and, drawing inspiration from the act of translation, creates an original Hebrew style.

In short, *Mase`ot ha-yam* contains two of the earliest modern narratives in Hebrew. Some readers may object to this judgment because the two stories are translations—or, more precisely, Hebrew adaptations of Campe's German versions of English and Dutch narratives. That provenance does not, however, diminish their place in literary history; regardless of origins, they are important works because of their unusual and effective Hebrew style. Lefin's originality lies in the unique power of his Hebrew writing. He is an important precursor of modern Hebrew writing and one of the most neglected. Where the hasidim often translated from Yiddish, Lefin translated from German, his fifth language after Yiddish, Hebrew, Polish, and French. Aware of Hebrew usages that had been shaped by Yiddish, Lefin avoided obvious calques from Yiddish phrases. He heightened the illusion of Hebrew as a living language by adding dialogue in place of third-person narrative.

Lefin uses a more biblical literary syntax than did the hasidim; in particular, he uses the Vav consecutive when describing a sequence of past events. This construction creates a hypotactic style, using more elaborate, complex sentences. Following ancient biblical norms, Lefin adds to the literary compression with compounded words (noun + pronoun suffix) such as *sefinatam* (their boat) or verb formations (including verb and direct object), such as *ve-yeḥabekum* (and they embraced them) and *ve-yenashekem* (and they kissed them).[13]

Whereas the Berlin Hebrew writers restricted their vocabulary by striving for supposedly "pure" biblical expression, Lefin did not strive for a questionable purity of biblical language; he instead drew from various historical layers of Hebrew usage. He expanded his active vocabulary by including postbiblical Hebrew and Aramaic, which were familiar to readers from Yiddish and from Talmudic study. He anticipated the synthetic approach that was later associated with "Mendele's *nusaḥ*." For example, he appropriately quotes from the Talmud to say that "the laughter did not leave the lips of the King" (לא פסקה חוכא מפומיה דמלכא).[14] In this way, Lefin pushed beyond the arbitrary limits set by the early *maskilim* in Berlin. Earlier *maskilim* generally used Aramaic when they wanted to mock pious characters. This trend is illustrated in Aharon Wolfsohn of Halle's play *Kalut da`at u-tzevi`ut* (Frivolity and False Piety, ca. 1794–96) and Joseph Perl's epistolary novel *Megale temirin* (Revealer of Secrets, 1819): the shift to Aramaic occurs primarily when corrupt rabbis are being satirized and their language parodied.[15] In contrast, Lefin takes a more positive approach to postbiblical Hebrew and includes some Hebrew usages that derived from Yiddish, such as the word *simḥa* to mean "a celebration."[16]

It would be possible to compile a long list of Lefin's Hebrew novelties, many of them based on Yiddish usages of Hebrew lexical items and Aramaic words. Whereas Lefin's friend Joseph Perl mocked the use of Yiddish-inflected Hebrew expressions by hasidim, Lefin was more tolerant and often used words in a postbiblical sense. *Mase`ot ha-yam* includes such terms as *mamesh* (really or precisely; as pronounced in Israel today, *mamash*); *bikhdei* (in order that); and *mistoma* (Aramaic, which derives from the Hebrew term *min ha-stam*, "probably," but Lefin embraces the later Talmudic and Yiddish usage).[17] In each of these cases, the postbiblical usage had been popularized in Yiddish and deemed suitable by Lefin. Another example is *shema*, which occurs frequently in the Talmud and which is also used in Yiddish to mean "lest."[18] Because Lefin is rarely included in the modern Hebrew canon, prominent lexicographers link the modern usage of *shema* to Bialik (Even-Shoshan) or Hazaz (Kena`ni). But the word occurs five times in *Mase`ot ha-yam*. Or consider the word אלא (only, but, except), which occurs about ninety-five times in *Mase`ot ha-yam* but never in *Oniya so'ara*. Aramaic words and phrases used by Lefin in *Mase'ot ha-yam* include אמבטיא (*'ambatia*, "bath"), חדא (*ḥada*, "one"), בעינא פקיחא (*be-'eina pekiḥa*, "with a sharp eye"), טינא (*tina*, "hatred"), דייסא (*daisa*, "porridge"), מלתא (*milta*, "word"), and פורתא (*purta*, "portion"). Lefin comfortably uses Talmudic words that derive from Greek, such as מטרפולין (*metropolin*) for "city," הדיוטות (*hediotot*) for "simple people," and אונקלאות (*'onkla'ot*) for "hooks"; one also finds the postbiblical term מתורגמן (*meturgeman)* for "translator" or "interpreter." Lefin sardonically asks in the afterword to his retranslation of Maimonides's work *Morei nevukhim* (Guide to the Perplexed), which he rendered in Mishnaic style, "Who authorized the young among proofreaders to shackle the making of blessings and prayers in the chains of biblical grammar?"[19] In his own unpretentious way, Lefin was an influential innovator.

Rewriting the Tradition

Lefin's original Hebrew style included a distinctive approach to biblical references. Nancy Sinkoff notes the use of quotations or paraphrases from Psalm 107 on the title page of *Mase'ot ha-yam* in three different editions: 1818, 1823 (printed together with *Oniya so'ara*), and 1859. She interprets them as containing a "covert message": "On the one hand, Lefin's use of the psalm as an introduction to his translation served to make the work more palatable to a traditional audience; its simple meaning suited the contents of the story well. But his choice was not merely literary; the decision to use this particular proof-text was part of his larger campaign against the mystification of traditional rabbinic Judaism."[20] Sinkoff explains that Lefin opposed an allegorical, mystical reading of Psalm 107 that was popular among hasidic readers of his time. Based on a work that was attributed to the Ba'al Shem Tov, *Sefer katan: pirush 'al Hodu* (1805, 1816),[21] the allegorical reading generalized beyond the concrete scene described in the Psalm. Noting that the kabbalistic, hasidic reading of Psalm 107 was known to *maskilim* such as Joseph Perl, Sinkoff argues that Lefin "deliberately appropriated verses 23–4 for his own purposes: by using the psalm and its paraphrase to open *Masaot hayam*, he was attempting to uproot the biblical text from the mystical matrix into which hasidism had placed it." Hence, Sinkoff writes that Lefin, unlike the hasidim, "read the psalm literally."[22]

This difference of interpretation divides hasidic from maskilic travel narratives. Especially in Nahman's fantasy tales, discussed in chapter 3, mundane travel is only the surface meaning. Such narratives are dominated by an allegorical level of meaning that involves a kabbalistic drama of spiritual life and redemption. The hagiographic accounts in *Shivḥei ha-Besht* and *Shivḥei ha-Ran* also tend to idealize and allegorize everyday events in the hasidic leaders' lives. By contrast, maskilic authors sought to represent the concreteness of actual travels. Describing scenes with greater immediacy, the *maskilim* differentiated their work from what they saw as hasidic mystifications.

The title page of *Mase`ot ha-yam* reflects Lefin's original approach in 1818, moving effectively beyond the reliance on exact biblical quotations. But the late edition printed in 1859 gives as an epigraph the frequently cited verses from Psalm 107:23–24:

> יוֹרְדֵי הַיָּם בָּאֳנִיּוֹת עֹשֵׂי מְלָאכָה בְּמַיִם רַבִּים׃
> הֵמָּה רָאוּ מַעֲשֵׂי יְהוָה וְנִפְלְאוֹתָיו בִּמְצוּלָה׃

> 23. Those who go down to the sea in ships, making it their trade in vast seas,
> 24. They have seen God's works and His wonders in the depths.

The publisher of the 1859 edition, by returning to an exact quotation of biblical verses, misconstrues Lefin's approach. The original 1818 edition follows a subtler method, paraphrasing these verses in prose and transforming them. After the title *Mase`ot ha-yam* (Sea Voyages), the title page announces:

> המה מעשי ה׳ ונפלאותיו אשר ראו יורדי ימים באניות האלאנדי ובריטאניא.

> These are tales of God and His wonders, which were seen by those who go down to the seas in ships from Holland and Britain.

This sentence recycles and alters the biblical language, retaining the mention of God but moving in a concrete, worldly direction by referring to Dutch and British ships. Similarly, early in the narrative when "the sky became dark with clouds," Lefin rephrases words from 1 Kings 18:45. The biblical passage reads:

וַיְהִי עַד־כֹּה וְעַד־כֹּה וְהַשָּׁמַיִם הִתְקַדְּרוּ עָבִים.

Meanwhile the sky darkened with clouds . . .

As noted in chapter 5, using the technique known as *shibbutz*, Moses Mendelsohn-Frankfurt often inserts biblical verses without modifying them; this biblical verse appears unaltered in *Metziat ha-aretz ha-ḥadasha.*[23] In contrast, Lefin alludes to the same source but transforms the verse into an original phrase:

בתוך שעה מועטת התקדרו השמים בעבים חשוכים.[24]

In a short while, the sky was obscured by dark clouds.

Without fanfare, Lefin pushes aside the maskilic penchant for unoriginal, inlaid biblical *melitza*. He changes the entire procedure and effect when he echoes biblical language while remaking it. Isaac Euchel seems to have anticipated a flexible approach to biblical citations in some narrative passages of his work, but Lefin takes that approach further.

With reference to Psalm 107, Sinkoff describes part of the ideological battle surrounding sea narratives in Hebrew. As mentioned, the hasidim often followed a kabbalistic interpretation of the Psalm; according to Sinkoff's paraphrase, based on works by Rivka Schatz-Uffenheimer, Isaiah Tishby, and Joseph Dan, "the mystical interpretation of verses 23–6 glosses the verbs 'descend' and 'ascend' in the psalm to address the dilemma faced by human souls inextricably mired in sin."[25] Sinkoff argues that the *maskilim* rejected this interpretive tradition, as is indicated by a parodic passage written by Joseph Perl, which she quotes: "In my limited opinion, it seems that the interpretation of 'they ascend to the Heavens, they go down again to the depths' (Psalm 107:26) is that sometimes the *tsadik* descends to *katnut* . . . in order to raise up the evil ones."[26] Paraphrasing the mystical interpretation of Psalm 107, Perl mocks one hasidic idea—especially familiar from Nahman's teachings—among many others that he attacks in *Megale temirin*. Sinkoff stresses the maskilic rejection of hasidic commentary: "While the Ba`al Shem Tov and his disciples used the psalm to encode the biblical text with the religious significance specific to hasidism and its leaders, Lefin cast it as an invitation for traditional Jews to gain a broader appreciation of the non-Jewish world, which he believed shared with them such fundamental beliefs as the concept of divine Providence. He read the psalm literally, that is as a *pashtan*, using its lyrical biblical poetry to introduce his translations of two treacherous sea-journeys."[27] In short, the hasidic tendency was to allegorize the psalm,[28] whereas Lefin literalized its metaphor of sea travel in *Mase`ot ha-yam*. Sinkoff discusses the introduction that Lefin wrote to *Mase`ot ha-yam*, which was not published until 2009: "Lefin informs his readers that he intended his translation to remind those who had fallen into dire straits, like the sailors of Campe's tales, of God's eternal vigilance."[29] This is, however, only part of the story. Lefin emphasizes Divine Providence in his sea narratives but also stresses the importance of human ingenuity. As Sinkoff observes, one of Lefin's key words is *taḥbula*—a strategy, stratagem, ruse, or tactic. A conspicuous element of these travel narratives is the ingenuity of the sailors who survive shipwreck. Lefin conceived reading these tales of adversity as the best possible way to prepare oneself for the inevitable misfortunes of life. As he emphasizes in the unpublished introduction to his translation, "Whoever does not educate himself to gird up his loins in the days of his tranquility does not have in him the strength to withstand a trial on a bad day."[30]

Lefin's Life and Works

Lefin was born in 1749 in Satanov, Russia. He may have been influenced by his elder townsman Isaac Satanov,[31] a prolific Hebrew writer and leading literary presence in Berlin who played a major role in the publishing house Ḥevrat ḥinukh ne`arim (associated with the Jewish Free School). Although it is difficult to characterize Satanov's multifaceted literary output, he was open to Mishnaic Hebrew and experimented with different Hebrew styles.[32] Directly or indirectly, he presumably encouraged Lefin's use of postbiblical Hebrew. Hillel Levine states that "while the Berlin Maskilim who wrote in Hebrew sought to imitate Biblical prose, Isaac Satanov turned to rabbinic Hebrew. Lefin too would appropriate rabbinic Hebrew because it was most understandable to the Jews that he wanted to reach as much as for aesthetic reasons."[33]

Lefin was deeply influenced by Moses Mendelssohn and his circle around the years 1780–84, when he lived in Berlin, though by the time he left Berlin, he was critical of the rising assimilation and antitraditionalism. At Mendelssohn's suggestion, Lefin translated S. A. Tissot's popular French medical handbook *Avis au peuple sur sa santé* (mainly from the German edition). When Lefin published his Hebrew adaptation under the title *Refu'ot ha-`am* (Remedies for the People) in 1789,[34] it included an approbation by Mendelssohn (apparently written shortly before his death) and was a popular success.

Lefin left Berlin in about 1784 and lived in Mikolayev (then in Russia, now located in western Ukraine). Early in the nineteenth century, after his wife died, he moved to Brody and then to Tarnopol, where he remained in close contact with Joseph Perl. Between 1809 and 1815, the Tarnopol region was in transition: as a consequence of the Napoleonic Wars, it was temporarily under Russian rule before being returned to Austria. During this period, Perl consulted with Lefin while establishing his Jewish school, which was based on the Berlin model.[35] Perl was deeply influenced by Lefin's Hebrew writing and is now remembered for his epistolary novel *Megale temirin*, which parodies the Hebrew style of hasidic authors.[36] Perl also emulated the pedagogues associated with the Berlin Jüdische Freischule by publishing books at the Tarnopol school—in particular, Lefin's translation of the Book of Proverbs (1814) and several annual calendars that collected Hebrew reading materials, called *Luaḥ ha-lev*.[37]

In 1808, Lefin published his philosophical, ethical work *Ḥeshbon ha-nefesh* (Moral Accounting or A Reckoning for the Soul), which achieved wider recognition after Israel Salanter (1810–83) reissued it for use by members of the Musar movement in 1844.[38] Despite Lefin's connections to the Berlin Enlightenment, his teachings were acceptable to Salanter, whose Lithuanian movement emphasized ethical conduct. In scholarly opinion, the importance of this book has been somewhat eclipsed by its association with the Musar movement, by the fact that only one copy of the first (1808) edition is extant, and by its direct borrowing from the method of self-improvement outlined in Benjamin Franklin's *Autobiography*, which Lefin appears to have read in French after the second volume was published in 1798.[39] Based on its fresh Hebrew style and clarity of thought, *Ḥeshbon ha-nefesh* merits a full-length study.

In his final years, Lefin focused his attention on a modern Hebrew translation of Maimonides's text *Guide to the Perplexed*, part of which was published posthumously. Although translation and adaptation were Lefin's primary literary modes, his satiric work "Der ershter khosid" (The First Hasid; in Hebrew "Maḥkimat peti," or Making the Fool Wise) at one point existed in manuscript.[40]

Lefin possessed remarkable linguistic and literary talent. His traditional Jewish education had given him a command of Hebrew and Aramaic, and during his years in Berlin he had improved his German. It is not clear how he learned French well enough to draft his early political reformist work "Essai d'un plan de réforme ayant pour objet d'éclairer la nation Juive en Pologne et de redresser par là ses mœurs" (1792),[41] although it is certain that Count Adam Kazimierz Czartoryski (1734–1823), who became his benefactor, played a role in this effort.[42] It is also possible that Czartoryski influenced Lefin's later decision to translate Campe.[43]

Avraham Gotlober tells a story of how Lefin came to the attention of Prince Czartoryski. At the time, Lefin was living in Mikolayev, which was inhabited by impoverished Jews who tried to support themselves as merchants:

> In one of these stores sat the wife of Mendel Lefin selling pots and pans. When the Prince and his companion passed this woman's store, he saw a large German book lying on her table. The Prince approached and saw that it was Wolf's mathematics, which was praised and exalted in those days. The Prince was astonished and asked the Jewish woman: "Whose book is this?" She answered: My husband studies it day and night, and sometimes when he comes to me here, he can't part from this book and brings it with him to the store, to study it here. The Prince said: Where is your husband? Hurry and call him so that I can make his acquaintance. Mendel Lefin came and stood before the Prince and his companion—though Mendel Lefin was neither handsome nor well-dressed; his face was covered with blemishes from smallpox. When he opened his mouth to speak, however, there came over him splendor, magnificence, and a spirit of knowledge; wisdom and intelligence hovered over his

> lips, which were full of grace. The Prince spoke with him and heard his great wisdom, and he also became aware that he had been a student and friend of the great scholar Moses Mendelssohn—who had already become famous among the honored wise men of Germany, and whom the Prince respected and exalted. From that time on until the end of his life, he gave Mendel Lefin what he needed to support his household, from the treasury of Count Czartoryski. He also received a monthly supply of wine and beer, until there was more than enough, and his wife sold the extra wine and beer. From the treasury he gave him a gold coin for expenses, in perpetuity; Mendel Lefin saved this money and, in a time of need, he gave it to the poor.[44]

This apocryphal account should be read with a measure of skepticism, but it draws attention to an important line of influence from Lefin to Mordechai Suchostober and Avraham Gotlober at the Zhitomir Rabbinical Seminary, which resulted in Lefin's indirect influence on Gotlober's pupil and friend S. Y. Abramovitsh. This lineage is also attested by the passing along of the manuscript of Lefin's Maimonides translation to Suchostober.[45]

As discussed in chapter 5, in 1779–80 Campe published an adaptation of Daniel Defoe's novel *Robinson Crusoe*, titling it *Robinson der Jüngere* (*Robinson the Younger*), which was very popular and was translated into many languages, including Hebrew. The most frequently translated work by Campe was *Die Entdeckung von Amerika* in three volumes (1781–82), as discussed in connection with Mendelsohn-Frankfurt's translation. Like his other works, Campe's twelve-volume work *Sammlung interessanter und durchgängig zweckmäßig abgefaßter Reisebeschreibungen für die Jugend* (Collection of Interesting and Always Purposefully Composed Travel Descriptions for the Young, 1786–93) is openly didactic. To promote the social and educational ideals of the Philanthropist movement, Campe sought to sway the German youth after commanding their attention with adventure stories.

Campe's work had been translated into Hebrew as early as in 1807, and thus Lefin clearly did not innovate in choosing to translate Campe. Campe knew Moses Mendelssohn and directly influenced the Haskala; Lefin almost certainly read Campe's early works in the 1780s, while he was in Berlin, and continued to follow Campe's later output. Volume 8 of Campe's *Reisebeschreibungen* is his *Briefe aus Paris zur Zeit der Revolution* (Letters from Paris at the Time of the Revolution).[46]

In his introduction to volume 9 of the *Reisebeschreibungen*, Campe explains what he understands as the message of Captain Wilson's travel narrative, as rendered by George Keate (1729–97). The encounter with Pacific Islanders in Palau—about six hundred miles east of the Philippines—becomes the basis for both an ethnographic adventure and a reflection on the so-called noble savage.[47] As one critic notes, "Keate's *Account* is the most thoroughgoing and elaborate presentation of the noble savage in the literature of the South Seas."[48] But Campe takes the British source one step further: a comparison to the original volume shows that Campe expanded the description of the people of Palau as "noble savages." In his introduction, for instance, he writes that the natives' behavior "appears to justify completely our highest notions of the original goodness of human nature." Moreover, it teaches that education is not necessarily at odds with virtuous simplicity. Campe states explicitly that this example supports the social goal of educating members of the lower classes.[49]

The Ideology behind Lefin's Adaptation of Campe

When Lefin translated Campe's texts, he kept to a simple, direct approach. Apart from the linguistic innovations, he effectively edited Campe's work, focusing on events and omitting many pedantic passages. He expressed his theological perspective in his unpublished introduction to *Mase'ot ha-yam* (see the appendix to this chapter), which was found in the Joseph Perl Archives at the National Library of Israel in Jerusalem; it is not known why this introduction was not published along with the two narratives. The introduction reflects Lefin's sophisticated literary and philosophical voice when he was not translating; he quotes so extensively from Hebrew and Aramaic sources that his erudition overwhelms the reader. It may be that an editor, or Lefin himself, deemed this introduction too difficult for the intended audience, which could explain why it was not published. The allusive, discursive introduction is completely unlike his sea narratives, which minimize quotations in favor of a concrete, descriptive translation-adaptation. The comparison suggests that translating from a source such as Campe's travel narratives provided concrete details and posed challenges that improved Lefin's writing.

The unpublished introduction to *Mase`ot ha-yam* is revealing in many respects. Lefin's piety may surprise readers who expect something else based on the reputation of the *maskilim* as reformers who criticized traditional Jewish practices. The opening paragraph combines an insistence on human diligence with a belief in Divine Providence:

> לעולם אל ימתין אדם שתשתנה הטבע בשבילו ע״י נס מבורר, ואל יתייאש אפי׳ [אפילו] כשהחרב מונחת על צווארו. אלא יעסוק בתחבולה ועבודה תמיד.[50]

> A person should never expect that nature will change for him by means of a *clear miracle*, and a person should not despair when the sword hangs over his head;[51] instead he should prepare a plan, pray, and work always [*ye-`asok be-taḥbula ve-`avoda tamid*].

The opposition to miracles is compatible with Lefin's rationalistic rejection of the hasidic movement.[52] Just a few years earlier, the collection *Shivḥei ha-Besht* had popularized many stories of the Ba`al Shem Tov's miracle cures. Although Lefin opposed belief in miracles, he did believe in God's Providence. Nevertheless, he emphasized the human obligation to "prepare a plan, pray, and work always," which formed his distinctive ideological position. Between the lines of his translated and adapted travel narratives, Lefin conveyed his conviction that even pious Jews need to take their fate into their own hands. This moralistic attitude was attractive to Israel Salanter, who based his Musar movement in part on Lefin's discursive writing.

Lefin's unpublished introduction expresses another purpose of his book. Although he urges self-reliance, he also encourages readers to appreciate God's benevolent guidance: "the person who has fallen into danger and been saved is obliged to give thanks and publicly tell of God's salvation, in order to teach them morality and faith in God, praised be He, in times of trouble."[53] Jewish tradition has established a specific prayer, the *Birkat ha-gomel*, for such occasions when a person has survived a life-threatening experience (such as sea travel). Beyond formulaic expressions of piety, the two narratives contained in *Mase`ot ha-yam* indirectly give thanks through Heemskerk's and Wilson's narratives of shipwreck and survival. From an even more pragmatic, stoical point of view, Lefin suggests that reading these tales will help people deal with future adversity:

> Whoever does not educate himself to gird up his loins in the days of his tranquility, does not have in him the strength to withstand a trial on a bad day: But he will lose his strength immediately, from the beginning, sit idle, and question God's ways, blessed be He; he gives himself up to wailing and curses and is lost in his wickedness, God forbid: For the good of our brethren, the Children of Israel, these [*Sea*] *Voyages* have now been translated into our language, in order to awaken the soul of the reader to train himself in this precious quality: In order that he will see from this to what lengths the force of perseverance and wisdom go—foreseeing the consequences [B. Tamid 32a] with which God has graced human beings—toward withstanding tremendous and enduring dangers, of cold and heat and hunger, thirst, wild animals, bandits, and severe illnesses.[54]

One of Lefin's stated motives for publishing *Mase`ot ha-yam*, then, is to prepare people to endure hardships without losing faith. This theme returns in the translation itself, when surviving adversity becomes a central motif, and both Campe and Lefin praise Captain Wilson. (See figure 12). When the shipwreck occurs, Wilson makes a speech to his crew emphasizing that to survive they will need all of their presence of mind (*Besonnenheit*) and strength: "you will be awakened to devote yourselves with all of your strength and strategy" (תתעוררו למסור נפשכם בכל עוז ותחבולה). In Lefin's version, based on Campe's translation of Keate's account, Wilson states that they should also renounce hard liquor.[55] This accords with the maskilic emphasis on intellect and scorn for individuals and groups (like the hasidim, according to a widespread stereotype) who indulged in alcoholic drinks to excess. Here and elsewhere, Lefin uses one of his favorite words, *taḥbula* (strategy), to indicate rational planning. In sum, the account celebrates the triumph of reason over almost impossible difficulties.

Lefin's introduction, in the midst of many biblical and Talmudic quotations, inserts a universalistic message drawn from the medieval

Fig. 12. Portrait of Captain Henry Wilson, from the frontispiece to Keate [and Wilson], *An Account of the Pelew Islands*, 1788 ed. Image from Google Books.

commentary *Eliahu Raba*, chapter 10: "Whether Gentile or Jew, whether slave or servant, the holy spirit rests on him in accordance with his deeds." Later, when retelling the exemplary conduct of the ordinary British sailors who survive shipwreck, Lefin prepares his readers for setbacks, emphasizing the virtues of "perseverance and wisdom."[56]

Lefin's message about enduring adversity merits further discussion. He had experienced a difficult life: he suffered from an eye ailment; he and his wife had no children; and his wife died long before he did. Apparently the stories of shipwreck gave him strength, encouraging him to come to terms with his own problems. His stoical worldview was characterized by the saying in Ecclesiastes 7:2: "It is better to go to a house of mourning than a house of feasting." He quotes this passage in the introduction (line 23) and seems to have lived accordingly.

Lefin's introduction is also significant on the literary level. It is extraordinarily erudite, with numerous quotations and allusions from traditional sources. But whereas the Berlin *maskilim* favored biblical inlays, Lefin included Talmudic and medieval references, which were more typical of rabbinic commentaries. This inclusiveness helped forge a modern Hebrew style that did not depend on biblical epigonism.

The introduction provides a clue to the success of *Mase`ot ha-yam*. When Lefin penned his introduction, he allowed full scope to his scholarly bent, resulting in a complex text that is difficult to follow. Translation took Lefin in a completely different direction, however, as he tried to parallel the original German while omitting Campe's excesses. Very rarely does he interpolate a quotation or allusion. One exception to this occurs in the first paragraph of Lefin's version, when—as in almost every Hebrew description of a storm at sea and as in the Book of Jonah—"the ship was on the verge of breaking up" (*ha-oniya ḥishva lehishaver*).

The contrast between the style of Lefin's introduction and the style of his translation shows how the task of translation contributed to the effectiveness of his Hebrew. Lefin's unusually clear style in *Mase`ot ha-yam* is the result of translation from German, whereas the erudite allusions in the introduction render his style opaque. In contrast to typical maskilic *shibbutz*, where biblical allusions and quotations predominate, a matrix of postbiblical literary relationships sometimes lies behind Lefin's writing. The connection between his opening sentence and traditional commentaries brings out another dimension of the unpublished text.

As mentioned earlier, Lefin's phrase "a person should not despair when the sword hangs over his neck" (אל יתייאש אפי׳ [אפילו] כשהחרב מונחת על צווארו) echoes traditional commentaries. The basic prooftext is in the Babylonian Talmud:[57]

> אפילו חרב חדה מונחת על צוארו של אדם אל ימנע עצמו מן הרחמים. (Berakhot 10a)
>
> Even if a sharp sword hangs over a person's neck, he should not give up on [God's] mercy.

Quoting the exact phrase in Berakhot while commenting on Genesis 18:22 (and probably alluding to the binding of Isaac in Genesis 22), Seforno wrote:

> אפ׳ חרב חדה מונחת על צוארו של אדם אל ימנע עצמו מן הרחמים.

Lefin's use of the phrase *'al yitya'esh* (should not depair) instead of *'al yimn'a 'atzmo* (should not give up on) can be traced to Rabbi Yona Gerondi's commentary on Proverbs 14:32, in which he writes, אפי׳ חרב מונחת בצוארו של אדם אל יתיאש מן הרחמים (Even if a sword hangs over a person's neck, he should not despair of [God's] mercy).[58] The most striking precursor of Lefin's text, however, is a passage in Baḥye's Torah commentary, which includes the two key phrases and refers to Psalm 107:

> וצריך אתה לדעת כי כח התפלה גדול אפילו לשנות הטבע. . . . אפילו חרב מונחת על צוארו של אדם אל ימנע עצמו מן הרחמים.[59]

> And you must know that the power of prayer is so great that it can even change nature. . . . Even if the sword is hanging over his neck, he should not deny himself [God's] mercy. (Commentary on Deuteronomy 11:13)

Lefin directly contradicted one aspect of this line of commentary, saying that people should *not* expect to be able to change nature by means of prayer. Although he accepts the notion of Divine Providence, he also has faith in modern science and human ingenuity and rejects the supernatural powers that are sometimes associated with prayer. The belief in the efficacy of petitionary prayer is an example of the antiscientific, mystical thinking that became common in hasidic circles, a way of thinking that Lefin opposed. His unpublished introduction to *Mase'ot ha-yam* therefore asserts that "a person should never expect nature to change for him by means of a *clear miracle*" and should rely on planning or tactics "when the sword hangs over his neck" (lines 1–2). Although Lefin echoes a line of Gemara and medieval commentaries, he transforms his sources to create a new meaning.[60] This rejection of the hasidic belief in miracles was already present in "Essai d'un plan de réforme" (1792), where Lefin attacked members of the "new sect" for their faith in miracles performed by their leaders.[61]

Setting Sail

Lefin's translation from Campe, published without any introduction, quickly enters stormy waters: "In the year 1783 in the month of Sivan, Captain Wilson—of the boat *Antelope*, loaded with about six hundred thousand pounds [of cargo], and with a crew of about fifty men, including sixteen from the people of China—came to the city of Macao, and after three weeks they were ordered to return from there to his country, the land of England, by means of the South Sea. Immediately, from the start, this journey appeared difficult to them, subject to very dangerous hardships."[62] Translating from German, Lefin uses a specificity that turns away from allegorized and biblicized sea narratives and instead describes an actual sea voyage leading to a real shipwreck.

Lefin's Hebrew description of a storm makes only a brief nod to the prophetic tradition:

> יום יום נתעוררה רוח סערה עם רעם וברקים ורבוי גשמים עד שנתרוממו גלי הים בזעף גדול **והאניה חשבה להשבר**, מימי הגשמים נכנסו מלמעלה ומימי הים מלמטה עד שנתלחלח הכל, ותתגעש ותרעש הספינה וימוכו כל הבהמה והחיה אשר בקרבה וימותו.[63]

> Day by day a storm wind was awakened, with thunder and lightning and a great amount of rain, until the waves of the sea rose up with great fury and **the ship was on the verge of breaking up**. The rainwater entered from above and the seawater from below until everything was wet, and the boat quaked and stormed until all of the animals and other living things inside it were struck down and died.

Lefin uses the phrase from Jonah, "the ship was on the verge of breaking up," but he translates most of the description directly from Campe. He sometimes uses the biblical Vav consecutive, but other aspects of his writing are Mishnaic. Lefin also compresses Campe's more verbose German account.[64] Some of the phrases, such as *ra`am ve-barakim* and *ribui geshamim*, are found in medieval commentaries. The former is not present in Campe; apparently Lefin adds the thunder and lightning for dramatic effect. He also describes damage to the ship's "sails, ropes, and masts" (*sedinim veha-ḥevelim veha-toranim*), using medieval Hebrew for nautical terms. In contrast, both Euchel and the author of *Oniya so`ara* use the biblical term *nes* to denote a sail. Lefin uses several different words, including the Talmudic term *kel`a* and the medieval term *sadin* or *vilon*.

Lefin's greatest contribution to literary history lies in his acceptance and popularization of postbiblical Hebrew writing.[65] Other *maskilim* who embraced biblical or "pure" language used this preference as a way to criticize rabbinic writers, especially the less literate hasidic authors. Lefin's views were more complex and inclusive, recognizing what is now called historical or diachronic linguistics. In a note to *Morei nevukhim*, his retranslation of Maimonides's *Guide to the Perplexed*, Lefin writes:

> As is known, languages change in their words in accordance with the time and the place (for example, the words *kasher, ve-pesher, tzarikh, zeman, tikein*, are not found in the early Prophets), and all the more so in their grammar. . . . And thus in the generation of the Tanaim, these words were invented [*nitḥadeshu*]: *reshut, ve-ḥova, shi`abud ve-shiḥarur ve-ḥeirut, 'efshar, 'i-'efshar*. . . . Who authorized the young among proofreaders to shackle the making of blessings and prayers in the chains of biblical grammar? If only they were wise, they would acquire wisdom to write a collection of the newly developed roots in accordance with Ezra, his court, the people of the great assembly, and the sages of the Mishna, in order to enrich our Holy Language for the sake of Shabbat songs and prayer [*hodaya*] and ethical proverbs [*mishlei musar ha-sekhl*].[66]

This is a clarion call to revive Hebrew inclusively instead of excluding postbiblical Hebrew as the Berlin *maskilim* were wont to do. Moreover, in mentioning *mishlei musar ha-sekhl*, Lefin may be alluding to his own work *Ḥeshbon ha-nefesh*, which was published in 1808. He had already begun developing a synthetic Hebrew that would bring together different historical layers of the language.

Lefin was also an innovator in Yiddish style; one reason for this success was his awareness of different linguistic registers. He asserted: "It is well known that there is a great difference between the language of the simple conversation between people and the language of poems and ornate writing [*melitzot*]. When one has to do with a similar person and a common interest, and especially when one is dealing with a servant, there language goes to its simplest."[67] Lefin wanted to reach simple readers, and he therefore translated biblical texts "into our Yiddish language, the way it is spoken among us today."[68] Lefin's sensitivity to linguistic registers is also evident in his Hebrew translations.

Nature and Divine Providence

Secularization has its limits in *Mase`ot ha-yam*. Following Campe, Lefin's translation refers often to Providence. But there is a clear distinction between working on human plans or strategies (*taḥbulot*) and relying on Divine Providence. Although Campe admires the crew members of Captain Wilson's ship for their ingenuity and perseverance, he also suggests that God lent a supporting hand in their survival. Because of the tension between these views, it is interesting to look closer at Campe's translation (and Lefin's retranslation) of Captain Wilson's speech to his crew. The captain advises them that "they cannot count on any means of salvation, other than those which they find in themselves."[69] This statement of self-reliance seems to have been a bit too extreme for Lefin, who added a clause: "apart from salvation from above [*milvad ha-teshu`ah mi-marom*], you cannot count on any help except that which is in your own hearts and in the exertions of your hands."[70] This change echoes similar changes in Lefin's translation of Tissot's medical handbook. Lefin expands horizons with his secularized Hebrew narratives of European travelers while retaining aspects of the traditional Jewish worldview.

Lefin preserves Campe's references to *die Vorsehung*, Providence. When the shipwrecked sailors see nearby islands, Campe's narrator comments that "this was the first consolation, which Providence sent to their anguished hearts, leading them to hope and trust in its further assistance."[71] Lefin translates closely that "this was the first consolation that was sent to them from Divine Providence [*hashgaḥa ha-Elohit*]." But then he goes further: "to plant in their hearts hope for assistance from God, blessed be He [*Ha-Shem yitbarakh*]."[72] In Lefin's translation, Campe's abstract Providence becomes more explicitly God's intervention. Lefin inserts elsewhere Hebrew phrases such as

בכל זאת נמלכו ונתנו לבם לאזור חיל ולאמץ בטחונם בהשגחת השם.[73]

> Nevertheless they took counsel and girded up their loins, taking courage in their confidence in God's Providence.

This mention of God's Providence (or Divine Supervision, *hashgaḥat Ha-Shem*) contrasts with Campe's humanistic emphasis on "masculine resolve" (*männlicher Standhaftigkeit*).[74] Later in *Mase`ot ha-yam*, "Providence from Above, may He be blessed" (השגחה העליונה יתברך) is Lefin's translation of the less-personalized phrase "benevolent Providence [*die gütige Vorsehung*]."[75] When one sailor can think of no way to save himself, he gives himself over to "the will of Providence [*den Willen der Vorsehung*]."[76] Lefin's character places his confidence in "the Providence of God, blessed be He [*be-hashgaḥat Ha-Shem yitbarakh*]."[77] Also in the second sea narrative of *Mase`ot ha-yam*, recounting Heemskerk and his crew's adventure in the Arctic, Lefin adds to Campe's references to Providence: where Campe refers to an action of the "all-ruling Providence," Lefin refers to "the Providence of God, blessed be He [*hashgaḥat Ha-Shem yitbarakh*]."[78] Where Campe mentions the ways of "the benevolent Providence [*die gütige Vorsehung*]," Lefin writes of the ways of "Providence from Above, may He be blessed [*hashgaḥa ha-'Eliona yitbarakh*]."[79] Later, describing sailors' efforts to save an ailing crew member, Campe writes that "Providence blessed this beautiful deed." Lefin refers to the intervention of "God, blessed be He [*Ha-Shem yitbarakh*], which rewards them.[80] Campe's rationalistic, Protestant views are transferred into traditional Jewish piety.

Given the dominant, universalist ideology of the Enlightenment, the particularity of separate religions never becomes an issue. In one passage of his description of Captain Wilson's adventures, Campe describes Christian prayer: "In the evening of this fortunately passed day, the Captain called the entire crew into the largest tent, in order to express the thanks of their moved hearts—in a collective prayer to the Creator of their existence, who had kept them alive until then. Never was there a more heartfelt and intimate prayer to God. At the end of this pious act it was established that in the future, every Sunday evening, it would be repeated."[81] This is Lefin's rendering:

> ויהי בערב אסף רב החובל את כל אנשיו בגדול שבאוהלים כדי להתפלל תפלה קצרה להודות להשגחה העליונה אשר עזרתם עד כה, ולבקש חסדו על העתיד, ולאחר שגמרו אותה, קבלו עליהן להוועץ כן בכל יום ראשון מימי השבוע, ומהיום ההוא נתקשרו כולם כאיש אחד.[82]

> And in the evening the Captain gathered all of the people in the largest of the tents in order to pray a short prayer giving thanks to Providence

> from Above, which had helped them until then, and to beg for His mercy in the future; after they finished it, they agreed to commune thus every Sunday, and from that day they were bound together as one person.

Lefin emphasizes the social effect of prayer—how it strengthens the bond between members of the crew. Instead of noting religious differences, he merges all religious sentiments. He includes Campe's extensive passages about the natives' customs and religion,[83] although he strengthens the flow of the narrative by moving them to the end of the book.[84] Lefin's Hebrew edition, following Campe's German edition, does not reproduce any of the remarkable images contained in the British editions of Wilson's adventure, such as *Abba Thulle King of Pelew*, *Lee Boo Second Son of Abba Thulle*, and *Capt. Wilson Invested with the Order of the Bone* (figures 13, 14, and 15).

One weakness of early Hebrew writing was its paucity of natural descriptions. The *maskilim* distinguished themselves by their greater

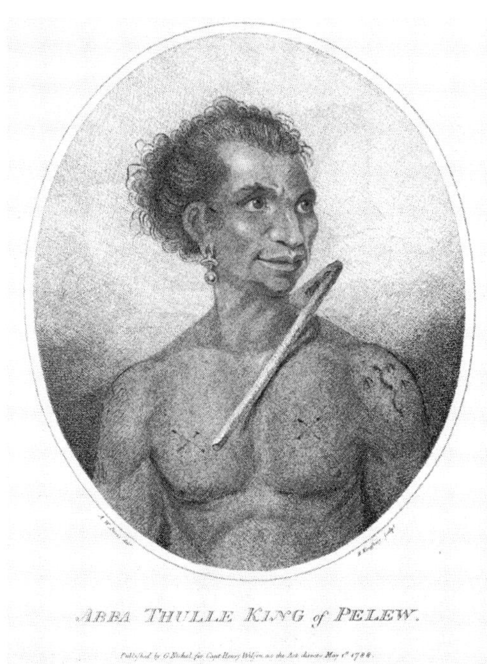

Fig. 13. Portrait of *Abba Thulle, King of Pelew*, from Keate [and Wilson], *An Account of the Pelew Islands*, 1788 ed., plate between pages 54 and 55. Courtesy of the British Library. © The British Library Board, W.7164.

Fig. 14. Portrait of *Lee Boo, Second Son of Abba Thulle*, drawn after he traveled to London with Captain Wilson, from Keate [and Wilson], *An Account of the Pelew Islands*, 1788 ed., plate between pages 338 and 339. Courtesy of the British Library. © The British Library Board, W.7164.

openness to nature.[85] Lefin confronts this limitation by closely following Campe's natural descriptions. For example, in the account of Wilson and his crew's shipwreck, translating word for word removes most of the temptation to rely on biblical phrases:

> . . . בתוך שעה מועטת <מועטה, 1859> התקדרו השמים בעבים חשוכים ונתעוררה מהומה רבה של גשמים רעמים וברקים. . . . פתאום נשמעה צעקת הצופה בראש התורן לאמר: משברי גלים! משברי גלים! . . . ובאותו רגע ממש נדחפה הספינה בכח גדול אל הסלע. . . . רעד ובהלה אחזה כל העם וגם רב החובל אשר נרדם **בירכתי הספינה**.[86]

> In a short time the skies were covered over by dark clouds, and there arose a great tumult of rains, thunder, and lightning. . . . Suddenly there was heard a shout from the scout at the top of the mast, saying: Breakwater! Breakwater! . . . and at exactly the same moment the boat thrust into the rocks with great force. . . . Trembling and fear gripped all of the people and also the Captain, who had fallen asleep **in the depths of the ship** [Jon. 1:5].

Fig. 15. Etching of *Capt. Wilson Invested with the Order of the Bone*, from George Keate, *Narrative of the Shipwreck of the* Antelope *East-India Pacquet on the Pelew Islands, Situated on the Western Part of the Pacific Ocean, in August 1783* (Perth: Morison, 1788), frontispiece. Courtesy of the British Library. © The British Library Board, 10492.bb.76.

This vivid description is captivating narrative on its own terms, for it does not appear to convey a message or a mystical allegory.[87] Only the final words echo the line in Jonah, where the prophet falls asleep "in the depths of the ship." "Breakwater" (*mishberei galim*, literally "breakers of waves") is a direct translation of the German term *Wogenbrecher* (wave-breakers).

Campe's description, as usual, is graphic: "Before long, a new storm arose; the heavens were suddenly covered over again with black clouds: thunder, lightning, and rain began . . . when suddenly from the crow's nest the watchman called down the terrible word: Breakers! Breakers! . . . as in the same moment the ship struck with force. Fright and horror fell upon the entire ship's crew. The Captain, and all those who were below deck, immediately leaped up." Placing the original German alongside Lefin's version is instructive:

> Nicht lange, so stieg ein neues Ungewitter auf; der Himmel hüllte sich plötzlich wieder in schwarze Wolken ein: es fing an zu blitzen, zu donnern und zu regnen ... als plötzlich die auf dem Mastkorbe ausgestellte Wache das schreckliche Wort: Wogenbrecher! Wogenbrecher! herabrief ... als das Schiff in dem nämlichen Augenblick mit Heftigkeit anstieß. Schrecken und Entsetzen überfielen die ganze Schiffsgesellschaft. Der Kapitan und Alle, welche unter dem Verdecke waren, sprangen augenblicklich hinauf.[88]

> ... בתוך שעה מועטת התקדרו השמים בעבים חשוכים ונתעוררה מהומה רבה של גשמים רעמים וברקים. . . . פתאום נשמעה צעקת הצופה בראש התורן לאמר: משברי גלים! משברי גלים! . . . ובאותו רגע ממש נדחפה הספינה בכח גדול אל הסלע. . . . רעד ובהלה אחזה כל העם וגם רב החובל אשר נרדם בירכתי הספינה דלג בבהלה לראות סבת הכשלון ההוא.[89]

Lefin's work as translator is precise, often following the syntax and punctuation of the German original. In one place, Lefin changes the perspective: in Campe's narrative, the watchman cries "Breakwater!" whereas Lefin brings out the experiential aspect when the watchman's cry "Breakwater!" is heard. His change works well with the next sentences, which refer to the sailors' reactions.[90] Lefin's graphic Hebrew descriptions, in contrast to any spiritualized or allegorized seascapes, continue the maskilic emphasis on the importance of learning about nature and geography.[91] This direction was already evident in some of his earliest Hebrew writing, which was published in the journal *Ha-me'asef*.[92]

Translators often diminish the source by creating a simpler version in translation, but when Lefin does so, he improves on Campe's original. An exemplary scene in *Mase'ot ha-yam* stems from this convoluted passage in Campe's narrative: "The day finally broke, and what some already thought they had seen during the night by the gleam of the lightning now appeared to all of them—a small island at a distance of three or four nautical miles to the south."[93] Lefin simplifies slightly to create a stronger picture of what the sailors thought they saw during the night and what they see now:

> לסוף הבריק השחר ואז נראה בעליל מה שנדמה להם לראות לאור הברקים בלילה: אי קטן ברוחב ג׳ או ד׳ פרסאות מצד צפון.[94]
>
> Finally dawn broke, and there appeared clearly what they thought they had seen in the flashes of lightning at night: a small island at a distance of three or four nautical miles to the south.

In other passages, Lefin improves on the logic of Campe's narrative. For example, after the seafarers catch sight of this island, a somber Campe writes proleptically: "But oh! how many new cares soon drove out the brief joy, which this sight had caused them!"[95] Lefin's narrator explains the psychology of the moment more clearly, without anticipating the sailors' future troubles:

> אולם אהה! כמה דאגות אחרות הפיגו את השמחה הקצרה הזאת מתוך לבם ע״י הספיקות הרבות שנשארו לפותרם עוד.[96]
>
> But oh! how many other worries weakened this brief joy in their hearts because of the numerous doubts that still remained to be resolved.

In *Mase`ot ha-yam*, Lefin avoids using Slavic words in his glosses, in contrast to the (anonymous) author of *Oniya so`ara*. Because of its hefty Slavic component, *Oniya so`ara* appears more similar to hasidic Hebrew writing. Lefin utilizes German and Yiddish in parenthetical glosses but almost entirely excludes Slavic words. In his translations into Yiddish, he embraces modern Ukrainian Yiddish and its Slavic component; however, in the main text of his Hebrew writings he seldom includes Yiddish, Polish, and Russian words. Nevertheless, he does use Hebrew expressions that had gained currency in Yiddish.[97]

Survival in the Arctic and with the Palau Islanders

The first narrative in *Mase`ot ha-yam*—from George Keate's account of Captain Wilson's shipwreck on the Palau Islands in 1783—praises the resourcefulness of the British and the simple virtues of the islanders. For most Hebrew readers in 1818, this narrative was their earliest exposure to something like an anthropological account of a distant people. Its favorable picture of European interactions with another culture is marred only when the Europeans introduce guns into two battles against enemies of the Palau Islanders.

The second narrative in *Mase'ot ha-yam* is from Campe's account of Willem Barents and Jacob Heemskerk's ill-fated attempt to discover a Northeast Passage and focuses on the Dutch sailors' perseverance and survival skills. (See figure 16.) In 1596–97, Heemskerk's crew may have been the first Europeans to survive a winter in the Arctic. Campe had raged against best-selling novels that took advantage of readers' "romantic expectations" and "Arcadian reveries." His travel narratives were therefore designed to wean young readers from such empty, imaginary fantasies. Campe hoped to instill a "desirable taste for serious and useful entertainments."[98] Nothing could be further from an idyllic Arcadia than the Arctic wasteland described in Campe's first *Reisebeschreibung*.

When their ship becomes trapped among icebergs, Heemskerk's crew is cut off from human society for the long Arctic winter. They are forced to abandon their ship, which is frozen in the ice; they rescue two lifeboats, build a house, and barely survive by burning driftwood and consuming supplies from the ship. The main encounters outside of their own small circle are with terrifying predators, polar bears.

All of this is a suitable backdrop for a lesson in overcoming adversity. Lefin hoped that his readers would "see from this to what lengths the force of perseverance and wisdom go . . . toward withstanding tremendous and enduring dangers, of cold and heat and hunger, thirst, wild animals, bandits, and severe illnesses."[99] The content of the story—translated from Dutch into German, adapted by Campe, and adapted again by Lefin—is less important than Lefin's original Hebrew style. An armchair explorer, Lefin was a pioneer of modern Hebrew writing.

Lefin's accomplishment was to create a pliant, vivid, naturalistic, and accessible Hebrew style. As discussed in chapters 2 and 3, Nathan Sternharz developed an expressive, readable Hebrew by translating explicitly and implicitly from Yiddish. The vocabulary and grammar remain close to Yiddish, lending the Hebrew the feel of a living language. Lefin uses

Fig. 16. Map of Nova Zembla showing the routes taken by Captains Willem Barents and Jacob Heemskerk, compiled by S. R. van Campen, from J. K. J. de Jonge, *Nova Zembla (1596–1597): The Barents Relics*, trans. Samuel Richard van Campen (London: Trübner, 1877), modified by Joseph Stoll, Syracuse University Cartographic Laboratory, in collaboration with Ken Frieden. Original map available from the British Library at https://www.flickr.com/photos/britishlibrary/11120205956 and made available in print by the Stony Brook University Library through Syracuse University Interlibrary Loan.

late Hebrew words such as *bikhdei* and *mamash*, which would have been familiar to Yiddish speakers. He also describes a sailor as having *mara shekhora* (a black, bitter mood), a medieval expression that occurs often in hasidic writings.[100] In spite of the hasidic associations, Lefin uses this phrase to translate *ernst und trockener Laune* (serious and dry disposition) in Campe's adaptation. Another colorful medieval expression that appears is *ma`ase shtut* (foolishness),[101] known from Yiddish usage as *mayse shtus*. Although Lefin's Hebrew writings usually relegate Yiddish words to parenthetical glosses, he was open to using all historical layers of Hebrew for the sake of greater expressiveness.

Lefin's translations from German, in spite of their precision, seldom echo that language. Lefin generally avoids German words, placing them in glosses where necessary. (An exception is the word *kapitan*, used frequently in the Heemskerk narrative; the Wilson narrative usually uses the term *rav ḥovel* for "captain.") But German remains present; for example, Lefin explains some less-familiar words using German and Yiddish glosses. A few dozen of these glosses appear in the first voyage in *Mase`ot ha-yam*. Sometimes indicating that they are *be-leshon 'Ashkenaz*, "in the language of Ashkenaz," Lefin retains (in Hebrew characters, usually in parentheses) the following German terms: *Steuermann*, *Verdeck*, *Zwieback*, *Kokosnuß*, *Engländer*, *Pulver*, *Hirschfänger*, *Bambus*, *Flutzeit*, *Schildkröte*, *Bootsmann*, *Schrott*, *Anker*, *Flagge*, *Pistolen*, *Pump*, *Kanal*, *Klavier*, *Miniatur*, *Pocken*, *Ratten*, *Flöte*, *Einhorn*, *Krebs*, *Schaltier*, *Teller*, *Treibholz*, *Schlitten*, *Steinkohlen*, *Schwindel*, *Skorbut*.[102] Some of Lefin's other explanatory gloss words—such as *biks*, *aptek*, *koyl*, *edel layt*, and *samet* (gun, pharmacy, bullet, nobility, and velvet, respectively)—are Yiddish rather than the cognate German words *Büchse*, *Apotheke*, *Kugel*, *Adelmann*, and *Samt*. After all, most of his target audience spoke Yiddish.

Elsewhere Lefin does not supply a Hebrew word but simply inserts a transliterated German word in parentheses, as if to admit that it is an unfortunate necessity. He gives in Hebrew characters, for example, the terms *Matrosen*, *Sirup*, *Yamus*, *Haifisch*, *Seebarbe*, *Eisschollen*, *Landkarke*, *Insel*, *Möwen* (*Mewen* in Campe), and *Kompaß*.[103] Foreign names and words (not transliterated) are sometimes placed in parentheses, as if to isolate the foreign presence: *Pizang*, *Spitz Bergen*, *Europa*, *Ostindien*, *Novo Zembla*, *Asia*.

This use of parentheses is familiar from other contemporary Hebrew writings, including hasidic books such as Nahman's *Sippurei ma`asiyot*. In Tale 10, for example, an unusually powerful storm is called a tempest, *se`ara she-korin (impet)*. Lefin avoids transliterating a word such as *Schaluppe*, instead using *oniya ketana* (small ship) in *Mase`ot ha-yam*; this avoidance distinguishes his translation from *Oniya so`ara*, which transliterates *Schaluppe*.

Thus, Lefin does not exclude German from his translation. Sometimes his glosses are Yiddish in addition to transliterated German, reflecting his openness and efforts to be accessible. A deeper question is whether his translation is influenced by German grammar. Does Lefin avoid following German sentence structures? *Maskilim* were wont to pillory hasidic authors who wrote Hebrew that sounded like a clumsy translation from Yiddish. Lefin sometimes closely follows the syntax of Campe's German, but on occasion he also lengthens sentences, as in the following passage from the second narrative in *Mase`ot ha-yam*:

> Nachdem sie die Schiffe vor Anker gebracht hatten, stieg ein Truppe von ihnen in die Schaluppe, und fuhr ans Land. Das erste, was sie hier erblickten, war eine große Menge Meweneier, die sie fleissig einsammelten, um einen Abendschmauß davon zu halten.[104]

> אחר כך תקעו את יתד הספינה (אנקער) ותיכף נסעו כמה אנשים בספינה קטנה ויצאו אל היבשה, בבואם מצאו סך עצום של ביצים ממין עוף ידוע הנקרא (מעוון) וליקטום <וילקטום, 1859> כולם להכין מהם סעודת ערב.[105]

> After they had anchored the ship, a group of them climbed into the sloop and rode to land. The first thing they glimpsed here was a great number of seagulls' eggs (*Meweneier*), which they diligently gathered, in order to hold an evening feast from them.[106]

> Afterward they dropped the ship's *yated* (*anker*) [literally, "stake" or "peg"; here *yated* is used to mean "anchor"], and immediately some of the men rode in the small ship and got off on land; when they arrived, they found a huge number of eggs from a kind of well-known bird that is called a *Mewen* and they gathered all of them to make an evening meal.

Lefin has some difficulties with maritime and ornithological terms: he does not find the available Hebrew noun *ogen* for "anchor" and has no word for "seagull."[107] He follows the syntactical order of the German but preserves a difference by using the Hebrew Vav consecutive (**ויצאו** and **וילקטום**) to connect a sequence of events. This enables him to break away from the Germanic sentence structure. He often uses hypotaxis to connect a sequence of phrases.

Describing an encounter with polar bears, Lefin remains close to the German word order but combines several sentences into one. He simplifies when, instead of writing that the bears "smell farther than they can see," he refers to their "sharp sense of smell." This phrasing enables him to compress several of Campe's sentences into one hypotactic Hebrew sentence:

> בתחלה קמו הדובים על רגליהם האחרונים לחקור ע״י חוש הריח החריף שלהם מה טיבם של בריאות <בריות, 1859> הללו, וכשהכירום שהם בני אדם רצו לקראתם בזעף ויבהלו המלחים מאוד מאוד ויחתרי לנוס ולהמלט באניה הקטנה.[108]

> At first the bears stood up on their hind legs to scrutinize, by means of their sharp sense of smell, what was the character of these creatures, and when they recognized that they were human beings, they ran toward them in fury, and the sailors were very, very frightened, and they rowed in the small boat to flee and find shelter.[109]

Lefin turns Campe's three sentences into one, with the help of connectives (-כש) and consecutive Vavs.

Lefin sometimes shifts the grammar and adds dialogue. Campe writes of the Heemskerk crew, "Our seafarers, who had to expect the complete destruction of the ship any moment, brought the sloop and a boat onto the ice, so that if it should be shattered, at least they would save these." Lefin adds dialogue to the sentence: "At this time of misfortune, they pulled two of the small boats onto the ice, for they said: Lest the ship break, these will be our means to escape."

> Unsere Seefahrer, welche die gänzliche Zerstörung ihres Schiffes alle Augenblicke erwarten mußten, brachten die Schaluppe und ein Boot aufs Eis, um wenn jenes zertrümmert werden sollte, wenigstens diese zu retten.[110]

בעת הצרה ההיא הוציאו שתי האניות הקטנות על פני הקרח כי אמרו פן תשבר הספינה והיו אלו לנו לפליטה.[111]

Lefin simplifies and compresses the text, turning two German phrases into one and anticipating the destruction of the ship in the sailors' words.

Authorship of *Mase`ot ha-yam* and *Oniya so`ara*

Several sources confirm that Mendel Lefin authored *Mase`ot ha-yam*, although the title page of the first edition lists the author only as הרבני המופלג החכם המפורסם מוהר"ר מ** ל**, "the prominent scholar, the famous wise man, our teacher, Reb M. L." The title page ends in German because the volume was published in Zholkva, near Lemberg, in Austrian eastern Galicia: "Gedruckt in Zolkiew bei Gerson Letteres, 1818."[112] The publisher's son, Meir Letteris, wrote briefly about this book in his memoir of 1869, commenting that because his initials are the same, מ** ל**, some people assumed he was the author.[113] He corrected the mistake, and in fact the 1859 edition had already listed Mendel Lefin as the author. There is also a list of Lefin's writings, including this work, among the papers in the Perl Archives. Moreover, Lefin's name was attached to *Mase`ot ha-yam* in several other contexts.

Some scholars have drawn another, less-definitive conclusion: that Lefin was also the author of *Oniya so`ara*. Nancy Sinkoff has summarized the arguments:

> It is also probable that Lefin was the author of the very rare *Oniyyah so'arah* (*The Raging Boat*), an anonymous bilingual (Hebrew and Yiddish) translation of Wilhelm Y. Bontekoe's tale of his voyage to the East Indies, which also appeared sometime in the second decade of the nineteenth century.... Catalog information about *Oniyyah so'arah* is contradictory and vague, although Samuel Poznanski claimed definitively [in 1897] that Lefin was its translator.... Evidence pointing to Lefin's hand in *Oniyyah so'arah* was its (probable) publication in Żółkiew, where *Masa'ot ha-yam* and *Di genarte velt* first appeared, its joint publication with one of the travelogues from *Masa'ot ha-yam* in the Vilna 1823 edition of that same title, its use of Slavic words in the Yiddish translation, and its being translated from the same source as those in *Masa'ot ha-yam*.[114]

For years I was convinced by these arguments. My certainty weakened, however, following careful stylistic comparisons and statistical analysis of word usage. It now seems to me unlikely that *Mase`ot ha-yam* and *Oniya so`ara* were written by the same author—although I would have liked to claim another important sea narrative for Mendel Lefin. In any event, it is probable that the translator of *Oniya so`ara* was among the small circle of Galician *maskilim* who knew Lefin and admired his Hebrew writings.

Comparing *Masa'ot ha-yam* and *Oniya so`ara* makes possible a deeper understanding of their distinctive stylistics. Evidence that they were not written by the same author includes a statistical count of terms used, especially nautical terminology, based on Captain Wilson's narrative in *Mase`ot ha-yam*. (The second story in *Mase`ot ha-yam*, about Heemskerk's adventure in the Arctic, confirms these statistics.) In the Wilson story, Lefin sometimes uses the word *oniya* (ship; 50 occurrences), but he far more often uses the postbiblical term *sefina* (boat; about 135 occurrences). In contrast, the author of *Oniya so`ara* seldom uses *sefina* (in the 1823 edition there are only 8 occurrences) and often uses *oniya* (in the 1823 edition, 121 occurrences). From this difference, it appears that the author of *Oniya so`ara* was trying to use mainly the biblical term, whereas Lefin often uses postbiblical vocabulary. The deck (German *Verdeck*) of a ship is a *gesher* (bridge) in *Mase`ot ha-yam*, perhaps influenced by English usage, but it is a vague *makhse* (covering) in *Oniya so`ara*. Another clear contrast relates to the use of two different terms for gunpowder (from German *Schießpulver*, literally "shooting powder"): the first story of *Mase`ot ha-yam* almost always uses the term that later took hold in modern Hebrew, *avak ha-serefa* (literally "fire powder"), whereas *Oniya so`ara* always uses the rare, idiosyncratic term *`afar ha-serefa* (literally "fire dust," except in one footnote, presumably added by a different hand). *Mase`ot ha-yam* uses *rav ha-ḥovel* more than 160 times to mean "the Captain," but *Oniya so`ara* uses it only a few times, favoring instead *kabarnit*. *Oniya so`ara* sometimes uses *nes* to mean "sail," whereas *Mase`ot ha-yam* always uses it to mean "banner" or "flag"; Lefin refers to a sail as a *kel`a*, *vilon*, or *sadin*. He also uses *sar* or *ha-sar* frequently (about 70 times each) when referring to one of the ship's officers or to a tribal chieftain, whereas *Oniya so`ara* uses the word only once. *Mase`ot ha-yam* uses *malaḥ* for "sailor," but *Oniya* *so`ara* uses *matroz* (as in German and Russian). A favorite word of Lefin's is *taḥbula* (stratagem, device), which occurs 15 times in *Mase`ot ha-yam* but only twice in *Oniya so`ara*.

We can also compare the use of common connective or transitional words. The expression *'aḥar kakh* (afterward) occurs 40 times in *Mase`ot ha-yam* but only once in *Oniya so`ara* (1823). Similarly, the connective *betokh kakh* (in the meantime) occurs 23 times in *Mase`ot ha-yam* but never in *Oniya so`ara*. *Mase`ot ha-yam* especially uses these connective words at the beginning of new paragraphs, indicating that Lefin gave more attention to transitions. I believe that the difference in incidence of these key words is conclusive in showing that Lefin was not the author of *Oniya so`ara*.

As already noted, Lefin distinguishes himself from the author of *Oniya so`ara* by relying less on biblical allusions. He strives to translate more literally, with fewer quotations. In Lefin's translation, there is nothing comparable to the following passage in *Oniya so`ara*: "**Before them the land was like Gan Eden** [Joel 2:3]. . . . There was nothing but **the sound of joy and rejoicing** [Jer. 7:34, 16:9, 25:10, 33:11], satisfaction and satiation · **No adversary · and no evil occurrence** [1 Kings 5:18]."

> **כגן עדן הארץ לפניהם** · . . . . אין שם כי אם **קול ששון וקול שמחה** · שבע ורויה, **אין שטן · ואין פגע רע.**[115]

This short passage includes at least three biblical quotations, which is characteristic of the author's work in *Oniya so`ara*, following accepted maskilic practices. In contrast, instead of transposing Campe's German into a Hebrew that is filled with biblical phrases, Lefin remains closer to the German words and avoids filling his sentences with quotations.

Another issue is the use of Slavic vocabulary in the Hebrew texts of *Oniya so`ara* and *Mase`ot ha-yam*. This makes for a one-sided comparison: whereas *Oniya so`ara* uses about ten Slavic words in parenthetical glosses, *Mase`ot ha-yam* seems to exclude all such words. Lefin uses a high proportion of Slavicisms in his Yiddish (e.g., in his 1814 translation of Proverbs), but he clearly avoids them in his Hebrew text. Here are some examples of the Slavic glosses in *Oniya so`ara*: סמאנד, טשאד, הארמאטי, פאצירקיש, חוואליש, פאר זאווירט, גלאווניש, טשערפחיש (*smand*, *tshad*, *hormate*, *patsherkes*, *khvalies*, *farzavirt*, *glavnis*, *tsherpakhes*).

Lefin excludes Slavic words from his Hebrew writing, instead using German and occasionally Yiddish in his glosses. His Hebrew in *Mase`ot ha-yam* sometimes uses biblical Hebrew and Aramaic, showing a far more sophisticated grasp of Hebrew philology than *Oniya so`ara*. With regard to the words for "sail," for example, *Oniya so`ara* usually relies on a questionable biblical usage of the term *nes*. *Mase`ot ha-yam* more accurately uses *nes* to mean "banner" or "flag." Referring to a small sail, in one passage Lefin uses *nes*, but elsewhere he refers to sails with a wide range of Talmudic and medieval terms such as *kel`a*, *sadin*, and *vilon*.

Biblical grammar, especially the Vav consecutive, appears hundreds of times in Lefin's *Mase`ot ha-yam* in appropriate connective contexts. The typical word *va-yehi*, "and it was" or "and it came to pass," occurs about 50 times. *Oniya so`ara* also uses the Vav consecutive hundreds of times, but *va-yehi* is less frequent (about 20 times). This seems to be one of the most obvious lines of separation between maskilic and hasidic Hebrew narrative: the *maskilim* far more consistently used the hypotactic Vav consecutive in past-time narration.

Lefin accomplished several difficult feats in his translated Hebrew narratives: (1) he moved away from the dominant maskilic Hebrew style, with its excessive biblical quotations (*melitza* and *shibbutz*); (2) he used a wide range of historical Hebrew, including biblical, Mishnaic, and medieval; and (3) he retained some Aramaic words and influences as well as Hebrew expressions that had become popular in Yiddish. At the same time, embracing a more inclusive conception of Hebrew, he included some Yiddish in glosses. Comparisons to the slightly earlier translations by Mendelsohn-Frankfurt and to later works by Mordechai Aaron Günzburg and David Zamość underscore his more flexible style. Lefin brought Hebrew closer to being a workable language of everyday speech.

God in Nature?

It is essential to understand both the formal qualities and the ideological underpinnings of major innovations in literary history.[116] In the case of Hebrew sea travel narratives, this book looks closely at linguistic elements by taking a diachronic approach to style while also attending to the shifting ideology of Hebrew authors. At key turning points in Hebrew literature, a Torah-centered Hebrew moved in tandem with a Zion-centered worldview. This parallel is evident in traditional pilgrimage narratives when authors quote incessantly from scripture and find order in the world by superimposing scripture on the landscape of Zion. They were scarcely capable of seeing beyond the limits of what the Hebrew Bible prepared them to see, and the New World did not fit onto their map of the globe. Heinrich Bünting pictured the world as a tripartite clover, with Jerusalem at its center (see figure 2, the Bünting map from 1581, *Die gantze Welt in ein Kleberblat*, reproduced at the beginning of chapter 1).

In contrast to traditional Jewish and Christian pilgrims, the *maskilim* emulated the Hebrew of the Torah but did not view the Land of Israel as the navel of the world. As they expanded their readers' geographical horizons by translating worldly travel narratives from Campe's adaptations, moderate *maskilim* such as Mendelsohn-Frankfurt, the author of *Oniya so'ara*, and Lefin gradually moved away from Torah-centered Hebrew. In addition to changing the geographical view of the world, these innovative authors also introduced shifting theological ideas. Whereas the hasidim rejected modern science, other travel writers embraced science and carried their convictions into novel ideas about the world, human existence, and God.

Near the end of Nahman of Bratslav's extraordinary Tale 6, "Of the Humble King," a wise man praises the hidden king who—because of his humility—shrinks until he ultimately becomes "nothing at all" (אין ממש or in Yiddish גאָר נישט). In Nahman's tales, kings often appear to represent God, but this vanishing act is unique. To explain how it happens, the narrator in Nahman's story alludes to a Talmudic passage about God, saying, "where His greatness [*gedulato*] is, there is His humility" (ובמקום גדולתו שם ענוותנותו).[117] Zvi Mark notes that this phrase derives from the passage in B. Megillah 31a: "Everywhere that you find God's might (*gevurato*), there you also find His humility."[118]

Decades earlier, in an introductory passage prefacing his accounts of nature in *Ha-me'asef*, Mendel Lefin also referred to God's greatness and humility but took this allusion to tractate B. Megillah in a very different direction:

> וכן מבואר בחכמת הטבע שהטביע השם יתעלה בכוחות כל מעשי בראשית · (א) שהיא כאיספקלריא מאירה להראות שלימותו: שם אתה מוצא גדולתו במקום ענוותנותו, שם חכמתו ושם שולטנותו, שם חמלתו וחנינותו לברואיו · וכו׳ וכו׳ אין קץ: (ב) ומכאן אמרו, שתכלית כוונת הבריאה שני דברים · לגלות שלימותו; ולהטיב לברואים:[119]

> And thus it is explained in natural science that God, may He be exalted, formed all of Creation with his power · (A) That it is like a shining mirror to reveal His perfection: There you find His greatness [*gedulato*] in the place of His humility [*ʿanvatanuto*]; where His wisdom and His authority are, there are His mercy and compassion toward His creatures · And so on, and so on, without end. (B) And from this it has been said that there are two purposes in the intention of the Creation · To reveal His perfection; and to perfect His creations.

Lefin anticipates Nahman's use of the Talmudic quotation when he substitutes the word *gedulato* (His greatness) for the original *gevurato* (His might).[120] Yet they interpret this passage in radically different ways. In "Of the Humble King," Nahman rejects the notion of a shining mirror in which nature reflects God. Instead of a homology or resemblance between God and the world, in Nahman's allegory there is a break or discontinuity because the truthful king is surrounded by a kingdom of lies. In many passages, Nahman and Nathan Sternharz flatly reject the God-in-nature concept.

Whereas Nahman represents the material world as degraded and as falling short of *imitatio Dei*, Lefin expresses his sense of the perfection of nature. According to Lefin, as Nancy Sinkoff writes, "scientific investigation of the natural world must sensitize the observer to the greatness and purposefulness of God's creative power."[121] Thus, one of his early articles describes the astonishing orderliness of a beehive.[122] Thirty years later in his translated account from Campe, *Maseʿot ha-yam*, Lefin describes Pacific Islanders in a kind of natural state, which to some extent conforms to Rousseau's notion of the "noble savage" (and to Campe's ideas on education).

For Nahman and Nathan Sternharz, the opposite of simple faith was philosophy or sophisticated inquiries (*ḥakirot* or, in the Ashkenazic pronunciation, *khakires*). To illustrate this view, Shmuel Feiner gives many examples from Sternharz's writings, including *Makhni`a zedim* and *Kin'at H' tzeva'ot*, two anonymously published works that have not been absolutely identified as his.[123] According to Feiner, in *Likutei halakhot* Sternharz "expresses total scorn of the natural sciences." Feiner points out that *maskilim* such as Shimon Bloch and Joseph Perl "recommended the study of the sciences in general and of the natural sciences in particular."[124] In *Tzir ne'eman*, a supplement to *Luaḥ ha-shana* of 1814–15, Perl alludes to Psalm 19 when he writes: "The Creator is exalted above our vision and our other senses, because He is holy and not visible to all living things, and so the Heavens and the Earth are full of his deeds, and they tell His honor and greatness."[125] Feiner adds that for Perl "science is therefore a first tool in the ascent to recognize the hidden God, distant unto Himself." In rejecting the natural sciences, Sternharz seems to have responded directly to Perl when he referred to "their calendars [*luḥot shelahem*], which they put together in their schools."[126] Sternharz also polemicized against Shmuel Romanelli, the author of the travel narrative *Mas'a be-`arav*, who defended the sciences and philosophy. In one of his published letters to his friend Shmuel Weinberg, Sternharz discusses Nahman's views: "his intention was not, God forbid, to know the natural world in accordance with the wisdom of the philosophers [*meḥakrim*] like Aristotle and Plato, may their names be blotted out." Some critics had mocked a passage on *da`at* (knowledge) in Nahman's *Sefer ha-middot* (*Sefer ha-'Alef Beit*, part 2), and Sternharz sets the record straight: "His only intention was to know the secret of nature, whence comes its root in the letters of the Torah and in their combinations."[127]

As discussed in chapters 2 and 3, Sternharz penned vivid accounts of both Nahman's pilgrimage and his own journey to the Land of Israel. But he never described nature for its own sake, which he probably would have considered an untoward step in the direction of idol worship. Nahman's travels were worth telling, according to Sternharz's worldview, because of their deeper or higher religious significance. For example, Nahman emphasized that before he could "ascend" and reach the Holy Land, he had to experience a descent into smallness (*katnut*); as part of this process, he exposed himself to humiliation and mockery during his stay in Istanbul.[128] In essence, along with all of the concrete scenes of travel, *Shivḥei ha-Ran* remains a hagiography.

Conclusion

Lefin advanced beyond prior Hebrew writers, and he did far more than just literalize where hasidic authors allegorized. He transcended the emphasis of the Berlin Haskala on "pure" biblical Hebrew and provided a new interpretation of what good Hebrew could be. The title pages of Lefin's books announced that they were written "in a simple and clean Mishnaic language [*leshon ha-Mishna ha-kala ve-ha-nekia*]"[129] or "in a pure and simple language [*be-lashon tzaḥ ve-kal*]."[130] Lefin wrote clear narrative Hebrew based heavily on Mishnaic Hebrew but also including biblical and postbiblical allusions. Although he seldom distinguished himself as an original thinker or author of Hebrew fiction,[131] he was an original and important early-modern Hebrew writer. He showed that the *maskilim* could match and even outdo the hasidim in the realm of Hebrew narrative. The hasidic narratives focused on spiritual events, ascent, and pilgrimage. In contrast, Lefin's translated narratives emphasized human ingenuity and the wider world, including an appreciation of distant cultures. Expanding far beyond a worldview that placed Jews and the Land of Israel at its center, Lefin published sea narratives that broadened horizons, and he adapted the German travel books to support his ideals. In place of narratives offering hasidic praises of the Rebbe or describing Jewish pilgrimages, he praised unpretentious sea travelers who worked together to overcome adversity. In contrast to Sternharz, who elicited only passing interest in landscapes and local populations, Lefin delighted in colorful descriptions of distant places and people.

Lefin was raised as a traditional Jewish man and received an outstanding education in rabbinic sources. He was able to transcend this milieu with the help of his maskilic friends in Berlin and his Polish sponsor, Count Czartoryski. Yet Lefin never left his origins behind and never separated himself from rabbinic traditions. From the beginning of his career as a translator from French and German, he avidly wrote books for the benefit of the broadest possible Jewish audience. First, he translated Tissot's popular medical handbook (1789–94), and later he adapted part of Benjamin Franklin's *Autobiography* into a method for moral self-improvement (1808). The result was so impressive that Israel Salanter reprinted Lefin's book *Ḥeshbon ha-nefesh* (Moral Accounting, or Reckoning of the Soul) in 1844 for use in his Musar movement.

Yiddishists have long appreciated Lefin's role as an innovator because of his remarkable Hebrew/Yiddish edition of the Book of Proverbs (1814); his posthumously published Hebrew/Yiddish version of Ecclesiastes was even more effective. Because of opposition from Hebraists such as Tuvia Feder, however, Lefin abandoned his Yiddish translations of the Tanakh. The time has come for a wider recognition of the importance of Lefin's writing.

During the final years of his life, Lefin lived in Tarnopol in close contact with Joseph Perl. While Perl produced the venomous satire *Megale temirin* in 1819, Lefin turned to his translation of Campe's sea narratives. For literary history, this neglected book, *Mase'ot ha-yam* (Sea Voyages), became Lefin's most important work because it provided a new model for Hebrew prose. In contrast, Perl chose to parody hasidic Hebrew writing, offering only a few positive counterexamples in fictional letters from *maskilim*. Lefin's alternative, based on Campe, was so accessible that it was reprinted and inspired further development of the travel narrative as a genre in modern Hebrew and Yiddish prose.

In sum, most rabbinic, hasidic, and maskilic travelers limited their Hebrew prose narratives by relying excessively on biblical quotations. As early as the fifteenth century, certain stock phrases became commonplaces in descriptions of sea travel. Two generations before S. Y. Abramovitsh wrote the short stories that were credited with creating the dominant *nusaḥ* (style) of modern Hebrew fiction, Lefin anticipated Abramovitsh's accomplishment by displacing the phenomenon of *melitza*.

Completing the hermeneutic circle by returning to the early part of this book, we can now recognize that there was a subtle kinship between Lefin and Sternharz. Both were inspired by a leading Jewish figure (Moses Mendelssohn in the years 1780–85 and Nahman of Bratslav in the years 1802–10), and both traveled at great expense and inconvenience to visit their mentors. Moreover, translation played a key role in their originality: Mendelssohn initially suggested to Lefin that he translate Tissot's medical work, and Lefin continued to translate from German and Hebrew until the end of his life; Nahman employed Sternharz to translate his teachings and stories from oral Yiddish into accessible Hebrew. After their mentors' deaths, Lefin and Sternharz carried on their legacy in spite of some dissent among the maskilic and hasidic groups that had formed around them. Working from Campe's German, Lefin moved through Yiddish and Aramaic when he created a newly pliant Hebrew in *Mase'ot ha-yam*. Working from Nahman's Yiddish stories and rabbinic commentaries, Sternharz created a folksy Hebrew that has aged better than almost any other Hebrew prose of the early nineteenth century.

Lefin and Sternharz, in spite of their mutual incomprehension and reciprocal scorn, were both innovators who helped to shape the evolving history of modern Hebrew prose. Hasidic circles have retained and exponentially widened readers' fascination for Nahman's works, seldom realizing that his scribe played a major role in translating them from Yiddish into innovative and accessible Hebrew. Unlike Hasidism, the maskilic movement has been in sharp decline since the disillusionment that followed the Russian pogroms of 1881. Moreover, the Zionist heirs to the Jewish Enlightenment have never adequately reclaimed the origins of the "revival of Hebrew" they championed starting in the 1880s. This book calls for a wide-ranging recognition, republication, translation, and critical analysis of the best Hebrew prose written early in the nineteenth century, starting with works by Mendel Lefin, Joseph Perl, and I. B. Levinsohn.[132]

Appendix

מנדל לפין, הקדמת המעתיק מסעות הים[133]

לעולם אל ימתין אדם שתשתנה הטבע בשבילו ע״י נס מבורר,
ואל יתייאש אפי׳ [אפילו] כשהחרב מונחת על צווארו · [134] אלא יעסוק בתחבולה
ועבודה תמיד שאין אדם נעשה חפשי מהן אלא במותו, ויהא בטוח
בהשי״ת שישלח ברכה במעשיו באופן הסמוי מן העין: והנה
מלתא דלא שכיחא היא שיעיז אדם לבטוח בצדקו כ״כ [כל כך] עד שיסמוך
על הנס · אבל מי שהוא שיכור בצרותיו עשוי לשכוח בהשגחתו
של הקב״ה, לכלות ידיו בחיקו ולאבד כל תוחלת ותקוה עוד:
וע״כ [ועל כן] מצוה לבקר את חבירו בצר לו אע״פ [אף על פי] שאין בידו לתומכו

בעצה וממון או מעשה, שעכ״פ [שעל כל פנים] יכול לזרזו ולאמץ בטחונו בברכת ד׳ · ע״פ [על פי] מוסר השכל ותנחומין של אמת מדוגמא של מאורעות קשות שניצול חביריו מהן לבסוף כשלא איבדו תוחלתם מן הישועה: ומי שנפל בסכנה וניצול חייב להודות ולספר ישועת ד׳ בקהל רב, בכדי ללמדם מוסר ובטחון בד׳ ישתבח לעתות הצרה: ומה גם שלפעמים מלמדם אגב זה איזו עצה ותחבולה, וענין אחר מעין המאורע שלו: וכל העם יטו אזנם וישמעו, ובפרט אותן מעוראות <מאורעות> של כמה מיני צרות תכופות בזו אחר זו, שהטה אדם אחד את שכמו לקבלם לשם פצעי אוהב הנאמן ית״ש [יתברך שמו]: בין ששרתה אח״כ [אחר כך] ברכת שמים על כחו לסובלם עד שכלו מאליהם, או על חכמתו להמציא לו מפלט מהם: ואפי׳ [ואפילו] לא נמלט מהם, אלא שנפטר מתוך בטחון בד׳ לבוא מיכאן לעולם שכולו עונג ומנוחה: שבין כך או כך חייב אדם לקבל דוגמא טובה מב״י [מבני ישראל] שכמותו, במדת הסבלנות ומנוחת הנפש שאין כל הרוחות מזיזות אותה ממקומה: כמש״ה [כמו שאמר הכתוב] הבוטחים בד׳ כהר ציון לא ימוט לעולם ועד,[135] ונאמר טוב ללכת אל בית אבל וכו׳:[136] ואמנם לא די להטות אוזן לסיפורי נצחונות שאירעו לפנינו, אלא שיש לרדוף ולהדר תמיד אחר מעשי אנשים כאילו יהיו מי שיהיו, [עמ׳ ב] לשומען מפיהם או מפי כתבם: כמשז״ל [כמו שאמרו חז״ל] איזהו חכם הלומד מכל אדם,[137] ואמרו בין גוי בין ישראל בין עבד ובין שפחה רוה״ק [רוח הקודש] שורה עליו לפי מעשיו:[138] ומסתמא גם אותם הגיבורים בסבלותם מלומדי מלחמה מנעוריהם היו, שהבא לטהר מסייעין לו[139] אבל לא יגעת ומצאת אל תאמין ·[140] ומי שאינו מחנך עצמו לחגור עוז במתניו בימי שלוותו, אין בו כח לעמוד בניסיון ליום רעה: אלא אובד עשתונותיו תיכף בתחלה, חובק את ידיו ומהרהר אחר מדותיו ב״ה [ברוך הוא], מוסר עצמו ליללות ולקללות ואובד ברשעו ח״ו: ולתועלת אחב״י [אחינו בני ישראל] נעתקו עתה מסעות הללו ללשונינו, בכדי להעיר נפש המעיין להתחנך במדה יקרה זו: כשיראה מיכאן, עד היכן מגיע כח ארך רוח וחכמה לראות הנולד[141] שחנן הש״י לאדם, לעמוד בסכנות עצומות וארוכות של קור וחום רעב צמאון חיה ולסטים וחלאים רעים: ולאחר שיתעורר להשגיח בנידון זה על כלל מקרי בני האדם בעוה״ז [בעולם הזה] ימצא שזהו מעשים בכל יום, שגיבורי כח לחסות בברכת ד׳ כול ניצולים ופחד חטאים תבואם: כמ״ש [כמו שכתוב] כי שבע יפול צדיק וקם ורשעים באחת יפולו:[142] ומאז והלאה יתן דעתו לאסוף זכרון מאורעות כאלו אחת אחת

למשמרת בלבו, והיו לכלי זיין מוכן בידו להגן על המוטטים,
ולנחמם במעשים שאירעו אפ׳ [אפילו] בימיהם בעירם לעיניהם: ובמדה
שהוא מקשט עצמו נעשה יותר מסוגל לקשט אחרים, שכשם שהוא
דובר אמת בפיו ובלבבו כך דבריו דוחקים למשכיות לב:
אבל בזכות זה תבא עליו ברכת אובדים להינצל מכל רע ונסיון,
כמש״ה [כמו שאמר הכתוב] רבים מכאובים לרשע והבוטח בד׳ חסד יסובבנו ·[143]

MENDEL LEFIN,
"TRANSLATOR'S INTRODUCTION TO *MASE`OT HA-YAM* (SEA VOYAGES)"

A person should never expect that nature will change for him by means of a clear miracle, and a person should not despair when the sword hangs over his head;[144] instead he should prepare a plan, pray, and work always—for a person is not made free of them except by his death, and he should trust that the Holy One, Blessed be He, will send a blessing on his deeds, in a manner that is hidden from the eye:

And the rabbis taught that it is an uncommon thing that a person dares to be so confident of His goodness that he trusts in the miracle. For a person who is drunk with his troubles may forget God's Providence, crossing his hands in his lap and losing all hope and expectation. Therefore, it is a commandment [*mitzvah*] to visit one's friend in adversity, even if it is not in one's power to support him with advice and money or deeds, because in any case one can encourage him and strengthen his faith

in God's blessings—by means of moral words and his true consolation on the example of harsh occurrences from which his friends were ultimately saved when they did not lose hope of salvation:

And the person who has fallen into danger and been saved is obliged to give thanks and publicly tell of God's salvation in order to teach them morality and faith in God, praised be He, in times of trouble. And what's more, sometimes one incidentally gives advice or teaches a plan of action regarding a similar situation:

And all of the people will bend their ears and hear, especially regarding events when several kinds of misfortune come in succession, and in which a person puts his shoulder to the wheel and accepts them as wounds delivered by the loving, faithful God: Whether Heaven's blessing will rest on him afterward by virtue of his being able to withstand them until they pass, or by his wisdom in finding a refuge from them: And even if he did not find refuge from them but perished with faith in God's assistance, coming from here to a world that is all delight and comfort: For either this way or that, a person is obliged to receive a good example from other people like him, with a measure of patience and spiritual calm—such that all of the winds do not move his soul from its place. As it is written, "Those who trust in the Lord are like Mount Zion and will never be moved for all eternity,"[145] and it is said, "Better to go to a house of mourning. . . ."[146] And indeed it is not enough to bend one's ear to stories of victory that have occurred before us; instead one should chase after and exalt, always speaking of the deeds of such people, whoever they are, to listen to them from their mouths or from their writings. As the sages said, "Who is wise? The one who learns from everyone."[147] And they said, "Whether Gentile or Jew, whether slave or servant, the holy spirit rests on him in accordance with his deeds."[148] And doubtless it was also about those heroes with their sufferings, the teachers of war from their youths, [that it is said] "The one who comes to purify is supported."[149] But do not believe [those who say], "I did not toil, and I found."[150] Whoever does not educate himself to gird up his loins in the days of his tranquility, does not have in him the strength to withstand a trial on a bad day: But he will lose his strength immediately, from the beginning, sit idle, and question God's ways, blessed be He; he gives himself up to wailing and curses and is lost in his wickedness, God forbid: For the good of our brethren, the Children of Israel, these [*Sea*] *Voyages* have now been translated into our language, in order to awaken the soul of the reader to train himself in this precious quality: In order that he will see from this to what lengths the force of perseverance and wisdom go—foreseeing the consequences[151] with which God has graced human beings—toward withstanding tremendous and enduring dangers, of cold and heat and hunger, thirst, wild

animals, bandits, and severe illnesses. And after he awakens to be aware in this regard, about all that happens to people in this world, he will find that these are everyday events,
when heroes of strength take shelter in God's blessing and are all saved, while fear overtakes sinners. As it is written, "For the righteous person falls seven times and stands up, while the wicked" fall at once:[152]
And from that time on, he [the reader] will put his mind to collecting memories of events like this, one by one to guard in his heart, and they will become weapons, ready to hand, to protect people from breakdowns, consoling them with events that have occurred even in their days and in their cities, before their eyes. And to the extent
that he adorns himself, he is made more capable of adorning others, for just as he is a speaker of truth in his mouth and heart, so do his words touch the depths of the heart:
But by virtue of this there will come to him the blessing of the lost, to be saved from all evil and temptation. As it is written, "Many are the sufferings of the wicked, but the person who trusts in the Lord will be surrounded by mercy."[153]

Transcribed and translated from Mendel Lefin, "Translator's Introduction to *Mase'ot ha-yam*," a manuscript in Folder 124 of the Joseph Perl Archives, printed by permission of the National Library of Israel, Jerusalem. First published as an appendix to Ken Frieden, "Neglected Origins of Modern Hebrew Prose: Hasidic and Maskilic Travel Narratives," *AJS Review* 33 (2009): 3–43. Where Lefin uses a colon, it is the equivalent of a *sof pasuk*, which marks the end of a verse in biblical texts.

Conclusion

In the decades after 1780, modern Hebrew entered the world from diverse sources, fostered by many distinctive writers. Sea travel narratives in Hebrew—from Jewish pilgrimage accounts to translated world travels by non-Jews—played a unique role. While bringing vital literary and linguistic qualities into focus, these travel narratives reveal their authors' contrasting ideologies and worldviews.

Three pathways guide *Travels in Translation*: (1) the development of narratives of sea travel as a seminal genre in Jewish literature; (2) the origins of modern Hebrew narrative in translations from German and Yiddish; and (3) the modernization of Jewish culture, leading away from the bookish world of Torah study and expanding the narrow horizons of a Zion-centered worldview. Jewish culture joined the modern world simultaneously in language and ideology, when the rise of modern Hebrew paralleled the emergence of modern Jewish life. As sea travels encompassed the modern world, so did the Hebrew that described them, inspiring readers who followed them to the ends of the earth. The modernization of Hebrew required a distancing from scripture to make naturalistic description possible.

This book reevaluates Berlin Hebrew writing (1780–1810), narratives of Hasidic pilgrimages (1815–22), and worldly travel narratives that were translated into Hebrew by enlightened authors in Galicia, Ukraine, and Lithuania (1815–24). The Hebraists in Berlin have been given too prominent a place in most literary histories, to the detriment of a balanced understanding. Not only German Jewish *maskilim* but also hasidim and their opponents, the *mitnagdim*, underwrote the early nineteenth-century origins of what eventually became modern Hebrew in the twentieth century. Moreover, moderate *maskilim* in Galicia and Ukraine extended the reach of Hebrew narrative. In a battle of books, Jewish men (because women were seldom taught Hebrew until the late nineteenth century) vied for prominence. Two seminal books of hasidic hagiography and fantasy tales were published in 1814–15 and served as a catalyst, pushing nonhasidic writers to match their accomplishment in a different vein.

After the decline of spoken Hebrew in ancient Palestine, written Hebrew was used continuously for almost two millennia in Jewish correspondence, legal decisions, study, and prayer. Although Jews seldom conversed spontaneously in Hebrew between about 200 CE and 1900,[1] educated men kept it alive in daily practice. Prior to the Enlightenment, many Ashkenazic Jews lived in a world that was circumscribed by the Hebrew Bible and Jewish law, with Jerusalem situated prominently at the center of that world. Their Torah-centered and Zion-centered tendencies motivated countless pilgrimages to the Holy Land, although scriptural accounts were incompatible with political and geographical realities in the Ottoman Empire. Pilgrims often superimposed their biblical expectations onto reality instead of consulting contemporary sources or relying on their own observations.

Modernization depended on a willingness to trust empirical evidence instead of placing unquestioning faith in scripture. Rabbis feared modern science, and for good reason: they suspected that it would challenge customary beliefs. Immersed in Bible and Talmud, they were archetypal textualists who resisted testing their sacred sources by applying to them a referential approach. In their pristine world of sacred texts, the ideal realm of "Jerusalem Above" transcended all comparison with mundane reality, or "Jerusalem Below." Until the present day, some ultra-Orthodox rabbis have dismissed paleontological and archaeological evidence that contests their fundamental belief in biblical events because their radical textualism places authoritative texts beyond the bounds of scrutiny.

Travel narratives posed unique challenges for Hebrew writers after Hebrew had lost touch with reality during the centuries when it was not a spoken language. Pilgrimage narratives often hovered ambiguously between intertextuality and reality as their authors mixed myth and observation while looking for the places they expected to find based on scriptural and rabbinic sources. Even educated, worldly authors such as Isaac Euchel and Shmuel Romanelli—who brought Hebrew back to reality by writing travelogues in Europe and Morocco—flooded their narratives with biblical allusions and quotations. In contrast, when a few outstanding authors such as Mendel Lefin imported J. H. Campe's *Reisebeschreibungen* into Hebrew, they pointed toward new possibilities. The inspiration provided by early-modern Hebrew travel narratives was decisive at the end of the nineteenth century, when S. Y. Abramovitsh's circle of Odessa writers advanced further.

Travels in Translation corrects a widespread misunderstanding about the origins of modern Hebrew. According to a founding myth, Eliezer Ben-Yehuda (Eliezer Yitzhak Perelman, 1858–1922) was an unprecedented man of letters who "revived" the Hebrew language—a figure of speech that evokes the resurrection of the dead (*teḥiyat ha-metim*) when the Messiah comes. Ben-Yehuda did indeed fight for the everyday use of Hebrew in Palestine, in connection with his Zionist convictions, during the 1880s and later. As the literary scholar Yosef Klausner writes, Ben-Yehuda believed that "the Jews could not hope to become a united people in their own land again unless their children revived Hebrew as their spoken tongue." This belief led to a linguistic experiment in child rearing that Klausner evidently viewed as heroic (though it has sometimes been reinterpreted as abusive): "In October 1881, they arrived in Jaffa where Ben-Yehuda informed his wife that henceforth they would converse only in Hebrew. The Ben-Yehuda household thus was the first Hebrew-speaking home established in Palestine, and his first son, Ben-Zion (later called Ithamar Ben-Avi), the first modern Hebrew-speaking child."[2] This anecdote about the Ben-Yehuda family is a commonplace that has been repeated countless times in Israeli and American Jewish schools.

Some basic outlines of the Ben-Yehuda story are plausible, but it misrepresents early-modern Hebrew by focusing almost entirely on the reanimation of *spoken* Hebrew. The first drawback of this one-sided account is that it underestimates the role of everyday Hebrew as it was given voice in prayer and study for more than a millennium. Moreover, long before Zionist ideology proposed the Jewish resettlement of Palestine and before avid Hebraists chose to speak Hebrew to support their return to Zion, thousands of writers in Europe and beyond had kept Hebrew alive in their poems, commentaries, legends, essays, newspaper articles, and books. (Although *Travels in Translation* focuses on the Yiddish- and German-speaking Ashkenazic communities, there were also significant contributions to Hebrew culture by Sephardim and Mizrahi Jews.) In short, the story of Eliezer Ben-Yehuda single-handedly importing spoken Hebrew to Palestine by forcing his wife and son to speak only Hebrew is a myth that should be corrected by juxtaposing it to a more realistic version of linguistic history.

Hebrew also survived orally in spoken Yiddish—and subsequently, to the extent that Hebrew lived, it lived as if haunted by Yiddish.[3] For several hundred years, Yiddish speakers throughout Europe passed down their implicit knowledge of an extensive Hebrew vocabulary. Some Israeli historians have been loath to accept that Yiddish, the widespread but often disparaged Diaspora language, played an instrumental role in the reanimation of Hebrew. This book shows that many early Hebrew authors translated into Hebrew, explicitly and implicitly, from their native German and Yiddish. Because modern Yiddish includes numerous Hebrew and Aramaic words and roots, Yiddish speakers readily incorporated many of those words into their Hebrew. When Nathan Sternharz translated from Nahman of Bratslav's Yiddish, he presumably thought in Yiddish while writing Hebrew. This made his Hebrew more accessible to a wide swath of readers—to uneducated men and virtually all women of the time—whose Hebrew was limited.

Although midrashic retellings of biblical stories have been known since ancient times, new Hebrew narrative literature was rare in the eighteenth century, leaving the field wide open for innovative efforts. Modern, secular stories scarcely existed in Jewish literature until the 1850s, and even Avraham Mapu's pathbreaking work *Ahavat Zion* (Love of Zion, 1853)—sometimes considered the first modern Hebrew novel—was set in biblical times to make the archaic language seem more credible.

The enigma remains, however: How did a small coterie of yeshiva-educated Jewish men, all of whom became autodidacts to receive scraps of a Western education, manage to create the foundations of a modern Jewish literature?[4] Unfortunately, H. N. Bialik's and S. Y. Abramovitsh's one-sided answers to this question have clouded literary history. In the period from 1885 to 1915, these leaders of the so-called revival (*ha-teḥiya*) of Hebrew minimized the accomplishments of their precursors and sometimes created the impression that they themselves were sui generis. Instead of acknowledging their teachers and their teachers' teachers, these giants of modern Hebrew showed their Oedipal "anxiety of influence" by slighting their forerunners and rendering it more difficult for subsequent critics to write an accurate cultural history. No author can single-handedly create an entirely novel style, yet Bialik essentially made this claim for Abramovitsh and "*nusaḥ* Mendele" (Mendele's style)—referring to the persona Mendele Mokher Sforim in Abramovitsh's Yiddish and Hebrew novels.

The notion of "the revival" (*ha-teḥiya*) is problematic because that name deceptively implies that Hebrew was formerly dead, which was certainly not the case. Is every language that is not used regularly for spontaneous, oral communication dead? Going back half a century to Jacques Derrida's early critique of phonocentrism may remind twenty-first-century readers that spoken language is not necessarily primary or more important than writing.[5] The case of Hebrew is particularly interesting in this regard because it was mainly a written language in Jewish communities for more than a millennium before devotees of the Zionist enterprise helped to renew efforts to speak it. Moreover, the absence of vowels in written Hebrew makes it the perfect example of a script that has primacy over voice and a powerful vehicle for interpretive word play involving slight changes. More than a thousand years of rabbinic commentary have shown how a written origin can spin off into innumerable rewritings and revoicings.

All of the Hebrew texts quoted and discussed in this book are pearls; the theme or topos of sea travel is the thread that connects them. The sequence of chapters is not entirely chronological but follows a progression in the emergence of early-modern Hebrew. My original design called for a general study of *innovation by translation* in works that were carried over from German into Hebrew and Yiddish, from Hebrew into Yiddish, and from Yiddish into Hebrew. This project proved unwieldy, however, and probably would have required three separate volumes. Moreover, without a focus on the travel motif, the study could have become too abstract and diffuse. Narratives of the sea came to my rescue, with the sounds of the waves and the smell of the salty mist.

This book rewrites literary history by returning to the origins of modern Hebrew narrative at the beginning of the nineteenth century. The maskilic use of *melitza*, which relied heavily on inlaid biblical quotations, was countered by other models that evolved with the help of parody and translation. Joseph Perl's parodies of hasidic writing, implicitly translated from Yiddish, began a new chapter in Hebrew literary history.[6] One distinctive pathway to revive Hebrew was to import phrases and calques from other languages instead of embedding biblical phrases, which often eclipsed authors' originality.

Simon Dubnow's insights hover over this book. He recognized the importance of translation for modern Hebrew writing when he observed S. Y. Abramovitsh around 1896, preparing the Hebrew version of *Be-`emek ha-bakha* (In the Valley of Tears). Dubnow noticed that when Abramovitsh translated the first part, working from the preexisting Yiddish version of *Dos vintshfingerl* (The Wishing-Ring), "he made the Hebrew translation—or rather, the reworking—masterfully and without any difficulties." But when he tried to continue writing the novel in Hebrew, without a Yiddish source, "he felt that it would not go easily." Dubnow explains that "one cannot create content and language together, but only one after the other; one must create the content first in the language of that life, which is portrayed in the artwork, and on this foundation one can then build the style of the revived Hebrew language."[7] With this observation, Dubnow stumbled upon the surprising idea that translation stimulated the re-creation of modern Hebrew. When the content was already present in Yiddish, the author could concentrate on making the linguistic innovations that were needed to express it in Hebrew.

"Mendele's *Nusaḥ*"—and the Grandfather of "the Grandfather"

On November 11, 1906, Abramovitsh misinformed his first literary biographer and misled future Hebrew literary historians. In a letter to Y. H. Ravnitzky, he claimed to have invented an utterly original Hebrew prose, a kind of mixed style, or *shatnez*, which Bialik would later dub "Mendele's *nusaḥ*." Abramovitsh—whom Sholem Aleichem had dubbed "the Grandfather" of modern Jewish literature—cagily denied having been influenced by any modern authors and referred only to medieval classics such as *'Akedat Yitzḥak* by Isaac ben Moses Arama, *Ha-kuzari* by Yehuda ha-Levi, and *Morei nevukhim* by Maimonides. These standard works, he says, gave him *leshon limudim*, a scholarly or learned language.[8] Elsewhere, he added the *Taḥkemoni* by Yehuda Al-Ḥarizi and *Beḥinat 'olam* by Jedaiah ben Abraham Bedersi.[9] In extant written sources, Abramovitsh never acknowledged having been influenced by any author who wrote later than 1600. One should be skeptical, however, regarding Abramovitsh's self-presentation and Bialik's adulatory depiction of "the creator of the *nusaḥ*,"[10] for the Hebrew of Abramovitsh's so-called *nusaḥ* was far less determinative than Bialik asserted. In his theory of the *nusaḥ*, Bialik expressed his wishful thinking that his own poetic style would shape the course of twentieth-century Hebrew poetry.

Thanks to the elite Hebrew authors of Odessa, the modernizing Haskala looms disproportionally large in Jewish literary history. According to their model of influence, Hebrew literary history followed a line that ran from the Berlin Enlightenment to the Odessa "revival." Some critics today continue to accept this premise, as if there were no major intermediaries or other influences between maskilic *melitza* and "Mendele's *nusaḥ*." Nevertheless, most Hebrew critics admit that the German Jewish attempt to write "pure" biblical Hebrew was, in literary terms, an ill-conceived detour that produced no masterpieces. In spite of this admission, some scholars continue to assume that modern Hebrew writing moved in a straight line—from the *neobiblical style* of the Haskala writers to Mendele's *synthetic style*. It is true that Abramovitsh conceived of his innovation in this framework as an advance beyond the wooden style of maskilic Hebrew—reflecting his own development from early efforts in the 1860s to his mature Hebrew writing after 1886. But even if we leave aside the influence of Abramovitsh's intervening Yiddish novels, this book demonstrates that there were other worthy sources of inspiration, such as Nathan Sternharz and Mendel Lefin. It would be naïve to think that the highbrow development from the Haskala to "Mendele's *nusaḥ*" was the only avant-garde, modernizing trend. There were many alternative literary pathways, including those pioneered by Abramovitsh's mentors and teachers at the Zhitomir Rabbinical Seminary.

Rewriting Hebrew Literary History

A new paradigm for Hebrew literary history should be based on the recognition that there was a continuous stream of rabbinic (and lowbrow) Hebrew prose, in many tributaries, from the Mishna and Maimonides until the modern period. One such tributary is exemplified by Jacob Emden, a rabbinic author who does not fit into the old model because, although not writing *melitza*, he was admired by the Berlin *maskilim*. Their one-sided, dogmatic approach to Hebrew style was not tenable; indeed, they acknowledged the importance of Emden's autobiographical writing and even printed some chapters from the manuscript of *Megillat sefer* in the journal *Ha-me'asef.* Nor was Emden unique; there were other exemplars of premodern Hebrew, such as the Hebrew writings of the wine merchant Ber of Bolekhov (Birkenthal).[11]

Moderate *maskilim* (such as Lefin) and hasidic authors, editors, and translators (such as Sternharz and the compilers of *Shivḥei ha-Besht*) contributed more than did the Berlin *maskilim* to what eventually became the Hebrew "revival." As we have seen, among moderate *maskilim* and the hasidim, translations from German and Yiddish played a specific role in superseding *melitza*. Long before Bialik referred to "Mendele's *nusaḥ*," a different strand was already emerging inspired by translation; like the hasidim, Abramovitsh traveled through Yiddish to escape *melitza*.[12] There is even a direct, traceable lineage from Lefin to Abramovitsh that runs through Abramovitsh's teachers at the Zhitomir Rabbinical Seminary in the 1860s: Mordechai Suchostober, Eliezer Tzvayfl, and Avraham Gotlober. All of them had admired Lefin's contributions to Hebrew writing in the previous decades, and all of them influenced the young Abramovitsh. Although Sholem Aleichem dubbed Abramovitsh "the Grandfather" of Jewish literature, Abramovitsh himself also had an unacknowledged grandfather: Mendel Lefin was a mentor to the teachers in Zhitomir who were Abramovitsh's symbolic parents.

Many rabbis and other traditionally educated men—such as Emden and Ber of Bolekhov—wrote accessible and effective Hebrew prose during the eighteenth century. Around 1780, however, there came a turning point when modernizing authors in Berlin tried to sever their ties to the conventions of postbiblical, rabbinic Hebrew writing by favoring neobiblical *melitza*. They tried to accomplish for Hebrew something analogous to what German neoclassical authors had done in emulating Greek writers. Ideologically, their modernizing program took a step forward, but their grammatical and lexical choices set their Hebrew off from ongoing developments and impeded the natural development of Hebrew literature.

As we have seen, quotation and translation were two of the basic devices that shaped the beginnings of Hebrew narrative. *Maskilim* almost invariably embedded countless biblical quotations in their Hebrew sea narratives, until Mendel Lefin joined the scene. Writing for Yiddish-speaking Jews in Ukraine, Lefin took advantage of the process of translation from German, which prompted him to move toward more naturalistic descriptions. Translating helped him escape from neobiblical *melitza*, with all of its limitations, as well as from his own tendency to quote rabbinic sources. Lefin's unpublished introduction to *Mase'ot ha-yam* (Sea Voyages) includes one quotation after another, overburdening it with erudition. Ultimately, the challenge of providing an accurate translation moved Lefin toward a more direct and less-allusive style.

This helps us understand why translated sea narratives played an important role in early-modern Hebrew writing. The task of the translator compelled authors such as Mendel Lefin to find concrete expressions in order to convey the minutiae of travel accounts. They had to break from their tendency to resort to biblical passages at every turn in order to cultivate Hebrew descriptive language. After all, what is the point of traveling to far-flung destinations if one only replicates the experience and language of prior travelers and narratives?

Secularization and Modernization

Around 1815, a two-pronged development occurred in modern Hebrew literature, which is easy to understand in connection with sea narratives. On the one hand, there was a secularization of content, when pilgrimages to the Holy Land were supplemented (and sometimes supplanted) by voyages to America and the Pacific. On the other hand, there was a modernization of the Hebrew language when some maskilic authors moved beyond biblical phrases, vocabulary, and grammar. Mendel Lefin's translations from German made a vital contribution by limiting the role of biblical sources, expanding the vocabulary to include many postbiblical words, and broadening horizons to the Pacific and the Arctic. Translating from German, he paradoxically shared some stylistic qualities with hasidic and other rabbinic authors who translated from Yiddish.

In Bratslav tradition, Nahman's pilgrimage epitomized the centrality of the Land of Israel. Nathan Sternharz followed in his master's footsteps in 1822 and wrote an account of the journey that was published posthumously, consolidating the Zion-centered worldview. In the twenty-first century, however, there are hints that among Bratslav hasidim the spiritual focus may be shifting. On Rosh Hashanah, thousands of Bratzlavers make a different kind of pilgrimage to the Rebbe's grave site and memorial (*tziun*) in Uman, Ukraine. One might say that for some disciples of Nahman the sacredness of this *tziun* has challenged the uniqueness of Zion.

Nathan Sternharz's and Mendel Lefin's Hebrew narratives presented an indirect dialogue and debate between hasidic and maskilic authors. These narratives were an important genre in the history of Hebrew literature, both stylistically and thematically. Lefin's translations from German might be understood as genre parodies of the prior Hebrew narratives of pilgrimage to the Land of Israel.

One axiom of this book is that the histories of Hebrew and Yiddish literature are interwoven. Following the rise of early-modern Hebrew literature, at a greater distance from the Hebrew Bible, the next step in the nineteenth century was to strengthen Yiddish literature, going beyond what could be accomplished in Hebrew. At a time when Hebrew was not a spoken language and could scarcely reflect lived experience, Yiddish became an accepted literary language that began to accomplish new feats of expression and representation.

Lefin's literary grandson, Abramovitsh, followed in his footsteps when he wrote an explicit parody and satire of hasidic pilgrimages in *Kitser masoes Binyumen ha-shlishi* and *Kitzur mase'ot Benyamin ha-shlishi* (*The Brief Travels of Benjamin the Third*; Yiddish, 1878; Hebrew, 1896). Abramovitsh invoked two previous world travelers, Benjamin of Tudela and Miguel de Cervantes's fictional Don Quixote, but the true object of his parody was hasidic writing.

Innovation by Translation

Translation played a key role in the reinvention of Hebrew as a modern literary language. Although the hasidic and maskilic practitioners of this art were worlds apart, they all benefited from the novelties made possible by translation. Nathan Sternharz developed something like oral-style Hebrew by emulating Yiddish; Mendel Lefin worked from German, simultaneously raising the level of Hebrew grammar and cultural sophistication. At odds with ethnocentric narratives of pilgrimage to the Holy Land, Lefin introduced universalistic tales of adventure, adversity, and survival.[13]

Sternharz and Lefin's contributions to the history of modern Hebrew narrative are, as we have seen, in part the result of their translations from Yiddish and German. Working in translation from living languages, both succeeded in writing simpler and more readable Hebrew in a way that calqued contemporary vernacular phrases. They sometimes wrote Hebrew using what sounded like an oral style, creating the impression that spoken Hebrew already existed in 1815–18. Whereas Perl parodied hasidic authors, Lefin outdid them by moving beyond tales of traveling to the Land of Israel, thereby expanding horizons and breaking the ethnocentrism of traditional Hebrew narratives.

The writings of Lefin and Sternharz directly influenced the course of modern Hebrew literature at about the same time as Joseph Perl's antihasidic parodies carried "folk Hebrew" into the stream of modern Hebrew literature.[14] In *Megale temirin* (Revealer of Secrets, 1819), Perl turned a parody of hasidic letters into the basis for an epistolary novel. In another way, Lefin's sea narratives helped create the context that made possible a new kind of mimesis in Hebrew. Influenced by Lefin's translated narratives and by I. B. Levinsohn's dialogue in *Divrei tzadikim* (Words of the Righteous, 1820–30), Perl showed in *Boḥen tzadik* (Test of the Righteous, 1838) that it was possible to create the illusion of an oral-style Hebrew that could convey spoken dialogue. Abramovitsh followed this tradition when he described Benjamin's mock-heroic journey, parodying hasidic narratives of pilgrimage. Around the same time, I. L. Peretz and M. Y.

Berdichevsky saw hasidic narrative as an alternative source of modern Jewish literature.

From another perspective, hasidic and maskilic writing can be understood as more than a neglected origin of modern Hebrew narrative. Authors such as Sternharz and Lefin anticipated the twentieth-century linguistic processes by which Israeli Hebrew emerged—adopting, adapting, and translating phrases from other languages.[15]

Textual Referentialism

This book began at the intersection of translation studies and Hebrew/Yiddish literary history. Later I found it necessary to supplement an abstract, formal approach with more meaningful content: narratives of sea travel facilitated a close comparison of Hebrew works by hasidim and *maskilim*. Sea narratives contain elements of literary development that might otherwise go unnoticed. In concrete terms, the language describing the realia of sea travel uncovers specific choices that maskilic and hasidic authors made around 1807–25. Furthermore, the topos of sea travel introduces unexpected thematics, bringing into play the conflicting worldviews of the hasidim and the *maskilim*. In contrast to the traditional Jewish conception that placed Zion at the center of the world and inspired pilgrimages to the Holy Land, the secularizing Enlightenment broadened horizons.

Hasidic and maskilic writing, when juxtaposed, reveal that the maskilic emphasis on biblical language had an unintended consequence. A rejection of rabbinic Hebrew writing implied a belittling of the cultural accomplishments of European Jewish communities, whereas a more positive view of the postbiblical evolution of Hebrew affirmed Jewish life and rabbinic writing in the Diaspora. The Berlin emphasis on biblical Hebrew was influenced by German neoclassicism, with a secular bent that pushed aside rabbinic writing, but it led in another direction. Although the Torah-centered *melitza* of the *maskilim* was supposed to help create a broader worldview, by a historical twist it ultimately contributed to the Zion-centered worldview.

When Hebrew was being "revived" at the end of the nineteenth century, it dovetailed with the beginnings of modern Zionism. One accomplishment of travel narratives in Hebrew had been to show that the Land of Israel was not the only worthy destination. Yet this progressive, modern viewpoint was in some ways undermined by the neobiblical bias, which led back to a Zion-centered conception. While returning to Hebrew, modern Zionism embraced the Zion-centered worldview.

Keyword Analysis

The Berlin writers in the journal *Ha-me'asef* tried to make a new start, favoring biblical Hebrew. They tried to distill a "pure language" (*lashon tzaḥ, lashon tzaḥa*) or a "language of purity" (*lashon tzaḥut*) that would limit postbiblical influences.[16] By rejecting postbiblical Hebrew, they set themselves apart from the dominant traditions of rabbinic writing and from a style of writing that was accessible to yeshiva-educated Jewish readers. In Berlin, the use of archaic language made it difficult to succeed in writing modern narrative because it was almost impossible to write natural-sounding speech or to describe contemporary life. Writers such as Naftali Hirsh Wessely concentrated on writing poetry, but even in this genre the Berlin writers have few readers today.

Google Books Ngram Viewer shows dramatically how the Berlin attempt to return to biblical Hebrew failed. Graph 1 charts the incidence of two words for "ship," the more prominently biblical term *oniya* and the almost completely postbiblical term *sefina*, in the Hebrew books from the years 1750–1900 scanned by Google. The maskilic writers' attempt to reintroduce the biblical word *oniya*, as represented by the large block in the period from 1775 to 1818, is unmistakable. Google Books Ngram Viewer is still a primitive tool—in part because the Optical Character Recognition for Hebrew characters is imperfect—but it illustrates that for centuries Hebrew writing primarily used the word *sefina*. The plural term *oniyot* had some popularity, as did *oni*.[17] Abruptly, at the end of the eighteenth century, maskilic writers apparently tried to impose the biblical term *oniya* as the main word to use for "ship," and its frequency of occurrence spiked. Yet the *maskilim* reached very few readers, and their preference never took hold. Around 1800, both words were legitimate, so the attempt to privilege *oniya* was untenable. Soon after, when Berlin collapsed as a center of Hebrew writing, their artificial preferences could not be maintained. Working at odds with centuries of postbiblical Hebrew,

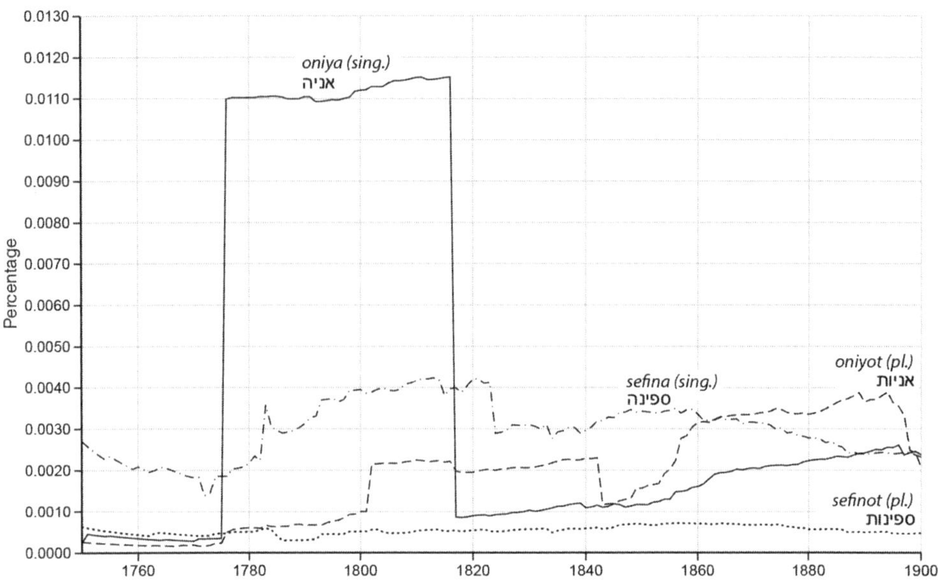

Graph 1. Results of a Google Books Ngram Viewer search for the incidence of two words meaning "boat" or "ship," singular (*oniya*, *sefina*) and plural (*oniyot*, *sefinot*) in Hebrew works published from 1750 to 1900, with a smoothing of 20. Reformatted by Joseph Stoll, Syracuse University Cartographic Laboratory, in collaboration with Ken Frieden.

the *maskilim* made themselves marginal, and they blocked the development toward a viable style of narrative realism. They have often dominated histories of modern Hebrew, perhaps because literary historians have recognized their contributions to modern Jewish education without noting their shortcomings in the area of Hebrew style.

The elite German Jewish writers missed the boat, so to speak. They wrote themselves into obscurity by insisting on an unrealistic "purity." They also tried to follow the rules of biblical grammar, for instance, when they insisted on using the biblical Vav consecutive instead of the Mishnaic past tense. Even Mendel Lefin relied on this archaic feature in spite of his commitment to Mishnaic Hebrew and to many other forward-looking innovations in Hebrew style.

Translations from living languages, especially German and Yiddish, formed an alternative to Berlin *melitza*. Although most authors who wrote for the elite journal *Ha-me'asef* insisted on gilding the biblical lily, a few—such as Isaac Satanov, Baruch Lindau, and Mendel Lefin—built a more practical prose style upon Mishnaic Hebrew. Some of them translated German scientific and philosophical sources, showing that Hebrew was capable of functioning as a modern language in different contexts. With encouragement from Moses Mendelssohn, Lefin translated S. A. Tissot's popular medical handbook into Hebrew as *Refu'at ha-`am* (Remedies for the People, 1789/1794). Well into the nineteenth century, Hebrew writers continued to link their innovations to the sciences, as did Abramovitsh when he adapted Harald Othmar Lenz's German work of natural history into Hebrew as *Sefer toldot ha-teva* (The Book of Natural History, 1862–72).

Paradoxes of Originality in Translation

There are several paradoxes in this literary history. One textual arc leads away from biblical quotation and toward more naturalistic writing about sea travel. Another arc is the movement from pilgrimage narratives to narratives of world travel. Yet the Hebrew narratives of world travel were translated from German by Jews who had never crossed an ocean or even the Mediterranean Sea. These armchair travelers expanded horizons by exploring new vistas in translation; although few of these German and Galician Jews continued to live in a Torah-centered world, they displaced their obsession with scripture onto another kind of text-centeredness.

Translators such as Moses Mendelsohn-Frankfurt and Mendel Lefin did not describe the world as they saw it; rather, they transferred texts from German to Hebrew. We may understand such translation biographically in the case of Lefin, who was going blind at the end of his life. Perhaps when failing vision cut him off from new experiences, translating travel narratives became a substitute.

This book shows a line of progression from the traditional, Torah- and Zion-centered worldview that characterizes Hasidic pilgrimages to a modern perspective that placed neither scripture nor Jerusalem at the center. The German *maskilim* moved geographically beyond the Jewish world, but linguistically they shackled their Hebrew to the Bible. Lefin translated worldly travels into a Hebrew that shed most of its religious and scriptural associations, writing innovative Hebrew that matched the non-Jewish travels. Yet nineteenth-century Hebrew writing never really became secular, never shook off its dependence on scripture. The next step toward secularization required the spoken vernacular, and some hasidic Hebrew writers were ahead of their time in using a folksy, colloquial, oral style. This was made possible by their implicit translations from everyday Yiddish. When hasidic Hebrew texts seemed to translate from Yiddish, this helped create a vernacular feel in modern Hebrew.

Yiddish-speaking settlers in Palestine who tried to adopt Hebrew translated many words and expressions from Yiddish into Hebrew. Haim Blanc focuses on these Yiddish influences, giving examples of Hebrew words that took on new meanings in Yiddish. He notes the "stylistic doublets," Hebrew words that have separate meanings in Ashkenazic and Sephardic pronunciation.[18] The grammatical borrowings are even more significant, and Blanc considers aspects of verbs. Israeli Hebrew often calqued Yiddish expressions, and complete phrases were carried over from Yiddish to Hebrew.[19] Hillel Halkin comments that "even slang, that most ephemeral of linguistic phenomena, is in Hebrew today still largely an exercise, if covert, in translation."[20]

Hasidic and maskilic translators of travel narratives, moving from their native Yiddish or German to Hebrew, anticipated the later process by which Jews "revived" Hebrew in Palestine. This was a startling turn of events because the initial impetus for maskilic translations was to expand the Jewish worldview. By importing narratives from German into Hebrew, *maskilim* sought to educate their readers and move them beyond Zion; however, the alliance between the Hebrew "revival" and Zionism eventually encouraged Israelis to forget the worldly, European connections. Instead of recognizing the hybrid character of Israeli speech, it was more ideologically acceptable to suppress awareness of German and Yiddish components.[21]

Premodern Hebrew, before its "rebirth" as a spoken language, was like a ship in a bottle. The ancient Hebrew of the Bible remained a constant source while the world changed. Most Hebrew writing—anchored to the scriptural and Mishnaic past yet propelled forward by poetry, prayer, commentaries, Midrashic retellings, hagiographies, and codes of Jewish law—kept a distance from the Jews' diaspora surroundings. Although postbiblical Hebrew evolved in rabbinic works, at the end of the eighteenth century many enlightened Jewish authors tried to return to what they understood as the pure Hebrew of the Bible. Their neobiblical Hebrew did not, however, facilitate representations of the modern milieu. Instead of describing the world around them, these writers often assembled countless quotations, creating a mosaic or patchwork. This intertextual tendency, arising from a self-imposed constraint, created a space for innovation through travel narratives: when they narrated real voyages, seminal Hebrew authors such as Sternharz and Lefin pulled the ship out of the bottle and sent modern Hebrew into the world.

The creative role of translation is a prominent subtext in this history of Hebrew travel narratives. By translating from Yiddish and German, the authors included here helped create the impression that Hebrew was a living language long before it achieved that status. The hasidic writers were ahead of their time when they wrote Hebrew that stayed close to Yiddish, almost breaking down the wall between the two. But Lefin came closest to creating a synthesis in the realm of sea narratives, inventing a workable language of everyday life and preparing the way for Hebrew to become a vernacular in the modern world.

Notes

⚓

Bibliography

⚓

Index

Notes

Preface

1. For a memoir describing the town and the Żyw/Frieden family history, see Menachem Mendel Frieden, *A Jewish Life on Three Continents: The Memoir of Menachem Mendel Frieden*, trans. and ed. Lee Shai Weissbach (Stanford, CA: Stanford Univ. Press, 2013), esp. 45–69.

2. I have always resisted using the term *Jewish literature* because, after all, only people can be Jewish. The most accurate description of my subject might be "Judaic traditions in literature," which is the first part of the title of the series I edit with Harold Bloom at Syracuse University Press. But if the word *Judaic* has gone out of fashion, it seems that we must accept the broadened meaning of the term *Jewish*.

3. Does this project necessarily involve nostalgia? I don't think so, even if David Roskies's book *A Bridge of Longing: The Lost Art of Yiddish Storytelling* (Cambridge, MA: Harvard Univ. Press, 1995) typifies one possible, alluring approach to Yiddish studies. Before a student of eastern European Jewish culture spends decades immersed in what could become "restorative nostalgia," required reading should be Svetlana Boym's book *The Future of Nostalgia* (New York: Basic Books, 2001), esp. 41–55.

4. I. L. Peretz, "Di toyte shtot," in *Ale verk*, vol. 6: *Far kleyn un groys* (Warsaw: Progress, 1909–13), 116, reprinted in *Ale verk fun I. L. Peretz*, vol. 6: *Far kleyn un groys* (Vilna: Kletzkin, 1925–29), 104.

Introduction

1. Other authors turned to writing travel narratives in Yiddish, which is a subject large enough to be the focus of a different book. Recent contributions to the study of Jewish travel narratives include Sidra DeKoven Ezrahi, *Booking Passage: Exile and Homecoming in the Modern Jewish Imagination* (Berkeley: Univ. of California Press, 2000), and Leah Garrett, *Journeys beyond the Pale: Yiddish Travel Writing in the Modern World* (Madison: Univ. of Wisconsin Press, 2003).

2. Sholem Aleichem immortalized the Jewish affinity for quotation in his character Tevye the Dairyman. For a study of this phenomenon, see my essay *A Century in the Life*

of Sholem Aleichem's Tevye, B. G. Rudolph Lectures in Judaic Studies, New Series, Lecture 1, 1993–94 (Syracuse, NY: Syracuse Univ. Press, 1997).

3. Economic and political difficulties in Ottoman Palestine undoubtedly also dissuaded many Jews who considered emigration there. During the same period, secularization enabled vast numbers of Jews to consider moving to North America.

4. Naftali Hirsh Wessely, *Divrei shalom ve-emet* (Berlin: n.p., 1782), letter 1, chaps. 1 and 9.

5. Ibid., letter 1, chap. 6. Joachim Heinrich Campe's best seller *Die Entdeckung von Amerika* (The Discovery of America, 1781) was based on William Robertson's work *The History of America*, 2 vols. (London: Strahan & Cadell, 1777). Campe's adaptation was preceded by Johann Friedrich Schiller's authorized translation, *Geschichte von Amerika* (History of America, 1777).

6. Yaacov Shavit, "A Duty Too Heavy to Bear: Hebrew in the Berlin Haskalah, 1783–1819: Between Classic, Modern, and Romantic," in *Hebrew in Ashkenaz: A Language in Exile*, ed. Lewis Glinert (New York: Oxford Univ. Press, 1993), p. 119.

7. On the "plain style," see the discussion by Margaret Cohen in *The Novel and the Sea* (Princeton, NJ: Princeton Univ. Press, 2010), pp. 42–45.

8. For a discussion of the reception history of *Robinson Crusoe*, see David Fishelov, *Dialogues with/and Great Books: The Dynamics of Canon Formation* (Brighton, UK: Sussex Academic Press, 2010), chap. 12.

9. Itamar Even-Zohar, *Polysystem Studies*, special issue of *Poetics Today* 11 (1990): 47.

10. Ibid.

11. George Steiner, *After Babel: Aspects of Language and Translation*, 3rd ed. (Oxford: Oxford Univ. Press, 1998), p. 314.

12. Naomi Seidman, *Faithful Renderings: Jewish-Christian Difference and the Politics of Translation* (Chicago: Univ. of Chicago Press, 2006), p. 250. Seidman refers to Seth L. Wolitz, "*Satan in Goray* as Parable," *Prooftexts* 9 (1989): 14, and to Irving H. Buchen, *Isaac Bashevis Singer and the Eternal Past* (New York: New York Univ. Press, 1968), p. ix.

13. See Eliezer Wiesel, . . . *Un di velt hot geshvign* / . . . *Y el mundo callaba* (. . . And the World Remained Silent) (Buenos Aires: Tsentral-farband fun Poylishe Yidn in Argentina, 1956). Compare Seidman, *Faithful Renderings*, chap. 5.

14. Restrictions on publishing in czarist Russia became more stringent after the Decembrist Revolt in 1825. In addition, because of opposition to rabbinic and especially hasidic texts, stemming in part from enlightened Jews during the 1820s, publication in Hebrew became substantially more difficult for hasidim, which slowed the reception of some essential works. For example, two important books by Nathan Sternharz—*Ḥayei Moharan* (The Life of Rabbi Nahman) and *Yemei Moharnat* (The Days of Rabbi Nathan)—were not printed until the 1870s, decades after the author's death.

15. I discuss the importance of parody as a vehicle for Hebrew literary innovation in my article "Joseph Perl's Escape from Biblical Epigonism through Parody of Hasidic Writing," *AJS Review* 29 (2005): 265–82.

16. My thesis on the role of translation in Hebrew literary history is based in part on my article "Neglected Origins of Modern Hebrew Prose: Hasidic and Maskilic Travel Narratives," *AJS Review* 33 (2009): 3–43.

17. On the distinction between biblical and Mishnaic Hebrew, see Aba Bendavid, *Leshon mikra ve-leshon ḥakhamim*, 2 vols. (Tel Aviv: Dvir, 1967–71).

18. Regarding mariners' belief in Providence, see Cohen, *The Novel and the Sea*, pp. 45–49.

19. See also Rebecca Wolpe, "The Sea and Sea Voyage in *Maskilic* Literature," PhD diss., Hebrew Univ. of Jerusalem, 2011.

20. Moshe Pelli, "The Literary Genre of the Travelogue in Hebrew Haskalah Literature: Shmuel Romanelli's Masa Ba'rav," *Modern Judaism* 11 (1991): 256, 257.

21. Nancy Sinkoff, "Strategy and Ruse in the Haskalah of Mendel Lefin of Satanow," in *New Perspectives on the Haskalah*, ed. Shmuel Feiner and David Sorkin (London: Litman Library of Jewish Civilization, 2001), p. 93.

22. Ibid.

23. Ernest Klein, *A Comprehensive Etymological Dictionary of the Hebrew Language for Readers of English* (Jerusalem: CARTA and Univ. of Haifa, 1987), p. 545, brackets in the original.

24. Robert Alter, trans., *The Book of Psalms: A Translation with Commentary* (New York: Norton, 2007), pp. 473–74.

25. Wallace Stevens, *The Collected Poems* (New York: Knopf, 1954), p. 10.

26. See Robert Alter, *The Invention of Hebrew Prose: Modern Fiction and the Language of Realism* (Seattle: Univ. of Washington Press, 1988): "Dov Sadan long ago proposed that there was a kind of imaginative logic which produced a compelling movement from literature to politics: after writers had succeeded in creating an 'as if' reality in Hebrew, the conditions of consciousness had been established in their readers for seeking to build an actual Hebrew reality, with all the requisite social institutions and political apparatus, in the real geography of this world" (p. 71).

1. Narratives of Sea Travel from Jonah to Yosef Sofer

1. As Rebecca Wolpe pointed out to me, this is less true of southern European Jewish culture. See also Noah Efron, *Judaism and Science: A Historical Introduction* (Westport, CT: Greenwood Press, 2007), and David Ruderman, *Jewish Thought and Scientific Discovery in Early Modern Europe* (New Haven, CT: Yale Univ. Press, 1995).

2. Among many studies of sea travel in biblical literature, see Raphael Patai, *The Children of Noah: Jewish Seafaring in Ancient Times* (Princeton, NJ: Princeton Univ. Press, 1998).

3. As noted earlier, unless otherwise indicated, all translations are my own. In the case of biblical passages, I have sometimes adapted translations from *JPS Hebrew–English Tanakh* (Philadelphia: Jewish Publication Society, 1999) and have consulted *The Jerusalem Bible*, ed. and trans. Harold Fisch (Jerusalem: Koren, 1983).

4. A. Cohen, *The Psalms* (London: Soncino, 1945), p. 358.

5. This discussion is adapted from my article "Neglected Origins of Modern Hebrew Prose: Hasidic and Maskilic Travel Narratives," *AJS Review* 33 (2009): 3–43, reprinted with permission from the Association for Jewish Studies.

6. Psalm 107 is therefore also the source of a halakhic discussion regarding the circumstances under which a traveling Jew should say the prayer after escaping danger (Berakhot 54b).

7. See, for example, the sixteenth-century commentator Tosefot Yom Tov on Tractate Demai, chap. 1, Mishna 1.

8. I return to the interpretation of Psalm 107 in chapter 6.

9. Adapted from the translation in *JPS Hebrew–English Tanakh* after consulting *The Jerusalem Bible*.

10. המוכר את הספינה מכר את התורן ואת הנס ואת העוגין ואת כל המנהיגין אותה (Babylonian Talmud, Mishna to Baba Batra, chap. 5, 1; cited in Daniel Sperber, *Nautica Talmudica* [Ramat Gan, Israel: Bar Ilan Univ. Press, 1986], p. 17). The pertinent biblical meaning of *nes* is "sail" and of *toran* is "mast," but Daniel Sperber argues that the Talmudic usage makes *nes* into "mast" and *toran* into "sailyard." Awareness of diachronic linguistics adds to the ambiguity of these terms.

11. Baraita di-Melekhet ha-mishkan 5, as cited in Sperber, *Nautica Talmudica*, p. 37.

12. Genesis Rabba 22, 6, as cited in ibid., p. 49.

13. Ibid., p. 18.

14. Beyond the scope of this analysis are Hebrew travel narratives that show the influence of Ladino and Arabic.

15. See Yehuda David Eisenstein, ed., *Otzar masa`ot: kovetz tiurim shel nose`im Yehudim be-Eretz Israel, Syria, Mitzrayim ve-artzot aḥerot* (New York: Eisenstein, 1926); the English title page lists the book as *Ozar Massaoth: A Collection of Itineraries by Jewish Travelers to Palestine, Syria, Egypt, and other Countries*. More reliable is Avraham Ya`ari, ed., *Mase`ot Eretz Israel shel `olim Yehudiim: mi-yemei ha-benayim ve-`ad reshit yemei shivat Tzion* (Tel Aviv: Ha-Histadrut ha-Tzionit, 1946). As editors of the anthologized texts, however, both Eisenstein and Ya`ari tacitly bring the punctuation into conformity with contemporary style. This approach obscures some of the pertinent linguistic and literary features; where possible, I have returned to Eisenstein's and Ya`ari's original Hebrew sources. Another issue not analyzed here is the ideological bias that guides both editors in the context of twentieth-century Zionism.

16. Elkan Nathan Adler, ed., *Jewish Travellers in the Middle Ages: 19 Firsthand Accounts* (1930; reprint, New York: Dover, 1987).

17. In Eisenstein, *Otzar masa`ot*, p. 98. In Avraham Ya`ari's collection *Mas`a Meshullam mi-Voltera be-Eretz Israel ba-shnat RM"A (1481)* (Jerusalem: Mossad Bialik, 1948), this passage reads differently: "The Cave of the Machpelah is on the outskirts [*`ibur*] of the land" (p. 68). "The navel of the land" can mean that it is at the center of the earth; the phrase *tabur ha-aretz* occurs in Judges 9:37 and Ezekiel 38:12, but the "center of the earth" idea may have been influenced by the Greek notion of the world's navel (*omphalos*).

18. In Eisenstein, *Otzar masa`ot*, p. 99, and in Ya`ari, *Mas`a Meshullam mi-Voltera*, p. 71.

19. Eisenstein, *Otzar masa`ot*, p. 100, and Ya`ari, *Mas`a Meshullam mi-Voltera*, p. 72.

20. In Ya`ari, *Mas`a Meshullam mi-Voltera*, p. 45, original orthography preserved.

21. Ibid., p. 117.

22. Meshullam's connections to biblical sources are also grammatical. Regarding his verbs, he variously uses (1) the simple past or perfective form that is common in Mishnaic writing (*ba'u, zarku*); (2) a compound form that may reflect the imperfect indicating a continuous past in Romance languages (*haya shokhev, hayu rotzim*); and (3) the biblical use of a consecutive Vav or conversive Vav to indicate a past or completed action (*va-yehi, va-tehi, ve-yeḥatru*). This trifold use of verb forms, reflecting linguistic shifts over the centuries, is typical of rabbinic Hebrew writing. Some prescriptive Hebrew linguists would later scorn this mixture of historical layers, although it was familiar and accessible to traditionally educated premodern readers.

23. In Ya`ari, *Mas`a Meshullam mi-Voltera*, p. 86.

24. Compare my translation here with the translation in Adler, ed., *Jewish Travellers in the Middle Ages*, p. 206.

25. The English translation I have seen is Ovadiah of Bartenura [Ovadia of Bertinoro], *Pathway to Jerusalem: The Travel Letters of Rabbi Ovadiah of Bartenura Written between 1488–1490 during His Journey to the Holy Land*, trans. Yaakov Dovid Shulman, ed. Avrohom Marmorstein (New York: CIS, 1992). Unfortunately, the translator sometimes opts to paraphrase instead of translate. I have retranslated the passages quoted from this text.

26. In Avraham Ya`ari, ed., *'Igrot Eretz Israel she-katvu ha-Yehudim ha-yoshvim ba-aretz la-aḥehem she-ba-gola mi-yemei galut Bavel ve-`ad shivat Tzion she-be-yamenu* (1943; reprint, Ramat-Gan: Massada, 1971), pp. 108–9.

27. מֵעִם יְהוָה צְבָאוֹת תִּפָּקֵד בְּרַעַם וּבְרַעַשׁ וְקוֹל גָּדוֹל סוּפָה וּסְעָרָה וְלַהַב אֵשׁ אוֹכֵלָה׃ Compare Isaiah 66:15: God's chariots are like a *sufa* that conveys God's anger; the divinely driven *sufa* is also linked to a punishing, flaming fire (*lahavei esh*).

28. Francis Brown, S. R. Driver, and Charles A. Briggs, eds., *A Hebrew and English Lexicon of the Old Testament* (Oxford: Clarendon Press, 1952), p. 227.

29. Ya`ari, *'Igrot Eretz Israel*, p. 109.

30. Or "Captain of the boat"; the transliterated Hebrew word הפאטרוני is probably intended to be *ha-padrone* because *patrone* means "patron" or "customer."

31. Moshe Basola, *Mase`ot Eretz-Israel le-Rabbi Moshe Basola*, 2nd ed., ed. Yitzhak ben-Tzvi (Jerusalem: Hebrew Society for Research on Eretz-Israel, 1939), p. 28. The passage can also be found in Ya`ari, *Mase`ot Eretz Israel*, pp. 128–29, with modernized punctuation and helpful footnotes.

32. In Ya`ari, *Mase`ot Eretz Israel*, p. 169.

33. Ibid., p. 170.

34. Ibid., pp. 170–71.

35. The difficulty Hebrew authors had in establishing a term for sails is a key marker of Hebrew writers' command of nautical Hebrew. Later, a sail was sometimes referred to as a *vilon*, and the plural was either *vilonot* or *vila'ot*. But this usage conflicted with the other meaning of *vilon* as "curtain."

36. In Ya`ari, *Mase`ot Eretz Israel*, p. 181.

37. For a pertinent discussion of Azulai, see Matthias B. Lehmann, "*Levantinos* and Other Jews: Reading H. Y. D. Azulai's Travel Diary," *Jewish Social Studies: History, Culture, Society*, New Series, 13 (2007): 1–34.

38. In Ya`ari, *Mase`ot Eretz Israel*, p. 376.

39. In ibid., p. 395. Ya`ari used different sources, eliminating what he said were additions by the *maskil* Solomon Dubno as editor of the first printing: Simḥa ben Yehoshua, *Ahavat Tzion* (Hordona: n.p., 1790). Dubno was the author's son-in-law.

40. Ya`ari, *'Igrot Eretz Israel*, p. 287.

41. A somewhat similar genre to the travel narratives under discussion here was the chronicle, as found in accounts of traumatic events such as *Yeven metzula* (Abyss of Mire or Abyss of Despair) by Nathan Hanover. Like travel narratives, chronicles of community misfortune sometimes presented clear observations in a direct, unadorned style.

42. Ya`ari, *'Igrot Eretz Israel*, p. 288.

43. Ibid.

44. The phrase עמד על דעתו derives from medieval commentators' usage; this is not the typical dictionary sense in modern Hebrew, where it usually means "to insist." For the medieval usage, see Ramban on Ex. 2:23, where he comments that Moses "gadal ve-`amad `al da`ato"; there are analogous Talmudic uses, such as in the Babylonian Talmud, Tractate Ḥullin 7b.

45. Aba Bendavid, *Leshon mikra ve-leshon ḥakhamim*, 2 vols. (Tel Aviv: Dvir, 1967), 1:187; 2:638–41.

46. Ibid., 1:246.

47. In Ya`ari, *'Igrot Eretz Israel*, pp. 288–89.

48. Ibid., p. 288.

49. *DBS Torah Treasures: The Computerized Torah Library*, version 13.0 (Brooklyn, NY: DBS, 2007), lists three other uses in the Tanakh, where the meaning is not "sail" but closer to the associated notion of opening or spreading.

50. Ernest Klein writes that the term פרס is "a later variant of פרשׂ" (*A Comprehensive Etymological Dictionary of the Hebrew Language for Readers of English* [Jerusalem: CARTA and Univ. of Haifa, 1987], p. 530).

51. Marcus Jastrow, *A Dictionary of the Targumim, the Talmud Babli and Yerushalmi, and the Midrashic Literature* (1903; reprint, New York: Judaica Press, 1992), p. 1232.

52. Along these lines, see Sidra DeKoven Ezrahi, *Booking Passage: Exile and Homecoming in the Modern Jewish Imagination* (Berkeley: Univ. of California Press, 2000).

53. Adapted from Harry Zohn's translation of Walter Benjamin, "The Task of the Translator," in *Illuminations* (New York: Schocken, 1969), p. 81, which is not entirely accurate; originally cited in Walter Benjamin, "Die Aufgabe des Übersetzers," in *Gesammelte Schriften*, vol. iv-1 (Frankfurt am Main: Suhrkamp, 1980), p. 20. The passage Benjamin quotes occurs in Rudolf Pannwitz, *Die Krisis der Europaeishen Kultur* (Munich: Hans Carl, 1921), p. 242: "Der grundsätzliche irrtum des übertragenden ist dass er den zufälligen stand der eignen sprache festhält anstatt sie durch die fremde sprache gewaltig bewegen zu lassen."

2. Nahman

1. Moshe Rosman, *Founder of Hasidism: A Quest for the Historical Ba`al Shem Tov* (Berkeley: Univ. of California Press, 1996).

2. Avraham Rubenstein, ed., *Shivḥei ha-Besht: mahadura mu`eret ve-mevu'eret* (Jerusalem: Reuven Mass, 1991), pp. 293, 361. In English, see Dan Ben-Amos and Jerome R. Mintz, eds., *In Praise of the Baal Shem Tov: The Earliest Collection of Legends about the Founder of Hasidism* (Northvale, NJ: Jason Aronson, 1993), Tale 231, p. 237. The Yiddish version contains more information about the failed trip to the Land of Israel, as discussed by Avraham Ya`ari in "Shtei mahadurot-yesod shel 'Shivḥei ha-Besht,'" *Kiryat sefer* 39 (1964): 559–61.

3. Compare Arthur Green, *Tormented Master: A Life of Rabbi Nahman of Bratslav* (New York: Schocken, 1981), p. 64.

4. Nathan Sternharz, *Likutei halakhot* (Jerusalem: Keren hadpasa de-ḥasidei Breslav, 1985), vol. 5, *Hilkhot mila* 3, 3, p. 140. Also cited at the beginning of Nathan Sternharz, *Yemei Moharnat*, parts 1 and 2 (1876/1904; reprint, New York: Rozenfeld and Berger, 1970), part 2, "Ma'amarim mi-*Likutei halakhot* mi-`inyan Eretz-Israel," §42, p. 152.

5. For a seminal reconsideration of the importance of hasidic *`aliya* to the Land of Israel, see Ben-Tzion Dinur, "Ha-yesodot ha-idiologiim shel ha-`aliyot be-shnot Tof"Kuf—Tof"Resh [1740–1840]," in *Be-mifne ha-dorot: meḥkarim ve-`iyunim be-reshitam shel ha-zmanim ha-ḥadashim be-toldot Israel*, vol. 1 (Jerusalem: Mossad Bialik, 1955), pp. 69–79.

6. Many books about Rabbi Nahman of Bratslav have focused on the details of his fascinating life—including the 1798–99 pilgrimage to Palestine—without emphasizing that most of our information is based on and mediated by a single source, Nathan

Sternharz. Although there are many fine studies of the Bratslaver Rebbe, the dominant methodology might be compared to reconstructing Socrates's life based solely on Plato's dialogues. From a current historiographic perspective, this approach appears somewhat naïve and misleading. On the one hand, historians of Hasidism now try to get behind the internal textual tradition by finding references to their subject in outside sources; on the other hand, following psychoanalytic models, some literary scholars employ a "hermeneutics of suspicion," reading between the lines and finding concealed meanings. I have learned from these new trends, but my approach has another goal: to understand the linguistic and literary contributions of Bratslav writings to literary history. Hence, the life of Nahman is less essential here than are the biographer's texts about him.

7. Itamar Even-Zohar discusses the significance of calques, when Yiddish has been embedded in Hebrew, in *Polysystem Studies*, special issue of *Poetics Today* 11 (1990): 126–27.

8. There are some indications that parts of *Likutei Moharan* and *Sefer ha-middot* (*Sefer ha-Aleph Beit*) were written by Nahman and another scribe, Abraham of Petersburg, before Sternharz became Nahman's scribe. Even more significant, as shown by Joseph Weiss, is the likelihood that *Ha-sefer ha-nisraf*—Nahman's "Burned Book"—was written by Nahman himself. Nevertheless, based on existing evidence, Weiss acknowledges that Nahman's Hebrew style was far inferior to Sternharz's (*Meḥkarim be-ḥasidut Breslav*, ed. M. Piekarz [Jerusalem: Mossad Bialik, 1974], pp. 223–24).

9. See Eliezer Schweid, *Moledet ve-aretz ye`uda: Eretz-Israel be-hagut shel `am Israel* (Tel Aviv: `Am `oved, 1979), chap. 1 (on the Land of Israel in the teachings of Rabbi Nahman of Bratslav).

10. Nahman of Bratslav, *Likutei Moharan* (Jerusalem: Keren hadpasa shel ḥasidei Breslav, 1988), §44.

11. Sternharz, *Likutei halakhot*, vol. 1, *Hilkhot beit ha-knesset* 5, 8, p. 474. Also cited in the collection of sayings at the beginning of Sternharz, *Yemei Moharnat*, 1970 ed., part 2, §12, p. 140.

12. Nathan Sternharz, *Likutei tefilot* (Jerusalem: Shilo and Keren hadpasa shel ḥasidei Breslav, 1943), §20, p. 73; also cited in Dinur, "Ha-yesodot ha-idiologiim," p. 78.

13. Nathan Sternharz, *Ḥayei Moharan* (Jerusalem: Keren hadpasa shel ḥasidei Breslav, 1981), §14.

14. Nathan Sternharz, *Shivḥei ha-Ran ha-menukad* (Jerusalem: Agudat "Meshekh ha-naḥal," 1981), §7.

15. Ibid., §10. In *Yemei Moharnat*, Sternharz also recalls a story by Nahman about overcoming obstacles in connection with traveling to the Land of Israel (1970 ed., part 1, p. 29). This passage may also be found in an autographed manuscript in the Schocken Library and at the National Library of Israel, Microfilm 47470, p. 2b. On *katnut* in Nahman of Bratslav's thought and during his travel to the Land of Israel, see Ada Rapoport-Albert, "'Katnut,' 'pshitut' ve-'eini yode`a' shel R. Nahman mi-Breslav," in *Studies in Jewish Religious and Intellectual History Presented to Alexander Altmann on the Occasion*

of His Seventieth Birthday, ed. Siegfried Stein and Raphael Loewe (Tuscaloosa: Univ. of Alabama Press, 1979), 7–33 (Hebrew pagination). See also Zvi Mark, "`Al matzevei katnut ve-gadlut be-haguto shel R. Naḥman mi-Breslav," *Da`at* (Winter 2001): 45–80.

16. Sternharz, *Shivḥei ha-Ran ha-menukad*, §30.

17. Green, *Tormented Master*, pp. 83–84.

18. See Nahman, *Likutei Moharan*, 1988 ed., §73, p. 89a, and Sternharz, *Ḥayei Moharan*, 1981 ed., "Nesi`ato le-Eretz Israel," p. 80.

19. Sternharz, *Yemei Moharnat*, 1970 ed., part 1, p. 12.

20. Sternharz, *Ḥayei Moharan*, 1981 ed., part 2, "Ma`alat torato ve-sfarav ha-kedoshim," §32, p. 38.

21. Ibid., §30.

22. For a good discussion of Nathan Sternharz, see Weiss, *Meḥkarim be-ḥasidut Breslav*, chap. 5.

23. Eliezer Steinman, "Tziun le-meshorer," *Ha-tekufa* 16 (1922): 500.

24. Compare Marcus Moseley, *Being for Myself Alone: Origins of Jewish Autobiography* (Stanford, CA: Stanford Univ. Press, 2006): "Not only do Nathan's *Shivhei haran* and *Hayyei moharan* remain the primary sources for Nahman's life to this day, but also virtually all of Nahman's teachings and tales were mediated through the person of Nathan and translated by him from Yiddish to Hebrew" (p. 315).

25. On the subject of Nahman's earlier scribe, Abraham of Petersburg, see Weiss, *Meḥkarim be-ḥasidut Breslav*, pp. 223–27.

26. The Dnieper River is too far from Osiatyn to be the one on which Nahman sailed. The text must be alluding to a different river, closer to Osiatyn and Medvedevke. In *Rebbe Nachman's Wisdom: Shevachay HaRan and Sichos HaRan* (Brooklyn, NY: Breslov Research Institute, 1973), translator Aryeh Kaplan writes that the town has been "confused by many later writers with the city of Gusyatin or Husyatin in the Western Ukraine." He corrects the record: "Ossatin was a small village near Medvedevka and Smela" (p. 245 n.; cf. p. 22 n.).

27. Mendel Lefin and some of his maskilic contemporaries introduced far more precise punctuation. See Lefin's note on punctuation in *Mod`a le-vina* (Berlin: Ḥevrat ḥinukh ne`arim, 1789), quoted and translated in my article "Neglected Origins of Modern Hebrew Prose: Hasidic and Maskilic Travel Narratives," *AJS Review* 33 (2009): app. I, p. 36. I. B. Levinsohn's satire *Divrei tzadikim* mocks the bewilderment of two hasidim when they encounter all of those unfamiliar markings. See I. B. Levinsohn and Joseph Perl, *Gilgulav shel megale sod: kuntras divrei tzadikim le-RIBaL ve-Yosef Perl*, ed. Jonatan Meir (Los Angeles: Cherub Press, 2004).

28. This passage was not included in the original text of *Shivḥei ha-Ran* or *Siḥot ha-Ran* (under the running header *Sippurei ma`asiyot*) that was printed at the back of Nahman of Bratslav [and Nathan Sternharz], *Sippurei ma`asiyot* ([Ostrog or Mohilev?]: n.p.) in 1815. The earliest edition I have found—in the Scholem Library of the National

Library of Israel, Jerusalem—that includes this passage is Nathan Sternharz, *Magid siḥot* (Zholkva: n.p., [1850?]). If this was the first expanded edition, then the additions were presumably based on manuscripts edited following Nathan Sternharz's death. The passages discussed here are quoted from that 1850 edition; the expanded section that includes this passage can be found in Nathan Sternharz, *Siḥot ha-Ran ha-menukad* (Jerusalem: Keren R. Israel Dov Odesser, [1981?]), §117, p. 20a.

29. It is possible that S. Y. Abramovitsh is alluding to this passage in his ironic description of preparations for the comical, quasi-heroic journey in *Kitser masoes Binyumin ha-shlishi* (The Brief Travels of Benjamin the Third) (Vilna: Romm, 1878).

30. *Hitbodedut* literally refers to isolating or secluding oneself, but in hasidic writings it denotes solitary prayer, contemplation, or meditation—including dialogues with God.

31. Nahman, *Likutei Moharan*, 1988 ed., part 2, §48, p. 27b.

32. Quoting from the original, Sternharz's *Magid siḥot*, p. 20a. See also Sternharz, *Siḥot ha-Ran ha-menukad*, 1981 ed., §117.

33. For another English rendering, see Nahman of Bratslav, *Rabbi Nachman's Wisdom: Shevachay HaRan and Sichos HaRan*, trans. Aryeh Kaplan, ed. Zvi Aryeh Rosenfeld (Brooklyn, NY: Breslov Research Institute, 1973), §117, pp. 245–46.

34. Sternharz, *Siḥot ha-Ran ha-menukad*, 1981 ed., §117.

35. This passage refers to the scene in "Seder ha-nesi`a shelo le-Eretz Israel," in Sternharz, *Shivḥei ha-Ran ha-menukad*, 1981 ed., §19, p. 39; Nahman [and Sternharz], *Sippurei ma`asiyot*, 1815 ed., supplementary section, p. 8a.

36. "Order of His Journey to the Land of Israel" was later included in the separate book *Shivḥei ha-Ran* (In Praise of Rabbi Nahman), as discussed later.

37. Nathan Sternharz, "Seder ha-nesi`a shelo le-Eretz Israel," Manuscript 16988, Schocken Library, Jerusalem, or Microfilm 45394, National Library of Israel, Jerusalem. The text of "Seder ha-nesi`a shelo le-Eretz Israel" begins on page 77b of the manuscript.

38. For an important analysis of this text, comparing it to the account in *Ḥayei Moharan*, see Ada Rapoport-Albert, "Shnei mekorot le-te'ur nesi`ato shel R. Nahman mi-Breslav le-Eretz-Israel," *Kiryat sefer* 46 (1971): 147–53. There does not seem to be an adequate English translation of "Seder ha-nesi`a shelo le-Eretz Israel." Aryeh Kaplan's translation "The Pilgrimage," in Nahman of Bratslav, *Rabbi Nachman's Wisdom* (pp. 33–102), takes too many liberties, paraphrasing some difficult passages and rendering some of the linguistic complexities invisible. By the same token, the translation of the later "Nesi`ato le-Eretz Israel" is also inexact: "Journey to the Holy Land," in Avraham Greenbaum, trans., and Moshe Mykoff, ed., *Tzaddik: (Chayey Moharan): A Portrait of Rabbi Nachman* (New York: Breslov Research Institute, 1987), pp. 45–60.

39. See Gershom Scholem, *Kuntras eile shemot: sifrei Moharan z"l mi-Breslav ve-sifrei talmidav ve-talmidei talmidav* (Jerusalem: n.p., 1928), p. 34, and David Assaf, *Breslav: bibliografiya mu`eret* (Jerusalem: Zalman Shazar Center, 2000), p. 16. Assaf points out that the title on the first page of *Magid siḥot* (1850? ed.) is "Shivḥei ha-Ran" (p. 15).

"Seder ha-nesi`a shelo le-Eretz Israel" was also printed under the title *Mase`ot ha-yam* or *Ma`agalei tzedek* (Warsaw: Lebenzohn, 1850). In his memoirs, Avraham Gotlober mentions an edition from Yosefov in 1846, and the database of the National Library of Israel also lists an edition of *Mase`ot ha-yam* (Yosefov: Shapiro, 1846), but this copy of the book has apparently been lost.

40. For more information about Nahman's followers, see Noah ha-Levi Sternfeld, ed., *Gidulei ha-naḥal* (Jerusalem: Meshekh ha-naḥal, 1984). Shimon of Krementshuk is described as Nahman's friend and first student, having become close to Nahman as early as 1785 (p. 107).

41. Marcus Moseley notes, referring to prior scholarship by Joseph Dan and Arthur Green, that although the obvious biographical model for Sternharz was *Shivḥei ha-Besht*, "there is . . . a marked distinction to be drawn between the classic mode of Hasidic hagiography as exemplified by *Shivhei habesht* and Nathan's accounts of the life of Nahman" (*Being for Myself Alone*, p. 316). Moseley points out, for example, that Sternharz almost completely omits suggestions of the "supernatural and/or the miraculous" (p. 316).

42. Nahman [and Sternharz], *Sippurei ma`asiyot*, 1815 ed., supplementary section, "Seder ha-nesi`a shelo le-Eretz Israel," new numbering, p. 4b; Sternharz, *Shivḥei ha-Ran ha-menukad*, 1981 ed., §5, p. 20.

43. See Rapoport-Albert, "Shnei mekorot," and Ada Rapoport-Albert, "The Problems of Succession in the Hasidic Leadership with Special Reference to the Circle of R. Nachman of Braslav," PhD diss., Univ. of London, 1974.

44. Nahman [and Sternharz], *Sippurei ma`asiyot*, 1815 ed., supplementary section, p. 4b; Sternharz, *Shivḥei ha-Ran ha-menukad*, 1981 ed., §6, pp. 20–21. Modern editions correct some of the grammatical errors, such as addressing one of his daughters in the masculine: "ata tis`a." The 1981 edition reads "at tis`i." Perl's hasidic characters in *Megale temirin* make similar mistakes.

45. Nahman [and Sternharz], *Sippurei ma`asiyot*, 1815 ed., supplementary section, p. 4b; Sternharz, *Shivḥei ha-Ran ha-menukad*, 1981 ed., §6, p. 21.

46. In Ashkenazic pronunciation, the Hebrew and Yiddish term רחמנות would have been pronounced identically, as *rakhmones*. Used in this sense, the Yiddish term *rakhmones* goes back to Talmudic and Midrashic usages (the Bar Ilan Judaic Library lists eighteen occurrences). This is an example of a phenomenon discussed by Max Weinreich ("the Way of the ShaS") in *History of the Yiddish Language*, 2 vols., trans. Shlomo Noble, ed. Paul Glasser (New Haven, CT: Yale Univ. Press, 2008), and by Dovid Katz in *Words on Fire: The Unfinished Story of Yiddish* (New York: Basic Books, 2004). In European Jewish life, study in Yiddish was a main vehicle for the transmission of Hebrew and Aramaic, from medieval Europe to the present. The abstract noun רחמנות is a good example of post-biblical Hebrew that spread by way of Yiddish. As a plural adjective, רחמניות occurs just once in the Hebrew Bible, in a horrible scene of bitter irony mentioned in Lamentations 4:10: "The hands of merciful women have cooked their children" (ידי נשים רחמניות בשלו

ילדיהן). Yiddish embraced the term *mercy* (*rakhmones*) perhaps because the similar Germanic words already carried strong Christian associations. The Jewish God might not be known prominently as *barmherzig* (compassionate, merciful) or represented as inclined to show something that sounds like Christian mercy (*Gnade*), but in discussing attributes of God, Yiddish speakers could talk about God's two basic pathways, *derekh ha-din* (the path of justice) and *derekh ha-raḥamim* (the path of mercy). By extension, people could show each other *rakhmones*, "mercy."

47. Yankev ben Yitskhok Ashkenazi, *Tsene-rene* (n.p., ca. 1670), e.g., pp. 63b, 67d, 90d. This early edition of *Tsene-rene* is available on Google Books at http://books.google.com/books?id=ZJlEAAAAcAAJ&pg=PT123&dq=%D7%A8%D7%97%D7%9E%D7%A0%D7%95%D7%AA&hl=en&sa=X&ei=5CQRUfvOAZLq0QH210GgAw&ved=0CDEQ6AEwAA (accessed Jan. 14, 2016).

48. Solomon Mandelkern, *Konkordantzia la-Tanakh* (Jerusalem: Schocken, 1986), p. 1087.

49. As mentioned earlier, Nathan Sternharz wrote two distinct accounts of Nahman's journey to Palestine in 1798. Although he did not meet Nahman until four years after the voyage took place, he was able to reconstruct it based on things he heard from Nahman and his followers. The early version was published in 1815 together with *Sippurey mayses* at the back of that volume; the second version, in *Ḥayei Moharan*, seems to have been written in the 1820s but not published until 1874. The long delay was the result of difficulties Sternharz had with the Russian authorities when he published Nahman's works. At odds with czarist censorship laws, he set up a printing press in his house in 1821 and published some books—such as the second edition of *Likutei Moharan* and *Likutei Moharan tenina* (part 2). He was arrested, forced to close his printing venture, and subsequently unable to publish most of his writings. This may have hastened his departure for Palestine in 1822; if so, his pilgrimage seems to echo the sea travel at the end of *Megale temirin*. At the end of his life, according to Gershom Scholem, Nathan Sternharz was able to send *Likutei halakhot* to the printer, but the first volume was not published until 1845, one year after he died (Scholem, *Kuntras eile shemot*, p. 10). Sternharz apparently also published *Likutei tefilot* secretly in 1827 (Scholem, *Kuntras eile shemot*, p. 19).

50. This section is based in part on my essay "Innovation by Translation: Yiddish and Hasidic Hebrew in Literary History," in *Arguing the Modern Jewish Canon: Essays on Literature and Culture in Honor of Ruth R. Wisse*, ed. Justin Cammy, Dara Horn, Alyssa Quint, and Rachel Rubinstein (Cambridge, MA: Center for Jewish Studies and Harvard Univ. Press, 2008), pp. 417–25.

51. Nahman [and Sternharz], *Sippurei ma`asiyot*, 1815 ed., supplementary section, p. 4b; Sternharz, *Shivḥei ha-Ran ha-menukad*, 1981 ed., §1, p. 19.

52. Ibid.

53. Nahman [and Sternharz], *Sippurei ma'asiyot*, 1815 ed., supplementary section, p. 4b; Sternharz, *Shivḥei ha-Ran ha-menukad*, 1981 ed., §3, p. 20.

54. One of the important phrases in Hebrew prayer is *'ad 'olam*, "forever." Yet this temporal usage of *'olam* was reframed in a spatial sense when popular belief called for the dichotomy between "this world" (*'olam ha-zeh*) and "the world to come" (*'olam ha-ba*). In Hebrew, this opposition can still be understood temporally. But translated into Yiddish, perhaps influenced by Christian beliefs, it became *di velt* and *yene velt*, "this world" and "that world," distinct spatially rather than temporally. The expression "the world to come" (*'olam ha-ba*), referring to the time after the Messiah comes, avoids imagining an ontologically separate other world.

55. Nahman [and Sternharz], *Sippurei ma'asiyot*, 1815 ed., supplementary section, p. 4b; Sternharz, *Shivḥei ha-Ran ha-menukad*, 1981 ed., §1, p. 20.

56. Martin Cunz rightly observes that the storm descriptions "are central to the literary structure" of *Shivḥei ha-Ran* and that the mortal danger presented by these storms sets the overarching narrative tone (*Die Fahrt des Rabbi Nachman von Brazlaw ins Land Israel [1798–1799]* [Tübingen: Mohr, 1997], p. 291). His analysis is also useful for its juxtaposition of the parallel passages in *Shivḥei ha-Ran* and *Ḥayei Moharan*.

57. Nahman [and Sternharz], *Sippurei ma'asiyot*, 1815 ed., supplementary section, p. 5a; Sternharz, *Shivḥei ha-Ran ha-menukad*, 1981 ed., §9, p. 22. I have preserved the original punctuation, which does not distinguish between commas and periods.

58. Of the three major storm accounts, this is the only one that has a direct parallel in *Ḥayei Moharan*, §5, "Nesi'ato le-Eretz Israel," para. 9 (see Cunz, *Die Fahrt des Rabbi Nachman*, p. 291).

59. One of the few studies of Nathan Sternharz's style is contained in Isaiah Rabinovitch, "Darko shel R. Nahman mi-Breslov el *Sippurei-ma'asiot* shelo," in *Shoreshim u-megamot: le-beḥinat mekoroteha shel ha-bikoret ha-ḥadasha ve-'iyunim be-darka shel ha-sifrut ha-'Ivrit* (Jerusalem: Mossad Bialik, 1967), chap. 6, pp. 163–218. Rabinovitch notes an "internal tension that does not tolerate any punctuation marks" in Sternharz's narrative voice (p. 165). Rabinovitch's commentary is more expressive in the Yiddish version of his essay, "Reb Nahman Braslavers veg tsu zayne sippurey mayses," *Di goldene keyt* 69–70 (1970): "Here the narrative style is dynamic, artistic: it is so taut that it does not have any intervening pauses, just as if it were rushing to reach the fateful fact that 'he [Nahman] wanted to see something and saw absolutely nothing'" (pp. 175–76).

60. In Nahman's Tale 10, the Hebrew text uses a rare meaning of a Yiddish word when a storm is called an *impet* (Nahman [and Sternharz], *Sippurei ma'asiyot*, 1815 ed., p. 48a; Nahman of Bratslav [and Nathan Sternharz], *Sippurei ma'asiyot* [Jerusalem: Keren hadpasa shel ḥasidei Breslav, 1979], p. 95). See Yudl Mark and Yuda A. Yoffe, eds., *Groyser verterbukh fun der Yidisher shprakh*, vol. 3 (New York: Yiddish Dictionary Committee, 1971), p. 1263, definition 6.

61. Nahman [and Sternharz], *Sippurei ma`asiyot*, 1815 ed., supplementary section, p. 6b; Sternharz, *Shivḥei ha-Ran ha-menukad*, 1981 ed., §14, pp. 30–31.

62. Nahman [and Sternharz], *Sippurei ma`asiyot*, 1815 ed., supplementary section, p. 6b, and Sternharz, *Shivḥei ha-Ran ha-menukad*, 1981 ed., §14, p. 30. Compare the descriptions of sea voyages in *Sippurei ma`asiyot*, Tale 2 and Tale 10; and see also Nahman, *Likutei Moharan*, 1988 ed., §12d, p. 17a.

63. Compare Cunz, *Die Fahrt des Rabbi Nachman*, p. 310.

64. Sternharz, *Shivḥei ha-Ran ha-menukad*, 1981 ed., §15, p. 31.

65. Nahman [and Sternharz], *Sippurei ma`asiyot*, 1815 ed., supplementary section, p. 7a; Sternharz, *Shivḥei ha-Ran ha-menukad*, 1981 ed., §15, p. 32.

66. Green, *Tormented Master*, pp. 172–75. In Nahman's experience of *katnut* prior to reaching the Land of Israel, he successively felt small, weak, and insignificant. The quick alternation of the Rebbe's moods suggests that he suffered from manic depression.

67. Sternharz, *Shivḥei ha-Ran ha-menukad*, 1981 ed., §20, p. 39.

68. Alexander Harkavy, *Yidish–English–Hebreyisher verterbukh* (New York: Hebrew Publishing, 1928), p. 373.

69. Nahman [and Sternharz], *Sippurei ma`asiyot*, 1815 ed., supplementary section, p. 9a; Sternharz, *Shivḥei ha-Ran ha-menukad*, 1981 ed., §21, pp. 43–44.

70. Nahman [and Sternharz], *Sippurei ma`asiyot*, 1815 ed., supplementary section, p. 9b; Sternharz, *Shivḥei ha-Ran ha-menukad*, 1981 ed., §21, p. 44.

71. Ibid.

72. Nahman [and Sternharz], *Sippurei ma`asiyot*, 1815 ed., supplementary section, pp. 9b–10a; Sternharz, *Shivḥei ha-Ran ha-menukad*, 1981 ed., §21, pp. 46–47.

73. In *A Dictionary of the Targumim, the Talmud Babli and Yerusahalmi, and the Midrashic Literature* (1903; reprint, New York: Judaica Press, 1992), Marcus Jastrow explains "bound together like a wasp and a scorpion," following Rashi: "as a bite of a wasp (requiring cold water) and one by a scorpion (requiring hot water)" (p. 390). See Rashi's gloss on the Babylonian Talmud, Tractate Ḥagiga 5a.

74. Nahman [and Sternharz], *Sippurei ma`asiyot*, 1815 ed., supplementary section, p. 10a; Sternharz, *Shivḥei ha-Ran ha-menukad*, 1981 ed., §21, pp. 47.

75. See Mendel Piekarz, *Ḥasidut Breslav: prakim be-ḥayei meḥolela, be-kitveha u-vesafiḥeha* (1972), 2nd ed. (Jerusalem: Mossad Bialik, 1995), app. 3, pp. 259–64. Piekarz refers to the earlier article by Joseph G. Weiss on the subject of internal rifts: "Ha-sefer ha-nisraf," in *Meḥkarim be-ḥasidut Breslav*, chap. 13. And compare the works by Rapoport-Albert cited earlier in this chapter: "'Katnut,' 'pshitut' ve-'eini yode`a'" and "Shnei mekorot le-te'ur nesi`ato."

76. Sternharz, "Nesi`ato le-Eretz Israel," in *Ḥayei Moharan*, 1981 ed., §1, p. 80.

77. Ibid.

78. Ibid., p. 81.

79. Nahman [and Sternharz], *Sippurei ma`asiyot*, 1815 ed., supplementary section, p. 1b; Sternharz, *Shivḥei ha-Ran ha-menukad*, 1981 ed., §6, p. 4.

80. Less-obvious examples of Yiddish influence might be in unusual uses of Nitpael verb form; for instance, "נשתדך עם בתו," "he arranged an engagement for his daughter," in Sternharz, *Ḥayei Moharan*, 1981 ed., p. 70b. This unusual Hebrew usage may be a translation of the Yiddish for "he became connected by marriage" (ער האט זיך משדך געווען).

81. Nahman [and Sternharz], *Sippurei ma`asiyot*, 1815 ed., supplementary section, p. 2b; Sternharz, *Shivḥei ha-Ran ha-menukad*, 1981 ed., §14, p. 9.

82. Sternharz, *Shivḥei ha-Ran ha-menukad*, 1981 ed., §20, p. 39.

83. Ibid., §§5, 19, 21.

84. Ibid., §§16, 21, 22. A related verbal form often appears in an imperfect or conditional construction. To say that as a young child Nahman would swallow his food without chewing it, Sternharz combines the future verb of being with the present tense of a verb, writing in the opening lines of *Shivḥei ha-Ran* that he יהיה בולע and לא יהיה לועס. "Nahman would say: how is it possible that he would transgress [יעשה עברה] unless he had become insane [אם לא שיהיה נעשה משוגע]?" Also, "Nahman יהיה מתחזק עצמו—" (Nahman would fortify himself) (Sternharz, *Shivḥei ha-Ran ha-menukad*, 1981 ed., §5, p. 4). This corresponds to the Yiddish ער האט זיך מתחזק געווען. This usage may have been influenced by the imperfect aspect of verbs in Slavic languages.

85. Iris Parush, "Mabat aḥer `al 'ḥayei ha-`Ivrit ha-«meita»: ha-ba`arut ha-mekuvenet ba-leshon ha-`Ivrit ba-ḥevra ha-Yehudit ha-mizraḥ eropit ba-me'ah ha-19 ve-hashpa`ata `al ha-sifrut ha-`Ivrit ve-kor'eha," *Alpayim* 13 (1996): 75, 80.

86. Ibid., p. 75.

3. Nahman's Fantasy Travels and Sternharz's Pilgrimage

1. Nahman of Bratslav [and Nathan Sternharz], *Sippurei ma`asiyot* ([Ostrog or Mohilev?]: n.p., 1815), introduction, p. 2b; in a standard twentieth-century edition, Nahman of Bratslav [and Nathan Sternharz], *Sippurei ma`asiyot* (Jerusalem: Keren hadpasa shel ḥasidei Breslav, 1979), introduction, p. 7. Although the title of the collection of Nahman's stories is usually translated *Tales*, it is worth looking closer at this title. First, we note that Nahman and Sternharz would have used the Ashkenazic pronunciation: *Sippurey mayses*. The term *sippur* is postbiblical Hebrew, meaning "story"; *ma`ase* (not the same as *ma`asiya*) is postbiblical Hebrew and means "event, incident." Based on these Hebrew meanings of *sippur* (story) and *ma`ase* (deed), the two words were combined as *sippur hamayse* in Yiddish and came to mean "narratives of events or deeds." The Hebrew title for Nahman's bilingual Hebrew/Yiddish masterpiece requires that we think simultaneously in both languages. Alone, the Yiddish word *mayse* means "story," as in the phrase *bobe-mayses* (derived from Stories of Bovo, but popularly understood to mean Grandmother Tales). But in medieval Hebrew the term *ma`asiya* came to mean "story," "folk tale," or

"fairy tale" (see Ya`akov Ken`ani, *Ha-milon ha-`Ivri ha-malei*, 4 vols. [n.p.: Milonim la`am, 2000], 2:1576), perhaps in connection with the Yiddish usage of *mayse*. Hence, "sippurei ma`asiyot" or "sippurey mayses" means roughly "stories of (folk) tales." Nahman did not just tell tales; he retold and redeemed folk tales.

2. Nathan Sternharz, *Yemei Moharnat*, part 1 (Lemberg: Ya`akov Meshullam Nik, 1876); Nathan Sternharz, *Yemei Moharnat*, part 1, edited by Israel Heilprin (Jerusalem: n.p., 1904); Nathan Sternharz, *Yemei Moharnat*, parts 1 and 2 (reprint, New York: Rozenfeld and Berger, 1970), part 2, "Ma'amarim mi-*Likutei halakhot* mi-`inyan Eretz-Israel," sec. 29, p. 148. The 1876 printing of the first part of *Yemei Moharnat* is extremely rare; I have found it only at the National Library of Israel and the British Library. The first edition of the second part of *Yemei Moharnat*, edited by Israel Heilprin, is also rare but available at the National Library of Israel.

3. Nathan Sternharz, *Ḥayei Moharan* (Jerusalem: Keren hadpasa shel ḥasidei Breslav, 1981), sec. 15, p. 18.

4. Today in Jewish circles it is far more common to hear the term *tikkun `olam* without the definite article. But the phrase *tikkun ha-`olam* was popular among hasidic writers. It uses *ha-`olam* in the postbiblical sense, meaning "world"; only in Ecclesiastes 3:11 is it possible to claim this as a biblical sense of the word, and experts doubt this interpretation even for that passage. The meanings of the postbiblical usage of *`olam* expanded to include "community" in the Middle Ages (possibly influenced by Yiddish *der oylem*). See Ernest Klein, *A Comprehensive Etymological Dictionary of the Hebrew Language for Readers of English* (Jerusalem: CARTA and Univ. of Haifa, 1987), p. 466.

5. Nahman of Bratslav [and Nathan Sternharz], *Likutei Moharan tinyana*, bound with *Likutei Moharan* (Jerusalem: Keren hadpasa shel ḥasidei Breslav, 1988), sec. 8, 10, p. 18a.

6. Nahman of Bratslav, *Likutei Moharan* (Jerusalem: Keren hadpasa shel ḥasidei Breslav, 1988), sec. 55, 2, p. 63a.

7. Ibid., sec. 81, p. 94a.

8. Sternharz, *Yemei Moharnat*, part 1, 1876 ed. In *Nave tzadikim* (Bnei Brak: n.p., 1969), Nathan Tzvi Kenig lists Nahman of Tcherin as editor (p. 138).

9. See Sternharz, *Yemei Moharnat*, part 1, 1876 ed., pp. 46b–48b; 1970 ed., pp. 111–15.

10. See Isaiah Rabinovitch, "Darko shel R. Naḥman mi-Breslav el *Sippurei-ma`asiyot* shelo," in *Shoreshim u-megamot: le-beḥinat mekoroteha shel ha-bikoret ha-ḥadasha ve-`iyunim be-darka shel ha-sifrut ha-`Ivrit* (Jerusalem: Mossad Bialik, 1967), pp. 163–218. He republished this chapter in Yiddish as "Reb Nakhmen Braslavers veg tsu zayne sippurey-mayses," *Di goldene keyt* 69–70 (1970): 174–220.

11. See Yosef Klausner, *Historiya shel ha-sifrut ha-`Ivrit ha-ḥadasha*, 6 vols. (Jerusalem: Hebrew Univ., 1930–50), 2:304–5.

12. Shmuel Werses, "Mi-lashon el lashon ba-'Sippurei ma`asiyot' shel R. Nahman mi-Breslav," *Ḥuliyot* 9 (2005): 31–35.

13. Joseph Perl, *Megale temirin* (Vienna: Strauss, 1819), and *Ma'asiyot ve-'igrot mi-tzadikim amitiim u-mi-anshei shlomeinu*, ed. Khone Shmeruk and Shmuel Werses (Jerusalem: Israel Academy of Sciences and Humanities, 1970).

14. See Mendel Piekarz, *Ḥasidut Breslav: prakim be-ḥayei meḥolela, be-kitveha u-ve-sefiḥeha*, 1972, 2nd ed. (Jerusalem: Mossad Bialik, 1995), p. 178.

15. The Hebrew reads:

זאת מצאנו באמתחת הכתבים והוא ענין התנצלות על שכתב ז״ל הספמ״ע על לשון פשוט כזה וזהו.

Even this single Hebrew line shows the influence of Yiddish: the implicit idiom *af aza poshetn loshn* (in such a simple language) is translated into *'al lashon pashut ke-zeh*. Some *mitnagdim* mocked this hasidic use of the preposition *'al* to translate Yiddish *af*, as in other expressions such as *'al shabbat* (translating *af shabbes*).

16. Nathan Sternharz, *Sippurei ma'asiyot*, 2nd ed. (n.p.: n.p., ca. 1845–50), "Hakdama shniya" (second preface), p. 2b; Nahman [and Sternharz], *Sippurei ma'asiyot*, 1979 ed., "Hakdama shniya," p. 14.

17. Although there is no typographic differentiation, it is also possible to conclude that the final sentence was added by the editor, indicating that he copied the note from Nathan Sternharz's manuscript just as he found it. (This ambiguity is made possible by the verb העתק, which can mean both "to copy" and "to translate.") It is possible that these lines were not written by Nathan Sternharz himself but that they do express the gist of what he might have written.

18. Sternharz, *Sippurei ma 'asiyot*, "Hakdama shniya," ca. 1845–50 ed., p. 2b; 1979 ed., p. 14.

19. Ibid.

20. In my translation, I have chosen a nonidiomatic phrase, "hurry himself," to mark the presence of a common feature of hasidic writing discussed in chapter 2: the use of *et 'atzmo* corresponding to the Yiddish reflexive *zikh*. The implicit Yiddish reflexive verb *aylen zikh* becomes *mezarez et 'atzmo*; here *'im eino mezarez et 'atzmo* (which occurs rarely in other hasidic writing) takes the place of the Hitpael form *'im eino mizdarez* (which occurs a few times in medieval, midrashic Hebrew).

21. Sternharz, *Sippurei ma 'asiyot*, "Hakdama shniya," 1845–50 ed., p. 2b; 1979 ed., p. 14.

22. For several incisive discussions of "foreignizing translation" since Friedrich Schleiermacher's essay "On the Different Methods of Translating," including Walter Benjamin's essay "The Task of the Translator," see Lawrence Venuti, ed., *The Translation Studies Reader*, 2nd ed. (London: Routledge, 2004). See also Lawrence Venuti, *The Scandals of Translation: Towards an Ethics of Difference* (London: Routledge, 1998).

23. As reported by Sternharz in his posthumously published biography of Nahman, *Ḥayei Moharan*, 2 vols. (Lemberg: Carl Budweiser, 1874), 1:part 1, p. 22b; 1981 ed., part 1, p. 87.

24. These are the *leshonot gasim* for which Sternharz apologizes in the posthumously published passage at the end of his second preface to *Sippurei ma'asiyot*.

25. See, for example, the analyses in Arnold Band's translation of Nahman of Bratslav, *The Tales* (New York: Paulist Press, 1978), and in Arthur Green, *Tormented Master: A Life of Rabbi Nahman of Bratslav* (New York: Schocken, 1981). See also Aryeh Kaplan's almost excessive tracing of the possible kabbalistic meanings in Aryeh Kaplan, trans., *Rabbi Nahman's Stories (Sippurey Ma`asioth)* (Jerusalem: Breslov Research Institute, 1983). The following works are also recommended: Yosef Dan, *Ha-sippur ha-ḥasidi* (Jerusalem: Keter, 1975), chap. 3; Piekarz, *Ḥasidut Breslav*; David Roskies, *A Bridge of Longing: The Lost Art of Yiddish Storytelling* (Cambridge, MA: Harvard Univ. Press, 1995), chap. 2; Ora Wiskind-Elper, *Tradition and Fantasy in the Tales of Reb Nahman of Bratslav* (Albany: State Univ. of New York Press, 1998); and Marianne Schleicher, *Intertextuality in the Tales of Rabbi Nahman of Bratslav: A Close Reading of* Sippurey Ma'asiyot (Leiden: Brill, 2007).

26. Nahman [and Sternharz] *Sippurei ma`asiyot*, 1815 ed., 7b; 1979 ed., pp. 10–11. From this point, citations to *Sippurei ma`asiyot* are given parenthetically in the text, using the abbreviation *SM* (for *Sippurei ma`asiyot*) with page numbers for the 1815 edition first and then the 1979 edition (e.g., *SM*, pp. 7b/10–11).

27. See Marcus Jastrow, *A Dictionary of the Targumim, the Talmud Babli and Yerushalmi, and the Midrashic Literature* (1903; reprint, New York: Judaica Press, 1992), p. 373.

28. See Avraham Even-Shoshan, *Ha-milon he-ḥadash*, 4 vols. (Jerusalem: Hotza'at Kiryat-sefer, 1985), 3:1298c.

29. This passage is used as an example in Yudl Mark and Yuda A. Yoffe, eds., *Groyser verterbukh fun der Yidisher shprakh*, 4 vols. (New York: Yiddish Dictionary Committee, 1961), 1:91.

30. The DBS database (*DBS Torah Treasures: The Computerized Torah Library*, version 13.0 [Brooklyn, NY: DBS, 2007]) shows, in writings associated with Rabbi Nahman, 206 occurrences of the term *sefina* or *ha-sefina* but no occurrences of *oniya* except for a few in the plural. In contrast, among hasidic texts more broadly conceived, DBS lists 417 instances of *sefina* or *ha-sefina* and 42 instances of *oniya*. In Sternharz's multivolume collection *Likutei halakha*, *sefina* appears 16 times, but *oniya* occurs in only a single passage. It is possible to resolve some mysteries of authorship using statistical data of this kind, as we see in chapter 7.

31. As discussed in chapter 1, the term *vilon* occasionally also appears in medieval glosses, where it means "sail." See Ken`ani, *Ha-milon ha-`Ivri ha-malei*, 1:484. Commenting on Isaiah 33:23, for example, Rashi explains that *bal parsu nes* means that they will not be able to spread sail (*lifros vilon*). Rashi and others may have taken the word *vilon* from Latin *vēlum*, one meaning of which is "sail," or from Old French (cognate with *voile*, "veil" or "sail").

32. Thanks go to Ghil`ad Zuckermann for his help refining this analysis. On the Israeli calquing of the Yiddish locution "ikh volt gevolt" (I would like to know), see Ghil`ad Zuckermann, *Israelit safa yafa: az eizu safa ha-Israelim medabrim?* trans. Maya Feldman (Tel Aviv: `Am `oved, 2008), p. 102.

33. In a private communication, this is the example Zuckermann gave: a French speaker who moves to Israel would be likely to say, "Ani ḥoshev ki ha-yeled yafe" (an acceptable but outmoded Hebrew grammatical form) instead of "Ani ḥoshev she-ha-yeled yafe" because of influence from the French word *que*. On "use intensification," see Ghil`ad Zuckermann, "Complement Clause Types in Israeli," in *Complementation: A Cross-Linguistic Typology*, ed. R. M. W. Dixon and A. Y. Aikhenvalt (Oxford: Oxford Univ. Press, 2006), pp. 72–92, and Ghil`ad Zuckermann, "Camouflaged Borrowing: Folk-Etymological Nativization in the Service of Puristic Language Engineering," PhD diss., Univ. of Oxford, 2000.

34. Hans Blumenberg, *Shipwreck with Spectator: Paradigm of a Metaphor for Existence*, trans. Steven Rendall (Cambridge, MA: MIT Press, 1997), p. 8. In the German original, Blumenberg writes: "Zwei Voraussetzungen bestimmen vor allem die Bedeutungslast der Metaphorik von Seefahrt und Schiffbruch: einmal das Meer als naturgegebene Grenze des Raumes menschlicher Unternehmungen und zum anderen seine Dämonisierung als Sphäre der Unberechenbarkeit, Gesetzlosigkeit, Orientierungswidrigkeit" (*Schiffbruch mit Zuschauer: Paradigma einer Daseinsmetapher* [Frankfurt am Main: Suhrkamp, 1979], p. 10). Rebecca Wolpe has referred me to other authors who discuss this motif, including Alan Corbin, *The Lure of the Sea: The Discovery of the Seaside in the Western World, 1750–1840*, trans. Jocelyn Phelps (Los Angeles: Univ. of California Press, 1994).

35. W. H. Auden, *The Enchafèd Flood or The Romantic Iconography of the Sea* (New York: Random House, 1950), p. 6.

36. "The Outlaw Ocean," *New York Times*, July 20, 2015; see also the front-page article "Men and Laws, Thrown Overboard: Crime Abounds on High Seas, and One Ship Offers a Case Study," *New York Times*, July 19, 2015.

37. The passage in Hebrew, quoted from the 1979 edition, is:

וילך ויעבור עד שבא אל הים וישב בספינה ועבר בים. ובא רוח סערה גדולה ונשא הספינה אל ספר א׳ שהי׳ שם מדבר. ומגודל הסערה שקורין (אומפיט) נשברה הספינה. אך האנשים שבה ניצולו ויצאו על היבשה.

38. Kaplan, *Rabbi Nahman's Stories*, p. 217.

39. See Sternharz, *Ḥayei Moharan*, "Sippurim ḥadashim" (New Stories), sec. 2, 1981 ed., pp. 66–67.

40. Sternharz, *Ḥayei Moharan*, "Nesi`ato le-Eretz Israel" (His Journey to the Land of Israel), sec. 7, 1981 ed., p. 82.

41. Rebecca Wolpe referred me to research indicating that the sea plays a similar role in other folklore: Albrecht Classen, "Storms, Sea Crossings, the Challenges of Nature, and the Transformation of the Protagonist in Medieval and Renaissance Literature," *Neohelicon* 30 (2003): 163, and Wayland D. Hand, "Crossing Water: A Folkloristic Motif," in *For Max Weinreich on His Seventieth Birthday: Studies in Jewish Languages, Literature, and Society* (The Hague: Morton, 1964), p. 83.

42. Sternharz, *Sippurei ma`asiyot*, "Hakdama shniya," ca. 1845–50 ed., p. 1a; 1979 ed., p. 8.

43. Sternharz, *Sippurei ma`asiyot*, "Hakdama shniya," ca. 1845–50 ed., p. 2b; 1979 ed., p. 14.

44. The only detailed literary analysis of *Yemei Moharnat* seems to be Marcus Moseley's discussion in *Being for Myself Alone: Origins of Jewish Autobiography* (Stanford, CA: Stanford Univ. Press, 2006). He astutely analyzes Sternharz's writings following a section on Jacob Emden's collection *Megillat sefer*, focusing on their characteristics as autobiographical writing. In this context, what links them is their impressive Hebrew style, building on centuries of rabbinic writing.

45. Mordechai Mantel surveys the complex textual history of *Yemei Moharnat* in "*Sefer yemei Moharnat* shel rebi Natan mi-Nemirov: `iyun bibliografi," *`Alei sefer* 14 (1987): 125–34. Mantel argues for a kind of unity between parts 1 and 2, but the publication history and existing manuscripts make clear that this posthumously published work is really a collection of writings rather than a book that was completed by the author. In the manuscripts, some segments bear the title *Yemei Natan*.

46. Sternharz, *Yemei Moharnat*, part 2, 1904 ed.

47. For example, passages from Sternharz's autobiography are extant in holograph manuscripts held by the Schocken Library in Jerusalem, with microfilms at the National Library of Israel (NLI). Three segments are as follows, with Schocken collection and microfilm numbers correlated to page numbers for the 1970 edition of *Yemei Moharnat*, part 1: (1) Schocken 70133, NLI Microfilm 47440, pp. 1–6 = pp. 28–33; (2) Schocken 70084, NLI Microfilm 46816, pp. 1–16 = pp. 33–53; (3) Schocken 47470, NLI Microfilm 47470, pp. 6–10 = pp. 53–58.

Moreover, two long manuscripts copied from Sternharz's papers that contain some variants merit study. Part 1 is contained in Schocken Manuscript 16990/2, NLI Microfilm 45444, pp. 72–133; part 2 is contained in two manuscripts: Schocken Manuscript 16989, NLI Microfilm 45446, pp. 1–72; and Schocken Manuscript 16990, NLI Microfilm 45444, numbered sheets 65–139.

48. See, for example, Nathan Sternharz, *Kitvei Rebbe Naḥman mi-Breslav: Ḥayei Moharan, Yemei Moharnat, Yemei ha-tela'ot* (Beit Shemesh: "Nekudot tovot," 2005).

49. Sternharz, *Yemei Moharnat*, 1970 ed., part 2, p. 273, sheet 137a. This book is numbered both by page (even-numbered pages) and by sheet (left-hand, facing pages); I list only the page numbers in citations. Subsequent citations to *Yemei Moharnat* are given parenthetically in the text, including the abbreviation *YM* and page numbers in the 1970 edition; all are from part 2.

50. This passage may be found in both of the full manuscripts of *Yemei Moharnat*, part 2, neither of them in Sternharz's hand. See Schocken Manuscript 16989, NLI Microfilm 45446, p. 10a, and Schocken Manuscript 16990, NLI Microfilm 45444, p. 15a. The first reads, "I am writing all of this on the ship" (*ve-ani kotev kol zeh `al ha-sefina*), but the latter

introduces an ambiguity. It gives a second reading of the final phrase as "at the library" (*'al ha-sifria*), but then above the word *sifria* (not deleted) it reads "on the ship" (*'al ha-sefina*). I assume that insertion reflects the copyist's confusion or a correction of the copyist's error.

51. T. V. Parfitt, "The Use of Hebrew in Palestine 1800–1882," *Journal of Semitic Studies* 17 (1972): 241.

52. Compare Ya'akov Yosef of Polonne, *Toldot Ya'akov Yosef* (Koretz: Tzvi Hirsh, 1780). This *mashal* appears in Parsha Ba-har Sinai, 13, and elsewhere. One edition of *Yemei Moharnat* (Jerusalem: "Meshekh ha-naḥal," 1982), part 2, refers to Ya'akov Yosef's commentaries on Parashot Kidushim, Shoftim, and Ki tis'a (p. 204).

53. See Joseph Perl, *'Al mahut kat ha-ḥasidim / Uiber das Wesen der Sekte Chassidim*, ed. Avraham Rubinstein (Jerusalem: Israeli Academy of Sciences and Humanities, 1977).

54. Perl, *Ma'asiyot ve-'igrot*.

55. An exception to this rule might be Tale 9, "Of the Sophisticate [*ḥakham*] and the Simpleton [*tam*]," as Shmuel Werses points out in his analysis of the Yiddish version in his article "Mi-lashon el lashon." Usually there is no mention of specific cities or towns, but in this tale Warsaw is named.

56. The significance of Zion has become less univocal in Bratslav Hasidism because Rabbi Nahman asked his followers to visit his grave—especially during Rosh Hashanah—in Uman, Russia (now in Ukraine). To some extent, this pilgrimage site shifted the focus of his hasidim away from the Land of Israel. The centrality of the Rebbe and pilgrimages to his grave have in the past two centuries somewhat weakened the disciples' Zion-centered worldview. There is a world center of Bratslav Judaism in Jerusalem, but Nahman's burial site in Uman is their pilgrimage site. Adulation of the Rebbe is one of the features of hasidic life that led to opposition from mainstream rabbis.

57. On Nahman and the *maskilim* of Uman, see Haim Liberman's article in Yiddish and Hebrew: "R. Nakhmen Bratslaver un di Umaner maskilim," *YIVO bleter* 29 (1947): 201–19, and "R. Nahman mi-Breslav u-maskilei Uman," in *Ohel Raḥel*, 3 vols. (New York: Liberman, 1980–84), 3:310–28. In *Ḥasidut Breslav*, chapter 2, Mendel Piekarz continues in the direction suggested by Liberman's analysis. See also Shmuel Feiner, "Be-'emunah bilvad! Ha-pulmus shel reb Natan mi-Nemirov neged ha-ateizm ve-ha-Haskalah," in *Meḥkerei ḥasidut*, vol. 15 of Meḥkerei Yerushalaim be-maḥshevet Yisrael, ed. Immanuel Etkes, David Assaf, and Joseph Dan (Jerusalem: Hebrew Univ., 1999), esp. pp. 93–97. Other pertinent primary texts can be found in Avraham Gotlober, *Zikronot u-ma'asiot*, ed. Reuven Goldberg (Jerusalem: Mossad Bialik, 1976), e.g., pp. 74–75.

58. Avraham Ḥazan, *Kokhvei 'or*, ed. Shmuel ha-Levi Hurvitz (1933; reprint, Jerusalem: Ḥasidei Breslov, 1987), the section entitled "Sippurim nifla'im," p. 8. Cited and discussed in Liberman, "R. Nahman Bratslaver un di Umaner Maskilim"; Piekarz, *Ḥasidut Breslav*; and Feiner, "Be-'emunah bilvad!" Feiner parses the acronyms as follows: רביז"ל = רבינו זכרונו לברכה; לאנ"ש = לאנשי שלומנו; ומכ"ש = ומכל שכן; למהרנ"ת = למורנו הרב ר' נתן; ע"כ = על כן; ופ"א = ופעם אחת; כ"כ = כל כך

59. The only known copy of the first edition of Hurwitz's translation is in the YIVO Library at the Center for Jewish History. It is listed in the catalog as Ḥaikil Horvits, *Tsafnat pa`neah*, 3 vols. (Berdichev: Bak, 1817); however, the YIVO copy is missing the beginning of part 1 and all of part 2. Zalman Reyzn describes this rare book and its later editions in his article "Campes 'Antdekung fun America' in Yiddish (bibliografishe notitsn)," *YIVO bleter* 5 (1933): 29–40. Israel Zinberg quotes two passages from the beginning and end of *Tsofnas paneakh* in *Di geshikhte fun der literature bay Yidn*, vol. 7, book 2: *Khasides un oyfklerung (1780–1820)*. New York: Sklarsky, 1943, app. 4, pp. 324–27. Using sophisticated methods of literary analysis, R. Lerner astutely analyzes the language of Hurwitz's book in his article "Tsu der geshikhte fun der literarisher sprakh onheyb 19-tn yorhundert (di shprakh fun H. Hurvitz's 'Tsofnas paneakh')," *Afn shprakhfront* 3 (1939): 165–90.

60. Reyzn, "Campes 'Antdekung fun America,'" p. 33, based on the memoirs of a Russian aristocrat (Reyzn cites the Russian *Evreiskaia entsiklopediia*, 6:848). Reyzn suggests, however, that the Russian memoirist confused Hebrew with Yiddish and that it was Khaikl Hurwitz (not his son) who had drafted his *Yiddish* translation by 1810. Another possibility is that there was a mix-up with the Hebrew translation by Moses Mendelsohn-Frankfurt, *Metziat ha-aretz ha-ḥadasha* (Altona: Bonn, 1807).

61. See M. Unger, "Khaikl Hurwitzes yikhes-briv," *Filologishe shriftn* 3 (1929): 86.

62. Nathan Sternharz, *`Alim le-trufa: mikhtevei Moharnat* (New York: Keren hadpasa shel ḥasidei Breslav, 1976), p. 16, letter 11, dated Friday, Parshat Va-yigash (Dec. 24, 1824). According to David Assaf, the letters from 1836–45 were edited by Rabbi Nahman of Tcherin, but the letters from 1822–34 were edited by Rabbi Nahman of Tulchin; they were first published in 1893 and 1896. See David Assaf, *Breslov: bibliografiya mu`eret* (Jerusalem: Zalman Shazar Center, 2000), entry 227, p. 68.

63. *Landkarte* was confused with *kronikes* in the first edition of *Sippurei ma`asiyot*, and Perl mocked this confusion in both *Megale temirin* and his posthumously published work *Ma`asiyot ve-'igrot*, p. 162 and note. See Khone Shmeruk, "Dvarim kehaviatam u-dvarim she-bedimion bi-'Megaleh temirin' shel Yosef Perl," in *Ha-kri'a le-navi: meḥkerei historia ve-sifrut*, ed. Israel Bartal (Jerusalem: Shazar Center, 1999), pp. 144–55.

64. On page 58a of the manuscript, an editor has excised the following sentences from Nathan's letter:

> נא בני להשתדל לשלוח לי [?] עם החתוכות שחותמין בהם אגרת בלי נר. וגם החותם מתוקן עם הגולקי כי מוכרח לי מאד והעיקר בשבילך = בשביל המכתבים שאני שולח לך שלא אצטרך להדליק נר בכל פעם. כי רצוני תמיד לחתום המכתבים נא לזרז בזה.

> Please, my son, make an effort to send me [illegible] with the cuttings that are used to stamp a letter without a candle. And also the stamp prepared with the ball because it is very necessary to me, and the main thing is for you—for the letters that I send you, so that I won't need to light a candle each time. For it is my intention always to stamp the letters please hurry in this.

Manuscript of letters, EVR IV 93, F 69530, Russian National Library (formerly the M. E. Saltykov-Shchedrin State Public Library), St. Petersberg, letter 4, dated Sunday, Parshat Vayera, 1840, p. 58a; in *`Alim le-trufa*, between letters 268 and 269, p. 229. I am grateful to Zvi Mark for lending me a microfilm of this little-known manuscript of the letters at the Russian National Library. Zinberg discusses this manuscript in *Di geshikhte fun der literatur bay Yidn*, vol. 7, book 2, pp. 315–18. Taking a more favorable view than Shimon Dubnov, Zinberg refers to R. Nathan's "flowing Hebrew" (p. 317).

65. See the letter of Monday, Parshat Shemot, 1841, from Teplik, manuscript page 59b, letter 14:

למען השם יזהיר מאד את כל מי שיודיעו עסק ישועה הזאת שיצפון הדבר ויגנוז מאד לבל יודע לזרים ח״ו.

66. In the manuscript of Nathan Sternharz's correspondence, p. 63a at the end of letter 3, dated Wednesday, the 36th day of the Counting of the Omer [12 May], 1841, Sternharz directed his son to "conceal these things from the mockers" (לגנוז דברים האלה מפני הליצנים). This letter was omitted by the editor (Nahman of Tcherin) between letters 323 and 324 in *`Alim le-trufa*, p. 271.

67. Feiner, "Be-'emunah bilvad!," pp. 89–124. In selecting examples from *Likutei halakhot*, Feiner builds on Ron Margolin's MA thesis, "Ha-'emunah ve-ha-kfirah be-torata shel ḥasidut Breslov `al pi ha-sefer Likutei halakhot le-R. Nathan Sternharz," Univ. of Haifa, 1991. See also Shmuel Romanelli of Mantua, *Mas'a be-`arav* (Berlin: Ḥevrat ḥinukh ne`arim, 1792). In English, see Samuel Romanelli, *Travail in an Arab Land*, trans. Yedida K. Stillman and Norman A. Stillman (Tuscaloosa: Univ. of Alabama Press, 1989). Romanelli's title plays on the similarity between the word *mas'a* (with final 'Aleph, "burden" or "travail") and *mas`a* (with final `Ayin, "journey"), as the Stillmans note in their introduction.

68. On Romanelli, see Moshe Pelli, "The Literary Genre of the Travelogue in Hebrew Haskalah Literature: Shmuel Romanelli's *Masa Ba`rav*," *Modern Judaism* 11 (1991): 241–60.

69. For accounts of this school, see Joseph Gutmann, "Geschichte der Knabenschule der jüdischen Gemeinde in Berlin," in *Festschrift zur Feier des hundertjährigen Bestehens der Knabenschule der jüdischen Gemeinde in Berlin* (Berlin: Phönix, 1926), part 1, pp. 3–138, and Peter Dietrich and Uta Lohmann, "'Daß die Kinder aller Confessionen sich kennen, ertragen und lieben lernen': Die jüdische Freischule in Berlin zwischen 1778 und 1825," in *Dialog zwischen den Kulture: Erziehungshistorische und religionspädagogische Gesichtspunkte interkultureller Bildung*, ed. Ingrid Lohmann and Wolfram Weiße (Münster: Waxmann, 1994), pp. 37–47. Initiated by Moses Mendelssohn and his disciples, the Knabenschule later came under the influence of Philanthropismus.

70. רשעים גמורים מפורסמים · ועשו לעצמן חברת חינוך נערים; Nathan Sternharz, *Likutei halakhot* (Jerusalem: Keren hadpasa de-ḥasidei Breslav, 1985), vol. 3, *Hilkhot Pesaḥ*, 7, 6, p. 298. Mendel Piekarz refers to this passage in "Reb Natan mi-Nemirov ba-aspaklariat sifro 'Likutei halakhot,'" *Tzion* 69 (2004): 203–40; the discussion of the publisher Ḥevrat

ḥinukh ne`arim occurs on p. 221. Thanks to Jonatan Meir for drawing my attention to this reference to the Berlin Jewish school. Haim Liberman cites pertinent passages from *Likutei halakhot* in his article on Rabbi Nahman and the *maskilim* of Uman ("R. Nakhmen Bratslaver un di Umaner maskilim").

71. From about 1780 to 1820, the press named Ḥevrat ḥinukh ne`arim (Society for Education of Youth) published dozens of books in Hebrew and a smaller number in German. As Zohar Shavit points out, however, there was a far greater supply of than a demand for Hebrew books in Berlin at this time ("From Friedländer's Lesebuch to the Jewish Campe: The Beginning of Hebrew Children's Literature in Germany," *Leo Baeck Institute Year Book* 33 [1988]: 385–415). After citing data on the number of pupils who attended the Berlin Jewish school, she refers to "the incredible discrepancy between the number of books and the number of their readers" (p. 388).

72. Nahman [and Sternharz], *Sippurei ma`asiyot*, 1815 ed., appended section with new numbering and subheading, "Seder ha-nesi`a shelo le-Eretz Israel," p. 5a; in the modern edition, Nathan Sternharz, *Shivḥei ha-Ran ha-menukad* (Jerusalem: Agudat "Meshekh ha-naḥal," 1981), sec. 9, p. 22. I have preserved the original punctuation, which does not distinguish between commas and periods.

73. Of the three major storm accounts, this is the only one that has a direct parallel in *Ḥayei Moharan*, sec. 5, "Nesi`ato le-Eretz Israel," para. 9. See also Martin Cunz, *Die Fahrt des Rabbi Nachman von Brazlaw ins Land Israel [1798–1799]* (Tübingen: Mohr, 1997), p. 291.

74. Perl, *Megale temirin*, 1819 ed., letter 151, 53a. See also the new, critical edition of *Megale temirin* edited by Jonatan Meir (Jerusalem: Mossad Bialik, 2013), p. 334.

75. Perl, *Megale temirin*, 2013 ed., letter 151, p. 334, note 1 (by Meir). Meir refers to Israel Bartal's essay "Ha-shikhiḥa ve-ha-zekhira: Eretz-Israel ba-toda`at tnu`at ha-Haskala be-mizraḥ Europa," in *Eretz-Israel ba-hagut ha-Yehudit ba-`et ha-ḥadasha*, ed. Aviezer Ravitzky (Jerusalem: Ben-Tzvi Institute, 1998), pp. 413–23.

4. Euchel

1. See Tal Kogman's study of writings in zoology and astronomy, "*Haskalah* Scientific Knowledge in Hebrew Garment: A General Statement and Two Examples," *Target* 19, no. 1 (2007): 69–83. One of the undisputed belletristic foci of the early *maskilim* was poetry; unfortunately for their place in Hebrew literary history, they adopted a baroque, neoclassical style that was soon swept aside by romanticism. I will not enter here into the debate over the influence of medieval Hebrew poetry from Spain—or of Renaissance and eighteenth-century Italian Hebrew authors, such as Immanuel ha-Romi and Moses Haim Luzzatto—on the German and Austrian Haskala. Although the Hebrew writers in Berlin were not absolutely original, they constituted a significant, new starting point. In modern Jewish education, the Jüdische Freischule in Berlin—and its ideological descendants to the east in Galicia and Russia—played a central, though not always explicit, role.

2. For simplicity, I view most maskilic Hebrew as attempting to follow biblical models. The reality was more complex, as is evident from writings by Isaac Satanov, Mendel Lefin, and others. See Boaz Shakhevitz, "'Arba` leshonot: `iyunim shel sifrut bi-leshon ha-maskilim `al pi *Ha-me'asef*," *Molad* 212 (1967): 236–42.

3. Ber of Bolekhov [Birkenthal], *Zikronot*, ed. M. Vizhnitzer (Berlin: Klal-Verlag, 1922).

4. See Marcus Moseley, *Being for Myself Alone: Origins of Jewish Autobiography* (Stanford, CA: Stanford Univ. Press, 2006).

5. Probably the most influential statement of this view is contained in Yosef Klausner, *Historiya shel ha-sifrut ha-`Ivrit ha-ḥadasha*, vol. 1 (Jerusalem: Hebrew Univ., 1930), lesson 2, pp. 33–87. Israeli literary criticism has since been redirected by scholars such as Dan Miron, Gershon Shaked, Hannan Hever, and Avner Holtzman, but—as I realized when I taught in the Hebrew Department at Tel Aviv University in 1997—many underlying assumptions about the centrality of the Haskala and its path to "Mendele's *nusaḥ*" have remained intact.

6. Israel Zinberg, *A History of Jewish Literature*, ed. and trans. Bernard Martin, vol. 8: *The Berlin Haskalah* (Cincinnati: Hebrew Union College and Ktav, 1976), pp. 82, 136, emphasis in original.

7. Klausner, *Historiya shel ha-sifrut ha-`Ivrit ha-ḥadasha*, 1:151–53. For a discussion of Isaac Satanov's writings, see Moshe Pelli, *Be-ma`avakei tmura: `iyunim ba-Haskala ha-`Ivrit be-Germania be-shilhei ha-me'a ha-Yod"Ḥet* (Tel Aviv: Tel Aviv Univ. Publishing, 1988), chap. 3.

8. Klausner, *Historiya shel ha-sifrut ha-`Ivrit ha-ḥadasha*, 1:154.

9. See my essays "'Nusaḥ Mendele' be-mabat bikorti" (in Hebrew), *Dappim le-meḥkar be-sifrut* 14–15 (2006): 89–103, and "Epigonism after Abramovitsh and Bialik," *Studia Rosenthaliana* 40 (2007–8): 159–81.

10. See H. N. Bialik, "Yotzer ha-nusaḥ," *Ha-`olam* 4, no. 50 (1910–11): 6–8, and "Mendele u-shloshet ha-kerakhim," in *Kol kitvei Mendele Moykher Sforim*, vol. 3 (Odessa: Va`ad ha-yovel, 1912), pp. 324–31. See also Y. H. Ravnitzky, "`Al ha-signon ha-`Ivri shel Mendele Moykher Sforim," in *Kol kitvei Mendele Moykher Sforim*, vol. 7 (Berlin: Dvir, 1922), p. 172, originally published in *Ha-`omer* 1 (1907): part 2, 23–31.

11. Moshe Pelli, "The Literary Genre of the Travelogue in Hebrew Haskalah Literature: Shmuel Romanelli's *Masa Ba`rav*," *Modern Judaism* 11 (1991): 249.

12. Compare Andreas Kennecke, *Isaac Abraham Euchel: Architekt der Haskala* (Göttingen: Wallstein, 2007), p. 288.

13. See Ingrid Lohmann, Britta L. Behm, and Uta Lohmann, eds., *Chevrat Chinuch Nearim: Die Jüdische Freischule in Berlin (1778–1825) im Umfeld preußischer Bildungspolitik und jüdischer Kultusreform. Eine Quellensammlung*, 2 vols. (Berlin: Waxmann Münster, 2001), 2:1324.

14. From an unpublished manuscript that Wolpe shared with me. She refers to Zohar Shavit, "From Friedländer's Lesebuch to the Jewish Campe: The Beginning of Hebrew Children's Literature in Germany," *Leo Baeck Institute Year Book* 33 (1988): 408. Wolpe adds that "in the discussions of a group of *maskilim* including Moses Mendelssohn, David Friedlander, and Shlomo Maimon on which works to translate for Jewish readers, there was no mention of *belles lettres*; the debate was between historical, moral or scientific works." In support of this statement, she cites Ḥayim Shoham, *Be-tzel haskalat Berlin* (Tel Aviv: Porter Institute, 1996), pp. 39–40.

15. This argument and the subsequent one are adapted from my article "Neglected Origins of Modern Hebrew Prose: Hasidic and Maskilic Travel Narratives," *AJS Review* 33 (2009): 3–43. See also Frieden, "'Nusaḥ Mendele' be-mabat bikorti."

16. An outstanding literary discussion of the maskilic Hebrew style is contained in Robert Alter, *The Invention of Hebrew Prose: Modern Fiction and the Language of Realism* (Seattle: Univ. of Washington Press, 1988), chap. 1, "From Pastiche to *Nusakh*." See also Robert Alter, *Hebrew and Modernity* (Bloomington: Indiana Univ. Press, 1994), chap. 3, "Inventing Hebrew Prose." On "folk Hebrew" (*`Ivrit `amamit*), Aharon Ben-Or (Orinovski) writes that "[Joseph] Perl points to it as a symbol of barbarism and ignorance, and we value it *as the beginning of popular Hebrew*, alive and natural" (*Toldot ha-sifrut ha-`Ivrit ha-ḥadasha*, vol. 1: *Tekufat ha-Haskala be-Israel* [Tel Aviv: "Yizreel," 1955], p. 77, emphasis in original). Compare my article "Joseph Perl's Escape from Biblical Epigonism through Parody of Hasidic Writing," *AJS Review* 29 (2005): 265–82.

17. See, for example, Raphael Mahler, *Hasidism and the Jewish Enlightenment: Their Confrontation in Galicia and Poland in the First Half of the Nineteenth Century*, trans. Eugene Orenstein, Aaron Klein, and Jenny Machlowitz Klein (Philadelphia: Jewish Publication Society of America, 1985). The Yiddish and (expanded) Hebrew originals of this book were published in 1942 and 1961. See also Mordecai Wilensky, *Hasidim ve-mitnagdim: le-toldot ha-pulmus she-beneihem ba-shanim 1772–1815*, 2 vols. (Jerusalem: Mosad Bialik, 1970). Another representative earlier work is Avraham Rubinstein's introduction to his edition of Joseph Perl, *`Al mahut kat ha-ḥasidim / Uiber das Wesen der Sekte Chassidim* (Jerusalem: Israeli Academy of Sciences and Humanities, 1977). Among excellent current books on the ideology of the Haskala, see Nancy Sinkoff, *Out of the Shtetl: Making Jews Modern in the Polish Borderlands* (Providence, RI: Brown Judaic Studies, 2004), and Shmuel Feiner, *Haskalah and History: The Emergence of a Modern Jewish Historical Consciousness*, trans. Chaya Naor and Sandra Silverston (Oxford: Littman Library of Jewish Civilization, 2002; originally published in Hebrew in 1990).

18. Numerous scholars—such as Israel Weinlös, Shmuel Werses, Khone Shmeruk, Dan Miron, Gershon Shaked, Moshe Pelli, Yehuda Friedlander, Jeremy Dauber, and Jonatan Meir—have written about Enlightenment satire in Hebrew and Yiddish prose, including studies of Aharon Wolfsohn of Halle, Joseph Perl, I. B. Levinsohn, S. Y. Abramovitsh, and others.

19. Jacob Emden, *Megillat sefer*, ed. David Kahana (Warsaw: Shuldberg, 1896), p. 187.

20. Robert Alter explains lucidly, in his introduction to Psalms, that "biblical Hebrew is what linguists call a synthetic language, as opposed to analytic languages such as English. Pronominal objects of verbs are usually indicated by an accusative suffix attached to the verb. . . . Instead of using possessive pronouns, nouns are declined with possessive suffixes." All of this contributes to what Alter calls a "terrific rhythmic compactness" in biblical Hebrew (*The Book of Psalms: A Translation with Commentary* [New York: Norton, 2007], p. xxix).

21. Both Euchel and Wolfsohn wrote satiric plays that followed in the footsteps of Molière's play *Tartuffe; ou l'Imposteur* (Tartuffe; or, The Impostor, 1664). Euchel's play is titled *Reb Chenokh; oder, Vos tut men damit*. The Berlin authors had probably read Molière in a contemporary German translation because *Tartuffe* achieved immense popularity in German in the half-century before their parodies were written. At least four different German versions appeared under several different titles in multiple editions between 1741 and 1788, including *Der Mucker; oder, Molierens Scheinheiliger betrüger Tartüffe* (1748); *Der Gleißner, oder Scheinheilige Betrüger* (1764); *Tartüffe, oder der scheinheilige Betrüger* (1780); and *Der Heuchler* (1788).

22. I have drawn this biographical sketch from Shmuel Feiner's excellent book *The Jewish Enlightenment*, trans. Chaya Naor (Philadelphia: Univ. of Pennsylvania Press, 2004), chap. 10.

23. Isaac Euchel, *Toldot rabenu ha-ḥakham Moshe ben Menaḥem* (Berlin: Ḥevrat ḥinukh ne`arim, 1789), dedicatory letter to Joel Brill (Loewe).

24. Feiner, *The Jewish Enlightenment*, pp. 225–26.

25. See Kennecke's discussion of Euchel's letters to Friedländer in *Isaac Abraham Euchel*, chap. 10.

26. Isaac Euchel, "'Igrot Yitzḥak Euchel," *Ha-me'asef* 2 (1785): 116–21 and 137–42, quote on p. 117 n.

27. Ibid., p. 118. Compare Kennecke, *Isaac Abraham Euchel*, p. 289.

28. Kennecke, *Isaac Abraham Euchel*, p. 288.

29. Euchel, "'Igrot Yitzḥak Euchel," p. 119.

30. Compare the discussion here with that in Rebecca Wolpe, "The True Way to Loving God: Nature in the *Haskala*," *Toronto Journal of Jewish Thought* 3 (2012), at http://tjjt.cjs.utoronto.ca/wp-content/uploads/2013/11/Rebecca-Wolpe-The-True-Way-to-Loving-God-Nature-in-the-Haskala-Vol.-3.pdf (accessed Jan. 11, 2016).

31. Euchel, "'Igrot Yitzḥak Euchel," p. 120.

32. Ibid., p. 139; this phrase alludes to Psalms 69:2.

33. See Shakhevitz, "'Arba` leshonot."

34. Kennecke, *Isaac Abraham Euchel*, p. 295.

35. Euchel, "'Igrot Yitzḥak Euchel," p. 118.

36. For a critical edition of Euchel's second travel narrative, with a helpful introduction and notes, see Isaac Euchel, "'Igrot Meshullam ben Uriah ha-Eshtemo`i," in *Prakim be-satira ha-`Ivrit*, vol. 1, ed. Yehuda Friedlander (Tel Aviv: Papyrus, 1979), pp. 19–61. Pelli gives a list of criticism on this work in *Sugot ve-sugiot be-sifrut ha-Haskala ha-`Ivrit* (Tel Aviv: Ha-kibbutz ha-me'uḥad, 1999), p. 299 n. Pelli's own approach emphasizes the creation of a "utopian" image by Euchel's fictional Meshullam. For another discussion by Moshe Pelli of this work, see his book *The Age of Haskalah: Studies in Hebrew Literature of the Enlightenment in Germany* (Leiden: Brill, 1979), pp. 215–27.

37. Moshe Pelli, "Le-reshito shel ha-zhenre ha-epistolari be-sifrut ha-`Ivrit he-ḥadasha: Isaac Euchel ve-'igrotav," *Bikoret u-farshanut* 16 (1981): 85.

38. See, for example, "Autobiography: On the Self-Understanding of the Maskilim," in Michael A. Meyer and Michael Brenner, eds., *German–Jewish History in Modern Times*, vol. 1: *Tradition and Enlightenment 1600–1780* (New York: Columbia Univ. Press, 1996), p. 316.

39. As Euchel himself admits, "The travel story itself is very thin, and it makes no real contribution to the narrative basis of the letters" ("'Igrot Meshullam ben Uriah ha-Eshtemo`i," in Friedlander, *Prakim be-satira ha-`Ivrit*, 1:23).

40. Isaac Euchel, "'Igrot Meshullam ben Uriah ha-Eshtemo`i," *Ha-me'asef* 6 (1790): 40, and in Friedlander, *Prakim be-satira ha-`Ivrit*, 1:42.

41. Moshe Pelli, "The Epistolary Story in Haskalah Literature: Isaac Euchel's ''Igrot Meshullam,'" *Jewish Quarterly Review* 93 (2003): 467.

42. Euchel, *Toldot rabenu ha-ḥakham Moshe ben Menaḥem*, introduction, 3 (my pagination).

43. See Shimshon ben Avraham of Shentz's commentary on the Babylonian Talmud, Tractate Nega`im, chapter 11, in *Bar Ilan's Judaic Library*, full version 18+, CD-ROM (Tel Aviv: Bar Ilan Univ., 2010).

44. Euchel, "'Igrot Meshullam ben Uriah ha-Eshtemo`i," *Ha-me'asef*, p. 41, and in Friedlander, *Prakim be-satira ha-`Ivrit*, 1:42.

45. In English, one meaning of the word *sheet* is "a rope (or chain) attached to either of the lower corners of a square sail"; however, there has been a metonymic or synecdochal use of the term to mean "sail" (*Compact Oxford English Dictionary*, 2nd ed., 1991).

46. This usage was evidently already firmly established in prestate Palestine. See the entry under מִפרשׂ in Yehuda Grozovski and David Yellin, eds., *Ha-milon ha-`Ivri* (Tel Aviv: Dvir, 1927), p. 314, where the definition is יריעות נס האניה. See also David Ettinger, *Sfatenu be-mar'ot: Milon histakluti be-tziurim* (Tel Aviv: Dvir, 1953), p. 226. In the fifth edition of his dictionary, *Milon `Ivri* (Tel Aviv: Dvir, 1950), Yehuda Gur (formerly Grozovski) revised the definition, avoiding the ambiguity of the word נס by revising the definition: יריעת האניה שמותחים על תֹּרן הספינה (p. 559).

47. See Francis Brown, S. R. Driver, and Charles A. Briggs, eds., *A Hebrew and English Lexicon of the Old Testament* (Oxford: Clarendon Press, 1952), entry *noseis*, meaning

3b on p. 652a: "since sails were the only ensign = sail"; see also Solomon Mandelkern, *Konkordantzia la-Tanakh* (Jerusalem: Schocken, 1986), entry *nes* under *noseis*, where one of the meanings listed is *velum navium*.

48. This is the tragic midrashic story of kidnapped women:

> אמרו מעשה בשבעים בתולות שנשבו, והושיבן בספינה להלוך ולהושיבן בקובות, והיו אותן הבתולות אומרות זו לזו בואו ונקדש שמו של הקב״ה אל יחללונו גוים ערלים, מה עשו, עלו לגג הספינה ונפלו לים וטבעו עצמם בים:

> They told a story of seventy virgins who were taken away and placed in a ship to take them and place them in houses of prostitution. These virgins spoke to one another: let us sanctify God's name and not let the uncircumcised defile us. What did they do? They climbed up to the roof [or deck] of the ship and fell into the sea and drowned themselves in the sea.

My translation from Lamentations Rabba in Shlomo Buber, *Midrash zuta: `Al Shir ha-shirim, Ruth, Eikha ve-Kohelet* (Berlin: Ḥevrat mekitsei nirdamim, 1895), parsha 1, 13 (36).

49. Euchel, "'Igrot Meshullam ben Uriah ha-Eshtemo`i," *Ha-me'asef*, p. 42, and in Friedlander, *Prakim be-satira ha-`Ivrit*, 1:43.

50. Note that Euchel shifts the preposition in the first phrase, ויהוה הטיל רוח־גדולה אל־הים, writing instead והאלהים הטיל רוח סערה על הים. The significance of this grammatical change is unclear.

51. The Berlin writers did not always succeed in finding biblical words for technical terms such as *anchor*. Thus, in "Letters of Meshullam," Euchel repeats his usage of *vav*, adding a footnote to explain what it means and then giving a German translation in parentheses ("'Igrot Meshullam ben Uriah ha-Eshtemo`i," *Ha-me'asef*, p. 40 n. 1, and in Friedlander, *Prakim be-satira ha-`Ivrit*, 1:59 n. 3.

52. As mentioned in chapter 3, Romanelli's title is a play on words, taking advantage of the similarity between the word *mas'a* (with final 'Aleph, "burden" or "travail") and *mas`a* (with final `Ayin, "journey").

53. ויהי היום והנה אני שיט באה טיטו״אן ויתן הסוחר שכרה וירדנו בה לבא עמה (Shmuel Romanelli, *Mas'a be-`arav: Hu sefer ha-korot* [Berlin: Ḥevrat ḥinukh ne`arim, 1792], chap. 1, p. 2). For a full English translation, see Samuel Romanelli, *Travail in an Arab Land*, trans. Yedida K. Stillman and Norman A. Stillman (Tuscaloosa: Univ. of Alabama Press, 1989), where this passage occurs on page 19.

54. Romanelli, *Mas'a be-`arav*, p. 25; see also the translation in Romanelli, *Travail in an Arab Land*, p. 55.

55. See Romanelli, *Mas'a be-`arav*, p. 26; for an alternate translation, see Romanelli, *Travail in an Arab Land*, p. 56.

56. Romanelli, *Mas'a be-`arav*, p. 26.

57. Pelli, "The Literary Genre of the Travelogue in Hebrew Haskalah Literature," p. 249. Ḥ. N. Shapiro takes a more favorable view of Romanelli's descriptive powers in *Toldot ha-sifrut ha-`Ivrit ha-ḥadasha*, vol. 1: *Sifrut ha-Haskala be-merkaz Germania (1784–1829)* (1939; reprint, Tel Aviv: Massada, 1967), pp. 493–97.

58. On this point, see Rebecca Wolpe's description of the *maskilim* in her dissertation, "The Sea and Sea Voyage in Maskilic Literature," Hebrew Univ. of Jerusalem, 2011: "The *maskilim* had no intention of detracting from religious faith but desired to restore the lost balance between Jewish and universal culture. They looked to medieval Jewish rationalist philosophy and interpretations, to critical views of antiquity and the authority of Kabbalah, seeking to glorify Hebrew as a vehicle of expression, no longer viewing non-Jewish culture as alien" (p. 13).

59. Chaim Rabin, "The Continuum of Modern Literary Hebrew," in *The Great Transition: The Recovery of the Lost Centers of Modern Hebrew Literature*, ed. Glenda Abramson and Tudor Parfitt (Totowa, NJ: Rowman & Allanheld, 1985), pp. 18, 19.

5. Mendelsohn-Frankfurt

1. For biographical information about Mendelsohn-Frankfurt and his father, see Noah H. Rosenblum, *Tradition in an Age of Reform: The Religious Philosophy of Samson Raphael Hirsch* (Philadelphia: Jewish Publication Society of America, 1976), pp. 51–53, 413. See also Eduard [Yeḥezkel] Dukesz, *Sefer ḥakhmei AH"W* [*Altona, Hamburg, and Wandsbeck*], part 2 (Hamburg: Goldschmidt, 1908), pp. 120–21.

2. See, for example, Mendelsohn-Frankfurt's letter from Hamburg, published in *Der Orient* 9 (Aug. 26, 1848): 275–76.

3. Moses Mendelsohn-Frankfurt, *Penei tevel: Musar ha-sekhel* (Amsterdam: Levisson, 1872). Although most of the contents of *Penei tevel* are belletristic poetry and prose, the subtitle roughly means "moral teachings." The title phrase *penei tevel* is itself taken from Job 37:12, as Ora Wiskind-Elper pointed out to me.

4. In a notebook, Mendelsohn-Frankfurt quotes his father's words: "When I was in Berlin I was a friend of Reb Moses Dessauer [Mendelssohn]; every week we also studied the Torah Portion with the learned Head of the Rabbinical Court in the community. Every Shabbat I prayed the morning prayers at the house of Reb Moses Dessauer, and when the service had ended, a few times he led me into his study to make Kiddush with him and to eat breakfast with him" (*Penei tevel*, p. 234; also cited and discussed in Noah Rosenblum, *`Iyunei sifrut ve-hagut: mi-shilhei ha-me'a ha-shmone `esre `ad yemenu* [Jerusalem: Reuven Mass, 1989], p. 56).

5. Rosenblum, *`Iyunei sifrut ve-hagut*, p. 57.

6. Mendelsohn-Frankfurt, *Penei tevel*, p. 17.

7. Quoted in ibid., p. 21.

8. Ibid., p. 22.

9. In the writing of Judeo-German, or German printed in Hebrew characters, Mendelsohn-Frankfurt was preceded by an adaptation called *Zeefahrer* (Prague, 1784). But this version, based on Campe's *Robinson der Jüngere*, follows that source almost slavishly.

10. Campe was at the forefront of efforts to reform the German language, and in some early editions the title of his book appeared as *Die Entdekkung von Amerika*.

11. See William Robertson, *Geschichte von Amerika*, trans. Johann Friedrich Schiller, 2 vols. (Leipzig: Weidmanns Erben & Reich, 1777). Johann Friedrich Schiller was an uncle and godfather to the now more renowned author (Johann Christoph) Friedrich von Schiller.

12. Review of Moses Mendelsohn-Frankfurt's translation *Metziat ha-aretz ha-ḥadasha*, *Ha-me'asef* 9 (1810): 101. The rare biblical phrase חדרי משׂכיתו can be found in Ezekiel 8:12 and in midrashic commentaries, but its meaning remains obscure.

13. Salomon Geßner, *Der Tod Abels* (Zürich: Geßner, 1759).

14. It is not entirely clear why *Metziat ha-aretz ha-ḥadasha* was aimed primarily at young readers. Perhaps the underlying assumption was that (mostly male, Jewish) adults—whose Hebrew was adequate to the task of reading this book—should be devoting their attention to something more serious in an area of traditional Jewish study, such as the Mishna and codes of Jewish law. On the title page, Moses Mendelsohn-Frankfurt notes that his book is written in Hebrew that is "clear and simple, to teach the youth of the Children of Israel the beauty of this language."

15. See Isaac Marcus Jost's recollections from the early nineteenth century: "je weiter wir im Deutschen vorrückten, gab er uns Campe's Kinderbibliothek und andere Jugendschriften in die Hand" (As we advanced further in German, he handed us Campe's Children's Library and other writings for young adults) (in Ingrid Lohmann, Britta L. Behm, and Uta Lohmann, eds., *Chevrat Chinuch Nearim: Die Jüdische Freischule in Berlin (1778–1825) im Umfeld preußischer Bildungspolitik und jüdischer Kultusreform. Eine Quellensammlung*, 2 vols. (Berlin: Waxmann Münster, 2001), 2:1324.

16. Review of *Metziat ha-aretz ha-ḥadasha*, 101.

17. "Mendelsohn-Frankfurt, Moses," in Getzel Kressel, *Leksikon ha-sifrut ha-`Ivrit*, vol. 2 (Merḥavia: Sifriat po`alim, 1967), p. 401. See also Moshe Pelli, *Haskala ve-modernizm* (Jerusalem: Ha-kibbutz ha-me'uḥad, 2008), pp. 100–102. The most thorough analysis of *Penei tevel* is Rosenblum's essay "He-`arakhot bikoretiot be-'Penei tevel,'" in *`Iyunei sifrut ve-hagut*, pp. 67–93. See also Shmuel Werses, "Ha-sefer *Penei tevel* be-zikato la-masoret ha-makama be-sifrutenu," in *Sefer Ḥayim Shirman: kovetz meḥkarim*, ed. Shraga Abramson and Aharon Mirski (Jerusalem: Schocken, 1970), pp. 135–48.

18. Mendelsohn-Frankfurt, *Penei tevel*, pp. 196–216.

19. Nurit Govrin, "Signon ha-makama be-sifrut ha-`Ivrit ba-dorot ha-aḥaronim," *Me'asef* 8–9 (1964–65): 407.

20. Of the many works on this subject, see, for example, Philip Edwards, *The Story of the Voyage* (Cambridge: Cambridge Univ. Press, 1994), and Percy G. Adams, *Travel Literature and the Evolution of the Novel* (Lexington: Univ. Press of Kentucky, 1983).

21. See Percy G. Adams, *Travelers and Travel Liars, 1660–1800* (1962; reprint, Berkeley: Univ. of California Press, 1980).

22. Georg Forster, *A Voyage round the World in His Britannic Majesty's Sloop,* Resolution (London: White, 1777); Georg Forster and Johann Reinhold Forster, *Johann Reinhold Forster's Reise um die Welt*, 3 vols. (Berlin: Haude and Spener, 1778–80); Johann Reinholt Forster, *Observations Made during a Voyage round the World* (London: Robinson, 1778).

23. Adams, *Travelers and Travel Liars*, p. 172.

24. Moses Mendelsohn-Frankfurt, *Metziat ha-aretz ha-ḥadasha* (Altona: The Author and Bonn, 1807), title page; subsequent page citations to this edition are given parenthetically in the text. The front matter of Mendelsohn-Frankfurt's book (the preface and glossary) lacks pagination, so in-text parenthetical references to the preface cite my roman numbering of these pages, starting at ii.

25. The title page advertises that the book was "collected and translated and supplemented from books of the nations [*sifrei ha-`amim*]."

26. Joachim Heinrich Campe, *Robinson der Jüngere, zur angenehmen und nützlichen Unterhaltung für Kinder*, 2 vols. (Frankfurt: n.p., 1781), 1:3b, my translation, which differs slightly from the contemporary edition, *Robinson the Younger* (Hamburg: Bohn, 1781).

27. The title page refers to the volume as "First Book," although no sequel appeared.

28. We came across earlier occurrences of *vilon* in chapter 1, but the usage here is one that Mendelsohn-Frankfurt shares with his contemporary, the hasidic writer Nathan Sternharz, as we saw in chapters 2 and 3.

29. See Ernest Klein, *A Comprehensive Etymological Dictionary of the Hebrew Language for Readers of English* (Jerusalem: CARTA and Univ. of Haifa, 1987), p. 84. Klein indicates that a third meaning of the phrase *naḥash bariaḥ* "is usually rendered by 'the slant serpent.'" See Job 26:13.

30. Review of *Metziat ha-aretz ha-ḥadasha*, pp. 100–101.

31. The words *Wendezirkel* and *Wendekreis* (tropical circle) were in competition in the late eighteenth century, as can be seen from scans and searches in Google Books Ngram Viewer. Until 1780, *Wendezirkel* was far more commonly used, after which *Wendekreis* became more common (except for around 1795–1805, when *Wendezirkel* was more common). Although in their dictionaries both Adelung and Campe prefer the term *Wendekreis* (which dominated after 1820), both Mendelsohn-Frankfurt and the *Ha-me'asef* reviewer of *Metziat ha-aretz ha-ḥadasha* use the older choice, *Wendezirkel*. In 1807–10, the two words were being used with similar frequency. See "Wendezirkel,Wendekreis," Google Books Ngram Viewer, at http://books.google.com/ngrams/graph?content=Wendezirkel%2CWendekreis&year_start=1750&year_end=2000&corpus=20&smoothing=3&share= (accessed Jan. 6, 2016).

32. Review of *Metziat ha-aretz ha-ḥadasha*, p. 100.

33. The name "the tropics" derives from the Greek *tropikos*, from the verb meaning "to turn." The latter is also the origin of the word *trope*, a turn of phrase.

34. Review of *Metziat ha-aretz ha-ḥadasha*, p. 100.

35. Joachim Heinrich Campe, *Wörterbuch zur Erklärung und Verdeutschung der unserer Sprache aufgedrungenen fremden Ausdrücke: Ein Ergänzungsband zu Adelungs Wörterbuche*, 2 vols. (Braunschweig: Schulbuchhandlung, 1801). The title of Campe's dictionary may be rendered *Dictionary for the Clarification and Germanification of Foreign Expressions That Have Intruded into Our Langauge: A Supplementary Volume to Adelung's Dictionary*. See the analysis of Campe's linguistic "purism" by Sibylle Orgeldinger in *Standardisierung und Purismus bei Joachim Heinrich Campe* (Berlin: Walter de Gruyter, 1999), pp. 25–27 and passim.

36. Campe writes that because of its foreign sound, the term *génie* should not be given German citizenship rights. Without acknowledging that he rejects the word, at least in part because of its association with romantic poets, he suggests that it can be replaced by *nature*, *ability*, or *creative spirit*. Here is the German passage: "Ungeachtet einige sehr achtungswürdige Schriftsteller, z. B. Garve in den Betrachtungen über Sprachverbesserungen (S. Beiträge zur Deutschen Sprachkunde, Berlin 1794), diesem Französischen Worte das Deutsche Bürgerrecht zuerkannt wissen wollen: so kann und wird es doch nie Deutsch werden, weil es unsere Sprach-ähnlichkeit verletzt. Der weiche Zischlaut, womit dieses Wort ausgesprochen werden muß, ist unserer Sprache so fremd, daß sie nicht einmahl unter ihren Buchstaben ein Zeichen dafür hat. Man gebraucht dieses fremde Wort bald in schlaffer (*sensu latiori*), bald in straffer (*strictiori*) Bedeutung. In jener genommen, kann es verdeutscht werden 1. durch Natur . . . , wofür wir auch das Wort Geist gebrauchen können. . . . 2. Durch Anlage oder Fähigkeit. . . . —In seiner engern Bedeutung genommen, bezeichnet das Wort einen mit außerordentlichen, besonders erfinderischen, Kräften begabten Geist, der sich neue Bahnen bricht . . . [and can be replaced by] erfinderischer Kopf oder schöpferischer Geist" (*Wörterbuch zur Erklärung und Verdeutschung*, 2:30).

37. The first published volume in the dictionary was Johann Christoph Adelung, *Versuch eines vollständigen grammatisch-kritischen Wörterbuches der Hochdeutschen Mundart* (Leipzig: Breitkopf, 1774), entries from A to E, available on Google Books at https://books.google.com/books?id=6q4_AAAAcAAJ&printsec=frontcover&source=gbs_ge_summary_r&cad=0#v=onepage&q&f=false (accessed Jan. 15, 2016).

38. See Johann Christoph Adelung, ed., *Vollständige Geschichte der Schiffarthen nach den noch gröstentheils unbekanten Südländern* (Halle: Gebauer, 1767), and Johann Christoph Adelung, ed., *Geschichte der Schiffahrten und Versuche welche zur Entdeckung des nordöstlichen Weges nach Japan und China von verschiedenen Nationen unternommen worden* (Halle: Gebauer, 1768). The inconsistent spelling of *Schiffarthen/Schiffahrten* is found in the originals, which on Jan. 15, 2016 were available from Google Books.

39. Campe uses the word *Vorgebirge* in chapter 7 of *Die Entdekkung von Amerika: Ein angenehmes und nützliches Lesebuch für Kinder und junge Leute*, 3 vols. (Hamburg: Bohn, 1781–82), 1:121, or *Die Entdeckung von Amerika: Ein Unterhaltungsbuch für Kinder und junge Leute*, vol. 1, 6th ed. (Braunschweig: Schulbuchhandlung, 1806), p. 105, but not in reference to the Cape of Good Hope.

40. See the interesting *Wikipedia* entry "Kap der guten Hoffnung" at http://de.wikipedia.org/wiki/Kap_der_Guten_Hoffnung (accessed Dec. 30, 2015).

41. In Google Ngram Viewer, compare the incidence of "Kap der guten Hoffnung" and "Vorgebirge der guten Hoffnung," at http://books.google.com/ngrams/graph?content=Kap+der+guten+Hoffnung%2CKap+der+Guten+Hoffnung%2CVorgebirge+der+Guten+Hoffnung%2CVorgebirge+der+guten+Hoffnung&year_start=1750&year_end=2000&corpus=8&smoothing=3 (accessed Jan. 15, 2016).

42. Joachim Heinrich Campe, *Wilhelm Isbrand Bonteku's merkwürdige Abentheuer auf einer Reise aus Holland nach Ostindien*, in vol. 5 of *Sammlung interessanter und durchgängig zweckmäßig abgefaßter Reisebeschreibungen für die Jugend* (Reutlingen: Grözinger, 1788), p. 15. Incidentally, modern Hebrew uses כף התקוה הטובה; the term כֵּף originally meant "rock" or "cliff," but because of the similarily in sound, *kef* was eventually used to designate a cape, the Cape of Good Hope in particular.

43. *Oniya so`ara* ([Zholkva?]: n.p., [1815–18?]), pages unnumbered; in the National Library of Israel copy, this page bears the handwritten number 5.

44. *Oniya so`ara* (Vilna: Menachem Mann Romm, 1823), 4.

45. See Campe, *Entdekkung von Amerika*, 1782 ed., p. 121, and *Entdeckung von Amerika*, 1806 ed., p. 45.

46. Review of *Metziat ha-aretz ha-ḥadasha*, p. 101.

47. Mendelsohn-Frankfurt, *Penei tevel*, pp. 241–52.

48. For a short, informative biographical sketch of Campe (1746–1818), see Sibylle Orgeldinger, *Standardisierung und Purismus bei Joachim Heinrich Campe* (Berlin: Walter de Gruyter, 1999), pp. 4–7.

49. Cendric Hentschel, "Campe and *The Discovery of America*," *German Life and Letters* 26 (1972–73): 1.

50. See Günther Ulbricht, "Spielpädogogik des Philanthropismus," in *Europa in der Frühen Neuzeit: Festschrift für Günther Mühlpfordt*, ed. Erich Donnert, vol. 6 (Cologne: Böhlau, 2002), p. 607.

51. On the Philanthropismus movement, see Rosemarie Ahrbeck-Wothge, ed., *Studien über den Philanthropismus und die Dessauer Aufklärung: Vorträge zur Geistesgeschichte des Dessau-Wörlitzer Kulturkreises* (Halle: Martin-Luther-Universität Halle-Wittenberg, 1970); and Günter Oesterle and Harald Tausch, eds., *Der imaginierte Garten* (Göttingen: Vandenhoeck and Ruprecht, 2001).

52. On relations between the Berlin *maskilim* and the Philanthropists, see Britta L. Behm, *Moses Mendelssohn und die Transformation der jüdischen Erziehung in Berlin: Eine*

bildungsgeschichtliche Analyse zur jüdischen Aufklärung im 18. Jahrhundert (Münster: Waxmann, 2002), pp. 176–89. For a general biographical sketch, see "Campe, Joachim Heinrich," in *Allgemeine Deutsche Biographie*, 56 vols. (Leipzig: Duncker & Humblot, 1876), 3:733–37.

53. See Wilhelm von Humboldt, *Briefe von Wilhelm von Humboldt an eine Freundin*, vol. 2 (Leipzig: Brockhaus, 1847), letter 38, Dec. 1832, p. 190: "Campe was, as I think that I have already told you, tutor in my father's house. . . . With him I learned writing and reading, and some history and geography in the manner of those times—the capitals, the so-called Seven Wonders of the World, and so on. Even then, he already had a very fortunate, natural ability to stimulate the child's understanding in a lively way."

54. M. Brann, "Aus H. Graetzens Lehr- und Wanderjahren," *Monatsschrift für Geschichte und Wissenschaft des Judenthums* 62 (1918): 231–65. This biographical article includes a significant note on Campe's travel narratives, which formed part of Graetz's early reading around 1833 (p. 242).

55. See Zohar Shavit, "Literary Interference between German and Jewish-Hebrew Children's Literature during the Enlightenment: The Case of Campe," *Poetics Today* 13 (1992): 41–61. Shavit writes that "the close relations between the Jewish Haskalah and German Enlightenment movements made German children's literature during the Enlightenment an ideal, if not *the* most desirable, model for imitation" (pp. 44–45, emphasis in original).

56. Israel Bartal, "Mordechai Aaron Günzburg: A Lithuanian *Maskil* Faces Modernity," trans. N. Greenwood and L. Schramm, in *From East and West: Jews in a Changing Europe, 1750–1870*, ed. Frances Malino and David Sorkin (Oxford: Blackwell, 1990), p. 143.

57. Zohar Shavit, "From Friedländer's Lesebuch to the Jewish Campe: The Beginning of Hebrew Children's Literature in Germany," *Leo Baeck Institute Year Book* 33 (1988): 405–6. See also Uriel Ofek, *Sifrut-yeledim ha-'Ivrit—ha-hatḥalot* (Tel Aviv: Porter Institute, 1979), esp. pp. 87–92, and compare Rebecca Wolpe, "The Sea Voyage Narrative as an Educational Tool in the Early Haskalah," MA thesis, Hebrew Univ. of Jerusalem, 2006, pp. 19–23.

58. Campe, *Robinson der Jüngere*, *Vorbericht* (preface), p. 4. Compare Susanne Barth, *Mädchenlektüren: Lesediskurse im 18. und 19. Jahrundert* (Frankfurt: Campus, 2002), p. 82, "Die Debatte um 'Empfindsamkeitsfieber,' 'Leselust,' und 'Lesezucht.'"

59. See Isaac Marcus Jost's recollections from the early nineteenth century in Lohmann, Behm, and Lohmann, *Chevrat Chinuch Nearim*, p. 1333.

60. See Moses Mendelssohn, "Schreiben, die philanthropinische Erziehung jüdischer Kinder betreffend," *Litteratur und Völkerkunde: Ein periodisches Werk* 2 (1783): 897–900, reprinted in *Moses Mendelssohn's gesammelte Schriften*, vol. 3, ed. G. B. Mendelssohn (Leipzig: Brockhaus, 1843), pp. 417–22.

61. See Campe, "An die jungen Leser," preface to *Wilhelm Isbrand Bonteku's merke würdige Abentheuer.*

62. Ibid., pp. 7–8. In the original German, the full passage reads: "Da ich aus guten Gründen mich verpflichtet fühle, euch allen, meine jungen Freunde und Freundinnen, das Lesen der Romane, so wie überhaupt solcher Bücher, welche nur darauf abzwecken, die Phantasie, die Einbildungskraft und die Empfindungen anzuregen, aus voller Ueberzeugung von ihrer groβen Schädlichkeit zu widerrathen: so muβ ich darauf denken, euch für dies kleine Opfer, welches ich zu eurem eigenen Besten von euch verlange, durch anderweitige Vergnügungen des Geistes schadlos zu halten. Deswegen habe ich mir bei der gegenwärtigen Sammlung von Reisebeschreibungen zur Regel gemacht, nich blos das Interessanteste dieses Fachs für euch auszusuchen, sondern auch noch überdem von Zeit zu Zeit eine und die andere von jenem ganz ausserordentlichen Reisebegebenheiten einzuweben, deren Geschichte an Annehmlichkeit und Wunderbarkeit den Romanen völlig gleichkommt, ohne daβ wir dadurch, wie von diesen, aus der wirklichen Welt in die der Phantasien und der Hirngespinnste hinausgeführt werden."

63. Ibid.

64. On Campe's opinions regarding the educational value of travel narratives, see David Blamires, *Telling Tales: The Impact of Germany on English Children's Books 1780–1918* (Cambridge: Open Book, 2009), chap. 2, "A World of Discovery: Joachim Heinrich Campe," p. 34.

65. George Keate [and Henry Wilson], *An Account of the Pelew Islands, Situated in the Western Part of the Pacific Ocean*, 2nd ed. (London: Nicol, 1788).

66. For a discussion of relevant publishing practices and copyright laws, see Bernhard Fabian, "English Books and Their Eighteenth-Century German Readers," in *The Widening Circle: Essays on the Circulation of Literature in Eighteenth-Century Europe*, ed. Paul J. Korshin (Philadelphia: Univ. of Pennsylvania Press, 1976), esp. p. 135. Fabian notes that "the travel book . . . appears to have been one of the most distinctive English contributions to eighteenth-century German reading" (p. 171).

67. Adams, *Travelers and Travel Liars*, p. 17.

68. I do not include Joseph Vitlin's book *Robinzon: Di geshikhte fun Alter Leb* here because the original from the 1820s has been lost. Compare David Roskies, "The Medium and the Message of the Maskilic Chapbook," *Jewish Social Studies* 41 (1979): 275–90, and *A Bridge of Longing: The Lost Art of Yiddish Storytelling* (Cambridge, MA: Harvard Univ. Press, 1995), pp. 62, 359 n. 20; Leah Garrett, "The Jewish Robinson Crusoe," *Comparative Literature* 54 (2002): 215–28; and Rebecca Wolpe, "The Sea and Sea Voyage in Maskilic Literature," PhD diss., Hebrew Univ. of Jerusalem, 2011.

69. Barth, *Mädchenlektüren*, esp. chap. 3, pp. 78–100.

70. Ibid., p. 79.

71. Campe, *Entdekkung von Amerika*, 1782 ed., 1:51, original orthography retained: "Wir sind verloren, schrien sie; wenn wir nicht stündlich wieder umkehren!"

72. Ibid., 1782 ed., 1:122: "Indes nun jederman in tiefen Schlaf versunken war, wurde das Schif von einem Meerstrome almählig gegen die Küste getrieben. Plötzlich erhielt es

einen so gewaltigen Stoß, daß dem erschrokkenen Schifsjungen das Steuer aus den Händen fuhr. . . . Alle gerieten in verzweifelnde Bestürzung."

73. Retaining the orthography of Campe's early editions, I quote the German passage:

> Schon wird es dunkel, und immer dunkler, und das bange Schifsvolk steht in ängstlicher Erwartung dessen, das da kommen sol, auf dem Verdekke, und hat seine Augen auf den Admiral gerichtet, welcher mit seiner gewöhnlichen Unerschrokkenheit die nötigen Verhaltungsbefehle austheilt.
>
> Jetzt beginnen die Wogen des weiten Ozeans almählig anzuschwellen; die Schiffe tanzen, das Tauwerk klappert, und der Sturmwind heult durch die Masten fürchterlich. Es blitzt un wird wider Nacht; es donnert und ein reichlicher Plazregen stürzt herab auf die taumelnden Schiffe. Jezt, jezt bricht die Wuth des heftigen Ungewitters mit allen seinen Schrekken hervor. Die Blize leuchten, der Donner kracht, die Wellen rauschen, die Winde brüllen, und die schwankenden Schiffe werden von mächtigen Wogen bald hoch in die Luft und bald in den tiefsten Abgrund hinabgeschleudert.
>
> Furcht und Entsezen hat sich der ganzen Manschaft bemächtiget. (Ibid., 1782 ed., 1:138–39)

74. Ibid., 1782 ed., 1:122.

75. Ibid., original spelling retained.

76. Ibid.

77. Ibid., 1:138.

78. See the discussion of this point in Wolpe, "The Sea and Sea Voyage in Maskilic Literature," p. 110. Wolpe writes that "Mendelsohn-Frankfurt also converts reported [speech] into direct speech wherever possible, a result of the change in structure of the book and the need to make the narrative more varied and entertaining." Because the Hebrew version dispenses with the frame narrative, the dialogue between the father and his children, "direct speech was to be used wherever possible," adding to "the dramatization of the account."

79. Campe, *Entdekkung von Amerika*, 1782 ed., 1:139.

80. Campe, *Entdeckung von Amerika*, 1806 ed., 1:155–56. Here I quote the later edition because the orthography of the 1782 edition is distracting.

81. H. N. Shapiro, *Toldot ha-sifrut ha-`Ivrit ha-ḥadasha*, vol. 1: *Sifrut ha-Haskala be-merkaz Germania (1784–1829)* (1939; reprint, Tel Aviv: Masada, 1967), pp. 491, 492.

82. Fishl Lachover, *Toldot ha-sifrut ha-`Ivrit ha-ḥadasha*, vol. 1 (Tel Aviv: Dvir, 1966), p. 136.

83. Part of the subsequent discussion is adapted from my article "Neglected Origins of Modern Hebrew Prose: Hasidic and Maskilic Travel Narratives," *AJS Review* 33 (2009): 3–43.

84. For further biographical information on Günzburg, see Baruch Karu, "Mordechai Aaron Günzburg," in *Yahadut Lita*, vol. 1, ed. Natan Goren (Tel Aviv: Hotza'at `am ha-sefer, 1959), pp. 419–21.

85. Bartal, "Mordechai Aaron Günzburg," p. 136.

86. Quoted in ibid., p. 132. I have modified the translation slightly from Mordechai Aaron Günzburg, *Aviezer* (Vilna: n.p., 1863), p. 66. See also Marcus Moseley's discussion of Günzburg in chapter 6 of *Being for Myself Alone: Origins of Jewish Autobiography* (Stanford, CA: Stanford Univ. Press, 2006).

87. M. A. Günzburg, *Glot ha-aretz ha-ḥadasha 'al yedei Kristof Kolumbus* (Vilna: Missionary Press, 1823), p. 8.

88. Ibid., p. 18.

89. *Ve-martiaḥ metzula ka-sir*: echoes Job 41:23, with a reversal of words. Thanks go to Ora Wiskind-Elper for helping track down some of the biblical echoes in this and the next passage.

90. *Mishberei yam 'adirim*: echoes Psalm 93:4.

91. *Le-ḥerdat 'Elokim*: echoes 1 Samuel 14:15.

92. Günzburg, *Glot ha-aretz ha-ḥadasha*, 23.

93. *Lo notar kol-neshama*: quoted from Joshua 11:11 but adding the word *bam* and changing the meaning of *neshama*. The biblical passage says that "not a soul remained," meaning in context that everyone was killed. Günzburg transforms the phrase by using it to refer to the psychological sense of "spirit" because no spirit is left in the sailors.

94. *Shav teshu'at 'adam*: echoing Ps. 60:13, where the text indicates that only God's assistance is worthy, for "the help of man is in vain."

95. David Zamość, *Robinzohn der yingere: eyn lezebukh fir kinder* (in Hebrew, in spite of the impression given by the title page) (Breslau: Zultzbakh, 1824), p. 10.

96. On this point, see Wolpe, "The Sea and Sea Voyage in Maskilic Literature," pp. 84–90.

97. See Mendelsohn-Frankfurt's *Penei tevel*, p. 42. Quoted in Dukesz, *Sefer Ḥakhmei AH"W*, part 2, p. 121.

6. Bontekoe

1. Part of this chapter is based on my article "Neglected Origins of Modern Hebrew Prose: Hasidic and Maskilic Travel Narratives," *AJS Review* 33 (2009): 3–43. Thanks to Rebecca Wolpe for her stimulating studies of sea travel in Hebrew and Yiddish.

2. *Oniya so'ara* was translated from Joachim Heinrich Campe, *Wilhelm Isbrand Bonteku's merkwürdige Abentheuer auf einer Reise aus Holland nach Ostindien*, in vol. 5 of *Sammlung interessanter und durchgängig zweckmäßig abgefaßter Reisebeschreibungen für die Jugend* (Reutlingen: Grözinger, 1788), pp. 12–58. The German title of this narrative translates as *Wilhelm Isbrand Bontekoe's Remarkable Adventure during a Trip from Holland to the East Indies*. The first narrative is based on Bontekoe's account of 1646. Campe Germanized the Dutch spelling "Bontekoe" to "Bonteku"; however, I follow the Dutch spelling. Campe intended the *Reisebeschreibungen* for young adults, to take the place of novels because of their potentially corrupting influence. From 1787 until 1799, some of

Campe's best-selling books were published through the school bookstore in Braunschweig. See the website of the Consortium for European Research Libraries at http://thesaurus.cerl.org/record/cni00027641 (accessed Jan. 15, 2016). The original orthography is preserved in all quotations from the 1788 edition of *Wilhelm Isbrand Bonteku's merkwürdige Abentheuer.*

3. More than one translator may have been responsible for the Hebrew and Yiddish texts of *Oniya so`ara*. Based on the availability of Hebrew education at this time, it is fair to assume that the author of the Hebrew translation was a man who had studied in a yeshiva but was influenced by the Haskala.

4. The Yiddish edition of this book, *Historiye: oder, fun shif brokh* (Vilna: n.p., [1823?]), was available and accessed by David Roskies at the National Library of Israel in Jerusalem in the early 1970s, but since then it has been reported lost. See David G. Roskies, "Ayzik-Meyer Dik and the Rise of Yiddish Popular Literature," PhD diss., Brandeis Univ., 1974. This is apparently the same narrative that was published previously as *Oniya so`ara*, an assumption based on a passage Roskies quotes in English translation (referring to page 11 in the Yiddish text): "Oh you deceived and blind people, how your hearts would have reacted differently" (Roskies, "Ayzik-Meyer Dik," p. 84). This narrative outcry occurs at the end of the first chapter in the bilingual edition of *Oniya so`ara* ([Zholkva?]: n.p., [1815–18?]), p. 15:

> אָֽה מענשין בלינדי שלימאזלניקי נעביך וויא גאנץ אנדרשט העט עש אייך דעמאלט גיוועזין אופֿין הערצין.

Pages are unnumbered, so the page numbers given in citations represent a past reader's numbering of the pages. The bilingual text is available online at http://web.nli.org.il/sites/nli/Hebrew/library/Pages/BookReader.aspx?pid=510414 (accessed Dec. 29, 2015).

5. See Rachel Elior's short entry on Aharon and Tsvi Hirsh Koidanover in the *YIVO Encyclopedia of Jews in Eastern Europe* (New Haven, CT: Yale Univ. Press, 2008), at http://www.yivoencyclopedia.org/article.aspx/Koidanover_Aharon_Shemuel_and_Tsevi_Hirsh (accessed Dec. 29, 2015). Jean Baumgarten has done extensive research on *Kav ha-yosher*; see, for example, his article "Yiddish Ethical Texts and the Diffusion of the Kabbalah in the 17th and 18th Centuries," *Bulletin du Centre de recherche français à Jérusalem* 18 (2007): 73–91, at http://bcrfj.revues.org/223 (accessed Dec. 29, 2015).

6. Tuvia Feder, *Kol meḥatzetzim*, in *Be-misterei ha-satira: prakim ba-satira ha-`Ivrit ha-ḥadasha be-me'ah ha-19*, vol. 1, ed. Yehuda Friedlander (Tel Aviv: Bar Ilan Univ., 1984).

7. See, for example, Nancy Sinkoff, *Out of the Shtetl: Making Jews Modern in the Polish Borderlands* (Providence, RI: Brown Judaic Studies, 2004), pp. 195–96 n.

8. See Meir Letteris's comments on a mix-up involving these initials in *Zikkaron be-sefer: Mémoiren. Ein Beitrag zur Literatur- und Culturgeschichte im XIX. Jahrhundert*, vol. 1: *Vom Jahre 1800 bis 1831* (Vienna: The Author and Schlossberg, 1869). Because of the identical initials and because Lefin's book was published by the press owned by Meir's

father, Gershon Letteris, Meir informs the reader that he was sometimes mistakenly thought to have been the author of *Mase`ot ha-yam* (p. 39 n.).

9. The title page is missing from the only extant copy of the bilingual edition of *Oniya so`ara*; it is sometimes cited as having been published in Zholkva in 1815, but the exact date is not known. Yitzhak Yudlov gives the date as "1818?" in entry 1299, on *Oniya so`ara* (Zholkva? 1818?), in *Sefer ginzei Israel: The Israel Mehlman Collection* (Jerusalem: National and Univ. Library, 1984), p. 208. Sinkoff cites Samuel Poznański's unequivocal but unsubstantiated claim that Lefin was the author of *Oniya so`ara* in "Wiener's 'Bibliotheca Friedlandiana,'" *Jewish Quarterly Review* 9 (1896–97): 159 (*Out of the Shtetl*, 195–96 n.). The catalog entry for the only known copy of the first edition, at the National Library of Israel, lists bibliographic details about the work as "(Zholkva?: 1815?)."

10. *Oniya so`ara* (Vilna: Menaḥem Mann Romm, 1823; reprints, Vilna-Horodna: Dfus ha-shutafim, 1825; Warsaw: Bomberg, 1854; and Warsaw: Unterhendler, 1878). There are many differences between the Hebrew/Yiddish edition of 1815–18 and the Hebrew edition of 1823, especially in the way the former uses parenthetical glosses, whereas the latter uses footnotes. The 1823 edition improved upon the earlier edition, but it is not known whether the author oversaw these revisions; pages in this edition are unnumbered, so the page numbers cited represent my numbering of the pages.

11. See Rebecca Wolpe's discussion of this point in "The Sea and Sea Voyage in Maskilic Literature," PhD diss., Hebrew Univ. of Jerusalem, 2011, p. 140.

12. Ibn Ezra's commentary says, רק בצעקת השם הוא לבדו יכול להצילם. . . . רק השם לבדו וכן המלחים וחובלי הים וכל חכמתם תתבלע (quoted from the *Bar Ilan's Judaic Library*, Full Version 18+, CD-ROM [Tel Aviv: Bar Ilan Univ., 2010]).

13. *Oniya so`ara*, 1815–18 ed., p. 52; quoted here from the 1823 ed., p. 30.

14. Campe: "während der Nacht machte sich ein heftiger Sturm auf, der uns gewaltig zusezte. Unser kleines Fahrzeug hielt sich indeß gut; und da wir den Sturm glüklich überlebten: so hatten wir Ursache auch in diesem Zufalle die Lenkung der göttlichen Vorsehung zu fahren" (*Wilhelm Isbrand Bonteku's merkwürdige Abentheuer*, p. 53).

15. See Gershom Scholem, "Merkaba Mysticism," in *Encyclopaedia Judaica*, vol. 11 (Jerusalem: Keter, 1972), pp. 1386–89.

16. As Yosef Dan writes in *Ha-sippur ha-ḥasidi* (Jerusalem: Keter, 1975), "Bratslav hasidim saw in this journey, in every single chapter of it, a hidden mystical meaning" (p. 187).

17. Nahman of Bratslav [and Nathan Sternharz], *Sippurei ma`asiyot* ([Ostrog or Mohilev?]: n.p., 1815), renumbered supplementary section, p. 9b. Waters reaching "the heart of the heavens" are an interesting transformation of the expected flames and smoke (from a ritual sacrifice) that reach the heavens.

18. Compare Rebecca Wolpe's analysis in "The Sea and Sea Voyage in Maskilic Literature," where she discusses ways in which *Oniya so`ara* and other maskilic translations "Judaize" the source; see, for example, pages 142–43.

19. *Oniya so`ara*, 1823 ed., opening paragraph, p. 2; Campe, *Wilhelm Isbrand Bonteku's merkwürdige Abentheuer*, pp. 12–13. The earlier Hebrew/Yiddish edition, in the collection of the National Library of Israel, is missing the first two pages, which would include this passage.

20. Campe, *Wilhelm Isbrand Bonteku's merkwürdige Abentheuer*, p. 13.

21. *Oniya so`ara*, 1823 ed., p. 2; the pages containing this passage are missing from the early, bilingual edition.

22. Campe, *Wilhelm Isbrand Bonteku's merkwürdige Abentheuer*, p. 13.

23. *Oniya so`ara*, 1823 ed., p. 2.

24. As discussed in chapter 1, *Oniya so`ara* was not the first Hebrew travel narrative to incorporate this phrase in the description of a storm at sea. A precursor came from Simḥa ben Yehoshua of Zalozitsh. See Avraham Ya`ari, ed., *Mase`ot Eretz-Israel shel `olim Yehudim: mi-yemei ha-benayim ve-`ad reishit yemei shivat Tzion* (Tel Aviv: Ha-Histadrut ha-Tzionit, 1946), p. 395. But *Oniya so`ara* does more with the phrase by modifying it to suit the crisis situation.

25. *Oniya so`ara*, 1823 ed., p. 3.

26. Campe, *Wilhelm Isbrand Bonteku's merkwürdige Abentheuer*, p. 14.

27. *Oniya so`ara*, 1823 ed., p. 3.

28. *Oniya so`ara*, 1815–18 ed., pp. 10–11; 1823 ed., p. 8. In the two editions, there are some differences in punctuation: the 1815–18 edition sprinkles in some commas between the bullets, whereas the 1823 edition uses only bullets.

29. Compare, for example, the commentary by Ralbag (Rabbi Levi ben Gershom, fourteenth century), on 2 Kings 12:18: אכלו ושבעו ממנו והותירו.

30. Campe, *Wilhelm Isbrand Bonteku's merkwürdige Abentheuer*, p. 24.

31. *Oniya so`ara*, 1823 ed., p. 10.

32. Campe, *Wilhelm Isbrand Bonteku's merkwürdige Abentheuer*, p. 24.

33. *Oniya so`ara*, 1823 ed., p. 10.

34. Campe's German reads: "Aber nunmehr mag der unglükliche Held meiner Geschichte selbst, und zwar größtentheils in seiner eigenen Manier reden" (*Wilhelm Isbrand Bonteku's merkwürdige Abentheuer*, p. 24). This acknowledgment that Campe is quoting enables him to borrow unabashedly from a prior German translation of the work.

35. *Oniya so`ara*, 1815–18 ed., p. 17.

36. Ibid., 1823 ed., pp. 10–11.

37. Ibid., 1815–18 ed., p. 18; Campe, *Wilhelm Isbrand Bonteku's merkwürdige Abentheuer*, p. 24.

38. *Oniya so`ara*, 1815–18 ed., p. 18.

39. The German lacks this direct address: "Das auf die Kohlen gegossene Wasser verursachte einen so dicken, schwefelichten und erstickenden Dampf, daß es fast unmöglich war, im Raume auszuhalten. Ich blieb demohngeachtet da; machte Anstalt, so viel es mir nur möglich war, und ließ die Leute einander ablösen, damit sie frische Luft schöpfen

konnten . . . Mir selbst wurde so schlimm, daß ich nicht mehr wußte wo ich war" (Campe, *Wilhelm Isbrand Bonteku's merkwürdige Abentheuer*, pp. 24–25).

40. Ibid., p. 25.

41. *Oniya so`ara*, 1815–18 ed., pp. 18–19; 1823 ed., p. 11.

42. Campe, *Wilhelm Isbrand Bonteku's merkwürdige Abentheuer*, p. 26.

43. *Oniya so`ara*, 1815–18 ed., pp. 19–20; the angle brackets indicate an emendation in the later edition.

44. Campe: "Als Roll dies bemerkte und seine Verwunderung darüber äußerte, riefen sie ihm zu: er möchte mit einsteigen; sie wollten in See stechen. Seine eigene Furcht bewog ihn, ihre Einladung anzunehmen. Er stieg hinab und sagte: lieben Leute, ihr müßt auf den Capitain warten!" (*Wilhelm Isbrand Bonteku's merkwürdige Abentheuer*, p. 26).

45. *Oniya so`ara*, 1815–18 ed., p. 20; 1823 ed., p. 12. The angle brackets indicate a typographical error that was corrected in the 1823 edition.

46. Campe, *Wilhelm Isbrand Bonteku's merkwürdige Abentheuer*, p. 26.

47. Ibid.

48. *Oniya so`ara*, 1815–18 ed., p. 21; 1823 ed., p. 12. See also Wolpe, "The Sea and Sea Voyage in Maskilic Literature," p. 143.

49. Campe, *Wilhelm Isbrand Bonteku's merkwürdige Abentheuer*, p. 28.

50. *Oniya so`ara*, 1815–18 ed., p. 23.

51. Ibid. This closely matches Lefin's lines, reproduced in the appendix to chapter 7: "And the person who has fallen into danger and been saved is obliged to give thanks and publicly tell of God's salvation": ומי שנפל בסכנה וניצול חייב להודות ולספר ישועת ד׳ בקהל רב (Mendel Lefin, "Translator's Introduction to *Mase`ot ha-yam*," Joseph Perl Archives, Folder 124, National Library of Israel, l. 12, as given in the appendix to chapter 7). These lines are also in the spirit of Psalm 40:10–12. Moreover, as Ora Wiskind-Elper pointed out to me, Lefin's sentence probably alludes to a passage in the Babylonian Talmud, Tractate Berakhot 54b, which refers to four specific situations of danger, after which people should give thanks to God: people who have sailed the sea, those who have crossed deserts, the sick who have been healed, and those who were imprisoned. This passage has been codified into Jewish law in connection with a prayer, thanking God for deliverance, that is recited after escaping a situation of danger, *bentshen gomel* (*birkat ha-gomel*).

52. Campe: "Mein Sohn, hier ist alle Hofnung aus! Es wird Nacht; die Schaluppe und das Boot sind weit von uns; wir können es unmöglich die ganze Nacht aushalten. Wir müßen Gott anrufen, und uns in seinen Willen ergeben" (*Wilhelm Isbrand Bonteku's merkwürdige Abentheuer*, p. 30).

53. Campe: "Wir fingen an, zu beten, und—unser armes Gebet wurde erhört! Denn kaum waren wir damit fertig: so waren die Schaluppe und das Boot nahe bei uns" (ibid.).

54. *Oniya so`ara*, 1815–18 ed., p. 25; 1823 ed., p. 16. Angle brackets indicate an emendation in the later edition.

55. Campe, *Wilhelm Isbrand Bonteku's merkwürdige Abentheuer*, p. 36.

56. *Oniya so'ara*, 1815–18 ed., p. 33.

57. Campe: "Ich rief zu Gott, er mögte unsere Noth nicht höher steigen lassen, als er wüßte, daß wir sie ertragen könnten . . . bedenket doch die Unmenschlichkeit und die Gottlosigkeit von dem, was ihr vorhabt, und haltet ein! Ruft den allmächtigen Gott an, der wird sich über euch erbarmen" (*Wilhelm Isbrand Bonteku's merkwürdige Abentheuer*, p. 37).

58. *Oniya so'ara*, 1815–18 ed., pp. 35–36; 1823 ed., p. 21. The Hebrew editions change the word בצרתה in Psalms to בצרתי.

59. Ibid., 1815–18 ed., p. 36; 1823 ed., p. 21.

60. Campe, *Wilhelm Isbrand Bonteku's merkwürdige Abentheuer*, p. 38.

7. Lefin

1. The full title of Campe's twelve-volume series of *Reisebeschreibungen* is *Sammlung interessanter und durchgängig zweckmäßig abgefaßter Reisebeschreibungen für die Jugend.* It was originally planned as a nine-volume series but then was extended to twelve, and additional travel volumes were added in a new series. Lefin's translations are based on volume 1, *Jacob Heemskerks und Wilhelm Barenz nördliche Entdeckungsreise und merkwüre dige Schicksale* (Wolfenbüttel: Schulbuchhandlung, 1786), and volume 9 (Braunschweig: Schulbuchhandlung, 1791). Volume 9 has no individual title indicating that it contains the Keate/Wilson narrative.

2. The two known editions of Mendel Lefin's travel book are *Mase'ot ha-yam* (Zholkva: Gerson Letteres, 1818) and *Mase'ot ha-yam* (Lemberg: D. H. Schrenzel, 1859); the copy of the first edition at the National Library of Israel is missing pages 37a–52b. Thanks to Google Books, I recently located a complete copy of the 1818 edition of *Mase'ot ha-yam* at the Austrian National Library in Vienna. The catalog listing incorrectly attributed it to Me'ir Halewi Letteris, and the title appeared as *Sepher mas coth hayam*. The shelf mark is 20.M.39. On Google Books, see https://play.google.com/books/reader?id=JyZiAAAAcAAJ&printsec=frontcover&output=reader&hl=en&pg=GBS.PA1 (accessed Jan. 18, 2016). The scanned original comes from the Kaiserliche Königliche Hofbibliothek in Vienna, now the Österreichische Nationalbibliothek: http://digital.onb.ac.at/OnbViewer/viewer.faces?doc=ABO_%2BZ204376208 (accessed Jan. 18, 2016).In *Mase'ot ha-yam*, Lefin translates and adapts two retold sea narratives, from volume 1 and volume 9 of Campe's *Reisebeschreibungen* (see note 1). Campe's adaptation in volume 1 is based on Captain Jacob van Heemskerk's account *Entdeckungsreise nach Spitzbergen und Nova Zembla*, published originally in Dutch but translated into German in Johann Christoph Adelung, ed., *Geschichte der Schiffahrten und Versuche welche zur Entdeckung des nordöstlichen Weges nach Japan und China von verschiedenen Nationen unternommen worden* (Halle: Gebauer, 1768). (This predecessor is listed at the end of Campe's *Vorbericht* [preface] to volume 1.) The adaptation in volume 9 was based on George Keate [and Henry Wilson], *An Account of the Pelew Islands, Situated in the Western Part of the Pacific*

Ocean, 2nd ed. (London: Nicol, 1788). Lefin's short, Arctic narrative was included with Bontekoe's narrative in two Hebrew reprints of *Oniya so'ara* (Vilna: Menachem Mann Romm, 1823) and (Vilna and Horodna: Ha-shutafim, 1825).

3. Israel Bartal, "Mordechai Aaron Günzburg: A Lithuanian *Maskil* Faces Modernity," trans. N. Greenwood and L. Schramm, in *From East and West: Jews in a Changing Europe, 1750–1870*, ed. Frances Malino and David Sorkin (Oxford: Basil Blackwell, 1990), p. 136.

4. Quoted in ibid., p. 132. I have modified the translation slightly from Mordechai Aaron Günzburg, *Aviezer* (Vilna: n.p., 1863), p. 66. See also Marcus Moseley's discussion of Günzburg in *Being for Myself Alone: Origins of Jewish Autobiography* (Stanford, CA: Stanford Univ. Press, 2006), chap. 6.

5. Israel Zinberg, *A History of Jewish Literature*, trans. and ed. Bernard Martin, vol. 6: *The German–Polish Cultural Center* (New York: Hebrew Union College Press and Ktav, 1975), p. 278. On Lefin, see also Israel Zinberg, *A History of Jewish Literature*, trans. and ed. Bernard Martin, vol. 9: *Hasidism and Enlightenment (1780–1820)* (New York: Hebrew Union College Press and Ktav, 1976), chap. 8; or, in the Yiddish edition, Israel Zinberg, *Di geshikhte fun der literatur bay Yidn*, vol. 7, book 2: *Khasides un oyfklerung (1780–1820)* (New York: Sklarsky, 1943).

6. Yosef Klausner, *Historiya shel ha-sifrut ha-`Ivrit ha-ḥadasha*, vol. 1 (Jerusalem: Hebrew Univ., 1930), lesson 6, chapter 4 on Mendel Lefin, pp. 199–225, and Yosef Klausner, "Meḥkarim be-toldot ha-sifrut ha-`Ivrit ha-ḥadasha: Lehishtalsheluto shel signon-ha-Mishna be-sifrut ha-ḥadasha," in *Kitvei ha-Universita ha-`Ivrit be-Yerushalaim: Mada`ei ha-Yahadut*, vol. 1: *Yedi`ot ha-makhon le-mada`ei ha-Yahadut*, vol. 3 (Jerusalem: Ha-madpis, 1926), pp. 163–78. For another appreciation of Lefin's Hebrew contribution, see Fishl Lachover, *Toldot ha-sifrut ha-`Ivrit ha-ḥadasha*, vol. 1 (Tel Aviv: Dvir, 1966), pp. 87–91. Jeremy Dauber also mentions the Mishnaic aspect of Lefin's style in *Antonio's Devils: Writers of the Jewish Enlightenment and the Birth of Modern Hebrew and Yiddish Literature* (Stanford, CA: Stanford Univ. Press, 2004), p. 217.

7. Uriel Ofek, *Sifrut-yeledim ha-`Ivrit—ha-hatḥalot* (Tel Aviv: Porter Institute, 1979), p. 93.

8. See Maks Erik, *Etyudn tsu der geshikhte fun der haskole (1789–1881)* (Minsk: Melukhe farlag fun Vaysrusland, 1934), p. 136.

9. Hillel Levine compares Lefin's views to those of Moses Mendelssohn regarding Providence in "Menahem Mendel Lefin: A Case Study of Judaism and Modernization," PhD diss., Harvard Univ., 1974. He refers to Mendelssohn's "natural theology in which God did not abandon the world to the mindless and amoral laws of nature" (p. 20).

10. Gerrit van Veer, *Nova Zembla: Vertelling van de derde zeiltocht om de noord en de overwintering in het Behouden Huis*, ed. Vibeke Roeper and Diederick Wildeman (Amsterdam: Athenaeum, 2011).

11. George Keate was a poet whose works included *The Monument in Arcadia: A Dramatic Poem in Two Acts* (London: Dodsley, 1773).

12. Mendel Lefin, "Translator's Introduction to *Mase'ot ha-yam*," Joseph Perl Archives, Folder 124, National Library of Israel, given in the appendix to this chapter.

13. The first example occurs several times in Captain Wilson's narrative (Lefin, *Mase'ot ha-yam*, 1818 ed.); the last two examples occur together at the end of chapter 12 in the narrative of Heemskerk's voyage (1818 ed., p. 54b). There are few substantive differences between the original 1818 edition and the 1859 reprint of *Mase'ot ha-yam*; quotations are cited from the first edition by page and side *a* or *b*.

14. *Mase'ot ha-yam*, 1818 ed., p. 28a; 1859 ed., p. 45, cited from Tractate Berakhot 9b.

15. See Joseph Perl, *Megale temirin* (Vienna: Anton Strauss, 1819), and Aharon Wolfsohn, *Kalut da'at u-tzevi'ut* [*R. Ḥanokh ve-R. Yosefkhe*], ed. Dan Miron (Tel Aviv: Siman kri'a and Mif'alim universitaiim le-hotza'a le-'or, 1977), which Wolfsohn seems to have translated himself around 1796–1800 from the Yiddish version of his play *Leykhtzin un fremelay* (ca. 1794). Again, translation played a part in an unusually innovative Hebrew work. For an English translation, see *Silliness and Sanctimony*, in *Landmark Yiddish Plays: A Critical Anthology*, ed. and trans. Joel Berkowitz and Jeremy Dauber (Albany: State Univ. of New York Press, 2006), pp. 81–111. Also interesting is the relationship between Wolfsohn's play and Isaac Euchel's similar work. See Isaak Euchel, *Reb Henoch, oder: Woß tut me damit: Eine jüdische Komödie der Aufklärungszeit*, ed. Marion Aptroot and Roland Gruschka (Hamburg: Buske, 2007).

16. This usage was discussed in chapter 2; compare Lefin, *Mase'ot ha-yam*, 1818 ed., p. 25a, and 1859 ed., p. 41.

17. In the first of Lefin's two sea narratives, there are more than a dozen occurrences of the Yiddishized term *mamesh*, nearly a hundred instances of the term *bikhdei*, and half-a-dozen appearances of the Aramaic and Yiddish term *mistome*. The use of Aramaic especially recalls one component of "Mendele's *nusaḥ*" as envisioned and in part invented by H. N. Bialik. I critique Abramovitsh's and Bialik's use of Aramaic in my essay "'Nusaḥ Mendele' be-mabat bikorti" (in Hebrew), *Dappim le-meḥkar be-sifrut* 14–15 (2006): 89–103.

18. See Yitskhok Niborski, Simon Neuberg, Eliezer Niborski, and Natalia Krynicka, eds., *Verterbukh fun loshn-koydesh-shtamike verter in Yidish*, 3rd ed. (Paris: Medem Bibliotek, 2012), p. 480.

19. Mendel Lefin, "Sium la-metargem *Sefer morei nevukhim*," translator's afterword to his posthumously published translation of *Morei nevukhim* (Zholkva: Saul Meyerhoffer, 1829), unnumbered pages, n. 11.

20. Nancy Sinkoff, "Strategy and Ruse in the Haskalah of Mendel Lefin of Satanow," in *New Perspectives on the Haskalah*, ed. Shmuel Feiner and David Sorkin (London: Littman Library of Jewish Civilization, 2001), pp. 94–95.

21. The National Library of Israel has digitized an earlier printing of *Sefer katan: pirush 'al Hodu*, listed as having been published in Koretz (?) in 1780 (?).

22. Sinkoff, "Strategy and Ruse," p. 97.

23. Moses Mendelsohn-Frankfurt, *Metziat ha-aretz ha-ḥadasha* (Altona: Bonn, 1807), p. 56.

24. Lefin, *Mase`ot ha-yam*, 1818 ed., p. 1a; 1859 ed., p. 3.

25. Sinkoff, "Strategy and Ruse," p. 95. See also Nancy Sinkoff, "Tradition and Transition: Mendel Lefin of Satanów and the Beginnings of the Jewish Enlightenment in Eastern Europe, 1749–1826," PhD diss., Columbia Univ., 1996, pp. 156–69, "The Anti-Hasidism in Journeys by Sea." Compare Martin Cunz, *Die Fahrt des Rabbi Nachman von Brazlaw ins Land Israel (1798–1799)* (Tübingen: Mohr, 1997), pp. 212–13.

26. Quoted in Sinkoff, "Strategy and Ruse," p. 96, citing a document from the Joseph Perl Archives at the National Library of Israel in Jerusalem.

27. Ibid., p. 97.

28. Pertinent to this allegorical bent is Nahman's interpretation of the verse "When you pass through the waters, I will be with you" (Isa. 43:2), in *Likutei Moharan*, teaching 73 (Jerusalem: Keren hadpasa shel ḥasidei Breslov, 1988), p. 89a.

29. Sinkoff, "Strategy and Ruse," p. 90.

30. Lefin, "Translator's Introduction to *Mase`ot ha-yam*," ll. 30–31 (see the appendix to this chapter).

31. Isaac Satanov moved to Berlin in 1771, published and edited many books in Hebrew, and worked in Mendelssohn's circle. For some years, starting in 1784, he managed the publishing house connected to the Jüdische Freischule. See Shmuel Feiner, *The Jewish Enlightenment*, trans. Chaya Naor (Philadelphia: Univ. of Philadelphia Press, 2004), pp. 243–51. Mendel Lefin may still have been in Berlin when the publisher Ḥevrat ḥinukh ne`arim was founded. The press published Lefin's first book: *Mod`a le-vina*, vol. 1: *Igeret ha-ḥokhma*, and [prospectus for] *Refu'at ha-`am* (Berlin: Ḥevrat ḥinukh ne`arim, 1789), based on his writings published in the journal *Ha-me'asef*. See Nancy Sinkoff, *Out of the Shtetl: Making Jews Modern in the Polish Borderlands* (Providence, RI: Brown Judaic Studies, 2004), pp. 38–39.

32. See Yosef Klausner, "Hishtalsheluto shel signon ha-Mishna be-sifrut ha-`Ivrit ha-ḥadasha," in *Be`ayot shel sifrut ve-med`a* (Tel Aviv: Massada, 1956), pp. 119–46.

33. See Levine, "Menahem Mendel Lefin," p. 15.

34. The fragmentary 1789 edition lists the title as *Refu'ot ha-`am*, whereas the complete 1794 edition was entitled *Refu'at ha-`am*, which might be more accurately translated as *Healing [for] the People*. Neither version of Lefin's title is a translation of Tissot's title *Avis au peuple sur sa santé* (Advice to the People Regarding Their Health). Lefin's title is a bilingual pun, starting in Hebrew but ending in French. Because the Hebrew term *ha-`am* sounds like the French term *l'âme* (the soul), the title *Refu'ot* or *Refu'at ha-`am* could suggest the interlinguistic meaning "remedies for the soul" or "healing the soul." This play on words anticipates the topic of Lefin's subsequent book, *Ḥeshbon ha-nefesh* (Moral Accounting, 1808; literally, An Accounting or a Reckoning of the Soul).

35. For a discussion of Perl's creation of the Israelite Free School in Tarnopol—the first modern Jewish school in Galicia—see Sinkoff, *Out of the Shtetl*, pp. 225–37. See also Filip Friedmann, "Yosef Perl vi a bildungs-tuer un zayn shul in Tarnopol," *YIVO bleter* 31–32 (1948): 131–90.

36. See my article "Joseph Perl's Escape from Biblical Epigonism through Parody of Hasidic Writing," *AJS Review* 29 (2005): 265–82.

37. The calendars were printed in 1813–14 and 1814–15; handwritten proofs for at least two later years were preserved in the Perl Library and Archives, but there are no known printed copies of the calendars, suggesting that they may not have been printed. See Joseph Perl, *Luaḥ ha-shana 1813–1814*, *Luaḥ ha-shana 1814–1815*, and *Luaḥ ha-shana 1815–1816* (Tarnopol), reprinted as *Luaḥ ha-lev*, ed. Menuḥa Gilboa (Tel Aviv: Department of Hebrew Literature, Tel Aviv Univ., 1973). These texts include descriptions of the natural world that clearly serve educational goals.

38. Mendel Lefin, *Ḥeshbon ha-nefesh* (Lemberg: Rubenstein, 1808; Vilna: Menachem Mann Romm, 1844). For a discussion of Israel Salanter in relation to Mendel Lefin, see Immanuel Etkes, *Rabbi Israel Salanter and the Mussar Movement: Seeking the Torah of Truth*, trans. Jonathan Chipman (Philadelphia: Jewish Publication Society, 1993), esp. chap. 9.

39. See Nancy Sinkoff, "Benjamin Franklin in Jewish Eastern Europe: Cultural Appropriation in the Age of the Enlightenment," *Journal of the History of Ideas* 61 (2000): 133–52. See also Levine, "Menahem Mendel Lefin."

40. See Israel Weinlös, "Mendel Lefin-Satanover: Biografishe shtudiye afn smakh fun handshriftlekhe materialn," *YIVO bleter* 2 (1931): 349; Erik, *Etyudn tsu der geshikhte fun der haskole*, pp. 148–49; and Shmuel Werses, "Be-`ekvotav shel ha-ḥibur 'Maḥkimat peti' ha-'avud," in *Megamot ve-tzurot be-sifrut ha-haskala* (Jerusalem: Magnes, 1990), pp. 319–37.

41. Mendel Lefin, "Essai d'un plan de réforme ayant pour objet d'éclairer la nation Juive en Pologne et de redresser par là ses mœurs" (1792), in *Materiały do dziejów sejmu czteroletniego*, vol. 6, ed. Artur Eisenbach, Jerzy Michałski, Emanuel Rostworowski, and Janusz Woliński (Warsaw: Instytut historii Polskiej akademii Nauk, 1969), p. 411.

42. For a discussion of Lefin's connections to Adam Kazimierz Czartoryski, see Sinkoff, *Out of the Shtetl*, chapter 2, "The *Maskil* and the Prince: Private Patronage and the Dissemination of the Jewish Enlightenment in Eastern Europe."

43. Sinkoff notes that both Adam Kazimierz Czartoryski and Joachim Heinrich Campe were Freemasons who "belonged to the Parisian Lodge, Les Neuf Soeurs" (*Out of the Shtetl*, p. 65).

44. My retranslation in consultation with Sinkoff's translation in *Out of the Shtetl*, pp. 51–52, from Avraham Gotlober, no title, *Ha-maggid* 17, no. 39 (1873): 356, which was reprinted in Avraham Gotlober, "Menahem Mendel Lefin of Satanov," in *Zikronot ve-masa`ot*, vol. 2, ed. Reuven Goldberg (Jerusalem: Mossad Bialik, 1976), pp. 201–2.

45. Roland Gruschka, *Übersetzungswissenschaftliche Aspekte von Mendel Lefin Satanowers Bibelübersetzungen* (Hamburg: Buske, 2007), p. 17.

46. *Briefe aus Paris zur Zeit der Revolution* (Braunschweig: Schulbuchhandlung, 1790). In the preface to volume 9 of the *Reisebeschreibungen*, Campe explains his decision not to continue publication of the *Briefe aus Paris* from volume 8. He comments that the public has been flooded with writings about France in the previous two years, so that he does not want to contribute any more to this excess (*Reisebeschreibungen*, vol. 9, *Vorrede* [preface]). He deliberately turns away from describing the revolutionary developments in Paris, choosing instead to tell the story of a sea adventure that contains a more conservative message. The maritime equivalent of revolution was mutiny, and Campe avoids that topic; instead, he shows a captain and crew who survive adversity by means of reason, ingenuity, and teamwork. He underplays the element of insubordination (and completely excludes any mention of desire or sexuality).

47. Thanks go to Rebecca Wolpe for sharing with me her unpublished manuscript on the idea of the "noble savage" in maskilic sea narratives. She also wrote to me that

> the "Noble Savage" has been defined by Ter Ellingson in his work *The Myth of the Noble Savage* as "a mythic personification of natural goodness by a romantic glorification of savage life." See Ter Ellingson, *The Myth of the Noble Savage* (Berkeley: Univ. of California Press, 2001), 1. Fairchild, in his 1928 study *The Noble Savage: A Study in Romantic Naturalism*, described the Noble Savage as any "free and wild being who draws directly from nature virtues which raise doubts as to the value of civilization." See Hoxie Neale Fairchild, *The Noble Savage: A Study in Romantic Naturalism* (New York: Columbia Univ. Press, 1928). The concept is often mistakenly attributed to Jean Jacques Rousseau. Not only is this attribution misleading, but as Ellingson demonstrates, the use of the term itself is highly flawed. Leaving aside issues of semantics, there is no doubt that from the Renaissance period onwards there were some poets, explorers, philosophers, and clerics that idealized non-European peoples, often interweaving depictions of them with depictions of utopia and references to the Golden Age. (Private correspondence, Aug. 27, 2013)

48. Bernard Smith, *European Vision and the South Pacific 1768–1850: A Study in the History of Art and Ideas* (London: Oxford Univ. Press, 1960), p. 99.

49. Campe, *Reisebeschreibungen*, vol. 9, p. 2.

50. Lefin, "Translator's Introduction to *Mase'ot ha-yam*," ll. 1–2, underlining in the original. I thank Jonatan Meir and Avraham Weizal for their help in deciphering Lefin's handwriting. A transcription and translation are contained in the appendix to this chapter.

51. Lefin's introduction is packed with quotations from ancient and medieval sources. This sentence alludes to a Talmudic passage in B. Berakhot 10a and to medieval commentators. See, for example, Seforno's commentary on Genesis 18:22 in *Ḥumash*

mikra'ot gedolot, and Rabbi Yona Gerondi's commentary on Proverbs 14:32 (in *Rabbenu Baḥye: bi'ur 'al ha-Torah*, ed. Ḥaim Dov Shevel [Jerusalem: Mossad ha-rav Kook, 1991], 3:314).

52. Compare Lefin's opposition to the hasidic belief in miracles, as performed by their leaders, in "Essai d'un plan de réforme," p. 411. Sinkoff discusses this opposition in *Out of the Shtetl*, pp. 89–90.

53. Lefin, "Translator's Introduction to *Mase`ot ha-yam*," ll. 12–14.

54. A facsimile of the introduction, followed by my Hebrew transcription and English translation, is included in my article "Neglected Origins of Modern Hebrew Prose: Hasidic and Maskilic Travel Narratives," *AJS Review* 33 (2009): 37–43. The appendix to this chapter provides the transcription and translation, modified slightly; the quoted passage occurs in lines 30–38.

55. In Lefin's Hebrew: להתאפק מכל מיני משקים משכרים (*Mase`ot ha-yam*, 1818 ed., p. 1b). In Keate's English: "it was strongly recommended to every individual not to drink any spirituous liquor" (Keate [and Wilson], *An Account of the Pelew Islands*, p. 12). See also Campe's German: "Eine nothwendige Bedingung hierzu sey, daß sie, um ihres Verstandes vollkommen mächtig zu bleiben, dem Genusse starker Getränke entsagen müßten" (*Reisebeschreibungen*, vol. 9, p. 13). This requirement does not preclude immediately serving two glasses of wine, as reported in English, German, and Hebrew.

56. Lefin, "Translator's Introduction to *Mase`ot ha-yam*," l. 36 (chapter appendix).

57. This idea became a commonplace of piety. Ora Wiskind-Elper has drawn my attention to two other early sources: Midrash Tanaim on Dvarim, chapter 3, and Pesikta zutarta (lekaḥ tov) on Exodus, Be-shalaḥ, chapter 16.

58. Avraham Löwenthal, ed., *Perush `al Mishlei le-rabbenu Yona Gerondi* (Berlin: Poppelauer, 1910), p. 70.

59. *Rabbenu Baḥye*, 3:314.

60. In *Out of the Shtetl*, Sinkoff briefly discusses Lefin's quotations from "the classical sayings of the Rabbinic Sages." She writes that his citations "not only gave Lefin's work a traditional imprimatur, but also expressed his ardent belief that there was nothing incompatible between a rationalized, renewed Judaism and the universal values common to all men" (p. 165).

61. Lefin, "Essai d'un plan de réforme," p. 411, nos. 20–22. See the analysis in N. M. Gelber, "Mendel Lefin-Satanover ve-hatza`otav le-tikun oraḥ-ḥayim shel Yehudei Polin bifnei ha-Seym ha-gadol (1788–1792)," in *The Abraham Weiss Jubilee Volume*, ed. Samuel Belkin (New York: Shulsinger, 1964), pp. 271–84, followed by a translation into Hebrew (pp. 287–301) and facsimiles from Hebrew and French memoranda (pp. 285–86, 302–5) connected to Lefin's appearance before the Polish council that had been established to consider issues regarding the Jewish community.

62. Lefin, *Mase`ot ha-yam*, 1818 ed., p. 1a; 1859 ed., p. 1.

63. Ibid.

64. "Man hatte fast täglich Sturm und Ungewitter, und das Schiff wurde von Wind und Wellen, unter heftigen Regengüssen, so sehr zerarbeitet, daß es mehr als einmal ganz das Ansehn hatte, daß es der Gewalt nicht länger würde widerstehen können. Der Regen drang von oben, das Seewasser von unten ein; alles wurde davon durchwässert; und das Schwanken und stoßen des von Sturmwinden geppeitschten und von ungeheurn Meereswogen geschaukelten Schiffes, war so gewaltsam, daß alles mitgenommene Rindvieh und die meisten andern an Bord befindlichen Thiere dadurch getödtet wurden" (Campe, *Reisebeschreibungen*, vol. 9, pp. 9–10).

65. On this assertion, see Dov Sadan, *'Al sifrutenu* (Jerusalem: Reuven Mass, 1950), p. 31.

66. Lefin, "Sium la-metargem *Sefer morei nevukhim*," sec. 7 n. 11.

67. From Lefin's introduction to his unpublished Yiddish translation of Psalms, quoted in Simḥa Katz, "Tirgumei Tanakh mi-et Menachem Mendel Lefin mi-Satanov," *Kiryat sefer* 16 (1939): 129. Leaving the prestandard spellings intact, the Yiddish reads:

> סיז ידוע דער גרוסר חילוק צ[וו]ישן דעם לשון פונים פראסטי שמוס ציווישן מענטשן צום דיבור פון שירים ומליצות: אז מיהאט מיט זיין גלייחן מענטשן אנגעמיינים אינטעריס צו טאהן, מכ״ש צו שאפן זיך מיט אדינסט, דא גייט דאס לשון גאר וויא צום פשוטסטן.

68. Lefin's introduction to his unpublished Yiddish translation of Psalms, quoted in Katz, "Tirgumei Tanakh mi-et Menachem Mendel Lefin mi-Satanov," pp. 129–30. The Yiddish phrase reads,

> אין אונזרן יודשן לשון אריין אזו וויא עס ווערט היינטיגן טאָג צווישן אונז גישמוסט.

For a discussion of Mendel Lefin's style of translation, see Gruschka, *Übersetzungswissenschaftliche Aspekte*. Gruschka quotes the full Yiddish introduction and provides a German translation (pp. 217–22). Compare Dror Mashbitz, "The Emergence of Modern Yiddish in Literature: Mendl Lefin's Translation of Ecclesiastes of 1819," MA thesis, Columbia Univ., 1970, pp. 13–14.

69. Campe, *Reisebeschreibungen*, vol. 9, p. 13.

70. Lefin, *Mase'ot ha-yam*, 1818 ed., p. 1b. Writing for a readership not limited to youth, Lefin excises Campe's patronizing addresses to his young audience. For example, he omits another long digression by Campe on Providence, *die Vorsehung* (*Reisebeschreibungen*, vol. 9, pp. 29–30). According to Campe, it was no coincidence that Captain Wilson brought aboard a Malaysian servant, nor was it an accident that about a year earlier another Malaysian arrived at the island as the result of another shipwreck. By these means, God enabled the British to communicate with the islanders with the help of interpreters. Campe comments: "Thus Providence guides the events of the world and the fate of people through its invisible hand, so that in the end everything leads to some intended, beneficial goal. . . . It is well for us that, in our own blindness toward what the future will

bring, our fate stands under such a wise and well-meaning direction" (p. 30). Although Lefin does repeatedly affirm the role of Providence, he omits this passage.

71. Campe, *Reisebeschreibungen*, vol. 9, p. 15.

72. Lefin, *Mase'ot ha-yam*, 1818 ed., p. 2a.

73. Ibid.

74. Campe, *Reisebeschreibungen*, vol. 9, p. 16.

75. Campe, *Reisebeschreibungen*, chapter 4.

76. Campe, *Reisebeschreibungen*, vol. 9, p. 51.

77. Lefin, *Mase'ot ha-yam*, 1818 ed., p. 7a; 1859 ed., p. 12.

78. Campe, *Jacob Heemskerks und Wilhelm Barenz*, p. 39; Lefin, *Mase'ot ha-yam*, 1818 ed., p. 57a, and 1859 ed., p. 76.

79. Campe, *Jacob Heemskerks und Wilhelm Barenz*, p. 46; Lefin, *Mase'ot ha-yam*, 1818 ed., p. 58b, and 1859 ed., p. 78.

80. Campe, *Jacob Heemskerks und Wilhelm Barenz*, p. 80; Lefin, *Mase'ot ha-yam*, 1818 ed., p. 53a, and 1859 ed., p. 53.

81. Campe, *Reisebeschreibungen*, vol. 9, p. 81, and passim.

82. Lefin, *Mase'ot ha-yam*, 1818 ed., p. 11b; 1859 ed., p. 19.

83. When the British are preparing to leave, one of the sailors decides he wants to remain on the island. Captain Wilson gives him advice before they depart: "In particular he recommended to him not to give up his religious practices, and also to celebrate a Sabbath [Sabbat] or a Sunday" (Campe, *Reisebeschreibungen*, vol. 9, p. 222). Lefin omits this sentence from chapter 15 (*Mase'ot ha-yam*, 1818 ed., p. 31b; 1859 ed., p. 51).

84. As noted in Rebecca Wolpe, "The Sea Voyage Narrative as an Educational Tool in the Early Haskalah," MA thesis, Hebrew Univ. of Jerusalem, 2006, pp. 75–76.

85. Rebecca Wolpe, "The True Way to Loving God: Nature in the *Haskala*," *University of Toronto Journal of Jewish Thought* 3 (2013), at http://tjjt.cjs.utoronto.ca/wp-content/uploads/2013/11/Rebecca-Wolpe-The-True-Way-to-Loving-God-Nature-in-the-Haskala-Vol.-3.pdf (accessed Jan. 7, 2015).

86. Lefin, *Mase'ot ha-yam*, 1818 ed., p. 1a.

87. In contrast, as we have seen, Nahman's tales are often subordinated to a kabbalistic allegory. Even one of Nathan Sternharz's accounts of a storm at sea culminates in Nahman's suggestion that leads to the calming of the storm. In his introduction to *Shivḥei ha-Ran*, Sternharz writes that his purpose is not to tell of miraculous events but to teach *musar*. The events are significant for their exemplary character and for their portrayal of Nahman's spiritual journey.

88. Campe, *Reisebeschreibungen*, vol. 9, pp. 10–11, ellipses added.

89. Lefin, *Mase'ot ha-yam*, 1818 ed., pp. 1a–1b; 1859 ed., p. 3, parallel ellipses added.

90. Another vivid storm description illustrates Lefin's art of translation: *Mase'ot ha-yam*, 1859, p. 39, from Campe, *Reisebeschreibungen*, vol. 9, p. 168.

91. In "Strategy and Ruse," Sinkoff writes: "Throughout the nineteenth century, east European *maskilim* answered Naphtali Herz Wessely's clarion call in *Divrei shalom ve'emet* (1782) that 'the forms of the lands and the oceans (geography)' should be an obligatory element of the secular curriculum" (p. 89).

92. See *Ha-me'asef* 5 (1789): 136–44.

93. Campe: "Der Tag brach endlich an; und was Einige schon während der Nacht beim Schein des Blitzes bemerkt haben wollten, das zeigte sich jetzt Allen—ein kleines Eiland in einer Entfernung von drei oder vier Seemeilen gegen Süden" (*Reisebeschreibungen*, vol. 9, p. 15).

94. Lefin, *Mase`ot ha-yam*, 1818 ed., p. 2a.

95. Campe: "Aber ach! wie viel neue Besorgnisse verdrängten bald darauf die kurze Freude, welche dieser Anblick ihnen verursacht hatte!" (*Reisebeschreibungen*, vol. 9, p. 15).

96. Lefin, *Mase`ot ha-yam*, 1818 ed., p. 2a.

97. Apart from the stylistic innovations, several ethical, ideological issues arise in *Mase`ot ha-yam* resulting from the British involvement in a war among islanders and the beginnings of a colonial presence. The narrative works hard to make both seem unproblematic: Campe appears oblivious, and Lefin does little better. An extension of the colonial question relates to the wisdom of bringing the king of Palau's son, Libo, back to London, where he dies of smallpox. Here the perspective changes in that George Keate came to know Libo in London and refers to Libo's impressions and experiences there.

98. Campe, *Jacob Heemskerks und Wilhelm Barenz*, unpaginated *Vorbericht* (preface).

99. Lefin, "Translator's Introduction to *Mase`ot ha-yam*," ll. 35–38.

100. Lefin, *Mase`ot ha-yam*, 1818 ed., p. 28a; 1859 ed., p. 45.

101. Lefin, *Mase`ot ha-yam*, 1818 ed., p. 38b; 1859 ed., p. 62.

102. The words in Hebrew that are glossed parenthetically are:

קברניטא (שטייער מאן), הגשר העליון (פערדעק), חרדה (צוויבאק), אגוזים (קאקוס ניסע), הבריטאנים (ענגלענדער), כדור עופרת (הנקרא קויל), אבק שריפה (הנקרא פולווער), מעט בגדי צמר (טוך אן וואנט), תיבת החובלין שבספינה הנקרא (שיפס אפטיק), חרב קצר אחד (הנקרא הירש פענגיר), קנה (באמבוס), לעת גאון המים (פלוהט צייט), צב אחד הנקרא (שילד קרעט), המלח הנקרא (באטסמאן), גרעיני העופרת (שרוט), העיגון הנקרא (אנקיר), הנס (ענגליש פלאגע), זוג קני השריפה קטנים הנקרא (פיסטולין), להוציא את המים ע״י קנה (הפומפ), מעברות המים (הנקרא קאנאל), מנגנת במצלתים (קלאויר), צלם דמות בקוטן הנקרא (מיניאטור), הצרעת (הנקרא פאקין), למשפחת השועים (עדיל לייט), עכברים גדולים (ראטען), החליל הנקרא (פלעטע), יש לו קרן גדול במצחו והבריטאנים היו קורין לו (איינהארין), סרטוני הים (קרעפס), מיני שאלין טירען (בעלי חיים בנרתק), הדולבקין (טעליר), הנקראים עצי שייטין (ובל״א טרייבהאלץ), שידה (שליטען), גחלי אבן (בל״א שטיין קולין), סיבוב המוח (בל״א שווינדיל), לחולי הנקרא (שקרובוט).

103. The phrases with German words that Lefin gives in parentheses, without a Hebrew equivalent, include

מכנסים של (מאטרזין), מים חמין מתוקים ממין (סירעפ), שרשי (יאמוס), (ההייא פיש), (זעע בארבע), עששיות גדולות של קרח הנקרא (אייז שאלן), בספרי רושמי המדינות (לאנד קארט), אי (אינזעל), עוף ידוע הנקרא (מעוון), הכלי הנקרא (קאמפעס).

104. Campe, *Jacob Heemskerks und Wilhelm Barenz*, p. 13.

105. Lefin, *Mase`ot ha-yam*, 1818 ed., p. 44b; 1859 ed., pp. 71–72.

106. Campe refers to a seagull as a *Mewe*, which was the more common eighteenth-century spelling of the now current term *Möwe*; Lefin transcribes it following the composite noun form *Meweneier*. Both spellings were used in the eighteenth and nineteenth centuries; the spelling *Möwe* displaced *Mewe* in the early twentieth century, according to the results of a search on Google Books Ngram Viewer (July 7, 2015).

107. Modern Hebrew authors later found the word שחף for "seagull," which makes an appearance as an unclean bird in Leviticus 11:16 and Deuteronomy 14:15.

108. Lefin, *Mase`ot ha-yam*, 1818 ed., p. 46a; 1859 ed., p. 74.

109. "Die Bären traten unterdeß auf die hinterbeine, um zu sehen, was es gäbe, weil sie weiter riechen, als sehen können. Sobald sie Menschen merkten, liefen sie ihnen entgegen, um sie anzugreifen. Nun standen den Matrosen die Haare vollends zu Berge, und sie liefen was sie laufen konnten, um die Schaluppe zu erreichen" (Campe, *Jacob Heemskerks und Wilhelm Barenz*, p. 32).

110. Ibid., p. 38.

111. Lefin, *Mase`ot ha-yam*, 1818 ed., p. 47a; 1859 ed., p. 75.

112. On Hebrew publishers in Zholkva, including the Letteris family, see N. M. Gelber and Y. Ben-Shem, eds., *Sefer Zholkiev* [*Kiria nisgava*] (Jerusalem: 'Entziklopediya shel galuyot, 1969), pp. 104–10.

113. M. [Meir] Letteris, *Zikkaron be-sefer: Mémoiren. Ein Beitrag zur Literatur- und Culturgeschichte im XIX. Jahrhundert* (in Hebrew), vol. 1 (Vienna: The Author and Schlossberg, 1869), p. 39 n. This error was also made by the Kaiserliche Königliche Hofbibliothek in Vienna, as explained in note 2 of this chapter.

114. Sinkoff, *Out of the Shtetl*, pp. 195–96 n.

115. *Oniya so`ara* ([Zholkva?]: n.p., [1815–18?]), p. 10.

116. This section is based on part of my article "Neglected Origins of Modern Hebrew Prose."

117. Nahman of Bratslav [and Nathan Sternharz], *Sippurei ma`asiyot* (Jerusalem: Keren hadpasa shel ḥasidei Breslav, 1979), p. 50.

118. בכל מקום שאתה מוצא גבורתו של הקב״ה שם אתה מוצא ענוותנותו. For an excellent discussion of this passage and tale, see Zvi Mark, *Mistika ve-shiga`on be-yetzirat R. Naḥman mi-Breslav* (Tel Aviv: `Am `oved, 2003), 359–70.

119. Mendel Lefin, "Mikhtavim shonim," *Ha-me'asef* 5 (1789): 83. Reprinted verbatim in Mendel Lefin, *Mod`a le-vina*, vol. 1, sec. 15, p. 2b. Original punctuation retained, in which the colon (:) is often used to end a paragraph and the bullet (·) is often used for

a period. Hebrew printers employed by both maskilic authors and hasidic authors commonly used the bullet where European languages used periods.

120. Mendel Lefin, Nahman of Bratslav, and Nathan Sternharz could have received the modified version of this phrase from many sources, such as *Rabbenu Baḥye* (commentary on Deut. 10:18) or the traditional Ashkenazic Motzei Shabbat prayers, as Zvi Mark has pointed out to me.

121. Sinkoff, *Out of the Shtetl*, p. 121.

122. Lefin, "Mikhtavim shonim," pp. 136–38.

123. In the second appendix to *Ḥasidut Breslav: prakim be-ḥayei meḥolela, be-kitveha u-ve-safiḥeha* (1972), 2nd ed. (Jerusalem: Mossad Bialik, 1995), Mendel Piekarz compares similar passages in works by Nathan Sternharz and argues that Lefin did write *Kin'at H' tzeva'ot.*

124. Shmuel Feiner, "Be-emunah bilvad! Ha-pulmus shel reb Natan mi-Nemirov neged ha-ateizm ve-ha-haskalah," in *Meḥkerei ḥasidut*, Meḥkerei Yerushalaim be-maḥshevet Yisrael, vol. 15, ed. Immanuel Etkes, David Assaf, and Joseph Dan (Jerusalem: Hebrew Univ., 1999), p. 107. See also Ron Margolin's thesis on *Likutei halakhot* ("Ha-'emunah ve-ha-kfirah be-torata shel ḥasidut Breslav `al pi ha-sefer Likutei halakhot le-R. Nathan Sternharz," Univ. of Haifa, 1991) and Hillel Levine's dissertation ("Menahem Mendel Lefin").

125. Quoted in Feiner, "Be-emunah bilvad!" p. 107.

126. Ibid., p. 108. Perl created the Israelitische Freischule under the influence of the Jüdische Freischule in Berlin. His admiration for the Berlin Haskala was so great that in his fiction he sometimes refers to his hometown Tarnopol as "Berlain." Sinkoff discusses Perl's activities, including his creation of the Israelite Free School in Tarnopol—the first modern Jewish school in Galicia—in *Out of the Shtetl* (pp. 225–37). According to some scholars, Mendel Lefin was more critical than Perl of the Berlin Haskala and *Ha-me'asef*; nevertheless, he did publish in that journal and at the Ḥinukh Ne`arim Press in 1789.

127. Nathan Sternharz, *`Alim le-trufa: mikhtevei Moharnat* (New York: Keren hadpasa shel ḥasidei Breslav, 1976), p. 176, letter of Wednesday, the twenty-fifth day of the counting the Omer (Apr. 27, 1836). The manuscript version (p. 11b) shows no significant passages excised from this letter.

128. Compare Zvi Mark, "`Al matzavei katnut ve-gadlut be-haguto shel R. Naḥman mi-Breslav," *Da`at*, Winter 2001, 45–80.

129. Lefin, *Morei nevukhim*, part 1; the same publisher printed Nathan Sternharz's *Likutei halakhot* in 1848!

130. Lefin, *Mase`ot ha-yam*, 1859 ed. The title page of the 1818 edition does not include this line, however, which suggests that it was added by the publisher.

131. Compare N. M. Gelber, "Mendel Satanower: Der Verbreiter der Haskala in Polen und Galizien," in *Aus zwei Jahrhunderten: Beiträge zur neueren Geschichte der Juden* (Vienna: Löwit, 1924), 49.

132. Jonatan Meir has contributed to realizing these desiderata with the following books: I. B. Levinsohn and Joseph Perl, *Gilgulav shel megale sod: kuntras divrei tzadikim le-RIBaL ve-Yosef Perl*, ed. Jonatan Meir (Los Angeles: Cherub Press, 2004); Joseph Perl, *Megale temirin*, 2 vols., ed. Jonatan Meir (Jerusalem: Mossad Bialik, 2013); and Jonatan Meir, *Ḥasidut meduma: 'Iyunim be-ketavav ha-satiriim shel Yosef Perl* (Jerusalem: Mossad Bialik, 2013). Together Jonatan Meir and I are pushing forward with a collection of short stories that are satires and parodies of the hasidim.

133. This transcription preserves Lefin's original punctuation. Although this is not a poetic text, I have retained the original line breaks in Lefin's manuscript. Thanks to the Department of Manuscripts at the National Library of Israel for granting permission to publish this important text; thanks to Jonatan Meir and Avraham Weizal for their assistance in deciphering Lefin's handwriting.

134. ברכות י, עמ׳ א; ספורנו על בראשית יח, כב; ר׳ יונה גרונדי על משלי יד, לב; רבינו בחיי, ביאור על התורה, עורך חיים דוב שוול (ירושלים: מוסד הרב קוק, תשנ״א), כרך ג, עמ׳ 314.

135. תהילים קכה, א.

136. קהלת ז, ב.

137. פרקי אבות ד, א.

138. אליהו רבה, פרק 10.

139. יומא לח עמ׳ ב.

140. מגילה ו עמ׳ ב.

141. מסכת תמיד לב עמ׳ א.

142. משלי כד, טז.

143. תהילים לב, י.

144. Babylonian Talmud, Tractate Berakhot 10a and medieval commentators: Seforno, commentary on Genesis 18:22, in *Humash mikra'ot gedolot*; R. Yona Gerondi's commentary on Proverbs 14:32; *Rabbenu Baḥye*, 3:314. Lefin's quotations and allusions seem designed to indicate that this translated book of sea adventure is compatible with pious beliefs and suitable for traditional Jewish readers. Lefin goes beyond the typical maskilic *shibbutz* by extending his quotations into postbiblical sources such as Mishna ('Avot), Gemara (Babylonian Talmud, Tractates Berakhot, Yoma, Megillah, and Tamid), and medieval commentaries (Seforno, Yona Gerondi, *Rabbenu Baḥye*). In the notes provided here, all Talmudic citations refer to the Babylonian Talmud.

145. Ps. 125:1.

146. "Better to go to a house of mourning than to go to a house of feasting" (Eccles. 7:2).

147. Mishna 'Avot 4:1.

148. Eliahu ben Shlomo Zalman, *Eliahu Raba* (Prague: Sommer, 1812), chap. 10.

149. B. Yoma 38b.

150. B. Megillah 6b.

151. B. Tamid 32a.

152. Prov. 24:16.

153. Ps. 32:10.

Conclusion

1. Firsthand sources do, however, note some rare nineteenth-century Hebrew conversations, as between traveling Jews who had no other common language. See, for example, Nathan Sternharz's account of his pilgrimage to the Land of Israel, discussed in chapter 3.

2. Yosef Klausner, "Ben-Yehuda, Eliezer," in *Encyclopedia Judaica*, 2nd ed., ed. Fred Skolnik and Michael Berenbaum (Detroit: Macmillan/Gale, 2007), 3:387.

3. Compare Dovid Katz, *Words on Fire: The Unfinished Story of Yiddish* (New York: Basic Books, 2004; rev. ed., 2007), esp. chap. 2, "The Three Languages of Ashkenaz." See also my article "Innovation by Translation: Yiddish and Hasidic Hebrew in Literary History," in *Arguing the Modern Jewish Canon: Essays on Literature and Culture in Honor of Ruth R. Wisse*, ed. Justin Cammy, Dara Horn, Alyssa Quint, and Rachel Rubinstein (Cambridge, MA: Center for Jewish Studies and Harvard Univ. Press, 2008), pp. 417–25.

4. Compare Robert Alter's excellent framing of this problem in *The Invention of Hebrew Prose: Modern Fiction and the Language of Realism* (Seattle: Univ. of Washington Press, 1988).

5. See, for example, Jacques Derrida's early works: *La voix et le phénomène: Introduction au problème du signe dans la phénoménologie de Husserl* (Paris: Presses Universitaires de France, 1967) and *De la grammatologie* (Paris: Editions de Minuit, 1967). In English, see *Voice and Phenomenon: Introduction to the Problem of the Sign in Husserl's Phenomenology*, trans. Leonard Lawlor (Evanston, IL: Northwestern Univ. Press, 2011) and *Of Grammatology*, trans. Gayatri Chakravorty Spivak (Baltimore: Johns Hopkins Univ. Press, 1976).

6. Ken Frieden, "Joseph Perl's Escape from Biblical Epigonism through Parody of Hasidic Writing," *AJS Review* 29 (2005): 265–82.

7. Simon Dubnow, *Fun "zhargon" tsu Yidish un andere artiklen: literarishe zikhroynes* (Vilna: Kletzkin, 1929), p. 46.

8. The letter from Abramovitsch to Ravnitzky is included in Khone Shmeruk, ed., *Ḥalifat 'igrot bein S. Y. Abramovitsh u-vein Ḥ. N. Bialik ve-Y. Ḥ. Ravnitzki ba-shanim 1905–1908* (Jerusalem: Israeli Academy of Sciences, 1976), p. 67.

9. Ibid., n. 4.

10. See my article "'Nusaḥ Mendele' be-mabat bikorti" (in Hebrew), *Dappim le-meḥkar be-sifrut* 14–15 (2006): 89–103; see also my essay "Epigonism after Abramovitsh and Bialik," *Studia Rosenthaliana* 40 (2007–8): 159–81.

11. See Ber of Bolekhov [Birkenthal], *Zikronot*, ed. M. Wischnitzer (Berlin: Klal-Verlag, 1922). In English, see *The Memoirs of Ber of Bolechow (1723–1805)*, trans. and

ed. M. Vishnitzer (London: Oxford Univ. Press, 1922). Gershon Hundert has brought to light more of Dov Ber Birkenthaler's writings; see "The Introduction to *Divrei Binah* by Dov Ber of Bolechów: An Unexamined Source for the History of Jews in the Lwów Region in the Second Half of the Eighteenth Century," *AJS Review* 33 (2009): 225–69.

12. In an early article, Menahem Perry discusses the indirect presence of Yiddish expressions in Mendele's Hebrew translation of *Mase'ot Benyamin ha-shlishi* (The Brief Travels of Benjamin the Third, 1896). For example, he refers to *firen in bod arayn* (duping someone), which happens literally when the antiheroes are taken to the bathhouse (a phrase Hillel Halkin translated as "taken to the cleaners"). See S. Y. Abramovitsh, *Tales of Mendele the Book Peddler*, ed. Dan Miron and Ken Frieden (New York: Schocken, 1996), p. 374; Menahem Perry, "Ha-'analogiya u-mekoma be-mivne ha-roman shel Mendele Mo"S [Mokher Sfarim]," *Ha-sifrut* 1 (1968): 65–100; and Menahem Perry, "Thematic and Structural Shifts in Autotranslations by Bilingual Hebrew–Yiddish Writers: The Case of Mendele Mokher Sforim," *Poetics Today* 2 (1981): 181–92.

13. In her MA thesis, "The Sea Voyage Narrative as an Educational Tool in the Early Haskalah" (Hebrew Univ. of Jerusalem, 2006), Rebecca Wolpe refers to Lefin's "somewhat universalist attitude." She cites the quotation בין עבד ובין שפחה רוה"ק שורה עליו לפי מעשיו (whether a slave or a maidservant, the spirit of God hovers over them in accordance with their deeds) in his unpublished introduction to *Mase'ot ha-yam* (Joseph Perl Archives, National Library of Israel, Folder 124; see the appendix in chapter 7). She comments: "It is clear that Lefin sought to combine traditional Jewish attitudes and the praise of G-d with Enlightenment concepts of morality and universalism" (p. 74).

14. Haim Liberman argues that it is more accurate to speak of "folk Hebrew" than of "hasidic Hebrew" ("R. Nakhmen Bratslaver un di Umaner maskilim," *YIVO bleter* 29 [1947]: 219).

15. Israeli Hebrew fiction and drama have also emerged under the star of translation—explicit or implicit—from European languages. In her book *Ha-lashon ba-drama ha-'Ivrit: ha-dialog ba-maḥaze ha-'Ivri ha-mekori ve-ha-meturgam mi-'Anglit u-mi-Tzarfatit*, 1948–1975 (Tel Aviv: Ha-kibbutz ha-me'uḥad, 1996), Rina Ben Shaḥar has shown how twentieth-century Hebrew drama developed with the help of translations from English and French.

16. After I published an essay on Joseph Perl in 2005, Robert Alter and I argued over whether the more common term around 1800 was *lashon tzaḥ* or *lashon tzaḥa*, and I sent him some results from the Bar Ilan Judaic Library database. Israeli Hebrew settled on the feminine, *lashon tzaḥa*. But thanks to Google Books NGram Viewer, based on the millions of scans stored by Google, a new tool quickly resolved the dispute. Graph 2 here shows the relative frequency of occurrence of these three terms over time: *lashon tzaḥ* or *lashon tzaḥa* (pure language) and *leshon tzaḥut* (language of purity).

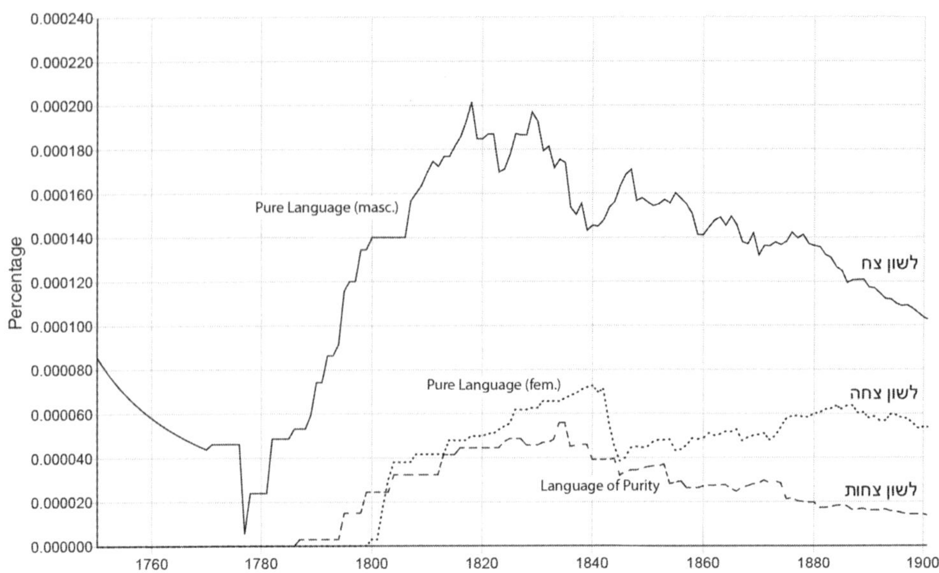

Graph 2. Results of a Google Books Ngram Viewer search for the incidence of three variant phrases meaning "pure language" in Hebrew works published from 1750 to 1900, with a smoothing of 20. Reformatted by Joseph Stoll, Syracuse University Cartographic Laboratory, in collaboration with Ken Frieden.

This graphing of "big data" by Google, based on the one hundred thousand or more scans from Hebrew books, is a delight for anyone interested in diachronic linguistics. It shows that there is no correct answer in Hebrew linguistic history: since the nineteenth century, these three terms have been in direct competition. One should approach these statistics cautiously, however, because at the present time Optical Character Recognition is sometimes inaccurate in dealing with Hebrew texts.

17. See, for example, Yehuda ha-Levi's poem "ʿAl ha-yam" (Upon the Sea). Unfortunately, I couldn't include the initial-stress word אני for "ship" in graph 1 because the numbers would have been completely skewed by the visually identical second-stress word *ani* (I).

18. For example: *khokhem* versus *ḥakham*, *khevre* versus *ḥevra*, and *tsures* versus *tzarot*. Haim Blanc, "Some Yiddish Influences in Israeli Hebrew," in *The Field of Yiddish*, vol. 2, ed. Uriel Weinreich (The Hague: Mouton, 1965), p. 189.

19. Israelis calqued *khapn* using *khataf* in verbal formulations such as *khataf siḥa* (*khapn a shmues*) and *khataf tnuma* (*khapn a driml*). Compare the phrases *le-ʿasot ʾet ha-mavet* (*makhn dem toyt*); *ʾata tzohek mimeni* (*du lakhst fun mir*), and *hu zarak ʿalav*

mabat (*er hot gevorfn af im a blik*). See Israel Rubin, "Vegn di virkung fun Yidish afn geredtn Hebreyish in Erets-Yisroel," *YIVO bleter* 25 (1945): 308.

20. Hillel Halkin, "Hebrew as She Is Spoke," *Commentary* 48 (July 1969): 59.

21. On this nonrecognition of the hybrid nature of Israeli speech, see Yael Chaver, *What Must Be Forgotten: The Survival of Yiddish Writing in Zionist Palestine* (Syracuse, NY: Syracuse Univ. Press, 2004).

Bibliography

Sea Narratives

Adelung, Johann Christoph, ed. *Geschichte der Schiffahrten und Versuche welche zur Entdeckung des nordöstlichen Weges nach Japan und China von verschiedenen Nationen unternommen worden*. Halle: Gebauer, 1768.

———. "Jacob Heemskerks und Wilhelm Barentz dritter Versuch im Nordost." In *Geschichte der Schiffahrten und Versuche welche zur Entdeckung des nordöstlichen Weges nach Japan und China von verschiedenen Nationen unternommen worden*, edited by Johann Christoph Adelung, 220–65. Halle: Gebauer, 1768.

———. *Vollständige Geschichte der Schiffarthen nach den noch gröstentheils unbekanten Südländern*. Halle: Gebauer, 1767.

Adler, Elkan Nathan, ed. *Jewish Travellers in the Middle Ages: 19 Firsthand Accounts*. 1930. Reprint. New York: Dover, 1987.

Adler, Marcus Nathan, trans. *The Itinerary of Benjamin of Tudela*. 1907. Reprint. Cold Spring, NY: NightinGale Resources, 2010.

Basola, Moshe. *Mase'ot Eretz-Israel le-Rabbi Moshe Basola*. 2nd ed. Edited by Yitzhak ben-Tzvi. Jerusalem: Hebrew Society for Research on Eretz-Israel, 1939.

Bontekoe, Willem Ysbrantsz. "Destruction by Fire of the Dutch East Indiaman the New Hoorn." In *The Mariner's Chronicle; Being a Collection of the Most Interesting Narratives of Shipwrecks, Fires, Famines*, vol. 2, edited by Archibald Duncan, 132–67. London: James Cundee, 1804.

———. *Journael ofte Gedenckwaerdige beschrijvinghe vande Oost-Indische Reyse*. Hoorn: Willemsz, 1646.

———. *Journael ofte Gedenckwaerdige beschrijvinghe van de Oost-Indische Reyse van Willem Ysbrantsz Bonte-Koe van Hoorn*. Amsterdam: Hartgers, 1648.

———. *Memorable Description of the East Indian Voyage 1618–25*. 1646. Translated by C. B. Bodde-Hodgkinson and Pieter Geyl. New York: McBride, 1929.

———. "Relation ou Iournal du voyage de Bontekoe aux Indes Orientales." In *Relations de divers voyages curieux qui n'ont point esté publiées*, new ed., vol. 1, edited by Melchisedec Thévenot, 1–49. Paris: Thomas Moette, 1696.

———. "Voyage de Guillaume Isbrantsz Bontekoe aus Indes Orientales." In *Histoire générale des voyages*, vol. 8, edited by Antoine François Prévost, 417–50. Paris: Didot, 1750.

———. "Wilhelm Isbrands Bontekoes Reise nach Ostindien." In *Allgemeine Historie der Reisen zu Wasser und zu Lande*, vol. 8, 378–411. Leipzig: Arkstee and Merkus, 1751.

Bontekoe, Willem Ysbrantsz, and Dirk Raven. *Journaal ofte Gedenckwaerdige beschrijvinge van de Oost-Indische Reyse van Willem Ysbrantsz Bonte-Koe van Hoorn*. Amsterdam: Brouwer, 1722.

Campe, Joachim Heinrich. *Die Entdekkung von Amerika: Ein angenehmes und nützliches Lesebuch für Kinder und junge Leute*. 2nd ed. 3 vols. Hamburg: Bohn, 1781–82.

———. *Die Entdeckung von Amerika: Ein Unterhaltungsbuch für Kinder und junge Leute*. 6th ed. Vol. 1. Braunschweig: Schulbuchhandlung, 1806.

———. *Jacob Heemskerks und Wilhelm Barenz nördliche Entdeckungsreise und merkwürdige Schicksale*. Vol. 1 of *Sammlung interessanter und durchgängig zweckmäßig abgefaßter Reisebeschreibungen für die Jugend*. Wolfenbüttel: Schulbuchhandlung, 1786.

———. *Robinson der Jüngerer, zur angenehmen und nützlichen Unterhaltung für Kinder*. 2 vols. Frankfurt: n.p., 1781.

———. *Robinson the Younger*. Hamburg: Bohn, 1781.

———. *Sammlung interessanter und durchgängig zweckmäßig abgefaßter Reisebeschreibungen für die Jugend*. Vol. 9. Braunschweig: Schulbuchhandlung, 1791. (Based on George Keate's account of Captain Wilson's voyage to Palau; no specific title was given to this volume.)

———. *Wilhelm Isbrand Bonteku's merkwürdige Abentheuer auf einer Reise aus Holland nach Ostindien*. In *Sammlung interessanter und durchgängig zweckmäßig abgefaßter Reisebeschreibungen für die Jugend*, vol. 5, 12–58. Reutlingen: Grözinger, 1788.

Eisenstein, Yehuda David, ed. *Otzar masa`ot: kovetz tiurim shel nosa`im Yehudiim be-Eretz Israel, Syria, Mitzrayim, ve-artzot aḥerot*. New York: Author, 1926.

Euchel, Isaac. "'Igrot Meshullam ben Uriah ha-Eshtemo`i." *Ha-me'asef* 6 (1790): 38–50, 80–85, 171–76, 245–49.

———. "'Igrot Meshullam ben Uriah ha-Eshtemo`i." In *Prakim ba-satira ha-`Ivrit*, vol. 1, edited by Yehuda Friedlander, 41–61. Tel Aviv: Papyrus, 1979.

———. "'Igrot Yitzḥak Euchel." *Ha-me'asef* 2 (1785): 116–21, 137–42.

Forster, Georg. *A Voyage round the World in His Britannic Majesty's Sloop,* Resolution. London: White, 1777.

Forster, Georg, and Johann Reinhold Forster. *Johann Reinhold Forster's Reise um die Welt.* 3 vols. Berlin: Haude and Spener, 1778–80.

Forster, Johann Reinholt. *Observations Made during a Voyage round the World.* London: Robinson, 1778.

Friedlander, Yehuda, ed. *Prakim ba-satira ha-`Ivrit.* Vol. 1. Tel Aviv: Papyrus, 1979.

Friedman, Philip. "Mikhtavim mi-Eretz Israel mi-shnot ha-Tof-Kuf-Ayin" Daled—ha-Tof-Kuf-Peh"Beit [1814–1822] (`Al ha-matzav ha-kalkali ve-ha-medini shel ha-Yehudim be-Eretz Israel be-snhot ha`esrim la-me'a ha-19)." *Tziyon* 3 (1937–38): 267–74.

Günzburg, M. A. *Di entdekung fun Amerika.* 3 vols. Vilna: Missionary Press, 1824.

———, trans. *Glot ha-aretz ha-ḥadasha `al yedei Kristof Kolumbus.* 3 vols. Vilna: Missionary Press, 1823.

Historiye fun den zeefahrer Robinzohn. Frankfurt an der Oder: Elsner, 1813.

Historiye: oder, fun shif brokh. Vilna: n.p., [1823?]. (Catalogued and researched by David Roskies at the National Library of Israel in Jerusalem in the early 1970s but now lost.)

Historiye oder zeltzame und vunderbahre begebenheiten eines yungen zee fahrers. Prague: Bak and Katz, 1784. (Adaptation of Daniel Defoe's novel *Robinson Crusoe*; German transliterated into Hebrew characters.)

Hurwitz, Khaikl. *Tsofnas paneakh.* Berdichev: Bak, 1817.

Jonge, J. K. J. de. *Nova Zembla (1596–1597): The Barents Relics.* Translated by Samuel Richard van Campen. London: Trübner, 1877.

Keate, George. *Narrative of the Shipwreck of the* Antelope *East-India Pacquet on the Pelew Islands, Situated on the Western Part of the Pacific Ocean, in August 1783.* Perth: Morison, 1788.

Keate, George [and Henry Wilson]. *An Account of the Pelew Islands, Situated in the Western Part of the Pacific Ocean.* 2nd ed. London: Nicol, 1788.

Lefin, Mendel, trans. and ed. *Mase`ot ha-yam.* Zholkva: Gerson Letteres, 1818.

———, trans. and ed. *Mase`ot ha-yam.* Lemberg: D. H. Schrenzel, 1859.

Mendelsohn-Frankfurt, Moshe, trans. and ed. *Metziat ha-aretz ha-ḥadasha.* Altona: Bonn, 1807. (No further volumes appeared.)

[Meshullam mi-Voltera]. *Mas`a Meshullam mi-Voltera be-Eretz Israel ba-shnat RM"A (1481)*. Edited by Avraham Ya`ari. Jerusalem: Mossad Bialik, 1948.

Oniya so`ara. [Zholkva?]: n.p., [1815–18?].

Oniya so`ara. Vilna: Menachem Mann Romm, 1823.

Oniya so`ara. Vilna and Horodna: Ha-shutafim, 1825.

*Oniya so`ara*. Warsaw: Tzvi Ya`akov Bamberg, 1854.

Oniya so`ara. Warsaw: Y. Unterhendler, 1878.

Ovadiah of Bartenura [Ovadia of Bertinoro]. *Pathway to Jerusalem: The Travel Letters of Rabbi Ovadiah of Bartenura Written between 1488–1490 during His Journey to the Holy Land*. Translated by Yaakov Dovid Shulman. Edited by Avrohom Marmorstein. New York: CIS, 1992.

Pesaro, Eliahu. "Mikhtav mi-Eliahu mi-`ir Pesaro asher be-Italia." In *Ḥayei `olam*, edited by M. Edelman, 7–25. Paris: Goldberg, 1879.

Simḥa ben Yehoshua of Zalozitsh. *Ahavat Tziyon*. Hordona: n.p., 1790.

Sobel, Samuel, ed. *Jewish Sea Stories*. Middle Village, NY: Jonathan David, 1985.

Sternharz, Nathan. *Mase`ot ha-yam*. Warsaw: Lebenzohn, 1850. (Includes "Seder nesi`ato le-Eretz Israel," based on the 1815 version from *Sippurei ma`asiyot*, later published in *Shivḥei ha-Ran*. Possibly not published by the Bratzlav hasidim.)

———. *Nesi`at ha-Ran le-Eretz ha-kedosha*. Mihalovitz: Deutsch, 1933. At http://www.hebrewbooks.org/34171.

———. "Nesi`ato le-Erets Israel." In *Ḥayei Moharan*, 80–87. Jerusalem: Keren hadpasa shel ḥasidei Breslav, 1981.

———. "Seder ha-nesi`a shelo le-Eretz Israel." In the supplementary sections appended to Nahman of Bratslav [and Nathan Sternharz], *Sippurei ma`asiyot*. [Ostrog or Mohilev?]: n.p., 1815.

———. "Seder ha-nesi`a shelo le-Eretz Israel." Manuscript 16988, Schocken Library, Jerusalem. Microfilm no. 45394, National Library of Israel, Jerusalem.

Veer, Gerrit van. *Nova Zembla: Vertelling van de derde zeiltocht om de noord en de overwintering in het Behouden Huis*. Edited by Vibeke Roeper and Diederick Wildeman. Amsterdam: Athenaeum, 2011.

Ya`ari, Avraham, ed. *The Goodly Heritage: Memoirs Describing the Life of the Jewish Community of Eretz Yisrael from the Seventeenth to the Twentieth Centuries*. Translated by Israel Schen. Jerusalem: Youth and Hechalutz Department of the Zionist Organization, 1958.

———, ed. *'Igrot Eretz Israel she-katvu ha-Yehudim ha-yoshvim ba-aretz la-aḥehem she-ba-gola mi-yemei galut Bavel ve-'ad shivat Tzion she-be-yamenu*. 1943. Reprint. Ramat-Gan: Massada, 1971.

———, ed. *Mase'ot Eretz Israel shel 'olim Yehudiim: mi-yemei ha-benayim ve-'ad reshit yemei shivat Tzion*. Tel Aviv: Ha-Histadrut ha-Tzioni, 1946.

———, ed. *Shluḥei Eretz Israel: toldot ha-shliḥut mi-ha-Aretz la-gola mi-ḥurban bait sheni 'ad ha-me'a ha-tsha' 'esrei*. Jerusalem: Mossad Ha-Rav Kook, 1951.

Zamość, David, trans. *Robinzohn der yingere: eyn lezebukh fir kinder* (in Hebrew). Breslau: Zultzbakh, 1824.

Zlotnik, Yehuda Leyb, ed. *Ma'ase Yerushalmi she-he-'atik R. Avraham ben Maimon*. Jerusalem: Ha-makhon ha-Eretz-Israeli le-folklor ve-etnologiya, 1946.

General, Primary, and Secondary Literature

Abramovitsh, S. Y. *Tales of Mendele the Book Peddler*. Edited by Dan Miron and Ken Frieden. New York: Schocken, 1996.

Adams, Percy G. *Travelers and Travel Liars, 1660–1800*. 1962. Reprint. New York: Dover, 1980.

———. *Travel Literature and the Evolution of the Novel*. Lexington: Univ. Press of Kentucky, 1983.

Adelung, Johann Christoph. *Versuch eines vollständigen grammatisch-kritischen Wörterbuches der Hochdeutschen Mundart*. Leipzig: Breitkopf, 1774.

Ahrbeck-Wothge, Rosemarie, ed. *Studien über den Philanthropismus und die Dessauer Aufklärung: Vorträge zur Geistesgeschichte des Dessau-Wörlitzer Kulturkreises*. Halle: Martin-Luther-Universität Halle-Wittenberg, 1970.

Alcalay, R. *The Complete Hebrew–English Dictionary*. New ed. Tel Aviv: Yedioth Ahronoth, 2000.

Alter, Robert, trans. *The Book of Psalms: A Translation with Commentary*. New York: Norton, 2007.

———. *Hebrew and Modernity*. Bloomington: Indiana Univ. Press, 1994.

———. *The Invention of Hebrew Prose: Modern Fiction and the Language of Realism*. Seattle: Univ. of Washington Press, 1988.

Aptroot, Marion, Andreas Kennecke, and Christoph Schulte, eds. *Isaac Euchel: Der Kulturrevolutionär der jüdischen Aufklärung*. Hanover: Wehrhahn, 2010.

Ashkenazi, Yankev ben Yitskhok. *Tsene-rene*. N.p.: n.p., ca. 1670.

Auden, W. H. *The Enchafèd Flood or The Romantic Iconography of the Sea*. New York: Random House, 1950.

Bar Ilan's Judaic Library. Full Version 18+. CD-ROM. Tel Aviv: Bar Ilan Univ., 2010.

Bartal, Israel. *Kozak ve-Bedoui: "`am" ve-"'aretz" be-le'umiut ha-Yehudit.* Tel Aviv: `Am `oved, 2007.

———. "Mordechai Aaron Günzburg: A Lithuanian *Maskil* Faces Modernity." Translated by N. Greenwood and L. Schramm. In *From East and West: Jews in a Changing Europe, 1750–1870*, edited by Frances Malino and David Sorkin, 126–47. Oxford: Blackwell, 1990.

———. "Ha-shikhiḥa ve-ha-zekhira: Eretz-Israel ba-toda`at tnu`at ha-Haskala be-mizraḥ Europa." In *Eretz-Israel ba-hagut ha-Yehudit ba-`et ha- ḥadasha*, edited by Aviezer Ravitzky, 413–23. Jerusalem: Ben-Tzvi Institute, 1998.

Barth, Susanne. *Mädchenlektüren: Lesediskurse im 18. und 19. Jahrhundert.* Frankfurt: Campus, 2002. (Chapter 3 on Joachim Heinrich Campe.)

Baumgarten, Jean. "Yiddish Ethical Texts and the Diffusion of the Kabbalah in the 17th and 18th Centuries." *Bulletin du Centre de recherche français à Jérusalem* 18 (2007): 73–91.

Behm, Britta L. *Moses Mendelssohn und die Transformation der jüdischen Erziehung in Berlin: Eine bildungsgeschichtliche Analyse zur jüdischen Aufklärung im 18. Jahrhundert.* Münster: Waxmann, 2002.

Beinfeld, Solon, Harry Bochner, Barry Goldstein, Yankl Salant, eds. *Comprehensive Yiddish–English Dictionary.* Bloomington: Indiana Univ. Press, 2013. (Based on the *Dictionnaire Yiddish–Français*, edited by Yitskhok Niborski, Bernard Vaisbrot, Simon Neuberg. Paris: Bibliothèque Medem, 2002.)

Bendavid, Aba. *Leshon mikra ve-leshon ḥakhamim.* 2 vols. Tel Aviv: Dvir, 1967–71.

Benjamin, Walter. "Die Aufgabe des Übersetzers." In *Gesammelte Schriften*, iv-1:9–21. Frankfurt am Main: Suhrkamp, 1980.

———. "The Task of the Translator." In *Illuminations*, translated by Harry Zohn, 69–82. New York: Schocken, 1969.

Ben-Or [Orinovski], Aharon. *Toldot ha-sifrut ha-`Ivrit ha-ḥadasha.* Vol. 1: *Tekufat ha-Haskala be-Israel.* Tel Aviv: "Yizreel," 1955.

Ben-Shaḥar, Rina. *Ha-leshon ba-drama ha-`Ivrit: ha-dialog ba-maḥaze ha-`Ivri ha-mekori ve-ha-meturgam mi-'Anglit u-mi-Tzarfatit, 1948–1975.* Tel Aviv: Ha-kibbutz ha-me'uḥad, 1996.

Ber of Bolekhov [Birkenthal]. *The Memoirs of Ber of Bolechow (1723–1805).* Translated and edited by M. Vishnitzer. London: Oxford Univ. Press, 1922.

———. *Zikronot.* Edited by M. Vizhnitzer. Berlin: Klal-Verlag, 1922.

Bialik, H. N. “Mendele u-shloshet ha-kerakhim.” In *Kol kitvei Mendele Moykher Sforim*, vol. 3, 324–31. Odessa: Va`ad ha-yovel, 1912.

———. “Yotzer ha-nusaḥ.” *Ha-olam* 4, no. 50 (1910–11): 6–8.

Blamires, David. *Telling Tales: The Impact of Germany on English Children's Books 1780-1918*. Cambridge: Open Book, 2009. (Especially chapter 2: “A World of Discovery: Joachim Heinrich Campe.”)

Blanc, Haim. “Some Yiddish Influences in Israeli Hebrew.” In *The Field of Yiddish*, vol. 2, edited by Uriel Weinreich, 185–201. The Hague: Mouton, 1965.

Blumenberg, Hans. *Schiffbruch mit Zuschauer: Paradigma einer Daseinsmetapher*. Frankfurt am Main: Suhrkamp, 1979.

———. *Shipwreck with Spectator: Paradigm of a Metaphor for Existence*. Translated by Steven Rendall. Cambridge, MA: MIT Press, 1997.

Boyarin, Daniel, and Jonathan Boyarin. “Diaspora: Generation and the Ground of Jewish Identity.” *Critical Inquiry* 20 (1993): 693–725.

———. *Powers of Diaspora: Two Essays on the Relevance of Jewish Culture*. Minneapolis: Univ. of Minnesota Press, 2002.

Boym, Svetlana. *The Future of Nostalgia*. New York: Basic Books, 2001.

Brann, M. “Aus H. Graetzens Lehr- und Wanderjahren.” *Monatsschrift für Geschichte und Wissenschaft des Judenthums* 62 (1918): 231–65.

Brown, Francis, S. R. Driver, and Charles A. Briggs, eds. *A Hebrew and English Lexicon of the Old Testament*. Oxford: Clarendon Press, 1952.

Buber, Shlomo. *Midrash zuta: `al Shir ha-shirim, Ruth, Eikha ve-Kohelet*. Berlin: Ḥevrat mekitsei nirdamim, 1895.

Buchen, Irving H. *Isaac Bashevis Singer and the Eternal Past*. New York: New York Univ. Press, 1968.

Campe, Joachim Heinrich. *Wörterbuch zur Erklärung und Verdeutschung der unserer Sprache aufgedrungenen fremden Ausdrücke: Ein Ergänzungsband zu Adelungs Wörterbuche*. 2 vols. Braunschweig: Schulbuchhandlung, 1801.

“Campe, Joachim Heinrich.” In *Allgemeine Deutsche Biographie*, 3:733–37. Leipzig: Duncker & Humblot, 1876.

Chaver, Yael. *What Must Be Forgotten: The Survival of Yiddish Writing in Zionist Palestine*. Syracuse, NY: Syracuse Univ. Press, 2004.

Classen, Albrecht. “Storms, Sea Crossings, the Challenges of Nature, and the Transformation of the Protagonist in Medieval and Renaissance Literature.” *Neohelicon* 30 (2003): 163–82.

Clifford, James. *Routes: Travel and Translation in the Late Twentieth Century*. Cambridge, MA: Harvard Univ. Press, 1997.

Cohen, A. *The Psalms*. London: Soncino, 1945.

Cohen, Margaret. *The Novel and the Sea*. Princeton, NJ: Princeton Univ. Press, 2010.

Corbin, Alan. *The Lure of the Sea: The Discovery of the Seaside in the Western World, 1750–1840*. Translated by Jocelyn Phelps. Los Angeles: Univ. of California Press, 1994.

DBS Torah Treasures: The Computerized Torah Library. Version 13.0. Brooklyn, NY: DBS, 2007.

Derrida, Jacques. *De la grammatologie*. Paris: Editions de Minuit, 1967.

———. "The Eyes of Language: The Abyss and the Volcano." Translated by Joseph Adamson and Jean Wilson. Revised by Gil Anidjar. In *Acts of Religion*, edited by Gil Anidjar, 191–227. New York: Routledge, 2002.

———. *Of Grammatology*. Translated by Gayatri Chakravorty Spivak. Baltimore: Johns Hopkins Univ. Press, 1976.

———. *Voice and Phenomenon: Introduction to the Problem of the Sign in Husserl's Phenomenology*. Translated by Leonard Lawlor. Evanston, IL: Northwestern Univ. Press, 2011.

———. *La voix et le phénomène: Introduction au problème du signe dans la phénoménologie de Husserl*. Paris: Presses Universitaires de France, 1967.

Dietrich, Peter, and Uta Lohmann. "'Daß die Kinder aller Confessionen sich kennen, ertragen und lieben lernen': Die Jüdische Freischule in Berlin zwischen 1778 und 1825." In *Dialog zwischen den Kulture: Erziehungshistorische und religionspädagogische Gesichtspunkte interkultureller Bildung*, edited by Ingrid Lohmann and Wolfram Weiße, 37–47. Münster: Waxmann, 1994.

Dinur, Ben-Tzion. *Be-mifne ha-dorot: meḥkarim ve-`iyunim be-reshitam shel ha-zmanim ha-ḥadashim be-toldot Israel*. Vol. 1. Jerusalem: Mossad Bialik, 1955.

Dubnov-Erlich, Sophie. *The Life and Work of S. M. Dubnov: Diaspora Nationalism and Jewish History*. Translated by Judith Vowles. Edited by Jeffrey Shandler. Bloomington: Indiana Univ. Press, 1991.

Dubnow, Simon. *Fun "zhargon" tsu Yidish un andere artiklen: literarishe zikhroynes*. Vilna: Kletzkin, 1929.

Dukesz, Eduard [Yeḥezkel]. *Sefer ḥakhmei AH"W* [*Altona, Hamburg, and Wandsbeck*]. Part 2. Hamburg: Goldschmidt, 1908. (Pp. 120–21 on Moses Mendelsohn-Frankfurt.)

Edwards, Philip. *The Story of the Voyage*. Cambridge: Cambridge Univ. Press, 1994.

Efron, Noah. *Judaism and Science: A Historical Introduction.* Westport, CT: Greenwood Press, 2007.

Elior, Rachel. "Aharon Koidanover." In *YIVO Encyclopedia of Jews in Eastern Europe.* New Haven, CT: Yale Univ. Press, 2008. At http://www.yivoencyclopedia.org/article.aspx/Koidanover_Aharon_Shemuel_and_Tsevi_Hirsh.

Emden, Jacob. *Megillat sefer.* Edited by David Kahana. Warsaw: Shuldberg, 1896.

Etkes, Immanuel. *Rabbi Israel Salanter and the Mussar Movement: Seeking the Torah of Truth.* Translated by Jonathan Chipman. Philadelphia: Jewish Publication Society, 1993.

Ettinger, David, ed. *Sfatenu be-mar'ot: milon histakeluti be-tziurim.* Tel Aviv: Dvir, 1953.

Euchel, Isaac. *Reb Henoch, oder: Woß tut me damit: Eine jüdische Komödie der Aufklärungszeit.* Edited by Marion Aptroot and Roland Gruschka. Hamburg: Buske, 2007.

———. *Toldot rabenu ha-ḥakham Moshe ben Menaḥem.* Berlin: Ḥevrat ḥinukh ne'arim, 1789.

Even-Shoshan, Avraham. *Ha-milon he-Ḥadash.* 4 vols. Jerusalem: Hotza'at kiryat-sefer, 1985.

Even-Zohar, Itamar. *Polysystem Studies.* Special issue of *Poetics Today* 11 (1990).

Ezrahi, Sidra DeKoven. *Booking Passage: Exile and Homecoming in the Modern Jewish Imagination.* Berkeley: Univ. of California Press, 2000.

Fabian, Bernhard. "English Books and Their Eighteenth-Century German Readers." In *The Widening Circle: Essays on the Circulation of Literature in Eighteenth-Century Europe,* edited by Paul J. Korshin. Philadelphia: Univ. of Pennsylvania Press, 1976.

Feiner, Shmuel. *Haskalah and History: The Emergence of a Modern Jewish Historical Consciousness.* Translated by Chaya Naor and Sondra Silverston. Oxford: Littman Library of Jewish Civilization, 2002.

———. *The Jewish Enlightenment.* Translated by Chaya Naor. Philadelphia: Univ. of Philadelphia Press, 2004.

Fishelov, David. *Dialogues with/and Great Books: The Dynamics of Canon Formation.* Brighton: Sussex Academic Press, 2010.

Friedberg, Ḥayim Dov, ed. *Toldot ha-dfus ha-'Ivri be-Polania.* Tel Aviv: n.p., 1950.

Frieden, Ken. *A Century in the Life of Sholem Aleichem's Tevye.* B. G. Rudolph Lectures in Judaic Studies, New Series, Lecture 1, 1993–94. Syracuse, NY: Syracuse Univ. Press, 1997.

———. "Epigonism after Abramovitsh and Bialik." *Studia Rosenthaliana* 40 (2007–8): 159–81.

———. "Innovation by Translation: Yiddish and Hasidic Hebrew in Literary History." In *Arguing the Modern Jewish Canon: Essays on Literature and Culture in Honor of Ruth R. Wisse*, edited by Justin Cammy, Dara Horn, Alyssa Quint, and Rachel Rubinstein, 417–25. Cambridge, MA: Center for Jewish Studies and Harvard Univ. Press, 2008.

———. "Joseph Perl's Escape from Biblical Epigonism through Parody of Hasidic Writing." *AJS Review* 29 (2005): 265–82.

———. "Literary Innovation in Yiddish Sea Travel Narratives, 1815–24." *Poetics Today* 35, no. 3 (2014–15): 357–82.

———. "Neglected Origins of Modern Hebrew Prose: Hasidic and Maskilic Travel Narratives." *AJS Review* 33 (2009): 3–43.

———. "'Nusaḥ Mendele' be-mabat bikorti" (in Hebrew). *Dappim le-meḥkar be-sifrut* 14–15 (2006): 89–103.

Frieden, Menachem Mendel. *A Jewish Life on Three Continents: The Memoir of Menachem Mendel Frieden*. Translated and edited by Lee Shai Weissbach. Stanford, CA: Stanford Univ. Press, 2013.

Friedmann, Filip. "Yosef Perl vi a bildungs-tuer un zayn shul in Tarnopol." *YIVO bleter* 31–32 (1948): 131–90.

Garrett, Leah. "The Jewish Robinson Crusoe." *Comparative Literature* 54 (2002): 215–28.

———. *Journeys beyond the Pale: Yiddish Travel Writing in the Modern World*. Madison: Univ. of Wisconsin Press, 2003.

Gelber, N. M., and Y. Ben-Shem, eds. *Sefer Zholkva* [*Kiria nisgava*]. Jerusalem: 'Entzikopediya shel galuyot, 1969. (On Hebrew publishing in Zholkva, pp. 104–10.)

Geßner, Salomon. *Der Tod Abels*. Zurich: Geßner, 1759.

Glinert, Lewis, ed. *Hebrew in Ashkenaz: A Language in Exile*. New York: Oxford Univ. Press, 1993.

Gotlober, Avraham. *Zikronot u-ma'asiot*. Edited by Reuven Goldberg. Jerusalem: Mossad Bialik, 1976.

Govrin, Nurit. "Signon ha-makama be-sifrut ha-'Ivrit ba-dorot ha-aḥaronim." *Me'asef* 8–9 (1964–65): 394–417.

Gries, Zeev. *The Book in the Jewish World 1700–1900*. Oxford: Littman Library of Jewish Civilization, 2007.

Grozovski, Yehuda, and David Yellin, eds. *Ha-milon ha-'Ivri*. Tel Aviv: Dvir, 1927.

Günzburg, Mordechai Aaron. *Aviezer.* Vilna: n.p., 1863.

Gur [Grozovski], Yehuda, ed. *Milon `Ivri.* Tel Aviv: Dvir, 1950.

Gutmann, Joseph. "Geschichte der Knabenschule der jüdischen Gemeinde in Berlin." In *Festschrift zur Feier des hundertjährigen Bestehens der Knabenschule der jüdischen Gemeinde in Berlin*, part 1, 3–138. Berlin: Phönix 1926.

Halkin, Hillel. "Hebrew as She Is Spoke." *Commentary* 48 (July 1969): 55–60.

Hand, Wayland D. "Crossing Water: A Folkloristic Motif." In *For Max Weinreich on His Seventieth Birthday: Studies in Jewish Languages, Literature, and Society*, 82–92. The Hague: Morton, 1964.

Harkavy, Alexander. *Yidish-English-Hebreyisher verterbukh.* New York: Hebrew Publishing, 1928.

Harshav, Benjamin. *Language in Time of Revolution.* Berkeley: Univ. of California Press, 1993.

Hebrew-English Edition of the Babylonian Talmud. London: Soncino, 1989.

Hentschel, Cedric. "Campe and *The Discovery of America.*" *German Life & Letters* 26 (1972–73): 1–13.

Humboldt, Wilhelm von. *Briefe von Wilhelm von Humboldt an eine Freundin.* Vol. 2. Leipzig: Brockhaus, 1847.

Hundert, Gershon. "The Introduction to *Divrei Binah* by Dov Ber of Bolechów: An Unexamined Source for the History of Jews in the Lwów Region in the Second Half of the Eighteenth Century." *AJS Review* 33 (2009): 225–69.

Jastrow, Marcus. *A Dictionary of the Targumim, the Talmud Babli and Yerushalmi, and the Midrashic Literature.* 1903. Reprint. New York: Judaica Press, 1992.

The Jerusalem Bible. Edited and translated by Harold Fisch. Jerusalem: Koren, 1983.

JPS Hebrew-English Tanakh. Philadelphia: Jewish Publication Society, 1999.

Karu, Baruch. "Mordechai Aaron Günzburg." In *Yahadut Lita*, vol. 1, edited by Natan Goren, 419–21. Tel Aviv: Hotza'at `am ha-sefer, 1959.

Katz, Dovid. *Words on Fire: The Unfinished Story of Yiddish.* New York: Basic Books, 2004; rev. ed., 2007.

Keate, George. *The Monument in Arcadia: A Dramatic Poem in Two Acts.* London: Dodsley, 1773.

Ken`ani, Ya`akov. *Ha-milon ha-`Ivri ha-malei.* 4 vols. N.p.: Milonim la`am, 2000.

Kennecke, Andreas. *Isaac Abraham Euchel: Architekt der Haskala.* Göttingen: Wallstein, 2007.

Kerler, Dov-Ber. *The Origins of Modern Literary Yiddish.* Oxford: Clarendon Press, 1999.

Khan, Geoffrey. *The Early Karaite Tradition of Hebrew Grammatical Thought.* Leiden: Brill, 2000.

Klausner, Yosef. "Ben-Yehuda, Eliezer." In *Encyclopedia Judaica*, 2nd ed., edited by Fred Skolnik and Michael Berenbaum, 3:386–88. Detroit: Macmillan/Gale, 2007.

———. *Historiya shel ha-sifrut ha-`Ivrit ha-ḥadasha.* 6 vols. Jerusalem: Hebrew Univ., 1930–50.

Klein, Ernest. *A Comprehensive Etymological Dictionary of the Hebrew Language for Readers of English.* Jerusalem: CARTA; Haifa: Univ. of Haifa, 1987.

Kogman, Tal. "*Haskalah* Scientific Knowledge in Hebrew Garment: A General Statement and Two Examples." *Target* 19, no. 1 (2007): 69–83.

———. *Ha-maskilim ba-mada`im: ḥinukh Yehudi le-mada`im be-merḥav dover ha-Germanit ba-`et ha-ḥadasha.* Jerusalem: Magnes, 2013.

Lehmann, Matthias B. "*Levantinos* and Other Jews: Reading H. Y. D. Azulai's Travel Diary." *Jewish Social Studies: History, Culture, Society*, New Series, 13 (2007): 1–34.

Lerner, R. "Tsu der geshikhte fun der literarisher sprakh onheyb 19-tn yorhundert (di shprakh fun H. Hurvitz's 'Tsofnas paneakh')." *Afn shprakhfront* 3 (1939): 165–90.

Levinsohn, I. B., and Joseph Perl. *Gilgulav shel megale sod: kuntras divrei tsadikim le-RIBaL ve-Yosef Perl.* Edited by Jonatan Meir. Los Angeles: Cherub Press, 2004.

Lohmann, Ingrid, Britta L. Behm, and Uta Lohmann, eds. *Chevrat Chinuch Nearim: Die Jüdische Freischule in Berlin (1778–1825) im Umfeld preußischer Bildungspolitik und jüdischer Kultusreform. Eine Quellensammlung.* 2 vols. Berlin: Waxmann Münster, 2001.

Löwenthal, Avraham, ed. *Perush `al Mishlei le-rabbenu Yona Gerondi.* Berlin: Poppelauer, 1910.

Mahler, Raphel. *Hasidism and the Jewish Enlightenment: Their Confrontation in Galicia and Poland in the First Half of the Nineteenth Century.* Translated by Eugene Orenstein, Aaron Klein, and Jenny Machlowitz Klein. Philadelphia: Jewish Publication Society of America, 1985.

———. *Ha-ḥasidut ve-ha-Haskala.* Merḥavia: Sifriat po`alim, 1961.

———. *Der kamf tsvishn haskole un khasides in Galitzia in der ershter helft fun 19tn yorhundert.* New York: YIVO, 1942.

Mandelkern, Solomon. *Konkordantzia la-Tanakh.* Jerusalem: Schocken, 1986.

Mark, Yudl, and Yuda A. Yoffe, eds. *Groyser verterbukh fun der Yidisher shprakh.* 4 vols. New York: Yiddish Dictionary Committee, 1961, 1966, 1971, 1980.

Matvejević, Predrag. *Mediterranean: A Cultural Landscape.* Translated by Michael Henry Heim. Berkeley: Univ. of California Press, 1999.

Meir, Jonatan. *Ḥasidut meduma: `iyunim be-ketavav ha-satiriim shel Yosef Perl.* Jerusalem: Mossad Bialik, 2013.

Mendelsohn-Frankfurt, Moses. *Penei tevel: musar ha-sekhel.* Amsterdam: Levisson, 1872.

———. *Schuschan-Eduth, das ist: Erklärung der fünf Bücher Mosche's.* Vol. 1. Stuttgart: Hallberger, 1840.

"Mendelsohn-Frankfurt, Moses." In Getzel Kressel, *Leksikon ha-sifrut ha-`Ivrit,* 2:401–2. Merḥavia: Sifriat po`alim, 1967.

Mendelssohn, Moses. "Schreiben, die philanthropinische Erziehung jüdischer Kinder betreffend." *Litteratur und Völkerkunde: Ein periodisches Werk* 2 (1783): 897–900. Reprinted in *Moses Mendelssohn's gesammelte Schriften,* vol. 3, edited by G. B. Mendelssohn, 417–22. Leipzig: Brockhaus, 1843. Also reprinted in *Gesammelte Schriften: Jubiläumsausgabe,* vol. 12.2, Briefwechsel 2.2, edited by Alexander Altmann, 85–88. Stuttgard-Bad Cannstatt: Friedrich Frommann, 1976.

Meyer, Michael A., and Michael Brenner, eds. *German–Jewish History in Modern Times.* Vol. 1: *Tradition and Enlightenment 1600–1780.* New York: Columbia Univ. Press, 1996.

Miron, Dan. *From Continuity to Contiguity: Toward a New Jewish Literary Thinking.* Stanford, CA: Stanford Univ. Press, 2010.

———. *A Traveler Disguised: The Rise of Modern Yiddish Fiction in the Nineteenth Century.* 1973. 2nd ed. Syracuse, NY: Syracuse Univ. Press, 1996.

Moseley, Marcus. *Being for Myself Alone: Origins of Jewish Autobiography.* Stanford, CA: Stanford Univ. Press, 2006.

Mosès, Stéphane. "Scholem and Rosenzweig: The Dialectics of History." Translated by Ora Wiskind. *History and Memory* 2, no. 2 (1990): 100–116.

Naveh, Hannah. *Nos`im ve-nos`ot: sippurei mas`a be-sifrut ha-`Ivrit ha-ḥadasha.* Jerusalem: Misrad ha-bitaḥon, 2002.

Niborski, Yitskhok, Simon Neuberg, Eliezer Niborski, and Natalia Krynicka, eds. *Verterbukh fun loshn-koydesh-shtamike verter in Yidish.* 3rd ed. Paris: Medem Bibliotek, 2012.

Oesterle, Günter, and Harald Tausch, eds. *Der imaginierte Garten.* Göttingen: Vandenhoeck and Ruprecht, 2001.

Ofek, Uriel. *Sifrut-yeledim ha-`Ivrit—ha-hatḥalot*. Tel Aviv: Porter Institute, 1979.

Orgeldinger, Sibylle. *Standardisierung und Purismus bei Joachim Heinrich Campe*. Berlin: Walter de Gruyter, 1999.

Pannwitz, Rudolf. *Die Krisis der Europaeishen Kultur*. Munich: Hans Carl, 1921.

Papirno, Avraham Ya`akov. "Zikronot." In *Sefer ha-shana*, vol. 1, edited by N. Sokolov, 60–75. Warsaw: Ha-tzefira, 1900.

Parfitt, T. V. "The Use of Hebrew in Palestine 1800–1882." *Journal of Semitic Studies* 17 (1972): 237–52.

Parush, Iris. "Mabat aḥer `al 'ḥayei ha-`Ivrit ha-«meita»": ha-ba`arut ha-mekuvenet ba-leshon ha-`Ivrit ba-ḥevra ha-Yehudit ha-mizraḥ Eropit ba-me'ah ha-19 ve-hashpa`ata `al ha-sifrut ha-`Ivrit ve-kor'eha." *Alpayim* 13 (1996): 65–106.

Patai, Raphael. *The Children of Noah: Jewish Seafaring in Ancient Times*. Princeton, NJ: Princeton Univ. Press, 1998.

Pelli, Moshe. *The Age of Haskalah: Studies in Hebrew Literature of the Enlightenment in Germany*. Leiden: Brill, 1979.

———. *Be-ma`avakei tmura: `iyunim ba-Haskala ha-`Ivrit be-Germania be-shilhei ha-me'a ha-Yod"Ḥet*. Tel Aviv: Tel Aviv Univ. Publishing, 1988.

———. *Dor ha-me'asefim be-shaḥar ha-Haskala*. Bnei Brak, Israel: Ha-kibbutz ha-me'uḥad, 2001.

———. "The Epistolary Story in Haskalah Literature: Isaac Euchel's 'Igrot Meshullam." *Jewish Quarterly Review* 93 (2003): 431–69.

———. *Haskala ve-modernizm*. Jerusalem: Ha-kibutz ha-me'uḥad, 2008.

———. *In Search of Genre: Hebrew Enlightenment and Modernity*. Lanham, MD: Univ. Press of America, 2005.

———. "Le-reshito shel ha-zhenre ha-epistolari be-sifrut ha-`Ivrit he-ḥadasha: Isaac Euchel ve-'iggarotav." *Bikoret u-farshanut* 16 (1981): 85–101.

———. "The Literary Genre of the Travelogue in Hebrew Haskalah Literature: Shmuel Romanelli's *Masa Ba`rav*." *Modern Judaism* 11 (1991): 241–60.

———. "On the Role of *Melitzah* in the Literature of Hebrew Enlightenment." In *Hebrew in Ashkenaz: A Language in Exile*, edited by Lewis Glinert, 99–110. New York: Oxford Univ. Press, 1993.

———. *Sha`ar la-Haskala: mafteaḥ mu`ar le-*Ha-me'asef*, ktav-ha-`et ha-rishon (1783–1811)*. Jerusalem: Magnes, 2001.

———. *Sugot ve-sugiot be-sifrut ha-Haskala ha-`Ivrit*. Tel Aviv: Ha-kibbutz ha-me'uḥad, 1999.

Peretz, I. L. "Di toyte shtot." In *Ale verk*, vol. 6: *Far kleyn un groys*, 116–29. Warsaw: Progress, 1909–13. Reprinted in *Ale verk fun I. L. Peretz*, vol. 6: *Far kleyn un groys*, 104–117. Vilna: Kletzkin, 1925–29.

Perl, Joseph. *Boḥen tzadik*. Prague: Landau, 1838.

———. *Luaḥ ha-shana 1813–1814*, *Luaḥ ha-shana 1814–1815*, and *Luaḥ ha-shana 1815–1816* (Tarnopol). Reprinted as *Luaḥ ha-lev*. Edited by Menuḥa Gilboa. Tel Aviv: Department of Hebrew Literature, Tel Aviv Univ., 1973.

———. *Megale temirin*. Vienna: Anton Strauss, 1819.

———. *Megale temirin*. 2 vols. Edited by Jonatan Meir. Jerusalem: Mossad Bialik, 2013.

———. *Yosef Perls Yidishe ksavim*. Edited by Israel Weinlös and Z. Kalmanovitsh. Vilna: YIVO, 1937.

Perry, Menahem. "Ha-analogiya u-mekoma be-mivne ha-roman shel Mendele Mo"S [Mokher Sfarim]." *Ha-sifrut* 1 (1968): 65–100.

———. "Thematic and Structural Shifts in Autotranslations by Bilingual Hebrew–Yiddish Writers: The Case of Mendele Mokher Sforim." *Poetics Today* 2 (1981):181–92.

Poznański, Samuel. "Wiener's 'Bibliotheca Friedlandiana.'" *Jewish Quarterly Review* 9 (1896–97): 157–61.

Rabbenu Baḥye: bi'ur 'al ha-Torah. Edited by Ḥaim Dov Shevel. Jerusalem: Mossad ha-rav Kook, 1991.

Rabin, Chaim. "The Continuum of Modern Literary Hebrew." In *The Great Transition: The Recovery of the Lost Centers of Modern Hebrew Literature*, edited by Glenda Abramson and Tudor Parfitt, 11–25. Totowa, NJ: Rowman & Allanheld, 1985.

Ravitzky, Aviezer, ed. *Eretz-Israel ba-hagut ha-Yehudit ba-`et ha-ḥadasha*. Jerusalem: Ben-Tzvi Institute, 1998.

Ravnitzky, Y. H. "`Al ha-signon ha-`Ivri shel Mendele Moykher Sforim." In *Kol kitvei Mendele Moykher Sforim*, vol. 7, 166–75. Berlin: Dvir, 1922. Originally published in *Ha-`omer* 1 (1907): part 2, 23–31.

Review of Moshe Mendelsohn-Frankfurt, *Metziat ha-aretz ha-ḥadasha*. *Ha-me'asef* 9 (1810): 97–101.

Reyzn, Zalman. "Kampes 'Antdekung fun Amerike' in Yidish (bibliografishe notitsn)." *YIVO bleter* 5 (1933): 29–40.

Robertson, William. *Geschichte von Amerika*. 2 vols. Translated by Johann Friedrich Schiller. Leipzig: Weidmanns Erben & Reich, 1777.

———. *The History of America.* 2 vols. London: Strahan & Cadell, 1777.

Romanelli, Shmuel [Samuel]. *Mas'a be-`arav: hu sefer ha-korot.* Berlin: Ḥevrat ḥinukh ne`arim, 1792.

———. *Travail in an Arab Land.* Translated by Yedida K. Stillman and Norman A. Stillman. Tuscaloosa: Univ. of Alabama Press, 1989.

Rosenblum, Noah Ḥ. *`Iyunei sifrut ve-hagut: mi-shilhei ha-me'a ha-shmone `esre `ad yemenu.* Jerusalem: Reuven Mass, 1989. (Includes essays on Moses Mendelsohn-Frankfurt and *Penei tevel.*)

———. *Tradition in an Age of Reform: The Religious Philosophy of Samson Raphael Hirsch.* Philadelphia: Jewish Publication Society of America, 1976.

Roskies, David G. "Ayzik-Meyer Dik and the Rise of Yiddish Popular Literature." PhD diss., Brandeis Univ., 1974.

———. *A Bridge of Longing: The Lost Art of Yiddish Storytelling.* Cambridge, MA: Harvard Univ. Press, 1995.

———. *The Genres of Yiddish Popular Literature 1790–1860.* Working Papers in Yiddish and East European Jewish Studies no. 8. New York: Max Weinreich Center for Advanced Jewish Studies, YIVO Institute for Jewish Research, 1975. (Discussion of "the sea adventure" on pp. 18–22.)

———. "The Medium and the Message of the Maskilic Chapbook." *Jewish Social Studies* 41 (1979): 275–90.

Rubin, Israel. "Vegn di virkung fun Yidish afn geredtn Hebreyish in Erets-Yisroel." *YIVO bleter* 25 (1945): 303–9.

Ruderman, David. *Jewish Thought and Scientific Discovery in Early Modern Europe.* New Haven, CT: Yale Univ. Press, 1995.

Sadan, Dov. *`Al sifrutenu.* Jerusalem: Reuven Mass, 1950.

Safran, William. "Diasporas in Modern Societies: Myths of Homeland and Return." *Diaspora: A Journal of Transnational Studies* 1 (1991): 83–99.

Satanov, Isaac. *Sefer ha-middot.* Berlin: Verlag der Jüdischen Freyschule, 1784.

———, trans. and ed. *Sefer ha-middot le-Aristoteles.* Berlin: Orientalische Buchdruckerey, 1790.

Scholem, Gershom. "Merkaba Mysticism." In *Encyclopaedia Judaica*, vol. 11, 1386–89. Jerusalem: Keter, 1972.

———. "On Our Language: A Confession." Translated by Ora Wiskind. *History and Memory* 2, no. 2 (1990): 97–99.

Schweid, Eliezer. *Moledet ve-aretz ye`uda: Eretz-Israel be-hagut shel `am Israel.* Tel Aviv: `Am `oved, 1979.

Seidman, Naomi. *Faithful Renderings: Jewish–Christian Difference and the Politics of Translation*. Chicago: Univ. of Chicago Press, 2006.

Shakhevitz, Boaz. "'Arba` leshonot: `iyunim shel sifrut bi-leshon ha-maskilim `al pi *Ha-me'asef*." *Molad* 212 (1967): 236–42.

Shapiro, Ḥ. N. *Toldot ha-sifrut ha-`Ivrit ha-ḥadasha*. Vol. 1: *Sifrut ha-Haskala be-merkaz Germania (1784–1829)*. 1939. Reprint. Tel Aviv: Massada, 1967.

Shavit, Yaacov. "A Duty Too Heavy to Bear: Hebrew in the Berlin Haskalah, 1783–1819: Between Classic, Modern, and Romantic." In *Hebrew in Ashkenaz: A Language in Exile*, edited by Lewis Glinert, 111–28. New York: Oxford Univ. Press, 1993.

Shavit, Zohar. "From Friedländer's Lesebuch to the Jewish Campe: The Beginning of Hebrew Children's Literature in Germany." *Leo Baeck Institute Year Book* 33 (1988): 385–415.

———. "Literarische Beziehungen zwischen der deutschen und der jüdisch-hebräischen Kinderliteratur in der Epoche der Aufklärung am Beispiel von J. H. Campe." In *Übersetzen, verstehen, Brücken bauen: Geisteswissenschaftliches und literarisches Übersetzen im internationalen Kulturaustausch*, edited by Armin Paul Frank. Berlin: E. Schmidt, 1993.

———. "Literary Interference between German and Jewish–Hebrew Children's Literature during the Enlightenment: The Case of Campe." *Poetics Today* 13, no. 1 (1992): 41–61.

Shmeruk, Khone. "Dvarim kehaviatam u-dvarim she-bedimion bi-'Megaleh temirin' shel Yosef Perl." In *Ha-kri'a le-navi: meḥkerei historia ve-sifrut*, edited by Israel Bartal, 144–55. Jerusalem: Shazar Center, 1999.

———, ed. *Ḥalifat 'igrot bein S. Y. Abramovitsh u-vein Ḥ. N. Bialik ve-Y. Ḥ. Ravnitzki ba-shanim 1905–1908*. Jerusalem: Israeli Academy of Sciences, 1976.

———. *Sifrut Yidish be-Polin: meḥkarim ve-`iyunim historiim*. Jerusalem: Magnes, 1981.

———. *Sifrut Yidish: prakim le-toldoteha*. Tel Aviv: Tel Aviv Univ. Press, 1978.

Shoḥam, Ḥayim. *Be-tzel haskalat Berlin*. Tel Aviv: Porter Institute, 1996.

Simon, E. A. [Akiba Ernst]. "Ha-filantropinizm ha-pedagogi ve-ha-ḥinukh ha-Yehudi." In *Sefer ha-yuvel likvod Mordechai Menachem Kaplan*, Hebrew Section, 149–85. New York: Jewish Theological Seminary, 1953.

Smith, Bernard. *European Vision and the South Pacific 1768–1850: A Study in the History of Art and Ideas*. London: Oxford Univ. Press, 1960.

Sperber, Daniel. *Nautica Talmudica*. Ramat-Gan: Bar Ilan Univ. Press, 1986.

Spivak, C. D., and Sol Bloomgarden (Yehoash), eds. *Yidish verterbukh*. New York: Yehoash, 1911.

Stampfer, Shaul. *Families, Rabbis, and Education: Traditional Jewish Society in Nineteenth-Century Eastern Europe*. Oxford: Littman Library of Jewish Civilization, 2010.

Steiner, George. *After Babel: Aspects of Language and Translation*. 3rd ed. Oxford: Oxford Univ. Press, 1998.

———. "Our Homeland, the Text." *Salmagundi* 66 (1985): 4–25.

Sternfeld, Noah ha-Levi, ed. *Gidulei ha-naḥal*. Jerusalem: Meshekh ha-naḥal, 1984.

Stevens, Wallace. *The Collected Poems*. New York: Knopf, 1954.

Tolkowsky, Samuel. *They Took to the Sea*. New York: Thomas Yoseloff, 1964.

Unger, Menashe. "Khaikl Hurwitzes yikhes-briv." *Filologishe shriftn* 3 (1929): 83–88.

Venuti, Lawrence. *The Scandals of Translation: Towards an Ethics of Difference*. London: Routledge, 1998.

———, ed. *The Translation Studies Reader*. 2nd ed. London: Routledge, 2004.

———. *The Translator's Invisibility: A History of Translation*. London: Routledge, 1995.

Viner [Weiner], M. *Tsu der geshikhte fun der Yidisher literatur in 19tn yorhundert*. 2 vols. New York: Yidisher Kultur Farband, 1945.

Weinreich, Uriel. *Ha-ʿIvrit ha-Ashkenazit ve-ha-ʿIvrit she-be-Yidish: beḥinatan ha-geografit*. Jerusalem: Raphel Ḥayim Ha-Cohen, 1965. (First published in *Leshonenu* 24 [1960]: 57–80, 180–96.)

"Wendezirkel,Wendekreis." Google Books Ngram Viewer, n.d. At http://books.google.com/ngrams/graph?content=Wendezirkel%2CWendekreis&year_start=1750&year_end=2000&corpus=20&smoothing=3&share=.

Werses, Shmuel. *Mi-lashon el lashon: yetzirot ve-gilguleihen be-sifrutenu*. Jerusalem: Magnes, 1996.

———. "Ha-sefer *Penei tevel* be-zikato la-masoret ha-makama be-sifrutenu." In *Sefer Ḥayim Shirman: kovetz meḥkarim*, edited by Shraga Abramson and Aharon Mirski, 135–48. Jerusalem: Schocken, 1970.

Wessely, Naftali Hirsh. *Divrei shalom ve-emet*. Berlin: n.p., 1782.

———. *Shirei tif'eret*. Berlin: Ḥevrat ḥinukh neʿarim, 1789.

Wiesel, Eliezer. *. . . Un di velt hot geshvign / . . . Y el mundo callaba*. Buenos Aires: Tsentral-farband fun Poylishe Yidn in Argentina, 1956.

Wolfsohn, R. Aharon. *Kalut da'at u-tzevi'ut* [*R. Khanokh ve–R. Yosefkhe*]. Edited by Dan Miron. Tel Aviv: Siman kri'a and Mif'alim universitaiim le-hotza'a le-'or, 1977.

———. *Silliness and Sanctimony*. In *Landmark Yiddish Plays: A Critical Anthology*, edited and translated by Joel Berkowitz and Jeremy Dauber, 81–111. Albany: State Univ. of New York Press, 2006.

Wolitz, Seth L. "*Satan in Goray* as Parable." *Prooftexts* 9 (1989): 13–25.

Wolpe, Rebecca. "From Slavery to Freedom: Abolitionist Expressions in Maskilic Sea Adventures." *AJS Review* 36 (2012): 43–70.

———. "The Sea and Sea Voyage in Maskilic Literature." PhD diss., Hebrew Univ. of Jerusalem, 2011.

———. "The Sea Voyage Narrative as an Educational Tool in the Early Haskalah." MA thesis, Hebrew Univ. of Jerusalem, 2006.

———. "The True Way to Loving God: Nature in the *Haskala*." *University of Toronto Journal of Jewish Thought* 3 (2012). At http://tjjt.cjs.utoronto.ca/wp-content/uploads/2013/11/Rebecca-Wolpe-The-True-Way-to-Loving-God-Nature-in-the-Haskala-Vol.-3.pdf.

Yudelov, Yitzhak. Entry 1299, on *Oniya so'ara* (Zholkva? 1818?). In *Sefer ginzei Israel: The Israel Mehlman Collection*, 208. Jerusalem: National and Univ. Library, 1984.

———. Entry 1310 on *Sefer mase'ot ha-yam*. In *Sefer ginzei Israel: The Israel Mehlman Collection*, 209. Jerusalem: National and Univ. Library, 1984.

Zalman, Eliahu ben Shlomo. *Eliahu Raba*. Prague: Sommer, 1812.

Zinberg, Israel. *Di geshikhte fun der literature bay yidn*. Vol. 7, book 1: *Berliner Haskole*. New York: Sklarsky, 1943.

———. *Di geshikhte fun der literature bay yidn*. Vol. 7, book 2: *Khasides un oyfklerung (1780–1820)*. New York: Sklarsky, 1943.

———. *A History of Jewish Literature*. Translated and edited by Bernard Martin. Vol. 8: *The Berlin Haskalah*. New York: Hebrew Union College and Ktav, 1976.

———. *A History of Jewish Literature*. Translated and edited by Bernard Martin. Vol. 9: *Hasidism and Enlightenment (1780–1820)*. New York: Hebrew Union College and Ktav, 1976.

Zuckermann, Ghil'ad. "Camouflaged Borrowing: Folk-Etymological Nativization in the Service of Puristic Language Engineering." PhD diss., Univ. of Oxford, 2000.

———. "Complement Clause Types in Israeli." In *Complementation: A Cross-Linguistic Typology*, edited by R. M. W. Dixon and A. Y. Aikhenvalt, 72–92. Oxford: Oxford Univ. Press, 2006.

———. "Hybridity versus Revivability: Multiple Causation, Forms, and Patterns." *Journal of Language Contact—VARIA* 2 (2009): 40–67.

———. *Israelit safa yafa: az eizu safa ha-Israelim medabrim?* Translated by Maya Feldman. Tel Aviv: `Am `oved, 2008.

———. *Language Contact and Lexical Enrichment in Israeli Hebrew*. New York: Palgrave Macmillan, 2003.

Hasidism

Alfasi, Yitzḥak. *Rebbe Naḥman mi-Breslav: ḥayav torato u-maḥsheveto*. Tel Aviv: "Netzaḥ," 1952–53.

Assaf, David. *Breslav: bibliografiya mu`eret*. Jerusalem: Zalman Shazar Center, 2000.

Barnai, Jacob. "`Aliyot ha-ḥasidim le-Eretz Israel." In *Historiografiya ve-le`umiut: magamot be-ḥeker Eretz-Israel ve-yishuva ha-Yehudi, 634–1881*, 140–59. Jerusalem: Magnes, 1995.

Ben-Amos, Dan, and Jerome R. Mintz, eds. *In Praise of the Baal Shem Tov: The Earliest Collection of Legends about the Founder of Hasidism*. Northvale, NJ: Jason Aronson, 1993.

Birnstein, Simḥa. "Moharan z"l mi-Breslav ve-Eretz Israel." *Darkenu* 1, no. 38 (1934–35): 10–11; no. 39: 14; no. 40: 11–12; no. 41: 12; no. 42: 6; no. 43: 11; no. 44: 9–10.

Cohen, Tova. "Ha-ḥasidut ve-Eretz-Israel—aspekt nosaf shel ha-satira be-'*Megale temirin*.'" *Tarbitz* 48 (1978–79): 332–40.

Cunz, Martin. *Die Fahrt des Rabbi Nachman von Brazlaw ins Land Israel (1798–1799)*. Tübingen: Mohr, 1997.

Dan, Yosef. *Ha-sippur ha-ḥasidi*. Jerusalem: Keter, 1975.

Dinur, Ben-Tzion. "Ha-yesodot ha-idiologiim shel ha-`aliyot be-shnot Tof"Kuf—Tof"Resh (1740–1840)." In *Be-mifne ha-dorot: meḥkarim ve-`iyunim be-reishitam shel ha-zmanim ha-ḥadashim be-toldot Israel*, vol. 1, 69–79. Jerusalem: Mossad Bialik, 1955.

Dubnov, Simon. *Toldot ha-ḥasidut: `al yesod mekorot rishonim, nidpasim ve-kit-vei-yad*. Tel Aviv: Dvir, 1975.

Feiner, Shmuel. "Be-'emunah bilvad! Ha-pulmus shel reb Natan mi-Nemirov neged ha-ateizm ve-ha-Haskalah." In *Meḥkerei ḥasidut*, vol. 15 of Meḥkerei

Yerushalaim be-maḥshevet Yisrael, edited by Immanuel Etkes, David Assaf, and Yosef Dan, 89–124. Jerusalem: Hebrew Univ., 1999.

———. "'Le-`akor et ha-ḥokhma miha-`olam'—oyevei ha-ne'orut ve-shorshei ha-`emda ha-ḥaredit." *Alpayim* 26 (2004): 166–90.

Geshuri, M. "Rebbe Nathan mi-Nemirov." *Talpiot* 6 (1955): 370–81, 730–38.

Glinert, Lewis. "The Hasidic Tale and the Sociolinguistic Modernization of the Jews of Eastern Europe." In *Ma`ase sippur: meḥkarim be-sipporet ha-Yehudit mugashim le-Yoav Elstein*, edited by Avidov Lipsker and Rella Kushelevsky, vii–xxxvi. Ramat-Gan: Bar Ilan Univ. Press, 2006.

Green, Arthur. *Tormented Master: A Life of Rabbi Nahman of Bratslav*. New York: Schocken, 1981.

Greenbaum, Avraham, trans., and Moshe Mykoff, ed. *Tzaddik (Chayey Moharan): A Portrait of Rabbi Nachman*. New York: Breslov Research Institute, 1987.

Ḥazan, Avraham (of Tulchin). *Kokhvei 'or*. Edited by Shmuel ha-Levi Horowitz. 1933. Reprint. Jerusalem: Ḥasidei Breslav, 1987.

———. *Yemei ha-tela'ot*. 1933. Reprint. Jerusalem: Yuval, 1968. [Describes the persecution of Bratslav hasidim and includes passages omitted from Nathan Sternharz, *Ḥayei Moharan*.]

Kenig, Nathan Tzvi. *Nave tzadikim*. Bnei Brak: n.p., 1969.

Kramer, Chaim. *Through Fire and Water: The Life of Reb Noson of Breslov*. Edited by Avraham Greenbaum. Jerusalem: Breslov Research Institute, 1992.

Liberman, Haim. *Ohel Raḥel*. 3 vols. New York: Liberman, 1980–84.

———. "R. Nakhmen Bratzlaver un di Umaner maskilim." *YIVO bleter* 29 (1947): 201–19.

Mantel, Mordechai. "*Sefer yemei Moharnat* shel rebi Natan mi-Nemirov: `iyun bibliografi." *`Alei sefer* 14 (1987): 125–34.

Margolin, Ron. "Ha-'emunah ve-ha-kfirah be-torata shel hasidut Breslov `al pi ha-sefer Likutei halakhot le-R. Nathan Sternharz." MA thesis, Univ. of Haifa, 1991.

Mark, Zvi. "`Al matzevei katnut ve-gadlut be-haguto shel R. Naḥman mi-Breslav." *Da`at*, Winter 2001, 45–80.

———. *Hitgalut ve-tikun be-ktevav ha-galuim ve-ha-sodiim shel R. Naḥman mi-Breslav*. Jerusalem: Magnes, 2011.

———. *Mistika ve-shiga`on be-yetzirat R. Naḥman mi-Breslav*. Tel Aviv: `Am `oved, 2003.

Nahman of Bratslav [see also "Sternharz, Nathan" in the "Sea Narratives" section]. *Likutei Moharan*. Ostrog, Slovenia: Segal, 1808.

———. *Likutei Moharan.* Jerusalem: Keren hadpasa shel ḥasidei Breslav, 1988. Bound with the second part, *Likutei Moharan tinyana* (1811), and a second title page listing the publication date as 1979.

———. *Magid siḥot.* Zholkva: n.p., [1850?].

———. *Rabbi Nachman's Stories (Sippurey Ma'asioth).* Translated by Aryeh Kaplan. Jerusalem: Breslov Research Institute, 1983.

———. *Rabbi Nachman's Wisdom: Shevachay HaRan and Sichos HaRan.* Translated by Aryeh Kaplan. Edited by Zvi Aryeh Rosenfeld. Brooklyn, NY: Breslov Research Institute, 1973.

———. *Siḥot ha-Ran ha-menukad.* Jerusalem: Keren R. Israel Dov Odesser, [1981?].

———. *The Tales.* Translated by Arnold J. Band. New York: Paulist Press, 1978.

Nahman of Bratslav [and Nathan Sternharz]. *Likutei Moharan tinyana.* Mohilev: n.p., 1811. Bound with *Likutei Moharan.* Jerusalem: Keren hadpasa shel ḥasidei Breslav, 1988.

———. *Sippurei ma'asiyot.* [Ostrog or Mohilev?]: n.p., 1815.

———. *Sippurei ma'asiyot.* Jerusalem: Keren hadpasa shel ḥasidei Breslav, 1979.

Nahman of Tcherin. *Parpara'ot le-ḥokhma.* Jerusalem: Keren hadpasa shel ḥasidei Breslav, 1983.

Nigal, Gedalyah. *The Hasidic Tale.* Translated by Edward Levin. Oxford: Littman Library of Jewish Civilization, 2008.

———. *Ha-sipporet ha-ḥasidit: toldoteha ve-nos'eha.* Jerusalem: Y. Markus, 1981.

Orián, Meir. "Masa'o shel R. Nahman mi-Breslav le-Eretz-Israel." *Mabbu'a* 14 (1979): 142–57.

Perl, Joseph. *'Al mahut kat ha-ḥasidim / Uiber das Wesen der Sekte Chassidim.* Edited by Avraham Rubinstein. Jerusalem: Israel Academy of Sciences and Humanities, 1977.

———. *Ma'asiyot ve-'igrot mi-tzadikim amitiim u-mi-anshei shlomeinu.* Edited by Khone Shmeruk and Shmuel Werses. Jerusalem: Israel Academy of Sciences and Humanities, 1970.

Piekarz, Mendel. *Ḥasidut Breslav: prakim be-ḥayei meḥolela, be-kitveha u-vesafiḥeha.* 1972. 2nd ed. Jerusalem: Mossad Bialik, 1995.

———. "Reb Natan mi-Nemirov ba-aspaklariat sifro 'Likutei halakhot.'" *Tzion* 69 (2004): 203–40.

Rabinovitch, Isaiah. "Darko shel R. Nahman mi-Braslav el *Sippurei-ma'asiot* shelo." In *Shoreshim u-megamot: le-beḥinat mekoroteha shel ha-bikoret* *ha-ḥadasha ve-`iyunim be-darka shel ha-sifrut ha-`Ivrit*, 163–218. Jerusalem: Mossad Bialik, 1967.

———. "Reb Nahman Braslavers veg tsu zayne sippurey mayses." *Di goldene keyt* 69–70 (1970): 174–220.

Rapoport-Albert, Ada. "'Katnut,' 'pshitut' ve-'eini yode`a' shel R. Nahman mi-Breslav." In *Studies in Jewish Religious and Intellectual History Presented to Alexander Altmann on the Occasion of His Seventieth Birthday*, edited by Siegfried Stein and Raphael Loewe, 7–33. Tuscaloosa: Univ. of Alabama Press, 1979. (Hebrew pagination.)

———. "The Problems of Succession in the Hasidic Leadership with Special Reference to the Circle of R. Nachman of Braslav." PhD diss., Univ. of London, 1974.

———. "Shnei mekorot le-te'ur nesi`ato shel R. Nahman mi-Breslav le-Eretz-Israel." *Kiryat sefer* 46 (1971): 147–53.

Rosman, Moshe. *Founder of Hasidism: A Quest for the Historical Ba`al Shem Tov.* Berkeley: Univ. of California Press, 1996.

Rubinstein, Avraham, ed. *Shivḥei ha-Besht: mahadura mu`eret ve-mevu'eret.* Jerusalem: Reuven Mass, 1991.

Schleicher, Marianne. *Intertextuality in the Tales of Rabbi Nahman of Bratslav: A Close Reading of* Sippurey Ma'asiyot. Leiden: Brill, 2007.

Scholem, Gershom. *Kuntras eile shemot: sifrei Moharan z"l mi-Breslav ve-sifrei talmidav ve-talmidei talmidav.* Jerusalem: n.p., 1928.

Shivḥei ha-Besht. Second printing. Berdichev: Shmuel Segal, 1815.

Steinman, Eliezer. "Tziun le-meshorer." *Ha-tekufa* 16 (1922): 499–501.

Sternharz, Nathan [see also the "Sea Narratives" section]. "`Alim le-trufa: mikhtevei Moharnat." Manuscript EVR IV 93, F 69530. Russian National Library, St. Petersberg (formerly the M. E. Saltykov-Shchedrin State Public Library).

———. *`Alim le-trufa: mikhtevei Moharnat.* New York: Keren hadpasa shel ḥasidei Breslav, 1976.

———. *Ḥayei Moharan.* 2 vols. Lemberg: Carl Budweiser, 1874.

———. *Ḥayei Moharan.* Jerusalem: Keren hadpasa shel ḥasidei Breslav, 1981.

———. *Kitvei Rebbe Nahman mi-Breslav: Ḥayei Moharan, Yemei Moharnat, Yemei ha-tela'ot.* Beit Shemesh: "Nekudot tovot," 2005. (With some additions based on manuscripts; the added passages are not clearly indicated in this edition.)

———. *Likutei halakhot.* Zholkva: Saul Meyerhoffer, 1848.

———. *Likutei halakhot.* 8 vols. Jerusalem: Keren hadpasa de-ḥasidei Breslav, 1985.

———. *Likutei tefilot.* Jerusalem: Shilo and Keren hadpasa shel ḥasidei Breslav, 1943.

———. *Magid siḥot.* Zholkva: n.p., [1850?]. (Includes supplementary sections from *Sippurei ma`asiyot* [1815], such as "Seder ha-nesi`a shelo le-Eretz Israel," later published in *Shivḥei ha-Ran.*)

———. *Sefer ha-middot.* Bratslav: n.p., 1821.

———. *Shivḥei ha-Ran ha-menukad.* Jerusalem: Agudat "Meshekh ha-naḥal," 1981.

———. *Siḥot ha-Ran ha-menukad.* Jerusalem: Keren R. Israel Dov Odesser, [1981?].

———. *Sippurei ma`asiyot.* [Ostrog or Mohilev?]: n.p., 1815.

———. *Sippurei ma`asiyot.* 2nd ed. N.p.: n.p., ca. 1845–50.

———. *Sippurei ma`asiyot.* Jerusalem: Keren hadpasa shel ḥasidei Breslav, 1979.

———. "Yemei Moharnat." Part 1. Manuscript 16990/2, Schocken Library, Jerusalem. Microfilm 45444, Sheets 72-133, National Library of Israel, Jerusalem.

———. "Yemei Moharnat." Part 2. Manuscript 16989, Schocken Library, Jerusalem. Microfilm 45446, Sheets 2-72, National Library of Israel, Jerusalem.

———. "Yemei Moharnat." Part 2. Manuscript 16990/1, Schocken Library, Jerusalem. Microfilm 45444, Sheets 65-139, National Library of Israel, Jerusalem.

———. *Yemei Moharnat.* Part 1. Lemberg: Ya`akov Meshullam Nik, 1876.

———. *Yemei Moharnat.* Part 1. Lublin: Shnaydmesser, 1919.

———. *Yemei Moharnat.* Part 2. Edited by Israel Heilprin. Jerusalem: n.p., 1904.

———. *Yemei Moharnat.* Parts 1 and 2. 1876/1904. Reprint. New York: Rozenfeld and Berger, 1970.

———. *Yemei Moharnat.* Jerusalem: "Meshekh ha-naḥal," 1982.

Ulbricht, Günther. "Spielpädogogik des Philanthropismus." In *Europa in der Frühen Neuzeit: Festschrift für Günther Mühlpfordt*, edited by Erich Donnert, vol. 6. Cologne: Böhlau, 2002.

Weiss, Joseph. *Meḥkarim be-ḥasidut Breslav.* Edited by M. Piekarz. Jerusalem: Mossad Bialik, 1974.

Werses, Shmuel. "Mi-lashon el lashon ba–'Sippurei ma`asiyot' shel R. Nahman mi-Breslav." *Ḥuliyot* 9 (2005): 9–47.

Wilensky, Mordecai. *Hasidim ve-mitnagdim: le-toldot ha-pulmus she-beneihem ba-shanim 1772–1815.* 2 vols. Jerusalem: Mosad Bialik, 1970.

Wiskind-Elper, Ora. *Tradition and Fantasy in the Tales of Reb Nahman of Bratslav.* Albany: State Univ. of New York Press, 1998.

Ya`akov Yosef of Polonne. *Toldot Ya`akov Yosef.* Koretz: Tzvi Hirsh, 1780.

Ya`ari, Avraham. "Shtei mahadurot-yesod shel 'Shivḥei ha-Besht.'" *Kiryat sefer* 39 (1964): 249–72, 394–407, 552–62.

Zeitlin, Hillel. *'Oro shel Meshiaḥ ba-torat ha-Breslavi.* In *Rabbi Nahman mi-Breslav: tza`ar ha-`olam ve-kisufei Meshiaḥ*, edited by Jonatan Meir, 69–99. Jerusalem: Orna Hass, 2006.

———. *Reb Nakhman Braslaver.* New York: Matones, 1952.

Zinberg, Israel. *A History of Jewish Literature.* Translated and edited by Bernard Martin. Vol. 9: *Hasidism and Enlightenment (1780–1820).* New York: Hebrew Union College Press and Ktav, 1976.

By and about (Menahem) Mendel Lefin of Satanov

Bik, Ya`akov Shmuel. Letter to Mendel Lefin and Joseph Perl (1811). In Israel Weinlös, "Mendel Lefin-Satanover." *YIVO bleter* 2 (1931): 342.

Birnboym, Yankev. "Lefin, (Menahem-) Mendel." In *Leksikon fun der nayer Yidisher literatur,* vol. 5, 349–54. New York: Congress for Jewish Culture, 1963.

Dauber, Jeremy. *Antonio's Devils: Writers of the Jewish Enlightenment and the Birth of Modern Hebrew and Yiddish Literature.* Stanford, CA: Stanford Univ. Press, 2004.

Erik, Maks. *Etyudn tsu der geshikhte fun der haskole (1789–1881).* Minsk: Melukhe farlag fun Vaysrusland, 1934. (Especially part 2, chapter 3, "Lefin and Bik," pp. 135–62.)

Feder, Tuvia. *Kol meḥatzetzim.* In *Be-misterei ha-satira: prakim ba-satira ha-`Ivrit ha-ḥadasha be-me'ah ha-19,* [vol. 1], edited by Yehuda Friedlander, 39–75. Tel Aviv: Bar Ilan Univ., 1984.

Friedkin, A. *Avraham-Ber Gotlober un zayn epokhe.* Vilna: Kletzkin, 1925.

Gelber, N. M. "Mendel Lefin-Satanover ve-hatza`otav la-tikun oraḥ ḥayim shel Yehudei Polin bifnei ha-Seym ha-gadol (1788–1792)." In *The Abraham Weiss Jubilee Volume,* edited by Samuel Belkin, 271–305. New York: Shulsinger, 1964.

———. "Mendel Satanower: Der Verbreiter der Haskala in Polen und Galizien." In *Aus zwei Jahrhunderten: Beiträge zur neueren Geschichte der Juden,* 39–57. Vienna: Lowit, 1924.

Gotlober, Avraham-Ber. ["Memories of Mendel Lefin."] *Ha-maggid* 17 (1873): nos. 32–41.

———. "Menahem Mendel Lefin of Satanov." In *Zikronot ve-masa'ot*, vol. 2, edited by Reuven Goldberg, 197–208. Jerusalem: Mossad Bialik, 1976.

———. "Zikhroynes: Erinerungen iber yudishe shrayber un sforim." *Di Yudishe folksbibliothek* 1 (1888): 250–53.

Gruschka, Roland. *Übersetzungswissenschaftliche Aspekte von Mendel Lefin Satanowers Bibelübersetzungen*. Hamburg: Buske, 2007.

Katz, Simkhe. "'Igrot maskilim bi-gnutam shel Hasidim." *Moznaim* 10 (1940): 266–76.

———. "Tirgumei Tanakh mi-et Menahem Mendel Lefin mi-Satanov." *Kiryat sefer* 19 (1939): 114–33. (Includes selections from Mendel Lefin's Yiddish translations of Lamentations, Job, and Psalms as well as the introduction to the translation of Psalms.)

Klausner, Yosef. *Be'ayot shel sifrut ve-med'a*. Tel Aviv: Massada, 1956.

———. *Historiya shel ha-sifrut ha-'Ivrit ha-ḥadasha*. Vol. 1. Jerusalem: Hebrew University, 1930.

———. "Meḥkarim be-toldot ha-sifrut ha-'Ivrit ha-ḥadasha: lehishtalsheluto shel signon-ha-Mishna be-sifrut ha-ḥadasha." In *Kitvei ha-Universita ha-'Ivrit be-Yerushalaim: mada'ei ha-Yahadut*, vol. 1, 163–78, Yedi'ot ha-makhon le-mada'ei ha-Yahadut, vol. 3. Jerusalem: Ha-madpis, 1926.

Lachover, Fishl. *Toldot ha-sifrut ha-'Ivrit ha-ḥadasha*. Vol. 1. Tel Aviv: Dvir, 1966.

Lefin, Mendel. "Essai d'un plan de réforme ayant pour objet d'éclairer la nation Juive en Pologne et de redresser par là ses mœurs" (1792). In *Materiały do dziejów sejmu czteroletniego*, vol. 6, edited by Artur Eisenbach, Jerzy Michałski, Emanuel Rostworowski, and Janusz Woliński, 409–21. Warsaw: Instytut historii Polskiej akademii Nauk, 1969.

———. *Ḥeshbon ha-nefesh*. Lemberg: Rubenstein, 1808.

———. *Ḥeshbon ha-nefesh*. Vilna: Menachem Mann Romm, 1844.

———. "Mikhtavim shonim." *Ha-me'asef* 5 (1789): 81–92, 136–44.

———. *Mod'a le-vina*. Vol. 1: *Igeret ha-ḥokhma*, and [prospectus for] *Refu'ot ha-'am*. Berlin: Ḥevrat ḥinukh ne'arim, 1789.

———, trans. *Morei nevukhim*. Zholkva: Saul Meyerhoffer, 1829. (A translation of Maimonides, *Guide to the Perplexed*, from the Tibbonic Hebrew into Mishnaic Hebrew. Includes the afterword "Sium la-metargem *Sefer morei nevukhim*.")

———, trans. *Refu'at ha-'am*. Zholkva: Mordechai Rabin Stein, 1794.

———, trans. *Refu'at ha-'am*. Lvov: Josef Schnayder, 1851. (Expanded edition with new material by M. Studentzki.)

———, trans. *Sefer Koheles im targum Yehudit u-viur.* Edited by Tzvi Ha-Cohen Reich. Odessa: Belinson, 1873.

———, trans. *Sefer Koheles Shlomo.* 1819. Reprint. Vilna: YIVO, 1930.

———, trans. *Sefer Mishlei Shlomo.* Tarnopol: n.p., 1814.

———. "'Tefilat hodaya' le-M. Lefin." With explanatory remarks by Avraham Rubinstein. *Kiryat sefer* 42 (1967): 403–4.

Letteris, M. [Meir]. *Zikkaron be-sefer: Mémoiren. Ein Beitrag zur Literatur- und Culturgeschichte im XIX. Jahrhundert* (in Hebrew). Vol. 1: *Vom Jahre 1800 bis 1831.* Vienna: The Author and Schlossberg, 1869.

Levine, Hillel. "Bein ḥasidut le-Haskala: `al pulmus anti-ḥasidi musve." In *Prakim be-toldot ha-ḥevra ha-yeudit bi-yemei ha-benaim u-ve-`et ha-ḥadasha.* Jerusalem: Magnes, 1980.

———. "Menahem Mendel Lefin: A Case Study of Judaism and Modernization." PhD diss., Harvard Univ., 1974.

Mahler, Raphael. *Divrei yemei Israel: dorot aḥaronim mi-shilhei ha-me`a ha-shmone-`esrei `ad yemenu.* Vol. 1. Merḥavia: Ha-shomer ha-tza'ir, 1962.

Mashbitz, Dror. "The Emergence of Modern Yiddish in Literature: Mendl Lefin's Translation of Ecclesiastes of 1819." MA thesis, Columbia Univ., 1970.

Meisl, Josef. *Haskalah: Geschichte der Aufklärungsbewegung unter den Juden in Russland.* Berlin: Schwetschke & Sohn, 1919.

Reyzn, Zalman. "Lefin (Levin), (Menahem-) Mendel." In *Leksikon fun der Yudisher literature un prese*, edited by S. Niger, 363–65. Warsaw: Tsentral, 1914.

———. "Mendel Lefin Satanover." In *Fun Mendelssohn biz Mendele*, 147–62. Warsaw: Kultur-lige, 1923.

Shmeruk, Khone. "Al `ikronot aḥadim shel tirgum Mishlei le-Mendel Lefin." In *Sifrut Yiddish be-Polin: meḥkarim ve-`iyunim historiim*, 165–83. Jerusalem: Magnes, 1981.

Shulman, Eliahu. "Mendel Satanover in Yiddish." *Yidishe shprakh* 24 (1964): 82–88.

Sinkoff, Nancy. "Benjamin Franklin in Jewish Eastern Europe: Cultural Appropriation in the Age of the Enlightenment." *Journal of the History of Ideas* 61 (2000): 133–52.

———. *Out of the Shtetl: Making Jews Modern in the Polish Borderlands.* Providence, RI: Brown Judaic Studies, 2004.

———. "Strategy and Ruse in the Haskalah of Mendel Lefin of Satanow." In *New Perspectives on the Haskalah*, edited by Shmuel Feiner and David Sorkin, 86–102. London: Littman Library of Jewish Civilization, 2001.

———. "Tradition and Transition: Mendel Lefin of Satanów and the Beginnings of the Jewish Enlightenment in Eastern Europe, 1749–1826." PhD diss., Columbia Univ., 1996.

Van Luit, Riety. "Hasidim, Mitnaggeddim, and the State in M. N. Lefin's *Essai d'un plan de réforme.*" *Zutot* 1 (2001): 188–95.

Weinlös, Israel. "Mendel Lefin-Satanover: biografishe shtudiye afn smakh fun handshriftlekhe materialn." *YIVO bleter* 2 (1931): 334–57.

Weinreich, Max. "Er hot gevolt iberzetsn dem Tanakh." *Afn shvel*, Oct.–Dec. 1999, 8–10, and Jan.–Mar. 2000, 9–11. (Originally published in *Forverts*, Apr. 1, 1928.)

———. *History of the Yiddish Language*. 2 vols. Translated by Shlomo Noble. Edited by Paul Glasser. New Haven, CT: Yale Univ. Press, 2008.

Weisberg, M. "Die neuhebraische Aufklarungsliteratur in Galizien." Part 3 on Mendel Levin [*sic*] and Hirz Homberg. *Monatsschrift für Geschichte und Wissenschaft des Judentums* 71, new series 35 (1927): 54–62.

Werses, Shmuel. "Ba-`ekevotav shel ha-ḥibur 'Maḥkimat peti' ha-'avud." In *Megamot ve-tzurot be-sifrut ha-Haskala*, 319–37. Jerusalem: Magnes, 1990.

Zinberg, Israel. *Di geshikhte fun der literature bay Yidn*. Vol. 7. Part 2. New York: Sklarsky, 1943.

———. *A History of Jewish Literature*. Translated and edited by Bernard Martin. Vol. 6: *The German–Polish Cultural Center*. New York: Hebrew Union College Press and Ktav, 1975. (Especially chapter 8 on Mendel Lefin, 275–81.)

Index

Italic page numbers denote illustrations.

Ken Frieden is the B. G. Rudolph Professor of Judaic Studies at Syracuse University. His books include *Genius and Monologue* (1985), *Freud's Dream of Interpretation* (1990), *Classic Yiddish Fiction* (1995), and anthologies of Yiddish literature in translation, such as *Tales of Mendele the Book Peddler* (1996) and *Classic Yiddish Stories* (2004). He has been a visiting professor at the universities in Tel Aviv, Haifa, and Heidelberg as well as at the University of California, Davis; he has been a research fellow at the Hebrew University in Jerusalem, the Free University of Berlin, and Harvard University. At Syracuse University Press, Frieden edits the series Judaic Traditions in Literature, Music, and Art. He translates from Yiddish and Hebrew and has edited collections of short stories by the Israeli authors Etgar Keret (*Four Stories*, 2010) and David Ehrlich (*Who Will Die Last*, 2013).